ISAAC ASIMOV

PRESENTS

THE GOLDEN YEARS OF SCIENCE FICTION

ISAAC ASIMOV

PRESENTS

THE GOLDEN YEARS OF SCIENCE FICTION

SECOND SERIES

28 STORIES AND NOVELLAS

Edited by ISAAC ASIMOV AND MARTIN H. GREENBERG

BONANZA BOOKS
NEW YORK

This 1983 edition is published by Bonanza Books, distributed by
Crown Publishers, Inc., by arrangement with Daw Books, Inc.

This book was previously published as two separate works entitled
Isaac Asimov Presents the Great SF Stories 3 (1941) and
Isaac Asimov Presents the Great SF Stories 4 (1942)

Manufactured in the United States of America

Library of Congress Cataloging in Publication Data
Main entry under title:

Isaac Asimov presents the golden years of science fiction.

  Previously published as two separate works entitled: Isaac Asimov
presents the great sf stories, III, 1941; and Isaac Asimov presents the
great sf stories, IV. 1942.
  1. Science fiction, American.   I. Asimov, Isaac, 1920–
PS648.S31794   1983   813'.0876'08   83-3840
ISBN: 0-517-413671

h g f e d c b a

Foreword

In the annals of science fiction the 1940s have come to be regarded as the Golden Era of the great sci-fi magazines. In this outstanding anthology, originally published as two separate volumes, Isaac Asimov and Martin H. Greenberg have brought together the truly outstanding stories and novellas published in the years 1941 and 1942. Each one is a fine and enduring example of creative imagination and vivid storytelling. They are all truly memorable classics.

—NRK

ACKNOWLEDGMENTS

Contents

Introduction

In the world outside reality, 1941 was yet another very bad year. On February 9 Field Marshal Rommel led his troops from Italy to Africa, where they soon began to blunt the British offensive designed to protect the Suez Canal. German U-boat attacks increased in intensity all through the year. On April 13 the U.S.S.R. signed an agreement with Japan promising neutrality and tacitly allowing Japanese expansionism to continue. The House of Commons was destroyed in a German air raid on May 10, the same day that Rudolf Hess flew on his mysterious "peace" mission to England. On May 24 the German pocket battleship *Bismarck* sank *H.M.S. Hood* and was itself sunk three days later by the Royal Navy.

Not unexpectedly, except by the Russians, Germany invaded the Soviet Union on June 22 in one of the most fateful moves of the war; by the end of the month they had control of a large portion of European Russia and the Ukraine. On August 11, Churchill and Roosevelt signed the "Atlantic Charter" on a ship in the ocean of the same name. On September 8, Leningrad was surrounded and a long siege had begun—German armies were sixty miles from Moscow by October 16. The Russian counteroffensive began on November 29.

On December 7, "a day that will live in infamy," Japanese carrier-based aircraft attacked Pearl Harbor and surrounding military installations. The United States declared war on Japan one day later and on Germany and Italy on the 11th, one day after *H.M.S. Prince of*

Wales and *Repulse* were sunk in the Indian Ocean. Hong Kong surrendered to the Japanese on Christmas Day.

During 1941 Edmund Wilson published his major study of utopian and socialist thought, *To The Finland Station.* The "Manhattan Project" leading to the atomic bomb was initiated at the end of the year. Léger painted "Divers Against a Yellow Background." Bruce Smith of the University of Minnesota won the Heisman Trophy as college football's outstanding player. Benjamin Britten composed his "Violin Concerto." *The Fall of Paris* by Ilya Ehrenburg was published. Brecht's *Mother Courage and Her Children* was produced. Minnesota repeated as National College Football Champion. The year's outstanding films included *Citizen Kane, How Green Was My Valley, the Big Store* (the Marx Brothers' last film) and *the First of the Few,* one of the last films of Leslie Howard, who was to die over the English Channel.

The population of the United States was 131,000,000; China's was estimated at 450,000,000. The record for the mile run was *still* the 4:06:4 set in 1937 by Sydney Wooderson of Great Britain. Nathaniel Micklem published *The Theology of Politics.* William Walton's "Scapino Overture" was performed. Bobby Riggs won the United States Tennis Association Championship. F. Scott Fitzgerald published *The Last Tycoon.* Noel Coward's *Blithe Spirit* was a hit. Whirlaway, with Eddie Arcaro on board, won the Kentucky Derby, while Wisconsin had the top basketball team. There were 38,800,000 private cars in the United States. The Yankees won the series from the Dodgers, Ted Williams led the majors with 37 home runs and an incredible .406 average, but Joe DiMaggio won the Most Valuable Player Award in the American League. Franze Werfel's *The Song of Bernadette* was published. Gary Cooper (for *Sergeant York)* and Joan Fontaine (for *Suspicion)* won Academy Awards. Joe Louis was still the heavyweight champion, but he almost lost the title to Billy Conn, saving his crown with a late-round knockout.

Death took Henri Bergson, James Joyce, Sherwood Anderson, Virginia Woolf, Kaiser Whilhelm II and Ignaz Paderewski.

Mel Brooks was still Melvin Kaminsky.

But in the real world, it was a super year.

In the real world the third World Science Fiction Convention (the Denvention) was held in Denver, Colorado, continuing (you should excuse the expression) its trek westward. The first "Boskone" was held in Boston. In the real world "Methuselah's Children" by Robert A. Heinlein and the long awaited "Second Stage Lensman" by "Doc" Smith appeared in *Astounding.*

More wondrous and sad things occurred in the real world: *Stirring*

Introduction

Science Stories and *Cosmic Stories* began their too brief lives, but *Comet Stories* died. *Unknown* changed its name to *Unknown Worlds* without damage or effect.

But as compensation, many more wonderful people made their maiden flights into reality: in January—Fredric Brown with "Not Yet The End"; in February—Cleve Cartmill with "Oscar," William Morrison with "Bad Medicine," and Damon Knight with "Resilience"; in May—Wilson Tucker (aka Bob) with "Interstellar Way-Station"; and in November—Ray Bradbury with the co-authored "Pendulum."

On August 1, while riding the subway to visit John Campbell, Isaac Asimov first thought about the fall and rise of intergalactic empires (with a little help from Gibbons) and the first hint of the Foundation rose mistily in his mind.

And distant wings were beating as Gregory Benford and Jane Gaskell were born.

Let us travel back to that honored year of 1941 and enjoy the best stories that the real world bequeathed to us.

And now on to 1942...

In the world outside reality, the year started out badly and then improved. On January 10 the Japanese invaded the East Indies and on the 19th launched their invasion of Burma. Even more ominously, Rommel's Africa Corps opened a new drive toward Egypt on January 21, threatening the entire Allied position in North Africa, and the British suffered another defeat when Singapore surrendered on February 15, two weeks after Vidkun Quisling was made Premier of Norway and added another word to the language of collaboration.

Japan continued its advance in the Pacific Theatre with the surrender of Bataan on April 9, the taking of Mandalay on May 1, and the surrender of the gallant garrison at Corregidor on May 6. Only the mixed results achieved by the U.S. Navy at the Battle of Midway on and about June 3 prevented an unbroken string of Japanese successes.

Rommel appeared invincible in North Africa as Tobruk fell on June 21, but then a series of events heralded the beginning of the end for the Axis forces: U.S. troops landed on Guadalcanal in the Pacific on August 7, the Germans' major drive against Stalingrad was bloodily stalled as the fall wore on and on October 23 the British counterattacked Rommel at El Alamein—by November 4 the Germans were in retreat, their fate sealed four days later when Allied forces landed in North Africa. By November 19 the German General Staff saw the handwriting on the wall.

On December 2, beneath the University of Chicago, a refugee scientist named Enrico Fermi achieved the first controlled chain reaction inside the world's first nuclear reactor, a major step on the road to the atomic age.

During 1942 John Steinbeck published *The Moon is Down,* while Dmitri Shostakovich composed the *Seventh Symphony.* The great Ted Williams led the major leagues in batting with a .351 average. The top films of the year were *How Green Was My Valley, Holiday Inn* and *Mrs. Miniver.*

The Beveridge Plan, which led directly to the present welfare state in Great Britain was published, as was James Burnham's classic study, *The Managerial Revolution.* Aaron Copland composed his beautiful *Lincoln Portrait* and Shut Out won the Kentucky Derby in a major upset. Albert Camus saw his *L'Etranger (The Stranger)* published and watched as it became one of the bibles of alienated man.

Some things did not change. Joe Louis was still the heavyweight boxing champion of the world and the world record for the mile run was still the 4:06.4 set by Sydney Wooderson in 1937.

1942 proved to be a remarkable year in science. In addition to Fermi's accomplishment, the first V-2 rocket was successfully tested by the Germans, while in the United States ENIAC (Electronic Numerical Integrator and Computer), the world's first real computer was assembled.

Greer Garson and James Cagney won Academy Awards. The Washington Redskins won the National Football League Championship and John Piper painted *Windsor Castle.* C.S. Lewis published *The Screwtape Letters.* The St. Louis Cardinals defeated the New York Yankees four games to one to take the World Series. Graham Sutherland painted his famous and non-ideological *Red Landscape.* T.S. Eliot published *Little Gidding,* while Erich Fromme's study *Escape From Freedom* seemed both appropriate and out of place in that totalitarian year. Stanford was the NCAA Basketball Champion.

Mel Brooks was still Melvin Kaminsky.

In the real world it was another good year, even though most of the top writers (and many fans) would soon be soldiers or working in war-related industries and/or research.

No new science fiction magazines were born, but all of the existing American ones made it through the year with the exception of *Stirring Science Stories,* which expired in March.

In the real world, more important people made their maiden voyages into reality: Hal Clement with "Proof" and Robert Abernathy with "Heritage" in June; in October, George O. Smith with "QRM-

Interplanetary," and in December, E(dna) Mayne Hull with "The Flight That Failed."

More wondrous things happened in the real world: Robert A. Heinlein (as Anson MacDonald) published "Beyond this Horizon" and "Waldo," Jack Williamson (as Will Stewart) published "Collision Orbit," the first of his excellent *Seetee* stories and Isaac Asimov began his classic *Foundation* series.

Death took Alexander Belyaev, one of the pioneer Russian science fiction writers.

But distant wings were beating as C. J. Cherryh, Samuel R. Delany, Langdon Jones, David Ketterer, Franz Rottensteiner, Douglas Trumbull, William Joe Watkins and Chelsea Quinn Yarbro were born.

Let us travel back to that honored year of 1942 and enjoy the best stories that the real world bequeathed to us.

ERRATA DEPARTMENT:

We would like to thank our readers for letting us know that five of the stories by Robert A. Heinlein that could not be included in Volumes 2 and 3 of this series are not in his *The Past Through Tomorrow*. These stories can be found in the following collections:

"And He Built a Crooked House" and "They"—THE UNPLEASANT PROFESSION OF JONATHAN HOAG
"Universe"—part of ORPHANS OF THE SKY
"Solution Unsatisfactory"—THE WORLDS OF ROBERT A. HEINLEIN
"By His Bootstraps"—THE MENACE FROM EARTH

ISAAC ASIMOV

PRESENTS

THE GOLDEN YEARS OF SCIENCE FICTION

And now on to 1942...

MECHANICAL MICE

Astounding Science Fiction
January

by Maurice A. Hugi
(Eric Frank Russell, 1905-1978)

The late Eric Frank Russell is the most underappreciated of the major science fiction writers of the "second generation" (his first story was published in 1937). His 1939 Unknown *novel* Sinister Barrier *thrust him into prominence for a time, and he did win the Hugo Award in 1955 for his story "Allamagoosa," but he has been badly neglected by the academic community.*

This clever story caused some confusion because Maurice G. Hugi was a real person, but the story was Russell's.

(I never could understand the trick of using pseudonyms. I know that there are reasons for it, like not wanting the neighbors to know you are disgracing yourself by displaying an imagination, or not wanting the Dean to know you are making money on the side—but, my goodness, you lose credit. For instance, I enormously enjoyed "The Mechanical Mice" when I first read it and I always thought of it as a beautifully crafted story and I never knew E. F. Russell had written it until quite recently. Terrible—I admit I wrote the Lucky Starr stories under a Paul French pseudonym, but I had over-riding reasons for that, and I put them under my own name as soon as I could. But then, I am so self-appreciative; I would never consent to give up an atom of credit.—I. A.)

It's asking for trouble to fool around with the unknown. Burman did it! Now there are quite a lot of people who hate like the very devil anything that clicks, ticks, emits whirring sounds, or generally behaves like an asthmatic alarm clock. They've got mechanophobia. Dan Burman gave it to them.

13

Who hasn't heard of the Burman Bullfrog Battery? The same chap! He puzzled it out from first to last and topped it with his now world-famous slogan: "Power in Your Pocket." It was no mean feat to concoct a thing the size of a cigarette packet that would pour out a hundred times as much energy as its most efficient competitor. Burman differed from everyone else in thinking it a mean feat.

Burman looked me over very carefully, then said, "When that technical journal sent you around to see me twelve years ago, you listened sympathetically. You didn't treat me as if I were an idle dreamer or a congenital idiot. You gave me a decent write-up and started all the publicity that eventually made me much money."

"Not because I loved you," I assured him, "but because I was honestly convinced that your battery was good."

"Maybe." He studied me in a way that conveyed he was anxious to get something off his chest. "We've been pretty pally since that time. We've filled in some idle hours together, and I feel that you're the one of my few friends to whom I can make a seemingly silly confession."

"Go ahead," I encouraged. We had been pretty pally, as he'd said. It was merely that we liked each other, found each other congenial. He was a clever chap, Burman, but there was nothing of the pedantic professor about him. Fortyish, normal, neat, he might have been a fashionable dentist to judge by appearances.

"Bill," he said, very seriously, "I didn't invent that damn battery."

"No?"

"No!" he confirmed. "I pinched the idea. What makes it madder is that I wasn't quite sure of what I was stealing and, crazier still, I don't know from whence I stole it."

"Which is as plain as a pikestaff," I commented.

"That's nothing. After twelve years of careful, exacting work I've built something else. It must be the most complicated thing in creation." He banged a fist on his knee, and his voice rose complainingly. "And now that I've done it, I don't know what I've done."

"Surely when an inventor experiments he knows what he's doing?"

"Not me!" Burman was amusingly lugubrious. "I've invented only one thing in my life, and that was more by accident than by good judgment." He perked up. "But that one thing was the key to a million notions. It gave me the battery. It has nearly given me things of greater importance. On several occasions it has nearly, but not quite, placed within my inadequate hands and half-understanding mind plans that would alter this world far beyond your conception." Leaning forward to lend emphasis to his speech, he said, "Now it has given me a mystery that has cost me twelve years of work and a nice sum of money. I finished it last night. I don't know what the devil it is."

"Perhaps if I had a look at it—"

"Just what I'd like you to do." He switched rapidly to mounting enthusiasm. "It's a beautiful job of work, even though I say so myself. Bet you that you can't say what it is, or what it's supposed to do."

"Assuming it can do something," I put in.

"Yes," he agreed. "But I'm positive it has a function of some sort." Getting up, he opened a door. "Come along."

It was a stunner. The thing was a metal box with a glossy, rhodium-plated surface. In general size and shape it bore a faint resemblance to an upended coffin, and had the same brooding, ominous air of a casket waiting for its owner to give up the ghost.

There were a couple of small glass windows in its front through which could be seen a multitude of wheels as beautifully finished as those in a first-class watch. Elsewhere, several tiny lenses stared with sphinx-like indifference. There were three small trapdoors in one side, two in the other, and a large one in the front. From the top, two knobbed rods of metal stuck up like goat's horns, adding a satanic touch to the thing's vague air of yearning for midnight burial.

"It's an automatic layer-outer," I suggested, regarding the contraption with frank dislike. I pointed to one of the trapdoors. "You shove the shroud in there, and the corpse comes out the other side reverently composed and ready wrapped."

"So you don't like its air, either," Burman commented. He lugged open a drawer in a nearby tier, hauled out a mass of drawings. "These are its innards. It has an electric circuit, valves, condensers, and something that I can't quite understand, but which I suspect to be a tiny, extremely efficient electric furnace. It has parts I recognize as cog-cutters and pinion-shapers. It embodies several small-scale multiple stampers, apparently for dealing with sheet metal. There are vague suggestions of an assembly line ending in that large compartment shielded by the door in front. Have a look at the drawings yourself. You can see it's an extremely complicated device for manufacturing something only little less complicated."

The drawings showed him to be right. But they didn't show everything. An efficient machine designer could correctly have deduced the gadget's function if given complete details. Burman admitted this, saying that some parts he had made "on the spur of the moment," while others he had been "impelled to draw." Short of pulling the machine to pieces, there was enough data to whet the curiosity, but not enough to satisfy it.

"Start the damn thing and see what it does."

"I've tried," said Burman. "It won't start. There's no starting handle, nothing to suggest how it can be started. I tried everything I could think of, without result. The electric circuit ends in those antennae at the top, and I even sent current through those, but nothing happened."

"Maybe it's a self-starter," I ventured. Staring at it, a thought struck me. "Timed," I added.

"Eh?"

"Set for an especial time. When the dread hour strikes, it'll go of its own accord, like a bomb."

"Don't be so melodramatic," said Burman, uneasily.

Bending down, he peered into one of the tiny lenses.

"Bz-z-z!" murmured the contraption in a faint undertone that was almost inaudible.

Burman jumped a foot. Then he backed away, eyed the thing warily, turned his glance at me.

"Did you hear that?"

"Sure!" Getting the drawings, I mauled them around. That little lens took some finding, but it was there all right. It has a selenium cell behind it. "An eye," I said. "It saw you, and reacted. So it isn't dead even if it does just stand there seeing no evil, hearing no evil, speaking no evil." I put a white handkerchief against the lens.

"Bz-z-z!" repeated the coffin, emphatically.

Taking the handkerchief, Burman put it against the other lenses. Nothing happened. Not a sound was heard, not a funeral note. Just nothing.

"It beats me," he confessed.

I'd got pretty fed up by this time. If the crazy article had performed, I'd have written it up and maybe I'd have started another financial snowball rolling for Burman's benefit. But you can't do anything with a box that buzzes whenever it feels temperamental. Firm treatment was required, I decided.

"You've been all nice and mysterious about how you got

hold of this brain wave," I said. "Why can't you go to the same source for information about what it's supposed to be?"

"I'll tell you—or, rather, I'll show you."

From his safe, Burman dragged out a box, and from the box he produced a gadget. This one was far simpler than the useless mass of works over by the wall. It looked just like one of those old-fashioned crystal sets, except that the crystal was very big, very shiny, and was set in a horizontal vacuum tube. There was the same single dial, the same cat's whisker. Attached to the lot by a length of flex was what might have been a pair of headphones, except in place of the phones were a pair of polished, smoothly rounded copper circles shaped to fit outside the ears and close against the skull.

"My one and only invention." said Burman, not without a justifiable touch of pride.

"What is it?"

"A time-traveling device."

"Ha, ha!" My laugh was very sour. I'd read about such things. In fact, I'd written about them. They were bunkum. Nobody could travel through time, either backward or forward. "Let me see you grow hazy and vanish into the future."

"I'll show you something very soon." Burman said it with assurance I didn't like. He said it with the positive air of a man who knows darned well that he can do something that everybody else knows darned well can't be done. He pointed to the crystal set. "It wasn't discovered at the first attempt. Thousands must have tried and failed. I was the lucky one. I must have picked a peculiarly individualistic crystal; I still don't know how it does what it does; I've never been able to repeat its performance even with a crystal apparently identical."

"And it enables you to travel in time?"

"Only forward. It won't take me backward, not even as much as one day. But it can carry me forward an immense distance, perhaps to the very crack of doom, perhaps everlastingly through infinity."

I had him now! I'd got him firmly entangled in his own absurdities. My loud chuckle was something I couldn't control.

"You can travel forward, but not backward, not even one day back. Then how the devil can you return to the present once you've gone into the future?"

"Because I never leave the present," he replied, evenly. "I don't partake of the future. I merely survey it from the vantage point of the present. All the same, it is time-traveling in the correct sense of the term." He seated himself. "Look here, Bill, what *are* you?"

"Who, me?"

"Yes, what are you." He went on to provide the answer. "Your name is Bill. You're a body and a mind. Which of them is Bill?"

"Both," I said, positively.

"True—but they're different parts of you. They're not the same even though they go around like Siamese twins." His voice grew serious. "Your body moves always in the present, the dividing line between the past and the future. But your mind is more free. It can think, and is in the present. It can remember, and at once is in the past. It can imagine, and at once is in the future, in its own choice of all the possible futures. *Your mind can travel through time!*"

He'd outwitted me. I could find points to pick upon and argue about, but I knew that fundamentally he was right. I'd not looked at it from this angle before, but he was correct in saying that anyone could travel through time within the limits of his own memory and imagination. At that very moment I could go back twelve years and see him in my mind's eyes as a younger man, paler, thinner, more excitable, not so cool and self-possessed. The picture was as perfect as my memory was excellent. For that brief spell I was twelve years back in all but the flesh.

"I call this thing a psychophone," Burman went on. "When you imagine what the future will be like, you make a characteristic choice of all the logical possibilities, you pick your favorite from a multitude of likely futures. The psychophone, somehow—the Lord alone knows how—tunes you into future *reality*. It makes you depict within your mind the future as it will be shaped in actuality, eliminating all the alternatives that will not occur."

"An imagination-stimulator, a dream-machine," I scoffed, not feeling as sure of myself as I sounded. "How do you know it's giving you the McCoy?"

"Consistency," he answered, gravely. "It repeats the same features and the same trends far too often for the phenomena to be explained as mere coincidence. Besides," he waved a persuasive hand, "I got the battery from the future. It works, doesn't it?"

"It does," I agreed, reluctantly. I pointed to his psychophone. "I, too, may travel in time. How about letting me have a try? Maybe I'll solve your mystery for you."

"You can try if you wish," he replied, quite willingly. He pulled a chair into position. "Sit here, and I'll let you peer into the future."

Clipping the headband over my cranium, and fitting the copper rings against my skull where it sprouted ears, Burman connected his psychophone to the mains, switched it on; or rather he did some twiddling that I assumed was a mode of switching on.

"All you have to do," he said, "is close your eyes, compose yourself, then try and permit your imagination to wander into the future."

He meddled with the cat's whisker. A couple of times he said, "Ah!" And each time he said it I got a peculiar dithery feeling around my unfortunate ears. After a few seconds of this, he drew it out to, "A-a-ah!" I played unfair, and peeped beneath lowered lids. The crystal was glowing like rats' eyes in a forgotten cellar. A furtive crimson.

Closing my own optics, I let my mind wander. Something was flowing between those copper electrodes, a queer, indescribable something that felt with stealthy fingers at some secret portion of my brain. I got the asinine notion that they were the dexterous digits of a yet-to-be-born magician who was going to shout, "Presto!" and pull my abused lump of think-meat out of a thirtieth-century hat—assuming they'd wear hats in the thirtieth century.

What was it like, or, rather, what would it be like in the thirtieth century? Would there be retrogression? Would humanity again be composed of scowling, fur-kilted creatures lurking in caves? Or had progress continued—perhaps even to the development of men like gods?

Then it happened! I swear it! I pictured, quite voluntarily, a savage, and then a huge-domed individual with glittering eyes—the latter being my version of the ugliness we hope to attain. Right in the middle of this erratic dreaming, those weird fingers warped my brain, dissolved my phantoms, and replaced them with a dictated picture which I witnessed with all the helplessness and clarity of a nightmare.

I saw a fat man spouting. He was quite an ordinary man as far as looks went. In fact, he was so normal that he looked henpecked. But he was attired in a Roman toga, and he wore a small, black box where his laurel wreath ought to have been. His audience was similarly dressed, and all were balancing their boxes like a convention of fish porters. What

Fatty was orating sounded gabble to me, but he said his piece
as if he meant it.

The crowd was in the open air, with great, curved rows of
seats visible in the background. Presumably an outside auditorium of some sort. Judging by the distance of the back
rows, it must have been a devil of a size. Far behind its
sweeping ridge a great edifice jutted into the sky, a cubical
erection with walls of glossy squares, like an immense glass-
house.

"F'wot?" bellowed Fatty, with obvious heat. "Wuk, wuk,
wuk, mor, noon'n'ni'! Bok onned, ord this, ord that." He
stuck an indignant finger against the mysterious object on his
cranium. "Bok onned, wuk, wuk, wuk. F'wot?" he glared
around. "F'nix!" The crowd murmured approval somewhat
timidly. But it was enough for Fatty. Making up his mind, he
flourished a plump fist and shouted, "Th'ell wit'm!" Then he
tore his box from his pate.

Nobody said anything, nobody moved. Dumb and wide-
eyed, the crowd just stood and stared as if paralyzed by the
sight of a human being sans box. Something with a long,
slender streamlined body and broad wings soared gracefully
upward in the distance, swooped over the auditorium, but still
the crowd neither moved nor uttered a sound.

A smile of triumph upon his broad face, Fatty bawled,
"Lem see'm make wuk now! Lem see'm—"

He got no further. With a rush of mistiness from its tail,
but in perfect silence, the soaring thing hovered and sent
down a spear of faint, silvery light. The light touched Fatty.
He rotted where he stood, like a victim of ultra-rapid leprosy.
He rotted, collapsed, crumbled within his sagging clothes, became dust as once he had been dust. It was horrible.

The watchers did not flee in utter panic; not one expression
of fear, hatred or disgust came from their tightly closed lips.
In perfect silence they stood there, staring, just staring, like a
horde of wooden soldiers. The thing in the sky circled to survey its handiwork, then dived low over the mob, a stubby antenna in its prow sparking furiously. As one man, the crowd
turned left. As one man it commenced to march, left, right,
left, right.

Tearing off the headband, I told Burman what I'd seen, or
what his contraption had persuaded me to think that I'd seen.
"What the deuce did it mean?"

"Automatons," he murmured. "Glasshouses and reaction
ships." He thumbed through a big diary filled with notations

in his own hands. "Ah, yes, looks like you were very early in the thirtieth century. Unrest was persistent for twenty years prior to the Antibox Rebellion."

"What rebellion?"

"The Antibox—the revolt of the automatons against the thirty-first century Technocrats. Jackson-Dkj-99717, a successful and cunning schemer with a warped box, secretly warped hundreds of other boxes, and eventually led the rebels to victory in 3047. His great-grandson, a greedy, thick-headed individual, caused the rebellion of the Boxless Freemen against his own clique of Jacksocrats."

I gaped at this recital, then said, "The way you tell it makes it sound like history."

"Of course it's history," he asserted. "History that is yet to be." He was pensive for a while. "Studying the future will seem a weird process to you, but it appears quite a normal procedure to me. I've done it for years, and maybe familiarity has bred contempt. Trouble is though, that selectivity is poor. You can pick on some especial period twenty times in succession, but you'll never find yourself in the same month, or even the same year. In fact, you're fortunate if you strike twice in the same decade. Result is that my data is very erratic."

"I can imagine that," I told him. "A good guesser can guess the correct time to within a minute or two, but never to within ten or even fifty seconds."

"Quite!" he responded. "So the hell of it has been that mine was the privilege of watching the panorama of the future, but in a manner so sketchy that I could not grasp its prizes. Once I was lucky enough to watch a twenty-fifth century power pack assembled from first to last. I got every detail before I lost the scene which I've never managed to hit upon again. But I made that power pack—and you know the result."

"So that's how you concocted your famous battery!"

"It is! But mine, good as it may be, isn't as good as the one I saw. Some slight factor is missing." His voice was suddenly tight when he added, "I missed something because I had to miss it!"

"Why?" I asked, completely puzzled.

"Because history, past or future, permits no glaring paradox. Because, having snatched this battery from the twenty-fifth century, I am recorded in that age as the twentieth-century inventor of the thing. They've made a mild improvement to it in those five centuries, but that improvement was automatically withheld from me. Future history is as fixed and unalterable by those of the present time as is the history of the past."

"Then," I demanded, "explain to me that complicated contraption which does nothing but say *bz-z-z.*"

"Damn it" he said, with open ire, "that's just what's making me crazy! It can't be a paradox, it just can't." Then, more carefully, "So it must be a seeming paradox."

"O.K. You tell me how to market a seeming paradox, and the commercial uses thereof, and I'll give it a first-class write up."

Ignoring my sarcasm, he went on, "I tried to probe the future as far as human minds can probe. I saw nothing, nothing but the vastness of a sterile floor upon which sat a queer machine, gleaming there in silent, solitary majesty. Somehow, it seemed aware of my scrutiny across the gulf of countless ages. It held my attention with a power almost hypnotic. For more than a day, for a full thirty hours, I kept that vision without losing it—the longest time I have ever kept a future scene."

"Well?"

"I drew it. I made complete drawings of it, performing the task with all the easy confidence of a trained machine draughtsman. Its insides could not be seen, but somehow they came to me, somehow I knew them. I lost the scene at four o'clock in the morning, finding myself with masses of very complicated drawings, a thumping head, heavy-lidded eyes, and a half-scared feeling in my heart." He was silent for a short time. "A year later I plucked up courage and started to build the thing I had drawn. It cost me a hell of a lot of time and hell of a lot of money. But I did it—it's finished."

"And all it does is buzz," I remarked, with genuine sympathy.

"Yes," he sighed, doubtfully.

There was nothing more to be said. Burman gazed moodily at the wall, his mind far, far away. I fiddled aimlessly with the copper ear-pieces of the psychophone. My imagination, I reckoned, was as good as anyone's, but for the life of me I could neither imagine nor suggest a profitable market for a metal coffin filled with watchmaker's junk. No, not even if it did make odd noises.

A faint, smooth *whir* came from the coffin. It was a new sound that swung us round to face it pop-eyed. *Whir-r-r!* it went again. I saw finely machined wheels spin behind the window in its front.

"Good heavens!" said Burman.

Bz-z-z! Whir-r! Click! The whole affair suddenly slid side-wise on its hidden casters.

The devil you know isn't half so frightening as the devil you don't. I don't mean that this sudden demonstration of life and motion got us scared, but it certainly made us leery, and our hearts put in an extra dozen bumps a minute. This coffin-thing was, or might be, a devil we didn't know. So we stood there, side by side, gazing at it fascinatedly, feeling apprehensive of we knew not what.

Motion ceased after the thing had slid two feet. It stood there, silent, imperturbable, its front lenses eyeing us with glassy lack of expression. Then it slid another two feet. Another stop. More meaningless contemplation. After that, a swifter and farther slide that brought it right up to the laboratory table. At that point it ceased moving, began to emit varied but synchronized ticks like those of a couple of sympathetic grandfather clocks.

Burman said, quietly, "Something's going to happen!"

If the machine could have spoken it would have taken the words right out of his mouth. He'd hardly uttered the sentence when a trapdoor in the machine's side fell open, a jointed, metallic arm snaked cautiously through the opening and reached for a marine chronometer standing on the table.

With a surprised oath, Burman dashed forward to rescue the chronometer. He was too late. The arm grabbed it, whisked it into the machine, the trapdoor shut with a hard snap, like the vicious clash of a sprung bear trap. Simultaneously, another trapdoor in the front flipped open, another jointed arm shot out and in again, spearing with ultra-rapid motion too fast to follow. That trapdoor also snapped shut, leaving Burman gaping down at his torn clothing from which his expensive watch and equally expensive gold chain had been ripped away.

"Good heavens!" said Burman, backing from the machine.

We stood looking at it a while. It didn't move again, just posed there ticking steadily as if ruminating upon its welcome meal. Its lenses looked at us with all the tranquil lack of interest of a well-fed cow. I got the idiotic notion that it was happily digesting a mess of cogs, pinions and wheels.

Because its subtle air of menace seemed to have faded away, or maybe because we sensed its entire preoccupation with the task in hand, we made an effort to rescue Burman's valuable timepiece. Burman tugged mightily at the trapdoor

through which his watch had gone, but failed to move it. I
tugged with him, without result. The thing was sealed as solidly as if welded in. A large screwdriver failed to pry it open.
A crowbar, or a good jimmy would have done the job, but at
that point Burman decided that he didn't want to damage the
machine which had cost him more than the watch.

Tick-tick-tick! went the coffin, stolidly. We were back
where we'd started, playing with our fingers, and no wiser
than before. There was nothing to be done, and I felt that the
accursed contraption knew it. So it stood there, gaping
through its lenses, and jeered *tick-tick-tick.* From its belly, or
where its belly would have been if it'd had one, a slow
warmth radiated. According to Burman's drawings, that was
the location of the tiny electric furnace.

The thing was functioning; there could be no doubt about
that! If Burman felt the same way as I did, he must have
been pretty mad. There we stood, like a couple of prize
boobs, not knowing what the machine was supposed to do,
and all the time it was doing under our very eyes whatever
it was designed to do.

From where was it drawing its power? Were those antennae sticking like horns from its head busily sucking current
from the atmosphere? Or was it, perhaps, absorbing radio
power? Or did it have internal energy of its own? All the evidence suggested that it was making something, giving birth to
something, but giving birth to what?

Tick-tick-tick! was the only reply.

Our questions were still unanswered, our curiosity was still
unsatisfied, and the machine was still ticking industriously at
the hour of midnight. We surrendered the problem until next
morning. Burman locked and double-locked his laboratory
before we left.

Police officer Burke's job was a very simple one. All he
had to do was walk around and around the block, keeping a
wary eye on the stores in general and the big jewel depot in
particular, phoning headquarters once per hour from the post
at the corner.

Night work suited Burke's taciturn disposition. He could
wander along, communing with himself, with nothing to
bother him or divert him from his inward ruminations. In
that particular section nothing ever happened at night,
nothing.

Stopping outside the gem-bedecked window, he gazed
through the glass and the heavy grille behind it to where a

low-power bulb shed light over the massive safe. There was a rajah's ransom in there. The guard, the grille, the automatic alarms and sundry ingenious traps preserved it from the adventurous fingers of anyone who wanted to ransom a rajah. Nobody had made the brash attempt in twenty years. Nobody had even made a try for the contents of the grille-protected window.

He glanced upward at a faintly luminescent path of cloud behind which lay the hidden moon. Turning, he strolled on. A cat sneaked past him, treading cautiously, silently, and hugging the angle of the wall. His sharp eyes detected its slinking shape even in the nighttime gloom, but he ignored it and progressed to the corner.

Back of him, the cat came below the window through which he just had stared. It stopped, one forefoot half-raised, its ears cocked forward. Then it flattened belly-low against the concrete, its burning orbs wide, alert, intent. Its tail waved slowly from side to side.

Something small and bright came skittering toward it, moving with mouselike speed and agility close in the angle of the wall. The cat tensed as the object came nearer. Suddenly, the thing was within range, and the cat pounced with lithe eagerness. Hungry paws dug at a surface that was not soft and furry, but hard, bright, and slippery. The thing darted around like a clockwork toy as the cat vainly tried to hold it. Finally, with an angry snarl, the cat swiped it viciously, knocking it a couple of yards where it rolled onto its back and emitted softly protesting clicks and tiny, urgent impulses that its feline attacker could not sense.

Gaining the gutter with a single leap, the cat crouched again. Something else was coming. The cat muscled, its eyes glowed. Another object slightly similar to the curious thing it had just captured, but a little bit bigger, a fraction noisier, and much different in shape. It resembled a small, gold-plated cylinder with a conical front from which projected a slender blade, and it slid along swiftly on invisible wheels.

Again the cat leaped. Down on the corner, Burke heard its brief shriek and following gurgle. The sound didn't bother Burke—he'd heard cats and rats and other vermin make all sorts of queer noises in the night. Phlegmatically, he continued on his beat.

Three quarters of an hour later, Police Officer Burke had worked his way around to the fatal spot. Putting his flash on the body, he rolled the supine animal over with his foot. Its throat was cut. Its throat had been cut with an utter savagery that had half-severed its head from its body. Burke scowled down at it. He was no lover of cats himself, but he found difficulty in imagining anyone hating like that!

"Somebody," he muttered, "wants flaying alive."

His big foot shoved the dead cat back into the gutter where street cleaners could cart it away in the morning. He turned his attention to the window, saw the light still glowing upon the untouched safe. His mind was still on the cat while his eyes looked in and said that something was wrong. Then he dragged his attention back to business, realized what was wrong, and sweated at every pore. It wasn't the safe, it was the window.

In front of the window the serried trays of valuable rings still gleamed undisturbed. To the right, the silverwares still shone untouched. But on the left had been a small display of delicate and extremely expensive watches. They were no longer here, not one of them. He remembered that right in front had rested a neat, beautiful calendar-chronometer priced at a year's salary. That, too, was gone.

The beam of his flash trembled as he tried the gate, found it fast, secure. The door behind it was firmly locked. The transom was closed, its heavy wire guard still securely fixed. He went over the window, eventually found a small, neat hole, about two inches in diameter, down in the corner on the side nearest the missing display.

Burke's curse was explosive as he turned and ran to the corner. His hand shook with indignation while it grabbed the telephone from its box. Getting headquarters, he recited his story. He thought he'd a good idea of what had happened, fancied he'd read once of a similar stunt being pulled elsewhere.

Looks like they cut a disk with a rotary diamond, lifted it out with a suction cup, then fished through the hole with a telescopic rod." He listened a moment, then said. "Yes, yes. That's just what gets me—the rings are worth ten times as much."

His still-startled eyes looked down the street while he paid attention to the voice at the other end of the line. The eyes wandered slowly, descended, found the gutter, remained fixed on the dim shape lying therein. Another dead cat! Still clinging to his phone, Burke moved out as far as the cord would allow, extended a boot, rolled the cat away from the curb. The flash settled on it. Just like the other—ear to ear!

"And listen," he shouted into the phone, "some maniac's wandering around slaughtering cats."

Replacing the phone, he hurried back to the maltreated window, stood guard in front of it until the police car rolled up. Four men piled out.

The first said, "Cats! I'll say somebody's got it in for cats! We passed two a couple of blocks away. They were bang in the middle of the street, flat in the headlights, and had been damn near guillotined. Their bodies were still warm."

The second grunted, approached the window, stared at the small, neat hole, and said, "The mob that did this would be too cute to leave a print."

"They weren't too cute to leave the rings," growled Burke.

"Maybe you've got something there," conceded the other. "If they've left the one, they might have left the other. We'll test for prints, anyway."

A taxi swung into the dark street, pulled up behind the police car. An elegantly dressed, fussy, and very agitated individual got out, rushed up to the waiting group. Keys jangled in his pale, moist hand.

"Maley, the manager—you phoned me," he explained, breathlessly. "Gentlemen, this is terrible, terrible! The window show is worth thousands, thousands! What a loss, what a loss!"

"How about letting us in?" asked one of the policemen, calmly.

"Of course, of course."

Jerkily, he opened the gate, unlocked the door, using about six keys for the job. They walked inside. Maley switched on the lights, stuck his head between the plateglass shelves, surveyed the depleted window.

"My watches, my watches," he groaned.

"It's awful, it's awful!" said one of the policemen, speaking with beautiful solemnity. He favored his companions with a sly wink.

Maley leaned farther over, the better to inspect an empty corner. "All gone, all gone," he moaned, "all my show of the finest makes in—*Yeeouw!*" His yelp made them jump. Maley bucked as he tried to force himself through the obstructing shelves toward the grille and the window beyond it. "My watch! My own watch!"

The others tiptoed, stared over his shoulders, saw the gold buckle of a black velvet fob go through the hole in the window. Burke was the first outside, his ready flash searching the concrete. Then he spotted the watch. It was moving rapidly along, hugging the angle of the wall, but it stopped dead as his beam settled upon it. He fancied he saw something else, equally bright and metalilc, scoot swiftly into the darkness beyond the circle of his beam.

Picking up the watch, Burke stood and listened. The noises of the others coming out prevented him from hearing clearly, but he could have sworn he'd heard a tiny whirring noise, and a swift, juicy ticking that was not coming from the instrument in his hand. Must have been only his worried fancy. Frowning deeply, he returned to his companions.

"There was nobody," he asserted. "It must have dropped out of your pocket and rolled."

Damn it, he thought, could a watch roll that far? What the devil was happening this night? Far up the street, something screeched, then it bubbled. Burke shuddered—he could make a shrewd guess at that! He looked at the others, but apparently they hadn't heard the noise.

The papers gave it space in the morning. The total was sixty watches and eight cats, also some oddments from the small stock of a local scientific instrument maker. I read about it on my way down to Burman's place. The details were fairly lavish, but not complete. I got them completely at a later time when we discovered the true significance of what had occurred.

Burman was waiting for me when I arrived. He appeared both annoyed and bothered. Over in the corner, the coffin was ticking away steadily, its noise much louder than it had been the previous day. The thing sounded a veritable hive of industry.

"Well?" I asked.

"It's moved around a lot during the night," said Burman. "It's smashed a couple of thermometers and taken the mercury out of them. I found some drawers and cupboards shut, some open, but I've an uneasy feeling that it's made a thorough search through the lot. A packet of nickel foil has vanished, a coil of copper wire has gone with it." He pointed an angry finger at the bottom of the door through which I'd just entered. "And I blame it for gnawing ratholes in that. They weren't there yesterday."

Sure enough, there were a couple of holes in the bottom of that door. But no rat made those—they were neat and smooth and round, almost as if a carpenter had cut them with a keyhole saw.

"Where's the sense in it making those?" I questioned. "It can't crawl through apertures that size."

"Where's the sense in the whole affair?" Burman countered. He glowered at the busy machine which stared back at him with its expressionless lenses and churned steadily on. *Tick-tick-tick!* persisted the confounded thing. Then, *whir-thump-click!*

I opened my mouth intending to voice a nice, sarcastic comment at the machine's expense when there came a very tiny, very subtle and extremely high-pitched whine. Something small, metallic, glittering shot through one of the rat holes, fled across the floor toward the churning monstrosity. A trapdoor opened and swallowed it with such swiftness that it had disappeared before I realized what I'd seen. The thing had been a cylindrical, polished object resembling the shuttle of a sewing machine, but about four times the size. And it had been dragging something also small and metallic.

Burman stared at me; I stared at Burman. Then he foraged around the laboratory, found a three-foot length of half-inch steel pipe. Dragging a chair to the door, he seated himself, gripped the pipe like a bludgeon, and watched the rat holes, Imperturbably, the machine watched him and continued to *tick-tick-tick.*

Ten minutes later, there came a sudden click and another tiny whine. Nothing darted inward through the holes, but the curious object we'd already seen—or another one exactly like it—dropped out of the trap, scooted to the door by which we were waiting. It caught Burman by surprise. He made a mad swipe with the steel as the thing skittered elusively past his feet and through a hole. It had gone even as the weapon walloped the floor.

"Damn!" said Burman, heartily. He held the pipe loosely in his grip while he glared at the industrious coffin. "I'd smash it to bits except that I'd like to catch one of these small gadgets first."

"Look out!" I yelled.

He was too late. He ripped his attention away from the coffin toward the holes, swinging up the heavy length of pipe, a startled look on his face. But his reaction was far too slow. Three of the little mysteries were through the holes and half-way across the floor before his weapon was ready to swing. The coffin swallowed them with the crash of a trapdoor.

The invading trio had rushed through in single file, and I'd got a better picture of them this time. The first two were golden shuttles, much like the one we'd already seen. The third was bigger, speedier, and gave me the notion that it could dodge around more dexterously. It had a long, sharp projection in front, a wicked, ominous thing like a surgeon's scalpel. Sheer speed deprived me of a good look at it, but I fancied that the tip of the scalpel had been tinged with red. My spine exuded perspiration.

Came an irritated scratching upon the outside of the door and a white-tipped paw poked tentatively through one of the holes. The cat backed to a safe distance when Burman opened the door, but looked lingeringly toward the laboratory. Its presence needed no explaining—the alert animal must have caught a glimpse of those infernal little whizzers. The same thought struck both of us; cats are quick on the pounce, very quick. Given a chance, maybe this one could make a catch for us.

We enticed it in with fair words and soothing noises. Its eagerness overcame its normal caution toward strangers, and it entered. We closed the door behind it; Burman got his length of pipe, sat by the door, tried to keep one eye on the holes and the other on the cat. He couldn't do both, but he tried. The cat sniffed and prowled around, mewed defeatedly. Its behavior suggested that it was seeking by sight rather than scent. There wasn't any scent.

With feline persistence, the animal searched the whole laboratory. It passed the buzzing coffin several times, but ignored it completely. In the end, the cat gave it up, sat on the corner of the laboratory table and started to wash its face.

Tick-tick-tick! went the big machine. Then *whir-thump!* A trap popped open, a shuttle fell out and raced for the door. A second one followed it. The first was too fast even for the cat, too fast for the surprised Burman as well. *Bang!* The length of the steel tube came down viciously as the leading shuttle bulleted triumphantly through a hole.

But the cat got the second one. With a mighty leap, paws extended, claws out, it caught its victim one foot from the door. It tried to handle the slippery thing, failed, lost it for an instant. The shuttle whisked around in a crazy loop. The cat got it again, lost it again, emitted an angry snarl, batted it against the skirting board. The shuttle lay there, upside down, four midget wheels in its underside spinning madly with a high, almost inaudible whine.

Eyes alight with excitement, Burman put down his weapon, went to pick up the shuttle. At the same time, the cat slunk toward it ready to play with it. The shuttle lay there, helplessly functioning upon its back. Before either could reach it the big machine across the room went *clunk!* opened a trap and ejected another gadget.

With astounding swiftness, the cat turned and pounced upon the newcomer. Then followed pandemonium. Its prey swerved agilely with a fitful gleam of gold; the cat swerved with it, cursed and spat. Black-and-white fur whirled around in a fighting haze in which gold occasionally glowed; the cat's hissings and spittings overlay a persistent whine that swelled and sank in the manner of accelerating or decelerating gears.

A peculiar gasp came from the cat, and blood spotted the floor. The animal clawed wildly, emitted another gasp followed by a gurgle. It shivered and flopped, a stream of crimson pouring from the great gash in its gullet.

We'd hardly time to appreciate the full significance of the ghastly scene when the victor made for Burman. He was standing by the skirting board, the still-buzzing shuttle in his hand. His eyes were sticking out with utter horror, but he retained enough presence of mind to make a frantic jump a second before the bulleting meance reached his feet.

He landed behind the thing, but it reversed in its own length and came for him again. I saw the mirrorlike sheen of its scalpel as it banked at terriffic speed, and the sheen was drowned in sticky crimson two inches along the blade. Burman jumped over it again, reached the lab table, got up on that.

"Lord!" he breathed.

By this time I'd got the piece of pipe which he'd discarded. I hefted it, feeling its comforting weight, then did my best to bat the buzzing lump of wickedness through the window and over the roofs. It was too agile for me. It whirled, accelerated, dodged the very tip of the descending steel, and flashed twice around the table upon which Burman had taken refuge. It ignored me completely. Somehow, I felt that it was responding entirely to some mysterious call from the shuttle Burman had captured.

I swiped desperately, missed it again, though I swear I missed by no more than a millimeter. Something whipped through the holes in the door, fled past me into the big machine. Dimly, I heard traps opening and closing and beyond all other sounds that steady, persistent *tick-tick-tick*. Another furious blow that accomplished no more than to dent the floor and jar my arm to the shoulder.

Unexpectedly, unbelievably, the golden curse ceased its insane gyrations on the floor and around the table. With a hard click, and a whir much louder than before, it raced easily up one leg of the table and reached the top.

Burman left his sanctuary in one jump. He was still clinging to the shuttle. I'd never seen his face so white.

"The machine!" he said, hoarsely. "Bash it to hell!"

Thunk! went the machine. A trap gaped, released another
demon with a scalpel. *Tzz-z-z!* a third shot in through the
holes in the door. Four shuttles skimmed through behind it,
made for the machine, reached it safely. A fifth came
through more slowly. It was dragging an automobile valve
spring. I kicked the thing against the wall even as I struck a
vain blow at one with a scalpel.

With another jump, Burman cleared an attacker. A second
sheared off the toe of his right shoe as he landed. Again he
reached the table from which his first toe had departed. All
three things with scalpels made for the table with a reckless
vim that was frightening.

"Drop that damned shuttle," I yelled.

He didn't drop it. As the fighting trio whirred up the legs,
he flung the shuttle with all his might at the coffin that had
given it birth. It struck, dented the casing, fell to the floor.
Burman was off the table again. The thrown shuttle lay battered and noiseless, its small motive wheels stilled.

The armed contraptions scooting around the table seemed
to change their purpose coincidently with the captured
shuttle's smashing. Together, they dived off the table, sped
through the holes in the door. A fourth came out of the
machine, escorting two shuttles, and those too vanished beyond the door. A second or two later, a new thing different
from the rest, came in through one of the holes. It was long,
round-bodied, snub-nosed, about half the length of a policeman's nightstick, had six wheels beneath, and a double row of
peculiar serrations in front. It almost sauntered across the
room while we watched it fascinatedly. I saw the serrations
jerk and shift when it climbed the lowered trap into the
machine. They were midget caterpillar tracks!

Burman had had enough. He made up his mind. Finding
the steel pipe, he gripped it firmly, approached the coffin. Its
lenses seemed to leer at him as he stood before it. Twelve
years of intensive work to be destroyed at a blow. Endless
days and nights of effort to be undone at one stroke. But Burman was past caring. With a ferocious swing he demolished
the glass, with a fierce thrust he shattered the assembly of
wheels and cogs behind.

The coffin shuddered and slid beneath his increasingly angry blows. Trapdoors dropped open, spilled out lifeless
samples of the thing's metallic brood. Grindings and raspings

came from the accursed object while Burman battered it to pieces. Then it was silent, a shapeless, useless mass of twisted and broken parts.

I picked up the dented shape of the object that had sauntered in. It was heavy, astonishingly heavy, and even after partial destruction its workmanship looked wonderful. It had a tiny, almost unnoticeable eye in front, but the miniature lens was cracked. Had it returned for repairs and overhaul?

"That," said Burman, breathing audibly, "is that!"

I opened the door to see if the noise had attracted attention. It hadn't. There was a lifeless shuttle outside the door, a second a yard behind it. The first had a short length of brass chain attached to a tiny hook projecting from its rear. The nose cap of the second had opened fanwise, like an iris diaphragm, and a pair of jointed metal arms were folded inside, hugging a medium-sized diamond. It looked as if they'd been about to enter when Burman destroyed the big machine.

Picking them up, I brought them in. Their complete inactivity, though they were undamaged, suggested that they had been controlled by the big machine and had drawn their motive power from it. If so, then we'd solved our problem simply, and by destroying the one had destroyed the lot.

Burman got his breath back and began to talk.

He said, "The Robot Mother! That's what I made—a duplicate of the Robot Mother. I didn't realize it, but I was patiently building the most dangerous thing in creation, a thing that is a terrible menace because it shares with mankind the ability to propagate. Thank Heaven we stopped it in time!"

"So," I remarked, remembering that he claimed to have got it from the extreme future, "that's the eventual master, or mistress, of Earth. A dismal prospect for humanity, eh?"

"Not necessarily. I don't know just how far I got, but I've an idea it was so tremendously distant in the future that Earth had become sterile from humanity's viewpoint. Maybe we'd emigrated to somewhere else in the cosmos, leaving our semi-intelligent slave machines to fight for existence or die. They fought—and survived."

"And then wangle things to try to alter the past in their favor." I suggested.

"No, I don't think so." Burman had become much calmer by now. "I don't think it was a dastardy attempt so much as an interesting experiment. The whole affair was damned in advance because success would have meant an impossible paradox. There are no robots in the next century, nor any knowledge of them. Therefore the intruders in this time must have been wiped out and forgotten."

"Which means," I pointed out, "that you must not only have destroyed the machine, but also all your drawings, all your notes, as well as the psychophone, leaving nothing but a few strange events and a story for me to tell."

"Exactly—I shall destroy everything. I've been thinking over the whole affair, and it's not until now I've understood that the psychophone can never be of the slightest use to me. It permits me to discover or invent only those things that history has decreed I shall invent, and which, therefore, I shall find with or without the contraption. I can't play tricks with history, past or future."

"Humph!" I couldn't find any flaw in his reasoning. "Did you notice," I went on, "the touch of bee psychology in our antagonists? You built the hive, and from it emerged workers, warriors, and"—I indicated the dead saunterer—"one drone."

"Yes," he said, lugubriously. "And I'm thinking of the honey—eighty watches! Not to mention any other items the late papers may report, plus any claims for slaughtered cats. Good thing I'm wealthy."

"Nobody knows you've anything to do with those incidents. You can pay secretly if you wish."

"I shall," he declared.

"Well," I went on, cheerfully, "all's well that ends well. Thank goodness we've got rid of what we brought upon ourselves."

With a sigh of relief, I strolled toward the door. A high whine of midget motors drew my startled attention downward. While Burman and I stared aghast, a golden shuttle slid easily through one of the rat holes, sensed the death of the Robot Mother and scooted back through the other hole before I could stop it.

If Burman had been shaken before, he was doubly so now. He came over to the door, stared incredulously at the little exit just used by the shuttle, then at the couple of other undamaged but lifeless shuttles lying about the room.

"Bill," he mouthed, "your bee analogy was perfect. Don't you understand? There's another swarm! A queen got loose!"

There was another swarm all right. For the next forty-eight hours it played merry hell. Burman spent the whole time down at headquarters trying to convince them that his evidence wasn't just a fantastic story, but what helped him to persuade the police of his veracity was the equally fantastic reports that came rolling in.

To start with, old Gildersome heard a crash in his shop at midnight, thought of his valuable stock of cameras and miniature movie projectors, pulled on his pants and rushed downstairs. A razor-sharp instrument stabbed him through the right instep when halfway down, and he fell the rest of the way. He lay there, badly bruised and partly stunned, while things clicked, ticked and whirred in the darkness and the gloom. One by one, all the contents of his box of expensive lenses went through a hole in the door. A quantity of projector cogs and wheels went with them.

Ten people complained of being robbed in the night of watches and alarm clocks. Two were hysterical. One swore that the bandit was "a six-inch cockroach" which purred like a toy dynamo. Getting out of bed, he'd put his foot upon it and felt its cold hardness wriggle away from beneath him. Filled with revulsion, he'd whipped his foot back into bed "just as another cockroach scuttled toward him." Burman did not tell that agitated complainant how near he had come to losing his foot.

Thirty more reports rolled in next day. A score of houses had been entered and four shops robbed by things that had the agility and furtiveness of rats—except that they emitted tiny ticks and buzzing noises. One was seen racing along the road by a homing railway worker. He tried to pick it up, lost his forefinger and thumb, stood nursing the stumps until an ambulance rushed him away.

Rare metals and fine parts were the prey of these ticking marauders. I couldn't see how Burman or anyone else could wipe them out once and for all, but he did it. He did it by baiting them like rats. I went around with him, helping him on the job, while he consulted a map.

"Every report," said Burman, "leads to this street. An alarm clock that suddenly sounded was abandoned near here. Two automobiles were robbed of small parts near here. Shuttles have been seen going to or from this area. Five cats were dealt with practically on this spot. Every other incident has taken place within easy reach."

"Which means," I guessed, "that the queen is somewhere near this point?"

"Yes." He stared up and down the quiet empty street over which the crescent moon shed a sickly light. It was two o'clock in the morning. "We'll settle this matter pretty soon!"

He attached the end of a reel of firm cotton to a small

piece of silver chain, nailed the reel to the wall, dropped the chain on the concrete. I did the same with the movement of a broken watch. We distributed several small cogs, a few clock wheels, several camera fitments, some small, tangled bunches of copper wire, and other attractive oddments.

Three hours later, we returned accompanied by the police. They had mallets and hammers with them. All of us were wearing steel leg-and-foot shields knocked up at short notice by a handy sheet-metal worker.

The bait had been taken! Several cotton strands had broken after being unreeled a short distance, but others were intact. All of them either led to or pointed to a steel grating leading to a cellar below an abandoned warehouse. Looking down, we could see a few telltale strands running through the window frame beneath.

Burman said, "Now!" and we went in with a rush. Rusty locks snapped, rotten doors collapsed, we poured through the warehouse and into the cellar.

There was a small, coffin-shaped thing against one wall, a thing that ticked steadily away while its lenses stared at us with ghastly lack of emotion. It was very similar to the Robot Mother, but only a quarter of the size. In the light of a police torch, it was a brooding, ominous thing of dreadful significance. Around it, an active clan swarmed over the floor, buzzing and ticking in metallic fury.

Amid angry whirs and the crack of snapping scalpels on steel, we waded headlong through the lot. Burman reached the coffin first, crushing it with one mighty blow of his twelve-pound hammer, then bashing it to utter ruin with a rapid succession of blows. He finished exhausted. The daughter of the Robot Mother was no more, nor did her alien tribe move or stir.

Sitting down on a rickety wooden case, Burman mopped his brow and said, "Thank heavens that's done!"

Tick-tick-tick!

. . . He shot up, snatched his hammer, a wild look in his eyes.

"Only my watch," apologized one of the policemen. "It's a cheap one, and it makes a hell of a noise." He pulled it out to show the worried Burman.

"Tick! tick!" said the watch, with mechanical aplomb.

AND HE BUILT
A CROOKED HOUSE

Astounding Science Fiction
February

by Robert A. Heinlein (1907-   )

*Robert A. Heinlein continued his dominance of
the science fiction world in 1941, which featured
his novel* Methuselah's Children, *which ran as a
three-part serial in* Astounding. *His short fiction
was every bit as good, and this volume contains
four of his stories.*

*"And He Built a Crooked House" represented
another innovative contribution by Heinlein. The
quality of a story is often a matter of perception,
and of course point of view is an important ingredient in all fiction, but it was never supposed to be
like this!*

(I appreciated Bob's work from the very beginning, from
his first story, but I must admit that I didn't actually decide
he was the best science fiction writer who ever was—and not
merely one of the best—till I read this one. It was so light-
hearted and so clever that I couldn't get it out of my mind.
Of course, what got me right in betwixt the short ribs was his
beginning and the knowledge that he had worked his way
down to the very address he was living at at the time.—I.A.)

SHOTTLE BOP

Unknown
February

by Theodore Sturgeon (1918-   )

*By the end of 1941 Theodore Sturgeon had a
spectacular string of stories to his credit. In less
than three years he had established himself as a
master of both science fiction and fantasy. Along
with Heinlein, he ruled over the peak of the Golden
Age.*
*Few writers could combine a feel for horror—
"Bianca's Hands," "It"—with a talent for comedy.
This story shows Sturgeon at his funniest.*

(I suppose that every once in a while as a story recedes
into the past but lives on in your memory, there is a chance
that you may confuse the author. You may attribute a story
of one man to another. Thus, I frequently notice that people
attribute one of Arthur C. Clarke's stories to me, which
pleases me, or one of my stories to him, which rouses my indignation. Here is one case in which I am guilty. I persist in
thinking that "Shottle Bop" was written by John Collier. I'm
wrong, of course, but Collier is a terrifically clever writer of
the gently fantastic—and so is Ted.—I. A.)

I'd never seen the place before, and I lived just down the
block and around the corner. I'll even give you the address, if
you like. "The Shottle Bop," between Twentieth and Twenty-
first Streets, on Tenth Avenue in New York City. You can
find it if you go there looking for it. Might even be worth
your while, too.

But you'd better not.

"The Shottle Bop." It got me. It was a small shop with a
weather-beaten sign swung from a wrought crane, creaking
dismally in the late fall wind. I walked past it, thinking of the
engagement ring in my pocket and how it had just been

38

handed back to me by Audrey, and my mind was far removed from such things as shottle bops. I was thinking that
Audrey might have used a gentler term than "useless" in
describing me: and her neatly turned remark about my being
a "constitutional psychopathic incompetent" was as un-called-
for as it was spectacular. She must have read it somewere,
balanced as it was by "And I wouldn't marry you if
you were the last man on earth!" which is a notably worn
cliché.

"Shottle Bop!" I muttered, and then paused, wondering
where I had picked up such oddly rhythmic syllables with
which to express myself. I'd seen it on that sign, of course,
and it had caught my eye. "And what," I asked myself,
"might be a Shottle Bop?" Myself replied promptly, "Dunno.
Toddle back and have a look." So toddle I did, back along
the east side of Tenth, wondering what manner of man might
be running such an establishment in pursuance of what kind
of business. I was enlightened on the second point by a sign
in the window, all but obscured by the dust and ashes of apparent centuries, which read:

WE SELL BOTTLES

There was another line of smaller print there. I rubbed at
the crusted glass with my sleeve and finally was able to make
out.

With things in them.

Just like that:

WE SELL BOTTLES
With things in them.

Well of course I went in. Sometimes very delightful things
come in bottles, and the way I was feeling, I could stand a
little delighting.

"Close it!" shrilled a voice, as I pushed through the door.
The voice came from a shimmering egg adrift in the air behind the counter, low-down. Peering over, I saw that it was
not an egg at all, but the bald pate of an old man who was
clutching the edge of the counter, his scrawny body streaming
away in the slight draft from the open door, as if he were
made of bubbles. A mite startled, I kicked the door with my

heel. He immediately fell on his face, and then scrambled
smiling to his feet.

"Ah, it's so good to see you again," he rasped.

I think his vocal cords were dusty, too. Everything else
here was. As the door swung to, I felt as if I were inside a
great dusty brain that had just closed its eyes. Oh yes, there
was light enough. But it wasn't the lamp light and it wasn't
daylight. It was like—like light reflected from the cheeks of
pale people. Can't say I enjoyed it much.

"What do you mean, 'again'?" I asked irritably. "You
never saw me before."

"I saw you when you came in and I fell down and got up
and saw you again," he quibbled, and beamed. "What can I
foo for do?"

"Huh?" I huhed, and then translated it into "What can I
do for you?"

"Oh, I said. "Well, I saw your sign. What have you got in
a bottle that I might like?"

"What do you want?"

"What've you got?"

He broke into a piping chant—I remember it yet, word for
word.

> *"For half a buck, a vial of luck*
> *Or a bottle of nifty breaks*
> *Or a flask of joy, or Myrna Loy*
> *For luncheon with sirloin steaks*
>
> *"Pour out a mug from this old jug,*
> *And you'll never get wet in rains.*
> *I've bottles of grins and racetrack wins*
> *and lotions to ease your pains.*
>
> *"Here's bottles of imps and wet-pack shrimps*
> *From a sea unknown to man,*
> *And an elixir to banish fear,*
> *And the sap from the pipes of Pan.*
>
> *"With the powdered horn of a unicorn*
> *You can win yourself a mate;*
> *With the rich hobnob; or get a job—*
> *It's yours at a lowered rate."*

"Now wait right there!" I snapped. "You mean you actually sell dragon's blood and ink from the pen of Friar Bacon
and all such mumbo-jum?"

He nodded rapidly and smiled all over his improbable face.
I went on—"The genuine article?"
He kept on nodding.

I regarded him for a moment. "You mean to stand there
with your teeth in your mouth and your bare face hanging
out and tell me that in this day and age, in this city and in
broad daylight, you sell such trash and then expect me—me,
an enlightened intellectual—"

"You are very stupid and twice as bombastic," he said quietly.

I glowered at him and reached for the doorknob—and
there I froze. And I mean froze. For the old man whipped
out an ancient bulb-type atomizer and squeezed a couple of
whiffs at me as I turned away; and so help me, *I couldn't
move!* I could cuss, though, and boy, did I.

The proprietor hopped over the counter and ran over to
me. He must have been standing on a box back there, for
now I could see he was barely three feet tall. He grabbed my
coat tails, ran up my back and slid down my arm, which was
extended doorward. He sat down on my wrist and swung his
feet and laughed up at me. As far as I could feel, he weighed
absolutely nothing.

When I had run out of profanity—I pride myself on never
repeating a phrase of invective—he said, "Does that prove
anything to you, my cocky and unintelligent friend? That was
the essential oil from the hair of the Gorgon's head. And until I give you an antidote, you'll stand there from now till a
week from text Nuesday!"

"Get me out of this," I roared, "or I smack you so hard
you lose your brains through the pores in your feet!"

He giggled.

I tried to tear loose again and couldn't. It was as if all my
epidermis had turned to high-carbon steel. I began cussing
again, but quit in despair.

"You think altogether too much of yourself," said the proprietor of the Shottle Bop. "Look at you! Why, I wouldn't
hire you to wash my windows. You expect to marry a girl
who is accustomed to the least of animal comfort, and then
you get miffed because she turns you down. Why does she
turn you down? Because you won't get a job. You're a no-
good. You're a bum. He, he! And you have the nerve to walk
around pelling teople where to get off. Now if I were in your
position I would ask politely to be released, and then I would
see if anyone in this shop would be good enough to sell you a
bottle full of something that might help out."

Now I never apologize to anybody, and I never back down, and I never take any guff from mere tradesmen. But this was different. I'd never been petrified before, nor had my nose rubbed in so many galling truths. I relented. "O.K., O.K.; let me break away then. I'll buy something."

"Your tone is sullen," he said complacently, dropping lightly to the floor and holding his atomizer at the ready. "You'll have to say 'Please. Pretty please.' "

He went back of the counter and returned with a paper of powder which he had me sniff. In a couple of seconds I began to sweat, and my limbs lost their rigidity so quickly that it almost threw me. I'd have been flat on my back if the man hadn't caught me and solicitously led me to a chair. As strength dribbled back into my shocked tissues, it occurred to me that I might like to flatten this hobgoblin for pulling a trick like that. But a strange something stopped me—strange because I'd never had the experience before. It was simply the idea that once I got outside I'd agree with him for having such a low opinion of me.

He wasn't worrying. Rubbing his hands briskly, he turned to his shelves. "Now, let's see . . . what would be best for you, I wonder? Hm-m-m. Success is something you couldn't justify. Money? You don't know how to spend it. A good job? You're not fitted for one." He turned gentle eyes on me and shook his head. "A sad case. *Tsk, tsk.*" I crawled. "A perfect mate? Uh-huh. You're too stupid to recognize perfection, too conceited to appreciate it. I don't think that I can— Wait!"

He whipped four or five bottles and jars off the dozens of shelves behind him and disappeared somewhere in the dark recesses of the store. Immediately there came sounds of violent activity—clinkings and little crashes; stirrings and then the rapid susurrant grating of a mortar and pestle; then the slushy sound of liquid being added to a dry ingredient during stirring; and at length, after quite a silence, the glugging of a bottle being filled through a filtering funnel. The proprietor reappeared triumphantly bearing a four-ounce bottle without a label.

"This will do it!" he beamed.

"That will do what?"

"Why, cure you!"

"Cure—" My pompous attitude, as Audrey called it, had returned while he was mixing. "What do you mean cure? I haven't got anything!"

"My dear little boy," he said offensively, "you most certainly have. Are you happy? Have you ever been happy? No. Well, I'm going to fix all that up. That is, I'll give you the start you need. Like any other cure, it requires your cooperation.

"You're in a bad way, young fellow. You have what is known in the profession as retrogressive metempsychosis of the ego in its most malignant form. You are a constitutional unemployable; a downright sociophagus. I don't like you. Nobody likes you."

Feeling a little bit on the receiving end of a blitz, I stammered, "W-what do you aim to do?"

He extended the bottle. "Go home. Get into a room by yourself—the smaller the better. Drink this down, right out of the bottle. Stand by for developments. That's all."

"But—what will it do to me?"

"It will do nothing *to* you. It will do a great deal *for* you. It can do as much for you as you want it to. But mind me, now. As long as you use what it gives you for your self-improvement, you will thrive. Use it for self-glorification, as a basis for boasting, or for revenge, and you will suffer in the extreme. Remember that, now."

"But what is it? How—"

"I am selling you a talent. You have none now. When you discover what kind of a talent it is, it will be up to you to use it to your advantage. Now go away. I still don't like you."

"What do I owe you?" I muttered, completely snowed under by this time.

"The bottle carries its own price. You won't pay anything unless you fail to follow my directions. Now will you go, or must I uncork a bottle of jinn—and I don't mean London Dry?"

"I'll go," I said. I'd seen something swirling in the depths of a ten-gallon carboy at one end of the counter, and I didn't like it a bit. "Good-by."

"Bood-gy," he returned.

I went out and I headed down Tenth Avenue and I turned east up Twentieth Street and I never looked back. And for many reasons I wish now that I had, for there was, without doubt, something very strange about that Shottle Bop.

I didn't simmer down until I got home; but once I had a cup of black Italian coffee under my belt I felt better. I was skeptical about it at last. I was actually inclined to scoff. But somehow I didn't want to scoff too loudly. I looked at the bottle a little scornfully, and there was a certain something about the glass of it that seemed to be staring back at me. I sniffed and threw it up behind some old hats on top of the closet, and then sat down to unlax. I used to love to unlax. I'd put my feet on the doorknob and slide down in the upholstery until I was sitting on my shoulder blades, and as the old saying has it, "Sometimes I sets and thinks, and sometimes I just sets." The former is easy enough, and is what even an accomplished loafer has to go through before he reaches the latter and more blissful state. It takes years of practice to relax sufficiently to be able to "just set." I'd learned it years ago.

But just as I was about to slip into the vegetable status, I was annoyed by something. I tried to ignore it. I manifested a superhuman display of lack of curiosity, but the annoyance persisted. A light pressure on my elbow, where it draped over the arm of the chair. I was put in the unpleasant predicament of having to concentrate on what it was; and realizing that concentration on anything was the least desirable thing there could be. I gave up finally, and with a deep sigh, opened my eyes and had a look.

It was the bottle.

I screwed up my eyes and then looked again, but it was still there. The closet door was open as I had left it, and its shelf almost directly above me. Must have fallen out. Feeling that if the damn thing were on the floor it couldn't fall any farther, I shoved it off the arm of the chair with my elbow.

It bounced. It bounced with such astonishing accuracy that it wound up in exactly the same spot it had started from—on the arm of the easy-chair, by my elbow. Startled, I shoved it violently. This time I pushed it hard enough to send it against the wall, from which it rebounded to the shelf under my small table, and thence back to the chair arm—and this time it perched cozily against my shoulder. Jarred by the bouncing, the stopper hopped out of the bottle mouth and rolled into my lap; and there I sat, breathing the bittersweet fumes of its contents, feeling frightened and silly as hell.

I grabbed the bottle and sniffed. I'd smelled that somewhere before—where was it? Uh—oh, yes; that mascara the Chinese honkytonk girls use in Frisco. The liquid was dark —smoky black. I tasted it cautiously. It wasn't bad. If it wasn't alcoholic, then the old man in the shop had found a darn good substitute for alcohol. At the second sip, I liked it and at the third I really enjoyed it and there wasn't any fourth because by then the little bottle was a dead marine.

That was about the time I remembered the name of the black
ingredient with the funny smell. Kohl. It is an herb the Ori-
entals use to make it possible to see supernatural beings. Silly
superstition!

And then the liquid I'd just put away, lying warm and
comfortable in my stomach, began to fizz. Then I think it began to swell. I tried to get up and couldn't. The room seemed
to come apart and throw itself at me piecemeal, and I passed
out.

Don't you ever wake up the way I did. For your own sake
be careful about things like that. Don't swim up out of a sodden sleep and look around you and see all those things fluttering and drifting and flying and creeping and crawling
around you—puffy things dripping blood, and filmy, legless
creatures, and little bits and snatches of pasty human anat-
omy. It was awful. There was a human hand afloat in the air
an inch away from my nose; and at my startled gasp it
drifted away from me, fingers fluttering in the disturbed air
from my breath. Something veined and bulbous popped out
from under my chair and rolled across the floor. I heard a
faint clicking, and looked up into a gnashing set of jaws without any face attached. I think I broke down and cried a little.
I know I passed out again.

The next time I awoke—must have been hours later, because it was broad daylight and my clock and watch had
both stopped—things were a little better. Oh, yes, there were
a few of the horrors around. But somehow they didn't bother
me much now. I was practically convinced that I was nuts;
now that I had the conviction, why worry about it? I dunno;
it must have been one of the ingredients in the bottle that
had calmed me down so. I was curious and excited, and
that's about all. I looked around me and I was almost
pleased.

The walls were green! The drab wallpaper had turned to
something breathtakingly beautiful. They were covered with
what seemed to be moss; but never moss like that grew for
human eyes to see before. It was long and thick, and it had a
slight perpetual movement—not that of a breeze, but of
growth. Fascinated, I moved over and looked closely.
Growing indeed, with all the quick magic of spore and cyst
and root and growth again to spore; and the swift magic of it
was only a part of the magical whole, for never was there
such a green. I put out my hand to touch and stroke it, but I
only felt the wallpaper. But when I closed my fingers, on it, I

could feel that light touch of it in the palm of my hand, the weight of twenty sunbeams, the soft resilience of jet-darkness in a closed place. The sensation was a delicate ecstasy, and never have I been happier than I was at that moment.

Around the baseboards were little snowy toadstools, and the floor was grassy. Up the hinged side of the closet door climbed a mass of flowering vines, and their petals were hued in tones indescribable. I felt as if I had been blind until now, and deaf, too; for now I could hear the whispering of scarlet, gauzy insects among the leaves and the constant murmur of growth. All around me was a new and lovely world, so delicate that the wind of my movements tore petals from the flowers, so real and natural that it defied its own impossibility. Awestruck, I turned and turned, running from wall to wall, looking under my old furniture, into my old books; and everywhere I looked I found newer and more beautiful things to wonder at. It was while I was flat on my stomach looking up at the bed springs, where a colony of jewellike lizards had nested, that I first heard the sobbing.

It was young and plaintive, and had no right to be in my room where everything was so happy. I stood up and looked around, and there in the corner crouched the translucent figure of a little girl. She was leaning back against the wall. Her thin legs were crossed in front of her, and she held the leg of a tattered toy elephant dejectedly in one hand and cried into the other. Her hair was long and dark, and it poured and tumbled over her face and shoulders.

I said, "What's the matter, kiddo?" I hate to hear a child cry like that.

She cut herself off in the middle of a sob and shook the hair out of her eyes, looking up and past me, all fright and olive skin and big, filled violet eyes. "Oh!" she squeaked.

I repeated, "What's the matter? Why are you crying?"

She hugged the elephant to her breast defensively, and whimpered, "W-where are you?"

Surprised, I said, "Right here in front of you, child. Can't you see me?"

She shook her head. "I'm scared. Who are you?"

"I'm not going to hurt you. I heard you crying, and I wanted to see if I could help you. Can't you see me at all?"

"No," she whispered. "Are you an angel?"

I guffawed. "By no means!" I stepped closer and put my hand on her shoulder. The hand went right through her and she winced and shrank away, uttering a little wordless cry.

"I'm sorry," I said quickly. "I didn't mean . . . you can't see me at all? I can see you."

She shook her head again. "I think you're a ghost," she said.

"Do tell!" I said. "And what are you?"

"I'm Ginny," she said. "I have to stay here, and I have no one to play with." She blinked, and there was a suspicion of further tears.

"Where did you come from?" I asked.

"I came here with my mother," she said. "We lived in lots of other rooming houses. Mother cleaned floors in office buildings. But this is where I got so sick. I was sick a long time. Then one day I got off the bed and came over here, but then when I looked back I was still on the bed. It was awful funny. Some men came and put the 'me' that was on the bed onto a stretcher-thing and took it—me—out. After a while Mummy left, too. She cried for a long time before she left, and when I called to her she couldn't hear me. She never came back, and I just got to stay here."

"Why?"

"Oh, I got to. I—don't know why. I just—got to."

"What do you do here?"

"I just stay here and think about things. Once a lady lived here, had a little girl just like me. We used to play together until the lady watched us one day. She carried on somethin' awful. She said her little girl was possessed. The girl kept callin' me, 'Ginny! Ginny! Tell Mamma you're here!'; an' I tried, but the lady couldn't see me. Then the lady got scared an' picked up her little girl an' cried, an' so I was sorry. I ran over here an' hid, an' after a while the other little girl forgot about me, I guess. They moved," she finished with pathetic finality.

I was touched. "What will become of you, Ginny?"

"I dunno," she said, and her voice was troubled. "I guess I'll just stay here and wait for Mummy to come back. I been here a long time. I guess I deserve it, too."

"Why, child?"

She looked guiltily at her shoes. "I couldn' stand feelin' so awful bad when I was sick. I got up out of bed before it was time. I shoulda stayed where I was. This is what I get for quittin'. But Mummy'll be back; just you see."

"Sure she will," I muttered. My throat felt tight. "You take it easy, kid. Any time you want someone to talk to, you just pipe up, I'll talk to you any time I'm around."

She smiled, and it was a pretty thing to see. What a raw deal for a kid! I grabbed my hat and went out.

Outside things were the same as in the room to me. The hallways, the dusty stair carpets wore new garments of brilliant, nearly intangible foliage. They were no longer dark, for each leaf had its own pale and different light. Once in a while I saw things not quite so pretty. There was a giggling thing that scuttled back and forth on the third-floor landing. It was a little indistinct, but it looked a great deal like Barrelhead Brogan, a shanty-Irish bum who'd returned from a warehouse robbery a year or so ago, only to shoot himself accidentally with his own gun. I wasn't sorry.

Down on the first floor, on the bottom step, I saw two youngsters sitting. The girl had her head on the boy's shoulder, and he had his arms around her, and I could see the banister through them. I stopped to listen. There voices were faint, and seemed to come from a long way away.

He said, "There's one way out."

She said, "Don't talk that way, Tommy!"

"What else can we do? I've loved you for three years, and we still can't get married. No money, no hope—no nothing. Sue, if we did do it, I just *know* we'd always be together. Always and always—"

After a long time she said, "All right, Tommy. You get a gun, like you said." She suddenly pulled him even closer. "Oh, Tommy, are you sure we'll always be together just like this?"

"Always," he whispered, and kissed her. "Just like this."

Then there was a long silence, while neither moved. Suddenly they were as I had first seen them, and he said:

"There's only one way out."

And she said, "Don't talk that way, Tommy!"

And he said, "What else can we do? I've loved you for three years—" It went on like that, over and over and over.

I felt lousy. I went on out into the street.

It began to filter through to me what had happened. The man in the shop had called it a "talent." I couldn't be crazy, could I? I didn't *feel* crazy. The draught from the bottle had opened my eyes on a new world. What was this world?

It was a thing peopled by ghosts. There they were—storybook ghosts, and regular haunts, and poor damned souls—all the fixings of a storied supernatural, all the things we have heard about and loudly disbelieve and secretly wonder about. So what? What had it all to do with me?

As the days slid by, I wondered less about my new, strange surroundings, and gave more and more thought to that question. I had bought—or been given—a talent. I could see ghosts. I could see all parts of a ghostly world, even the vegetation that grew in it. That was perfectly reasonable—the trees and birds and fungi and flowers. A ghost world is a world as we know it, and a world as we know it must have vegetation. Yes, I could see them. But they couldn't see me!

O.K.; what could I get out of it? I couldn't talk about it or write about it because I wouldn't be believed; and besides, I had this thing exclusive, as far as I knew; why cut a lot of other people in on it?

On what, though?

No, unless I could get a steer from somewhere, there was no percentage in it for me that I could see. And then, about six days after I took that eye-opener, I remembered the one place where I might get that steer.

The Shottle Bop!

I was on Sixth Avenue at the time, trying to find something in a five-and-dimie that Ginny might like. She couldn't touch anything I brought her but she enjoyed things she could look at—picture books and such. By getting her a little book of photographs of trains since the "De Witt Clinton," and asking her which of them was like ones she had seen, I found out approximately how long it was she'd been there. Nearly eighteen years. Anyway, I got my bright idea and headed for Tenth Avenue and the Shottle Bop. I'd ask that old man—he'd tell me.

At the corner of Ninth Avenue I bumped into Happy Sam Healy and Fred Bellew. Fred was good people, but I never had much use for Happy Sam. He went for shaggy hats and lapelled vests, and he had patent-leather hair and too much collar-ad good looks. I was in a hurry and didn't want to talk to anyone, but Sam grabbed me by the arm.

"Slow down, mug, slow down! Long time no see. Where you bound in such a hurry?"

"Going over to Tenth to see a man about you."

Sam quit grinning and Fred walked over. "Why can't you guys quit knocking each other?" he asked quietly.

If it weren't for Fred, Sam and I would have crossed bows even more than we did, which was still altogether too much.

"I'll always speak civilly to a human being," I said. "Sam's different."

Sam said, "Don't set yourself up, chum. I'm cutting some ice with a certain party that froze you out."

"If you say exactly what you mean, I'll probably rap you for it," I flared.

Fred pushed hastily between us. "I'll see you later, Sam," he said. He pushed me with some difficulty away from the scene.

Sam stood staring after us for a minute and then put his hands in his pockets, shrugged, grinned, and went jauntily his own way.

"Aw, why do you always stand in front of that heel when I want to scrape him off the sidewalk?" I complained.

"Calm down, you big lug," Fred grinned. "That bantam wants trouble with you because of Audrey. If you mess him up, he'll go running to her about it, and you'll be really out."

"I am already, so what?"

He glanced at me. "That's up to you." Then, seeing my face, he said quickly, "O.K., don't tell me. It's none of my business. I know. How've you been?"

I was quiet for a while, walking along. Fred was a darn good egg. You could tell a guy like that practically anything. Finally, I said, "I'm looking for a job, Fred."

He nodded. "Thought you would. Doing what?" Anybody else, knowing me, would have hooted and howled.

"Well, I—" Oh, what the hell, I thought, I'll tell him. If he thinks I'm nuts, he won't say so to anyone but me. Old Fred didn't look like much, with his sandy hair and his rimless specs and those stooped shoulders that too much book reading gave him, but he had sense.

"I was walking down Tenth," I began—

By the time I had come to the part about the ghost of the kid in my room, we had reached Tenth Avenue in the late Twenties, and turned south. I wasn't paying much attention to where we were, to tell you the truth, and that's why what happened did happen.

Before I had a chance to wind up with the question that was bothering me—"I have it . . . what will I do with it?" Fred broke in with "Hey! Where is this place of yours?"

"Why—between Nineteenth and Twentieth," I said. "Holy smoke—we're at Eighteenth! We walked right past it!"

Fred grinned and swung around. We went back up the avenue with our eyes peeled, and not a sign of the Shottle Bop did we see. For the first time a doubtful look crept onto Fred's bland face. He said:

"You wouldn't kid me, would you, lug?"

"I tell you—" I began.

Then I saw a penny lying on the sidewalk. I bent to pick it up, and heard him say, "Hey! There it is! Come on."

"Ah! I knew it was on this block!" I said, and turned toward Fred. Or where Fred had been. Facing me was a blank wall. The whole side of the block was void of people. There was no sign of a shop or of Fred Bellew.

I stood there for a full two minutes not even daring to think. Then I walked downtown toward Twentieth, and then uptown to Twenty-first. Then I did it again. No shop. No Bellew.

I stood frothing on the uptown corner. What had that guy done; hopped a passing truck or sunk into the ground or vanished into the shop? Yeah; and no shop there! A wise guy after all. I trod the beat once more with the same results. Then I headed for home. I hadn't gone twenty feet when I heard the pound of someone running, and Fred came panting up and caught my shoulder. We both yelped at once—"Hey! Where've you been?"

I said, "What was the idea of ducking out like that? Man, you must've covered a hundred yards in about six seconds to get away from me while I picked up a penny off the sidewalk!"

"Duck out nothing!" said Bellow, angrier than I'd ever seen him. "I saw the store and went in. I thought you were right behind me. I look around and you're outside, staring at the shop like it was something you didn't believe. Then you walk off. Meanwhile the little guy in the store tries to sell me some of his goods. I stall him off, still looking for you. You walk past two or three times, looking in the window. I call you; you don't bat an eyelash. I tell the little guy: 'Hold on—I'll be back in a second with my friend there.' He rears back on his heels and laughs like a maniac and waves me out. Come on, dope. Let's go back. That old man really has something there. I'd say I was in the market for some of that stuff of his!"

"O.K., O.K.," I said. "But Fred—I'll swear I didn't see the place. Come on then; lead me to it. I must be going really screwball."

"Seems like," said Fred.

So we went back, and there was no shop at all. Not a sign of one. And then and there we had one pip of an argument. He said I'd lied about it in the first place, and I said, well, why did he give me that song-and-dance about his seeing it, and he said it was some kind of a joke I'd pulled on him; and then we both said, "Oh yeah?" a couple of times and began

to throw punches. I broke his glasses for him. He had them
in his pocket and fell down on them. I wound up minus a
very good friend and without my question answered—what
was I going to do with this "talent?"

I was talking to Ginny one afternoon about this and that
when a human leg, from the knee down, complete and puffy,
drifted between us. I recoiled in horror, but Ginny pushed it
gently with one hand. It bent under the touch, and started
toward the window, which was open a little at the bottom.
The leg floated toward the crack and was sucked through like
a cloud of cigarette smoke, reforming again on the other side.
It bumbled against the pane for a moment and then balooned
away.

"My gosh!" I breathed. "What *was* that?"

Ginny laughed. "Oh, just one of the Things that's all 'e
time flying around. Did it scare you? I used to be scared, but
I saw so many of them that I don't care any more, so's they
don't light on me."

"But what in the name of all that's disgusting are they?"

"Parts." Ginny was all childish savoir-faire.

"Parts of what?"

"People, silly. It's some kind of a game, *I* think. You see,
if someone gets hurt and loses something—a finger or an ear
or something, why, the ear—the *inside* part of it, I mean, like
me being the inside of the 'me' they carried out of here—it
goes back to where the person who owned it lived last. Then
it goes back to the place before that, and so on. It doesn't go
very fast. Then when something happens to a whole person,
the 'inside' part comes looking for the rest of itself. It picks
up bit after bit—Look!" She put out a filmy forefinger and
thumb and nipped a flake of gossamer out of the air.

I leaned over and looked closely; it was a small section of
semitransparent human skin, ridged and whorled.

"Somebody must have cut his finger," said Ginny matter-
of-factly, "while he was living in this room. When something
happens to um—you see! He'll be back for it!"

"Good heavens!" I said. "Does this happen to everyone?"

"I dunno. Some people have to stay where they are—like
me. But I guess if you haven't done nothing to deserve bein'
kept in one place, you have to come all around pickin' up
what you lost."

I'd thought of more pleasant things in my time.

For several days I'd noticed a gray ghost hovering up and
down the block. He was always on the street, never inside.

He whimpered constantly. He was—or had been—a little inoffensive man of the bowler hat and starched collar type. He paid no attention to me—non of them did, for I was apparently invisible to them. But I saw him so often that pretty soon I realized that I'd miss him if he went away. I decided I'd chat with him the next time I saw him.

I left the house one morning and stood around for a few minutes in front of the brownstone steps. Sure enough, pressing through the flotsam of my new, weird coexistent world, came the slim figure of the wraith I had noticed, his rabbit face screwed up, his eyes deep and sad, and his swallowtail coat and striped waistcoat immaculate. I stepped up behind him and said, "Hi!"

He started violently and would have run away, I'm sure, if he'd known where my voice was coming from.

"Take it easy, pal," I said. "I won't hurt you."

"Who are you?"

"You wouldn't know if I told you," I said. "Now stop shivering and tell me about yourself."

He mopped his ghostly face with a ghostly handkerchief, and then began fumbling nervously with a gold toothpick. "My word," he said. "No one's talked to me for years. I'm not quite myself, you see."

"I see," I said. "Well, take it easy. I just happen to've noticed you wandering around here lately. I got curious. You looking for somebody?"

"Oh, no," he said. Now that he had a chance to talk about his troubles, he forgot to be afraid of this mysterious voice from nowhere that had accosted him. "I'm looking for my home."

"Hm-m-m," I said. "Been looking a long time?"

"Oh, yes." His nose twitched. "I left for work one morning a long time ago, and when I got off the ferry at Battery Place I stopped for a moment to watch the work on that newfangled elevated railroad they were building down there. All of a sudden there was a loud noise—my goodness! It was terrible—and the next thing I knew I was standing back from the curb and looking at a man who looked just like me! A girder had fallen, and—my word!" He mopped his face again. "Since then I have been looking and looking. I can't seem to find anyone who knows where I might have lived, and I don't understand all the things I see floating around me, and I never thought I'd see the day when grass would grow on lower Broadway—oh, it's terrible." He began to cry.

I felt sorry for him. I could easily see what had happened. The shock was so great that even his ghost had amnesia! Poor little egg—until he was whole, he could find no rest. The thing interested me. Would a ghost react to the usual cures for amnesia? If so, then what would happen to him?

"You say you got off a ferryboat?"

"Yes."

"Then you must have lived on the Island . . . Staten Island, over there across the bay!"

"You really think so?" He stared through me, puzzled and hopeful.

"Why sure! Say, how'd you like me to take you over there? Maybe we could find your house."

"Oh, that would be splendid! But—oh, my, what will my wife say?"

I grinned. "She might want to know where you've been. Anyway, she'll be glad to have you back, I imagine. Come on; let's get going!"

I gave him a shove in the direction of the subway and strolled down behind him. Once in a while I got a stare from a passerby for walking with one hand out in front of me and talking into thin air. It didn't bother me very much. My companion, though, was very self-conscious about it, for the inhabitants of his world screeched and giggled when they saw him doing practically the same thing. Of all humans, only I was invisible to them, and the little ghost in the bowler hat blushed from embarrassment until I thought he'd burst.

We hopped a subway—it was a new experience for him, I gathered—and went down to South Ferry. The subway system in New York is a very unpleasant place to one gifted as I was. Everything that enjoys lurking in the dark hangs out there, and there is quite a crop of dismembered human remains. After this day I took the bus.

We got a ferry without waiting. The little gray ghost got a real kick out of the trip. He asked me about the ships in the harbor and their flags, and marveled at the dearth of sailing vessels. He *tsk, tsked* at the Statue of Liberty; the last time he had seen it, he said, was while it still had its original brassy gold color, before it got its patina. By this I placed him in the late '70s; he must have been looking for his home for over sixty years!

We landed at the Island, and from there I gave him his head. At the top of Fort Hill he suddenly said, "My name is John Quigg. I live at 45 Fourth Avenue!" I've never seen anyone quite so delighted as he was by the discovery. And from then on it was easy. He turned left, and then right, and then left again, straight down for two blocks and again right. I noticed—he didn't—that the street was marked "Winter Avenue." I remembered vaguely that the streets in this section had been numbered years ago.

He trotted briskly up the hill and then suddenly stopped and turned vaguely. "I say, are you still with me?"

"Still here," I said.

"I'm all right now. I can't tell you how much I appreciate this. Is there anything I could do for you?"

I considered. "Hardly. We're of different times, you know. Things change."

He looked, a little pathetically, at the new apartment house on the corner and nodded. "I think I know what happened to me," he said softly. "But I guess it's all right. . . . I made a will, and the kids were grown." He sighed. "But if it hadn't been for you I'd still be wandering around Manhattan. Let's see—ah; come with me!"

He suddenly broke into a run. I followed as quickly as I could. Almost at the top of the hill was a huge old shingled house, with a silly cupola and a complete lack of paint. It was dirty and it was tumble-down, and at the sight of it the little fellow's face twisted sadly. He gulped and turned through a gap in the hedge and down beside the house. Casting about in the long grass, he spotted a boulder sunk deep into the turf.

"This is it," he said. "Just you dig under that. There is no mention of it in my will, except a small fund to keep paying the box rent. Yes, a safety-deposit box, and the key and an authorization are under that stone. I hid it"—he giggled— "from my wife one night, and never did get a chance to tell her. You can have whatever's any good to you." He turned to the house, squared his shoulders, and marched in the side door, which banged open for him in a convenient gust of wind. I listened for a moment and then smiled at the tirade that burst forth. Old Quigg was catching real hell from his wife, who'd sat waiting for over sixty years for him! It was a bitter stream of invective, but—well, she must have loved him. She couldn't leave the place until she was complete, if Ginny's theory was correct, and she wasn't really complete until her husband came home! It tickled me. They'd be all right now!

I found an old pinchbar in the drive and attacked the

ground around the stone. It took quite a while and made my
hands bleed, but after a while I pried the stone up and was
able to scrabble around under it. Sure enough, there was an
oiled silk pouch under there. I caught it up and carefully un-
wrapped the strings around it. Inside was a key and letter
addressed to a New York bank, designating only "Bearer"
and authorizing use of the key. I laughed aloud. Little old
meek and mild John Quigg, I'd bet, had set aside some "mad
money." With a layout like that, a man could take a powder
without leaving a single sign. The son-of-a-gun! I would never
know just what it was he had up his sleeve, but I'll bet there
was a woman in the case. Even fixed it up with his will! Ah,
well—I should kick!

It didn't take me long to get over to the bank. I had a little
trouble getting into the vaults, because it took quite a while
to look up the box in the old records. But I finally cleared the
red tape, and found myself the proud possessor of just under
eight thousand bucks in small bills—and not a yellowback
among 'em!

Well, from then on I was pretty well set. What did I do?
Well, first I bought clothes, and then I started out to cut ice
for myself. I clubbed around a bit and got to know a lot of
people, and the more I knew the more I realized what a lot
of superstitious dopes they were. I couldn't blame anyone for
skirting a ladder under which crouched a genuine basilisk, of
course, but what the heck—not one in a thousand have beasts
under them! Anyway, my question was answered. I dropped
two grand on an elegant office with drapes and dim indirect
lighting, and I got a phone installed and a little quiet sign on
the door—Psychic Consultant. And, boy, I did all right.

My customers were mostly upper crust, because I came
high. It was generally no trouble to get contact with people's
dead relatives, which was usually what they wanted. Most
ghosts are crazy to get in contact with this world anyway.
That's one of the reasons that almost anyone can become a
medium of sorts if he tries hard enough; Lord knows that it
doesn't take much to contact the average ghost. Some, of
course, were not available. If a man leads a pretty square
life, and kicks off leaving no loose ends, he gets clear. I never
did find out where these clear spirits went to. All I knew was
that they weren't to be contacted. But the vast majority of
people have to go back and tie up those loose ends after they
die—righting a little wrong here, helping someone they've
hindered, cleaning up a bit of dirty work. That's where luck

itself comes from, I do believe. You don't get something for nothing.

If you get a nice break, it's been arranged that way by someone who did you dirt in the past, or someone who did wrong to your father or your grandfather or your great uncle Julius. Everything evens up in the long run, and until it does, some poor damned soul is wandering around the earth trying to do something about it. Half of humanity is walking around crabbing about its tough breaks. If you and you and you only knew what dozens of powers were begging for the chance to help you if you'll let them! And if you let them, you'll help clear up the mess they've made of their lives here, and free them to go wherever it is they go when they're cleaned up. Next time you're in a jam, go away somewhere by yourself and open your mind to these folks. They'll cut in and guide you all right, if you can drop your smugness and your mistaken confidence in your own judgment.

I had a couple of ghostly stooges to run errands for me. One of them, an ex-murderer by the name of One-eye Rachuba, was the fastest spook ever I saw, when it came to locating a wanted ancestor; and then there was Professor Grafe, a frog-faced teacher of social science who'd embezzled from a charity fund and fallen into the Hudson trying to make a getaway. He could trace the most devious genealogies in mere seconds, and deduce the most likely whereabouts of the ghost of a missing relative. The pair of them were all the office force I could use, and although every time they helped out one of my clients they came closer to freedom for themselves, they were both so entangled with their own sloppy lives that I was sure of their services for years.

But do you think I'd be satisfied to stay where I was, making money hand over fist without really working for it? Oh, no. Not me. No, I had to bigtime. I had to brood over the events of the last few months, and I had to get dramatic about that screwball Audrey, who really wasn't worth my trouble. I had to lie awake nights thinking about Happy Sam and his gibes. It wasn't enough that I'd proved Audrey wrong when she said I'd never amount to anything. I wasn't happy when I thought about Sam and the eighteen a week he pulled down driving a light delivery truck. Uh-huh. I had to show them up.

I even remembered what the little man in the Shottle Bop had said to me about using my "talent" for bragging or for revenge. That didn't make any difference to me. I figured I had the edge on everyone, everything. Cocky, I was. Why, I could send one of my ghostly stooges out any time and find out exactly what anyone had been doing three hours ago come Michaelmas. With the shade of the professor at my shoulder, I could back-track on any far-fetched statement and give immediate and logical reasons for back-tracking. No one had anything on me, and I could out-talk, out-maneuver, and out-smart anyone on earth. I was really quite a feller. I began to think, "What's the use of my doing as well as this when the gang on the West Side don't know anything about it?" and "Man, would that half-wit Happy Sam burn up if he saw me drifting down Broadway in my new eight-thousand-dollar roadster!" and "To think I used to waste my time and tears on a dope like Audrey!" In other words, I was tripping up on an inferiority complex. I acted like a veridam fool, which I was. I went over to the West Side.

It was a chilly, late winter night. I'd taken a lot of trouble to dress myself and my car so we'd be bright and shining and would knock some eyes out. Pity I couldn't brighten my brains up a little.

I drove up in front of Casey's pool room, being careful to do it too fast, and concentrating on shrieks from the tires and a shuddering twenty-four-cylinder roar from the engine before I cut the switch. I didn't hurry to get out of the car, either. Just leaned back and lit a fifty-cent cigar, and then tipped my hat over one ear and touched the horn button, causing it to play "Tuxedo Junction" for forty-eight seconds. Then I looked over toward the pool hall.

Well, for a minute I thought that I shouldn't have come, if that was the effect my return to the fold was going to have. And from then on I forgot about anything except how to get out of here.

There were two figures slouched in the glowing doorway of the pool room. It was up a small side street, so short that the city had depended on the place, and old institution, to supply the street lighting. Looking carefully, I made out one of the silhouetted figures as Happy Sam, and the other was Fred Bellew. They just looked out at me; they didn't move; they didn't say anything, and when I said, "Hiya, small fry— remember me?" I noticed that along the darkened walls flanking the bright doorway were ranked the whole crowd of them—the whole gang. It was a shock; it was a little too casually perfect. I didn't like it.

"Hi," said Fred quietly. I knew he wouldn't like the big-timing. I didn't expect any of them to like it, of course, but Fred's dislike sprang from distaste, and the others' from resentment, and for the first time I felt a little cheap. I climbed out over the door of the roadster and let them have a gander at my fine feathers.

Sam snorted and said, "Jellybean!" very clearly. Someone else giggled, and from the darkness beside the building came a high-pitched, "Woo-woo!"

I walked up to Sam and grinned at him. I didn't feel like grinning. "I ain't seen you in so long I almost forgot what a heel you were," I said. "How you making?"

"I'm doing all right," he said, and added offensively, "I'm still *working* for a living."

The murmur that ran through the crowd told me that the really smart thing to do was to get back into that shiny new automobile and hoot along out of there. I stayed.

"Wise, huh?" I said weakly.

They'd been drinking, I realized—all of them. I was suddenly in a spot. Sam put his hands in his pockets and looked at me down his nose. He was the only short man that ever could do that to me. After a thick silence he said:

"Better get back to yer crystal balls, phony. We like guys that sweat. We even like guys that have rackets, if they run them because they're smarter or tougher than the next one. But luck and gab ain't enough. Scram."

I looked around helplessly. I was getting what I'd begged for. What had I expected, anyway? Had I thought that these boys would crowd around and shake my hand off for acting this way? There was something missing somewhere, and when I realized what it was, it hit me. Fred Bellew—he was just standing there saying nothing. The old equalizer wasn't functioning any more. Fred wasn't aiming to stop any trouble between me and Sam. I was never so alone in my life!

They hardly moved, but they were all around me suddenly. If I couldn't think of something quickly, I was going to be mobbed. And when those mugs started mobbing a man, they did it up just fine. I drew a deep breath.

"I'm not asking for anything from you, Sam. Nothing; that means advice, see?"

"You're gettin' it!" he flared. "You and your seeanses. We heard about you. Hanging up widow-women for fifty bucks a throw to talk to their 'dear departed'! P-sykik investigator! With a line! Go on; beat it!"

I had a leg to stand on now. "A phony, huh? Why you

gabby Irishman, I'll bet I could put a haunt on you that would make that hair of yours stand up on end, if you have guts enough to go where I tell you to."

"You'll bet? That's a laugh. Listen at that, gang." He laughed, then turned to me and talked through one side of his mouth. "All right, you wanted it. Come on, rich guy; you're called. Fred'll hold the stakes. How about ten of your lousy bucks for every one of mine? Here, Fred—hold this sawbuck."

"I'll give you twenty to one," I said half hysterically. "And I'll take you to a place where you'll run up against the home-liest, plumb-meanest old haunt you ever heard of."

The crowd roared. Sam laughed with them, but didn't try to back out. With any of that gang, a bet was a bet. He'd taken me up, and he'd set odds, and he was bound. I just nodded and put two century notes into Fred Bellew's hand. Fred and Sam climbed into the car, and just as we started, Sam leaned out and waved.

"See you in hell, fellas," he said. "I'm goin' to raise me a ghost, and one of us is going to scare the other one to death!"

I honked my horn to drown out the whooping and holler-ing from the sidewalk and got out of there. I turned up the parkway and headed out of town.

"Where to?" Fred asked after a while.

"Stick around," I said, not knowing.

There must be some place not far from here where I could find an honest-to-God haunt, I thought, one that would make Sam back-track and set me up with the boys again. I opened the compartment in the dashboard and let Ikey out. Ikey was a little twisted imp who'd got his tail caught in between two sheets of steel when they were assembling the car, and had to stay there until it was junked.

"Hey, Ike," I whispered. He looked up, the gleam of the compartment light shining redly in his bright little eyes. "Whistle for the professor, will you? I don't want to yell for him because those mugs in the back seat will hear me. They can't hear you."

"O.K., boss," he said; and putting his fingers to his lips, he gave vent to a blood-curdling, howling scream.

That was the prof's call-letters, as it were. The old man flew ahead of the car, circled around and slid in beside me through the window, which I'd opened a crack for him.

"My goodness," he panted, "I wish you wouldn't summon me to a location which is traveling with this high degree of celerity. It was all I could do to catch up with you."

"Don't give me that, professor," I whispered. "You can catch a stratoliner if you want to. Say, I have a guy in the back who wants to get a real scare from a ghost. Know of any around here?"

The professor put on his ghostly pince-nez. "Why, yes. Remember my telling you about the Wolfmeyer place?"

"Golly—he's bad."

"He'll serve your purpose admirably. But don't ask me to go there with you, None of us ever associates with Wolfmeyer. And for Heaven's sake, be careful."

"I guess I can handle him. Where is it?"

He gave me explicit directions, bade me good night and left. I was a little surprised; the professor traveled around with me a great deal, and I'd never seen him refuse a chance to see some new scenery. I shrugged it off and went my way. I guess I just didn't know any better.

I headed out of town and into the country to a certain old farmhouse. Wolfmeyer, a Pennsylvania Dutchman, had hanged himself there. He had been, and was, a bad egg. Instead of being a nice guy about it all, he was the rebel type. He knew perfectly well that unless he did plenty of good to make up for the evil, he'd be stuck where he was for the rest of eternity. That didn't seem to bother him at all. He got surly and became a really bad spook. Eight people had died in that house since the old man rotted off his own rope. Three of them were tenants who had rented the place, and three were hobos, and two were psychic investigators. They'd all hanged themselves. That's the way Wolfmeyer worked. I think he really enjoyed haunting. He certainly was thorough about it anyway.

I didn't want to do any real harm to Happy Sam. I just wanted to teach him a lesson. And look what happened!

We reached the place just before midnight. No one had said much, except that I told Fred and Sam about Wolfmeyer, and pretty well what was to be expected from him. They did a good deal of laughing about it, so I just shut up and drove. The next item of conversation was Fred's, when he made the terms of the bet. To win, Sam was to stay in the house until dawn. He wasn't to call for help and he wasn't to leave. He had to bring in a coil of rope, tie a noose in one end and string the other up on "Wolfmeyer's Beam"—the great oaken beam on which the old man had hung himself, and eight others after him. This was as an added temptation to Wolfmeyer to work on Happy Sam, and

was my idea. I was to go in with Sam, to watch him in case
the thing became dangerous. Fred was to stay in the car a
hundred yards down the road and wait.

I parked the car at the agreed distance and Sam and I got
out. Sam had my tow rope over his shoulder, already noosed.
Fred had quieted down considerably, and his face was dead
serious.

"I don't think I like this," he said, looking up the road at
the house. It hunched back from the highway, and looked
like a malign being deep in thought.

I said, "Well, Sam? Want to pay up now and call it quits?"

He followed Fred's gaze. It sure was a dreary-looking
place, and his liquor had fizzed away. He thought a minute,
then shrugged and grinned. I had to admire the rat. "Hell, I'll
go through with it. Can't bluff me with scenery, phony."

Surprisingly, Fred piped up, "I don't think he's a phony,
Sam. He showed me something one day, over on Tenth Avenue. A little store. There was something funny about it. We
had a little scrap afterward, and I was sore for a long time,
but—I think he has something there."

The resistance made Sam stubborn, though I could see by
his face that he knew better. "Come on, phony," he said and
swung up the road.

We climbed into the house by way of a cellar door that
slanted up to a window on the first floor. I hauled out a flash-
light and lit the way to the beam. It was only one of many
that delighted in turning the sound of one's footsteps into
laughing whispers that ran round and round the rooms and
halls and would not die. Under the famous beam the dusty
floor was dark-stained.

I gave Sam a hand in fixing the rope, and then clicked
off the light. It must have been tough on him then. I didn't
mind, because I knew I could see anything before it got to
me, and even then, no ghost could see me. Not only that, for
me the walls and floors and ceilings were lit with the phos-
phorescent many-hued glow of the ever-present ghost plants.
For its eerie effect I wished Sam could see the ghost-molds
feeding greedily on the stain under the beam.

Sam was already breathing heavily, but I knew it would
take more than just darkness and silence to get his goat. He'd
have to be alone, and then he'd have to have a visitor or so.

"So long, kid," I said, slapping him on the shoulder; and I
turned and walked out of the room.

I let him hear me go out of the house and then I crept

silently back. It was without doubt the most deserted place I have ever seen. Even ghosts kept away from it, excepting, of course, Wolfmeyer's. There was just the luxurious vegetation, invisible to all but me, and the deep silence rippled by Sam's breath. After ten minutes or so I knew for certain that Happy Sam had more guts than I'd ever have credited him with. He had to be scared. He couldn't—or wouldn't—scare himself.

I crouched down against the wall of an adjoining room and made myself comfortable. I figured Wolfmeyer would be along pretty soon. I hoped earnestly that I could stop the thing before it got too far. No use in making this any more than a good lesson for a wiseacre. I was feeling pretty smug about it all, and I was totally unprepared for what happened.

I was looking toward the doorway opposite when I realized that for some minutes there had been the palest of pale glows there. It brightened as I watched; brightened and flickered gently. It was green, the green of things moldy and rotting away; and with it came a subtly harrowing stench. It was the smell of flesh so very dead that it had ceased to be really odorous. It was utterly horrible, and I was honestly scared out of my wits. It was some moments before the comforting thought of my invulnerability came back to me, and I shrank lower and closer to the wall and watched.

And Wolfmeyer came in.

His was the ghost of an old, old man. He wore a flowing, filthy robe, and his bare forearms thrust out in front of him were stringy and strong. His head, with its tangled hair and beard, quivered on a broken, ruined neck like the blade of a knife just thrown into soft wood. Each slow step as he crossed the room set his head to quivering again. His eyes were alight; red they were, with deep green flames buried in them. His canine teeth had lengthened into yellow, blunt tusks, and they were like pillars supporting his crooked grin. The putrescent green glow was a horrid halo about him. He was a bright and evil thing.

He passed me, completely unconscious of my presence, and paused at the door of the room where Sam waited by the rope. He stood just outside it, his claws extended, the quivering of his head slowly dying. He stared in at Sam, and suddenly opened his mouth and howled. It was a quiet, deadly sound, one that might have come from the throat of a distant dog, but, though I couldn't see into the other room, I knew that Sam had jerked his head around and was staring at the ghost. Wolfmeyer raised his arms a trifle, seemed to totter a bit, and then moved into the room.

I snapped myself out of the crawling terror that gripped me and scrambled to my feet. If I didn't move fast—

Tiptoeing swiftly to the door, I stopped just long enough to see Wolfmeyer beating his arms about erratically over his head, a movement that made his robe flutter and his whole figure pulsate in the green light; just long enough to see Sam on his feet, wide-eyed, staggering back and back toward the rope. He clutched his throat and opened his mouth and made no sound, and his head tilted, his neck bent, his twisted face gaped at the ceiling as he clumped backward away from the ghost and into the ready noose. And then I leaned over Wolfmeyer's shoulder, put my lips to his ear, and said: "*Boo!*"

I almost laughed. Wolfmeyer gave a little squeak, jumped about ten feet, and, without stopping to look around, high-tailed out of the room so fast that he was just a blur. That was one scared old spook!

At the same time Happy Sam straightened, his face relaxed and relieved, and sat down with a bump under the noose. That was as close a thing as ever I want to see. He sat there, his face soaking wet with cold sweat, his hands between his knees, staring limply at his feet.

"That'll show you!" I exulted, and walked over to him. "Pay up, scum, and may you starve for that week's pay!" He didn't move. I guess he was plenty shocked.

"Come on!" I said, "Pull yourself together, man! Haven't you seen enough? That old fellow will be back any second now. On your feet!"

He didn't move.

"Sam!"

He didn't move.

"*Sam!*" I clutched at his shoulder. He pitched over sideways and lay still.

He was quite dead.

I didn't do anything and for a while I didn't say anything. Then I said hopelessly, as I knelt there. "Aw, Sam. Sam— cut it out, fella."

After a minute I rose slowly and started for the door. I'd taken three steps when I stopped. Something was happening! I rubbed my hand over my eyes. Yes, it—it was getting dark! The vague luminescence of the vines and flowers of the ghost-world was getting dimmer, fading, fading—

But that had never happened before!

No difference. I told myself desperately, it's happening now, all right. *I got to get out of here!*

See? You see? It was the stuff—that damn stuff from the Shottle Bop. It was wearing off! When Sam died it . . . it stopped working on me! Was this what I had to pay for the bottle? Was this what was to happen if I used it for revenge?

The light was almost gone—and now it was gone. I couldn't see a thing in the room but one of the doors. Why could I see that doorway? What was that pale-green light that set off its dusty frame?

Wolfmeyer!

I got to get out of here!

I couldn't see ghosts any more. Ghosts could see me now. I ran. I darted across the dark room and smashed into the wall on the other side. I reeled back from it, blood spouting from between the fingers I slapped to my face. I ran again. Another wall clubbed me. Where was that other door? I ran again, and again struck a wall. I screamed and ran again. I tripped over Sam's body. My head went through the noose. It whipped down on my windpipe, and my neck broke with an agonizing crunch. I floundered there for half a minute, and then dangled.

Dead as hell, I was. Wolfmeyer, he laughed and laughed.

Fred found me and Sam in the morning. He took our bodies away in the car. Now I've got to stay here and haunt this damn old house. Me and Wolfmeyer.

THE ROCKET OF 1955

Stirring Science Stories
April

by C. M. Kornbluth (1923-1958)

*C. M. Kornbluth was a member of the legend-
ary Futurians, that group of New York kids who
were in at the beginning of fandom and from
whose ranks came many of the major writers and
editors in the field. Kornbluth's solo stories were often grim, reflecting his personality and generally
cynical attitude toward the world as he saw it. His
collaborations with Frederik Pohl have become
classics, but he was a very important individual
voice in science fiction, and he has never really
been replaced.*

*The short-short is one of the most difficult of
literary forms, but not for Cyril Kornbluth*

(I'm sure that Marty never met Cyril Kornbluth, who died
of a heart attack at a tragically young age, but I did. He was,
I believe, the youngest of the Futurians, three years younger
than myself so that he was only fifteen when the organization
was born with both him and myself as members. He was also
perhaps the most brilliant of us all—but erratically and
morosely brilliant. Of us all, he was closest to Fred Pohl. To
me, he was never close at all. As I look back at it. I think he
never liked me: because, I think, I was loud and cheerful and
so self-centered that I never noticed he never liked me. After
he died and I worked it out, I felt bad that I had made no effort to make him like me better, but, of course, it was too
late—I.A.)

The scheme was all Fein's, but the trimmings that made it
more than a pipe dream and its actual operation depended on
me. How long the plan had been in incubation I do not
know, but Fein, one spring day, broke it to me in crude

form. I pointed out some errors, corrected and amplified on
the thing in general, and told him that I'd have no part of
it—and changed my mind when he threatened to reveal certain indiscretions committed by me some years ago.

It was necessary that I spend some months in Europe, con-
ducting research work incidental to the scheme. I returned
with recorded statements, old newspapers, and photostatic
copies of certain documents. There was a brief, quiet interview with that old, bushy-haired Viennese worshipped incon-
tinently by the mob; he was convinced by the evidence I had
compiled that it would be wise to assist us.

You all know what happened next—it was the professor's
historic radio broadcast. Fein had drafted the thing, I had
rewritten it, and told the astronomer to assume a German accent while reading. Some of the phrases were beautiful:
"American dominion over the very planets! . . . veil at last
ripped aside . . . man defies gravity . . . travel through limitless space . . . plant the red-white-and-blue banner in the soil
of Mars!"

The requested contributions poured in. Newspapers and
magazines ostentatiously donated yard-long checks of a few
thousand dollars; the government gave a welcome half-mil-
lion; heavy sugar came from the "Rocket Contribution
Week" held in the nation's public schools; but independent
contributions were the largest. We cleared seven million dollars, and then started to build the spaceship.

The virginium that took up most of the money was tin
plate; the monoatomic fluorine that gave us our terrific speed
was hydrogen. The takeoff was a party for the newsreels: the
big, gleaming bullet extravagant with vanes and projections;
speeches by the professor; Farley, who was to fly it to Mars,
grinning into the cameras. He climbed an outside ladder to
the nose of the thing, then dropped into the steering compartment. I screwed down the soundproof door, smiling as he
hammered to be let out. To his surprise, there was no duplicate of the elaborate dummy controls he had been practicing
on for the past few weeks.

I cautioned the pressmen to stand back under the shelter,
and gave the professor the knife switch that would send the
rocket on its way. He hesitated too long—Fein hissed into his
ear: "Anna Pareloff of Cracow, Herr Professor . . ."

The triple blade clicked into the sockets. The vaned projectile roared a hundred yards into the air with a wobbling
curve—then exploded.

A photographer, eager for an angle shot, was killed; so

were some kids. The steel roof protected the rest of us. Fein and I shook hands, while the pressmen screamed into the telephones which we had provided.

But the professor got drunk, and, disgusted with the part he had played in the affair, told all and poisoned himself. Fein and I left the cash behind and hopped a freight. We were picked off it by a vigilance committee (headed by a man who had lost fifty cents in our rocket). Fein was too frightened to talk or write so they hanged him first, and gave me a paper and pencil to tell the story as best I could.

Here they come, with an insulting thick rope.

THEY

Unknown
April

by Robert A. Heinlein

Robert Heinlein's popularity and skill as a science-fiction writer has obscured his real talent and feel for fantasy. "They" is a stunning accomplishment and one of his finest efforts. It is a story in the tradition of Robert Sheckley and Philip K. Dick before there was one.

(Do you know what "solipsism" is? Any person with a spark of introversion has gone through a period of solipsism and wondered what he (or she) was and how it had happened that he (or she) was *the* living thing for whom the whole illusion had been created. Generally, as one grows up and becomes involved with the world, one forgets, unless one is "paranoid" in the morbid sense. Well Bob Heinlein has here written the classical tale of solipsism. It can never be done again, and no one who has read this would even dream of trying.—I.A.)

EVOLUTION'S END

Thrilling Wonder Stories
April

by Robert Arthur (1909-1969)

*Robert Arthur (born Robert A. Feder) became a
well known Hollywood screenwriter, but he was
also a talented (and sadly neglected) author of
..mystery, fantasy, and science fiction, whose "Mur-
chison Morks" series in* Argosy *had a devoted following. He was also a neglected editor who
"ghosted" several of the books credited to Alfred
..Hitchcock and (under his own name) edited the
excellent anthology* Davy Jones' Haunted Locker
*(1965). Unfortunately, his best short fiction has
never been collected.*

*"Evolution's End" addresses several profound
questions, including The Purpose of Man and The
Future of Mankind. It also happens to be one of
the very best stories of 1941.*

(Such is science fiction these days that its stars, and even a
number of its second-raters, have no trouble whatever in getting exposure. The world gets to know them and to make
much of them.

Forty years ago, however, even the greatest writers were
obscure. The conventions were few and small, and outside the
immediate field of science fiction all was dark.

So it was that Robert Arthur labored without applause. I
never met him and knew him only as a name attached to stories. My opinion of his abilities can be measured by this,
however. In the first decade of television when I noted that
some screenplays were written by Robert Alan Aurthur, I
had the vague feeling that it was "my" Robert Arthur with
his last name unaccountably misspelled. I.A.)

Aydem was pushing the humming vacuum duster along the
endless stone corridors of the great underground Repository

of Natural Knowledge when Ayveh, coming up quietly behind him, put her hands over his eyes.

He whirled, to see Ayveh's laughing face, mischief dancing on it.

"Ayveh!" he exclaimed eagerly. "But what are you doing here? It is forbidden any woman—"

"I know." Ayveh threw back her head, her long hair, richly golden, rippling down her shoulders to contrast with the pale apple-green of the shapeless linen robe she wore—a robe identical to Aydem's, the universal garb of the human slaves of the more-than-human Masters who ruled the world. It was an underground world. Generations since, the Masters, their great, thin-skulled heads and mighty brains proving uncomfortably vulnerable to the ordinary rays of the sun, had retreated underground.

"But Dmu Dran wishes to see you, Aydem," the girl Ayveh went on, "and he sent me to fetch you. There are visitors arriving, and you must convey them from the tube station to his demonstration chambers. They are very important visitors."

"But why did he not transmit the order to me by directed thinking?" Aydem asked, puzzled. "He knows that even out here, in the Exhibit Section, I would receive it."

"Perhaps he sent me because he knew I wished to see you." Ayveh suggested happily. "And because he knew you hungered for the sight of me. There are times, Aydem, when Dmu Dran actually seems to understand what feelings are."

"A Master understand feelings?" Aydem's tone was scornful. "The Masters are nothing but brains. Great machines for thought, which know nothing of joy or sorrow or hunger for another."

"Shh!" Frightened, Ayveh put her fingers to his lips. "You must not say such things. Generous as Dmu Dran is, he is still a Master, and if his mind should chance to be listening, he would have to punish you. It might even mean the fuel chambers."

Aydem kissed the fingers that had stopped his speech. Then, seeing the mingled fear and longing in her face, he drew her close and kissed her savagely, tasting the sweetness of her lips until a pulse was beating like a hammer in his throat.

Shaken, Ayveh freed herself and looked about, fearful that someone might have seen. There was no one. The corridors of the exhibit chambers of this tremendous museum of natural history of which their Master, Dmu Dran, was curator, wound endlessly away in darkness except for the tiny lighted area that enclosed them.

"There is no one to see," Ayden reassured her. "I alone tend the exhibit chambers, and only I am permitted to leave the Master's quarters without orders. And if any did see, who would tell?"

"Ekno," the girl whispered. "He would tell. He would like to see you sent into the fuel chambers, because he knows that we—that we—"

Her voice faltered and trailed off at the look of grimness in the man's face. Aydem stared down at her, at her loveliness, before he spoke. He himself stood nearly six feet tall, and his dark hair was a shaggy mane dropping almost to his shoulders. He was beardless, for all facial hair had been removed by an unguent when he was a youth—a whim of Dmu Dran's, though many Masters were less fastidious.

His body held the sturdiness of the trunk of an oak— which he had never seen. And though his duties were light in this mechanized, sub-surface world to which man's life on Mother Earth had retreated with the evolution of the Masters, muscles corded his body and were but lightly hidden by the green robe that swathed him.

And there was a tension in those muscles now, as if they would explode into action if only they had something to seize upon and rend and tear.

"Ayveh," he said, "I have seen the mating papers. I took them from the machine to the Master a period ago. Our request to be assigned as each other's mate has been denied. On the basis of the Selector Machine rating, I have been assigned to Teema, your assistant in overseeing the Master's household, and you to Ekno, who tends to minor repairs."

"That ugly hairy one?" Horror almost robbed Ayveh of her voice. "Who smells so bad and is always looking after me when I pass? No! I—I would rather kill myself first."

"I"—there was savagery in Ayden's words—"would rather kill the Masters!"

"Oh, no!" the girl whispered in terror. "You must not speak it. If you harmed Dmu Dran—if it became known even that you wished to—we should all be destroyed. Not in the fuel chambers. We should go to the example cells. And we would not die—for a long time."

"Better that," Aydem said stonily, "than to be slaves, to be mated to those we despise, to keep forever our silence and obey orders, to live and die like beasts!"

Then, at Ayveh's sudden gasp of terror, Aydem whirled.

His own features paled as he drew himself to attention. For Dmu Dran, their Master, had come silently up behind them as they spoke, the air-suspended chair which carried him making no sound.

And Dmu Dran, his great round face blank, his large popping eyes unreadable, stared at Aydem with an unusual intensity. Yet no thoughts were coming from the mind within the huge globular, thin-walled skull over which only a little wispy hair, like dried hay, was plastered.

Had Dmu Dran heard? Had he caught the emanations of violent emotion which must have been spreading all over the vicinity from Aydem? Was he now probing into their minds for the words they had just spoken? If he knew or guessed them, their fate would be a terrible one.

But when Dmu Dran spoke—for mental communication with the undeveloped slave mind was fatiguing for a Master—his voice was mild.

"I fear," he said, in a thin piping tone, "that my servants are not happy. Perhaps they are upset by the mating orders that have arrived?"

Aydem of course was supposed to know nothing of the contents of the orders, having in theory no ability to read. But since Dmu Dran evidently knew he *could* read—he had been taught in his boyhood by a wise old slave long dead— boldness seemed the only course.

"Master," he said, "the girl Ayveh and I hoped to be mates. It is true we are not happy, because we have been assigned to others."

"Happiness." Dmu Dran spoke the word reflectively. "Unhappiness. Mmm. Those are things not given us to feel. You are aware emotion is not a desirable characteristic in a slave?"

"Aye, Master," Aydem agreed submissively.

"The selector machine," Dmu Dran went on, "shows both you and the girl Ayveh to be capable of much emotion. It also indicates in both of you a brain capacity large for a slave. It is for these reasons you have been denied each other. It is desired that slaves should be strong and healthy, intelligent, but not too intelligent, and lacking in emotion so they will not become discontented. You understand these things, do you not?"

"Aye, Master," Aydem agreed in some astonishment. Ayveh pressed close to him, frightened by the strange conduct of Dmu Dran—for no Master ever spoke so familiarly with a slave.

Dmu Dran was silent, as if thinking. While he waited, Aydem reflected that Dmu Dran was not exactly as other Masters were. To an untrained eye, all Masters looked much alike—a great, globular head set upon a small neckless body, the neck having disappeared in the course of evolution of the great head, so that the weight might be better rested on the stronger back and shoulder muscles.

But Dmu Dran was perceptibly taller than other Masters Aydem had seen. Aydem had not seen many—there were only some thousand of them, and they lived in small groups in far-flung underground Centers, if not entirely alone, as did Dmu Dran. Dmu Dran's cranium was also slightly smaller in diameter.

Now an odd expression touched the flat countenance of the Master.

"Aydem," he said, "You have seen the contents of these halls many times. But Ayveh has not. So come with me now, both of you. We have a little time, and I wish to view some specimens. It is many years since I last examined them."

He turned his chair, and Aydem, exchanging a look of puzzlement with Ayveh, followed him down the corridor between the great, glass-enclosed, hermetically sealed exhibits.

As they went, light sprang on alongside them, activated by the heat of their bodies on thermo-couples, and died away behind them. The Master led them several hundred yards, and halted at last in a section devoted to ancient animals of the Earth's youth.

There were here many beasts, huge and ferocious in appearance, reproduced in their natural environment, seen, save by Aydam, not more than half a dozen times a year. Only six or eight Masters were born each year, just enough to keep the total of a thousand from dwindling. They visited the Repository of Natural Knowledge in the course of their educational studies.

In the glass cases that lined the miles of corridors were exhibits, many of them animated so cunningly that the artificial replicas of man and animal of the past seemed endowed with life, encompassing all the natural history of the world from the mists of the unknown, millions of years before, to the present day. But since the great brains of the Masters needed to be apprised of a fact but once to make it theirs forever, there was never really occasion for a Master to come here twice.

Now Dmu Dran, Aydem and Ayveh stood before a great, orange-colored beast with black stripes, a snarl frozen upon his features, huge fangs, many inches in length, protruding from his jaws. Even though he was but a model of a beast dead many millennia, Ayveh instinctively drew closer to Aydem, as if the creature were indeed about to leap, and as if they were part of that group of men and women, much like themselves, that faced it in desperation with long, pointed sticks in their hands.

"The saber-tooth tiger," Dmu Dran said. "When it reigned on this Earth uncounted years ago, it was Master of Aiden, the world above, a scourge feared and hated by all other animals. For many thousands of years it grew more and more powerful, its dominance contested by few. By its great teeth it was known—terrible weapons for rending and tearing its prey. But in the end it ceased to be. Why did a beast like that, which no natural enemy could oppose, die, think you?"

"It must indeed have been a fearful opponent that conquered it, Master," Ayveh ventured uncertainly.

What might have been a smile, had a Master known smiling, rippled over the pale moon-face.

"Nature killed it," Dmu Dran informed them. "Nature destroyed it by her very generosity. Those tusks you see that gave it its name—Nature continued to add to their length and strength. But, alas! In her enthusiasm, she made them so long in the course of time that their possessor could not close its mouth, could not eat, and so eventually starved to death. Aye, Nature evolved her great and dread child right out of existence."

"That was indeed strange." Aydem frowned. "I do not understand. Why did she do so?"

"Nature has curious ways." Dmu Dran shrugged. "And having an infinity of time, she can afford an infinity of experiments. What she is not satisfied with, though she has made it supreme, she destroys."

Dmu Dran shot his chair a few yards to the left.

"And here," he said, "is another great beast that was once master of the world when it was young."

The creature he now indicated stood far above a man's head, even a slave's. Three times, four times, five times higher than a slave did it tower.

"The great dinosaur of the Earth's infancy," Dmu Dran told them. "The hugest beast ever to shake the world with its tread. That one"—he pointed—"the largest land animal ever evolved. The enemies that could conquer it were few or none. Unmolested by the lesser denizens of the day and the night, it ruled the Earth by its very bulk. Yet it too passed. Why, think you?"

Aydem and Ayveh were silent, so Dmu Dran explained.

"Again Nature was overgenerous. To this creature whose bulk made it sovereign, it added still more bulk. Alack! In time she so increased the size of the beast that it could not get enough to eat, though it fed twenty-four hours of the day. It simply could not ingest fuel enough for its huge body. So in the end it too passed."

The man and the girl were still silent, their eyes wide with wonder. Dmu Dran abruptly shot his air car a hundred yards down the corridor and stopped again, the lights coming on automatically the moment he paused.

He was now before the section devoted to the evolution of man himself, beginning with a creature half man, half beast, and rising to a reproduction of the Masters who now ruled the world.

Uneducated though they were, Aydem and Ayveh saw and understood the procession of figures, each more erect, each less hairy, each larger-headed than the one before it.

Near the end of the line was an upright figure which caused Ayveh to gasp, it was so like Aydem.

"Man of the Early Machine Age"

Dmu Dran read the inscription on the imperishable metal plate at the foot of the figure. "Aye, your Aydem does look like him. For it was man of that period, balanced between ignorance and knowledge, that we Masters thought it best our slaves should resemble. But here is the exhibit that I have most pondered upon."

He moved a few feet, and they stood before the last half dozen figures.

"There"—and Dmu Dran, with one short arm, indicated a figure as tall as Aydem, but differing from the one just before it in that its head was half again as large—"there is the first of the Masters. A mutant, with a brain-weight double anything ever known in man before. John Master, his name was, and it was appropriate. For in the last ten thousand years, all humankind save slaves have been his descendants—not men now, but Masters. I have often speculated upon the chance that saw him born, and wondered if, had he never been conceived and brought to issue, the human species might not have turned in quite another direction."

Dmu Dran was silent, thinking, and the two slaves did not intrude upon his thoughts. Instead they studied the figures following this John Master of the large head. Each was larger-headed than the one before it, each smaller-bodied, shorter-necked, until the last figure might have been Dmu Dran himslf.

"It is an interesting point on which to wonder," Dmu Dran said after a time. "How would mankind have evolved had not my ancestor been born? The old records show that he was a cold and ruthless man, without sentiment. That by the power of his logical mind, and with the aid of his children, he seized the rule of the world and made his descendants supreme forever. Forever? Well—supreme ever since. So that now we Masters, the highest species of animal ever to evolve, are despotic rulers of the world, and if we wished, of the Solar System—even of the Universe.

"But we do not wish. The Solar System, save for this world, is lifeless, and it has never been worth our while to consider whether the stars beyond were worth reaching. We feel nothing, we enjoy nothing, for the capacity for those things has been bred out of us—evolved away in the course of yesterday's eons. We merely think, with our almost perfect brains, here in the bowels of the Earth, served by our slaves in a world almost effortless even for them.

"We are, so far as we know—and there is little we do not know—the Masters, nature's final product, evolution's end!"

Abruptly Dmu Dran's piping voice ceased, leaving tiny echoes rustling in the corridors. Aydem and Ayveh were alarmed and uneasy. Could Dmu Dran by chance be mad? Madness did sometimes afflict a Master, though rarely one of Dmu Dran's age. Usually they were much younger or much older, when the unexplainable insanity that was the only ailment the Masters had not conquered, took them.

"I sometimes think," Dmu Dran said after a moment, in a quieter tone now, "that though we consider ourselves the last step in evolution's chain, we may be wrong. Who knows what plans nature has for us? None of us. But we shall. I am going to put it to the test, the momentous test that may decide the whole future of the world, aye, of the Universe itself. For know, my servants, that my visitors today are the Masters of the Supreme Council, come at my invitation to examine a machine that I have made my life's work.

"It is a matter of electricity and rays that will stimulate the latent change that lies in all plants and animals. So that in one generation, an animal may progress from the form it was born with to the form its descendants a thousand generations away would have. Aye—in less than a generation, in a few periods!

"And I am going to propose to the Supreme Council that a chosen few of us Masters subject ourselves to the influence of this machine, that we may know what we are to become, in Nature's hidden scheme, in the persons of our grandchildren many times removed. I shall propose to them we raise ourselves now to the glories of the final form destined to the Masters, and I think they will agree.

"For we Masters, the favored children of nature, will hardly be loath to rise to the final position scarcely lower than gods that our philosophers have foreseen as ultimately ours!"

Excitement shone in Dmu Dran's popping eyes. But in a moment it died. He gestured.

"Return to your quarters, my servants. I shall meet my visitors myself, Aydem. Say nothing to anyone, and worry not for the moment concerning the mating assignments. Nothing will be done about such matters until I—know."

With that cryptic remark, he shot away down the corridor in his air-chair as Aydem and Ayveh stared at each other in perplexity and mounting hope.

In the periods of waiting that followed, there was tension in the slaves' quarters. All knew of the unprecedented visit of the Supreme Council, and somehow word got about that the mating assignments had come, but had not yet been announced by Dmu Dran.

Curiosity regarding these matters, however, was not as strong as it might have been had not slaves been for so many generations bred for docility and lack of emotion. Aydem and Ayveh's fellow servants exhibited only mild curiosity about any occurrence, and when not working, for the most part contented themselves with eating, sleeping, and playing simple games.

Only Ekno, the hairy one who coveted Ayveh, had a brain that busied itself with affairs outside its immediate concern. And Ekno, hatred in his face as he watched Aydem covertly, knew that something of great import was transpiring. He could scarcely contain himself to know what, and even took the great risk, unthinkable to the others, of snooping about Dmu Dran's private quarters under the pretense of making repairs, hoping to pick up some scrap of information.

In time, after many secret sessions in Dmu Dran's demonstration chambers, the Supreme Council left, each Master boarding his private air-car and being shot away through the great maze of tunnels that honeycombed the earth to his home center. With the President of the Council, the oldest living Master, went a large, heavy package which Aydem transported to his car with great care, little dreaming that the destiny of himself and Ayveh and countless millions of their unborn descendants lay within those careful wrappings.

After this, for some periods more, nothing happened. The other slaves almost forgot anything unusual had occurred. Only Ekno still watched Aydem's every move, eager for some evidence of wrong-doing he could present to Dmu Dran, or even to the Board of Slave Mating, supreme authority in regard to all slaves.

But with Dmu Dran's strange words ringing in his mind, Aydem made no move Ekno could seize upon. Save when outside the living quarters, to which Ekno by the nature of his duties was usually confined, Aydem and Ayveh did not even exchange words.

But Aydem's chief duty was to keep the interminable corridors of the exhibit section free from the natural rock dust that gathered, and only he was permitted to enter it. Ekno dared not follow him there, so it was there he and Ayveh met.

It was a great risk Ayveh took, for no woman was permitted to leave the living quarters at all. But Dmu Dran's words had given them courage. And it was possible for her, since she was chief of the women, to slip away from her duties for stolen moments from time to time.

On these occasions they exchanged few words. Their hearts spoke for them, and their tongues could be silent. Aydem eagerly showed the girl through the multitudinous exhibits that traced man's life on the planet.

Long years these had fascinated him. Countless periods he had spent studying them, and scanning the engraved metal placards that explained each detail of what he saw.

Though Ayveh could not read, he could interpret for her. And many of the exhibits spoke for themselves. Almost all were animated. A touch of a button set them in motion, and countless replicas of countless types of men who had walked the world and vanished, went through the acts of life again.

In engrossed silence, Aydem and Ayveh watched hairy men of the Earth's infancy defend themselves with fire and spear and arrow against the attacks of wild animals. They saw other men, higher in the scale of evolution, build simple dwellings, strike fire from flints or produce it from spun sticks, hunt, plant seed, weave cloth, cook, and do all the multitudinous acts that were necessary to existence.

Most of all, Aydem was fascinated not by the exhibits

showing the machine world just before the coming of the
Masters, but by the reproductions of man in his younger
days. Haltingly he tried to explain to Ayveh that he felt
within himself a kinship to those long dead men who had
made bows and arrows, planted and reaped their crops with
their hands, had tamed wild horses and on their backs ridden
down the wild boar and the wolf, had, with spear and arrow,
defended themselves against their enemies.

He stretched his arms, and his mighty muscles coiled and
knotted.

"Sometimes in my sleep," he told Ayveh, his eyes burning,
"I am no longer within these underground dominions of the
Masters, but am free upon Aiden, the Earth's surface. I know
what it must be like, for I can see it all in my dreams. I can
feel the warm touch of what they call the sun, and underfoot
the roughness of the growing things called grass. Animals, not
artificial like these, but alive, roam the land, and in my
dreams I combat them."

"It must be a wonderful place," Ayveh whispered wistfully.
"So strange and different from this."

"Sometimes I feel as if I were going to burst, forever
locked away within these walls of rock where the Masters
choose to live!" Aydem burst out. "I wish to work, to fight, to
conquer—"

Somewhere nearby there was a scraping noise. Ayveh
gasped with terror, and Aydem whirled instantly. The sound
of running footsteps sprang up several corridors away. Aydem dashed in that direction, caught a glimpse of a man running toward the living quarters.

He put on a burst of speed, but the other outdistanced him
and ducked through a door before Aydem could get close
to identify the spying one.

"But it was Ekno," he said, his voice grim, as he hurried
back to take the frightened Ayveh to her quarters. "It was
Ekno, and he was spying on us. He overheard. He will report
to Dmu Dran."

"But the Master," Ayveh faltered, "he did not mind before—"

Aydem took her hand.

"There is no telling what a Master will do," he growled.
"He may have been amusing himself. We must be prepared.
Do not sleep this period. Wait for me behind this door that
leads from the quarters to the exhibits. Come if I call. Have
food with you."

"But Aydem!" Ayveh exclaimed, wide-eyed. "You would not question the decree of a Master?"

"If Dmu Dran condemns me to the fuel chamber," Aydem answered, "I will kill him and we will try to escape. See!"

From beneath his tunic he withdrew a knife with a long gleaming blade and a heavy handle.

"I have had this long," he boasted. "It is part of an exhibit that became out of order. I fixed it under Dmu Dran's direction. And stole this unnoticed. I will kill Dmu Dran with it if I must. There are many tunnels that may have been abandoned leading out from this center. I have heard it whispered, by old Temu who taught me when I was young, that one leads to the world above. We will seek it. We will seek escape. If we must, we will die. But I will not go to the fuel chambers."

He looked at her white face.

"But I can go alone—" he began.

Ayveh flung herself into his arms.

"No, Aydem, no!" she whispered. "Where you go, I will go. If you live, I will live. If you die, I will die."

He kissed her then strongly, passionately. And as he kissed her, the command came. By directed thinking. To report at once to Dmu Dran.

With unfaltering stride Aydem entered Dmu Dran's personal quarters. As he went in, he passed Ekno, and there was a smirk of triumph on the hairy one's features. Aydem did not deign to glance at the other. He closed the door behind him, and was in the presence of Dmu Dran.

The flat, pop-eyed face of the Master was as blank as ever.

"Aydem, my servant," he piped, "a charge has been placed against you. A serious charge. You merit punishment. If I do not punish you, the charge may come to the attention of the Board of Slave Mating. It will wish to know why. It will send for you, and when you are placed beneath the instruments, it will know I have been guilty of a crime too. It will know that you are far above the allowed intelligence quotient for a slave, and that I have falsified your records since childhood, as I have falsified those of the servant Ayveh."

Aydem stared at him in speechless astonishment.

"You are startled, Servant Aydem," the Master said. "But it is true I, a Master, have violated one of the most rigid rules of the few that Masters must observe. I have deliberately preserved from destruction in the fuel chambers a man and a woman of as high a physical and mental level as the world has known since the days of the first Master.

"I have done this for reasons of my own. I think we shall soon know whether I have been right to—"

He did not finish, for behind him a section of the wall grew luminous, and a figure began to appear, seemingly within it.

Dmu Dran made a gesture. Aydem withdrew quickly to one side, beyond the seeing range of the communicator panel, and the Master turned. A voice, piping but stern, spoke from the wall:

"Dmu Dran! Nalu Tah, president of the Supreme Council, speaks."

"Dmu Dran listens."

"Dmu Dran! Of the ten subjects upon whom the Supreme Council has been testing the apparatus devised by you for the precipitating of evolutionary change, the last has just gone mad. The brain capacity of all increased by fifty per cent, and the skulls enlarged during their subjection to the rays of your apparatus. Each, however, after reaching an increase of approximately fifty per cent in brain size, was afflicted by the dread madness. All have been destroyed. Dmu Dran, you are ordered to report at once to Judicial Center to make explanation, and be judged."

"Dmu Dran hears."

The glow in the wall died. The great-headed figure of the president of the Supreme Council vanished. Dmu Dran let out a little sigh.

"Mad," he whispered. "All went mad. As some are going mad already, and as in a hundred thousand years all will, the entire race of Masters. So that they will be no more. In a hundred thousand years, the supreme creation of Nature, the mightiest thinking machine she has ever produced, will be destroyed. By the irresistible force of Nature herself, adding always to the gift she has given, until the weight of it crushes us out of existence. Yes, crushes us literally out of existence."

He turned, faced the wondering Aydem.

"Aydem, my servant," he said, "I have been right. I have feared a certain thing, and I have learned that my fears are well founded. I have concentrated the evolutionary development of a hundred thousand years in certain selected Masters, and all have gone mad. The reason I can easily guess. Their brains grew in size, until the very weight of the brain crushed many of its own cells. The very multiplicity of the cells piled layer upon top of layer destroyed the more delicate. The process can already be seen at work occasionally now. In time it will encompass all.

"The bulk of the dinosaur, which made it supreme, killed it. The teeth of the saber-tooth tiger destroyed it. And the brain of the Masters, which has made them supreme, is fore-destined to destroy them just as utterly.

"Aydem, you are a man as men were before the sudden branching that produced the Masters. A branching that I now know was but another experiment on Nature's part, leading nowhere. Hark you—the ultimate evolution of man is yet to come. Yes, yet to come.

"Yet, if the Masters live out their existence, Nature may well be foiled, or at the least, set back a thousand million years in her plans. For in a hundred thousand years, when the Masters are gone, man may well be gone too.

"Yet, if the Masters were to vanish now, while you and Ayveh lived, from *your* loins might spring the line that will yet reach upward to the stars."

Dmu Dran's voice piped off into silence. But he was not finished speaking, for after a moment he shook himself and continued.

"What man will be like in the end I do not know. He will not be a great-headed thinking machine, I am sure. He will have a mind, yes, but soul too, and body, all balanced into a whole that will far surpass us, the Masters.

"What I am going to do is hard. Yet perhaps I am but a tool of Nature's too. Perhaps she designed me for this very purpose—to put evolution back upon its proper track.

"Aydem, you may never understand. That does not matter. These are my last orders. Take Ayveh. Go to the very end of the exhibit section. There, in a section where the rooms have been crushed by falling rock, you will find one stone perfectly round and seemingly too great for a thousand men to move. Upon one side is a red spot. Push at this spot. The rock will roll aside and you will see an entrance. Descend. A passage-way will lead you upward and in time you will come out upon Aiden, the surface of the Earth above—a region into which we Masters have not chosen to venture save but fleet-ingly for a thousand years.

"You will have the half of one period in which to do this. Then I will press a button here beside me. The details you would not understand. But when I do, every inch of these vast tunnels that we Masters have created throughout the Earth's interior will collapse. Every Master will die at the same instant. And every slave—for there are none living save yourselves whose blood may go into the lifestream of the Man to come. It would take centuries for them to evolve

again as a group to your level. So you two, Aydem and
Ayveh, will be, to all historical appearance, the first man and
woman. The gap between you and your ancestors will be
broken when I press this button.

"You will not understand my reasons, I say. But you will
survive above, for you have long studied the great exhibit
chambers and know what you must do to wrest a living from
Nature. In time you will forget that such things as Masters
ever existed. And your kind will mount upward toward the
stars, on a true course which has been sidetracked for only a
little while."

Dmu Dran fell silent, as if musing, and his pale round face
seemed sad. Aydem, in truth, understood but little. Yet he
understood Dmu Dran's instructions, and his heart leaped
within his breast.

Dmu Dran looked up.

"Go now," he ordered.

Aydem forced his way through the tangle of weeds and
roots that choked the entrance of the cave, in which the long
tunnel he and Ayveh had traversed for an interminable time
ended. He stood upright, and drew Ayveh after him.

They had emerged upon the surface of the Earth at night.
The moon, a thing of wondrous beauty to them, rode the
heavens low in the east, a great orange ball. A summer
night's wind breathed through the great masses of tangled
vegetation that surrounded them, and the scent of flowers was
carried by it.

The man and the woman breathed deep, speechless with
wonder and joy. Somewhere near a nightbird was trilling, and
from farther away came the cry of an unknown animal. Both
sounds alike were music to their ears.

"Free!" Aydem whispered exultingly. "Ayveh, we are free!
We are slaves no more!"

Bathed by the moonlight, caressed by the night breeze,
they stood close together, his arm about her, and feasted their
eyes and ears on the world.

"The knife I stole," Aydem said, "I will keep. With it we
will make what we need, kill what we need. Ayveh, Ayveh—"

His words broke off. Of a sudden the very earth beneath
them had begun to tremble. It seemed to shudder. One long-
drawn puff of air, like a hollow death-gasp, seemed forced
from the cavern before which they stood, and the ground under them shook, Ayveh was thrown into Aydem's arms, and
he held her close until the violent tremor had passed.

"Dmu Dran has pressed the button," he said, understanding. "The Masters are no more. Ayveh, my mate, the Masters are no more! We are free, and there is no one to come after us. We will know struggle and conflict and labor, but we are free!"

He held her close and kissed her. Then at last, hand in hand, they set out together into the world Dmu Dran had given them. Aydem—the first man. And Ayveh—the first woman.

MICROCOSMIC GOD

Astounding Science Fiction
April

by Theodore Sturgeon

*There are many who feel that this is the finest
story to come from the typewriter of Theodore
Sturgeon. It was selected by the Science Fiction
Writers of America for their* Hall of Fame *short
story volume, and it has received critical acclaim
from numerous quarters.*

The theme of survival *has a long history in
science fiction, but no one ever surpassed the Sturgeon who wrote this inventive and convincing
story.*

(Finest story? Yes, I am among those that Marty refers to
as "many." However, truth is truth. I think this is the best of
his *science fiction* stories. I placed both "It" and "Bianca's
Hands" above it, but they are both fantasies. I must say that
what struck me most about the story, was pity and sorrow for
the small creatures and indignation at the "god" who, in my
mind, at the time I read the book was very much like the
"God" we were so busily taught to love and admire. Remember what 1941 was like!—I.A.)

Here is a story about a man who had too much power, and
a man who took too much, but don't worry; I'm not going
political on you. The man who had the power was named
James Kidder, and the other was his banker.

Kidder was quite a guy. He was a scientist and he lived on
a small island off the New England coast all by himself. He
wasn't the dwarfed little gnome of a mad scientist you read
about. His hobby wasn't personal profit, and he wasn't a meg-
alomaniac with a Russian name and no scruples. He wasn't
insidious, and he wasn't even particularly subversive. He kept
his hair cut and his nails clean and lived and thought like a
reasonable human being. He was slightly on the baby-faced

side; he was inclined to be a hermit; he was short and plump and—brilliant. His specialty was biochemistry, and he was always called *Mr.* Kidder. Not Dr." Not "Professor." Just Mr. Kidder.

He was an odd sort of apple and always had been. He had never graduated from any college or university because he found them too slow for him, and too rigid in their approach to education. He couldn't get used to the idea that perhaps his professors knew what they were talking about. That went for his texts, too. He was always asking questions, and didn't mind very much when they were embarrassing. He considered Gregor Mendel a bungling liar, Darwin an amusing philosopher, and Luther Burbank a sensationalist. He never opened his mouth without leaving his victim feeling breathless. If he was talking to someone who had knowledge, he went in there and got it. If he was talking to someone whose knowledge was already in his possession, he only asked repeatedly, "How do you know?" His most delectable pleasure was taken in cutting a fanatical eugenicist into conversational ribbons. So people left him alone and never, never asked him to tea. He was polite, but not politic.

He had a little money of his own, and with it he leased the island and built himself a laboratory. Now I've mentioned that he was a biochemist. But being what he was, he couldn't keep his nose in his own field. It wasn't too remarkable when he made an intellectual excursion wide enough to perfect a method of crystallizing Vitamin B_1 profitably by the ton—if anyone wanted it by the ton. He got a lot of money for it. He bought his island outright and put eight hundred men to work on an acre and a half of his ground, adding to his laboratory and building equipment. He got messing around with sisal fiber, found out how to fuse it, and boomed the banana industry by producing a practically unbreakable cord from the stuff.

You remember the popularizing demonstration he put on at Niagara, don't you? That business of running a line of the new cord from bank to bank over the rapids and suspending a ten-ton truck from the middle of it by razor edges resting on the cord? That's why ships now moor themselves with what looks like heaving line, no thicker than a lead pencil, that can be coiled on reels like garden hose. Kidder made cigarette money out of that, too. He went out and bought himself a cyclotron with part of it.

After that money wasn't money any more. It was large numbers in little books. Kidder used to use little amounts of it to have food and equipment sent out to him, but after a while that stopped, too. His bank dispatched a messenger by seaplane to find out if Kidder was still alive. The man returned two days later in a mused state, having been amazed something awesome at the things he'd seen out there. Kidder was alive, all right, and he was turning out a surplus of good food in an astonishingly simplified synthetic form. The bank wrote immediately and wanted to know if Mr. Kidder, in his own interest, was willing to release the secret of his dirtless farming. Kidder replied that he would be glad to, and enclosed the formulas. In a P. S. he said that he hadn't sent the information ashore because he hadn't realized anyone would be interested. That from a man who was responsible for the greatest sociological change in the second half of the twentieth century—factory farming. It made him richer; I mean it made his bank richer. He didn't give a rap.

But Kidder didn't really get started until about eight months after the bank messenger's visit. For a biochemist who couldn't even be called "Dr." he did pretty well. Here is a partial list of the things that he turned out:

A commercially feasible plan for making an aluminum alloy stronger than the best steel so that it could be used as a structural metal.

An exhibition gadget he called a light pump, which worked on the theory that light is a form of matter and therefore subject to physical and electromagnetic laws. Seal a room with a single light source, beam a cylindrical vibratory magnetic field to it from the pump, and the light will be led down it. Now pass the light through Kidder's "lens"—a ring which perpetuates an electric field along the lines of a high-speed iris-type camera shutter. Below this is the heart of the light pump—a ninety-eight-percent efficient light absorber, crystalline, which, in a sense, *loses* the light in its internal facets. The effect of darkening the room with this apparatus is slight but measurable. Pardon my layman's language, but that's the general idea.

Synthetic chlorophyll—by the barrel.

An airplane propeller efficient at eight times sonic speed.

A cheap goo you brush on over old paint, let harden, and then peel off like strips of cloth. The old paint comes with it. That one made friends fast.

A self-sustaining atomic disintegration of uranium's isotope 238, which is two hundred times as plentiful as the old standby, U-235.

That will do for the present. If I may repeat myself; for a

biochemist who couldn't even be called "Dr.," he did pretty well.

Kidder was apparently unconscious of the fact that he held power enough on his little island to become master of the world. His mind simply didn't run to things like that. As long as he was left alone with his experiments, he was well content to leave the rest of the world to its own clumsy and primitive devices. He couldn't be reached except by a radiophone of his own design, and its only counterpart was locked in a vault of his Boston bank. Only one man could operate it—the bank president. The extraordinarily sensitive transmitter would respond only to President Conant's own body vibrations. Kidder had instructed Conant that he was not to be disturbed except by messages of the greatest moment. His ideas and patents, when Conant could pry one out of him, were released under pseudonyms known only to Conant—Kidder didn't care.

The result, of course, was in infiltration of the most astonishing advancements since the dawn of civilization. The nation profited—the world profited. But most of all, the bank profited. It began to get a little oversize. It began getting its fingers into other pies. It grew more fingers and had to bake more figurative pies. Before many years had passed, it was so big that, using Kidder's many weapons, it almost matched Kidder in power.

Almost.

Now stand by while I squelch those fellows in the lower left-hand corner who've been saying all this while that Kidder's slightly improbable; that no man could ever perfect himself in so many ways in so many sciences.

Well, you're right. Kidder was a genius—granted. But his genius was not creative. He was, to the core, a student. He applied what he knew, what he saw, and what he was taught. When first he began working in his new laboratory on his island he reasoned something like this:

"Everything I know is what I have been taught by the sayings and writings of people who have studied the sayings and writings of people who have—and so on. Once in a while someone stumbles on something new and he or someone cleverer used the idea and disseminates it. But for each one that finds something really new, a couple of million gather and pass on information that is already current. I'd know more if I could get the jump on evolutionary trends. It takes too long to wait for the accidents that increase man's knowledge—my knowledge. If I had ambition enough now to figure out how to travel ahead in time, I could skim the surface of the future and just dip down when I saw something interesting. But time isn't that way. It can't be left behind or tossed ahead. What else is left?

"Well, there's the proposition of speeding intellectual evolution so that I can observe what it cooks up. That seems a bit inefficient. It would involve more labor to discipline human minds to that extent than it would to simply apply myself along those lines. But I can't apply myself that way. No one man can.

"I'm licked. I can't speed myself up, and I can't speed other men's minds up. Isn't there an alternative? There must be—somewhere, somehow, there's got to be an answer."

So it was to this, and not to eugenics, or light pumps, or botany, or atomic physics, that James Kidder applied himself. For a practical man, the problem was slightly on the metaphysical side, but he attacked it with typical thoroughness, using his own peculiar brand of logic. Day after day he wandered over the island, throwing shells impotently at sea gulls and swearing richly. Then came a time when he sat indoors and brooded. And only then did he get feverishly to work.

He worked in his own field, biochemistry, and concentrated mainly on two things—genetics and animal metabolism. He learned, and filed away in his insatiable mind, many things having nothing to do with the problem in hand, and very little of what he wanted. But he piled that little on what little he knew or guessed, and in time had quite a collection of known factors to work with. His approach was characteristically unorthodox. He did things on the order of multiplying by pears, and balancing equations by adding log $\sqrt{-1}$ to one side and ∞ to the other. He made mistakes, but only one of a kind, and later, only one of a species. He spent so many hours at his microscope that he had to quit work for two days to get rid of a hallucination that his heart was pumping his own blood through the mike. He did nothing by trial and error because he disapproved of the method as sloppy.

And he got results. He was lucky to begin with, and even luckier when he formularized the law of probability and reduced it to such low terms that he knew almost to the item what experiments not to try. When the cloudy, viscous semifluid on the watch glass began to move of itself he knew he was on the right track. When it began to seek food on its own he began to be excited. When it divided and, in a few hours, redivided, and each part grew and divided again, he was triumphant, for he had created life.

He nursed his brain children and sweated and strained over them, and he designed baths of various vibrations for them, and inoculated and dosed and sprayed them. Each move he made taught him the next. And out of his tanks and tubes and incubators came amoebalike creatures, and then ciliated animalcules, and more and more rapidly he produced animals with eye spots, nerve cysts, and then—victory of victories—a real blastopod, possessed of many cells instead of one. More slowly he developed a gastropod, but once he had it, it was not too difficult for him to give it organs, each with a specified function, each inheritable.

Then came cultured mollusklike things, and creatures with more and more perfected gills. The day that a nondescript thing wriggled up an inclined board out of a tank, threw flaps over its gills and feebly breathed air, Kidder quit work and went to the other end of the island and got disgustingly drunk. Hangover and all, he was soon back in the lab, forgetting to eat, forgetting to sleep, tearing into his problem.

He turned into a scientific byway and ran down his other great triumph—accelerated metabolism. He extracted and refined the stimulating factors in alcohol, cocoa, heroin, and Mother Nature's prize dope runner, *cannabis indica*. Like the scientist who, in analyzing the various clotting agents for blood treatments, found that oxalic acid and oxalic acid alone was the active factor, Kidder isolated the accelerators and decelerators, the stimulants and soporifics, in every substance that ever undermined a man's morality and/or caused a "noble experiment." In the process he found one thing he needed badly—a colorless elixir that made sleep the unnecessary and avoidable waster of time it should be. Then and there he went on a twenty-four-hour shift.

He artifically synthesized the substances he had isolated, and in doing so sloughed away a great many useless components. He pursued the subject along the lines of radiations and vibrations. He discovered something in the longer reds which, when projected through a vessel full of air vibrating in the supersonics, and then polarized, speeded up the heartbeat of small animals twenty to one. They ate twenty times as much, grew twenty times as fast, and—died twenty times sooner than they should have.

Kidder built a huge hermetically sealed room. Above it was another room, the same length and breadth but not quite so high. This was his control chamber. The large room was

divided into four sealed sections, each with its individual heat
and atmosphere controls. Over each section were miniature
cranes and derricks—handling machinery of all kinds. There
were also trapdoors fitted with air locks leading from the upper to the lower room.

By this time the other laboratory had produced a warm-
blooded, snake-skinned quadruped with an astonishingly rapid
life cycle—a generation every eight days, a life span of about
fifteen. Like the echidna, it was oviparous and mammalian.
Its period of gestation was six hours; the eggs hatched in
three; the young reached sexual maturity in another four
days. Each female laid four eggs and lived just long enough
to care for the young after they hatched. The males generally
died two or three hours after mating. The creatures were
highly adaptable. They were small—not more than three
inches long, two inches to the shoulder from the ground.
Their forepaws had three digits and a triple-jointed, opposed
thumb. They were attuned to life in an atmosphere with a
large ammonia content. Kidder bred four of the creatures
and put one group in each section of the sealed room.

Then he was ready. With his controlled atmospheres he
varied temperatures, oxygen content, humidity. He killed
them off like flies with excesses of, for instance, carbon dioxide, and the survivors bred their physical resistance into the
next generation. Periodically he would switch the eggs from
one sealed section to another to keep the strains varied. And
rapidly, under these controlled conditions, the creatures began
to evolve.

This, then, was the answer to his problem. He couldn't
speed up mankind's intellectual advancement enough to have
it teach him the things his incredible mind yearned for. He
couldn't speed himself up. So he created a new race—a race
which would develop and evolve so fast that it would surpass
the civilization of man; and from them he would learn.

They were completely in Kidder's power. Earth's normal
atmosphere would poison them, as he took care to demonstrate to every fourth generation. They would make no attempt to escape from him. They would live their lives and
progress and make their little trial-and-error experiments
hundreds of times faster than man did. They had the edge on
man, for they had Kidder to guide them. It took man six
thousand years to really discover science, three hundred to
really put it to work. It took Kidder's creatures two hundred
days to equal man's mental attainments. And from then

on—Kidder's spasmodic output made the late, great Tom Edison look like a home handicrafter.

He called them Neoterics, and he teased them into working for him. Kidder was inventive in an ideological way; that is, he could dream up impossible propositions providing he didn't have to work them out. For example, he wanted the Neoterics to figure out for themselves how to build shelters out of porous material. He created the need for such shelters by subjecting one of the sections to a high-pressure rainstorm which flattened the inhabitants. The Neoterics promptly devised waterproof shelters out of the thin waterproof material he piled in one corner. Kidder immediately blew down the flimsy structures with a blast of cold air. They built them up again so that they resisted both wind and rain. Kidder lowered the temperature so abruptly that they could not adjust their bodies to it. They heated their shelters with tiny braziers. Kidder promply turned up the heat until they began to roast to death. After a few deaths, one of their bright boys figured out how to build a strong insulant house by using three-ply rubberoid, with the middle layer perforated thousands of times to create tiny air pockets.

Using such tactics, Kidder forced them to develop a highly advanced little culture. He caused a drought in one section and a liquid surplus in another, and then opened the partition between them. Quite a spectacular war was fought, and Kidder's notebooks filled with information about military tactics and weapons. Then there was the vaccine they developed against the common cold—the reason why that affliction has been absolutely stamped out in the world today, for it was one of the things that Conant, the bank president, got hold of. He spoke to Kidder over the radiophone one winter afternoon with a voice so hoarse from laryngitis that Kidder sent him a vial of the vaccine and told him briskly not ever to call him again in such a disgustingly inaudible state. Conant had it analyzed and again Kidder's accounts—and the bank's —swelled.

At first Kidder merely supplied them with the materials he thought the Neoterics might need, but when they developed an intelligence equal to the task of fabricating their own from the elements at hand, he gave each section a stock of raw materials. The process for really strong aluminum was developed when he built in a huge plunger in one of the sections, which reached from wall to wall and was designed to descend at the rate of four inches a day until it crushed whatever was at the bottom. The Neoterics, in self-defense, used what strong material they had in hand to stop the inexorable death that threatened them. But Kidder had seen to it that they had nothing but aluminum oxide and a scattering of other elements, plus plenty of electric power. At first they ran up dozens of aluminum pillars; when these were crushed and twisted they tried shaping them so that the soft metal would take more weight. When that failed they quickly built stronger ones; and when the plunger was halted, Kidder removed one of the pillars and analyzed it. It was hardened aluminum, stronger and tougher than molybd steel.

Experience taught Kidder that he had to make certain changes to increase his power over his Neoterics before they got too ingenious. There were things that could be done with atomic power that he was curious about; but he was not willing to trust his little superscientists with a thing like that unless they could be trusted to use it strictly according to Hoyle. So he instituted a rule of fear. The most trivial departure from what he chose to consider the right way of doing things resulted in instant death of half a tribe. If he was trying to develop a Diesel-type power plant, for instance, that would operate without a flywheel starter, and a bright young Neoteric used any of the materials for architectural purposes, half the tribe immediately died. Of course, they had developed a written language; it was Kidder's own. The teletype in a glass-enclosed area in a corner of each section was a shrine. Any directions that were given on it were obeyed, or else—. After this innovation, Kidder's work was much simpler. There was no need for any more indirection. Anything he wanted done was done. No matter how impossible his commands, three or four generations of Neoterics could find a way to carry them out.

This quotation is from a paper that one of Kidder's high-speed telescopic cameras discovered being circulated among the younger Neoterics. It is translated from the highly simplified script of the Neoterics.

"These edicts shall be followed by each Neoteric upon pain of death, which punishment will be inflicted by the tribe upon the individual to protect the tribe against him.

"Priority of interest and tribal and individual effort is to be given the commands that appear on the word machine.

"Any misdirection of material or power, or use thereof for any other purpose than the carrying out of the machine's commands, unless no command appears, shall be punishable by death.

"Any information regarding the problem at hand, or ideas

or experiments which might conceivably bear upon it, are to become the property of the tribe.

"Any individual failing to cooperate in the tribal effort, or who can be termed guilty of not expending his full efforts in the work; or the suspicion thereof, shall be subject to the death penalty."

Such are the results of complete domination. This paper impressed Kidder as much as it did because it was completely spontaneous. It was the Neoterics' own creed, developed by them for their own greatest good.

And so at last Kidder had his fulfillment. Crouched in the upper room, going from telescope to telescope, running off slowed-down films from his high-speed cameras, he found himself possessed of a tractable, dynamic source of information. Housed in the great square building with its four half-acre sections was a new world, to which he was god.

President Conant's mind was similar to Kidder's in that its approach to any problem was along the shortest distance between any two points, regardless of whether that approach was along the line of most or least resistance. His rise to the bank presidency was a history of ruthless moves whose only justification was that they got him what he wanted. Like an overefficient general, he would never vanquish an enemy through sheer force of numbers alone. He would also skillfully flank his enemy, not on one side, but on both. Innocent bystanders were creatures deserving no consideration.

The time he took over a certain thousand-acre property, for instance, from a man named Grady, he was not satisfied with only the title to the land. Grady was an airport owner—had been all his life, and his father before him. Conant exerted every kind of pressure on the man and found him unshakable. Finally judicious persuasion led the city officials to dig a sewer right across the middle of the field, quite efficiently wrecking Grady's business. Knowing that this would supply Grady, who was a wealthy man, with motive for revenge, Conant took over Grady's bank at half again its value and caused it to fold up. Grady lost every cent he had and ended his life in an asylum. Conant was very proud of his tactics.

Like many another who has had Mammon by the tail, Conant did not know when to let go. His vast organization yielded him more money and power than any other concern in history, and yet he was not satisfied. Conant and money were like Kidder and knowledge. Conant's pyramided enterprises were to him what the Neoterics were to Kidder. Each had made his private world; each used it for his instruction and profit. Kidder, though, disturbed nobody but his Neoterics. Even so, Conant was not wholly villainous. He was a shrewd man, and had discovered early the value of pleasing people. No man can rob successfully over a period of years without pleasing the people he robs. The technique for doing this is highly involved, but master it and you can start your own mint.

Conant's one great fear was that Kidder would some day take an interest in world events and begin to become opinionated. Good heavens—the potential power he had! A little matter like swinging an election could be managed by a man like Kidder as easily as turning over in bed. The only thing he could do was to call him periodically and see if there was anything that Kidder needed to keep himself busy. Kidder appreciated this. Conant, once in a while, would suggest something to Kidder that intrigued him, something that would keep him deep in his hermitage for a few weeks. The light pump was one of the results of Conant's imagination. Conant bet him it couldn't be done. Kidder did it.

One afternoon Kidder answered the squeal of the radiophone's signal. Swearing mildly, he shut off the film he was watching and crossed the compound to the old laboratory. He went to the radiophone, threw a switch. The squealing stopped.

"Well?"

"Hello, Kidder," said Conant. "Busy?"

"Not very," said Kidder. He was delighted with the pictures his camera had caught, showing the skillful work of a gang of Neoterics synthesizing rubber out of pure sulphur. He would rather have liked to tell Conant about it, but somehow he had never got around to telling Conant about the Neoterics, and he didn't see why he should start now.

Conant said, "Er . . . Kidder, I was down at the club the other day and a bunch of us were filling up an evening with loose talk. Something came up which might interest you."

"What?"

"Couple of the utilities boys there. You know the power setup in this country, don't you? Thirty percent atomic, the rest hydroelectric, diesel and steam?"

"I hadn't known," said Kidder, who was as innocent as a babe of current events.

"Well, we were arguing about what chances a new power source would have. One of the men there said it would be smarter to produce a new power and then talk about it. Another one waived that; said he couldn't name that new power, but he could describe it. Said it would have to have everything that present power sources have, plus one or two more things. It could be cheaper, for instance. It could be more efficient. It might supersede the others by being easier to carry from the power plant to the consumer. See what I mean? Any one of these factors might prove a new source of power competitive to the others. What I'd like to see is a new power with *all* of these factors. What do you think of it?"

"Not impossible."

"Think not?"

"I'll try it."

"Keep me posted." Conant's transmitter clicked off. The switch was a little piece of false front that Kidder had built into the set, which was something that Conant didn't know. The set switched itself off when Conant moved from it. After the switch's sharp crack, Kidder heard the banker mutter, "If he does it, I'm all set. If he doesn't, at least the crazy fool will keep himself busy on the isl—"

Kidder eyed the radiophone for an instant with raised eyebrows, and then shrugged them down again with his shoulders. It was quite evident that Conant had something up his sleeve, but Kidder wasn't worried. Who on earth would want to disturb him? He wasn't bothering anybody. He went back to the Neoterics' building, full of the new power idea.

Eleven days later Kidder called Conant and gave specific instructions on how to equip his receiver with a facsimile set which would enable Kidder to send written matter over the air. As soon as this was done and Kidder informed, the biochemist for once in his life spoke at some length.

"Conant—you implied that a new power source that would be cheaper, more efficient and more easily transmitted than any now in use did not exist. You might be interested in the little generator I have just set up.

"It has power, Conant—unbelievable power. Broadcast. A beautiful little tight beam. Here—catch this on the facsimile recorder." Kidder slipped a sheet of paper under the clips on his transmitter and it appeared on Conant's set. "Here's the wiring diagram for a power receiver. Now listen. The beam is so tight, so highly directional, that not three thousandths of one percent of the power would be lost in a two-thousand-mile transmission. The power system is closed. That is, any drain on the beam returns a signal along it to the transmitter, which automatically steps up to increase the power output. It has a limit, but it's way up. And something else. This little gadget of mine can send out eight different beams with a total horsepower output of around eight thousand per minute per beam. From each beam you can draw enough power to turn the page of a book or fly a superstratosphere plane. Hold on—I haven't finished yet. Each beam, as I told you before, returns a signal from receiver to transmitter. This not only controls the power output of the beam, but directs it. Once contact is made, the beam will never let go. It will follow the receiver anywhere. You can power land, air or water vehicles with it, as well as any stationary plant. Like it?"

Conant, who was a banker and not a scientist, wiped his shining pate with the back of his hand and said, "I've never known you to steer me wrong yet, Kidder. How about the cost of this thing?"

"High," said Kidder promptly. "As high as an atomic plant. But there are no high-tension lines, no wires, no pipelines, no nothing. The receivers are little more complicated than a radio set. The transmitter is—well, that's quite a job."

"Didn't take you long," said Conant.

"No," said Kidder, "it didn't, did it?" It was the lifework of nearly twelve hundred highly cultured people, but Kidder wasn't going into that. "Of course, the one I have here's just a model."

Conant's voice was strained. "A—model? And it delivers—"

"Over sixty-thousand horsepower," said Kidder gleefully.

"Good heavens! In a full-sized machine—why, one transmitter would be enough to—" The possibilities of the thing choked Conant for a moment. "How is it fueled?"

"It isn't," said Kidder. "I won't begin to explain it. I've tapped a source of power of unimaginable force. It's—well, big. So big that it can't be misused."

"What?" snapped Conant. "What do you mean by that?"

Kidder cocked an eyebrow. Conant *had* something up his sleeve, then. At this second indication of it, Kidder, the least suspicious of men, began to put himself on guard. "I mean just what I say," he said evenly. "Don't try too hard to understand me—I barely savvy it myself. But the source of this power is a monstrous resultant caused by the unbalance of two previously equalized forces. Those equalized forces are cosmic in quantity. Acutally, the forces are those which make suns, crush atoms the way they crushed those that compose the companion of Sirius. It's not anything you can fool with."

"I don't—" said Conant, and his voice ended puzzledly.

"I'll give you a parallel of it," said Kidder. "Suppose you take two rods, one in each hand. Place their tips together and push. As long as your pressure is directly along their long axes, the pressure is equalized; right and left hands cancel each other out. Now I come along; I put out one finger and touch the rods ever so lightly where they come together. They snap out of line violently; you break a couple of knuckles. The resultant force is at right angles to the original force you exerted. My power transmitter is on the same principle. It takes an infinitesimal amount of energy to throw those forces out of line. Easy enough when you know how to do it. The important question is whether or not you can control the resultant when you get it. I can."

"I—see." Conant indulged in a four-second gloat. "Heaven help the utility companies. I don't intend to. Kidder—I want a full-size transmitter."

Kidder clucked into the microphone. "Ambitious, aren't you? I haven't a staff out here, Conant—you know that. And I can't be expected to build four or five thousand tons of apparatus myself."

"I'll have five hundred engineers and laborers out there in forty-eight hours."

"You will not. Why bother me with it? I'm quite happy here, Conant, and one of the reasons is that I've no one to get in my hair."

"Oh, now, Kidder—don't be like that. I'll pay you—"

"You haven't got that much money," said Kidder briskly. He flipped the switch on his set. *His* switch worked.

Conant was furious. He shouted into the phone several times, then began to lean on the signal button. On his island, Kidder let the thing squeal and went back to his projection room. He was sorry he had sent the diagram of the receiver to Conant. It would have been interesting to power a plane or a car with the model transmitter he had taken from the Neoterics. But if Conant was going to be that way about it—well, anyway, the receiver would be no good without the transmitter. Any radio engineer would understand the diagram, but not the beam which activated it. And Conant wouldn't get his beam.

Pity he didn't know Conant well enough.

Kidder's days were endless sorties into learning. He never slept, nor did his Neoterics. He ate regularly every five hours, exercised for half an hour in every twelve. He did not keep track of time, for it meant nothing to him. Had he wanted to know the date, or the year, even, he knew he could get it from Conant. He didn't care, that's all. The time that was not spent in observation was used in developing new problems for the Neoterics. His thoughts just now ran to defense. The idea was born in his conversation with Conant; now the idea was primary, its motivation something of no importance. The Neoterics were working on a vibration field of quasi-electrical nature. Kidder could see little practical value in such a thing—an invisible wall which would kill any living thing which touched it. But still—the idea was intriguing.

He stretched and moved away from the telescope in the upper room through which he had been watching his creations at work. He was profoundly happy here in the large control room. Leaving it to go to the old laboratory for a bite to eat was a thing he hated to do. He felt like bidding it good-bye each time he walked across the compound, and saying a glad hello when he returned. A little amused at himself, he went out.

There was a black blob—a distant power boat—a few miles off the island, toward the mainland. Kidder stopped and stared distastefully at it. A white petal of spray was affixed to each side of the black body—it was coming toward him. He snorted, thinking of the time a yacht load of silly fools had landed out of curiosity one afternoon, spewed themselves over his beloved island, peppered him with lamebrained questions, and thrown his nervous equilibrium out for days. Lord, how he hated *people!*

The thought of unpleasantness bred two more thoughts that played half-consciously with his mind as he crossed the compound and entered the old laboratory. One was that perhaps it might be wise to surround his buildings with a field of force of some kind and post warnings for trespassers. The other thought was of Conant and the vague uneasiness the man had been sending to him through the radiophone these last weeks. His suggestion, two days ago, that a power plant be built on the island—horrible idea!

Conant rose from his seat on a laboratory bench as Kidder walked in.

They looked at each other wordlessly for a long moment. Kidder hadn't seen the bank president in years. The man's presence, he found, made his scalp crawl.

"Hello," said Conant genially. "You're looking fit."

Kidder grunted. Conant eased his unwieldy body back onto

the bench and said, "Just to save you the energy of asking questions, Mr. Kidder, I arrived two hours ago on a small boat. Rotten way to travel. I wanted to be a surprise to you; my two men rowed me the last couple of miles. You're not very well equipped here for defense, are you? Why, anyone could slip up on you the way I did."

"Who'd want to?" growled Kidder. The man's voice edged annoyingly into his brain. He spoke too loudly for such a small room; at least, Kidder's hermit's ears felt that way. Kidder shrugged and went about preparing a light meal for himself.

"Well," drawled the banker, "I might want to." He drew out a Dow-metal cigar case. "Mind if I smoke?"

"I do," said Kidder sharply.

Conant laughed easily and put the cigars away. "I might," he said, "want to urge you to let me build that power station on this island."

"Radiophone work?"

"Oh, yes. But now that I'm here you can't switch me off. Now—how about it?"

"I haven't changed my mind."

"Oh, but you should, Kidder, you should. Think of it— think of the good it would do for the masses of people that are now paying exorbitant power bills!"

"I hate the masses! Why do you have to build here?"

"Oh, that. It's an ideal location. You own the island; work could begin here without causing any comment whatsoever. The plant would spring full-fledged on the power markets of the country, having been built in secret. The island can be made impregnable."

"I don't want to be bothered."

"We wouldn't bother you. We'd build on the north end of the island—a mile and a quarter from you and your work. Ah—by the way—where's the model of the power transmitter?"

Kidder, with his mouth full of synthesized food, waved a hand at a small table on which stood the model, a four-foot, amazing intricate device of plastic and steel and tiny coils.

Conant rose and went over to look at it. "Actually works, eh?" He sighed deeply and said, "Kidder, I really hate to do this, but I want to build that plant rather badly. Corson! Robbins!"

Two bull-necked individuals stepped out from their hiding places in the corners of the room. One idly dangled a revolver by its trigger guard. Kidder looked blankly from one to the other of them.

"These gentlemen will follow my orders implicitly, Kidder. In half an hour a party will land here—engineers, contractors. They will start surveying the north end of the island for the construction of the power plant. These boys here feel about the same way I do as far as you are concerned. Do we proceed with your cooperation or without it? It's immaterial to me whether or not you are left alive to continue your work. My engineers can duplicate your model."

Kidder said nothing. He had stopped chewing when he saw the gunmen, and only now remembered to swallow. He sat crouched over his plate without moving or speaking.

Conant broke the silence by walking to the door. "Robbins—can you carry that model there?" The big man put his gun away, lifted the model gently, and nodded. "Take it down to the beach and meet the other boat. Tell Mr. Johansen, the engineer, that this is the model he is to work from." Robbins went out. Conant turned to Kidder. "There's no need for us to anger ourselves," he said oilily. "I think you are stubborn, but I don't hold it against you. I know how you feel. You'll be left alone; you have my promise. But I mean to go ahead on this job, and a small thing like your life can't stand in my way."

Kidder said, "Get out of here." There were two swollen veins throbbing at his temples. His voice was low, and it shook.

"Very well. Good day, Mr. Kidder. Oh—by the way—you're a clever devil." No one had ever referred to the scholastic Mr. Kidder that way before. "I realize the possibility of your blasting us off this island. I wouldn't do it if I were you. I'm willing to give you what you want—privacy. I want the same thing in return. If anything happens to me while I'm here, the island will be bombed by someone who is working for me. I'll admit they might fail. If they do, the United States government will take a hand. You wouldn't want that, would you? That's rather a big thing for one man to fight. The same thing goes if the plant is sabotaged in any way after I go back to the mainland. You might be killed. You will most certainly be bothered interminably. Thanks for your . . . er . . . cooperation." The banker smirked and walked out, followed by his taciturn gorilla.

Kidder sat there for a long time without moving. Then he shook his head, rested it in his palms. He was badly frightened; not so much because his life was in danger, but because his privacy and his work—his world—were threatened. He was hurt and bewildered. He wasn't a businessman. He couldn't handle men. All his life he had run away from humans and what they represented to him. He was like a frightened child when men closed in on him.

Cooling a little, he wondered vaguely what would happen when the power plant opened. Certainly the government would be interested. Unless—unless by then Conant was the government. That plant was an unimaginable source of power, and not only the kind of power that turned wheels. He rose and went back to the world that was home to him, a world where his motives were understood, and where there were those who could help him. Back at the Neoterics' building, he escaped yet again from the world of men into his work.

Kidder called Conant the following week, much to the banker's surprise. His two days on the island had gotten the work well under way, and he had left with the arrival of a shipload of laborers and material. He kept in close touch by radio with Johansen, the engineer in charge. It had been a blind job for Johansen and all the rest of the crew on the island. Only the bank's infinite resources could have hired such a man, or the picked gang with him.

Johansen's first reaction when he saw the model had been ecstatic. He wanted to tell his friends about this marvel; but the only radio set available was beamed to Conant's private office in the bank, and Conant's armed guards, one to every two workers, had strict orders to destroy any other radio transmitter on sight. About that time he realized that he was a prisoner on the island. His instant anger subsided when he reflected that being a prisoner at fifty thousand dollars a week wasn't too bad. Two of the laborers and an engineer thought differently, and got disgruntled a couple of days after they arrived. They disappeared one night—the same night that five shots were fired down on the beach. No questions were asked, and there was no more trouble.

Conant covered his surprise at Kidder's call and was as offensively jovial as ever. "Well, now! Anything I can do for you?"

"Yes," said Kidder. His voice was low, completely without expression. "I want you to issue a warning to your men not to pass the white line I have drawn five hundred yards north of my buildings, right across the island."

"Warning? Why, my dear fellow, they have orders that you are not to be disturbed on any account."

"You've ordered them. All right. Now warn them. I have an electric field surrounding my laboratories that will kill anything living which penetrates it. I don't want to have murder on my conscience. There will be no deaths unless there are trespassers. You'll inform your workers?"

"Oh, now, Kidder," the banker expostulated. "That was totally unnecessary. You won't be bothered. Why—" But he found he was talking into a dead mike. He knew better than to call back. He called Johansen instead and told him about it. Johansen didn't like the sound of it, but he repeated the message and signed off. Conant liked that man. He was, for a moment, a little sorry that Johansen would never reach the mainland alive.

But that Kidder—he was beginning to be a problem. As long as his weapons were strictly defensive he was no real menace. But he would have to be taken care of when the plant was operating. Conant couldn't afford to have genius around him unless it was unquestionably on his side. The power transmitter and Conant's highly ambitious plans would be safe as long as Kidder was left to himself. Kidder knew that he could, for the time being, expect more sympathetic treatment from Conant than he could from a horde of government investigators.

Kidder only left his own enclosure once after the work began on the north end of the island, and it took all of his unskilled diplomacy to do it. Knowing the source of the plant's power, knowing what could happen if it were misused, he asked Conant's permission to inspect the great transmitter when it was nearly finished. Insuring his own life by refusing to report back to Conant until he was safe within his own laboratory again, he turned off his shield and walked up to the north end.

He saw an awe-inspiring sight. The four-foot model was duplicated nearly a hundred times as large. Inside a massive three-hundred-foot tower a space was packed nearly solid with the same bewildering maze of coils and bars that the Neoterics had built so delicately into their machine. At the top was a globe of polished golden alloy, the transmitting antenna. From it would stream thousands of tight beams of force, which could be tapped to any degree by corresponding thousands of receivers placed anywhere at any distance. Kidder learned that the receivers had already been built, but his informant, Johansen, knew little about that end of it and was saying less. Kidder checked over every detail of the structure, and when he was through he shook Johansen's hand admiringly.

"I didn't want this thing here," he said shyly, "and I don't. But I will say that it's a pleasure to see this kind of work."

"It's a pleasure to meet the man that invented it."

Kidder beamed. "I didn't invent it," he said. "Maybe some day I'll show you who did. I—well, good-bye." He turned before he had a chance to say too much and marched off down the path.

"Shall I?" said a voice at Johansen's side. One of Conant's guards had his gun out.

Johansen knocked the man's arm down. "No." He scratched his head. "So that's the mysterious menace from the other end of the island. Eh! Why, he's a hell of a nice little feller!"

Built on the ruins of Denver, which was destroyed in the great Battle of the Rockies during the Western War, stands the most beautiful city in the world—our nation's capital, New Washington. In a circular room deep in the heart of the White House, the president, three army men, and a civilian sat. Under the president's desk a dictaphone unostentatiously recorded every word that was said. Two thousand and more miles away, Conant hung over a radio receiver, tuned to receive the signals of the tiny transmitter in the civilian's side pocket.

One of the officers spoke.

"Mr. President, the 'impossible claims' made for this gentleman's product are absolutely true. He has proved beyond doubt each item on his prospectus."

The president glanced at the civilian, back at the officer. "I won't wait for your report," he said. "Tell me—what happened?"

Another of the army men mopped his face with a khaki bandanna. "I can't ask you to believe us, Mr. President, but it's true all the same. Mr. Wright here has in his suitcase three or four dozen small . . . er . . . bombs—"

"They're not bombs," said Wright casually.

"All right. They're not bombs. Mr. Wright smashed two of them on an anvil with a sledge hammer. There was no result. He put two more in an electric furnace. They burned away like so much tin and cardboard. We dropped one down the barrel of a field piece and fired it. Still nothing." He paused and looked at the third officer, who picked up the account.

"We really got started then. We flew to the proving

grounds, dropped one of the objects and flew to thirty thousand feet. From there, with a small hand detonator no bigger than your fist, Mr. Wright set the thing off. I've never seen anything like it. Forty acres of land came straight up at us, breaking up as it came. The concussion was terrific—you must have felt it here, four hundred miles away."

The president nodded. "I did. Seismographs on the other side of the Earth picked it up."

"The crater it left was a quarter of a mile deep at the center. Why, one plane load of those things could demolish any city! There isn't even any necessity for accuracy!"

"You haven't heard anything yet," another officer broke in. "Mr. Wright's automobile is powered by a small plant similar to the others. He demonstrated it to us. We could find no fuel tank of any kind, or any other driving mechanism. But with a power plant no bigger than six cubic inches, that car, carrying enough weight to give it traction, outpulled an army tank!"

"And the other test!" said the third excitedly. "He put one of the objects into a replica of a treasury vault. The walls were twelve feet thick, super-reinforced concrete. He controlled it from over a hundred yards away. He . . . he burst that vault! It wasn't an explosion—it was as if some incredibly powerful expansive force inside filled it and flattened the walls from inside. They cracked and split and powdered, and the steel girders and rods came twisting and shearing out like . . . like—*whew!* After that he insisted on seeing you. We knew it wasn't usual, but he said he has more to say and would say it only in your presence."

The president said gravely, "What is it, Mr. Wright?"

Wright rose, picked up his suitcase, opened it and took out a small cube, about eight inches on a side, made of some light-absorbent red material. Four men edged nervously away from it.

"These gentlemen," he began, "have seen only part of the things this device can do. I'm going to demonstrate to you the delicacy of control that is possible with it." He made an adjustment with a tiny knob on the side of the cube, set it on the edge of the president's desk.

"You have asked me more than once if this is my invention or if I am representing someone. The latter is true. It might also interest you to know that the man who controls this cube is right now several thousand miles from here. He, and he alone, can prevent it from detonating now that I"—he pulled his detonator out of the suitcase and pressed a button—"have done this. It will explode the way the one we dropped from the plane did, completely destroying this city and everything in it, in just four hours. It will also explode"—he stepped back and threw a tiny switch on his detonator—"if any moving object comes within three feet of it or if anyone leaves this room but me—it can be compensated for that. If, after I leave, I am molested, it will detonate as soon as a hand is laid on me. No bullets can kill me fast enough to prevent me from setting it off."

The three army men were silent. One of them swiped nervously at the beads of cold sweat on his forehead. The others did not move. The president said evenly,

"What's your proposition?"

"A very reasonable one. My employer does not work in the open, for obvious reasons. All he wants is your agreement to carry out his orders; to appoint the cabinet members he chooses, to throw your influence in any way he dictates. The public—Congress—anyone else—need never know anything about it. I might add that if you agree to this proposal, this 'bomb,' as you call it, will not go off. But you can be sure that thousands of them are planted all over the country. You will never know when you are near one. If you disobey, it means instant annihilation for you and everyone else within three or four square miles.

"In three hours and fifty minutes—that will be at precisely seven o'clock—there is a commercial radio program on station RPRS. You will cause the announcer, after his station identification, to say 'Agreed.' It will pass unnoticed by all but my employer. There is no use in having me followed; my work is done. I shall never see or contact my employer again. That is all. Good afternoon, gentlemen!"

Wright closed his suitcase with a businesslike snap, bowed, and left the room. Four men sat frozen, staring at the little red cube.

"Do you think he can do all he says?" asked the president.

The three nodded mutely. The president reached for his phone.

There was an eavesdropper to all of the foregoing. Conant, squatting behind his great desk in the vault, where he had his sanctum sanctorum, knew nothing of it. But beside him was the compact bulk of Kidder's radiophone. His presence switched it on, and Kidder, on his island, blessed the day he had thought of that device. He had been meaning to call Conant all morning, but was very hesitant. His meeting with the young engineer Johansen had impressed him strongly. The man was such a thorough scientist, possessed of such complete delight in the work he did, that for the first time in his life Kidder found himself actually wanting to see someone again. But he feared for Johansen's life if he brought him to the laboratory, for Johansen's work was done on the island, and Conant would most certainly have the engineer killed if he heard of his visit, fearing that Kidder would influence him to sabotage the great transmitter. And if Kidder went to the power plant he would probably be shot on sight.

All one day Kidder wrangled with himself, and finally determined to call Conant. Fortunately he gave no signal, but turned up the volume on the receiver when the little red light told him that Conant's transmitter was functioning. Curious, he heard everything that occurred in the president's chamber three thousand miles away. Horrified, he realized what Conant's engineers had done. Built into tiny containers were tens of thousands of power receivers. They had no power of their own, but, by remote control, could draw on any or all of the billions of horsepower the huge plant on the island was broadcasting.

Kidder stood in front of his receiver, speechless. There was nothing he could do. If he devised some means of destroying the power plant, the government would certainly step in and take over the island, and then—what would happen to him and his precious Neoterics?

Another sound grated out of the receiver—a commercial radio program. A few bars of music, a man's voice advertising stratoline fares on the installment plan, a short silence, then:

"Station RPRS, voice of the nation's Capital, District of South Colorado."

The three-second pause was interminable.

"The time is exactly . . . er . . . *agreed*. The time is exactly seven p. m., Mountain Standard Time."

Then came a half-insane chuckle. Kidder had difficulty believing it was Conant. A phone clicked. The banker's voice:

"Bill? All set. Get out there with your squadron and bomb up the island. Keep away from the plant, but cut the rest of it to ribbons. Do it quick and get out of there."

Almost hysterical with fear, Kidder rushed about the room and then shot out the door and across the compound. There were five hundred innocent workmen in barracks a quarter mile from the plant. Conant didn't need them now, and he didn't need Kidder. The only safety for anyone was in the plant itself, and Kidder wouldn't leave his Neoterics to be bombed. He flung himself up the stairs and to the nearest teletype. He banged out, "Get me a defense. I want an impenetrable shield. Urgent!"

The words rippled out from under his fingers in the functional script of the Neoterics. Kidder didn't think of what he wrote, didn't really visualize the thing he ordered. But he had done what he could. He'd have to leave them now, get to the barracks; warn those men. He ran up the path toward the plant, flung himself over the white line that marked death to those who crossed it.

A squadron of nine clip-winged, mosquito-nosed planes rose out of a cove on the mainland. There was no sound from the engines, for there were no engines. Each plane was powered with a tiny receiver and drew its unmarked, light-absorbent wings through the air with power from the island. In a matter of minutes they raised the island. The squadron leader spoke briskly into a microphone.

"Take the barracks first. Clean 'em up. Then work south."

Johansen was alone on a small hill near the center of the island. He carried a camera, and though he knew pretty well that his chances of ever getting ashore again were practically nonexistent, he liked angle shots of his tower, and took innumerable pictures. The first he knew of the planes was when he heard their whining dive over the barracks. He stood transfixed, saw a shower of bombs hurtled down and turn the barracks into a smashed ruin of broken wood, metal and bodies. The picture of Kidder's earnest face flashed into his mind. Poor little guy—if they ever bombed his end of the island he would—But his tower! Were they going to bomb the plant?

He watched, utterly appalled, as the planes flew out to sea, cut back and dove again. They seemed to be working south. At the third dive he was sure of it. Not knowing what he could do, he nevertheless turned and ran toward Kidder's place. He rounded a turn in the trail and collided violently with the little biochemist. Kidder's face was scarlet with exertion, and he was the most terrified-looking object Johansen had ever seen.

Kidder waved a hand northward. "Conant!" he screamed over the uproar. "It's Conant! He's going to kill us all!"

"The plant?" said Johansen, turning pale.

"It's safe. He won't touch *that!* But . . . my place . . what about all those men?"

"Too late!" shouted Johansen.

"Maybe I can—Come on!" called Kidder, and was off down the trail, heading south.

Johansen pounded after him. Kidder's little short legs became a blur as the squadron swooped overhead, laying its eggs in the spot where they had met.

As they burst out of the woods, Johansen put on a spurt, caught up with the scientist and knocked him sprawling not six feet from the white line.

"Wh . . . wh—"

"Don't go any farther, you fool! Your own damned force field—it'll kill you!"

"Force field? But—I came through it on the way up— Here. Wait. If I can—" Kidder began hunting furiously about in the grass. In a few seconds he ran up to the line, clutching a large grasshopper in his hand. He tossed it over. It lay still.

"See?" said Johansen. "It—"

"Look! It jumped! Come on! I don't know what went wrong, unless the Neoterics shut it off. They generated that field—I didn't."

"Neo—huh?"

"Never mind," snapped the biochemist, and ran.

They pounded gasping up the steps and into the Neoterics' control room. Kidder clapped his eyes to a telescope and shrieked in glee. "They've done it! They've done it!"

"Who's—"

"My little people! The Neoterics! They've made the impenetrable shield! Don't you see—it cut through the lines of force that start up that field out there! Their generator is still throwing it up, but the vibrations can't get out! They're safe! They're safe!" And the overwrought hermit began to cry. Johansen looked at him pityingly and shook his head.

"Sure—your little men are all right. But we aren't," he added as the floor shook at the detonation of a bomb.

Johansen closed his eyes, got a grip on himself and let his curiosity overcome his fear. He stepped to the binocular telescope, gazed down it. There was nothing there but a curved sheet of gray material. He had never seen a gray quite like that. It was absolutely neutral. It didn't seem soft and it didn't seem hard, and to look at it made his brain reel. He looked up.

Kidder was pounding the keys on a teletype, watching the blank yellow tape anxiously.

"I'm not getting through to them," he whimpered. "I don't know what's the mat—Oh, Of *course!*"

"What?"

"The shield is absolutely impenetrable! The teletype impulses can't get through or I could get them to extend the screen over the building—over the whole island! There's nothing those people can't do!"

"He's crazy," Johansen said under his breath. "Poor little—"

The teletype began clicking sharply. Kidder dove at it, practically embraced it. He read off the tape as it came out. Johansen saw the characters, but they meant nothing to him.

"Almighty," Kidder read falteringly, "pray have mercy on us and be forebearing until we have said our say. Without orders we have lowered the screen you ordered us to raise. We are lost, O great one. Our screen is truly impenetrable, and so cut off your words on the word machine. We have never, in memory of any Neoteric, been without your word before. Forgive us our action. We will eagerly await your answer."

Kidder's fingers danced over the keys. "You can look now," he gasped. "Go on—the telescope!"

Johansen, trying to ignore the whine of sure death from above, looked.

He saw what looked like land—fantastic fields under cultivation, a settlement of some sort, factories, and—beings. Everything moved with incredible rapidity. He couldn't see one of the inhabitants except as darting pinky-white streaks. Fascinated, he stared for a long minute. A sound behind him made him whirl. It was Kidder, rubbing his hands together briskly. There was a broad smile on his face.

"They did it," he said happily. "You see?"

Johansen didn't see until he began to realize that there was a dead silence outside. He ran to a window. It was night outside—the blackest night—when it should have been dusk. "What happened?"

"The Neoterics," said Kidder, and laughed like a child. "My friends downstairs there. They threw up the impenetrable shield over the whole island. We can't be touched now!"

And at Johansen's amazed questions, he launched into a description of the race of beings below them.

Outside the shell, things happened. Nine airplanes suddenly went dead-stick. Nine pilots glided downward, powerless, and some fell into the sea, and some struck the miraculous gray shell that loomed in place of an island; slid off and sank.

And ashore, a man named Wright sat in a car, half dead with fear, while government men surrounded him, approached cautiously, daring instant death from a now-dead source.

In a room deep in the White House, a high-ranking army officer shrieked, "I can't stand it any more! I can't!" and leaped up, snatched a red cube off the president's desk, ground it to ineffectual litter under his shining boots.

And in a few days they took a broken old man away from the bank and put him in an asylum, where he died within a week.

The shield, you see, was truly impenetrable. The power plant was untouched and sent out its beams; but the beams could not get out, and anything powered from the plant went dead. The story never became public, although for some years there was heightened naval activity off the New England coast. The navy, so the story went, had a new target range out there—a great hemi-ovoid of gray material. They bombed it and shelled it and rayed it and blasted all around it, but never even dented its smooth surface.

Kidder and Johansen let it stay there. They were happy enough with their researches and their Neoterics. They did not hear or feel the shelling, for the shield was truly impenetrable. They synthesized their food and their light and air from the materials at hand, and they simply didn't care. They were the only survivors of the bombing, with the exception of three poor maimed devils that died soon afterward.

All this happened many years ago, and Kidder and Johansen may be alive today, and they may be dead. But that doesn't matter too much. The important thing is that the great gray shell will bear watching. Men die, but races live. Someday the Neoterics, after innumerable generations of inconceivable advancement, will take down their shield and come forth. When I think of that I feel frightened.

JAY SCORE

Astounding Science Fiction
May

by Eric Frank Russell (1905-1978)

*"Jay Score" was somewhat overshadowed when it
first appeared because the May, 1941 Astounding
happened to contain two important Heinlein stories, "Universe" (too long for inclusion here), and
"Solution Unsatisfactory" (in his "Anson MacDonald" persona). In addition, there was "Liar!" by
one of your editors, and as a bonus, Heinlein provided a guide and outline to his still-in-process Future History. Sorry, Isaac, but they don't make sf
magazines like this any more.*

*Russell's contribution is a fine story and was the
first of a series of four, finally collected as* Men,
Martians and Machines *in 1955.*

(No, they don't, Marty. And I'm the first to agree. To this
day, people speak of the 1927 Yankees as the greatest ball
team of all time, and I agree. And my feeling is that the
1939-1941 *Astoundings* were the greatest science fiction magazines of all time, including my own, and that the May, 1941
issue and September, 1941 issue may be the greatest individual issues of all time. I'm surprised, looking back on it, that
John Campbell published *two* robot stories in the May issue,
but "Jay Score" was *so* good. In fact, from my own self-centered viewpoint it was the best robot story not written by myself since "Helen O'Loy" by Lester Del Rey—I.A.)

There are very good reasons for everything they do. To the
uninitiated some of their little tricks and some of their regulations seem mighty peculiar—but rocketing through the cosmos isn't quite like paddling a bathtub across a farm pond,
no, sir!

For instance, this stunt of using mixed crews is pretty sensible when you look into it. On the outward runs toward

Mars, the Asteroids, or beyond, they have white Terrestrials to tend the engines because they're the ones who perfected modern propulsion units, know most about them and can nurse them like nobody else. All ships' surgeons are black Terrestrials because for some reason none can explain no Negro gets gravity-bends or space nausea. Every outside repair gang is composed of Martians, who use very little air, are tiptop metal workers, and fairly immune to cosmic-ray burn.

As for the inward trips to Venus, they mix them similarly except that the emergency pilot is always a big clunker like Jay Score. There's a motive behind that; he's the one who provided it. I'm never likely to forget him. He sort of sticks in the mind, for keeps. What a character!

Destiny placed me at the top of the gangway the first time he appeared. Our ship was the *Upskadaska City*, a brand new freighter with limited passenger accommodation, registered in the Venusian spaceport from which she took her name. Needless to say she was known among hardened spacemen as the *Upsydaisy*.

We were lying in the Colorado Rocket Basin, north of Denver, with a fair load aboard, mostly watchmaking machinery, agricultural equipment, aeronautical jigs, and tools for Upskadaska, as well as a case of radium needles for the Venusian Cancer Research Institute. There were eight passengers, all emigrating agriculturalists planning on making hay thirty million miles nearer the sun. We had ramped the vessel and were waiting for the blow-brothers-blow siren, due in forty minutes, when Jay Score arrived.

He was six feet nine, weighed at least three hundred pounds yet toted this bulk with the easy grace of a ballet dancer. A big guy like that, moving like that, was something worth watching. He came up the duralumin gangway with all the nonchalance of a tripper boarding the bus for Jackson's Creek. From his hamlike right fist dangled a rawhide case not quite big enough to contain his bed and maybe a wardrobe or two.

Reaching the top, he paused while he took in the crossed swords on my cap, said, "Morning, Sarge. I'm the new emergency pilot. I have to report to Captain McNulty."

I knew we were due for another pilot now that Jew Durkin had been promoted to the snooty Martial scent bottle *Prometheus*. So this was his successor. He was a Terrestrial all right, but neither black nor white. His expressionless but capable face looked as if covered with old, well-seasoned leather. His eyes held fires resembling phosphorescence.

There was an air about him that marked him an exceptional individual the like of which I'd never met before.

"Welcome, Tiny," I offered, getting a crick in the neck as I stared up at him. I did not offer my hand because I wanted it for use later on. "Open your satchel and leave it in the sterilizing chamber. You'll find the skipper in the bow."

"Thanks," he responded without the glimmer of a smile. He stepped into the airlock, hauling the rawhide haybarn with him.

"We blast in forty minutes," I warned.

Didn't see anything more of Jay Score until we were two hundred thousand out, with Earth a greenish moon at the end of our vapor-trail. Then I heard him in the passage asking someone where he could find the sergeant-at-arms. He was directed through my door.

"Sarge," he said, handing over his official requisition, "I've come to collect the trimmings." Then he leaned on the barrier, the whole framework creaked and the top tube sagged in the middle.

"Hey!" I shouted.

"Sorry!" He unleaned. The barrier stood much better when he kept his mass to himself.

Stamping his requisition, I went into the armory, dug out his needle-ray projector and a box of capsules for same. The biggest Venusian mud-skis I could find were about eleven sizes too small and a yard too short for him, but they'd have to do. I gave him a can of thin, multipurpose oil, a jar of graphite, a Lepanto power-pack for his microwave radiophone and, finally, a bunch of nutweed pellicules marked: "Compliments of the Bridal Planet Aromatic Herb Corporation."

Shoving back the spicy lumps, he said, "You can have 'em—they give me the staggers." The rest of the stuff he forced into his side-pack without so much as twitching an eyebrow. Long time since I'd seen anyone so poker-faced.

All the same, the way he eyed the spacesuits seemed strangely wistful. There were thirty bifurcated ones for the Terrestrials, all hanging on the wall like sloughed skins. Also there were six head-and-shoulder helmets for the Martians, since they needed no more than three pounds of air. There wasn't a suit for him. I couldn't have fitted him with one if my life had depended upon it. It'd have been like trying to can an elephant.

Well, he lumbered out lightly, if you get what I mean. The

casual, loose-limbed way he transported his tonnage made me think I'd like to be some place else if ever he got on the rampage. Not that I thought him likely to run amok; he was amiable enough though sphinxlike. But I was fascinated by his air of calm assurance and by his motion, which was fast, silent, and, eerie. Maybe the latter was due to his habit of wearing an inch of sponge rubber under his big dogs.

I kept an interested eye on Jay Score while the *Upsydaisy* made good time on her crawl through the void. Yes, I was more than curious about him because his type was a new one on me despite that I've met plenty in my time. He remained uncommunicative but kind of quietly cordial. His work was smoothly efficient and in every way satisfactory. McNulty took a great fancy to him, though he'd never been one to greet a newcomer with love and kisses.

Three days out, Jay made a major hit with the Martians. As everyone knows, those goggle-eyed, tententacled, half-breathing kibitzers have stuck harder than glue to the Solar System Chess Championship for more than two centuries. Nobody outside of Mars will ever pry them loose. They are nuts about the game and many's the time I've seen a bunch of them go through all the colors of the spectrum in sheer excitement when at last somebody has moved a pawn after thirty minutes of profound cogitation.

One rest-time Jay spent his entire eight hours under three pounds pressure in the starboard airlock. Through the lock's phones came long silences punctuated by wild and shrill twitterings as if he and the Martians were turning the place into a madhouse. At the end of the time we found our tentacled outside crew exhausted. It turned out that Jay had consented to play Kli Yang and had forced him to a stalemate. Kli had been sixth runner-up in the last Solar melee, had been beaten only ten times—each time by a brother Martian, of course.

The red-planet gang had a finger on him after that, or I should say a tentacle-tip. Every rest-time they waylaid him and dragged him into the airlock. When we were eleven days out he played the six of them simultaneously, lost two games, stalemated three, won one. They thought he was a veritable whizzbang—for a mere Terrestrial. Knowing their peculiar abilities in this respect, I thought so, too. So did McNulty. He went so far as to enter the sporting data in the log.

You may remember the stunt that the audiopress of 2270 boosted as "McNulty's Miracle Move"? It's practically a legend of the spaceways. Afterward, when we'd got safely home, McNulty disclaimed the credit and put it where it rightfully belonged. The audiopress had a good excuse, as usual. They said he was the captain, wasn't he? And his name made the headline alliterative, didn't it? Seems that there must be a sect of audio-journalists who have to be alliterative to gain salvation.

What precipitated that crazy stunt and whitened my hair was a chunk of cosmic flotsam. Said object took the form of a gob of meteoric nickel-iron ambling along at the characteristic speed of *pssst!* Its orbit lay on the planetary plane and it approached at right angles to our sunward course.

It gave us the business. I'd never have believed anything so small could have made such a slam. To the present day I can hear the dreadful whistle of air as it made a mad break for freedom through that jagged hole.

We lost quite a bit of political juice before the auto-doors sealed the damaged section. Pressure already had dropped to nine pounds when the compensators held it and slowly began to build it up again. The fall didn't worry the Martians; to them nine pounds was like inhaling pig-wash.

There was one engineer in that sealed section. Another escaped the closing doors by the skin of his left ear. But the first, we thought, had drawn his fateful number and eventually would be floated out like so many spacemen who've come to the end of their duty.

The guy who got clear was leaning against a bulwark, white-faced from the narrowness of his squeak. Jay Score came pounding along. His jaw was working, his eyes were like lamps, but his voice was cool and easy.

He said, "Get out. Seal this room. I'll try to make a snatch. Open up and let me out fast when I knock."

With that he shoved us from the room, which we sealed by closing its autodoor. We couldn't see what the big hunk was doing but the telltale showed he'd released and opened the door to the damaged section. Couple of seconds later the light went out, showing the door had been closed again. Then came a hard, urgent knock. We opened. Jay plunged through hell-for-leather with the engineer's limp body cuddled in his huge arms. He bore it as if it were no bigger and heavier than a kitten and the way he took it down the passage threatened to carry him clear through the end of the ship.

Meanwhile we found we were in a first-class mess. The rockets weren't functioning any more. The venturi tubes were okay and the combustion chambers undamaged. The injectors worked without a hitch—providing that they were pumped by hand. We had lost none of our precious fuel and the shell was intact save for that one jagged hole. What made us useless was the wrecking of our coordinated feeding and firing controls. They had been located where the big bullet went through and now they were so much scrap.

This was more than serious. General opinion called it certain death though nobody said so openly. I'm pretty certain that McNulty shared the morbid notion even if his official report did under-describe it as "an embarrassing predicament." That is just like McNulty. It's a wonder he didn't define our feelings by recording that we were somewhat nonplussed.

Anyway, the Martial squad poured out, some honest work being required of them for the first time in six trips. Pressure had crawled back to fourteen pounds and they had to come into it to be fitted with their head-and-shoulder contraptions.

Kli Yang sniffed offensively, waved a disgusted tentacle and chirruped, "I could swim!" He eased up when we got his dingbat fixed and exhausted it to his customary three pounds. That is the Martian idea of sarcasm: whenever the atmosphere is thicker than they like they make sinuous backstrokes and claim, "I could swim!"

To give them their due, they were good. A Martian can cling to polished ice and work continuously for twelve hours on a ration of oxygen that wouldn't satisfy a Terrestrial for more than ninety minutes. I watched them beat it through the airlock, eyes goggling through inverted fishbowls, their tentacles clutching power lines, sealing plates and quasi-arc welders. Blue lights made little auroras outside the ports as they began to cut, shape and close up that ragged hole.

All the time we continued to bullet sunward. But for this accursed misfortune we'd have swung a curve into the orbit of Venus in four hours' time. Then we'd have let her catch us up while we decelerated to a safe landing.

But when that peewee planetoid picked on us we were still heading for the biggest and brightest furnace hereabouts. That was the way we continued to go, our original velocity being steadily increased by the pull of our fiery destination.

I wanted to be cremated—but not yet!

Up in the bow navigation room Jay Score remained in constant conference with Captain McNulty and the two astro-computator operators. Outside, the Martians continued to crawl around, fizzing and spitting with flashes of ghastly blue light. The engineers, of course, weren't waiting for them to finish their job. Four in spacesuits entered the wrecked section and started the task of creating order out of chaos.

I envied all those busy guys and so did many others. There's a lot of consolation in being able to do something even in an apparently hopeless situation. There's a lot of misery in being compelled to play with one's fingers while others are active.

Two Martians came back through the lock, grabbed some more sealing-plates and crawled out again. One of them thought it might be a bright idea to take his pocket chess set as well, but I didn't let him. There are times and places for that sort of thing and knight to king's fourh on the skin of a busted boat isn't one of them. Then I went along to see Sam Hignett, our Negro surgeon.

Sam had managed to drag the engineer back from the rim of the grave. He'd done it with oxygen, adrenalin and heart-massage. Only his long, dexterous fingers could have achieved it. It was a feat of surgery that has been brought off before, but not often.

Seemed that Sam didn't know what had happened and didn't much care, either. He was like that when he had a patient on his hands. Deftly he closed the chest incision with silver clips, painted the pinched flesh with iodized plastic, cooled the stuff to immediate hardness with a spray of ether.

"Sam," I told him. "You're a marvel."

"Jay gave me a fair chance," he said. "He got him here in time."

"Why put the blame on him?" I joked, unfunnily.

"Sergeant," he answered, very serious, "I'm the ship's doctor. I do the best I can. I couldn't have saved this man if Jay hadn't brought him when he did."

"All right, all right," I agreed. "Have it your own way."

A good fellow, Sam. But he was like all doctors—you know, ethical. I left him with his feebly breathing patient.

McNulty came strutting along the catwalk as I went back. He checked the fuel tanks. He was doing it personally, and that meant something. He looked worried, and that meant a devil of a lot. It meant that I need not bother to write my last will and testament because it would never be read by anything living.

His portly form disappeared into the bow navigation room and I heard him say, "Jay, I guess you—" before the closing door cut off his voice.

He appeared to have a lot of faith in Jay Score. Well, that

individual certainly looked capable enough. The skipper and the new emergency pilot continued to act like cronies even while heading for the final frizzle.

One of the emigrating agriculturalists came out of his cabin and caught me before I regained the armory. Studying me wide-eyed, he said, "Sergeant, there's a half-moon showing through my port."

He continued to pop them at me while I popped mine at him. Venus showing half her pan meant that we were now crossing her orbit. He knew it too—I could tell by the way he bugged them.

"Well," he persisted, with ill-concealed nervousness, "how long is this mishap likely to delay us?"

"No knowing." I scratched my head, trying to look stupid and confident at one and the same time. "Captain McNulty will do his utmost. Put your trust in him—Poppa knows best."

"You don't think we are . . . er . . . in any danger?"

"Oh, not at all."

"You're a liar," he said.

"I resent having to admit it," said I.

That unhorsed him. He returned to his cabin, dissatisfied, apprehensive. In short time he'd see Venus in three-quarter phase and would tell the others. Then the fat would be in the fire.

Our fat in the solar fire.

The last vestiges of hope had drained away just about the time when a terrific roar and violent trembling told that the long-dead rockets were back in action. The noise didn't last more than a few seconds. They shut off quickly, the brief burst serving to show that repairs were effective and satisfactory.

The noise brought out the agriculturalist at full gallop. He knew the worst by now and so did the others. It had been impossible to conceal the truth for the three days since he'd seen Venus as a half-moon. She was far behind us now. We were cutting the orbit of Mercury. But still the passengers clung to desperate hope that someone would perform an unheard-of-miracle.

Charging into the armory, he yipped, "The rockets are working again. Does that mean?"

"Nothing," I gave back, seeing no point in building false hopes.

"But can't we turn round and go back?" He mopped perspiration trickling down his jowls. Maybe a little of it was forced out by fear, but most of it was due to the unpleasant fact that interior conditions had become anything but arctic.

"Sir," I said, feeling my shirt sticking to my back, "we've got more pull than any bunch of spacemen ever enjoyed before. And we're moving so goddam fast that there's nothing left to do but hold a lily."

"My ranch," he growled, bitterly. "I've been allotted five thousand acres of the best Venusian tobacco-growing territory, not to mention a range of uplands for beef."

"Sorry, but I think you'll be lucky ever to see it."

Crrrump! went the rockets again. The burst bent me backward and made him bow forward like he had a bad bellyache. Up in the bow, McNulty or Jay Score or someone was blowing them whenever he felt the whim. I couldn't see any sense in it.

"What's that for?" demanded the complainant, regaining the perpendicular.

"Boys will be boys," I said.

Snorting his disgust, he went to his cabin. A typical Terrestrial emigrant, big, healthy and tough, he was slow to crack and temporarily too peeved to be really worried in any genuinely soul-shaking way.

Half an hour later the general call sounded on buzzers all over the boat. It was a ground signal, never used in space. It meant that the entire crew and all other occupants of the vessel were summoned to the central cabin. Imagine guys being called from their posts in full flight!

Something unique in the history of space navigation must have been behind that call, probably a compose-yourselves-for-the-inevitable-end speech by McNulty.

Expecting the skipper to preside over the last rites, I wasn't surprised to find him standing on the tiny dais as we assembled. A faint scowl lay over his plump features but it changed to a ghost of a smile when the Martians mooched in and one of them did some imitation shark-dodging.

Erect beside McNulty, expressionless as usual, Jay Score looked at that swimming Martian as if he were a pane of glass. Then his strangely lit orbs shifted their aim as if they'd seen nothing more boring. The swim-joke was getting stale, anyway.

"Men and vedras," began McNulty—the latter being the Martian word for "adults" and, by implication, another piece of Martian sarcasm—"I have no need to enlarge upon the awkwardness of our position." That man certainly could pick his words—awkward! "Already we are nearer the sun than any vessel has been in the whole history of cosmic navigation."

"Comic navigation," murmured Kli Yang, with tactless wit.

"We'll need your humor to entertain us later," observed Jay Score in a voice so flat that Kli Yang subsided.

"We are moving toward the luminary," went on McNulty, his scowl reappearing, "faster than any ship moved before. Bluntly, there is not more than one chance in ten thousand of us getting out of this alive." He favored Kli Yang with a challenging stare but that tentacled individual was now subdued. "However, there *is* that one chance—and we are going to take it."

We gaped at him, wondering what the devil he meant. Every one of us knew our terrific velocity made it impossible to describe a U-turn and get back without touching the sun. Neither could we fight our way in the reverse direction with all that mighty drag upon us. There was nothing to do but go onward, onward, until the final searing blast scattered our disrupted molecules.

"What we intend is to try a cometary," continued McNulty. "Jay and myself and the astro-computators think it's remotely possible that we might achieve it and pull through."

That was plain enough. The stunt was a purely theoretical one frequently debated by mathematicians and astro-navigators but never tried out in grim reality. The idea is to build up all the velocity that can be got and at the same time to angle into the path of an elongated, elliptical orbit resembling that of a comet. In theory, the vessel might then skim close to the sun so supremely fast that it would swing pendulumlike far out to the opposite side of the orbit whence it came. A sweet trick—but could we make it?

"Calculations show our present condition fair enough to permit a small chance of success," said McNulty. "We have power enough and fuel enough to build up the necessary velocity with the aid of the sun-pull, to strike the necessary angle and to maintain it for the necessary time. The only point about which we have serious doubts is that of whether we can survive at our nearest to the sun." He wiped perspiration, unconsciously emphasizing the shape of things to come. "I won't mince words, men. It's going to be a choice sample of hell!"

"We'll see it through, Skipper," said someone. A low murmur of support sounded through the cabin.

Kli Yang stood up, simultaneously waggled four jointless arms for attention, and twittered, "It is an idea. It is excellent. I, Kli Yang, endorse it on behalf of my fellow vedras. We shall cram ourselves into the refrigerator and suffer the Terrestrial stink while the sun goes past."

Ignoring that crack about human odor, McNulty nodded and said, "Everybody will be packed into the cold room and endure it as best they can."

"Exactly," said Kli. "Quite," he added with bland disregard of superfluity. Wiggling a tentacle-tip at McNulty, he carried on, "But we cannot control the ship while squatting in the icebox like three and a half dozen strawberry sundaes. There will have to be a pilot in the bow. One individual can hold her on course—until he gets fried. So somebody has to be the fryee."

He gave the tip another sinuous wiggle, being under the delusion that it was fascinating his listeners into complete attention. "And since it cannot be denied that we Martians are far less susceptible to extremes of heat, I suggest that—"

"Nuts!" snapped McNulty. His gruffness deceived nobody. The Martians were nuisances—but grand guys.

"All right." Kli's chirrup rose to a shrill, protesting yelp. "Who else is entitled to become a crisp?"

"Me," said Jay Score. It was queer the way he voiced it. Just as if he were a candidate so obvious that only the stone-blind couldn't see him.

He was right, at that! Jay was the very one for the job. If anyone could take what was going to come through the fore observations ports it was Jay Score. He was big and tough, built for just such a task as this. He had a lot of stuff that none of us had got and, after all, he was a fully qualified emergency pilot. And most definitely this was an emergency, the greatest ever.

But it was funny the way I felt about him. I could imagine him up in front, all alone, nobody there, our lives depending on how much hell he could take, while the tremendous sun extended its searing fingers—

"You!" ejaculated Kli Yang, breaking my train of thought. His goggle eyes bulged irefully at the big, laconic figure on the dais. "You would! I am ready to mate in four moves, as you are miserably aware, and promptly you scheme to lock yourself away."

"Six moves," contradicted Jay, airily. "You cannot do it in less than six."

"Four!" Kli Yang fairly howled. "And right at this point you—"

It was too much for the listening McNulty. He looked as if on the verge of a stroke. His purple face turned to the semaphoring Kli.

"To hell with your blasted chess!" he roared. "Return to your stations, all of you. Make ready for maximum boost. I will sound the general call immediately it becomes necessary to take cover and then you will all go to the cold room." He stared around, the purple gradually fading as his blood pressure went down.

"That is, everyone except Jay."

More like old times with the rockets going full belt. They thundered smoothly and steadily. Inside the vessel the atmosphere became hotter and hotter until moisture trickled continually down our backs and a steaminess lay over the gloss of the walls. What it was like in the bow navigation-room I didn't know and didn't care to discover. The Martians were not inconvenienced yet; for once their whacky composition was much to be envied.

I did not keep check on the time but I'd had two spells of duty with one intervening sleep period before the buzzers gave the general call. By then things had become bad. I was no longer sweating: I was slowly melting into my boots.

Sam, of course, endured it most easily of all the Terrestrials and had persisted long enough to drag his patient completely out of original danger. That engineer was lucky, if it's luck to be saved for a bonfire. We put him in the cold room right away, with Sam in attendance.

The rest of us followed when the buzzer went. Our sanctuary was more than a mere refrigerator; it was the strongest and coolest section of the vessel, a heavily armored, triple-shielded compartment holding the instrument lockers, two sick bays and a large lounge for the benefit of space-nauseated passengers. It held all of us comfortably.

All but the Martians. It held them, but not comfortably. They are never comfortable at fourteen pounds pressure, which they regard as not only thick but also smelly—something like breathing molasses impregnated with aged goat.

Under our very eyes Kli Yang produced a bottle of *hooloo* scent, handed it to his half-parent, Kli Morg. The latter took it, stared at us distastefully, then sniffed the bottle in an ostentatious manner that was positively insulting. But nobody said anything.

All were present excepting McNulty and Jay Score. The skipper appeared two hours later. Things must have been raw up front, for he looked terrible. His haggard face was beaded and glossy, his once-plump cheeks sunken and blistered. His usually spruce, well-fitting uniform hung upon him sloppily. It needed only one glance to tell that he'd had a darned good roasting, as much as he could stand.

Walking unsteadily, he crossed the floor, went into the first-aid cubby, stripped himself with slow, painful movements. Sam rubbed him with tannic jelly. We could hear the tormented skipper grunting hoarsely as Sam put plenty of pep into the job.

The heat was now on us with a vengeance. It pervaded the walls, the floor, the air and created a multitude of fierce stinging sensations in every muscle of my body. Several of the engineers took off their boots and jerkins. In short time the passengers followed suit, discarding most of their outer clothing. My agriculturalist sat a miserable figure in tropical silks, moody over what might have been.

Emerging from the cubby, McNulty flopped onto a bunk and said, "If we're all okay in four hours' time, we're through the worst part."

At that moment the rockets faltered. We knew at once what was wrong. A fuel tank had emptied and a relay had failed to cut in. An engineer should have been standing by to switch the conduits. In the heat and excitement, someone had blundered.

The fact barely had time to register before Kli Yang was out through the door. He'd been lolling nearest to it and was gone while we were trying to collect our overheated wits. Twenty seconds later the rockets renewed their steady thrum.

An intercom bell clanged right in my ear. Switching its mike, I croaked a throaty, "Well?" and heard Jay's voice coming back to me from the bow.

"Who did it?"

"Kli Yang," I told him. "He's still outside."

"Probably gone for their domes," guessed Jay. "Tell him I said thanks."

"What's it like around where you live?" I asked.

"Fierce. It isn't so good . . . for vision." Silence a moment, then, "Guess I can stick it . . . somehow. Strap down or hold on ready for the next time I sound the . . . bell."

"Why?" I half yelled, half rasped.

"Going to rotate her. Try . . . distribute . . . the heat."

A faint squeak told that he'd switched off. I told the others to strap down. The Martians didn't have to bother about that because they owned enough saucer-sized suckers to weld them to a sunfishing meteor.

Kli came back, showed Jay's guess to be correct; he was dragging the squad's head-and-shoulder pieces. The load was as much as he could pull now that temperature had climbed to the point where even he began to wilt.

The Martian moochers gladly donned their gadgets, sealing the seams and evacuating them down to three pounds pressure. It made them considerably happier. Remembering that we Terrestrials use spacesuits to keep air inside, it seemed queer to watch those guys using theirs to keep it outside.

They had just finished making themselves comfortable and had laid out a chessboard in readiness for a minor journey when the bell sounded again. We braced ourselves. The Martians clamped down their suckers.

Slowly and steadily the *Upsydaisy* began to turn upon her longitudinal axis. The chessboard and pieces tried to stay put, failed, crawled along the floor, up the wall and across the ceiling. Solar pull was making them stick to the sunward side.

I saw Kli Morg's strained, heat-ridden features glooming at a black bishop while it skittered around, and I suppose that inside his goldfish bowl were resounding some potent samples of Martian invective.

"Three hours and a half," gasped McNulty.

That four hours estimate could only mean two hours of approach to the absolute deadline and two hours of retreat from it. So the moment when we had two hours to go would be the moment when we were at our nearest to the solar furnace, the moment of greatest peril.

I wasn't aware of that critical time, since I passed out twenty minutes before it arrived. No use enlarging upon the horror of that time. I think I went slightly nuts. I was a hog in an oven, being roasted alive. It's the only time I've ever thought of the sun as a great big shining bastard that ought to be extinguished for keeps. Soon afterward I became incapable of any thought at all.

I recovered consciousness and painfully moved in my straps ninety minutes after passing the midway point. My dazed mind had difficulty in realizing that we had now only half an hour to go to reach theoretical safety.

What had happened in the interim was left to my imagination and I didn't care to try to picture it just then. The sun blazing with a ferocity multi-million times greater than that of a tiger's eye, and a hundred thousand times as hungry for our blood and bones. The flaming corona licking out toward this shipload of half-dead entities, imprisoned in a steel bottle.

And up in front of the vessel, behind its totally inadequate quartz observation-ports, Jay Score sitting alone, facing the mounting inferno, staring, staring, staring—

Getting to my feet, I teetered uncertainly, went down like a bundle of rags. The ship wasn't rotating any longer and we appeared to be bulleting along in normal fashion. What dropped me was sheer weakness. I felt lousy.

The Martians already had recovered. I knew they'd be the first. One of them lugged me upright and held me steady while I regained a percentage of my former control. I noticed that another had sprawled right across the unconscious McNulty and three of the passengers. Yes, he'd shielded them from some of the heat and they were the next ones to come to life.

Struggling to the intercom, I switched it but got no response from the front. For three full minutes I hung by it dazedly before I tried again. Nothing doing. Jay wouldn't or couldn't answer.

I was stubborn about it, made several more attempts with no better result. The effort cost me a dizzy spell and down I flopped once more. The heat was still terrific. I felt more dehydrated than a mummy dug out of sand a million years old.

Kli Yang opened the door, crept out with dragging, pain-stricken motion. His air-helmet was secure on his shoulders. Five minutes later he came back, spoke through the helmet's diaphragm.

"Couldn't get near the bow navigation room. At the midway catwalk the autodoors are closed, the atmosphere sealed off, and it's like being inside a furnace." He stared around, met my gaze, answered the question in my eyes. "There's no air in the bow."

No air meant the observation ports had gone *phut*. Nothing else could have emptied the navigation room. Well, we carried spares for that job and could make good the damage once we got into the clear. Meanwhile here we were roaring along, maybe on correct course and maybe not, with an empty, airless navigation room and with an intercom system that gave nothing but ghastly silence.

Sitting around, we picked up strength. The last to come out of his coma was the sick engineer. Sam brought him through again. It was about then that McNulty wiped sweat, showed sudden excitement.

"Four hours, men," he said, with grim satisfaction. "We've done it!"

We raised a hollow cheer. By Jupiter, the super-heated atmosphere seemed to grow ten degrees cooler with the news. Strange how relief from tension can breed strength; in one minute we had conquered former weakness and were ready to go. But it was yet another four hours before a quartet of spacesuited engineers penetrated the forward hell and bore their burden from the airless navigation room.

They carried him into Sam's cubbyhole, a long, heavy, silent figure with face burned black.

Stupidly I hung around him saying, "Jay, Jay, how're you making out?"

He must have heard, for he moved the fingers of his right hand and emitted a chesty, grinding noise. Two of the engineers went to his cabin, brought back his huge rawhide case. They shut the door, staying in with Sam and leaving me and the Martians fidgeting outside. Kli Yang wandered up and down the passage as if he didn't know what to do with his tentacles.

Sam came out after more than an hour. We jumped him on the spot.

"How's Jay?"

"Blind as a statue." He shook his woolly head. "And his voice isn't there any more. He's taken an awful beating."

"So that's why he didn't answer the intercom." I looked him straight in the eyes. "Can you . . . can you do anything for him, Sam?"

"I only wish I could." His sepia face showed his feelings. "You know how much I'd like to put him right. But I can't." He made a gesture of futility. "He is completely beyond my modest skill. Nobody less than Johannsen can help him. Maybe when we get back to Earth—" His voice petered out and he went back inside.

Kli Yang said, miserably, "I am saddened."

A scene I'll never forget to my dying day was that evening we spent as guests of the Astro Club in New York. That club was then—as it is today—the most exclusive group of human beings ever gathered together. To qualify for membership one had to perform in dire emergency a feat of astro-navigation tantamount to a miracle. There were nine members in those days and there are only twelve now.

Mace Waldron, the famous pilot who saved that Martian liner in 2263, was the chairman. Classy in his soup and fish, he stood at the top of the table with Jay Score sitting at his side. At the opposite end of the table was McNulty, a broad smirk of satisfaction upon his plump pan. Beside the skipper was old, white-haired Knud Johannsen, the genius who designed the J-series and a scientific figure known to every spaceman.

Along the sides, manifestly self-conscious, sat the entire crew of the *Upsydaisy,* including the Martians, plus three of our passengers who'd postponed their trips for this occasion. There were also a couple of audio-journalists with scanners and mikes.

"Gentlemen and vedras," said Mace Waldron, "this is an event without precedent in the history of humanity, an event never thought of, never imagined by this club. Because of that I feel it doubly an honor and a privilege to propose that Jay Score, Emergency Pilot, be accepted as a fully qualified and worthy member of the Astro Club."

"Seconded!" shouted three members simultaneously.

"Thank you, gentlemen." He cocked an inquiring eyebrow. Eight hands went up in unison. "Carried," he said. "Unanimously." Glancing down at the taciturn and unmoved Jay Score, he launched into a eulogy. It went on and on and on, full of praise and superlatives, while Jay squatted beside him with a listless air.

Down at the other end I saw McNulty's gratified smirk grow stronger and stronger. Next to him, old Knud was gazing at Jay with a fatherly fondness that verged on the fatuous. The crew likewise gave full attention to the blank-faced subject of the talk, and the scanners were fixed upon him too.

I returned my attention to where all the others were looking, and the victim sat there, his restored eyes bright and glittering, but his face completely immobile despite the talk, the publicity, the beam of paternal pride from Johannsen.

But after ten minutes of this I saw J.20 begin to fidget with obvious embarrassment.

Don't let anyone tell you that a robot can't have feelings!

UNIVERSE

Astounding Science Fiction
May

by Robert A. Heinlein

Another SFWA HALL OF FAME story, "Universe" is justly famous, both as a story and as the prototype (if not the actual first) treatment of a self-contained, confined world, in this case an enormous spaceship whose inhabitants have forgotten who they were, what they were doing, and even the nature of their existence.

It is truly one of the most influential and important stories in science fiction.

(There was no one like Bob Heinlein for getting there first. The self-contained world is now not only a staple of science fiction, but a recognized part of science itself. I have written frequently of "star-ships" as representing the serious future of humanity in my non-fiction, and I tell you quite unabashedly that the idea came to me from "Universe." I can't say that Gerard O'Neill got the notion of his "space settlements" from "Universe," but if it turned out he had, I would be pleased, but not surprised. Ah, that golden year of 1941.—I.A.)

LIAR!

Astounding Science Fiction
May

by Isaac Asimov (1920-   )

(I was very fortunate to have squeezed a story into the May, 1941, *Astounding*, if only that I found myself in company with giants, though I must admit it was frightening to feel that I was in competition with them.

"Liar!" was only the fourth story I had sold to Campbell and the second positronic robot story I had placed with him. The first was "Reason." "Liar!" was also the first that John had taken without requesting revision of any sort.

I wish he had, though. There were parts that were embarrassingly amateurish, and that I carefully revised nine years later when I prepared the story for inclusion in *I, Robot*. Here, however, because of the necessity of playing fair with the reader and with the historical imperative, the story appears as it had appeared in the magazine. If you snicker at my clumsiness here and there, please remember that I wrote it when I was only 20.—I.A.)

Alfred Lanning lit his cigar carefully, but the tips of his fingers were trembling slightly. His gray eyebrows hunched low as he spoke between puffs.

"It reads minds all right—damn little doubt about that! But why?" He looked at mathematician Peter Bogert. "Well?"

Bogert flattened his black hair down with both hands, "That was the thirty-fourth RB model we've turned out, Lanning. All the others were strictly orthodox."

The third man at the table frowned. Milton Ashe was the youngest officer of U. S. Robot & Mechanical Men, Inc., and proud of his post.

"Listen, Bogert. There wasn't a hitch in the assembly from start to finish. I guarantee that."

Bogert's thick lips spread in a patronizing smile, "Do you? If you can answer for the entire assembly line, I recommend your promotion. By exact count, there are seventy-five thou-

131

sand, two hundred and thirty-four operations necessary for the manufacture of a single positronic brain, each separate operation depending for successful completion upon any number of factors, from five to a hundred and five. If any one of them goes seriously wrong, the 'brain' is ruined. I quote our own information folder, Ashe."

Milton Ashe flushed, but a fourth voice cut off his reply.

"If we're going to start by trying to fix the blame on one another, I'm leaving." Susan Calvin's hands were folded tightly in her lap, and the little lines about her thin, pale lips deepened. "We've got a mind-reading robot on our hands and it strikes me as rather important that we find out just why it reads minds. We're not going to do that by saying, 'Your fault! My fault!' "

Her cold gray eyes fastened upon Ashe, and he grinned.

Lanning grinned too, and, as always at such times, his long white hair and shrewd little eyes made him the picture of a biblical patriarch, "True for you, Dr. Calvin."

His voice became suddenly crisp, "Here's everything in pill-concentrate form. We've produced a positronic brain of supposedly ordinary vintage that's got the remarkable property of being able to tune in on thought waves. It would mark the most important advance in robotics in decades if we knew how it happened. We don't, and we have to find out. Is that clear?"

"May I make a suggestion?" asked Bogert.

"Go ahead!"

"I'd say that until we do figure out the mess—and as a mathematician I expect it to be a very devil of a mess—we keep the existence of RB-34 a secret. I mean even from the other members of the staff. As heads of the departments, we ought not to find it an insoluble problem, and the fewer know about it—"

"Bogert is right," said Dr. Calvin. "Ever since the Interplanetary Code was modified to allow robot models to be tested in the plants before being shipped out to space, anti-robot propaganda has increased. If any word leaks out about a robot being able to read minds before we can announce complete control of the phenomenon, pretty effective capital could be made out of it."

Lanning sucked at his cigar and nodded gravely. He turned to Ashe, "I think you said you were alone when you first stumbled on this thought-reading business."

"I'll say I was alone—I got the scare of my life. RB-34 had just been taken off the assembly table and they sent him down to me. Obermann was off somewheres, so I took him down to the testing room myself—at least I started to take him down." Ashe paused, and a tiny smile tugged at his lips, "Say, did any of you ever carry on a thought conversation without knowing it?"

No one bothered to answer, and he continued, "You don't realize it at first, you know. He just spoke to me—as logically and sensibly as you can imagine—and it was only when I was most of the way down to the testing rooms that I realized that I hadn't said anything. Sure, I thought lots, but that isn't the same thing, is it? I locked that thing up and ran for Lanning. Having it walking beside me, calmly peering into my thoughts and picking and choosing among them gave me the willies."

"I imagine it would," said Susan Calvin thoughtfully. Her eyes fixed themselves upon Ashe in an oddly intent manner. "We are so accustomed to considering our own thoughts private."

Lanning broke in impatiently, "Then only the four of us know. All right! We've got to go about this systematically. Ashe, I want you to check over the assembly line from beginning to end—everything. You're to eliminate all operations in which there was no possible chance of an error, and list all those where there were, together with its nature and possible magnitude."

"Tall order," grunted Ashe.

"Naturally! Of course, you're to put the men under you to work on this—every single one if you have to, and I don't care if we go behind schedule, either. But they're not to know why, you understand."

"Hm-m-m, yes!" The young technician grinned wryly. "It's still a lulu of a job."

Lanning swiveled about in his chair and faced Calvin, "You'll have to tackle the job from the other direction. You're the robopsychologist of the plant, so you're to study the robot itself and work backward. Try to find out how he ticks. See what else is tied up with his telepathic powers, how far they extend, how they warp his outlook, and just exactly what harm it has done to his ordinary RB properties. You've got that?"

Lanning didn't wait for Dr. Calvin to answer.

"I'll coordinate the work and interpret the findings mathematically." He puffed violently at his cigar and mumbled the rest through the smoke, "Bogert will help me there, of course."

Bogert polished the nails of one pudgy hand with the other and said blandly, "I dare say. I know a little in the line."

"Well! I'll get started." Ashe shoved his chair back and rose. His pleasantly youthful face crinkled in a grin, "I've got the darnedest job of any of us, so I'm getting out of here and to work."

He left with a slurred, "B' seein' ye!"

Susan Calvin answered with a barely perceptible nod, but her eyes followed him out of sight and she did not answer when Lanning grunted and said, "Do you want to go up and see RB-34 now, Dr. Calvin?"

RB-34's photoelectric eyes lifted from the book at the muffled sound of hinges turning and he was upon his feet when Susan Calvin entered.

She paused to readjust the huge "No Entrance" sign upon the door and then approached the robot.

"I've brought you the texts upon hyperatomic motors, Herbie—a few anyway. Would you care to look at them?"

RB-34—otherwise known as Herbie—lifted the three heavy books from her arms and opened to the title page of one:

"Hm-m-m! 'Theory of Hyperatomics.'" He mumbled inarticulately to himself as he flipped the pages and then spoke with an abstracted air, "Sit down, Dr. Calvin! This will take me a few minutes."

The psychologist seated herself and watched Herbie narrowly as he took a chair at the other side of the table and went through the three books systematically.

At the end of half an hour, he put them down, "Of course, I know why you brought these."

The corner of Dr. Calvin's lip twitched, "I was afraid you would. It's difficult to work with you, Herbie. You're always a step ahead of me."

"It's the same with these books, you know, as with the others. They just don't interest me. There's nothing to your textbooks. Your science is just a mass of collected data plastered together by makeshift theory—and all so incredibly simple, that it's scarcely worth bothering about.

"It's your fiction that interests me. Your studies of the interplay of human motives and emotions." His mighty hand gestured vaguely as he sought the proper words.

Dr. Calvin whispered, "I think I understand."

"I see into minds, you see," the robot continued, "and you have no idea how complicated they are. I can't begin to understand everything because my own mind has so little in common with them—but I try, and your novels help."

"Yes, but I'm afraid that after going through some of the harrowing emotional experiences of our present-day sentimental novel"—there was a tinge of bitterness in her voice—"you find real minds like ours are dull and colorless."

"But I don't!"

The sudden energy in the response brought the other to her feet. She felt herself reddening, and thought wildly, "He must know!"

Herbie subsided suddenly, and muttered in a low voice from which the metallic timbre departed almost entirely. "But, of course, I know about it, Dr. Calvin. You think of it always, so how can I help but know?"

Her face was hard. "Have you—told anyone?"

"Of course not!" This, with genuine surprise. "No one has asked me."

"Well, then," she flung out, "I suppose you think I am a fool."

"No! It is a normal emotion."

"Perhaps that is why it is so foolish." The wistfulness in her voice drowned out everything else. Some of the woman peered through the layer of doctorhood. "I am not what you would call—attractive."

"If you are referring to mere physical attraction, I couldn't judge. But I know, in any case, that there are other types of attraction."

"Nor young." Dr. Calvin had scarcely heard the robot.

"You are not yet forty." An anxious insistence had crept into Herbie's voice.

"Thirty-eight as you count the years; a shriveled sixty as far as my emotional outlook on life is concerned. Am I a psychologist for nothing?"

She drove on with bitter breathlessness, "And he's barely thirty-five and looks and acts younger. Do you suppose he ever sees me as anything but . . . but what I am?"

"You are wrong!" Herbie's steel fist struck the plastic-topped table with a strident clang. "Listen to me—"

But Susan Calvin whirled on him now and the hunted pain in her eyes became a blaze, "Why should I? What do you know about it all, anyway, you . . . you machine. I'm just a specimen to you; an interesting bug with a peculiar mind spread-eagled for inspection. It's a wonderful example of frustration, isn't it? Almost as good as your books." Her voice, emerging in dry sobs, choked into silence.

The robot cowered at the outburst. He shook his head pleadingly. "Won't you listen to me, please? I could help you if you would let me."

"How?" Her lips curled. "By giving me good advice?"

"No, not that. It's just that I know what other people think—Milton Ashe, for instance."

There was a long silence, and Susan Calvin's eyes dropped. "I don't want to know what he thinks," she gasped. "Keep quiet."

"I think you would want to know what he thinks."

Her head remained bent, but her breath came more quickly. "You are talking nonsense," she whispered.

"Why should I? I am trying to help. Milton Ashe's thoughts of you—" he paused.

And then the psychologist raised her head, "Well?"

The robot said quietly, "He loves you."

For a full minute, Dr. Calvin did not speak. She merely stared. Then, "You are mistaken! You must be. Why should he?"

"But he does. A thing like that cannot be hidden, not from me."

"But I am so . . . so—" she stammered to a halt.

"He looks deeper than the skin, and admires intellect in others. Milton Ashe is not the type to marry a head of hair and a pair of eyes."

Susan Calvin found herself blinking rapidly and waited before speaking. Even then her voice trembled, "Yet he certainly never in any way indicated—"

"Have you ever given him a chance?"

"How could I? I never thought that—"

"Exactly!"

The psychologist paused in thought and then looked up suddenly. "A girl visited him here at the plant half a year ago. She was pretty, I suppose—blond and slim. And, of course, could scarcely add two and two. He spent all day puffing out his chest, trying to explain how a robot was put together." The hardness had returned, "Not that she understood! Who was she?"

Herbie answered without hesitation, "I know the person you are referring to. She is his first cousin, and there is no romantic interest there, I assure you."

Susan Calvin rose to her feet with a vivacity almost girlish. "Now isn't that strange? That's exactly what I used to pretend to myself sometimes, though I never really thought so. Then it all must be true."

She ran to Herbie and seized his cold, heavy hand in both hers. "Thank you, Herbie." Her voice was an urgent, husky whisper. "Don't tell anyone about this. Let it be our secret— and thank you again." With that, and a convulsive squeeze of Herbie's unresponsive metal fingers, she left.

Herbie turned slowly to his neglected novel, but there was no one to read *his* thoughts.

Milton Ashe stretched slowly and magnificently, to the tune of cracking joints and chorus of grunts, and then glared at Peter Bogert, Ph.D.

"Say," he said, "I've been at this for a week now with just about no sleep. How long do I have to keep it up? I thought you said the positronic bombardment in Vac Chamber D was the solution."

Bogert yawned delicately and regarded his white hands with interest. "It is. I'm on the track."

"I know what *that* means when a mathematician says it. How near the end are you?"

"It all depends."

"On what?" Ashe dropped into a chair and stretched his long legs out before him.

"On Lanning. The old fellow disagrees with me." He sighed, "A bit behind the times, that's the trouble with him. He clings to matrix mechanics as the all in all, and this problem calls for more powerful mathematical tools. He's so stubborn."

Ashe muttered sleepily, "Why not ask Herbie and settle the whole affair?"

"Ask the robot?" Bogert's eyebrows climbed.

"Why not? Didn't the old girl tell you?"

"You mean Calvin?"

"Yeah! Susie herself. That robot's a mathematical wiz. He knows all about everything plus a bit on the side. He does triple integrals in his head and eats up tensor analysis for dessert."

The mathematician stared skeptically, "Are you serious?"

"So help me! The catch is that the dope doesn't like math. He would rather read slushy novels. Honest! You should see the tripe Susie keeps feeding him: 'Purple Passion' and 'Love in Space.'"

"Dr. Calvin hasn't said a word of this to us."

"Well, she hasn't finished studying him. You know how she is. She likes to have everything just so before letting out the big secret."

"She told *you*."

"We sort of got to talking. I have been seeing a lot of her lately." He opened his eyes wide and frowned, "Say, Bogie, have you been noticing anything queer about the lady lately?"

Bogert relaxed into an undignified grin, "She's using lipstick, if that's what you mean."

"Hell, I know that. Rouge, powder and eye shadow, too. She's a sight. But it's not that. I can't put my finger on it. It's the way she talks—as if she were happy about something." He thought a little, and then shrugged.

The other allowed himself a leer, which, for a scientist past fifty, was not a bad job, "Maybe she's in love."

Ashe allowed his eyes to close again, "You're nuts, Bogie. You go speak to Herbie; I want to stay here and go to sleep."

"Right! Not that I particularly like having a robot tell me my job, nor that I think he can do it!"

A soft snore was his only answer.

Herbie listened carefully as Peter Bogert, hands in pockets, spoke with elaborate indifference.

"So there you are. I've been told you understand these things, and I am asking you more in curiosity than anything else. My line of reasoning, as I have outlined it, involves a few doubtful steps, I admit, which Dr. Lanning refuses to accept, and the picture is still rather incomplete."

The robot didn't answer, and Bogert said, "Well?"

"I see no mistake." Herbie studied the scribbled figures.

"I don't suppose you can go any further than that?"

"I daren't try. You are a better mathematician than I, and—well, I'd hate to commit myself."

There was a shade of complacency in Bogert's smile, "I rather thought that would be the case. It is deep. We'll forget it." He crumpled the sheets, tossed them down the waste shaft, turned to leave, and then thought better of it.

"By the way—"

The robot waited.

Bogert seemed to have difficulty. "There is something— that is, perhaps you can—" He stopped.

Herbie spoke quietly. "Your thoughts are confused, but there is no doubt at all that they concern Dr. Lanning. It is silly to hesitate, for as soon as you compose yourself, I'll know what it is you want to ask."

The mathematician's hand went to his sleek hair in the familiar smoothing gesture. "Lanning is nudging seventy," he said, as if that explained everything.

"I know that."

"And he's been director of the plant for almost thirty years." Herbie nodded.

"Well, now," Bogert's voice became ingratiating, "you would know whether . . . whether he's thinking of resigning. Health, perhaps, or some other—"

"Quite," said Herbie, and that was all.

"Well, do you know?"

"Certainly."

"Then—uh—could you tell me?"

"Since you ask, yes." The robot was quite matter-of-fact about it. "He has already resigned!"

"What!" The exclamation was an explosive, almost inarticulate, sound. The scientist's large head hunched forward, "Say that again!"

"He has already resigned," came the quiet repetition, "but it has not yet taken effect. He is waiting, you see, to solve the problem of—er—myself. That finished, he is quite ready to turn the office of director over to his successor."

Bogert expelled his breath sharply, "And this successor? Who is he?" He was quite close to Herbie now, eyes fixed fascinated on those unreadable dull-red photoelectric cells that were the robot's eyes.

Words came slowly, "You are the next director."

And Bogert relaxed into a tight smile. "This is good to know. I've been hoping and waiting for this. Thanks, Herbie."

Peter Bogert was at his desk until five that morning and he was back at nine. The shelf just over the desk emptied of its row of reference books and tables, as he referred to one after the other. The pages of calculations before him increased microscopically and the crumpled sheets at his feet mounted into a hill of scribbled paper.

At precisely noon, he stared at the final page, rubbed a blood-shot eye, yawned, and shrugged. "This is getting worse each minute. Damn!"

He turned at the sound of the opening door and nodded at Lanning, who entered, cracking the knuckles of one gnarled hand with the other.

The director took in the disorder of the room and his eyebrows furrowed together.

"New lead?" he asked.

"No," came the defiant answer. "What's wrong with the old one?"

Lanning did not trouble to answer, nor to do more than

bestow a single cursory glance at the top sheet upon Bogert's desk. He spoke through the flare of a match as he lit a cigar.

"Has Calvin told you about the robot? It's a mathematical genius. Really remarkable."

The other snorted loudly, "So I've heard. But Calvin had better stick to robopsychology. I've checked Herbie on math, and he can scarcely struggle through calculus."

"Calvin didn't find it so."

"She's crazy."

"And I don't find it so." The director's eyes narrowed dangerously.

"You!" Bogert's voice hardened. "What are you talking about?"

"I've been putting Herbie through his paces all morning, and he can do tricks you never heard of."

"Is that so?"

"You sound skeptical!" Lanning flipped a sheet of paper out of his vest pocket and unfolded it. "That's not my handwriting, is it?"

Bogert studied the large angular notation covering the sheet, "Herbie did this?"

"Right! And if you'll notice, he's been working on your time integration of Equation 22. It comes"—Lanning tapped a yellow fingernail upon the last step—"to the identical conclusion I did, and in a quarter the time. You had no right to neglect the Linger Effect in positronic bombardment."

"I didn't neglect it. For Heaven's sake, Lanning, get it through your head that it would cancel out—"

"Oh, sure, you explained that. You used the Mitchell Translation Equation, didn't you? Well—it doesn't apply."

"Why not?"

"Because you've been using hyper-imaginaries, for one thing."

"What's that to do with?"

"Mitchell's Equation won't hold when—"

"Are you crazy? If you'll reread Mitchell's original paper in the *Transactions of the Far*—"

"I don't have to. I told you in the beginning that I didn't like his reasoning, and Herbie backs me in that."

"Well, then," Bogert shouted, "let that clockwork contraption solve the entire problem for you. Why bother with nonessentials?"

"That's exactly the point. Herbie can't solve the problem. And if he can't, we can't—alone. I'm submitting the entire question to the National Board. It's gotten beyond us."

Bogert's chair went over backward as he jumped up a-snarl, face crimson. "You're doing nothing of the sort."

Lanning flushed in his turn, "Are you telling me what I can't do?"

"Exactly," was the gritted response. "I've got the problem beaten and you're not to take it out of my hands, understand? Don't think I don't see through you, you desiccated fossil. You'd cut your own nose off before you'd let me get the credit for solving robotic telepathy."

"You're a damned idiot, Bogert, and in one second I'll have you suspended for insubordination"—Lanning's lower lip trembled with passion.

"Which is one thing you won't do, Lanning. You haven't any secrets with a mind-reading robot around, so don't forget that I know all about your resignation."

The ash on Lanning's cigar trembled and fell, and the cigar itself followed, "What . . . what—"

Bogert chuckled nastily, "And I'm the new director, be it understood. I'm very aware of that; don't think I'm not. Damn your eyes, Lanning, I'm going to give the orders about here or there will be the sweetest mess that you've ever been in."

Lanning found his voice and let it out with a roar. "You're suspended, d'ye hear? You're relieved of all duties. You're broken, do you understand?"

The smile on the other's face broadened, "Now, what's the use of that? You're getting nowhere. I'm holding the trumps. I know you've resigned. Herbie told me, and he got it straight from you."

Lanning forced himself to speak quietly. He looked an old, old man, with tired eyes peering from a face in which the red had disappeared, leaving the pasty yellow of age behind, "I want to speak to Herbie. He can't have told you anything of the sort. You're playing a deep game, Bogert, but I'm calling your bluff. Come with me."

Bogert shrugged, "To see Herbie? Good! Damned good!"

It was also precisely at noon that Milton Ashe looked up from his clumsy sketch and said, "You get the idea? I'm not too good at getting this down, but that's about how it looks. It's a honey of a house, and I can get it for next to nothing."

Susan Calvin gazed across at him with melting eyes. "It's really beautiful," she sighed. "I've often thought that I'd like to—" Her voice trailed away.

"Of course," Ashe continued briskly, putting away his pencil, "I've got to wait for my vacation. It's only two weeks off, but this Herbie business has everything up in the air." His eyes dropped to his fingernails. "Besides, there's another point—but it's a secret."

"Then don't tell me."

"Oh, I'd just as soon, I'm just busting to tell someone— and you're just about the best—er—confidante I could find here." He grinned sheepishly.

Susan Calvin's heart bounded, but she did not trust herself to speak.

"Frankly," Ashe scraped his chair closer and lowered his voice into a confidential whisper, "the house isn't to be only for myself. I'm getting married!"

And then he jumped out of his seat, "What's the matter?"

"Nothing!" The horrible spinning sensation had vanished, but it was hard to get words out. "Married? You mean—"

"Why, sure! About time, isn't it? You remember that girl who was here last summer. That's she! But you *are* sick. You—"

"Headache!" Susan Calvin motioned him away weakly. "I've . . . I've been subject to them lately. I want to . . . to congratulate you, of course. I'm very glad—" The inexpertly applied rouge made a pair of nasty red splotches upon her chalk-white face. Things had begun spinning again. "Pardon me—please—"

The words were a mumble, as she stumbled blindly out the door. It had happened with the sudden catastrophe of a dream—and with all the unreal horror of a dream.

But how could it be? Herbie had said—

And Herbie knew! He could see into minds!

She found herself leaning breathlessly against the door jamb, staring into Herbie's metal face. She must have climbed the two flights of stairs, but she had no memory of it. The distance had been covered in an instant, as in a dream.

As in a dream!

And still Herbie's unblinking eyes stared into hers and their dull red seemed to expand into dimly shining nightmarish globes.

He was speaking, and she felt the cold glass pressing against her lips. She swallowed and shuddered into a certain awareness of her surroundings.

Still Herbie spoke, and there was agitation in his voice—as if he were hurt and frightened and pleading.

The words were beginning to make sense. "This is a dream," he was saying, "and you mustn't believe in it. You'll

wake into the real world soon and laugh at yourself. He loves
you, I tell you. He does, he does! But not here! Not now!
This is an illusion."

Susan Calvin nodded, her voice a whisper, "Yes! Yes!" She
was clutching Herbie's arm, clinging to it, repeating over and
over, "It isn't true, is it? It isn't, is it?"

Just how she came to her senses, she never knew—but it
was like passing from a world of misty unreality to one of
harsh sunlight. She pushed him away from her, pushed hard
against that steely arm, and her eyes were wide.

"What are you trying to do?" Her voice rose to a harsh
scream. "What are you trying to do?"

Herbie backed away, "I want to help."

The psychologist stared, "Help? By telling me this is a
dream? By trying to push me into schizophrenia?" An hysterical tenseness seized her, "This is no dream! I wish it were!"

She drew her breath sharply, "Wait! Why . . . why, I understand. Merciful Heavens, it's so obvious."

There was horror in the robot's voice, "I had to!"

"And I believed you! I never thought—"

Loud voices outside the door brought her to a halt. She
turned away, fists clenching spasmodically, and when Bogert
and Lanning entered, she was at the far window. Neither of
the men paid her the slightest attention.

They approached Herbie simultaneously; Lanning angry
and impatient, Bogert, coolly sardonic. The director spoke
first.

"Here now, Herbie. Listen to me!"

The robot brought his eyes sharply down upon the aged
director, "Yes, Dr. Lanning."

"Have you discussed me with Dr. Bogert?"

"No, sir." The answer came slowly, and the smile on Bogert's face flashed off.

"What's that?" Bogert shoved in ahead of his superior and
straddled the ground before the robot. "Repeat what you told
me yesterday."

"I said that—" Herbie fell silent. Deep within him his
metallic diaphragm vibrated in soft discords.

"Didn't you say he had resigned?" roared Bogert. "Answer
me!"

Bogert raised his arm frantically, but Lanning pushed him
aside, "Are you trying to bully him into lying?"

"You heard him, Lanning. He began to say 'Yes' and

stopped. Get out of my way! I want the truth out of him, understand!"

"I'll ask him!" Lanning turned to the robot. "All right, Herbie, take it easy. Have I resigned?"

Herbie stared, and Lanning repeated anxiously, "Have I resigned?" There was the faintest trace of a negative shake of the robot's head. A long wait produced nothing further.

The two men looked at each other and the hostility in their eyes was all but tangible.

"What the devil," blurted Bogert, "has the robot gone mute? Can't you speak, you monstrosity?"

"I can speak," came the ready answer.

"Then answer the question. Didn't you tell me Lanning had resigned? Hasn't he resigned?"

And again there was nothing but dull silence, until from the end of the room, Susan Calvin's laugh rang out suddenly, high-pitched and semi-hysterical.

The two mathematicians jumped, and Bogert's eyes narrowed, "You here? What's so funny?"

"Nothing's funny." Her voice was not quite natural. "It's just that I'm not the only one that's been caught. There's irony in three of the greatest experts in robotics in the world falling into the same elementary trap, isn't there?" Her voice faded, and she put a pale hand to her forehead. "But it isn't funny!"

This time the look that passed between the two men was one of raised eyebrows. "What trap are you talking about?" asked Lanning stiffly. "Is something wrong with Herbie?"

"No." She approached them slowly. "Nothing is wrong with him—only with us." She whirled suddenly and shrieked at the robot, "Get away from me! Go to the other end of the room and don't let me look at you."

Herbie cringed before the fury of her eyes and stumbled away in a clattering trot.

Lanning's voice was hostile, "What is all this, Dr. Calvin?"

She faced them and spoke sarcastically, "Surely you know the fundamental First Law of Robotics."

The other two nodded together. "Certainly," said Bogert, irritably, "a robot may not injure a human being, or through inaction, allow him to come to harm."

"How nicely put," sneered Calvin. "But what kind of harm?"

"Why—any kind."

"Exactly! Any kind! But what about hurt feelings? What

about deflation of one's ego? What about the blasting of one's hopes? Is that injury?"

Lanning frowned, "What would a robot know about—" And then he caught himself with a gasp.

"You've caught on, have you? *This* robot reads minds. Do you suppose it doesn't know everything about mental injury? Do you suppose that if asked a question, it wouldn't give exactly that answer that one wants to hear? Wouldn't any other answer hurt us, and wouldn't Herbie know that?"

"Good Heavens!" muttered Bogert.

The psychologist cast a sardonic glance at him, "I take it you asked him whether Lanning had resigned. You wanted to hear that he had resigned and so that's what Herbie told you."

"And I suppose that is why," said Lanning, tonelessly, "it would not answer a little while ago. It couldn't answer either way without hurting one of us."

There was a short pause in which the men looked thoughtfully across the room at the robot, crouching in the chair by the bookcase, head resting in one hand.

Susan Calvin stared steadfastly at the floor, "He knew of all this. That . . . that devil knows everything—including what went wrong in his assembly." Her eyes were dark and brooding.

Lanning looked up, "You're wrong there, Dr. Calvin. He doesn't know what went wrong. I asked him."

"What does that mean?" cried Calvin. "Only that you didn't want him to give you the solution. It would puncture your ego to have a machine do what you couldn't. Did you ask him?" she shot at Bogert.

"In a way." Bogert coughed and reddened. "He told me he knew very little about mathematics."

Lanning laughed, not very loudly, and the psychologist smiled caustically. She said, "I'll ask him! A solution by him won't hurt my ego." She raised her voice into a cold, imperative, "Come here!"

Herbie rose and approached with hesitant steps.

"You know, I suppose," she continued, "just exactly at what point in the assembly an extraneous factor was introduced or an essential one left out."

"Yes," said Herbie, in tones barely heard.

"Hold on," broke in Bogert angrily. "That's not necessarily true. You want to hear that, that's all."

"Don't be a fool," replied Calvin. "He certainly knows as

much math as you and Lanning together, since he can read minds. Give him his chance."

The mathematician subsided, and Calvin continued, "All right, then, Herbie, give! We're waiting." And in an aside, "Get pencils and paper, gentlemen."

But Herbie remained silent, and there was triumph in the psychologist's voice, "Why don't you answer, Herbie?"

The robot blurted out suddenly, "I cannot. You know I cannot! Dr. Bogert and Dr. Lanning don't want me to."

"They want the solution."

"But not from me."

Lanning broke in, speaking slowly and distinctly, "Don't be foolish, Herbie. We do want you to tell us."

Bogert nodded curtly.

Herbie's voice rose to wild heights, "What's the use of saying that? Don't you suppose that I can see past the superficial skin of your mind? Down below, you don't want me to. I'm a machine, given the imitation of life only by virtue of the positronic interplay in my brain—which is man's device. You can't lose face to me without being hurt. That is deep in your mind and won't be erased. I can't give the solution."

"We'll leave," said Dr. Lanning. "Tell Calvin."

"That would make no difference," cried Herbie, "since you would know anyway that it was I that was supplying the answer."

Calvin resumed, "But you understand, Herbie, that despite that, Drs. Lanning and Bogert want that solution."

"By their own efforts!" insisted Herbie.

"But they want it, and the fact that you have it and won't give it hurts them. You see that, don't you?"

"Yes! Yes!"

"And if you tell them that will hurt them, too."

"Yes! Yes!" Herbie was retreating slowly, and step by step Susan Calvin advanced. The two men watched in frozen bewilderment.

"You can't tell them," droned the psychologist slowly, "because that would hurt and you mustn't hurt. But if you don't tell them, you hurt, so you must tell them. And if you do, you will hurt and you mustn't, so you can't tell them; but if you don't, you hurt, so you must; but if you do, you hurt, so you mustn't; but if you don't, you hurt, so you must; but if you do, you—"

Herbie was up against the wall, and here he dropped to his knees. "Stop!" he shrieked. "Close your mind! It is full of pain and frustration and hate! I didn't mean it, I tell you! I tried to help! I told you what you wanted to hear. I had to!"

The psychologist paid no attention. "You must tell them, but if you do, you hurt, so you mustn't; but if you don't, you hurt, so you must; but—"

And Herbie screamed!

It was like the whistling of a piccolo many times magnified—shrill and shriller till it keened with the terror of a lost soul and filled the room with the piercingness of itself.

And when it died into nothingness, Herbie collapsed into a huddled heap of motionless metal.

Bogert's face was bloodless, "He's dead!"

"No!" Susan Calvin burst into body-racking gusts of wild laughter. "Not dead—merely insane. I confronted him with the insoluble dilemma, and he broke down. You can scrap him now—because he'll never speak again."

Lanning was on his knees beside the thing that had been Herbie. His fingers touched the cold, unresponsive metal face and he shuddered. "You did that on purpose." He rose and faced her, face contorted.

"What if I did? You can't help it now." And in a sudden access of bitterness, "He deserved it."

The director seized the paralysed, motionless Bogert by the wrist, "What's the difference. Come, Peter." He sighed, "A thinking robot of this type is worthless anyway." His eyes were old and tired, and he repeated, "Come, Peter!"

It was minutes after the two scientists left that Dr. Susan Calvin regained part of her mental equilibrium. Slowly, her eyes turned to the living-dead Herbie and the tightness returned to her face. Long she stared while the triumph faded and the helpless frustration returned—and of all her turbulent thoughts only one infinitely bitter word passed her lips.

"*Liar!*"

That finished it for then, naturally. I knew I couldn't get any more out of her after that. She just sat there behind her desk, her white face cold and—remembering.

I said, "Thank you, Dr. Calvin!" but she didn't answer. It was two days before I could get to see her again.

SOLUTION UNSATISFACTORY

Astounding Science Fiction
May

by Robert A. Heinlein

*What an issue. Writing as "Anson MacDonald"
Robert Heinlein contributed this fine novelette of a
war of the future. It is a powerful story of man's
creation out of control, and it helped to establish
science fiction's popular reputation for "accurate"
prediction.*

*In this case, one that we hope never happens
again.*

(I don't know how many times I have used "Solution Unsatisfactory" in my talks about science fiction prophecy. In a
sense, Bob predicted the Manhattan Project before anyone
else dreamed of it. Predicting an actual nuclear weapon
wasn't difficult and Bob at least avoided the too-obvious
bomb and went straight to fallout. The real tickler, though,
was predicting the nuclear stalemate in perfect detail. As far
as I am concerned this story is the all-time record for an un-
clouded crystal ball.—I.A.)

TIME WANTS A SKELETON

Astounding Science Fiction
June

by Ross Rocklynne (1913-   )

Ross Rocklynne contributed two stories to Volume 1 of this series ("Into the Darkness," June Astonishing Stories *and "Quietus," from the September issue of* Astounding), *exceptional stories that point up the relative neglect suffered during the "Golden Age" by this talented and innovative writer, who labored in the shadow of Heinlein, Sturgeon, van Vogt, and others. Two relatively recent collections that feature the best of his early work are* The Sun Destroyers *and* The Men and the Mirror *(both 1973). His fiction continues to appear, but only infrequently.*

This powerful story was one of four that constituted his "Darkness" series, published over an eleven year period: "Daughter of Darkness" in the November, 1941 Astounding; *"Abyss of Darkness" in the December, 1942,* Astounding; *and after a long hiatus, "Revolt of the Devil Star" in the February, 1951,* Imagination.

(Sometimes one does think that a certain weariness gets into one's bones with age; that the good old days weren't good at all, but that you were merely young then. In fact, I go around saying this all the time. Every once in a while, however, I am shaken.

I do read science fiction these days with not quite the eager avidity of youth. Sometimes I would almost say I was jaded. When I reread "Time Wants a Skeleton," however, I suddenly felt all the old excitement. I tried for a long time to put my feelings into a phrase that wasn't a cliche and then gave up. The cliche it had to be.

I said, "They don't write stories like that any more." —I.A.)

Asteroid No. 1007 came spinning relentlessly up.

Lieutenant Tony Crow's eyes bulged. He released the choked U-bar frantically, and pounded on the auxiliary underjet controls. Up went the nose of the ship, and stars, weirdly splashed across the heavens, showed briefly.

Then the ship fell, hurling itself against the base of the mountain. Tony was thrown from the control chair. He smacked against the wall, grinning twistedly. He pushed against it with a heavily shod foot as the ship teetered over, rolled a bit, and then was still—still, save for the hiss of escaping air.

He dived for a locker, broke out a pressure suit, perspiration pearling his forehead. He was into the suit, buckling the helmet down, before the last of the air escaped. He stood there, pained dismay in his eyes. His roving glance rested on the wall calendar.

"Happy December!" he snarled.

Then he remembered. Johnny Braker was out there, with his two fellow outlaws. By now, they'd be running this way. All the more reason why Tony should capture them now. He'd need their ship.

He acted quickly, buckling on his helmet, working over the air lock. He expelled his breath in relief as it opened. Nerves humming, he went through, came to his feet, enclosed by the bleak soundlessness of a twenty-mile planetoid more than a hundred million miles removed from Earth.

To his left the mountain rose sharply. Good. Tony had wanted to put the ship down there anyway. He took one reluctant look at the ship. His face fell mournfully. The stern section was caved in and twisted so much it looked ridiculous. Well, that was *that*.

He quickly drew his Hampton and moved soundlessly around the mountain's shoulder. He fell into a crouch as he saw the gleam of the outlaw ship, three hundred yards distant across a plain, hovering in the shadow thrown by an overhanging ledge.

Then he saw the three figures leaping toward him across the plain. His Hampton came viciously up. There was a puff of rock to the front left of the little group. They froze.

Tony left his place of concealment, snapping his headset on.

"Stay where you are!" he bawled.

The reaction was unexpected. Braker's voice came blasting back.

"The hell you say!"

A tiny crater came miraculously into being to Tony's left. He swore, jumped behind his protection, came out a second later to send another projectile winging its way. One of the figures pitched forward, to move no more, the balloon rotundity of its suit suddenly lost. The other two turned tail, only to halt and hole up behind a boulder gracing the middle of the plain. They proceeded to pepper Tony's retreat.

Tony shrank back against the mountainside, exasperated beyond measure. His glance, roving around, came to rest on a cave, a fault in the mountain that tapered out a hundred feet up.

He stared at the floor of the cave unbelievingly.

"I'll be double-damned," he muttered.

What he saw was a human skeleton.

He paled. His stomach suddenly heaved. Outrageous, haunting thoughts flicked through his consciousness. The skeleton was—horror!

And it had existed in the dim, unutterably distant past, before the asteroids, before the human race had come into existence!

The thoughts were gone, abruptly. Consciousness shuddered back. For a while, his face pasty white, his fingers trembling, he thought he was going to be sick. But he wasn't. He stood there, staring. Memories! If he knew where they came from— His very mind revolted suddenly from probing deeper into a mystery that tore at the very roots of his sanity!

"It existed before the human race," he whispered. "Then where did the skeleton come from?"

His lips curled. Illusion! Conquering his maddening revulsion, he approached the skeleton, knelt near it. It lay inside the cave. Colorless starlight did not allow him to see it as well as he might. Yet, he saw the gleam of gold on the long, tapering finger. Old yellow gold, untarnished by atmosphere; and inset with an emerald, with a flaw, a distinctive, ovular air bubble, showing through its murky transparency.

He moved backward, away from it, face set stubbornly. "Illusion," he repeated.

Chips of rock, flaked off the mountainside by the exploding bullets of a Hampton, completed the transformation. He risked stepping out, fired.

The shot struck the boulder, split it down the middle. The two halves parted. The outlaws ran, firing back to cover their hasty retreat. Tony waited until the fire lessened, then stepped out and sent a shot over their heads.

Sudden dismay showed in his eyes. The ledge overhanging the outlaw ship cracked—where the bullet had struck it.

"What the hell—" came Braker's gasp. The two outlaws stopped stock-still.

The ledge came down, its ponderousness doubled by the absence of sound. Tony stumbled panting across the plain as the scene turned into a churning hell. The ship crumbled like clay. Another section of the ledge descended to bury the ship inextricably under a small mountain.

Tony Crow swore blisteringly. But ship or no ship, he still had a job to do. When the outlaws finally turned, they were looking into the menacing barrel of his Hampton.

"Get 'em up," he said impassively.

With studied insolence, Harry Jawbone Yates, the smaller of the two, raised his hands. A contemptuous sneer merely played over Braker's unshaved face and went upward to his smoky eyes.

"Why should I put my hands up? We're all pals, now—theoretically." His natural hate for any form of the law showed in his eyes. "You sure pulled a prize play, copper. Chase us clear across space, and end up getting us in a jam it's a hundred-to-one shot we'll get out of."

Tony held them transfixed with the Hampton, knowing what Braker meant. No ship would have reason to stop off on the twenty-mile mote in the sky that was Asteroid 1007.

He sighed, made a gesture. "Hamptons over here, boys. And be careful." The weapons arced groundward. "Sorry. I was intending to use your ship to take us back. I won't make another error like that one, though. Giving up this early in the game, for instance. Come here, Jawbone."

Yates shrugged. He was blond, had pale, wide-set eyes. By nature, he was conscienceless. A broken jawbone, protruding at a sharp angle from his jawline, gave him his nickname.

He held out his wrists. "Put 'em on." His voice was an effortless affair which did not go as low as it could; rather womanish, therefore. Braker was different. Strength, nerve, and audacity showed in every line of his heavy, compact body. If there was one thing that characterized him it was his violent desire to live. These were men with elastic codes of ethics. A few of their more unscrupulous activities had caught up with them.

Tony put cuffs over Yates' wrist.

"Now you, Braker."

"Damned if I do," said Braker.

"Damned if you don't," said Tony. He waggled the Hampton, his normally genial eyes hardening slightly. "I mean it, Braker," he said slowly.

Braker sneered and tossed his head. Then, as if resistance was below his present mood, he submitted.

He watched the cuffs click silently. "There isn't a hundred-to-one chance, anyway," he growled.

Tony jerked slightly, his eyes turned skyward. He chuckled.

"Well, what's so funny?" Braker demanded.

"What you just said." Tony pointed. "The hundred-to-one shot—there she is!"

Braker turned.

"Yeah," he said. "Yeah. Damnation!"

A ship, glowing faintly in the starlight, hung above an escarpment that dropped to the valley floor. It had no visible support, and, indeed, there was no trace of the usual jets.

"Well, that's an item!" Yates muttered.

"It is at that," Tony agreed.

The ship moved. Rather, it simply disappeared, and next showed up a hundred feet away on the valley floor. A valve in the side of the cylindrical affair opened and a figure dropped out, stood looking at them.

A metallic voice said, "Are you the inhabitants or just people?"

The voice was agreeably flippant, and more agreeably feminine. Tony's senses quickened.

"We're people," he explained. "See?" He flapped his arms like wings. He grinned. "However, before you showed up, we had made up our minds to be—inhabitants."

"Oh. Stranded." The voice was slightly chilly. "Well, that's too bad. Come on inside. We'll talk the whole thing over. Say, are those handcuffs?"

"Right."

"Hm-m-m. Two outlaws—and a copper. Well, come on inside and meet the rest of us."

An hour later, Tony, agreeably relaxed in a small lounge, was smoking his third cigarette, pressure suit off. Across the room was Braker and Yates. The girl, whose name, it developed, was Laurette, leaned against the door jamb, clad in jodhpurs and white silk blouse. She was blond and had clear, deep-blue eyes. Her lips were pursed a little and she looked angry. Tony couldn't keep his eyes off her.

Another man stood beside her. He was dark in complexion

and looked as if he had a short temper. He was snapping the fingernails of two hands in a manner that showed characteristic impatience and nervousness. His name was Erle Masters.

An older man came into the room, fitting glasses over his eyes. He took a quick look around the room. Tony came to his feet.

Laurette said tonelessly, "Lieutenant, this is my father. Daddy, Lieutenant Tony Crow of the IPF. Those two are the outlaws I was telling you about."

"Outlaws, eh?" said Professor Overland. His voice seemed deep enough to count the separate vibrations. He rubbed at a stubbled jaw. "Well, that's too bad. Just when we had the De-Tosque strata 1007 fitting onto 70. And there were ample signs to show a definite dovetailing of apex 1007 into Morrell's fourth crater on Ceres, which would have put 1007 near the surface, if not on it. If we could have followed those up without an interruption—"

"Don't let this interrupt you," Masters broke in. His nails clicked. "We'll let these three sleep in the lounge. We can finish up the set of indications we're working on now, and then get rid of them."

Overland shook his graying head doubtfully. "It would be unthinkable to subject those two to cuffs for a full month."

Masters said irritably, "We'll give them a parole. Give them their temporary freedom if they agree to submit to handcuffs again when we land on Mars."

Tony laughed softly. "Sorry. You can't trust those two for five minutes, let alone a month." He paused. "Under the circumstances, professor, I guess you realize I've got full power to enforce my request that you take us back to Mars. The primary concern of the government in a case like this would be placing these two in custody. I suggest if we get under way now, you can devote more time to your project."

Overland said helplessly, "Of course. But it cuts off my chances of getting to the Christmas banquet at the university." Disappointment showed in his weak eyes. "There's a good chance they'll give me Amos, I guess, but it's already December third. Well, anyway, we'll miss the snow."

Laurette Overland said bitterly, "I wish we hadn't landed on 1007. You'd have got along without us then, all right."

Tony held her eyes gravely. "Perfectly, Miss Overland. Except that we would have been inhabitants. And, shortly, very, very dead ones."

"So?" She glared.

Erle Masters grabbed the girl's arm with a muttered word and led her out of the room.

Overland grasped Tony's arm in a friendly squeeze, eyes twinkling. "Don't mind them, son. If you or your charges need anything, you can use my cabin. But we'll make Mars in forty-eight hours, seven or eight of it skimming through the Belt."

Tony shook his head dazedly. "Forty-eight hours?"

Overland grinned. His teeth were slightly tobacco-stained. "That's it. This is one of the new ships—the H-H drive. They zip along."

"Oh! The Fitz-Gerald Contraction?"

Overland nodded absently and left. Tony stared after him. He was remembering something now—the skeleton.

Braker said indulgently, "What a laugh."

Tony turned.

"What," he asked patiently, "is a laugh?"

Braker thrust out long, heavy legs. He was playing idly with a gold ring on the third finger of his right hand.

"Oh," he said carelessly, "a theory goes the rounds the asteroids used to be a planet. They're not sure the theory is right, so they send a few bearded long faces out to trace down faults and strata and striations on one asteroid and link them up with others. The girl's old man was just about to nail down 1007 and 70 and Ceres. Good for him. But what the hell! They prove the theory and the asteroids still play ring around the rosy and what have they got for their money?"

He absently played with his ring.

Tony as absently watched him turning it round and round on his finger. Something peculiar about— He jumped. His eyes bulged.

That ring! He leaped to his feet, away from it.

Braker and Yates looked at him strangely.

Braker came to his feet, brows contracting. "Say, copper, what ails you? You gone crazy? You look like a ghost."

Tony's heart began a fast, insistent pounding. Blood drummed against his temples. So he looked like a ghost? He laughed hoarsely. Was it imagination that suddenly stripped the flesh from Braker's head and left nothing but—a skull?

"I'm not a ghost." He chattered senselessly, still staring at the ring.

He closed his eyes tight, clenched his fists.

"He's gone bats!" said Yates, incredulously.

"Bats! Absolutely bats!"

Tony opened his eyes, looked carefully at Braker, at Yates, at the tapestried walls of the lounge. Slowly, the tensity left him. Now, no matter what developed he would have to keep a hold on himself.

"I'm all right, Braker. Let me see that ring." His voice was low, controlled, ominous.

"You take a fit?" Braker snapped suspiciously.

"I'm all right." Tony deliberately took Braker's cuffed hands into his own, looked at the gold band inset with the flawed emerald. Revulsion crawled in his stomach, yet he kept his eyes on the ring.

"Where'd you get the ring, Braker?" He kept his glance down.

"Why—'29, I think it was; or '28." Braker's tone was suddenly angry, resentful. He drew away. "What is this, anyway? I got it legal, and so what?"

"What I really wanted to know," said Tony, "was if there was another ring like this one—ever. I hope not . . . I don't know if I do. Damn it!"

"And I don't know what you're talking about," snarled Braker. "I still think you're bats. Hell, flawed emeralds are like fingerprints, never two alike. You know that yourself."

Tony slowly nodded and stepped back. Then he lighted a cigarette, and let the smoke inclose him.

"You fellows stay here," he said, and backed out and bolted the door behind him. He went heavily down the corridor, down a short flight of stairs, then down another short corridor.

He chose one of two doors, jerked it open. A half dozen packages slid from the shelves of what was evidently a closet. Then the other door opened. Tony staggered backward, losing his balance under the flood of packages. He bumped into Laurette Overland. She gasped and started to fall. Tony managed to twist around in time to grab her. They both fell anyway. Tony drew her to him on impulse and kissed her.

She twisted away from him, her face scarlet. Her palm came around, smashed into his face with all her considerable strength. She jumped to her feet, then the fury in her eyes died. Tony came erect, smarting under the blow.

"Sportsmanlike," he snapped angrily.

"You've got a lot of nerve," she said unsteadily. Her eyes went past him. "You clumsy fool. Help me get these packages back on the shelves before daddy or Erle come along. They're Christmas presents, and if you broke any of the wrappings— Come on, can't you help?"

Tony slowly hoisted a large carton labeled with a "Do Not Open Before Christmas" sticker, and shoved it onto the lower rickety shelf, where it stuck out, practically ready to fall again. She put the smaller packages on top to balance it.

She turned, seeming to meet his eyes with difficulty.

Finally she got out, "I'm sorry I hit you like that, lieutenant. I guess it was natural—your kissing me I mean." She smiled faintly at Tony, who was ruefully rubbing his cheek. Then her composure abruptly returned. She straightened.

"If you're looking for the door to the control room, that's it."

"I wanted to see your father," Tony explained.

"You can't see him now. He's plotting our course. In fifteen minutes—" She let the sentence dangle. "Erle Masters can help you in a few minutes. He's edging the ship out of the way of a polyhedron."

"Polyhedron?"

"Many-sided asteroid. That's the way we designate them." She was being patronizing now.

"Well, of course. But I stick to plain triangles and spheres and cubes. A polyhedron is a sphere to me. I didn't know we were on the way. Since when? I didn't feel the acceleration."

"Since ten minutes ago. And naturally there wouldn't be any acceleration with an H-H drive. Well, if you want anything, you can talk to Erle." She edged past him, went swinging up the corridor. Tony caught up with her.

"You can help me," he said, voice edged. "Will you answer a few questions?"

She stopped, her penciled brows drawn together. She shrugged. "Fire away, lieutenant."

She leaned against the wall, tapping it patiently with one manicured fingernail.

Tony said, "All I know about the Hoderay-Hammond drive, Miss Overland, is that it reverses the Fitz-Gerald Contraction principle. It makes use of a new type of mechanical advantage. A moving object contracts in the direction of motion. Therefore a stationary object, such as a ship, can be made to move if you contract it in the direction you want it to move. How that's accomplished, though, I don't know."

"By gravitons—Where have you been all your life?"

"Learning," said Tony, "good manners."

She flushed. Her fingers stopped drumming. "If you realized you were interrupting important work, you'd know why I forget my manners. We were trying to finish this up so daddy could get back to his farewell dinner at the university.

I guess the professors guessed right when they sent his—
Well, why should I explain that to you?"

"I'm sure," said Tony, "I don't know."

"Well, go on," she said coldly.

Tony lighted a cigarette, offered her one with an apology.
She shook her head impatiently.

Tony eyed her through the haze of smoke. "Back there on
1007 I saw a skeleton with a ring on its finger."

She seemed nonplused. "Well. Was it a pretty ring?"

Tony said grimly, "The point is, Braker never got near that
skeleton after I saw it, but that same ring is now on his finger."

Startlement showed in her eyes. "That doesn't sound very
plausible, lieutenant!"

"No, of course it doesn't. Because then the same ring is in
two different places at the same time."

"And of course," she nodded, "that would be impossible.
Go on. I don't know what you're getting at, but it certainly is
interesting."

"Impossible?" said Tony. "Except that it happens to be the
truth. I'm not explaining it away, Miss Overland, if that's
your idea. Here's something else. The skeleton is a human
skeleton, but it existed before the human race existed."

She shoved herself away from her indolent position. "You
must be crazy."

Tony said nothing.

"How did you know?" she said sharply.

"I *know*. Now *you* explain the H-H drive, if you will."

"I will!" She said: "Gravitons are the ultimate particle of
matter. There are 1846 in a proton, one in an electron, which
is the reason why a proton is 1846 times as heavy as an electron.

"Now you can give me a cigarette, lieutenant. I'm curious
about this thing, and if I can't get to the bottom of it, my father certainly will."

After a while, she blew out smoke nervously.

She continued, speaking rapidly: "A Wittenberg disrupter
tears atoms apart. The free electrons are shunted off into ac-
cumulators, where we get power for lighting, cooking, heating
and so forth. The protons go into the proton analyzer, where
the gravitons are ripped out of them and stored in a special
type of spherical field. When we want to move the ship, the
gravitons are released. They spread through the ship and everything in the ship.

"The natural place for a graviton is in a proton. The gravitons rush for the protons—which are already saturated with 1846 gravitons. Gravitons are unable to remain free in three-dimensional space. They escape along the time line, into the past. The reaction contracts the atoms of the ship and everything in the ship, and shoves it forward along the opposite space-time line—forward into the future and forward in space. In the apparent space of a second, therefore, the ship can travel thousands of miles, with no acceleration effects.

"Now, there you have it, lieutenant. Do what you can with it."

Tony said, "What would happen if the gravitons were forced into the future rather than the past?"

"Lieutenant, I would have been surprised if you hadn't said that! Theoretically, it's an impossibility. Anybody who knows gravitons would say so. But if Braker is wearing a ring that a skeleton older than the human race is also wearing—*Ugh!*"

She put her hands to her temples in genuine distaste. "We'll have to see my father," she said wearily. "He'll be the one to find out whether or not you make this up as you go along."

Erle Masters looked from Tony to Laurette.

"You believe this bilge he's been handing you?"

"I'm not interested in what you think, Erle. But I am in what you do, Daddy."

Overland looked uneasy, his stubbled jaws barely moving over a wad of rough-cut.

"It does sound like . . . er . . . bilge," he muttered. "If you weren't an IPF man, I'd think you were slightly off-center. But—one thing, young man. How did you know the skeleton was older than the human race?"

"I said it existed *before* the human race."

"Is there any difference?"

"I think there is—somehow."

"Well," said Overland patiently, "how do you know it?"

Tony hesitated. "I don't really know. I was standing at the mouth of the cave, and something—or someone—told me."

"*Someone!*" Masters blasted the word out incredulously.

"I don't know!" said Tony. "All I know is what I'm telling you. It couldn't have been supernatural—could it?"

Overland said quickly, "Don't let it upset you, son. Of course it wasn't supernatural. There's a rational explanation somewhere, I guess. But it's going to be hard to come by."

He nodded his head abstractedly, and kept on nodding it like a marionette. Then he smiled peculiarly.

"I'm old now, son—you know? And I've seen a lot. I don't disbelieve anything. There's only one logical step for a scientist to take now, and that's to go back and take a look at that skeleton."

Masters' breath sounded. "You can't do that!"

"But we're going to. And remember that I employ *you*, because Laurette asked me to. Now turn this ship back to 1007. This might be more important than patching up a torn-up world at that." He chuckled.

Laurette shook her blond head. "You know," she said musingly, "this might be the very thing we *shouldn't* do, going back like this. On the other hand, if we went on our way, *that* might be the thing we shouldn't do."

Masters muttered, "You're talking nonsense, Laurette."

He ostentatiously grabbed her bare arm, and led her from the room after her father, throwing Tony a significant glance as he passed.

Tony expelled a long breath. Then, smiling twistedly, he went back to the lounge, to wait—for what? His stomach contracted again with revulsion—or was it a premonition?

Braker came sharply to his feet. "What's up, Crow?"

"Let me see that ring again," Tony said. After a minute he raised his eyes absently. "It's the same ring," he muttered.

"I wish to hell," Braker exploded, "I knew what you were talking about!"

Tony looked at him obliquely, and said under his breath, "Maybe it's better you don't."

He sat down and lighted a cigarette. Braker swore, and finally wandered to the window. Tony knew what he was thinking: of Earth; of the cities that teemed; of the vast stretches of open space between the planets. Such would be his thoughts. Braker, who loved life and freedom.

Braker, who wore a ring—

Then the constellations showing through the port abruptly changed pattern.

Braker leaped back, eyes bulging. "What the—"

Yates, sitting sullenly in the corner, came alertly to his feet. Braker mutely pointed at the stars.

"I could have sworn," he said thickly.

Tony came to his feet. He had seen the change. But his thoughts flowed evenly, coldly, a smile frozen on his lips.

"You saw right, Braker," he said coldly, then managed to grab the guide rail as the ship bucked. Braker and Yates sailed across the room, faces ludicrous with surprise. The ship turned the other way. The heavens spun, the stars blurring. Something else Tony saw besides blurred stars: a dull-gray, monstrous landscape, a horizon cut with mountains, a bright, small sun fringing tumbled clouds with reddish, ominous silver. Then stars again, rushing past the port, simmering through an atmosphere—

Blackness crushed its way through Tony Crow's consciousness, occluding it until, finally, his last coherent thought had gone. Yet he seemed to know what had happened. There was a skeleton in a cave on an asteroid—millions of years from now. And the ship had struck.

Tony moved, opened his eyes. The lights were out, but a pale shaft of radiance was streaming through the still-intact port. Sounds insinuated themselves into his consciousness. The wet drip of rain, the low murmur of a spasmodic wind, a guttural *kutakikchkut* that drifted eerily, insistently, down the wind.

Tony slowly levered himself to his feet. He was lying atop Braker. The man was breathing heavily, a shallow gash on his forehead. Involuntarily, Tony's eyes dropped to the ring. It gleamed—a wicked eye staring up at him. He wrenched his eyes away.

Yates was stirring, mumbling to himself. His eyes snapped open, stared at Tony.

"What happened?" he said thickly. He reeled to his feet. *"Phew!"*

Tony smiled through the gloom. "Take care of Braker," he said, and turned to the door, which was warped off its hinges. He loped down the corridor to the control room, slowing down on the lightless lower deck ramp. He felt his way into the control room. He stumbled around until his foot touched a body. He stooped, felt a soft, bare arm. In sudden, stifling panic, he scooped Laurette's feebly breathing body into his arms. She might have been lead, as his feet seemed made of lead. He forced himself up to the upper corridor, kicked open the door of her father's room, placed her gently on the bed. There was light here, probably that of a moon. He scanned her pale face anxiously, rubbing her arms toward the heart. Blood came to her cheeks. She gasped, rolled over. Her eyes opened.

"Lieutenant," she muttered.

"You all right?"

Tony helped her to her feet.

"Thanks, lieutenant. I'll do." She tensed. "What about my father?"

"I'll bring him up," said Tony.

Five minutes later, Overland was stretched on the bed, pain in his open eyes. Three ribs were broken. Erle Masters hovered at the foot of the bed, dabbing at one side of his face with a reddened handkerchief, a dazed, scared look in his eyes. Tony knew what he was scared of, but even Tony wasn't playing with that thought now.

He found a large roll of adhesive in the ship's medicine closet. He taped Overland's chest. The breaks were simple fractures. In time, they would do a fair job of knitting. But Overland would have to stay on his back.

Masters met Tony's eyes reluctantly.

"We'll have to get pressure suits and take a look outside."

Tony shrugged. "We won't need pressure suits. We're already breathing outside air, and living under this planet's atmospheric pressure. The bulkheads must be stowed in some place."

Overland's deep voice sounded, slowly. "I think we've got an idea where we are, Erle. You can feel the drag of this planet—a full-size planet, too. Maybe one and a half gravities. I can feel it pulling on my ribs." A bleak expression settled on his stubbled face. He looked at Tony humorlessly. "Maybe I'm that skeleton, son."

Tony caught his breath. "Nonsense. Johnny Braker's wearing the ring. If anybody's that skeleton, he is. *Not* that I wish him any bad luck, of course." He nodded once, significantly, then turned toward the door with a gesture at Masters. Masters, plainly resenting the soundless command, hesitated, until Laurette made an impatient motion at him.

They prowled through the gloomy corridor toward the small engine room, pushed the door open. The overpowering odor of ozone and burning rubber flung itself at them.

Masters uttered an expressive curse as Tony played a beam over what was left of the reversed Fitz-Gerald Contraction machinery. His nails clicked startlingly loud in the heavy silence.

"Well, that's that," he muttered.

"What d'you mean—that's that?" Tony's eyes bored at him through the darkness.

"I mean that we're stuck here, millions of years ago." He laughed harshly, unsteadily.

Tony said without emotion, "Cut it out. Hasn't this ship got auxiliary rocket blasts?"

"Naturally. But this is a one and a half gravity planet. Anyway, the auxiliary jets won't be in such good condition after a fifty-foot drop."

"Then we'll fix 'em," said Tony sharply. He added, "What makes you so sure it's millions of years ago, Masters?"

Masters leaned back against the door jamb, face as cold and hard as stone.

"Don't make me bow to you any more than I have to, lieutenant," he said ominously. "I didn't believe your story before, but I do now. You predicted this crack-up—it had to happen. So I'm ready to concede it's millions of years ago; mainly because there wasn't any one and a half gravity planet within hundreds of millions of miles of the asteroid belt. But there *used* to be one."

Tony said, lips barely moving, "Yes?"

"There used to be one—*before the asteroids.*"

Tony smiled twistedly. "I'm glad you realize that."

He turned and went for the air lock, but, since the entire system of electric transmission had gone wrong somewhere, he abandoned it and followed a draft of wet air. He jerked open the door of a small storage bin, and crawled through. There was a hole here, that had thrust boxes of canned goods haphazardly to one side. Beyond was the open night.

Tony crawled out, stood in the lee of the ship, occasional stinging drops of rain lashing at their faces. Wind soughed across a rocky plain. A low roar heralded a nearby, swollen stream. A low *kutakikchkut* monotonously beat against the night, night-brooding bird, Tony guessed, nested in the heavy growth flanking a cliff that cut a triangular section from a heavily clouded sky. Light from a probable moon broke dimly through clouds on the leftward horizon.

Masters' teeth chattered in the cold.

Tony edged his way around the ship, looking the damage over. He was gratified to discover that although the auxiliary rocket jets were twisted and broken, the only hole was in the storage bin bulkheads. That could be repaired, and so, in time, could the jets.

They started to enter the ship when Masters grasped his arm. He pointed up into the sky, where a rift in the clouds showed.

Tony nodded slowly. Offsetting murkily twinkling stars, there was another celestial body, visible as a tiny crescent.

"A planet?" muttered Tony.

"Must be." Masters' voice was low.

They stared at it for a moment, caught up in the ominous, baleful glow. Then Tony shook himself out of it, went for the storage bin.

Walking down the corridor with Masters, Tony came upon Braker and Yates.

Braker grinned at him, but his eyes were ominous.

"What's this I hear about a skeleton?"

Tony bit his lip. "Where'd you hear it?"

"From the girl and her old man. We stopped outside their room a bit. Well, it didn't make sense, the things they were saying. Something about an emerald ring and a skeleton and a cave." He took one step forward, an ugly light in his smoky eyes. "Come clean, Crow. How does this ring I've got on my finger tie up with a skeleton?"

Tony said coldly, "You're out of your head. Get back to the lounge."

Braker sneered. "Why? You can't make us stay there with the door broken down."

Masters made an impatient sound. "Oh, let them go, lieutenant. We can't bother ourselves about something as unimportant as this. Anyway, we're going to need these men for fixing up the ship."

Tony said to Yates, "You know anything about electricity? Seems to me you had an E.E. once."

Yates' thin face lighted, before he remembered his sullen pose. "O. K., you're right," he muttered. He looked at Braker interrogatively.

Braker said: "Sorry. We're not obligated to work for you. As prisoners, you're responsible for us and our welfare. We'll help you or whoever's bossing the job *if* we're not prisoners."

Tony nodded. "Fair enough. But tonight, you stay prisoners. Tomorrow, maybe not," and he herded them back into the lounge. He cuffed them to the guide rail, and so left them, frowning a little. Braker had been too acquiescent.

The reason for that struck Tony hard. Walking back along the corridor, he saw something gleaming on the floor. He froze. Revulsion gripping him, he slowly picked up the ring.

Masters turned, said sharply, "What's up?"

Tony smiled lopsidedly, threw the ring into the air twice, speculatively, catching it in his palm. He extended it to Masters.

"Want a ring?"

Masters' face went white as death. He jumped back.

"Damn you!" he said violently. "Take that thing away!"

"Braker slipped it off his finger," said Tony, his voice edging into the aching silence. Then he turned on his heel, and walked back to the lounge. He caught Braker's attention.

He held the ring out.

"You must have dropped it," he said.

Braker's lips opened in a mirthful, raucous laugh.

"You can have it, copper," he gasped. "*I* don't want to be any damned skeleton!"

Tony slipped the ring into his pocket and walked back down the corridor with a reckless swing to his body.

He knocked on the door to Overland's room, opened it when Laurette's voice sounded.

Masters and Laurette looked at him strangely.

Overland looked up from the bed.

"Lieutenant," he said, an almost ashamed look on his face, "sometimes I wonder about the human mind. Masters seems to think that now *you've* got the ring, *you're* going to be the skeleton."

Masters' nails clicked. "It's true, isn't it? The outlaws know about the ring. We know about it. But Crow *has* the ring, and it's certain none of us is going to take it."

Overland made an exasperated clicking sound.

"It's infantile," he snapped. "Masters, you're acting like a child, not like a scientist. There's only one certainty, that one of us is going to be the skeleton. But there's no certainty which one. And there's even a possibility that all of us will die." His face clouded angrily. "And the most infantile viewpoint possible seems to be shared by all of you. You've grown superstitious about the ring. Now it's—a ring of death! Death to him who wears the ring! *Pah!*"

He stretched forth an imperative hand.

"Give it to me, lieutenant! I'll tell you right now that no subterfuge in the universe will change the fact of my being a skeleton if I *am* the skeleton; and vice versa."

Tony shook his head. "I'll be keeping it—for a while. And you might as well know that no scientific argument will convince anybody the ring is not a ring of death. For, you see, it is."

Overland sank back, lips pursed. "What are you going to do with it?" he charged. When Tony didn't answer, he said pettishly, "Oh, what's the use! On the face of it, the whole situation's impossible." Then his face lighted. "What did you find out?"

Tony briefly sketched his conclusions. It would be two or

three weeks before they could repair the rocket jets, get the electric transmission system working properly.

Overland nodded absently. "Strange, isn't it!" he mused. "All that work DeTosque, Bodley, Morrell, Haley, the Farr brothers and myself have done goes for nothing. Our being here proves the theory they were working on."

Laurette smiled lopsidedly at Tony.

"Lieutenant," she said, "maybe the skeleton was a woman."

"A woman!" Masters' head snapped around, horror on his face. "Not you, Laurette!"

"Why not? Women have skeletons, too—or didn't you know?" She kept her eyes on Tony. "Well, lieutenant? I put a question up to you."

Tony kept his face impassive. "The skeleton," he said, without a tremor, "was that of a man."

"Then," said Laurette Overland, stretching out her palm, cup-shaped, "give me the ring."

Tony froze, staring. That his lie should have this repercussion was unbelievable. Out of the corner of his eye he saw Overland's slowly blanching face. On Masters, Laurette's statement had the most effect.

"Damn you, Crow!" he said thickly. "This is just a scheme of yours to get rid of the ring!" He lunged forward.

The action was unexpected. Tony fell backward under the impact of the man's fist. He sprawled on his back. Masters threw himself at him.

"Erle, you utter fool!" That was Laurette's wail.

Disgust settled on Tony's face. He heaved, by sheer muscular effort, and threw Masters over on his back. His fist came down with a brief but pungent *crack*. Masters slumped, abruptly lifeless.

Tony drew himself to his feet, panting. Laurette was on her knees beside Masters, but her dismayed eyes were turned upward to Tony.

"I'm sorry, lieutenant!" she blurted.

"What have you got to be sorry about?" he snapped. "Except for being in love with a fool like that one."

He was sorry for it the second he said it. He didn't try to read Laurette's expression, but turned sullen eyes to Overland.

"It's night," he said abruptly, "and it's raining. Tomorrow, when the sun comes up, it'll probably be different. We can figure out the situation then, and start our plans for—" He let the sentence dangle. Plans for what? He concluded, "I suggest we all get some sleep," and left.

He arranged some blankets on the floor of the control room, and instantly went to sleep, though there were times when he stirred violently. The skeleton was in his dreams—

There were five of them at the breakfast table. Laurette serving; Masters beside her, keeping his eyes sullenly on the food; Braker, eating as heartily as his cuffed hands would allow; Yates, picking at his food with disinterest.

Tony finished his second cup of coffee, and scraped his chair back.

"I'll be taking a look around," he told Laurette in explanation. He turned to the door.

Braker leaned back in his chair until it was balanced on two legs, and grinned widely.

"Where you going, Mr. Skeleton?"

Tony froze.

"After a while, Braker," he said, eyes frigid, "the ring will be taken care of."

Yates' fork came down. "If you mean you're going to try to get rid of it, you know you can't do it. It'll come back." His eyes were challenging.

Masters looked up, a strange, milling series of thoughts in his sullen eyes. Then he returned to his food.

Tony, wondering what that expression had meant, shrugged and left the room; and shortly, the ship, by way of the cavity in the storage bin.

He wandered away from the ship, walking slowly, abstractedly, allowing impressions to slip into his mind without conscious resistance. There was a haunting familiarity in this tumbled plain, though life had no place in the remembrance. There was some animal life, creatures stirring in the dank humus, in long, thick grass, in gnarled tree tops. This was mountain country and off there was a tumbling mountain stream.

He impelled himself toward it, the tiny, yet phenomenally bright sun throwing a shadow that was only a few inches long. It was high "noon."

He stood on the brink of the rocky gorge, spray prismatically alive with color, dashing up into his face. His eyes followed the stream up to the mountain fault where water poured downward to crush at the rocks with the steady, pummeling blow of a giant. He stood there, lost in abstraction, other sounds drowned out.

All except the grate of a shoe behind him. He tried to whirl; too late! Hands pushed against his back—in the next second, he had tumbled off the brink of the chasm, clutching wildly, vainly, at thick spray. Then, an awful moment of freezing cold, and the waters had enclosed him. He was borne away, choking for air, frantically flailing with his arms.

He was swept to the surface, caught a chaotic glimpse of sun and clouded sky and rock, and then went under again, with a half lungful of air. He tensed, striving to sweep away engulfing panic. A measure of reason came back. Hands and feet began to work in purposeful unison. The surface broke around him. He stayed on top. But that was only because the stream was flowing darkly, swiftly, evenly. He was powerless to force himself against this current.

He twisted, savagely looking for some sign of release. A scaly, oily tree limb came at him with a rush. One wild grab, and the limb was bending downstream, straining against the pressure his body was exerting. He dashed hair from his eyes with one trembling hand, winced as he saw the needle-bed of rapids a hundred feet downstream. If that limb hadn't been there— His mind shuddered away from the thought.

Weakly, he drew himself hand over hand upward, until the tree trunk was solidly below him. He dropped to the ground, and lay there, panting. Then he remembered the hands on his back. With a vicious motion, he jerked out his key ring. That was the answer—the key to the cuffs was gone, taken during the night, of course! Erle Masters, then, had pulled this prize play, or perhaps one of the outlaws, after Masters released him.

After a while, he came to his feet, took stock of his surroundings. Off to his left, a cliff side, and scarcely a half-mile distant, the pathetically awry hulk of the ship, on the top of the slope that stretched away.

The cliff side came into his vision again. A fault in the escarpment touched a hidden spot in his memory. He involuntarily started toward it. But he slowed up before he got to the fault—which was really a cave that tapered out to nothingness as its sides rose.

The cave!

And this sloping plain, these mountains, composed the surface of Asteroid 1007, millions of years from now.

Tony dropped emotionlessly to his knees at the mouth of the cave. Not so long ago, he had done the same thing. Then there had been a complete, undisjointed skeleton lying there.

Somehow, then, he had known the skeleton existed before the human race—as if it were someone—the skeleton?—that had spoken to him across the unutterable years. The skeleton? That could not be! Yet, whence had come the memory?

He took the ring from his pocket and put it on his finger. It gleamed.

He knelt there for minutes, like a man who worships at his own grave, and he was not dead. Not dead! He took the ring from his finger, then, a cold, bleak smile growing on his face.

He came to his feet, a rising wind whipping at his hair. He took a half dozen running steps toward the river, brought his arm over his shoulder in a throwing gesture.

Somehow the ring slipped from his fingers and fell.

He stooped, picked it up. This time, he made it leave his hand. It spun away, twinkling in the faint sunlight. But the gravity had hold of it, and it fell on the brink of the river, plainly visible.

A dry, all-gone feeling rose in Tony's throat. Grimly, he went forward, picked it up again. Keeping his eyes on it, he advanced to the brink of the river gorge. He held the ring over the darkly swirling waters, slowly released it.

It struck the river like a plummet. The waters enclosed it and it was gone. He looked at the spot where it had disappeared, half expecting it to spring back up into his hand. But it was gone. Gone for good!

He started dazedly back to the ship, moving in an unreal dream. Paradoxical that he had been able to get rid of it. It had dropped from his hand once, fallen short of the river once. The third time it had given up trying!

When he came up to the ship, Masters was standing at the stern, looking at the broken rocket jets. He turned, and saw Tony, water still dripping from his uniform. He fell back a step, face turned pallid.

Tony's lips curled. "Who did it?"

"D-did what?"

"You know what I mean," Tony bit out. He took three quick steps forward.

Masters saw that, and went reckless. Tony side-stepped him, brought his left arm around in a short arc. Masters went down cursing. Tony knelt, holding Masters down by the throat. He felt through his pockets, unearthed the key to the cuffs. Then he hauled Masters to his feet and shook him. Masters' teeth clicked.

"Murderer!" Tony snapped, white with rage.

Masters broke loose. "I'd do it again," he said wildly, and

swung. He missed. Tony lashed out with the full power of his open palm, caught Masters on the side of the head. Masters went reeling back, slammed against the side of the ship. Tony glared at him, and then turned on his heel.

He met Laurette Overland coming down the stairs to the upper corridor.

"Lieutenant!" Her eyes danced with excitement. "I've been looking for you. Where in the world have you been?"

"Ask Masters." He urged himself down the corridor, jaw set. She fell into step beside him, running to keep up with his long strides.

"You're all wet!" she exclaimed. "Can't you tell me what happened? Did you go swimming?"

"Involuntarily." He kept on walking.

She grabbed his arm, and slowed him to a stop. An ominous glint replaced her excitement.

"What," she said, "did you mean when you said I should ask Erle about it? Did he push you in? If he did, I'll—" She was unable to speak.

Tony laughed humorlessly. "He admitted it. He stole my key to the handcuffs with the idea that it would be easier to free Braker and Yates that way after I was . . . uh . . . properly prepared to be a skeleton."

Her head moved back and forth. "That's horrible," she said lowly. "Horrible."

He held her eyes. "Perhaps I shouldn't have told you about it," he said, voice faintly acid. "He's your fiancé, isn't he?"

She nodded, imperceptibly, studying him through the half gloom. "Yes. But maybe I'll change my mind, lieutenant. Maybe I will. But in the meantime, come along with me. Daddy's discovered something wonderful."

Professor Overland's head was propped up. He had a pencil and paper on his pyramided legs.

"Oh. Lieutenant! Come in." His face lighted. "Look here! Gravitons *can* thrust their way through to the future, giving the ship a thrust into the past. But only if it happened to enter the spherical type of etheric vacuum. This vacuum would be minus everything—electrons, photons, cosmic rays and so forth, except under unusual circumstances. At some one time, in either the past or future, there might be a stream of photons bridging the vacuum. Now, when gravitons are ejected into the past, they grab hold of light photons, and become ordinary negative electrons. Now say the photons are farther away in the past than they are in the future. The gravitons therefore follow the line of least resistance and hook up with photons of the future. The photons in this case were perhaps hundreds of millions of years away in the vacuum. In traveling that time-distance, the gravitons kicked the ship back for a proportionate number of years, burned up our machinery, and wrecked us on this suddenly appearing before-the-asteroid world."

Laurette said brightly, "But that isn't the important part, daddy."

"I can find another of those etheric vacuums," Overland went on, preoccupiedly, pointing out a series of equations. "Same type, same structure. But we have to go to the planet Earth in order to rebuild the reversed contraction machinery. We'll find the materials we need there." He glanced up. "But we have to get off this world before it cracks up, lieutenant."

Tony started. "Before this world cracks up?"

"Certainly. Naturally. You can—" His heavy brows came down abruptly. "You didn't know about that, did you? Hmm-m." He stroked his jaw, frowning. "You recall the crescent planet you and Masters saw? Well, he took some readings on that. It's wonderful, son!" His eyes lighted. "It's an ill wind that blows nobody good. Not only do we know now that the asteroid evolved from a broken-up planet, but we also know the manner in which that planet broke up. Collision with a heavy, smaller body."

Tony paled. "You mean—" he said huskily. "Good heavens!" Sweat stood out on his forehead. "How soon will that happen?" he said ominously.

"Well, Erle has the figures. Something over eighteen or nineteen days. It'll be a crack-up that'll shake the sun. And we'll be here to witness it." He smiled wryly. "I'm more scientist than man, I guess. I never stop to think we might die in the crack-up, and furnish six skeletons instead of one."

"There'll be no skeletons," Tony said, eyes narrowed. "For one thing, we can repair the ship, though we'll have to work like mad. For another—I threw the ring into the river. It's gone."

Laurette seemed to pale. "I . . . I don't see how that could be done," she stammered. "You couldn't get rid of it, not really—could you?"

"It's gone," Tony said stubbornly. "For good. And don't forget it. There'll be no skeleton. And you might try to impress that on Masters, so he doesn't try to produce one," he added significantly.

He left the room with a nod, a few seconds later stepped

into the lounge. Braker and Yates turned around. Both were cuffed.

Tony took the key from his pocket and the cuffs fell away. In brief, pungent tones, then, he explained the situation, the main theme being that the ship had to be well away from the planet before the crack-up. Yates would go over the wiring system. Braker, Masters and Tony would work with oxyacetylene torches and hammers over the hole in the hull and the rocket jets.

Then he explained about the ring.

Yates ran a thin hand through his yellow hair.

"You don't do it that easy," he said in his soft, effortless voice. "There's a skeleton up there, and it's got Braker's ring on its finger. It's got to be accounted for, don't it? It's either me or you or Braker or the girl or her old man or Masters. There ain't any use trying to avoid it, either." His voice turned sullen. He looked at Braker, then at Tony. "Anyway, I'm keeping my back turned the right way so there won't be any dirty work."

Braker's breath sounded. "Why, you dirty rat," he stated. He took a step toward Yates. "You would think of that. And probably you'd try it on somebody else, too. Well, don't go pulling it on me, understand." He scowled. "And you better watch him, too, Crow. He's pure poison—in case you got the idea we were friends."

"Oh, cut it out," Tony said wearily. He added, "If we get the ship in working order, there's no reason why all six of us shouldn't get off—alive." He turned to the door, waved Braker and Yates after him. Yet he was sickeningly aware that *his* back was turned to men who admittedly had no conscience to speak of.

A week passed. The plain rang with sledgehammer strokes directed against the twisted tubes. Three were irreplaceable.

Tony, haggard, tired, unbelievably grimed from his last trip up the twisted, hopeless-looking main blast tube, was suddenly shocked into alertness by sounds of men's voices raised in fury outside the ship. He ran for the open air lock, and urged himself toward the ship's stern. Braker and Yates were tangling it.

"I'll kill him!" Braker raged. He had a rock the size of his fist in his hand. He was attempting, apparently, to knock Jawbone Yates' brains out. Erle Masters stood near, chewing nervously at his upper lip.

With an oath, Tony wrenched the rock from Braker's

hand, and hauled the man to his feet. Yates scrambled erect, whimpering, mouth bleeding.

Braker surged wildly toward him. "The dirty—!" he snarled. "Comes up behind me with an oxy torch!"

Yates shrilled, backing up, "That's a lie!" He pointed a trembling hand at Braker. "It was *him* that was going to use the torch on *me!*"

"Shut up!" Tony bawled. He whirled on Masters. "You've got a nerve to stand there," he snarled. "But then you *want* a skeleton! Damned if you're going to get one! Which one did it?"

Masters stammered, "I didn't see it! I . . . I was just—"

"The hell you say!" Tony whirled on the other two, transfixing them with cold eyes.

"Cut it out," he said, lips barely moving. "Either you're letting your nerves override you, or either one or both of you is blaming the other for a move he made himself. You might as well know the skeleton I saw was intact. What do you think a blow torch would do to a skeleton?" His lips curled.

Braker slowly picked up his torch with a poisonous glance at Yates. Yates as slowly picked his sledgehammer. He turned on Tony.

"You said the skeleton was intact?" Eagerness, not evident from his carefully sullen voice, was alive in his eyes.

Tony's glance passed over the man's broken, protruding jaw.

"The head," he replied, "was in shadow."

He winced. The passing of hope was a hard thing to watch, even in a man like Jawbone Yates.

He turned, releasing his breath in a long, tired sigh. What a man-sized job this was. Outwitting fate—negating what *had* happened!

Tony worked longer than he expected that day, tracing down the web of asbestos-covered rocket fuel conduits, marking breaks down on the chart. The sun sank slowly. Darkness swept over the plain, along with a rising wind. He turned on the lights, worked steadily on, haggard, nerves worn. Too much work to allow a slowing up. The invading planet rose each night a degree or more larger. Increasing tidal winds and rainstorms attested to a growing gravitational attraction.

He put an x-mark on the check—and then froze. A scream had gone blasting through the night.

Tony dropped pencil and chart, went flying up the ramp to the upper corridor. He received the full impact of Masters' second scream. Masters had left his room, was running up the corridor, clad in pajamas. There was a knife sticking out of his shoulder.

Tony, gripped with horror, impelled himself after the man, caught up with him as he plunged face downward. He dropped to one knee, staring at a heavy meat knife that had been plunged clear through the neck muscles on Masters' left shoulder, clearly a bid for a heart stroke.

Masters turned on his side. He babbled, face alive with horror. Tony rose, went with the full power of his legs toward the lounge.

A figure showed, running ahead of him. He caught up with its, whipped his arm around the man's neck.

"You!"

Yates squirmed tigerishly. He turned, broke loose, face alive with fury. Tony's open palm lashed out, caught Yates full on the face. Yates staggered and fell. He raised himself to one elbow.

"Why'd you do it?" Tony rasped, standing over him.

Yates' face was livid. "Because I'd rather live than anything else I can think of!" His booted foot lashed out. Tony leaped back. Yates rose. Tony brought his bunched fist up from his knees with all the ferocity he felt. Yates literally rose an inch off the floor, sagged, and sopped to the floor.

Tony picked him up in one arm, and flung him bodily into the lounge.

Braker rose from his sleeping position on a cushioned bench, blinking.

Tony said cuttingly, "Your pal ran a knife through Masters shoulder."

"Huh?" Braker was on his feet. "Kill him?" In the half-light his eyes glowed.

"You'd be glad if he did!"

Braker looked at Yates. Then, slowly, "Listen, copper. Don't make the mistake of putting me in the same class with a rat like Yates. I don't knife people in the back. But if Masters was dead, I'd be glad of it. It might solve a problem that's bothering the rest of us. What you going to do with him?"

"I already did it. But tell Yates he better watch out for Masters, now."

Braker grunted scornfully. "Huh. Masters'll crack up and down his yellow back."

Tony left.

Laurette and Overland were taking care of Masters in his room. The wound was clean, hardly bleeding.

Overland, somewhat pale, was hanging onto the door. "It's not serious, honey," he said, as her fingers nimbly wound bandages.

"Not serious?" She turned stricken eyes up to Tony. "Look at him. And Daddy says it's not serious!"

Tony winced. Masters lay face down on the bed, babbling hysterically to himself, his eyes preternaturally wide. His skin was a pasty white, and horror had etched flabby lines around his lips.

"Knifed me," he gasped. "Knifed me. I was sleeping, that was the trouble. But I heard him—" He heaved convulsively, and buried his face in his pillow.

Laurette finished her job, face pale.

"I'll stay here the rest of the night," Tony told her.

Overland gnawed painfully at his lower lip.

"Who did it?"

Tony told him.

"Can't we do something about it?"

"What?" Tony laughed scornfully. "Masters had the same trick pulled on him that he pulled on me. He isn't any angel himself."

Overland nodded wearily. His daughter helped him out of the room.

During the night, Masters tossed and babbled. Finally he fell into a deep sleep. Tony leaned back in a chair, moodily listening to the sough of the wind, later on watching the sun come up, staining the massed clouds with running, changing streaks of color.

Masters awoke. He rolled over. He saw Tony, and went rigid. He came to his feet, and huddled back against the wall.

"Get out," he gasped, making a violent motion with his hand.

"You're out of your head," said Tony angrily. "It was Yates."

Masters panted, "I know it was. What difference does it make? You're all in the same class. I'm going to watch myself after this. I'm going to keep my back turned the right way. I'm going to be sure that none of you—"

Tony put his hands on his hips, eyes narrowed.

"If you've got any sense, you'll try to forget this and act like a human being. Better to be dead than the kind of man you'll turn into."

"Get out. Get out!" Masters waved his hand again, shuddering.

Tony left, shaking his head slowly.

Tony stood outside the ship, smoking a cigarette. It was night. He heard a footstep behind him. He fell back a step, whirling.

"Nerves getting you, too?" Laurette Overland laughed shakily, a wool scarf blowing back in the heavy, unnatural wind.

Tony relaxed. "After two weeks of watching everybody watching everybody else, I guess so."

She shivered. He sensed it was not from the bite of the wind. "I suppose you mean Erle."

"Partly. Your father's up and around today, isn't he? He shouldn't have gotten up that night."

"He can get around all right."

"Maybe he better lock himself in his room." He smiled with little amusement. "The others are certain the ring will come back."

She was silent. Through the ominous gloom, lit now by a crescent planet that was visible as a small moon, and growing steadily larger, he saw a rueful, lopsided smile form on her face. Then it was gone.

She said, "Erle was telling me the jets are in bad condition. A trial blast blew out three more."

"That's what happened."

She went on: "He also told me there was a definite maximum weight the jets could lift in order to get us free of the gravity. We'll have to throw out everything we don't need. Books, rugs, clothing, beds." She drew a deep breath. "And in the end, maybe a human being."

Tony's smile was frozen. "Then the prophecy would come true."

"Yes. It is a prophecy, isn't it?" She seemed childishly puzzled. She added, "And it looks like it has to come true. Because— Excuse me, lieutenant," she said hurriedly, and vanished toward the air lock.

Tony stared after her, his mind crawling with unpleasant thoughts. It was unbelievable, fantastic. So you couldn't outwit fate. The ship would have to be lightened. Guesswork might easily turn into conviction. There might be one human being too many—

Professor Overland came slowly from the air lock, wincing from the cold after his two weeks of confinement. His hag-

gard eyes turned on Tony. He came forward, looking up at
the growing planet of destruction.

"Erle has calculated three days, eight hours and a few
minutes. But it's ample time, isn't it, lieutenant?"

"One jet will straighten out with some man-size labor.
Then we can start unloading extra tonnage. Lots of it."

"Yes. Yes. I know." He cleared his throat. His eyes turned
on Tony, filled with a peculiar kind of desperation. "Lieutenant," he said huskily, "there's something I have to tell you.
The ring came back."

Tony's head jerked. "It came back?" he blurted.

"In a fish."

"Fish?"

Overland ran a trembling hand across his brow. "Yesterday
a week ago, Laurette served fried fish. She used an old dress
for a net. I found the ring in what she brought to my room.
Well, I'm not superstitious about the ring. One of us *is* the
skeleton—up there. We can't avoid it. I put the ring on—
more bravado than anything else. But this morning"—his
voice sank to a whisper—"the ring was gone. Now I'm becoming superstitious, unscientifically so. Laurette is the only
one who could—or would—have taken it. The others would
have been glad it was on my finger rather than theirs. Even
Erle."

Tony stared through him. He was remembering Laurette's
peculiar smile. Abruptly, he strode toward the ship, calling
back hurriedly:

"Better go inside, sir."

In the ship, he knocked sharply on Laurette's door.

She answered nervously, "Yes."

"May I come in?"

"No. No. Do you have to?"

He thought a moment, then opened the door and stepped
inside. She was standing near her bed, her eyes haunted.

Tony extended a hand imperatively. "Give me the ring."

She said, her voice low, controlled, "Lieutenant, I'll keep
the ring. You tell that to the others. Then there won't be any
of this nervous tension and this murder plotting."

He said ominously, "You may wind up a skeleton."

"You said the skeleton was not a woman."

"I was lying."

"You mean," she said, "it *was* a woman?"

Tony said patiently, "I mean that I don't know. I couldn't
tell. Do I get the ring, or don't I?"

She drew a deep breath. "Not in the slightest can it decide who will eventually die."

Tony advanced a step. "Even your father doesn't believe that now," he grated.

She winced. "I'll keep the ring and stay in my room except when I cook. You can keep everybody out of the ship. Then there won't be anybody to harm me."

Footsteps sounded in the corridor. Masters entered the room. Tension had drawn hollow circles under eyes that refused to stay still.

"You," he said to Tony, his voice thin, wavering. He stood with his back to the wall. He wet his lips. "I was talking with your father."

"All right, all right," she said irritably. "I've got the ring, and I'm keeping it."

"No, you can't, Laurette. We're going to get rid of it, this time. The six of us are going to watch."

"You can't get rid of it!" Then, abruptly, she snatched it off her finger. "Here!"

Imperceptibly, he shrank back against the wall.

"There's no use transferring it now. You've got it, you might as well carry it." His eyes swiveled, lighted with a sudden burst of inspiration. "Better yet, let Crow carry it. He represents the law. That would make it proper."

She seemed speechless.

"Can you imagine it? Can you imagine a sniveling creature like him— I'll keep the ring. First my father gets weak in the knees, and then—" She cast a disdainful look at Masters. "I wish you'd both leave me alone, please."

Tony shrugged, left the room, Masters edging out after him.

Tony stopped him.

"How much time have we got left?"

Masters said jerkily, "We've been here fourteen days. It happens on the twenty-fifth. That's eleven days from now, a few hours either way."

"How reliable are your figures?"

Masters muttered, "Reliable enough. We'll have to throw out practically everything. Doors, furniture, clothes. And then—"

"Yes?"

"I don't know," Masters muttered, and slunk away.

It was the twenty-fourth of December.

Tidal winds increased in savagery in direct proportion to

the growing angular diameter of the invading planet. Heavy, dully colored birds fought their way overhead. On the flanks of abruptly rising cliff edges, gnarled trees lashed. Rain fell spasmodically. Clouds moved in thoroughly indiscriminate directions. Tentacular leaves whirlpooled. Spray, under the wind's impact, cleared the river gorge. The waterfall was muted.

Rushing voluminous air columns caught at the growing pile emerging from the ship's interior, whisked away clothing, magazines, once a mattress. It did not matter. Two worlds were to crash in that momentous, before-history forming of the asteroids. There was but one certainty. This plain, these mountains—and a cave—were to stay intact through the millions of years.

Inside the air lock, Masters stood beside a heavy weight scale. Light bulbs, dishes, silverware, crashed into baskets indiscriminately, the results weighed, noted, discarded. Doors were torn off their hinges, floors ripped up. Food they would keep, and water, for though they eventually reached Earth, they could not know whether it yet supported life.

The ship, devoid of furnishings, had been a standard eleven tons for an H-H drive. Furnishing, food, et cetera, brought her to over thirteen tons. Under a one and a half gravity, it was twenty tons. Masters' figures, using the firing area the ship now had, with more than half the jets beyond use, were exact enough. The maximum lift the jets would or could afford was plus or minus a hundred pounds of ten and three quarter tons.

Masters looked up from his last notation, eyes red-rimmed, lips twitching. Braker and Yates and Tony were standing in the air lock, watching him.

Fear flurried in Masters' eyes. "What are you looking at me like that for?" he snarled. Involuntarily, he fell back a step.

Yates giggled.

"You sure do take the fits. We was just waiting to see how near we was to the mark. There ain't anything else to bring out."

"Oh, there isn't?" Masters glared. "We're still eight hundred pounds on the plus side. How about the contraction machinery?"

Tony said: "It's our only hope of getting back to the present. Overland needs it to rebuild the drive."

"Pressure suits!"

"We're keeping six of them, in case the ship leaks."

"Doors!" said Masters wildly. "Rugs!"

"All," said Tony, "gone."

Masters' nails clicked. "Eight hundred pounds more," he said hoarsely. He looked at his watch, said, "Eleven hours plus or minus," took off his watch and threw it out. He made a notation on his pad, grinning crookedly. "Another ounce gone."

"I'll get Overland," Tony decided.

"Wait!" Masters thrust up a pointing finger. "Don't leave me alone with those two wolves. They're waiting to pounce on us. Four times one hundred and fifty is six hundred."

"You're bats," said Braker coldly.

"Besides," said Yates, "where would we get the other two hundred pounds?"

Masters panted at Tony, "You hear that? He wants to know where they'd get the other two hundred pounds!"

"I was joking," said Yates.

"Joking! *Joking!* When he tried to knife me once!"

"Because," concluded Yates, "the cards call for only one skeleton. *I'll* get him."

He came back shortly with Laurette and her father.

Overland fitted his glasses over his weak eyes while he listened, glancing from face to face.

"It would be suicidal to get rid of the machinery, what's left of it. I have another suggestion. We'll take out all the direct-vision ports. They might add up to eight hundred pounds."

"Not a bad idea," said Braker slowly. "We can wear pressure suits. The ship might leak anyway."

Masters waved a hand. "Then get at it! Laurette, come here. You've got the ring. *You* don't want to be the skeleton, do you? Put your back to this wall with me."

"Oh, Erle," she said in disgust, and followed her father out.

Tony brought three hack saws from the pile of discarded tools. Working individual rooms, the three of them went through the ship, sawing the ports off at the hinges, pulling out the port packing material. The ship was now a truly denuded spectacle, the floors a mere grating of steel.

The ports and packing were placed on the scale.

"Five hundred—five twenty-five—five sixty-one. That's all!" Masters sounded as if he were going to pieces.

Tony shoved him aside. "Five sixty-one it is. There may be

a margin of error, though," he added casually. "Braker, Yates—out with this scale."

The two stooped, heaved. The scale, its computed weight already noted, went out—

Tony said, "Come on, Masters."

Masters trotted behind, doglike, as if he had lost the power of thought. Tony got the six pressure suits out of the corner of the control room, and gestured toward them. Everybody got into the suits.

Tony buckled his helmet down. "Now give her the gun."

Masters stood at the auxiliary rocket control board, face pale, eyes unnaturally wide.

He made numerous minor adjustments. He slowly depressed a plunger. A heavy, vibrating roar split the night. The ship leaped. There was a sensation of teetering motion. In the vision plates, the plain moved one step nearer, as if a new slide had been inserted in a projector. The roar swept against them voluminously. The picture remained the same.

Masters wrenched up the plunger, whirled.

"You see?" he panted. "I could have told you!"

Professor Overland silenced him with a wave of the hand, pain showing in his eyes.

"I make this admission almost at the expense of my sanity," he said slowly. "Events have shaped themselves—incredibly. Backward. In the future, far away, in a time none of us may ever see again, lies a skeleton with a ring on its finger.

"Now which causes which—the result or its cause?"

He took off his glasses, blinked, fitted them back on.

"You see," he said carefully, "some of the things that have happened to us are a little bit incredible. There is Lieutenant Crow's—*memory* of these events. He saw the skeleton and it brought back memories. From where? From the vast storehouse of the past? That does not seem possible. Thus far it is the major mystery, how he *knew* that the skeleton existed before the human race.

"Other things are perhaps more incredible. Three shipwrecks! Incredible coincidence! Then there is the incident of the ring. It is—a ring of death. I say it who thought I would never say it. Lieutenant Crow even had some difficulty throwing it into the river. A fish swallowed it and it came back to me. Then my daughter stole it from me. And she refused to give it up, or let us know what her plans for disposition of it are.

"I do not know whether we are shaping a future that is, or whether a future that is is shaping us.

"And finally we come to the most momentous occurrence of this whole madness. An utterly ridiculous thing like two hundred or two hundred and fifty pounds.

"So we must provide a skeleton. The future that *is* says so."

Silence held. The roar of the river, and the growing violence of the tidal wind rushed in at them. Braker's breath broke loose.

"He's right. Somebody has to get off—and stay off! And it isn't going to be the old man, him being the only one knows how to get us back."

"That's right," said Yates. "It ain't going to be the old man."

Masters shrank back. "Well, don't look at me!" he snarled.

"I wasn't looking at you," Yates said mildly.

Tony's stomach turned rigid. This was what you had to go through to choose a skeleton to die on an asteroid, its skin and flesh to wear and evaporate away and finally wind up millions of years later as a skeleton in a cave with a ring on its finger. These were some of the things you had to go through before you became that skeleton yourself—

"Laurette," he said, "isn't in this lottery."

Braker turned on him. "The hell she isn't!"

Laurette said, voice edged, "I'm in. I might be the straw that broke the camel's back."

Overland said painfully, "Minus a hundred and five might take us over the escarpment. Gentlemen, I'll arrange this lottery, being the only nonparticipant."

Masters snarled, eyes glittering, "You're prejudiced in favor of your daughter!"

Overland looked at him mildly, curiously, as he would some insect. He made a clicking sound with his lips.

Masters pursued his accusation.

"We'll cut for high man, low card to take the rap!"

"Yah!" jeered Yates. "With your deck, I suppose."

"Anybody's deck!" said Masters.

"All the cards were thrown out. Why weren't yours?"

"Because I knew it would come to this."

"Gentlemen," said Overland wearily. "It won't be a deck. Laurette, the ring."

She started, paled. She said, "I haven't got it."

"Then," said her father, without surprise, "we'll wait around until it shows up."

Braker whirled on him. "You're crazy! We'll draw lots anyway. Better still, we'll find where she put the ring."

"I buried it," said the girl, and her eyes fluttered faintly. "You better leave it buried. You're just proving—"

"Buried it!" blasted Masters. "When she could have used a hammer on it. When she could have melted it in an oxyacetylene torch. When she could—"

"When she could have thrown it in the river and have a fish bring it back! Shut up, Masters." Braker's jawline turned ominous. "Where's the ring? The skeleton's got to have a ring and it's going to have one."

"I'm not going to tell you." She made a violent motion with her hand. "This whole thing is driving me crazy. We don't need the ring for the lottery. Leave it there, can't you?" Her eyes were suddenly pleading. "If you dig it up again, you'll just complete a chain of coincidence that couldn't possibly—"

Overland said, "We won't use the ring in the lottery. It'll turn up later and the skeleton will wear it. We don't have to worry about it, Braker."

Yates said, "Now we're *worrying* about it!"

"Well, it has to be there, doesn't it?" Braker charged.

Tony interrupted by striking a match. He applied flame to a cigarette, sucked in the nerve-soothing smoke.

His eyes were hard, watchful. "Ten hours to get out of range of the collision," his lips said.

"Then we'll hold the lottery now," said Overland. He turned and left the room. Tony heard his heavy steps dragging up the ramp.

The five stood statuesque until he came back. He had a book in one hand. Five straws stuck out from between the pages, their ends making an even line parallel with the book.

Overland's extended hand trembled slightly.

"Draw," he said. "My daughter may draw last, so you may be sure I am not tricking anybody. Lieutenant? Braker? Anybody. And the short straw loses."

Tony pulled a straw.

"Put it down on the floor at your feet," said Overland, "since someone may have previously concealed a straw."

Tony put it down, face stony.

The straw was as long as the book was wide.

Braker said, in an ugly tone, "Well, I'll be damned!"

Braker drew a shorter one. He put it down.

Yates drew a still shorter one. His smile of bravado vanished. Sweat stood suddenly on his pale forehead.

"Go ahead, Masters!" he grated. "The law of averages says you'll draw a long one."

"I don't believe in the law of averages," said Masters sulkily. "Not on this planet, anyway— I'll relinquish the chance to Laurette."

"That," said Laurette, "is sweet of you."

She took a straw without hesitation.

Masters said nervously, "It's short, isn't it?"

"Shorter than mine." Yates breath came out in a long sigh. "Go ahead, Masters. Only one straw left, so you don't have to make a decision."

Masters jerked it out.

He put it on the floor. It was long.

A cry burst from Overland's lips. "Laurette!"

She faced their silent stares with curled lips.

"That's that. I hope my hundred and five helps."

Tony dropped his cigarette. "It won't," he snapped. "We were fools for including you."

Suddenly he was watching Braker out of the corner of his eye, his nerves tense.

Overland said in a whisper, "How could I suggest leaving my daughter out? I said a hundred pounds *might* be the margin. If I'd have suggested leaving her out, you'd have accused me of favoritism."

Braker said casually, "There's only going to be one lottery held here."

Yates looked dumfounded. "Why, you blasted fool," he said. "What if we're stuck back here before the human race and there ain't any women?"

"That's what I mean. I thought we'd include the girl. If she was drawn, then we could ask some gentleman to volunteer in her place."

He made a sudden motion. Tony made a faster one. His Hampton came out and up.

"Drop it!" he rasped. "I said—*drop it!*"

Braker's eyes bulged. He looked at the Hampton as if he were unable to comprehend it. He cursed rackingly and dropped the automatic as if it were infested with a radioactive element. It clattered on the metal grating of the denuded floor.

A smile froze on Tony's lips. "Now you can explain where you got that automatic."

Braker, eyes fuming like those of a trapped animal, involuntarily shot a glance at Masters.

Tony turned his head slightly toward Masters. "It would be you," he said bitterly.

He whirled—too late. Yates hurtled toward him, struck him in a flying tackle. Tony fell audibly. He tangled furiously with Yates. No good! Braker, face contorted with glee, leaped on top of him, struggled mightily, and then with the main force of his two gloved hands wrenched the Hampton away, rolled from Tony's reach, then snapped himself to his feet, panting.

"Thanks, Yates!" he exclaimed. "Now get up, Crow. Get up. What a man. What a big hulking man. Weighs two hundred if he weighs an ounce." His lips curled vengefully. "Now get up and get out!"

Overland made a step forward, falteringly.

Braker waved the weapon all-inclusively.

"Back, you," he snarled. "This is my party, and it's a bad-taste party, too. Yates, corner the girl. Masters, stand still— you're my friend if you want to be. All right, lieutenant, get going—and dig! For the ring!" His face screwed up sadistically. "Can't disappoint that skeleton, can we?"

Tony came to his feet slowly, heart pounding with what seemed like long-spaced blows against his ribs. Painfully, his eyes ran from face to face, finally centered on Laurette's.

She surged forward against Yates' retaining grip.

"Don't let them do it, lieutenant," she cried. "It's a dirty trick. You're the one person out of the four who doesn't deserve it. I'll—" She slumped back, her voice fading, her eyes burning. She laughed jerkily. "I was just remembering what you did when all the Christmas packages came tumbling down on us. You kissed me, and I slapped you, but I really wanted you to kiss me again."

Yates laughed nastily. "Well, would you listen to that. Masters, you going to stand there and watch them two making love?"

Masters shuddered, his face graying. He whispered, "It's all right. I wish—"

"Cut out the talk!" Braker broke in irritably.

Tony said, as if the other conversation had not intervened, "I wanted to kiss you again, too." He held her wide, unbelieving eyes for a long moment, then dropped his and bit at his shuddering lower lip. It seemed impossible to stand here and realize that this was defeat and that there was no defense against it! He shivered with an unnatural jerk of the shoulders.

"All right," Braker said caustically, "get going."

Tony stood where he was. Braker and everybody else except Laurette Overland faded. Her face came out of the mist, wild, tense, lovely and lovable. Tears were coming from her eyes, and her racking sobs were muted. For a long moment, he hungrily drank in that last glimpse of her.

"Lieutenant!"

He said dully, his eyes adding what his lips did not, "Good-bye, Laurette."

He turned, went toward the air lock with dragging feet, like a man who leaves the death house only to walk toward a worse fate. He stopped at the air lock. Braker's gun prodded him.

He stood faintly in the air lock until Braker said, "Out, copper! Get moving."

And then he stepped through, the night and the wild wind enclosing him, the baleful light of the invading planet washing at him.

Faintly he heard Braker's jeering voice, "So long, copper." Then, with grim, ponderous finality, came the wheeze of the closing air lock.

He wandered into the night for a hundred feet, somehow toward the vast pile that had been extracted from the ship's interior. He seemed lost in unreality. This was the pain that went beyond all pains, and therefore numbed.

He turned. A blast of livid flame burst from the ship's main tube. Smaller parallels of fire suddenly ringed it. The ship moved. It slid along the plain on its runners, hugged the ground for two hundred feet, plummeting down the slope. Tony found himself tense, praying staccato curses. Another hundred feet. The escarpment loomed.

He thrust his arms forcefully upward.

"Lift!" he screamed. *"Lift!"*

The ship's nose turned up, as her short wings caught the force of the wind. Then it roared up from the plain, cleared the escarpment by a scant dozen feet. The echoes of the blast muted the very howl of the wind. The echoes died. Then there was nothing but a bright jewel of light receding. Then there was—nothing.

Tony looked after it, conscious that the skin was stretched dry and tight across his cheekbones. His upflung arms dropped. A little laugh escaped his lips. He turned on his heels. The wind was so furious he could lean against it. It was night, and though the small moon this before-the-asteroids world boasted was invisible, the heavens overflowed with the baleful, pale-white glow of the invading planet.

It was still crescent. He could clearly see the ponderous immensity the lighted horns embraced. The leftward sky was occluded a full two-fifths by the falling monster, and down in the seas the shores would be overborne by tidal waves.

He stood motionless. He was at a loss in which direction to turn. An infinity of directions, and there could be no purpose in any. What type of mind could choose a direction?

That thought was lost. He moved toward the last link he had with humanity—with Laurette. He stood near the trembling pile. There was a cardboard carton, addressed to Professor Henry Overland, a short chain of canceled stamps staring up at him, pointing to the nonexistence of everything that would be. America and Christmas and the post office.

He grinned lopsidedly. The grin was lost. It was even hard to know what to do with one's face. He was the last man on a lost world. And even though he was doomed to death in this unimaginably furious crack-up, he should have some goal, something to live for up to the very moment of death!

He uttered a soft, trapped cry, dashed his gloves to his helmeted face. Then a thought simmered. Of course! The ring! He had to find that ring, and he would. The ring went with the skeleton. And the skeleton went with the ring. Lieutenant Tony Crow—and there could be no doubt of this whatsoever—was to be that skeleton which had grinned up at him so many years ago—no, not ago, acome.

A useless task, of course. The hours went past, and he wandered across the tumbled, howling plain, traversing each square foot, hunting for a telltale, freshly turned mound of earth. He went to the very brink of the river gorge, was immersed in leaping spumes of water. Of the ring that he must have there was no trace.

Where would she have buried it? How would her mind work? Surely, she could not have heartlessly buried the ring, hiding it forever, when Tony Crow needed it for the skeleton he was to turn into!

He knew the hours were flying. Yet, better to go mad with this tangible, positive purpose, than with the intangible, negative one of waiting spinelessly for death from the lowering monster who now owned the heavens.

How convenient this was. One time-traveled. One witness to the origin of the asteroids. Similarly, one might time-travel and understand at last the unimaginable, utterly baffling process by which the solar system came into being. Nothing as simple as a collision. Or a binary sweeping past a single. Or a whirling nebula. It would be connected with the expanding universe, in some outrageously simple manner. But everything was simple once one knew the answer. For instance—

The ring! Yes, it was as simple as that. Even Laurette Overland would be forced to yield to the result that was influencing its own cause!

Tenseness gave way to relief. One could not baffle the future. Naturally, she'd buried the ring in the cave. Unless she wanted to be perverse. But she would *not* be perverse in a matter like this. Future and present demanded co-operation, if there was to be a logical future!

Forcing himself against a wind that blew indiscriminately, he reached the funnel in the mountainside. The skeleton was not here, naturally. But it would be—with the necessary ring on its finger. Unbelievable how the future shapes its own past! It was as if his own skeleton, which existed millions of years *acome,* on which his own healthy flesh rode *now,* were plainly telling him what he should do.

He dug with a cold methodicity, starting from the rear of the cave. No sign of the ring, and no sign of recently turned earth. He discarded his gloves, placed them carefully to one side, and dug with a sharp rock.

No sign of the ring! The hours passed. What was he to do? His thoughts sharpened with desperation. An hour, little more, remained. Then would come the smash—and death.

He was in the cave! He, the skeleton!

He lay on his back, head propped up in locked hands. Trees and limbs and leaves hurtled by in a tempestuous wind. Soon, out in the sky, would float the remnants of this very substantial world. The millions of years would pass. A Lieutenant Tony Crow, on the trail of three criminals, would land here, look into this cave, and see his own skeleton—only he would not know it.

He lay there, tense, waiting. The wind would dig up the ring, whip it through the air. He would hear a tinkling sound. That would be the ring, striking against the wall of the cave. He would pick it up and put it on his finger. In a few moments after that would come the sound—the heavy vibration—the ear-splitting concussion—the cosmic clash—the ... the ... *bang* of a world breaking up. *Bang!*

He listened, waiting for the ring.

He listened, and heard a voice, screaming down the wind.

He impelled himself to his feet, in one surge of motion. He stood there, blood pounding against his temples, his lips parted and trembling. There could be no sound like that. Not when he was the last human being on this world. Not when the scream could be that of Laurette Overland, calling to him.

Of course, it was not she. Of course, it could not be. This was merely one of those things previewing the preparation of a skeleton with a ring in a— *Stop!*

He moved from the cave, out into the wind, and stood there. He heard nothing—did he? A pound of feet—such as death running might make.

A scream!

He ran around the shoulder of the mountain, stood there, panting, clasping his helmeted head between his trembling, cold hands.

"Lieutenant!"

A voice, whipped into his imagination by the ungodly wind!

He would not believe it.

A form, stumbling out of the pale night! Running toward him, its lips moving, saying words that the wind took away. And it was Laurette Overland, forming in his imagination now that he had gone completely mad.

He waited there, in cold amusement. There was small use in allowing himself to be fooled. And yet—and yet—the ring had to come back; to him. This was Laurette Overland, and she was bringing it—for him to wear. That was selfish of her. If *she* had the ring, if *she* had dug it up, why didn't *she* wear it?

Then she would be the skeleton.

Then there would be two skeletons!

His mind froze, then surged forward into life and sanity. A cold cry of agony escaped him. He stumbled forward and caught the girl up in his arms. He could feel the supple firmness of her body even through the folds of her undistended pressure suit.

Laurette's lips, red and full against the ghastly induced paleness of her face, parted and words came out. Yet he could make no sense of it, for the unimaginable wind, and the cold horror lancing through his mind occluded words and sentences.

"—had to . . . out. A hundred pounds." He felt her hysterical laugh. So the ship had started to fall. She had bailed out, had swept to solid ground on streams of flame shooting from the rocket jets in the shoulders of her suit. This much he knew. Hours and hours she had fought her way—toward the plain. Because she remembered something. The ship was gone. Safe. She remembered something that was important and it had to do with the skeleton and the ring. She had to get out. It was her part in the ghastly across-the-millions-of-years stage play. She had to dig up the ring.

He held her out at arm's length and looked down at her gloved hands. Yes, there was mud on them. So the ring had not been in the cave.

His eyes shuddered upward to hers.

"Give me the ring." His lips formed the words slowly.

"No, no, lieutenant," she blurted out. "It's not going to be *that* way. Don't you see? It's Amos! Amos!"

"You must be crazy to have come back!" he panted. He shook in sudden overwhelming, maddening fury. "You're crazy anyway!"

He suddenly wrenched at her hands, forced them open. But there was no ring. He shook her madly.

"Where's the ring? Give it to me, you damned little fool! If you're wearing it—if you think for one moment—you can't do this—"

The wind whipped the words away from her, she knew, even as that which she was saying was lost to him.

He stopped talking, and with a cold ferocity wrapped one arm around her, and with the other started to unbuckle her gloves with his own bare hands. She struggled suddenly, tigerishly. She wrenched herself away from him. She ran backward three steps. She looked up into the sky for one brief second, at the growing monster. He could see the cold, frantic horror settling on her face. Collision! And it was a matter of moments! And he, the true skeleton, did not have the ring!

He moved toward her, one slow step at a time, his eyes wild, his jaw set with purpose.

She darted past him. He whirled, panting, went frantically after her. And every step he took grew more leaden, for the moment was here. The collision was about to occur. And the girl was running toward the cave.

Laurette vanished around the shoulder of the mountain. The cave swallowed her. His steps slowed down. He stood there, drew a deep, tremulous breath. Then he entered the cave, and stood facing her, the wind's howl diminishing.

She said, coldly, "We haven't much time to talk or fight, lieutenant. You're acting like a madman. Here." She stooped and picked up his gloves. She held them out. "Put these on."

He said, "Give me the ring."

She stared at him through the gloom, at his preternaturally wide eyes.

"All right," she said. She unbuckled the glove of her right hand. She moved close to him, holding his eyes with her own. "If you want to be the skeleton, you may."

He felt her fingers touch his right hand. He felt something cold traveling up his fingers. He felt the ring enclosing his finger. Yes, the ring was on there, where it should be. He felt it—coldly. It could not very well be his imagination—could it? Of course not. She would not try to fool him. Yet her eyes were hypnotic, and he was in a daze. Feebly, he knew he should resist. But she forced his glove over his right hand, and he heard the buckles click. Then the left hand glove went on, and was buckled.

Her arms crept up around his neck. Tears glinted unashamedly in her eyes.

"Hold me tight, lieutenant," she whispered huskily. "You know . . . you know, there may be a chance."

"No, there isn't, Laurette. There can't be. I've got the ring on my finger."

He could feel her drawing a deep breath. "Of course— you've got the ring on your finger! I think it can't be very far away, lieutenant. Hold me." Her voice was a whimper. "Maybe we'll live."

"Not I. Perhaps you."

"This cave, this very mountain, lived through the holocaust. And perhaps we will, too. Both of us."

She was being illogical, he knew. But he had sunk into a dull, apathetic state of mind. Let her try to believe what was impossible. He had the ring on his finger. He *did*.

Did he?

He jerked. He had felt the cold of its metal encircling his finger. He had *thought* he had felt it! His fingers moved. A dull, sickening sense of utter defeat engulfed him. This was defeat. *She* had the ring! *She* was the skeleton!

And there was no time to change it. There would be no time. The blood rushed in his head, giddily. He caught her eyes, and held them, and tried to let her know in that last moment that he knew what she had done. She bit her lip and smiled. Then—her face clouded. Clouded as his thoughts clouded. It was like that.

He heard no monstrous sound, for here was sound that was no sound. It was simply the ponderous headlong meeting of two planets. They had struck. They were flattening out against each other, in the immeasurable second when consciousness was whipped away, and fragments of rock, some large, some small, were dribbling out in a fine frothy motion from underneath the circle of collision. The planet was yawning mightily. A jigsaw of pieces, a Humpty Dumpty that all the king's horses and all the king's men could never put together again. This was the mighty prelude to the forming of an asteroid belt, and of a girl skeleton on Asteroid No. 1007.

He was alive.
Alive and thinking.
It did not seem possible.
He was wedged into the back of the cave. A boulder shut off light, and a projecting spur of it reached out and pinioned him with gentle touch against the wall at his back. He was breathing. His suit was inflated with ten pounds of pressure. Electric coils were keeping his body warm. He was alive and the thoughts were beginning in his brain. Slow, senseless thoughts. Thoughts that were illogical. He could not even bring himself to feel emotion. He was pinioned here in the darkness, and out there was an asteroid of no air, small gravity, and a twenty-mile altitude.

Laurette Overland would be dead, and she would be wearing the ring. Tears, unashamed, burned at his eyes.

How long had he been here, wedged in like this: minutes, hours, days? Where were Overland, Masters, Braker and Yates? Would they land and move this boulder away?

Something suddenly seemed to shake the mountain. He felt the vibration rolling through his body. What had caused that? Some internal explosion, an aftermath of the collision? That did not seem likely, for the vibration had been brief, barely perceptible.

He stood there, wedged, his thoughts refusing to work except with a monotonous regularity. Mostly he thought of the skeleton; so that skeleton *had* existed before the human race!

After a while, it might have been five minutes or an hour or more, he became aware of arms and legs and a sluggishly beating heart. He raised his arms slowly, like an automaton that has come to life after ages of motionlessness, and pushed against the boulder that hemmed him in. It seemed to move away from him easily. He stepped to one side and imparted a ponderous, rocking motion to the boulder. It fell forward and stopped. Light, palely emanating from the starry, black night that overhung Asteroid No. 1007, burst through over the top of the boulder. Good. There was plenty of room to crawl through—after a while. He leaned against the boulder, blood surging weakly in his veins.

He felt a vibration so small that it might have been imagination. Then again, it might have been the ship, landing on the asteroid. At least, there was enough likelihood of that to warrant turning his headset receiver on.

He listened, and heard the dull undertone of a carrier wave; or was that the dull throb of blood against his temples? No, it couldn't be. He strained to listen, coherent thoughts at last making headway in his mind.

Then:

"Go on, professor—Masters." That was Braker's voice! "We'll all go crazy if we don't find out who the skeleton is."

Then Braker had landed the ship, after escaping the holocaust that had shattered that before-the-asteroids world! Tony almost let loose a hoarse breath, then withheld it, savagely. If Braker heard that, he might suspect something. Whatever other purpose Tony had in life now, the first and most important was to get the Hampton away from Braker.

Overland muttered, his voice lifeless, "If it's my daughter, I'd rather you'd go first, Braker."

Masters spoke. "I'll go ahead, professor. I'd do anything to—" His voice broke.

Overland muttered, "Don't take it so hard, son. We all have our bad moments. It couldn't be a skeleton, anyway."

"Why not?" That was Yates. Then, "Oh, hell, yes! It couldn't be, could it, professor? You know, this is just about the flukiest thing that has ever happened I guess. Sometimes it makes me laugh! On again, off again!"

"Finnegan," finished Braker absently. "Say, I don't get it. This time business. You say the gravity of that planet was holding us back in time like a rubber band stretched tight. When the planet went, the rubber band broke—there wasn't that gravity any more. And then we snapped back to our real time. But what if Crow and your daughter weren't released like that? Then we ought to find the skeleton—maybe two of 'em."

"The gravity of the asteroid would not be enough to hold them back," Overland said wearily.

"Then I don't get it," Braker snapped with exasperation. "This is the present, our real present. Back there is the ledge that cracked our ship up, so it has to be the present. Then how come Crow said he saw a skeleton? Say," he added, in a burst of anger, "do you think that copper was pulling the wool over our eyes? Well, I'll be—"

Yates said, "Grow up! Crow was telling the truth."

Overland said, "The skeleton will be there. The lieutenant saw it."

Masters: "Maybe he saw his own skeleton."

Yates: "Say, that's right!"

Braker: "Well, why not? The same ring was in two different places at the same time, so I guess the same skeleton could be in Crow at the same time as in the cave. It's a fact, and you don't talk yourself out of it."

Tony's head was whirling. What in heaven were they talking about? Were they intimating that the release of gravity, when the planet broke up, released everything back to the real present, as if some sort of bond had been broken? His hands started to tremble. Of course. It was possible. The escapage of gravitons had thrust them back into the past. Gravitons, the very stuff of gravity, had held them there. And when that one and a half gravity had dispersed, when the gravitons were so far distant that they no longer exerted that tension, everything had snapped back—to the present!

Everything! His thoughts turned cold. Somewhere, somehow, something was terribly wrong. His head ached. He clenched his hands, and listened again. For a full minute, there was no voice. Tony could envision them walking along, Masters and Overland in front, Braker and Yates behind, making their slow way to the cave, Overland dreading what he was to find there.

Then: "Hurry it up, professor. Should be right around here."

Overland whispered, throatily, "There it is, Braker. My God!" He sounded as if he were going all to pieces.

"The skeleton!" Yates blurted out, burrs in his voice. "Ye gods, professor, d'you suppose— Why sure—they just weren't snapped back."

Shaking, pasty white of face, Tony clawed his way halfway up the boulder. He hung there, just able to look outside. The whole floor of the cave was visible. And the skeleton lay there, gleaming white, and the ring shone on its tapering finger!

Laurette.

He lifted his head, conscious that his eyes were smarting painfully. Through a blur, he saw Braker, Yates, Masters and

Overland, standing about thirty feet distant from the cave, silent, speechless, staring at the skeleton.

Braker said, his voice unsteady, "It's damned strange, isn't it? We knew it was going to be there, and there it is, and it robs you of your breath."

Yates cleared his throat, and said firmly, "Yeah, but who is it? Crow or the girl?"

Overland took a step forward, his weak eyes straining.

"It's not a very long skeleton, is it?" he whispered.

Braker said, harshly, "Now don't try talking yourself into anything, professor. You can't see the skeleton well enough from here to tell who it is. Masters, stop shaking." His words were implicit with scorn. "Move over there and don't try any funny stuff like you did on the ship a while ago. I should have blasted you then. I'm going to take a look at that skeleton."

He went forward sideways, hand on his right hip where the Hampton was holstered.

He came up to the mouth of the cave, stood looking down on the skeleton, frowning. Then he knelt. Tony could see his face working with revulsion, but still he knelt there, as if fascinated.

Tony's lips stretched back from his teeth. Here's where Braker got his! He worked his way up to the top of the boulder, tensed, slid over to the other side on his feet. He took one step forward and bent his knees.

Braker raised his head.

His face contorted into a sudden mask of horror.

"You!" he screamed. His eyes bulged.

Tony leaped.

Braker fell backward, face deathly pale, clawing at the Hampton. Tony was on top of him before he could use it. He pinned Braker down, going for the Hampton with hands, feet, and blistering curses. His helmet was a sudden madhouse of consternated voices. Overland, Masters, and Yates swept across his vision. And Yates was coming forward.

He caught hold of the weapon, strained at it mightily, the muscles of his stomach going rigid under the exertion.

Braker kicked at Tony's midriff with heavy boots, striving to puncture the pressure suit. Tony was forced over on his back, saw Braker's sweating face grinning mirthlessly into his.

Stars were suddenly occluded by Yates' body. The man fell to his knees, pinned Tony down, and with Braker's help broke Tony's hold on the Hampton.

"Give it to me!" That was Masters' voice, blasting out shrilly. By sheer surprise, he wrenched the weapon from Yates. Tony flung himself to his feet as the outlaw hurled himself at Masters with a snarl, made a grab for Yates' foot. Yates tried to shake him off, hopped futilely, then stumbled forward, falling. But he struck against Masters. Masters' hold on the weapon was weak. It went sailing away in an arc, fell at the mouth of the cave.

"Get it!" Braker's voice blasted out as he struggled to his feet. Masters was ahead of him. Wildly, he thrust Braker aside. Yates reached out, tripped Masters. Braker went forward toward the Hampton, and then stopped, stock-still.

A figure stepped from the cave, picked up the weapon, and said, in cold, unmistakable tones, "Up with them. You, Braker. Yates!"

Braker's breath released in a long shuddering sigh, and he dropped weakly, helplessly to his knees.

His voice was horrible. "I'm crazy," he said simply, and continued to kneel there and continued to look up at the figure as if it were a dead figure come to life at which he stared.

The blood drummed upward in Tony's temples, until it was a wild, crazy, diapason. His shuddering hands raised to clasp his helmet.

Then:

"Laurette," he whispered brokenly. *"Laurette!"*

There were six human beings here.

And *one skeleton on the floor of the cave.*

How long that tableau held, Tony had no way of knowing. Professor Overland, standing off to Tony's left, arms half raised, a tortured, uncomprehending look on his face. Masters, full length on his stomach, pushing at the ground with his clawed hands to raise his head upward. Yates, in nearly the same position, turned to stone. Braker, his breath beginning to sound out in little, bottled-up rasps.

And the girl, Laurette, she who should have been the skeleton, standing there at the mouth of the cave, her face indescribably pale, as she centered the Hampton on Braker and Yates.

Her voice edged into the aching silence.

"It's Amos," she said. She was silent, looking at her father's haggard face, smiling twistedly.

"Amos," said Overland hoarsely, saying nothing else, but in that one word showing his utter, dismaying comprehension. He stumbled forward three steps. "We thought— We thought—" He seemed unable to go on. Tears sounded in his voice. He said humbly, "We thought you were the— But no. It's Amos!" His voice went upward hysterically.

"Stop it!" Laurette's voice lashed out. She added softly, tenderly, "No, I'm not the skeleton. Far from it, Daddy. Amos is the skeleton. He was the skeleton all along. I didn't realize it might be that way until the ship lifted. Then it seemed that the ship was going to fall and I thought my hundred and five might help after all and anyway, I decided that the lieutenant was all alone down there. And that somehow made me think of the time all the Christmas packages tumbled down on him and how I slapped him." She laughed unsteadily. "That made me remember that the university sent your present with a 'Do Not Open Before Christmas' sticker on it. I remembered you were leaving the university and they were giving you a combination farewell gift and Christmas present. You didn't know, but I did, that the professors decided you couldn't possibly be back before Christmas and so they sent it to the ship. You had always told them you admired—Amos. He hung on the biology classroom wall. It seemed I suddenly knew how things *had* to be. I put two and two together and I took a chance on it."

She fell silent, and the silence held for another full, shocking minute. She went on, as if with an effort.

"We threw everything out of the ship, remember? The Christmas presents, too. When I dropped from the ship later, I reached the plain and I broke open the carton with the 'Do Not Open' sticker on it, and there was Amos, as peaceful as you please. I put the ring on his finger and left him there, because I knew that some way the wind or crack-up or *something* would drop him in the cave. He *had* to turn up in the cave.

"Anyway," she added, her lips quirking roguishly, "by our time, back there, it was December 25th."

Masters clawed his way to his knees, his lips parted unnaturally.

"A Christmas present!" he croaked. "A Christmas present!" His face went white.

The girl said unsteadily, "Cut it out, Erle!"

She leaned weakly against the wall of the cave. "Now come up here, lieutenant, and take this gun out of my hands and don't stare at me as if you've lost your senses."

Tony forced himself to his feet, and like an automaton skirted around Braker and Yates and took the suddenly shaking weapon from her.

She uttered a weary sigh, smiled at him faintly, bemusedly, and whispered, "Merry Christmas, lieutenant!" She slumped slowly to the ground.

Tony gestured soundlessly at Masters. Masters, face abject and ashamed, picked her up in tender arms.

"Come up here, professor," Tony said dully. He felt as if all the life had been pumped from his bones.

Overland came forward, shaking his head with emotion. "Amos!" he whispered. He broke in a half-hysterical chuckle, stopped himself. He hovered around Laurette, watching her tired face. "At least my girl lives," he whispered brokenly.

"Get up, Braker," said Tony. "You, too, Yates."

Yates rose, vaguely brushing dust from his pressure suit, his lips working over words that refused to emerge.

Braker's voice was a hoarse, unbelieving whisper. His eyes were abnormally wide and fixed hypnotically on the skeleton. "So that's what we went through—for a damned classroom skeleton." He repeated it. "For a damned classroom skeleton!"

He came to his feet, fighting to mold his strained face back to normal. "Just about back where we started, eh? Well," he added in a shaking, bitter tone, "Merry Christmas." He forced his lips into half-hearted cynicism.

Tony's face relaxed. He drew in a full, much-needed breath of air. "Sure. Sure— Merry Christmas. Everybody. Including Amos—whoever he used to be."

Nobody seemed to have anything to say. Or perhaps their thoughts were going back for the moment to a pre-asteroid world. Remembering. At least Masters was remembering, if the suffering, remorseful look on his face meant anything.

Tony broke it. "That's that, isn't it? Now we can go back to the ship. From there to Earth. Professor—Masters—start off." He made a tired gesture.

Masters went ahead, without a backward look, carrying the gently breathing, but still unconscious girl. Overland stole a last look at the skeleton, at Amos, where he lay, unknowing of the chaos the mere fact of his being there, white and perfect and wired together, and with a ring on his perfect tapering finger, had caused. Overland walked away hurriedly after Masters. Amos would stay where he was.

Tony smiled grimly at Braker. He pointed with his free hand.

"Want your ring back, Braker?"

Braker's head jerked minutely. He stared at the ring, then back at Tony. His fists clenched at his sides. *"No!"*

Tony grinned—for the first time in three weeks.

"Then let's get going."

He made a gesture. Braker and Yates, walking side by side, went slowly for the ship, Tony following behind. He turned only once, and that was to look at his wrecked patrol ship, where it lay against the base of the mountain. A shudder passed down his spine. There was but one mystery that remained now. And its solution was coming to Tony Crow, in spite of his effort to shove its sheerly maddening implications into the back of his mind—

Professor Overland and Masters took Laurette to her room. Tony took the two outlaws to the lounge, wondering how he was going to secure them. Masters solved his problem by entering with a length of insulated electric wire. He said nothing, but wordlessly went to work securing Braker and Yates to the guide rail while Tony held the Hampton on them. After he had finished, Tony bluntly inspected the job. Masters winced, but he said nothing.

After they were out in the hall, going toward Laurette's room, Masters stopped him. His face was white, strained in the half-darkness.

"I don't know how to say this," he began huskily.

"Say what?"

Masters' eyes shifted, then, as if by a deliberate effort of will, came back.

"That I'm sorry."

Tony studied him, noted the lines of suffering around his mouth, the shuddering pain in his eyes.

"Yeah, I know how you feel," he muttered. "But I guess you made up for it when you tackled Braker and Yates. They might have been using electric wire on us by now." He grinned lopsidedly, and clapped Masters on the arm. "Forget it, Masters. I'm with you all the way."

Masters managed a smile, and let loose a long breath. He fell into step beside Tony's hurrying stride. "Laurette's O. K."

"Well, lieutenant," said Laurette, stretching lazily, and smiling up at him, "I guess I got weak in the knees at the last minute."

"Didn't we all!" He smiled ruefully. He dropped to his knees. She was still in her pressure suit and lying on the floor. He helped her to a sitting position, and then to her feet.

Overland chuckled, though there was a note of uneasy

reminiscence in his tone. "Wait till I tell the boys at Lipton
U. about this."

"You'd better not," Laurette warned. She added, "You
broke down and admitted the ring was an omen. When a
scientist gets superstitious—"

Tony broke in. "Weren't we all?"

Masters said, dropping his eyes, "I guess we had good
enough reason to be superstitious about it." His hand went
absently upward to his shoulder.

Overland frowned, and, hands behind his back, walked to
the empty porthole. "All that work DeTosque, the Farr
brothers, Morrell, and myself put in. There's no reason to
patch up the asteroids and try to prove they were all one
world. But at the same time, there's no proof—no absolute
proof—" He clicked his tongue. Then he swung on Tony, biting speculatively at his lower lip, his eyes sharpening.

"There's one thing that needs explaining which probably
never will be explained, I guess. It's too bad. Memory? Bah!
That's not the answer, lieutenant. You stood in the cave
there, and you saw the skeleton, and somehow you *knew* it
had existed before the human race, but was not *older* than
the human race. It's something else. You didn't pick up the
memory from the past—not over a hundred million years.
What then?" He turned away, shaking his head, came back
abruptly as Tony spoke, eyes sharpening.

"I'll tell you why," Tony said evenly.

His head moved up and down slowly, and his half-lidded
eyes looked lingeringly out the porthole toward the mountain
where his wrecked patrol ship lay. "Yes, I'll tell you why."

Laurette, Masters and Overland were caught up in tense
silence by the strangeness of his tone.

He said faintly: "Laurette and I were trapped alive in the
back of the cave when the two worlds crashed. We lived
through it. I didn't know she was back there, of course; she
recovered consciousness later—at the right time, I'd say!" He
grinned at her obliquely, then sobered again. "I saw the
skeleton and somehow I was too dazed to realize it couldn't
be Laurette. Because when the gravity was dispersed, the tension holding everything back in time was released, and everything went back to the present—just a little less than the
present. I'll explain that later."

He drew a long breath.

"This is hard to say. I was in the back of the cave. I felt
something strike the mountainside.

"That was my patrol ship—with me in it."

His glance roved around. Overland's breath sucked in audibly.

"Careful now, boy," he rumbled warningly, alarm in his eyes.

Tony's lips twisted. "It happens to be the truth. After my ship crashed I got out. A few minutes later I stood at the mouth of the cave, looking at the skeleton. For a minute, I—remembered. Fragmentary things. The skeleton was—horror.

"And why not? I was also in the back of the cave, thinking that Laurette was dead and that she was the skeleton. The Tony Crow at the mouth of the cave and the Tony Crow trapped in the rear of the cave were *en rapport* to an infinite degree. They were the same person, in two different places at the same time, and their brains were the same."

He stopped.

Masters whispered through his clenched teeth, "Two Tony Crows. It couldn't be."

Tony leaned back against the wall. "There were two rings, at the same time. There were two skeletons, at the same time. Braker had the skeleton's ring on his finger. Amos was wrapped up in a carton with a Christmas sticker on it. They were both some place else. You all know that and admit it. Well, there were two Tony Crows, and if I think about it much longer, it'll drive me—"

"Hold it, boy!" Overland's tone was sharp. Then he said mildly, "It's nothing to get excited about. The mere fact of time-travel presupposes duplicity of existence. Our ship and everything in it was made of electrons that existed somewhere else at the same time—a hundred million years ago, on the pre-asteroid world. You can't get away from it. And you don't have to get scared just because two Tony Crows were a few feet distant from each other. Remember that all the rest of us were duplicated, too. Ship A was thrust *back* into time just an hour or so before Ship B landed here after being thrust *forward*. You see?"

Laurette shuddered. "It's clear, but it's—" She made a confused motion.

Overland's tired, haggard eyes twinkled. "Anyway, there's no danger of us running across ourselves again. The past is done for. That's the main thing."

Neither Laurette nor Tony said anything. They were studying each other, and a smile was beginning at the corner of Laurette's lips. Erle Masters squirmed uncomfortably.

Overland continued, speculatively: "There was an energy loss some place. We weren't snapped back to the real present at all. We should have come back to the present that we left, *plus* the three weeks we stayed back in time. Back there it was Christmas—and Laurette was quite correct when she broke open my package." He grinned crookedly. "But it's still more than three weeks to Christmas here. It was a simple energy loss, I guess. If I had a penc—"

Erle Masters broke in on him, coughing uncomfortably and grinning wryly at the same time. "We'd better get down to the control room and plot out our course, professor."

"What?" Overland's eyes widened. He looked around at the man and girl. "Oh." He studied them, then turned, and clapped Masters on the back. "You're dead right, son. Let's get out!"

"I'm glad you weren't Amos," Tony told the girl.

"I couldn't very well have been, lieutenant."

He grinned, coloring slightly.

Then he took her hands in his, and put his head as close to hers as the helmets would allow.

He said, "When we get back to Earth, I'm going to put a r—" He stopped, biting at his lip. Remembrances of another time, on a pre-asteroid world, flooded back with the thought.

She started, paled. Involuntarily, her eyes turned to the open port, beyond which was a mountain, a cave, a skeleton, a ring.

She nodded, slowly, faintly. "It's a good idea," she murmured. She managed a smile. "But not—an emerald."

1941

THE WORDS OF GURU

Stirring Science Stories
June

by C. M. Kornbluth

*Another short but wonderful story by the very
young Kornbluth. It appeared in* Stirring Science
Stories, *a short-lived but exciting magazine edited
by Cyril's friend Donald A. Wollheim, which was a
major market for a number of young New York
fans-to-be-writers. Many of the stories in its pages
were collaborations (regardless of whose name was
on them) but this one was Kornbluth's.*

(When Don Wollheim edited *Stirring* and its companion
magazine *Cosmic,* he had an operating budget that included
zero dollars for writers—if I recall correctly. He had to call
upon the members of the Futurians therefore to supply him
with the material to keep going till the magazines caught on
and he could afford to pay. Even I submitted a story called
"The Secret Sense"—one of my lesser works, I think. Cyril
was by far the most active contributor, I think, and the best.
It wasn't Don's fault that the combination of no budget *and*
World War II made continuation impossible. And, by the
way, since I whined in the previous introduction about being
only 20 as an excuse for imperfection, *this* story appeared
when Cyril was only 18.—I.A.)

Yesterday, when I was going to meet Guru in the woods a
man stopped me and said: "Child, what are you doing out at
one in the morning? Does your mother know where you are?
How old are you, walking around this late?"

I looked at him, and saw that he was white-haired, so I
laughed. Old men never see; in fact men hardly see at all.
Sometimes young women see part, but men rarely ever see at
all. "I'm twelve on my next birthday," I said. And then, because I would not let him live to tell people, I said, "and I'm
out this late to see Guru."

"Guru?" he asked. "Who is Guru? Some foreigner, I suppose? Bad business mixing with foreigners, young fellow. Who is Guru?"

So I told him who Guru was, and just as he began talking about cheap magazines and fairy tales I said one of the words that Guru taught me and he stopped talking. Because he was an old man and his joints were stiff he didn't crumple up but fell in one piece, hitting his head on the stone. Then I went on.

Even though I'm going to be only twelve on my next birthday I know many things that old people don't. And I remember things that other boys can't. I remember being born out of darkness, and I remember the noises that people made about me. Then when I was two months old I began to understand that the noises meant things like the things that were going on inside my head. I found out that I could make the noises too, and everybody was very much surprised. "Talking!" they said, again and again. "And so very young! Clara, what do you make of it?" Clara was my mother.

And Clara would say: "I'm sure I don't know. There never was any genius in my family, and I'm sure there was none in Joe's." Joe was my father.

Once Clara showed me a man I had never seen before, and told me that he was a reporter—that he wrote things in newspapers. The reporter tried to talk to me as if I were an ordinary baby; I didn't even answer him, but just kept looking at him until his eyes fell and he went away. Later Clara scolded me and read me a little piece in the reporter's newspaper that was supposed to be funny—about the reporter asking me very complicated questions and me answering with baby noises. It was not true, of course. I didn't say a word to the reporter, and he didn't ask me even one of the questions.

I heard her read the little piece, but while I listened I was watching the slug crawling on the wall. When Clara was finished I asked her: "What is that gray thing?"

She looked where I pointed, but couldn't see it. "What gray thing, Peter?" she asked. I had her call me by my whole name, Peter, instead of anything silly like Petey. "What gray thing?"

"It's as big as your hand, Clara, but soft. I don't think it has any bones at all. It's crawling up, but I don't see any face on the topwards side. And there aren't any legs."

I think she was worried, but she tried to baby me by putting her hand on the wall and trying to find out where it was. I called out whether she was right or left of the thing. Finally she put her hand right through the slug. And then I realized that she really couldn't see it, and didn't believe it was there. I stopped talking about it then and only asked her a few days later: "Clara, what do you call a thing which one person can see and another person can't?"

"An illusion, Peter," she said. "If that's what you mean." I said nothing, but let her put me to bed as usual, but when she turned out the light and went away I waited a little while and then called out softly. "Illusion! Illusion!"

At once Guru came for the first time. He bowed, the way he always has since, and said: "I have been waiting."

"I didn't know that was the way to call you," I said.

"Whenever you want me I will be ready. I will teach you, Peter—if you want to learn. Do you know what I will teach you?"

"If you will teach me about the gray thing on the wall," I said, "I will listen. And if you will teach me about real things and unreal things I will listen."

"These things," he said thoughtfully, "very few wish to learn. And there are some things that nobody ever wished to learn. And there are some things that I will not teach."

Then I said: "The things nobody has ever wished to learn I will learn. And I will even learn the things you do not wish to teach."

He smiled mockingly. "A master has come," he said, half-laughing. "A master of Guru."

That was how I learned his name. And that night he taught me a word which would do little things, like spoiling food.

From that day to the time I saw him last night he has not changed at all, though now I am as tall as he is. His skin is still as dry and shiny as ever it was, and his face is still bony, crowned by a head of very coarse, black hair.

When I was ten years old I went to bed one night only long enough to make Joe and Clara suppose I was fast asleep. I left in my place something which appears when you say one of the words of Guru and went down the drainpipe outside my window. It always was easy to climb down and up, ever since I was eight years old.

I met Guru in Inwood Hill Park. "You're late," he said.

"Not too late," I answered. "I know it's never too late for one of these things."

"How do you know?" he asked sharply. "This is your first."

"And maybe my last," I replied. "I don't like the idea of it.

If I have nothing more to learn from my second than my first I shan't go to another."

"You don't know," he said. "You don't know what it's like—the voices, and the bodies slick with unguent, leaping flames; mind-filling ritual! You can have no idea at all until you've taken part."

"We'll see," I said. "Can we leave from here?"

"Yes," he said. Then he taught me the word I would need to know, and we both said it together.

The place we were in next was lit with red lights, and I think that the walls were of rock. Though of course there was no real seeing there, and so the lights only seemed to be red, and it was not real rock.

As we were going to the fire one of them stopped us. "Who's with you?" she asked, calling Guru by another name. I did not know that he was also the person bearing that name, for it was a very powerful one.

He cast a hasty, sidewise glance at me and then said: "This is Peter of whom I have often told you."

She looked at me then and smiled, stretching out her oily arms. "Ah," she said, softly, like the cats when they talk at night to me. "Ah, this is Peter. Will you come to me when I call you, Peter? And sometimes call for me—in the dark— when you are alone?"

"Don't do that!" said Guru, angrily pushing past her. "He's very young—you might spoil him for his work."

She screeched at our backs: "Guru and his pupil—fine pair! Boy, he's no more real than I am—you're the only real thing here!"

"Don't listen to her," said Guru. "She's wild and raving. They're always tight-strung when this time comes around."

We came near the fires then, and sat down on rocks. They were killing animals and birds and doing things with their bodies. The blood was being collected in a basin of stone, which passed through the crowd. The one to my left handed it to me. "Drink," she said, grinning to show me her fine, white teeth. I swallowed twice from it and passed it to Guru.

When the bowl had passed all around we took off our clothes. Some, like Guru, did not wear them, but many did. The one to my left sat closer to me, breathing heavily at my face. I moved away. "Tell her to stop, Guru," I said. "This isn't part of it, I know."

Guru spoke to her sharply in their own language, and she changed her seat, snarling.

Then we all began to chant, clapping our hands and

beating our thighs. One of them rose slowly and circled about the fires in a slow pace, her eyes rolling wildly. She worked her jaws and flung her arms about so sharply that I could hear the elbows crack. Still shuffling her feet against the rock floor she bent her body backwards down to her feet. Her belly muscles were bands nearly standing out from her skin, and the oil rolled down her body and legs. As the palms of her hands touched the ground, she collapsed in a twitching heap and began to set up a thin wailing noise against the steady chant and hand beat that the rest of us were keeping up. Another of them did the same as the first, and we chanted louder for her and still louder for the third. Then, while we still beat our hands and thighs, one of them took up the third, laid her across the altar, and made her ready with a stone knife. The fire's light gleamed off the chipped edge of obsidian. As her blood drained down the groove, cut as a gutter into the rock of the altar, we stopped our chant and the fires were snuffed out.

But still we could see what was going on, for these things were, of course, not happening at all—only seeming to happen, really, just as all the people and things there only seemed to be what they were. Only I was real. That must be why they desired me so.

As the last of the fires died Guru excitedly whispered: "The Presence!" He was very deeply moved.

From the pool of blood from the third dancer's body there issued the Presence. It was the tallest one there, and when it spoke its voice was deeper, and when it commanded its commands were obeyed.

"Let blood!" it commanded, and we gashed ourselves with flints. It smiled and showed teeth bigger and sharper and whiter than any of the others.

"Make water!" it commanded, and we all spat on each other. It flapped its wings and rolled its eyes, which were bigger and redder than any of the others.

"Pass flame!" it commanded, and we breathed smoke and fire on our limbs. It stamped its feet, let blue flames roar from its mouth, and they were bigger and wilder than any of the others.

Then it returned to the pool of blood and we lit the fires again. Guru was staring straight before him; I tugged his arm. He bowed as though we were meeting for the first time that night.

"What are you thinking of?" I asked. "We shall go now."

"Yes," he said heavily. "Now we shall go." Then we said the word that had brought us there.

The first man I killed was Brother Paul, at the school where I went to learn the things that Guru did not teach me.

It was less than a year ago, but it seems like a very long time. I have killed so many times since then.

"You're a very bright boy, Peter," said the brother.

"Thank you, brother."

"But there are things about you that I don't understand. Normally I'd ask your parents but—I feel that they don't understand either. You were an infant prodigy, weren't you?"

"Yes, brother."

"There's nothing very unusual about that—glands, I'm told. You know what glands are?"

Then I was alarmed. I had heard of them, but I was not certain whether they were the short, thick green men who wear only metal or the things with many legs with whom I talked in the woods.

"How did you find out?" I asked him.

"But Peter! You look positively frightened, lad! I don't know a thing about them myself, but Father Frederick does. He has whole books about them, though I sometimes doubt whether he believes them himself."

"They aren't good books, brother," I said. "They ought to be burned."

"That's a savage thought, my son. But to return to your own problem—"

I could not let him go any further knowing what he did about me. I said one of the words Guru taught me and he looked at first very surprised and then seemed to be in great pain. He dropped across his desk and I felt his wrist to make sure, for I had not used that word before. But he was dead.

There was a heavy step outside and I made myself invisible. Stout Father Frederick entered, and I nearly killed him too with the word, but I knew that that would be very curious. I decided to wait, and went through the door as Father Frederick bent over the dead monk. He thought he was asleep.

I went down the corridor to the book-lined office of the stout priest and, working quickly, piled all his books in the center of the room and lit them with my breath. Then I went down to the schoolyard and made myself visible again when there was nobody looking. It was very easy. I killed a man I passed on the street the next day.

There was a girl named Mary who lived near us. She was

fourteen then, and I desired her as those in the Cavern out of Time and Space had desired me.

So when I saw Guru and he had bowed, I told him of it, and he looked at me in great surprise. "You are growing older, Peter," he said.

"I am, Guru. And there will come a time when your words will not be strong enough for me."

He laughed. "Come, Peter," he said. "Follow me if you wish. There is something that is going to be done—" He licked his thin, purple lips and said: "I have told you what it will be like."

"I shall come," I said. "Teach me the word." So he taught me the word and we said it together.

The place we were in next was not like any of the other places I had been to before with Guru. It was No-place. Always before there had been the seeming passage of time and matter, but here there was not even that. Here Guru and the others cast off their forms and were what they were, and No-place was the only place where they could do this.

It was not like the Cavern, for the Cavern had been out of Time and Space, and this place was not enough of a place even for that. It was No-place.

What happened there does not bear telling, but I was made known to certain ones who never departed from there. All came to them as they existed. They had not color or the seeming of color, or any seeming of shape.

There I learned that eventually I would join with them; that I had been selected as the one of my planet who was to dwell without being forever in that No-place.

Guru and I left, having said the word.

"Well?" demanded Guru, staring me in the eye.

"I am willing," I said. "But teach me one word now—"

"Ah," he said grinning. "The girl?"

"Yes," I said. "The word that will mean much to her."

Still grinning, he taught me the word.

Mary, who had been fourteen, is now fifteen and what they call incurably mad.

Last night I saw Guru again and for the last time. He bowed as I approached him. "Peter," he said warmly.

"Teach me the word," said I.

"It is not too late."

"Teach me the word."

"You can withdraw—with what you master you can master also this world. Gold without reckoning; sardonyx and gems, Peter! Rich crushed velvet—stiff, scraping, embroidered tapestries!"

"Teach me the word."

"Think, Peter, of the house you could build. It could be of white marble, and every slab centered by a winking ruby. Its gate could be of beaten gold within and without and it could be built about one slender tower of carven ivory, rising mile after mile into the turquoise sky. You could see the clouds float underneath your eyes."

"Teach me the word."

"Your tongue could crush the grapes that taste like melted silver. You could hear always the song of the bulbul and the lark that sounds like the dawnstar made musical. Spikenard that will bloom a thousand thousand years could be ever in your nostrils. Your hands could feel the down of purple Himalayan swans that is softer than a sunset cloud."

"Teach me the word."

"You could have women whose skin would be from the black of ebony to the white of snow. You could have women who would be as hard as flints or as soft as a sunset cloud."

"Teach me the word."

Guru grinned and said the word.

Now, I do not know whether I will say that word, which was the last that Guru taught me, today or tomorrow or until a year has passed.

It is a word that will explode this planet like a stick of dynamite in a rotten apple.

THE SEESAW

Astounding Science Fiction
July

by A. E. van Vogt (1912-   ) .

*This is a good story, one of the best of 1941,
but it is also important for what it led to. "The
Seesaw" became* The Weapon Makers, *which led to*
The Weapon Shops of Isher.

*The slogan in the story, "The Right to Buy
Weapons Is the Right to be Free," found few dis-
senters in that war-torn year of 1941. Van Vogt remains one of the field's most influential and least
understood practitioners.*

(I shouldn't allow my personal opinions to intrude too
much in this series of anthologies, for we are selecting stories
that are not so much our favorites—although most of them
are—but stories that are of historic significance in the development of science fiction. I liked "The Seesaw" enormously, but looking back on van Vogt's writing now, it seems
to me that "The Seesaw" was almost the last piece I worshipped. I found that as the years of World War II
progressed his stories got progressively more difficult to follow. I think he was trying to top himself each time and make
each story successively more complex. This can be dangerous.
E. E. Smith fell into the trap and in the case of the *Foundation Stories*, I stopped when I thought there was no longer
any way I could avoid falling into the trap myself.—I. A.)

MAGICIAN BELIEVED TO HAVE
HYPNOTIZED CROWD!

June 11, 1941—Police and newspapermen believe that Middle City will shortly be advertised as
the next stopping place of a master magician, and
they are prepared to extend him a hearty welcome
if he will condescend to explain exactly how he

211

fooled hundreds of people into believing they saw a strange building, apparently a kind of gun shop.

The building seemed to appear on the space formerly, and still, occupied by Aunt Sally's Lunch and Patterson Tailors. Only employees were inside the two aforementioned shops, and none noticed any untoward event. A large, brightly shining sign featured the front of the gun shop, which had been so miraculously conjured out of nothingness; and the sign constituted the first evidence that the entire scene was nothing but a masterly illusion. For from whichever angle one gazed at it, one seemed to be staring straight at the words, which read:

FINE WEAPONS
THE RIGHT TO BUY WEAPONS
IS THE RIGHT TO BE FREE

The window display was made up of an assortment of rather curiously shaped guns, rifles as well as small arms; and a glowing sign in the window stated:

THE FINEST ENERGY WEAPONS
IN THE KNOWN UNIVERSE

Inspector Clayton of the Investigation Branch attempted to enter the shop, but the door seemed to be locked; a few moments later, C. J. (Chris) McAllister, reporter of the *Gazette-Bulletin,* tried the door, found it opened, and entered.

Inspector Clayton attempted to follow him, but discovered that the door was again locked. McAllister emerged after some time, and was seen to be in a dazed condition. All memory of the action had apparently been hypnotized out of him, for he could make no answer to the questions of the police and spectators.

Simultaneous with his reappearance, the strange building vanished as abruptly as it had appeared.

Police state they are baffled as to how the master magician created so detailed an illusion for so long a period before so large a crowd. They are prepared to recommend his show, when it comes, without reservation.

Author's Note: The foregoing account did not mention that the police, dissatisfied with the affair, attempted to contact McAllister for a further interview, but were unable to locate him. Weeks passed, and he was still not to be found.

Herewith follows the story of what happened to McAllister from the instant that he found the door of the gun shop unlocked.

There was a curious quality about the gun shop door. It was not so much that it opened at his first touch as that, when he pulled, it came away like a weightless thing. For a bare instant, McAllister had the impression that the knob had freed itself into his palm.

He stood quite still, startled. The thought that came finally had to do with Inspector Clayton, who a minute earlier had found the door locked.

The thought was like a signal. From behind him boomed the voice of the inspector: "Ah, McAllister, I'll handle this now."

It was dark inside the shop beyond the door, too dark to see anything, and somehow his eyes wouldn't accustom themselves to the intense gloom. . . .

Pure reporter's instinct made him step forward toward the blackness that pressed from beyond the rectangle of door. Out of the corner of one eye, he saw Inspector Clayton's hand reaching for the door handle that his own fingers had let go a moment before; and quite simply he knew that if the police officer could prevent it, no reporter would get inside that building.

His head was still turned, his gaze more on the police inspector than on the darkness in front; and it was as he began another step forward that the remarkable thing happened.

The door handle would not allow Inspector Clayton to touch it. It twisted in some queer way, in some *energy* way, for it was still there, a strange, blurred shape. The door itself, without visible movement, so swift it was, was suddenly touching McAllister's heel.

Light, almost weightless, was that touch; and then, before he could think or react to what had happened, the momentum of his forward movement had carried him inside.

As he breasted the darkness, there was a sudden, enormous tensing along his nerves. Then the door shut tight, the brief, incredible agony faded. Ahead was a brightly lit shop; behind—were unbelievable things!

For McAllister, the moment that followed was one of
blank impression. He stood, body twisted awkwardly, only
vaguely conscious of the shop's interior, but tremendously
aware, in the brief moment before he was interrupted, of
what lay beyond the transparent panels of the door through
which he had just come.

There was no unyielding blackness anywhere, no Inspector
Clayton, no muttering crowd of gaping spectators, no dingy
row of shops across the way.

It wasn't even remotely the same street. There was *no*
street.

Instead, a peaceful park spread there. Beyond it, brilliant
under a noon sun, glowed a city of minarets and stately towers—

From behind him, a husky, musical, woman's voice said,
"You will be wanting a gun?"

McAllister turned. It wasn't that he was ready to stop feast-
ing his eyes on the vision of the city. The movement was automatic reaction to a sound. And because the whole affair
was still like a dream, the city scene faded almost instantly;
his mind focused on the young woman who was advancing
slowly from the rear section of the store.

Briefly, his thought wouldn't come clear. A conviction that
he ought to say something was tangled with first impressions
of the girl's appearance. She had a slender, well-shaped body;
her face was creased into a pleasant smile. She had brown
eyes, neat, wavy brown hair. Her simple frock and sandals
seemed so normal at first glance that he gave them no other
thought.

He was able to say: "What I can't understand is why the
police officer who tried to follow me couldn't get in. And
where is he now?"

To his surprise, the girl's smile became faintly apologetic.
"We know that people consider it silly of us to keep harping
on that ancient feud."

Her voice grew firmer: "We even know how clever the
propaganda is that stresses the silliness of our stand. Meanwhile, we never allow any of *her* men in here. We continue
to take our principles very seriously."

She paused as if she expected dawning comprehension
from him, but McAllister saw from the slow puzzlement
creeping into her eyes that his face must look as limp as were
the thoughts behind it.

Her men! The girl had spoken the word as if she were
referring to some personage, and in direct reply to his use of

the words, police officer. That meant *her* men, whoever she was, were policemen; and they weren't allowed in this gun shop. So the door was hostile, and wouldn't admit them.

A strange emptiness struck into McAllister's mind, matching the hollowness that was beginning to afflict the pit of his stomach, a sense of unplumbed depths, the first, staggering conviction that all was not as it should be.

The girl was speaking in sharper tone: "You mean you know nothing of all this, that for generations the gunmaker's guild has existed in this age of devastating energies as the common man's only protection against enslavement. The right to buy guns—"

She stopped again, her narrowed eyes searching him; then: "Come to think of it, there's something very illogical about you. Your outlandish clothes—you're not from the northern farm plains, are you?"

He shook his head dumbly, more annoyed with his reactions every passing second. But he couldn't help it. A tightness was growing in him, becoming more unbearable instant by instant, as if somewhere a vital mainspring were being wound to the breaking point.

The young woman went on more swiftly: "And come to think of it, it is astounding that a policeman should have tried the door and there was no alarm."

Her hand moved; metal flashed in it, metal as bright as steel in blinding sunlight. There was not the faintest hint of the apologetic in her voice as she said, "You will stay where you are, sir, till I have called my father. In our business, with our responsibility, we never take chances. Something is very wrong here."

Curiously, it was at that point that McAllister's mind began to function clearly; the thought that came paralleled hers: How had this gun shop appeared on a 1941 street? How had he come here into this fantastic world?

Something was very wrong indeed!

It was the gun that held his attention. A tiny thing it was, shaped like a pistol, but with three cubes projecting in a little half circle from the top of the slightly bulbous firing chamber.

And as he stared, his mind began to quiver on its base; for that wicked little instrument, glittering there in her browned fingers, was as real as she herself.

"Good Heaven!" he whispered. "What the devil kind of gun is it? Lower that thing and let's try to find out what all this is about."

She seemed not to be listening; and abruptly he noticed that her gaze was flicking to a point on the wall somewhat to his left. He followed her look—in time to see seven miniature white lights flash on.

Curious lights! Briefly, he was fascinated by the play of light and shade, the waxing and waning from one tiny globe to the next, a rippling movement of infinitesimal increments and decrements, an incredibly delicate effect of instantaneous reaction to some supersensitive barometer.

The lights steadied; his gaze reverted to the girl. To his surprise, she was putting away her gun. She must have noticed his expression.

"It's all right," she said coolly. "The automatics are on you now. If we're wrong about you, we'll be glad to apologize. Meanwhile, if you're still interested in buying a gun, I'll be happy to demonstrate."

So the automatics were on him, McAllister thought ironically. He felt no relief at the information. Whatever the automatics were, they wouldn't be working in his favor; and the fact that the young woman could put away her gun in spite of her suspicions spoke volumes for the efficiency of the new watchdogs.

There was absolutely nothing he could do but play out this increasingly grim and inexplicable farce. Either he was mad, or else he was no longer on Earth, at least not the Earth of 1941—which was utter nonsense.

He'd have to get out of this place, of course. Meanwhile, the girl was assuming that a man who came into a gun shop would, under ordinary circumstances, want to buy a gun.

It struck him suddenly that, of all the things he could think of, what he wanted to see was one of those strange guns. There were implications of incredible things in the very shape of the instruments. Aloud he said, "Yes, by all means show me."

Another thought occurred to him. He added: "I have no doubt your father is somewhere in the background making some sort of study of me."

The young woman made no move to lead him anywhere. Her eyes were dark pools of puzzlement, staring at him.

"You may not realize it," she said finally, slowly, "but you have already upset our entire establishment. The lights of the automatics should have gone on the moment father pressed the buttons, as he did when I called to him. They didn't! That's unnatural, that's alien.

"And yet"—her frown deepened—"if you were one of

them, how did you get through that door? Is it possible that *her* scientists have discovered human beings who do not affect the sensitive energies? And that you are one of many such, sent as an experiment to determine whether or not entrance could be gained?

"Yet that doesn't make logic either.

"If they had even a hope of success, they would not risk so lightly the chance of an overwhelming surprise. Instead you would be the entering wedge of an attack on a vast scale. She is ruthless, she's brilliant; and she craves all power during her lifetime over poor saps like you who have no more sense than to worship her amazing beauty and the splendor of the Imperial Court."

The young woman paused, with the faintest of smiles. "There I go again, off on a political speech. But you can see that there are at least a few reasons why we should be careful about you."

There was a chair over in one corner; McAllister started for it. His mind was calmer, cooler.

"Look," he began, "I don't know what you're talking about. I don't even know how I came to be in this shop. I agree with you that the whole thing requires explanation, but I mean that differently than you do. In fact . . ."

His voice trailed. He had been half lowered over the chair, but instead of sinking into it, he came erect like an old, old man. His eyes fixed on lettering that shone above a glass case of guns behind her. He said hoarsely, "Is that—a calendar?"

She followed his gaze, puzzled: "Yes, it's June third. What's wrong?"

"I don't mean that. I mean—" He caught himself with a horrible effort. "I mean those figures above that. I mean—what year is this?"

The girl looked surprised. She started to say something, then stopped and backed away. Finally: "Don't look like that! There's nothing wrong. This is eighty-four of the four thousand seven hundredth year of the Imperial House of the Isher. It's quite all right."

There was no real feeling in him. Quite deliberately he sat down, and the conscious wonder came: exactly how *should* he feel?

Not even surprise came to his aid. Quite simply, the whole pattern of events began to make a sort of distorted logic.

The building front superimposed on those two 1941 shops; the way the door had acted; the great exterior sign with its odd linking of freedom with the right to buy weapons; the actual display of weapons in the window, *the finest energy weapons in the known universe!*

He grew aware that minutes had passed while he sat there in slow, dumb thought. And that the girl was talking earnestly with a tall, gray-haired man who was standing on the open threshold of the door through which she had originally come.

There was an odd, straining tenseness in the way they were talking. Their low-spoken words made a curious blur of sound in his ears, strangely unsettling in effect—McAllister could not quite analyze the meaning of it until the girl turned; and, in a voice dark with urgency, said, "Mr. McAllister, my father wants to know what year you're from!"

Briefly, the sense of the sentence was overshadowed by that stark urgency; then: "Huh!" said McAllister. "Do you mean that you're responsible for— And how the devil did you know my name?"

The older man shook his head. "No, we're not responsible." His voice quickened but lost none of its gravity. "There's no time to explain. What has happened is what we gunmakers have feared for generations: that sooner or later would come one who lusted for unlimited power; and who, to attain tyranny, must necessarily seek first to destroy us.

"Your presence here is a manifestation of the energy force that she has turned against us—something so new that we did not even suspect it was being used against us. But now—I have no time to waste. Get all the information you can, Lystra, and warn him of his own personal danger."

The man turned. The door closed noiselessly behind his tall figure.

McAllister asked, "What did he mean—personal danger?"

He saw that the girl's brown eyes were uneasy as they rested on him.

"It's hard to explain," she began in an uncomfortable voice. "First of all, come to the window, and I'll try to make everything clear. It's all very confusing to you, I suppose."

McAllister drew a deep breath. "Now we're getting somewhere."

His alarm was gone. The older man seemed to know what it was all about; that meant there should be no difficulty getting home again. As for all this danger to the gunmakers' guild, that was their worry, not his. Meanwhile—

He stepped forward, closer to the girl. To his amazement, she cringed away as if he had struck at her.

As he stared blankly, she turned, and laughed a humorless,

uncertain laugh; finally she breathed, "Don't think I'm being silly, don't be offended—but for your life's sake don't touch any human body you might come into contact with."

McAllister was conscious of a chill. It struck him with a sudden, sharp dismay that the expression of uneasiness in the girl's face was—fear!

His own fear fled before a wave of impatience. He controlled himself with an effort.

"Now, look," he began. "I want to get things clear. We can talk here without danger, providing I don't touch you or come near you. Is that straight?"

She nodded. "The floor, the walls, every piece of furniture, in fact the entire shop is made of perfect nonconducting material."

McAllister had a sudden sense of being balanced on a tightrope over a bottomless abyss. The way this girl could imply danger without making it clear what the danger was almost petrified him.

He forced calm into his mind. "Let's start," he said, "at the beginning. How did you and your father know my name, and that I was not of"—he paused before the odd phrase, then went on—"of this time?"

"Father X-rayed you," the girl said, her voice as stiff as her body. "He X-rayed the contents of your pockets. That was how he first found out what was the matter. You see, the X-rays themselves became carriers of the energy with which you're charged. That's what was the matter; that's why the automatics wouldn't focus on you, and—"

"Just a minute!" said McAllister. His brain was a spinning world. "Energy—charged?"

The girl was staring at him. "Don't you understand?" she gasped. "You've come across five thousand years of time; and of all the energies in the universe, time is the most potent. You're charged with trillions of trillions of time-energy units. If you should step outside this shop, you'd blow up this city of the Isher and half a hundred miles of land beyond.

"You"—she finished on an unsteady, upward surge of her voice—"you could conceivably destroy the Earth!"

He hadn't noticed the mirror before; funny, too, because it was large enough, at least eight feet high, and directly in front of him on the wall where a minute before—he could have sworn—had been solid metal.

"Look at yourself," the girl was saying soothingly. "There's nothing so steadying as one's own image. Actually your body is taking the mental shock very well."

It was! He stared in dimly gathering surprise at his image. There was a paleness in the lean face that stared back at him; but the body was not actually shaking as the whirling in his mind had suggested.

He grew aware again of the girl. She was standing with one finger on one of a series of wall switches. Abruptly, he felt better.

"Thank you," he said quietly. "I certainly needed that."

She smiled encouragingly; and he was able now to be amazed at her conflicting personality. There had been on the one hand her complete inability a few minutes earlier to get to the point of his danger, a distinct incapacity for explaining things with words; yet obviously her action with the mirror showed a keen understanding of human psychology. He said, "The problem now is, from your point of view, to circumvent this—Isher—woman, and to get me back to 1941 before I blow up the Earth of . . . of whatever year this is."

The girl nodded. "Father says that you can be sent back, but—as for the rest: watch!"

He had no time for relief at the knowledge that he could be returned to his own time. She pressed another button. Instantly the mirror was gone into the metallic wall. Another button clicked—and the wall vanished.

Literally vanished. Before him stretched a park similar to the one he had already seen through the front door—obviously an extension of the same garden-like vista. Trees were there, and flowers, and green, green grass in the sun.

There was also the city again, nearer from this side, but not so pretty, immeasurably grimmer.

One vast building, as high as it was long, massively dark against the sky, dominated the entire horizon. It was a good quarter-mile away; and incredibly, it was at least that long and that high.

Neither near that monstrous building nor in the park was a living person visible. Everywhere was evidence of man's dynamic labor—but no men, not a movement; even the trees stood motionless in that strangely breathless sunlit day.

"Watch!" said the girl again, more softly.

There was no click this time. She made an adjustment on one of the buttons; and suddenly the view was no longer so clear. It wasn't that the sun had dimmed its bright intensity. It wasn't even that glass was visible where a moment before there had been nothing.

There was still no apparent substance between them and the gemlike park. But—

The park was no longer deserted!

Scores of men and machines swarmed out there. McAllister stared in frank amazement; and then as the sense of illusion faded, and the dark menace of those men penetrated, his emotion changed to dismay.

"Why," he said at last, "those men are soldiers, and the machines are—"

"Energy guns!" she said. "That's always been their problem: how to get their weapons close enough to our shops to destroy us. It isn't that the guns are not powerful over a very great distance. Even the rifles we sell can kill unprotected life over a distance of miles; but our gun shops are so heavily fortified that, to destroy us, they must use their biggest cannon at point-blank range.

"In the past, they could never do that because we own the surrounding park; and our alarm system was perfect—until now. The new energy they're using affects none of our protective instruments; and—what is infinitely worse—affords them a perfect shield against our own guns. Invisibility, of course, has long been known; but if you hadn't come, we would have been destroyed without ever knowing what happened."

"But," McAllister exclaimed sharply, "what are you going to do? They're still out there working—"

Her brown eyes burned with a fierce, yellow flame. "Where do you think Father is?" she asked. "He's warned the guild; and every member has now discovered that similar invisible guns are being set up outside his place by invisible men. Every member is working at top speed for some solution. They haven't found it yet."

She finished quietly: "I thought I'd tell you."

McAllister cleared his throat, parted his lips to speak— then closed them as he realized that no words were even near his lips. Fascinated, he watched the soldiers connecting what must have been invisible cables that led to the vast building in the background: foot-thick cables that told of the titanic power that was to be unleashed on the tiny weapon shop.

There was actually nothing to be said. The deadly reality out there overshadowed all conceivable sentences and phrases. Of all the people here, he was the most useless, his opinion the least worthwhile.

Oddly, he must have spoken aloud, but he did not realize that until the familiar voice of the girl's father came from one side of him. The older man said, "You're quite mistaken, McAllister. Of all the people here you are the *most* valuable.

Through you we discovered that the Isher were actually attacking us. Furthermore, our enemies do not know of your existence, therefore have not yet realized the full effect produced by the new blanketing energy they have used.

"You, accordingly, constitute the unknown factor—our only hope, for the time left to us is incredibly short. Unless we can make immediate use of the unknown quantity you represent, all is lost!"

The man looked older, McAllister thought; there were lines of strain in his lean, sallow face as he turned toward his daughter; and his voice, when he spoke, was edged with harshness: "Lystra, number seven!"

As the girl's fingers touched the seventh button, her father explained swiftly to McAllister: "The guild supreme council is holding an immediate emergency session. We must choose the most likely method of attacking the problem, and concentrate individually and collectively on that method. Regional conversations are already in progress, but only one important idea has been put forward as yet . . . ah, gentlemen!"

He spoke past McAllister, who turned with a start, then froze.

Men were coming out of the solid wall, lightly, easily, as if it were a door and they were stepping across a threshold. One, two, three—twelve.

They were grim-faced men, all except one who glanced at McAllister, started to walk past, then stopped with a half-amused smile.

"Don't look so blank. How else do you think we could have survived these many years if we hadn't been able to transmit material objects through space? The Isher police have always been only too eager to blockade our sources of supply. Incidentally, my name is Cadron—Peter Cadron!"

McAllister nodded in a perfunctory manner. He was no longer genuinely impressed by the new machines. Here were endless products of the machine age; science and invention so stupendously advanced that men made scarcely a move that did not involve a machine. He grew aware that a heavy-faced man near him was about to speak.

The man began: "We are gathered here because it is obvious that the source of the new energy is the great building just outside this shop—"

He motioned toward the wall where the mirror had been a few minutes previously, and the window through which McAllister had gazed at the monstrous structure in question.

The speaker went on: "We've known, ever since that build-

ing was completed five years ago, that it was a power building aimed against us; and now from it new energy has flown
out to engulf the world, immensely potent energy, so strong
that it broke the very tension of time, fortunately only at this
nearest gun shop. Apparently it weakens when transmitted
over distance. It—"

"Look, Dresley!" came a curt interruption from a small,
thin man. "What good is all this preamble? You have been
examining the various plans put forward by regional groups.
Is there, or isn't there, a decent one among them?"

Dresley hesitated. To McAllister's surprise, the man's eyes
fixed doubtfully on him, his heavy face worked for a moment, then hardened.

"Yes, there is a method, but it depends on compelling our
friend from the past to take a great risk. You all know what
I'm referring to. It will gain us the time we need so desperately."

"Eh!" said McAllister, and stood stunned as all eyes turned
to stare at him.

The seconds fled; and it struck McAllister that what he
really needed again was the mirror—to prove to him that his
body was putting up a good front. Something, he thought,
something to steady him.

His gaze flicked over the faces of the men. The gunmakers
made a curious, confusing pattern in the way they sat, or
stood, or leaned against glass cases of shining guns; and there
seemed to be fewer than he had previously counted. One,
two—ten, including the girl. He could have sworn there had
been fourteen.

His eyes moved on, just in time to see the door of the back
room closing. Four of the men had obviously gone to the laboratory or whatever lay beyond the door. Satisfied, he forgot
them.

Still, he felt unsettled; and briefly his eyes were held by the
purely mechanical wonder of this shop, here in this vastly future world, a shop that was an intricate machine in itself
and—

He discovered that he was lighting a cigarette; and
abruptly realized that that was what he needed most. The first
puff tingled deliciously along his nerves. His mind grew calm;
his eyes played thoughtfully over the faces before him.

He said, "I can't understand how any one of you could
even think of compulsion. According to you, I'm loaded with
energy. I may be wrong, but if any of you should try to

thrust me back down the chute of time, or even touch me, that energy in me would do devastating things—"

"You're damned right!" chimed in a young man. He barked irritably at Dresley: "How the devil did you ever come to make such a psychological blunder? You know that McAllister will have to do as we want, to save himself; and he'll have to do it fast!"

Dresley grunted under the sharp attack. "Hell," he said, "the truth is we have no time to waste, and I just figured there wasn't time to explain, and that he might scare easily. I see, however, that we're dealing with an intelligent man."

McAllister's eyes narrowed over the group. There was something phony here. They were talking too much, wasting the very time they needed, as if they were marking time, waiting for something to happen.

He said sharply, "And don't give me any soft soap about being intelligent. You fellows are sweating blood. You'd shoot your own grandmothers and trick me into the bargain, because the world you think right is at stake. What's this plan of yours that you were going to compel me to participate in?"

It was the young man who replied: "You are to be given insulated clothes and sent back into your own time—"

He paused. McAllister said, "That sounds okay, so far. What's the catch?"

"There is no catch!"

McAllister stared. "Now, look here," he began, "don't give me any of that. If it's as simple as that, how the devil am I going to be helping you against the Isher energy?"

The young man scowled blackly at Dresley. "You see," he said to the other, "you've made him suspicious with the talk of yours about compulsion."

He faced McAllister. "What we have in mind is an application of a sort of an energy lever and fulcrum principle. You are to be a 'weight' at the long end of a kind of energy 'crowbar,' which lifts the greater 'weight' at the short end. You will go back five thousand years in time; the machine in the great building to which your body is tuned, and which has caused all this trouble, will move ahead in time about two weeks."

"In that way," interrupted another man before McAllister could speak, "we shall have time to find a counteragent. There must be a solution, else our enemies would not have acted so secretly. Well, what do you think?"

McAllister walked slowly over to the chair that he had oc-

cupied previously. His mind was turning at furious speed, but
he knew with a grim foreboding that he hadn't a fraction of
the technical knowledge necessary to safeguard his interests.

He said slowly, "As I see it, this is supposed to work something like a pump handle. The lever principle, the old idea
that if you had a lever long enough, and a suitable fulcrum,
you could move the Earth out of its orbit."

"Exactly!" It was the heavy-faced Dresley who spoke.
"Only this works in time. You go five thousand years, the
building goes a few wee . . ."

His voice faded, his eagerness drained from him as he
caught the expression on McAllister's face.

"Look!" said McAllister, "there's nothing more pitiful than
a bunch of honest men engaged in their first act of dishonesty. You're strong men, the intellectual type, who've spent
your lives enforcing an idealistic conception. You've always
told yourself that if the occasion should ever require it, you
would not hesitate to make drastic sacrifices. But you're not
fooling anybody. *What's the catch?*"

It was quite startling to have the suit thrust at him. He
hadn't observed the men emerge from the back room; and it
came as a distinct shock to realize that they had actually
gone for the insulated clothes before they could have known
that he would use them.

McAllister stared grimly at Peter Cadron, who held the
dull, grayish, limp thing toward him. A very flame of abrupt
rage held him choked; before he could speak, Cadron said in
a tight voice, "Get into this, and get going! It's a matter of
minutes, man! When those guns out there start spraying energy, you won't be alive to argue about our honesty."

Still he hesitated; the room seemed insufferably hot; and he
was sick—sick with the deadly uncertainty. Perspiration
streaked stingingly down his cheeks. His frantic gaze fell on
the girl, standing silent and subdued in the background, near
the front door.

He strode toward her; and either his glare or presence was
incredibly frightening, for she cringed and turned white as a
sheet.

"Look!" he said. "I'm in this as deep as hell. What's the
risk in this thing? I've got to feel that I have some chance.
Tell me, what's the catch?"

The girl was gray now, almost as gray and dead-looking as
the suit Peter Cadron was holding. "It's the friction," she

mumbled finally, "you may not get all the way back to 1941. You see, you'll be a sort of 'weight' and—"

McAllister whirled away from her. He climbed into the soft, almost flimsy suit, crowding the overall-like shape over his neatly pressed clothes. "It comes tight over the head, doesn't it?" he asked.

"Yes!" It was Lystra's father who answered. "As soon as you pull that zipper shut, the suit will become completely invisible. To outsiders it will seem just as if you have your ordinary clothes on. The suit is fully equipped. You could live on the moon inside it."

"What I don't get," complained McAllister, "is why I have to wear it. I got here all right without it."

He frowned. His words had been automatic, but abruptly a thought came: "Just a minute. What becomes of the energy with which I'm charged when I'm bottled up in this insulation?"

He saw by the stiffening expressions of those around him that he had touched on a vast subject.

"So that's it!" he snapped. "The insulation is to prevent me losing any of that energy. That's how it can make a 'weight.' I have no doubt there's a connection from this suit to that other machine. Well, it's not too late. It's—"

With a desperate twist, he tried to jerk aside, to evade the clutching hands of the four men who leaped at him. Hopeless movement! They had him instantly; and their grips on him were strong beyond his power to break.

The fingers of Peter Cadron jerked the zipper tight, and Peter Cadron said, "Sorry, but when we went into that back room, we also dressed in insulated clothing. That's why you couldn't hurt us. Sorry, again!

"And remember this: There's no certainty that you are being sacrificed. The fact that there is no crater in *our* Earth proves that you did not explode in the past, and that you solved the problem in some other way. *Now, somebody open the door, quick!*"

Irresistibly he was carried forward. And then—

"Wait!"

It was the girl. The colorless gray in her face was a livid thing. Her eyes glittered like dark jewels; and in her fingers was the tiny, mirror-bright gun she had pointed in the beginning at McAllister.

The little group hustling McAllister stopped as if they had been struck. He was scarcely aware; for him there was only the girl, and the way the muscles of her lips were working, and the way her voice suddenly flamed: "This is utter outrage. Are we such cowards—is it possible that the spirit of liberty can survive only through a shoddy act of murder and gross defiance of the rights of the individual? I say no! Mr. McAllister must have the protection of the hypnotism treatment, even if we die during the wasted minutes."

"Lystra!" It was her father; and McAllister realized in the swift movement of the older man what a brilliant mind was there, and how quickly the older man grasped every aspect of the situation.

He stepped forward and took the gun from his daughter's fingers—the only man in the room, McAllister thought flashingly, who could dare approach her in that moment with the certainty she would not fire. For hysteria was in every line of her face, and the racking tears that followed showed how dangerous her stand might have been against the others.

Strangely, not for a moment had hope come. The entire action seemed divorced from his life and his thought; there was only the observation of it. He stood there for a seeming eternity and, when emotion finally came, it was surprise that he was not being hustled to his doom. With the surprise came awareness that Peter Cadron had let go his arm and stepped clear of him.

The man's eyes were calm, his head held proudly erect; he said, "Your daughter is right, sir. At this point we rise above our petty fears, and we say to this unhappy man: 'Have courage! You will not be forgotten. We can guarantee nothing, cannot even state exactly what will happen to you. But we say: if it lies in our power to help you, that help you shall have.' And now—we must protect you from the devastating psychological pressures that would otherwise destroy you, simply but effectively."

Too late, McAllister noticed that the others had turned faces away from that extraordinary wall—the wall that had already displayed so vast a versatility. He did not even see who pressed the activating button for what followed.

There was a flash of dazzling light. For an instant he felt as if his mind had been laid bare; and against that nakedness the voice of Peter Cadron pressed like some ineradicable engraving stamp: "To retain your self-control and your sanity—this is your hope: this you will do in spite of everything! And, for your sake, speak of your experience only to scientists or to those in authority who you feel will understand and help. Good luck!"

So strong remained the effect of that brief flaring light that he felt only vaguely the touch of their hands on him, propelling him. He must have fallen, but there was no pain—

He grew aware that he was lying on a sidewalk. The deep, familiar voice of Police Inspector Clayton boomed over him: "Clear the way; no crowding now!"

McAllister climbed to his feet. A pall of curious faces gawked at him; and there was no park, no gorgeous city. Instead, a bleak row of one-story shops made a dull pattern on either side of the street.

He'd have to get away from here. These people didn't understand. Somewhere on Earth must be a scientist who could help him. After all, the record was that he hadn't exploded. Therefore, somewhere, somehow—

He mumbled answers at the questions that beat at him; and then he was clear of the disappointed crowd. There followed purposeless minutes of breakneck walking; the streets ahead grew narrower, dirtier—

He stopped, shaken. What was happening?

It was night, in a brilliant, glowing city. He was standing on an avenue that stretched jewel-like into remote distance.

A street that lived, flaming with a soft light that gleamed up from its surface—a road of light, like a river flowing under a sun that shone nowhere else, straight and smooth and—

He walked along for uncomprehending minutes, watching the cars that streamed past—and wild hope came!

Was this again the age of the Isher and the gunmakers? It could be; it looked right, and it meant they had brought him back. After all, they were not evil, and they would save him if they could. For all he knew, weeks had passed in their time and—

Abruptly, he was in the center of a blinding snowstorm. He staggered from the first, mighty, unexpected blow of that untamed wind, then, bracing himself, fought for mental and physical calm.

The shining, wondrous night city was gone; gone too the glowing road—both vanished, transformed into this deadly, wilderness world.

He peered through the driving snow. It was daylight; and he could make out the dim shadows of trees that reared up through the white mist of blizzard less than fifty feet away.

Instinctively he pressed toward their shelter, and stood finally out of that blowing, pressing wind.

He thought: One minute in the distant future; the next— where?

There was certainly no city. Only trees, an uninhabited forest and winter—

The blizzard was gone. And the trees. He stood on a sandy beach; before him stretched a blue, sunlit sea that rippled over broken white buildings. All around, scattered far into that shallow, lovely sea, far up into the weed-grown hills, were the remnants of a once tremendous city. Over all clung an aura of incredible age; and the silence of the long-dead was broken only by the gentle, timeless lapping of the waves—

Again came that instantaneous change. More prepared this time, he nevertheless sank twice under the surface of the vast, swift river that carried him on and on. It was hard swimming, but the insulated suit was buoyant with the air it manufactured each passing second; and, after a moment, he began to struggle purposefully toward the tree-lined shore a hundred feet to his right.

A thought came, and he stopped swimming. "What's the use!"

The truth was as simple as it was terrible. He was being shunted from the past to the future; he was the "weight" on the long end of an energy seesaw; and in some way he was slipping farther ahead and farther back each time. Only that could explain the catastrophic changes he had already witnessed. In a minute would come another change and—

It came! He was lying face downward on green grass, but there was no curiosity in him. He did not look up, but lay there hour after hour as the seesaw jerked on: past—future—past—future—

Beyond doubt, the gunmakers had won their respite; for at the far end of this dizzy teeter-totter was the machine that had been used by the Isher soldiers as an activating force; it too teetered up, then down, in a mad seesaw.

There remained the gunmakers' promise to help him, vain now; for they could not know what had happened. They could not find him even in this maze of time.

There remained the mechanical law that forces must balance.

Somewhere, sometime, a balance would be struck, probably in the future—because there was still the fact that he hadn't exploded in the past. Yes, somewhere would come the balance when he would again face *that* problem. But now—

On, on, on the seesaw flashed; the world on the one hand grew bright with youth, and on the other dark with fantastic age.

Infinity yawned blackly ahead.

Quite suddenly it came to him that he knew where the seesaw would stop. It would end in the very remote past, with the release of the stupendous temporal energy he had been accumulating with each of those monstrous swings.

He would not witness, but he would cause, the formation of the planets.

ARMAGEDDON

Unknown
August

by Fredric Brown (1906-1972)

Fredric Brown was one of the most talented professionals in the history of science fiction. A well known mystery writer (he was a winner of the Edgar Award of the MWA), in the sf field he is best remembered for his short-shorts, but he produced excellent work at all lengths. His novel What Mad Universe *(book form, 1949) remains one of the outstanding satires on the science fiction field— and much of it still hurts!*

There have been too many end-of-the-world stories. Here is a beautiful example of the rare almost-the-end-of-the-world tale, told as only Brown could tell it—with his tongue firmly in his cheek.

(I suppose Fred Brown is the acknowledged master of the short-short. When Marty and I, along with Joe Olander, put out our recent *One Hundred S. F. Short Short Stories*, there were none included by Fred Brown for the simple reason that we could not get permissions for any. —That was the reason, wasn't it, Marty?—In any case, more than one reviewer shook his head over the omission, feeling it was a measure of our lack of good taste, and I couldn't help but feel that that was the way it indeed looked.—I. A.)

It happened—of all places—in Cincinnati. Not that there is anything wrong with Cincinnati, save that it is not the center of the Universe, nor even of the State of Ohio. It's a nice old town and, in its way, second to none. But even its Chamber of Commerce would admit that it lacks cosmic significance. It must have been mere coincidence that Gerber the Great— what a name!—was playing Cincinnati when things slipped elsewhere.

Of course, if the episode had become known, Cincinnati would be the most famous city of the world, and little Herbie

231

would be hailed as a modern St. George and get more acclaim than a quiz kid. But no member of that audience in the
Bijou Theater remembers a thing about it. Not even little
Herbie Westerman, although he had the water pistol to show
for it.

He wasn't thinking about the water pistol in his pocket as
he sat looking up at the prestidigitator on the other side of
the footlights. It was a new water pistol, bought en route to
the theater when he'd inveigled his parents into a side trip
into the five-and-dime on Vine Street, but at the moment,
Herbie was much more interested in what went on upon the
stage.

His expression registered qualified approval. The front-
and-back palm was no mystery to Herbie. He could do it
himself. True, he had to use pony-sized cards that came with
his magic set and were just right for his nine-year-old hands.
And true, anyone watching could see the card flutter from
the front-palm position to the back as he turned his hand.
But that was a detail.

He knew, though, that front-and-back palming seven cards
at a time required great finger strength as well as dexterity,
and that was what Gerber the Great was doing. There wasn't
a telltale click in the shift, either, and Herbie nodded ap-
probation. Then he remembered what was coming next.

He nudged his mother and said, "Ma, ask Pop if he's gotta
extra handkerchief."

Out of the corner of his eyes, Herbie saw his mother turn
her head and in less time than it would take to say, "Presto,"
Herbie was out of his seat and skinning down the aisle. It
had been, he felt, a beautiful piece of misdirection and his
timing had been perfect.

It was at this stage of the performance—which Herbie had
seen before, alone—that Gerber the Great asked if some little
boy from the audience would step to the stage. He was
asking it now.

Herbie Westerman had jumped the gun. He was well in
motion before the magician had asked the question. At the
previous performance, he'd been a bad tenth in reaching the
steps from aisle to stage. This time he'd been ready, and he
hadn't taken any chances with parental restraint. Perhaps his
mother would have let him go and perhaps not; it had
seemed wiser to see that she was looking the other way. You
couldn't trust parents on things like that. They had funny
ideas sometimes.

"—will please step up on the stage?" And Herbie's foot

touched the first of the steps upward right smack on the interrogation point of that sentence. He heard the disappointed scuffle of other feet behind him, and grinned smugly as he went on up across the footlights.

It was the three-pigeon trick, Herbie knew from the previous performance, that required an assistant from the audience. It was almost the only trick he hadn't been able to figure out. There *must*, he knew, have been a concealed compartment somewhere in that box, but where it could be he couldn't even guess. But this time he'd be holding the box himself. If from that range he couldn't spot the gimmick, he'd better go back to stamp collecting.

He grinned confidently up at the magician. Not that he, Herbie, would give him away. He was a magician, too, and he understood that there was a freemasonry among magicians and that one never gave away the tricks of another.

He felt a little chilled, though, and the grin faded as he caught the magician's eyes. Gerber the Great, at close range, seemed much older than he had seemed from the other side of the footlights. And somehow different. Much taller, for one thing.

Anyway, here came the box for the pigeon trick. Gerber's regular assistant was bringing it in on a tray. Herbie looked away from the magician's eyes and he felt better. He remembered, even, his reason for being on the stage. The servant limped. Herbie ducked his head to catch a glimpse of the under side of the tray, just in case. Nothing there.

Gerber took the box. The servant limped away and Herbie's eyes followed him suspiciously. Was the limp genuine or was it a piece of misdirection?

The box folded out flat as the proverbial pancake. All four sides hinged to the bottom, the top hinged to one of the sides. There were little brass catches.

Herbie took a quick step back so he could see behind it while the front was displayed to the audience. Yes, he saw it now. A triangular compartment built against one side of the lid, mirror-covered, angles calculated to achieve invisibility. Old stuff. Herbie felt a little disappointed.

The prestidigitator folded the box, mirror-concealed compartment inside. He turned slightly. "Now, my fine young man—"

What happened in Tibet wasn't the only factor; it was merely the final link of a chain.

The Tibetan weather had been unusual that week, highly unusual. It had been warm. More snow succumbed to the gentle warmth than had melted in more years than man could count. The streams ran high, they ran wide and fast.

Along the streams some prayer wheels whirled faster than they had ever whirled. Others, submerged, stopped altogether. The priests, knee-deep in the cold water, worked frantically, moving the wheels nearer to shore where again the rushing torrent would turn them.

There was one small wheel, a very old one that had revolved without cease for longer than any man knew. So long had it been there that no living lama recalled what had been inscribed upon its prayer plate, nor what had been the purpose of that prayer.

The rushing water had neared its axle when the lama Klarath reached for it to move it to safety. Just too late. His foot slid in the slippery mud and the back of his hand touched the wheel as he fell. Knocked loose from its moorings, it swirled down with the flood, rolling along the bottom of the stream, into deeper and deeper waters.

While it rolled, all was well.

The lama rose, shivering from his momentary immersion, and went after other of the spinning wheels. What, he thought, could one small wheel matter? He didn't know that—now that other links had broken—only that tiny thing stood between Earth and Armageddon.

The prayer wheel of Wangur Ul rolled on, and on, until— a mile farther down—it struck a ledge, and stopped. That was the moment.

"And now, my fine young man—"

Herbie Westerman—we're back in Cincinnati now—looked up, wondering why the prestidigitator had stopped in mid-sentence. He saw the face of Gerber the Great contorted as though by a great shock. Without moving, without changing, his face began to change. Without appearing different, it became different.

Quietly, then, the magician began to chuckle. In the overtones of that soft laughter was all of evil. No one who heard it could have doubted who he was. No one did doubt. The audience, every member of it, knew in that awful moment who stood before them, knew it—even the most skeptical among them—beyond shadow of doubt.

No one moved, no one spoke, none drew a shuddering breath. There are things beyond fear. Only uncertainty causes fear, and the Bijou Theater was filled, then, with a dreadful certainty.

The laughter grew. Crescendo, it reverberated into the far dusty corners of the gallery. Nothing—not a fly on the ceiling—moved.

Satan spoke.

"I thank you for your kind attention to a poor magician." He bowed, ironically low. "The performance is ended."

He smiled. "All performances are ended."

Somehow the theater seemed to darken, although the electric lights still burned. In dead silence, there seemed to be the sound of wings, leathery wings, as though invisible Things were gathering.

On the stage was a dim red radiance. From the head and from each shoulder of the tall figure of the magician there sprang a tiny flame. A naked flame.

There were other flames. They flickered along the proscenium of the stage, along the footlights. One sprang from the lid of the folded box little Herbie Westerman still held in his hands.

Herbie dropped the box.

Did I mention that Herbie Westerman was a Safety Cadet? It was purely a reflex action. A boy of nine doesn't know much about things like Armageddon, but Herbie Westerman should have known that water would never have put out that fire.

But, as I said, it was purely a reflex action. He yanked out his new water pistol and squirted it at the box of the pigeon trick. And the fire *did* vanish, even as a spray from the stream of water ricocheted and dampened the trouser leg of Gerber the Great, who had been facing the other way.

There was a sudden, brief hissing sound. The lights were growing bright again, and all the other flames were dying, and the sound of wings faded, blended into another sound—rustling of the audience.

The eyes of the prestidigitator were closed. His voice sounded strangely strained as he said: "This much power I retain. None of you will remember this."

Then, slowly, he turned and picked up the fallen box. He held it out to Herbie Westerman. "You must be more careful, boy," he said. "Now hold it so."

He tapped the top lightly with his wand. The door fell open. Three white pigeons flew out of the box. The rustle of their wings was not leathery.

Herbie Westerman's father came down the stairs and, with

a purposeful air, took his razor strop off the hook on the kitchen wall.

Mrs. Westerman looked up from stirring the soup on the stove. "Why, Henry," she asked, "are you really going to punish him with that—just for squirting a little water out of the window of the car on the way home?"

Her husband shook his head grimly. "Not for that, Marge. But don't you remember we bought him that water gun on the way downtown, and that he wasn't near a water faucet after that? Where do you think he filled it?"

He didn't wait for an answer. "When we stopped in at the cathedral to talk to Father Ryan about his confirmation, that's when the little brat filled it. Out of the baptismal font! Holy water he uses in his water pistol!"

He clumped heavily up the stairs, strop in hand.

Rhythmic thwacks and wails of pain floated down the staircase. Herbie—who had saved the world—was having his reward.

ADAM AND NO EVE

Astounding Science Fiction
September

by Alfred Bester (1913-   )

Alfred Bester really came into his own after World War II, with stories like "The Men Who Murdered Mohammed," "Time Is the Traitor," and the spectacular novels, The Demolished Man *(in* Galaxy, *1952) and* The Stars My Destination *(1956), both considered among the finest in modern science fiction. Bester had (he is still writing) a varied career, dropping in and out of the sf field while working for the comics, television, and* Holiday *magazine. An astute observer of science fiction, he was one of the field's best critics as book reviewer for* The Magazine of Fantasy and Science Fiction *from 1960 to 1962. Alfred Bester was a "New Wave" writer long before the term became fashionable.*

"Adam and No Eve" remains one of his best stories, and one of the finest early tales of "inner space."

(I didn't meet Alfie Bester till long after this story was written—and goodness, how it impressed me. I can still quote the formula. When I did meet him, I instantly found he could be classified into the group of "Writers who have personalities like the stories they write." Others are L. Sprague de Camp and Lester Del Rey. Of course, there is the group of "Writers who don't have personalities like the stories they write," such as Frederic Brown and Theodore Sturgeon. Naturally, I realize that this is subjective and that other people will group different writers into each of the two groups. I don't know which group I belong, by the way.—I.A.)

Crane knew this must be the seacoast. Instinct told him; but more than instinct, the few shreds of knowledge that clung to his torn, feverish brain told him; the stars that had shown at night through the rare breaks in the clouds, and his compass that still pointed a trembling finger north. That was strangest of all, Crane thought. Though a welter of chaos, the Earth still retained its polarity.

It was no longer a coast; there was no longer any sea. Only the faint line of what had been a cliff, stretching north and south for endless miles. A line of gray ash. The same gray ash and cinders that lay behind him; the same gray ash that stretched before him. Fine silt, knee-deep, that swirled up at every motion and choked him. Cinders that scudded in dense mighty clouds when the mad winds blew. Cinders that were churned to viscous mud when the frequent rains fell.

The sky was jet overhead. The black clouds rode high and were pierced with shafts of sunlight that marched swiftly over the Earth. Where the light struck a cinder storm, it was filled with gusts of dancing, gleaming particles. Where it played through rain it brought the arches of rainbows into being. Rain fell; cinder storms blew; light thrust down—together, alternately and continually in a jigsaw of black and white violence. So it had been for months. So it was over every mile of the broad Earth.

Crane passed the edge of the ashen cliffs and began crawling down the even slope that had once been the ocean bed. He had been traveling so long that all sense of pain had left him. He braced elbows and dragged his body forward. Then he brought his right knee under him and reached forward with elbows again. Elbows, knee, elbows, knee— He had forgotten what it was to walk.

Life, he thought dazedly, is wonderful. It adapts itself to anything. If it must crawl, it crawls. Callus forms on the elbows and knees. The neck and shoulders toughen. The nostrils learn to snort away the ashes before they inhale. The bad leg swells and festers. It numbs, and presently it will rot and fall off.

"I beg pardon," Crane said, "I didn't quite get that—"

He peered up at the tall figure before him and tried to understand the words. It was Hallmyer. He wore his stained lab jacket and his gray hair was awry. Hallmyer stood delicately on top of the ashes and Crane wondered why he could see the scudding cinder clouds through his body.

"How do you like your world, Stephen?" Hallmyer asked.

Crane shook his head miserably.

"Not very pretty, eh?" said Hallmyer. "Look around you.

Dust, that's all; dust and ashes. Crawl, Stephen, crawl. You'll find nothing but dust and ashes—"

Hallmyer produced a goblet of water from nowhere. It was clear and cold. Crane could see the fine mist of dew on its surface and his mouth was suddenly coated with dry grit.

"Hallmyer!" he cried. He tried to get to his feet and reach for the water, but the jolt of pain in his right leg warned him. He crouched back.

Hallmyer sipped and then spat in his face. The water felt warm.

"Keep crawling," said Hallmyer bitterly. "Crawl round and round the face of the Earth. You'll find nothing but dust and ashes—" He emptied the goblet on the ground before Crane. "Keep crawling. How many miles? Figure it out for yourself. Pi-R-Square. The radius is eight thousand or so—"

He was gone, jacket and goblet. Crane realized that rain was falling again. He pressed his face into the warm sodden cinder mud, opened his mouth and tried to suck the moisture. He groaned and presently began crawling.

There was an instinct that drove him on. He had to get somewhere. It was associated, he knew, with the sea—with the edge of the sea. At the shore of the sea something waited for him. Something that would help him understand all this. He had to get to the sea—that is, if there was a sea any more.

The thundering rain beat his back like heavy planks. Crane paused and yanked the knapsack around to his side where he probed in it with one hand. It contained exactly three things. A pistol, a bar of chocolate and a can of peaches. All that was left of two months' supplies. The chocolate was pulpy and spoiled. Crane knew he had best eat it before all value rotted away. But in another day he would lack the strength to open the can. He pulled it out and attacked it with the opener. By the time he had pierced and pried away a flap of tin, the rain had passed.

As he munched the fruit and sipped the juice, he watched the wall of rain marching before him down the slope of the ocean bed. Torrents of water were gushing through the mud. Small channels had already been cut—channels that would be new rivers some day. A day he would never see. A day that no living thing would ever see. As he flipped the empty can aside, Crane thought: The last living thing on Earth eats its last meal. Metabolism plays its last act.

Wind would follow the rain. In the endless weeks that he

had been crawling, he had learned that. Wind would come in a few minutes and flog him with its clouds of cinders and ashes. He crawled forward, bleary eyes searching the flat gray miles for cover.

Evelyn tapped his shoulder.

Crane knew it was she before he turned his head. She stood alongside, fresh and gay in her bright dress, but her lovely face was puckered with alarm.

"Stephen," she cried, "you've got to hurry!"

He could only admire the way her smooth honey hair waved to her shoulders.

"Oh, darling!" she said, "you've been hurt!" Her quick gentle hands touched his legs and back. Crane nodded.

"Got it landing," he said. "I wasn't used to a parachute. I always thought you came down gently—like plumping onto a bed. But the gray earth came up at me like a fist—And Umber was fighting around in my arms. I couldn't let him drop, could I?"

"Of course not, dear—" Evelyn said.

"So I just held on to him and tried to get my legs under me," Crane said. "And then something smashed my legs and side—"

He paused, wondering how much she knew of what really had happened. He didn't want to frighten her.

"Evelyn, darling—" he said, trying to reach up his arms.

"No dear," she said. She looked back in fright. "You've got to hurry. You've got to watch out behind!"

"The cinder storms?" He grimaced. "I've been through them before."

"Not the storms!" Evelyn cried. "Something else. Oh, Stephen—"

Then she was gone, but Crane knew she had spoken the truth. There was something behind—something that had been following him all those weeks. Far in the back of his mind he had sensed the menace. It was closing in on him like a shroud. He shook his head. Somehow that was impossible. He was the last living thing on Earth. How could there be a menace?

The wind roared behind him, and an instant later came the heavy clouds of cinders and ashes. They lashed over him, biting his skin. With dimming eyes, he saw the way they coated the mud and covered it with a fine dry carpet. Crane drew his knees under him and covered his head with his arms. With the knapsack as a pillow, he prepared to wait out the storm. It would pass as quickly as the rain.

The storm whipped up a great bewilderment in his sick head. Like a child he pushed at the pieces of his memory, trying to fit them together. Why was Hallmyer so bitter toward him? It couldn't have been that argument, could it?

What argument?

Why, that one before all this happened.

Oh, that!

Abruptly, the pieces fit themselves together.

Crane stood alongside the sleek lines of his ship and admired it tremendously. The roof of the shed had been removed and the nose of the ship hoisted so that it rested on a cradle pointed toward the sky. A workman was carefully burnishing the inner surfaces of the rocket jets.

The muffled sounds of an argument came from within the ship and then a heavy clanking. Crane ran up the short iron ladder to the port and thrust his head inside. A few feet beneath him, two men were buckling the long tanks of ferrous solution into place.

"Easy there," Crane called. "Want to knock the ship apart?"

One looked up and grinned. Crane knew what he was thinking. That the ship would tear itself apart. Everyone said that. Everyone except Evelyn. She had faith in him. Hallmyer never said it either. But Hallmyer thought he was crazy in another way. As he descended the ladder, Crane saw Hallmyer come into the shed, lab jacket flying.

"Speak of the devil!" Crane muttered.

Hallmyer began shouting as soon as he saw Crane. "Now listen—"

"Not all over again," Crane said.

Hallmyer dug a sheaf of papers out of his pocket and waved it under Crane's nose.

"I've been up half the night," he said, "working it through again. I tell you I'm right. I'm absolutely right—"

Crane looked at the tight-written equations and then at Hallmyer's bloodshot eyes. The man was half mad with fear.

"For the last time," Hallmyer went on. "You're using your new catalyst on iron solution. All right. I grant that it's a miraculous discovery. I give you credit for that."

Miraculous was hardly the word for it. Crane knew that without conceit, for he realized he'd only stumbled on it. You had to stumble on a catalyst that would induce atomic disintegration of iron and give 10×10^{10} foot-pounds of energy for every gram of fuel. No man was smart enough to think all that up by himself.

"You don't think I'll make it?" Crane asked.

"To the moon? Around the moon? Maybe. You've got a fifty-fifty chance." Hallmyer ran fingers through his lank hair. "But for God's sake, Stephen, I'm not worried about you. If you want to kill yourself, that's your own affair. It's the Earth I'm worried about—"

"Nonsense. Go home and sleep it off."

"Look"—Hallmyer pointed to the sheets of paper with a shaky hand—"no matter how you work the feed and mixing system you can't get one hundred percent efficiency in the mixing and discharge."

"That's what makes it a fifty-fifty chance," Crane said. "So what's bothering you?"

"The catalyst that will escape through the rocket tubes. Do you realize what it'll do if a drop hits the Earth? It'll start a chain of iron disintegrations that'll envelope the globe. It'll reach out to every iron atom—and there's iron everywhere. There won't be any Earth left for you to return to—"

"Listen," Crane said wearily, "we've been through all this before."

He took Hallmyer to the base of the rocket cradle. Beneath the iron framework was a two-hundred-foot pit, fifty feet wide and lined with firebrick.

"That's for the initial discharge flames. If any of the catalyst goes through, it'll be trapped in this pit and taken care of by the secondary reactions. Satisfied now?"

"But while you're in flight," Hallmyer persisted, "you'll be endangering the Earth until you're beyond Roche's limit. Every drop of non-activated catalyst will eventually sink back to the ground and—"

"For the very last time," Crane said grimly, "the flame of the rocket discharge takes care of that. It will envelop any escaped particles and destroy them. Now get out. I've got work to do."

As he pushed him to the door, Hallmyer screamed and waved his arms. "I won't let you do it!" he repeated over and over. "I'll find some way to stop you. I won't let you do it—"

Work? No, it was sheer intoxication to labor over the ship. It had the fine beauty of a well-made thing. The beauty of polished armor, of a balanced swept-hilt rapier, of a pair of matched guns. There was no thought of danger and death in Crane's mind as he wiped his hands with waste after the last touches were finished.

She lay in the cradle ready to pierce the skies. Fifty feet of slender steel, the rivet heads gleaming like jewels. Thirty feet were given over to fuel the catalyst. Most of the forward compartment contained the spring hammock Crane had devised to take up the initial acceleration shock. The ship's nose was a solid mass of natural quartz that stared upward like a cyclopian eye.

Crane thought: She'll die after this trip. She'll return to the Earth and smash in a blaze of fire and thunder, for there's no way yet of devising a safe landing for a rocket ship. But it's worth it. She'll have had her one great flight, and that's all any of us should want. One great beautiful flight into the unknown—

As he locked the workshop door, Crane heard Hallmyer shouting from the cottage across the fields. Through the evening gloom he could see him waving frantically. He trotted through the crisp stubble, breathing the sharp air deeply, grateful to be alive.

"It's Evelyn on the phone," Hallmyer said.

Crane stared at him. Hallmyer was acting peculiarly. He refused to meet his eyes.

"What's the idea?" Crane asked. "I thought we agreed that she wasn't to call—wasn't to get in touch with me until I was ready to start? You been putting ideas into her head? Is this the way you're going to stop me?"

Hallmyer said, "No—" and studiously examined the indigo horizon.

Crane went into his study and picked up the phone.

"Now, listen, darling," he said without preamble, "there's no sense getting alarmed now. I explained everything very carefully. Just before the ship crashes, I take to a parachute and float down as happy and gentle as Wynken, Blynken and Nod. I love you very much and I'll see you Wednesday when I start. So long—"

"Good-bye, sweetheart," Evelyn's clear voice said, "and is that what you called me for?"

"Called you!"

A brown hulk disengaged itself from the hearth rug and lifted itself to strong legs. Umber, Crane's Great Dane, sniffed and cocked an ear. Then he whined.

"Did you say I called you?" Crane shouted.

Umber's throat suddenly poured forth a bellow. He reached Crane in a single bound, looked up into his face and whined and roared all at once.

"Shut up, you monster!" Crane said. He pushed Umber away with his foot.

"Give Umber a kick for me," Evelyn laughed. "Yes, dear. Someone called and said you wanted to speak to me."

"They did, eh? Look, honey, I'll call you back—"

Crane hung up. He arose doubtfully and watched Umber's uneasy actions. Through the windows, the late evening glow sent flickering shadows of orange light. Umber gazed at the light, sniffed and bellowed again. Suddenly struck, Crane leaped to the window.

Across the fields a solid mass of flame thrust high into the air, and within it was the fast-crumbling walls of the workshop. Silhouetted against the blaze, the figure of half a dozen men darted and ran.

"Good heavens!" Crane cried.

He shot out of the cottage and with Umber hard at his heels, sprinted toward the shed. As he ran he could see the graceful nose of the spaceship within the core of heat, still looking cool and untouched. If only he could reach it before the flames softened its metal and started the rivets.

The workmen trotted up to him, grimy and panting. Crane gaped at them in a mixture of fury and bewilderment.

"Hallmyer!" he shouted. "Hallmyer!"

Hallmyer pushed through the crowd. His eyes were wild and gleamed with triumph.

"Too bad," he said. "I'm sorry, Stephen—"

"You swine!" Crane shouted. "You frightened old man!" He grasped Hallmyer by the lapels and shook him just once. Then he dropped him and started into the shed.

Hallmyer cried something and an instant later a body hurtled against Crane's calves and spilled him to the ground. He lurched to his feet, fists swinging. Umber was alongside, growling over the roar of the flames. Crane smashed a man in the face, and saw him stagger back against a second. He lifted a knee in a vicious drive that sent the last man crumpling to the ground. Then he ducked his head and plunged into the shop.

The scorch felt cool at first, but when he reached the ladder and began mounting to the port, he screamed with the agony of his burns. Umber was howling at the foot of the ladder, and Crane realized that the dog could never escape from the rocket blasts. He reached down and hauled Umber into the ship.

Crane was reeling as he closed and locked the port. He retained consciousness barely long enough to settle himself in the spring hammock. Then instinct alone prompted his hands to reach out toward the control board. Instinct and the frenzied refusal to let his beautiful ship waste itself in the flames. He would fail— Yes. But he would fail, trying.

His fingers tripped the switches. The ship shuddered and roared. And blackness descended over him.

How long was he unconscious? There was no telling. Crane awoke with cold pressing against his face and body, and the sound of frightened yelps in his ears. Crane looked up and saw Umber tangled in the springs and straps of the hammock. His first impulse was to laugh; then suddenly he realized. He had looked *up!* He had looked up at the hammock.

He was lying curled in the cup of the quartz nose. The ship had risen high—perhaps almost to Roche's zone, to the limit of the Earth's gravitational attraction, but then without guiding hands at the controls to continue its flight, had turned and was dropping back toward Earth. Crane peered through the crystal and gasped.

Below him was the ball of the Earth. It looked three times the size of the moon. And it was no longer his Earth. It was a globe of fire mottled with black clouds. At the northernmost pole there was a tiny patch of white, and even as Crane watched, it was suddenly blotted over with hazy tones of red, scarlet and crimson. Hallmyer had been right.

He lay frozen in the cup of the nose for hours as the ship descended, watching the flames gradually fade away to leave nothing but the dense blanket of black around the Earth. He lay numb with horror, unable to understand—unable to reckon up a billion people snuffed out, a green fair planet reduced to ashes and cinders. His family, home, friends, everything that was once dear and close to him—gone. He could not think of Evelyn.

Air, whistling outside, awoke some instinct in him. The few shreds of reason left told him to go down with his ship and forget everything in the thunder and destruction, but the instinct of life forced him to his feet. He climbed up to the store chest and prepared for the landing. Parachute, a small oxygen tank—a knapsack of supplies. Only half aware of what he was doing he dressed for the descent, buckled on the 'chute and opened the port. Umber whined pathetically, and he took the heavy dog in his arms and stepped out into space.

But space hadn't been so clogged, the way it was now. Then it had been difficult to breathe. But that was because the air had been rare—not filled with dry clogging grit like now.

Every breath was a lungful of ground glass—or ashes—or cinders—

The pieces of memory sagged apart. Abruptly he was in the present again—a dense black present that hugged him with soft weight and made him fight for breath. Crane struggled in mad panic, and then relaxed.

It had happened before. A long time past he'd been buried deep under ashes when he'd stopped to remember. Weeks ago—or days—or months. Crane clawed with his hands, inching forward through the mound of cinders that the wind had thrown over him. Presently he emerged into the light again. The wind had died away. It was time to begin his crawl to the sea once more.

The vivid pictures of his memory scattered again before the grim vista that stretched out ahead. Crane scowled. He remembered too much, and too often. He had the vague hope that if he remembered hard enough, he might change one of the things he had done—just a very little thing—and then all this would become untrue. He thought: It might help if everyone remembered and wished at the same time—but there isn't any more everyone. I'm the only one. I'm the last memory on Earth. I'm the last life.

He crawled. Elbows, knee, elbows, knee— And then Hallmyer was crawling alongside and making a great game of it. He chortled and plunged in the cinders like a happy sea lion.

Crane said; "But why do we have to get to the sea?"

Hallmyer blew a spume of ashes.

"Ask her," he said, pointing to Crane's other side.

Evelyn was there, crawling seriously, intently; mimicking Crane's smallest action.

"It's because of our house," she said. "You remember our house, darling? High on the cliff. We were going to live there forever and ever, breathing the ozone and taking morning dips. I was there when you left. Now you're coming back to the house at the edge of the sea. Your beautiful flight is over, dear, and you're coming back to me. We'll live together, just we two, like Adam and Eve—"

Crane said: "That's nice."

Then Evelyn turned her head and screamed: "Oh, Stephen! Watch out!" and Crane felt the menace closing in on him again. Still crawling, he stared back at the vast gray plains of ash, and saw nothing. When he looked at Evelyn again he saw only his shadow, sharp and black. Presently, it, too, faded away as the marching shaft of sunlight passed.

But the dread remained. Evelyn had warned him twice, and she was always right. Crane stopped and turned, and settled himself to watch. If he was really being followed, he would see whatever it was, coming along his tracks.

There was a painful moment of lucidity. It cleaved through his fever and bewilderment, bringing with it the sharpness and strength of a knife.

I'm going mad, he thought. The corruption in my leg has spread to my brain. There is no Evelyn, no Hallmyer, no menace. In all this land there is no life but mine—and even ghosts and spirits of the underworld must have perished in the inferno that girdled the planet. No—there is nothing but me and my sickness. I'm dying—and when I perish, everything will perish. Only a mass of lifeless cinders will go on.

But there was a movement.

Instinct again. Crane dropped his head and played dead. Through slitted eyes he watched the ashen plains, wondering if death was playing tricks with his eyes. Another façade of rain was beating down toward him, and he hoped he could make sure before all vision was obliterated.

Yes. There.

A quarter mile back, a gray-brown shape was flitting along the gray surface. Despite the drone of the distant rain, Crane could hear the whisper of trodden cinders and see the little clouds kicking up. Stealthily he groped for the revolver in the knapsack as his mind reached feebly for explanations and recoiled from fear.

The thing approached, and suddenly Crane squinted and understood. He recalled Umber kicking with fear and springing away from him when the 'chute landed them on the ashen face of the Earth.

"Why, it's Umber," he murmured. He raised himself. The dog halted. "Here boy!" Crane croaked gayly. "Here, boy!"

He was overcome with joy. He realized that a miserable loneliness had hung over him, almost a horrible sensation of oneness in emptiness. Now his was not the only life. There was another. A friendly life that could offer love and companionship. Hope kindled again.

"Here, boy!" he repeated. "Come on, boy—"

After a while he stopped trying to snap his fingers. The Great Dane hung back, showing fangs and a lolling tongue. The dog was emaciated to a skeleton and its eyes gleamed red and ugly in the dusk. As Crane called once more, mechanically, the dog snarled. Puffs of ash leaped beneath its nostrils.

He's hungry, Crane thought, that's all. He reached into the knapsack and at the gesture the dog snarled again. Crane withdrew the chocolate bar and laboriously peeled off the paper and silver foil. Weakly he tossed it toward Umber. It fell far short. After a minute of savage uncertainty, the dog advanced slowly and gobbled up the food. Ashes powdered its muzzle. It licked its chops ceaselessly and continued to advance on Crane.

Panic jerked within him. A voice persisted: This is no friend. He has no love or companionship for you. Love and companionship have vanished from the land along with life. Now there is nothing left but hunger.

"No—" Crane whispered. "That isn't right. We're the last of life on Earth. It isn't right that we should tear at each other and seek to devour—"

But Umber was advancing with a slinking sidle, and his teeth showed sharp and white. And even as Crane stared at him, the dog snarled and lunged.

Crane thrust up an arm under the dog's muzzle, but the weight of the charge carried him backward. He cried out in agony as his broken, swollen leg was struck by the weight of the dog. With his free right hand he struck weakly, again and again, scarcely feeling the grind of teeth gnawing his left arm. Then something metallic was pressed under him and he realized he was lying on the revolver he had let fall.

He groped for it and prayed the cinders had not clogged its mechanism. As Umber let go his arm and tore at his throat, Crane brought the gun up and jabbed the muzzle blindly against the dog's body. He pulled and pulled the trigger until the roars died away and only empty clicks sounded. Umber shuddered in the ashes before him, his body nearly shot in two. Thick scarlet stained the gray.

Evelyn and Hallmyer looked down sadly at the broken animal. Evelyn was crying, and Hallmyer reached nervous fingers through his hair in the same old gesture.

"This is the finish, Stephen," he said. "You've killed part of yourself. Oh—you'll go on living, but not all of you. You'd best bury that corpse, Stephen. It's the corpse of your soul."

"I can't," Crane said. "The wind will blow the ashes away."

"Then burn it—"

It seemed that they helped him thrust the dead dog into his

knapsack. They helped him take off his clothes and pack them underneath. They cupped their hands around the matches until the cloth caught fire, and blew on the weak flame until it sputtered and burned limply. Crane crouched by the fire and nursed it until nothing was left but more gray ash. Then he turned and once again began crawling down the ocean bed. He was naked now. There was nothing left of what-had-been but his flickering little life.

He was too heavy with sorrow to notice the furious rain that slammed and buffeted him, or the searing pains that were shooting through his blackened leg and up his hip. He crawled. Elbows, knee, elbows, knee— Woodenly, mechanically, apathetic to everything. To the latticed skies, the dreary ashen plains and even the dull glint of water that lay far ahead.

He knew it was the sea—what was left of the old, or a new one in the making. But it would be an empty, lifeless sea that some day would lap against a dry lifeless shore. This would be a planet of rock and stone, of metal and snow and ice and water, but that would be all. No more life. He, alone, was useless. He was Adam, but there was no Eve.

Evelyn waved gayly to him from the shore. She was standing alongside the white cottage with the wind snapping her dress to show the clean, slender lines of her figure. And when he came a little closer, she ran out to him and helped him. She said nothing—only placed her hands under his shoulders and helped him lift the weight of his heavy pain-ridden body. And so at last he reached the sea.

It was real. He understood that. For even after Evelyn and the cottage had vanished, he felt the cool waters bathe his face. Quietly— Calmly—

Here's the sea, Crane thought, and here am I. Adam and no Eve. It's hopeless.

He rolled a little farther into the waters. They laved his torn body. Quietly— Calmly—

He lay with face to the sky, peering at the high menacing heavens, and the bitterness within him welled up.

"It's not right!" he cried. "It's not right that all this should pass away. Life is too beautiful to perish at the mad act of one mad creature—"

Quietly the waters laved him. Quietly— Calmly—

The sea rocked him gently, and even the agony that was reaching up toward his heart was no more than a gloved hand. Suddenly the skies split apart—for the first time in all those months—and Crane stared up at the stars.

Then he knew. This was not the end of life. There could never be an end to life. Within his body, within the rotting tissues that were rocking gently in the sea was the source of ten million-million lives. Cells—tissues—bacteria—endamœba— Countless infinities of life that would take new root in the waters and live long after he was gone.

They would live on his rotting remains. They would feed on each other. They would adapt themselves to the new environment and feed on the minerals and sediments washed into this new sea. They would grow, burgeon, evolve. Life would reach out to the lands once more. It would begin again the same old re-repeated cycle that had begun perhaps with the rotting corpse of some last survivor of interstellar travel. It would happen over and over in the future ages.

And then he knew what had brought him back to the sea. There need be no Adam—no Eve. Only the sea, the great mother of life was needed. The sea had called him back to her depths that presently life might emerge once more, and he was content.

Quietly the waters rocked him. Quietly—Calmly—the mother of life rocked the last-born of the old cycle who would become the first-born of the new. And with glazing eyes Stephen Crane smiled up at the stars, stars that were sprinkled evenly across the sky. Stars that had not yet formed into the familiar constellations, nor would not for another hundred million centuries.

SOLAR PLEXUS

Astonishing Stories
September
by James Blish (1921-1975)

*The late James Blish made several notable con-
tributions to science fiction. As a writer, his novel*
A Case of Conscience *(1958) remains one of the
most fascinating and provoking treatments of reli-
gion in sf. His "Okie" series (collected as* Cities in
Flight, *1969) was a most original contribution to
the classic quest theme, while his "Pantropy" stories
were uniformly excellent accounts of human and
more-than-human biological change.*

*As a commentator, Blish was among the pioneer
critical voices from within the genre, and his two
collections* The Issue at Hand *and* More Issues at
Hand *(both published as "William Atheling, Jr.")
are insightful and perceptive. Finally, Blish was a
creative editor—the one and only issue of* Van-
guard Science Fiction *produced under his editorship
is one of the most sought after collector's items in
sf while* New Dreams This Morning *(1966) is still
the definitive anthology on the portrayal of the arts
in science fiction.*

*"Solar Plexus" is one of his earliest stories, and
the best early discussion of what a cyborg might be
like, and what the effect on the human component
might be.*

(Jim Blish is one of the most endearing of all the science
fiction writers. Indeed, a photograph exists—which Jay Kay
Klein shows at all available opportunities, of him planting a
juicy kiss right on my cheek. I must admit, though, that my
fondness for him was shaken when I discovered he was
William Atheling, Jr. I don't particularly like critics and
Atheling hadn't always been kind to me.—However, I recovered and decided I would forgive that rat, Atheling, for Jim's
sake. —I.A.)

Brant Kittinger did not hear the alarm begin to ring. Indeed, it was only after a soft blow had jarred his free-floating observatory that he looked up in sudden awareness from the interferometer. Then the sound of the warning bell reached his consciousness.

Brant was an astronomer, not a spaceman, but he knew that the bell could mean nothing but the arrival of another ship in the vicinity. There would be no point in ringing a bell for a meteor—the thing could be through and past you during the first cycle of the clapper. Only an approaching ship would be likely to trip the detector, and it would have to be close.

A second dull jolt told him how close it was. The rasp of metal which followed, as the other ship slid along the side of his own, drove the fog of tensors completely from his brain. He dropped his pencil and straightened up.

His first thought was that his year in the orbit around the new trans-Plutonian planet was up, and that the Institute's tug had arrived to tow him home, telescope and all. A glance at the clock reassured him at first, then puzzled him still further. He still had the better part of four months.

No commercial vessel, of course, could have wandered this far from the inner planets; and the UN's police cruisers didn't travel far outside the commercial lanes. Besides, it would have been impossible for anyone to find Brant's orbital observatory by accident.

He settled his glasses more firmly on his nose, clambered awkwardly backwards out of the prime focus chamber and down the wall net to the control desk on the observation floor. A quick glance over the boards revealed that there was a magnetic field of some strength nearby, one that didn't belong to the invisible gas giant revolving half a million miles away.

The strange ship was locked to him magnetically; it was an old ship, then, for that method of grappling had been discarded years ago as too hard on delicate instruments. And the strength of the field meant a big ship.

Too big. The only ship of that period that could mount generators that size, as far as Brant could remember, was the Cybernetics Foundation's *Astrid*. Brant could remember well the Foundation's regretful announcement that Murray Bennett had destroyed both himself and the *Astrid* rather than turn the ship in to some UN inspection team. It had happened only eight years ago. Some scandal or other . . .

Well, who then?

He turned the radio on. Nothing came out of it. It was a simple transistor set tuned to the Institute's frequency, and since the ship outside plainly did not belong to the Institute, he had expected nothing else. Of course he had a photophone also, but it had been designed for communication over a reasonable distance, not for cheek-to-cheek whispers.

As an afterthought, he turned off the persistent alarm bell. At once another sound came through: a delicate, rhythmic tapping on the hull of the observatory. Someone wanted to get in.

He could think of no reason to refuse entrance, except for a vague and utterly unreasonable wonder as to whether or not the stranger was a friend. He had no enemies, and the notion that some outlaw might have happened upon him out here was ridiculous. Nevertheless, there was something about the anonymous, voiceless ship just outside which made him uneasy.

The gentle tapping stopped, and then began again, with an even, mechanical insistence. For a moment Brant wondered whether or not he should try to tear free with the observatory's few maneuvering rockets—but even should he win so uneven a struggle, he would throw the observatory out of the orbit where the Institute expected to find it, and he was not astronaut enough to get it back there again.

Tap, tap. Tap, tap.

"All right," he said irritably. He pushed the button which set the airlock to cycling. The tapping stopped. He left the outer door open more than long enough for anyone to enter and push the button in the lock which reversed the process; but nothing happened.

After what seemed to be a long wait, he pushed his button again. The outer door closed, the pumps filled the chamber with air, the inner door swung open. No ghost drifted out of it; there was nobody in the lock at all.

Tap, tap. Tap, tap.

Absently he polished his glasses on his sleeve. If they didn't want to come into the observatory, they must want him to come out of it. That was possible: although the telescope had a Coudé focus which allowed him to work in the ship's air most of the time, it was occasionally necessary for him to exhaust the dome, and for that purpose he had a space suit. But he had never been outside the hull in it, and the thought alarmed him. Brant was nobody's spaceman.

Be damned to them. He clapped his glasses back into place and took one more look into the empty airlock. It was still empty, with the outer door now moving open very slowly. . . .

A spaceman would have known that he was already dead,
but Brant's reactions were not quite as fast. His first move
was to try to jam the inner door shut by sheer muscle-power,
but it would not stir. Then he simply clung to the nearest
stanchion, waiting for the air to rush out of the observatory,
and his life after it.

The outer door of the airlock continued to open, placidly,
and still there was no rush of air—only a kind of faint, un-
ticketable inwash of odor, as if Brant's air were mixing with
someone else's. When both doors of the lock finally stood
wide apart from each other, Brant found himself looking
down the inside of a flexible, airtight tube, such as he had
once seen used for the transfer of a small freight-load from a
ship to one of Earth's several space stations. It connected the
airlock of the observatory with that of the other ship. At the
other end of it, lights gleamed yellowly, with the unmistakable, dismal sheen of incandescent overheads.

That was an old ship, all right.

Tap. Tap.

"Go to hell," he said aloud. There was no answer.

Tap. Tap.

"Go to hell," he said. He walked out into the tube, which
flexed sinuously as his body pressed aside the static air. In the
airlock of the stranger, he paused and looked back. He was
not much surprised to see the outer door of his own airlock
swinging snugly shut against him. Then the airlock of the
stranger began to cycle; he skipped on into the ship barely in
time.

There was a bare metal corridor ahead of him. While he
watched, the first light bulb over his head blinked out. Then
the second. Then the third. As the fourth one went out, the
first came on again, so that now there was a slow ribbon of
darkness moving away from him down the corridor. Clearly,
he was being asked to follow the line of darkening bulbs
down the corridor.

He had no choice, now that he had come this far. He followed the blinking lights.

The trail led directly to the control room of the ship. There
was nobody there, either.

The whole place was oppressively silent. He could hear the
soft hum of generators—a louder noise than he ever heard on
board the observatory—but no ship should be this quiet.
There should be muffled human voices, the chittering of communications systems, the impacts of soles on metal. Someone

had to operate a proper ship—not only its airlocks, but its
motors—and its brains. The observatory was only a barge,
and needed no crew but Brant, but a real ship had to be
manned.

He scanned the bare metal compartment, noting the apparent age of the equipment. Most of it was manual, but
there were no hands to man it.

A ghost ship for true.

"All right," he said. His voice sounded flat and loud to
him. "Come on out. You wanted me here—why are you hiding?"

Immediately there was a noise in the close, still air, a thin,
electrical sigh. Then a quiet voice said, "You're Brant Kittinger."

"Certainly," Brant said, swiveling fruitlessly toward the apparent source of the voice. "You know who I am. You
couldn't have found me by accident. Will you come out? I've
no time to play games."

"I'm not playing games," the voice said calmly. "And I
can't come out, since I'm not hiding from you. I can't see
you; I needed to hear your voice before I could be sure of
you."

"Why?"

"Because I can't see inside the ship. I could find your observation boat well enough, but until I heard you speak I
couldn't be sure that you were the one aboard it. Now I
know."

"All right," Brant said suspiciously. "I still don't see why
you're hiding. Where are you?"

"Right here," said the voice. "All around you."

Brant looked all around himself. His scalp began to creep.
"What kind of nonsense is that?" he said.

"You aren't seeing what you're looking at, Brant. You're
looking directly at me, no matter where you look. *I am the
ship.*"

"Oh," Brant said softly. "So that's it. You're one of Murray Bennett's computer-driven ships. Are you the *Astrid*, after
all?"

"This is the *Astrid*," the voice said. "But you miss my
point. I am Murray Bennett, also."

Brant's jaw dropped open. "Where are you?" he said after
a time.

"Here," the voice said impatiently. "I am the *Astrid*. I am
also Murray Bennett. Bennett is dead, so he can't very well
come into the cabin and shake your hand. I am now Murray

Bennett; I remember you very well, Brant. I need your help, so I sought you out. I'm not as much Murray Bennett as I'd like to be."

Brant sat down in the empty pilot's seat.

"You're a computer," he said shakily. "Isn't that so?"

"It is and it isn't. No computer can duplicate the performance of a human brain. I tried to introduce real human neural mechanisms into computers, specifically to fly ships, and was outlawed for my trouble. I don't think I was treated fairly. It took enormous surgical skill to make the hundreds and hundreds of nerve-to-circuit connections that were needed—and before I was half through, the UN decided that what I was doing was human vivisection. They outlawed me, and the Foundation said I'd have to destroy myself; what could I do after that?

"I did destroy myself. I transferred most of my own nervous system into the computers of the *Astrid*, working at the end through drugged assistants under telepathic control, and finally relying upon the computers to seal the last connections. No such surgery ever existed before, but I brought it into existence. It worked. Now I'm the *Astrid*—and still Murray Bennett too, though Bennett is dead."

Brant locked his hands together carefully on the edge of the dead control board. "What good did that do you?" he said.

"It proved my point. I was trying to build an almost living spaceship. I had to build part of myself into it to do it—since they made me an outlaw to stop my using any other human being as a source of parts. But here is the *Astrid*, Brant, as almost alive as I could ask. I'm as immune to a dead spaceship—a UN cruiser, for instance—as you would be to an infuriated wheelbarrow. My reflexes are human-fast. I feel things directly, not through instruments. I fly myself: I am what I sought—the ship that almost thinks for itself."

"You keep saying 'almost,'" Brant said.

"That's why I came to you," the voice said. "I don't have enough of Murray Bennett here to know what I should do next. You knew me well. Was I out to try to use human brains more and more, and computer-mechanisms less and less? It seems to me that I was. I can pick up the brains easily enough, just as I picked you up. The solar system is full of people isolated on research boats who could be plucked off them and incorporated into efficient machines like the *Astrid*. But I don't know. I seem to have lost my creativity. I have a base where I have some other ships with beautiful computers

in them, and with a few people to use as research animals I
could make even better ships of them than the *Astrid* is. But
is that what I want to do? Is that what I set out to do? I no
longer know, Brant. Advise me."

The machine with the human nerves would have been
touching had it not been so much like Bennett had been. The
combination of the two was flatly horrible.

"You've made a bad job of yourself, Murray," he said.
"You've let me inside your brain without taking any real
thought of the danger. What's to prevent me from stationing
myself at your old manual controls and flying you to the
nearest UN post?"

"You can't fly a ship."

"How do you know?"

"By simple computation. And there are other reasons.
What's to prevent me from making you cut your own throat?
The answer's the same. You're in control of your body; I'm
in control of mine. My body is the *Astrid*. The controls are
useless, unless I actuate them. The nerves through which I do
so are sheathed in excellent steel. The only way in which you
could destroy my control would be to break something necessary to the running of the ship. That, in a sense, would kill
me, as destroying your heart or your lungs would kill you.
But that would be pointless, for then you could no more nav-
igate the ship than I. And if you made repairs, I would be—
well, resurrected."

The voice fell silent a moment. Then it added, matter-of-
factly, "Of course, I can protect myself."

Brant made no reply. His eyes were narrowed to the squint
he more usually directed at a problem in Milne transforma-
tions.

"I never sleep," the voice went on, "but much of my navi-
gating and piloting is done by an autopilot without requiring
my conscious attention. It is the same old Nelson autopilot
which was originally on board the *Astrid,* though, so it has to
be monitored. If you touch the controls while the autopilot is
running, it switches itself off and I resume direction myself."

Brant was surprised and instinctively repelled by the steady
flow of information. It was a forcible reminder of how much
of the computer there was in the intelligence that called itself
Murray Bennett. It was answering a question with the almost
mindless wealth of detail of a public-library selector—and
there was no "Enough" button for Brant to push.

"Are you going to answer my question?" the voice said
suddenly.

"Yes," Brant said. "I advise you to turn yourself in. The *Astrid* proves your point—and also proves that your research was a blind alley. There's no point in your proceeding to make more *Astrids;* you're aware yourself that you're incapable of improving on the model now."

"That's contrary to what I have recorded," the voice said. "My ultimate purpose as a man was to build machines like this. I can't accept your answer: it conflicts with my primary directive. Please follow the lights to your quarters."

"What are you going to do with me?"

"Take you to the base."

"What for?" Brant said.

"As a stock of parts," said the voice. "Please follow the lights, or I'll have to use force."

Brant followed the lights. As he entered the cabin to which they led him, a disheveled figure arose from one of the two cots. He started back in alarm. The figure chuckled wryly and displayed a frayed bit of gold braid on its sleeve.

"I'm not as terrifying as I look," he said. "Lt. Powell of the UN scout *Iapetus,* at your service."

"I'm Brant Kittinger, Planetary Institute astrophysicist. You're just the faintest bit battered, all right. Did you tangle with Bennett?"

"Is that his name?" the UN patrolman nodded glumly. "Yes. There's some whoppers of guns mounted on this old tub. I challenged it, and it cut my ship to pieces before I could lift a hand. I barely got into my suit in time—and I'm beginning to wish I hadn't."

"I don't blame you. You know what he plans to use us for, I judge."

"Yes," the pilot said. "He seems to take pleasure in bragging about his achievements—God knows they're amazing enough, if even half of what he says is true."

"It's all true," Brant said. "He's essentially a machine, you know, and as such I doubt that he can lie."

Powell looked startled. "That makes it worse. I've been trying to figure a way out—"

Brant raised one hand sharply, and with the other he patted his pockets in search of a pencil. "If you've found anything, write it down, don't talk about it. I think he can hear us. Is that so, Bennett?"

"Yes," said the voice in the air. Powell jumped. "My hearing extends throughout the ship."

There was silence again. Powell, grim as death, scribbled on a tattered UN trip ticket.

Doesn't matter, can't think of a thing.

Where's the main computer? Brant wrote. *There's where personality residues must lie.*

Down below. Not a chance without blaster. Must be 8" of steel around it. Control nerves the same.

They sat hopelessly on the lower cot. Brant chewed on the pencil. "How far is his home base from here?" he asked at length.

"Where's here?"

"In the orbit of the new planet."

Powell whistled. "In that case, his base can't be more than three days away. I came on board from just off Titan, and he hasn't touched his base since, so his fuel won't last much longer. I know this type of ship well enough. And from what I've seen of the drivers, they haven't been altered."

"Umm," Brant said. "That checks. If Bennett in person never got around to altering the drive, this ersatz Bennett we have here will never get around to it, either." He found it easier to ignore the listening presence while talking; to monitor his speech constantly with Bennett in mind was too hard on the nerves. "That gives us three days to get out, then. Or less."

For at least twenty minutes Brant said nothing more, while the UN pilot squirmed and watched his face hopefully. Finally the astronomer picked up the piece of paper again.

Can you pilot this ship? he wrote.

The pilot nodded and scribbled: *Why?*

Without replying, Brant lay back on the bunk, swiveled himself around so that his head was toward the center of the cabin, doubled up his knees, and let fly with both feet. They crashed hard against the hull, the magnetic studs in his shoes leaving bright scars on the metal. The impact sent him sailing like an ungainly fish across the cabin.

"What was that for?" Powell and the voice in the air asked simultaneously. Their captor's tone was faintly curious, but not alarmed.

Brant had his answer already prepared. "It's part of a question I want to ask," he said. He brought up against the far wall and struggled to get his feet back to the desk. "Can you tell me what I did then, Bennett?"

"Why, not specifically. As I told you, I can't see inside the ship. But I get a tactual jar from the nerves of the controls, the lights, the floors, the ventilation system, and so on, and also a ringing sound from the audios. These things tell me that you either stamped on the floor or pounded on the wall.

From the intensity of all the impressions, I compute that you stamped."

"You hear and you feel, eh?"

"That's correct," the voice said. "Also I can pick up your body heat from the receptors in the ship's temperature control system—a form of seeing, but without any definition."

Very quietly, Brant retrieved the worn trip ticket and wrote on it: *Follow me.*

He went out into the corridor and started down it toward the control room, Powell at his heels. The living ship remained silent only for a moment.

"Return to your cabin," the voice said.

Brant walked a little faster. How would Bennett's vicious brain child enforce his orders?

"I said, go back to your cabin," the voice said. Its tone was now loud and harsh, and without a trace of feeling; for the first time, Brant was able to tell that it came from a voder, rather than from a tape-vocabulary of Bennett's own voice. Brant gritted his teeth and marched forward.

"I don't want to have to spoil you," the voice said. "For the last time—"

An instant later Brant received a powerful blow in the small of his back. It felled him like a tree and sent him skimming along the corridor deck like a flat stone. A bare fraction of a second later there was a hiss and a flash, and the air was abruptly hot and choking with the sharp odor of ozone.

"Close," Powell's voice said calmly. "Some of these rivet heads in the walls evidently are high-tension electrodes. Lucky I saw the nimbus collecting on that one. Crawl, and make it snappy."

Crawling in a gravity-free corridor was a good deal more difficult to manage than walking. Determinedly, Brant squirmed into the control room, calling into play every trick he had ever learned in space to stick to the floor. He could hear Powell wriggling along behind him.

"He doesn't know what I'm up to," Brant said aloud. "Do you, Bennett?"

"No," the voice in the air said. "But I know of nothing you can do that's dangerous while you're lying on your belly. When you get up, I'll destroy you, Brant."

"Hmmm," Brant said. He adjusted his glasses, which he had nearly lost during his brief, skipping carom along the deck. The voice had summarized the situation with deadly precision. He pulled the now nearly pulped trip ticket out of his shirt pocket, wrote on it, and shoved it across the desk to Powell.

How can we reach the autopilot? Got to smash it.

Powell propped himself up on one elbow and studied the scrap of paper, frowning. Down below, beneath the deck, there was an abrupt sound of power, and Brant felt the cold metal on which he was lying sink beneath him. Bennett was changing course, trying to throw them within range of his defenses. Both men began to slide sidewise.

Powell did not appear to be worried; evidently he knew just how long it took to turn a ship of this size and period. He pushed the piece of paper back. On the last free space on it, in cramped letters, was: *Throw something at it.*

"Ah," said Brant. Still sliding, he drew off one of his heavy shoes and hefted it critically. It would do. With a sudden convulsion of motion he hurled it.

Fat, crackling sparks criss-crossed the room; the noise was ear-splitting. While Bennett could have had no idea what Brant was doing, he evidently had sensed the sudden stir of movement and had triggered the high-tension current out of general caution. But he was too late. The flying shoe plowed heel-foremost into the autopilot with a rending smash.

There was an unfocused blare of sound from the voder—more like the noise of a siren than like a human cry. The *Astrid* rolled wildly, once. Then there was silence.

"All right," said Brant, getting to his knees. "Try the controls, Powell."

The UN pilot arose cautiously. No sparks flew. When he touched the boards, the ship responded with an immediate purr of power.

"She runs," he said. "Now, how the hell did you know what to do?"

"It wasn't difficult," Brant said complacently, retrieving his shoe. "But we're not out of the woods yet. We have to get to the stores fast and find a couple of torches. I want to cut through every nerve-channel we can find. Are you with me?"

"Sure."

The job was more quickly done than Brant had dared to hope. Evidently the living ship had never thought of lightening itself by jettisoning all the equipment its human crew had once needed. While Brant and Powell cut their way enthusiastically through the jungle of efferent nerve-trunks running from the central computer, the astronomer said:

"He gave us too much information. He told me that he had connected the artificial nerves of the ship, the control nerves, to the nerve-ends running from the parts of his own brain that he had used. And he said that he'd had to make *hundreds* of such connections. That's the trouble with allowing a computer to act as an independent agent—it doesn't know enough about interpersonal relationships to control its tongue. . . . There we are. He'll be coming to before long, but I don't think he'll be able to interfere with us now."

He set down his torch with a sigh. "I was saying? Oh, yes. About those nerve connections: if he had separated out the pain-carrying nerves from the other sensory nerves, he would have had to have made *thousands* of connections, not hundreds. Had it really been the living human being, Bennett, who had given me that cue, I would have discounted it, because he might have been using understatement. But since it was Bennett's double, a computer, I assumed that the figure was of the right order of magnitude. Computers don't understate.

"Besides, I didn't think Bennett could have made thousands of connections, especially not working telepathically through a proxy. There's a limit even to the most marvelous neurosurgery. Bennett had just made general connections, and had relied on the segments from his own brain which he had incorporated to sort out the impulses as they came in—as any human brain could do under like circumstances. That was one of the advantages of using parts from a human brain in the first place."

"And when you kicked the wall—" Powell said.

"Yes, you see the crux of the problem already. When I kicked the wall, I wanted to make sure that he could *feel* the impact of my shoes. If he could, then I could be sure that he hadn't eliminated the sensory nerves when he installed the motor nerves. And if he hadn't, then there were bound to be pain axons present, too."

"But what has the autopilot to do with it?" Powell asked plaintively.

"The autopilot," Brant said, grinning, "is a center of his nerve-mesh, an important one. He should have protected it as heavily as he protected the main computer. When I smashed it, it was like ramming a fist into a man's solar plexus. It hurt him."

Powell grinned too. "K.O.," he said.

NIGHTFALL

Astounding Science Fiction
September
by Isaac Asimov

(Well, here it is. "Nightfall" was my sixteenth published story, but the thirty-second I had written. I wrote it in March 1941, when I was 21¼ years old. It was the first story of mine that Campbell paid me a bonus for. It was the first story of mine that placed as the lead novelet in an issue of *Astounding*. It was the first story of mine that rated an *Astounding* cover.

It was a milestone for me, obviously.

I was not aware at the time just exactly how much of a milestone it was.

At the time, it was just another story I had written, and it didn't make a terribly big splash, but as the months and years passed, it seemed to get bigger and bigger in retrospect until now there is not only a general consensus that it is the best short piece I have ever written, but there seems to be a general consensus that it is the best short piece of science fiction ever written. At least it placed first in several polls, including one of the membership of the Science Fiction Writers of America.

I hasten to say that I disagree. In my own opinion I have written three short pieces that are better and I shall see to it that each is included in this series when the appropriate year is reached. In fact, I think "Nightfall" has serious flaws and crudities as far as writing style is concerned. However—after it appeared I never again wrote another science fiction story that remained unpublished, and very few that weren't accepted by the first editor to whom it was offered—so I guess "Nightfall," not quite three years after I had begun to submit stories for publication, marked the end of my apprenticeship—I.A.)

*"If the stars should appear one night in a thousand years,
how would men believe and adore, and preserve for many
generations the remembrance of the city of God!"—Emerson*

Aton 77, director of Saro University, thrust out a belliger-
ent lower lip and glared at the young newspaperman in a hot
fury.

Theremon 762 took that fury in his stride. In his earlier
days, when his now widely syndicated column was only a
mad idea in a cub reporter's mind, he had specialized in "impossible" interviews. It had cost him bruises, black eyes, and
broken bones; but it had given him an ample supply of
coolness and self-confidence.

So he lowered the outthrust hand that had been so
pointedly ignored and calmly waited for the aged director to
get over the worst. Astronomers were queer ducks, anyway,
and if Aton's actions of the last two months meant anything,
this same Aton was the queer-duckiest of the lot.

Aton 77 found his voice, and though it trembled with re-
strained emotion, the careful, somewhat pedantic, phraseology for which the famous astronomer was noted, did not
abandon him.

"Sir," he said, "you display an infernal gall in coming to
me with that impudent proposition of yours."

The husky telephotographer of the Observatory, Beenay
25, thrust a tongue's tip across dry lips and interposed nervously, "Now, sir, after all—"

The director turned to him and lifted a white eyebrow.
"Do not interfere, Beenay. I will credit you with good intentions in bringing this man here; but I will tolerate no insubordination now."

Theremon decided it was time to take a part. "Director
Aton, if you'll let me finish what I started saying I think—"

"I don't believe, young man," retorted Aton, "that anything
you could say now would count much as compared with your
daily columns of these last two months. You have led a vast
newspaper campaign against the efforts of myself and my colleagues to organize the world against the menace which it is
now too late to avert. You have done your best with your
highly personal attacks to make the staff of this Observatory
objects of ridicule."

The director lifted the copy of the Saro City *Chronicle* on
the table and shook it at Theremon furiously. "Even a person
of your well-known impudence should have hesitated before

coming to me with a request that he be allowed to cover to-day's events for his paper. Of all newsmen, you!"

Aton dashed the newspaper to the floor, strode to the window and clasped his arms behind his back.

"You may leave," he snapped over his shoulder. He stared moodily out at the skyline where Gamma, the brightest of the planet's six suns, was setting. It had already faded and yellowed into the horizon mists, and Aton knew he would never see it again as a sane man.

He whirled. "No, wait, come here!" He gestured peremptorily. "I'll give you your story."

The newsman had made no motion to leave, and now he approached the old man slowly. Aton gestured outward, "Of the six suns, only Beta is left in the sky. Do you see it?"

The question was rather unnecessary. Beta was almost at zenith; its ruddy light flooding the landscape to an unusual orange as the brilliant rays of setting Gamma died. Beta was at aphelion. It was small; smaller than Theremon had ever seen it before, and for the moment it was undisputed ruler of Lagash's sky.

Lagash's own sun, Alpha, the one about which it revolved, was at the antipodes; as were the two distant companion pairs. The red dwarf Beta—Alpha's immediate companion—was alone, grimly alone.

Aton's upturned face flushed redly in the sunlight. "In just under four hours," he said, "civilization, as we know it, comes to an end. It will do so because, as you see, Beta is the only sun in the sky." He smiled grimly. "Print that! There'll be no one to read it."

"But if it turns out that four hours pass—and another four—and nothing happens?" asked Theremon softly.

"Don't let that worry you. Enough will happen."

"Granted! And *still*—if nothing happens?"

For a second time, Beenay 25 spoke, "Sir, I think you ought to listen to him."

Theremon said, "Put it to a vote, Director Aton."

There was a stir among the remaining five members of the Observatory staff, who till now had maintained an attitude of wary neutrality.

"That," stated Aton flatly, "is not necessary." He drew out his pocket watch. "Since your good friend, Beenay, insists so urgently, I will give you five minutes. Talk away."

"Good! Now, just what difference would it make if you allowed me to take down an eyewitness account of what's to come? If your prediction comes true, my presence won't hurt; for in that case my column would never be written. On the other hand, if nothing comes of it, you will just have to expect ridicule or worse. It would be wise to leave that ridicule to friendly hands."

Aton snorted. "Do you mean yours when you speak of friendly hands?"

"Certainly!" Theremon sat down and crossed his legs. "My columns may have been a little rough at times, but I gave you people the benefit of the doubt every time. After all, this is not the century to preach 'the end of the world is at hand' to Lagash. You have to understand that people don't believe the 'Book of Revelations' any more, and it annoys them to have scientists turn about face and tell us the Cultists are right after all—"

"No such thing, young man," interrupted Aton. "While a great deal of our data has been supplied us by the Cult, our results contain none of the Cult's mysticism. Facts are facts, and the Cult's so-called 'mythology' *has* certain facts behind it. We've exposed them and ripped away their mystery. I assure you that the Cult hates us now worse than you do."

"I don't hate you. I'm just trying to tell you that the public is in an ugly humor. They're angry."

Aton twisted his mouth in derision. "Let them be angry."

"Yes, but what about tomorrow?"

"There'll be no tomorrow!"

"But if there is. Say that there is—just to see what happens. That anger might take shape into something serious. After all, you know, business has taken a nose dive these last two months. Investors don't really believe the world is coming to an end, but just the same they're being cagy with their money until it's all over. Johnny Public doesn't believe you, either, but the new spring furniture might as well wait a few months—just to make sure.

"You see the point. Just as soon as this is all over, the business interests will be after your hide. They'll say that if crackpots—begging your pardon—can upset the country's prosperity any time they want simply by making some cockeyed prediction—it's up to the planet to prevent them. The sparks will fly, sir."

The director regarded the columnist sternly. "And just what were you proposing to do to help the situation?"

"Well," grinned Theremon, "I was proposing to take charge of the publicity. I can handle things so that only the ridiculous side will show. It would be hard to stand, I admit, because I'd have to make you all out to be a bunch of gibbering idiots, but if I can get people laughing at you, they might forget to be angry. In return for that, all my publisher asks is an exclusive story."

Beenay nodded and burst out, "Sir, the rest of us think he's right. These last two months we've considered everything but the million-to-one chance that there is an error somewhere in our theory or in our calculations. We ought to take care of that, too."

There was a murmur of agreement from the men grouped about the table, and Aton's expression became that of one who found his mouth full of something bitter and couldn't get rid of it.

"You may stay if you wish, then. You will kindly refrain, however, from hampering us in our duties in any way. You will also remember that I am in charge of all activities here, and in spite of your opinions as expressed in your columns, I will expect full co-operation and full respect—"

His hands were behind his back, and his wrinkled face thrust forward determinedly as he spoke. He might have continued indefinitely but for the intrusion of a new voice.

"Hello, hello, hello!" It came in a high tenor, and the plump cheeks of the newcomer expanded in a pleased smile. "What's this morgue-like atmosphere about here? No one's losing his nerve, I hope."

Aton started in consternation and said peevishly, "Now what the devil are you doing here, Sheerin? I thought you were going to stay behind in the Hideout."

Sheerin laughed and dropped his tubby figure into a chair. "Hideout be blowed! The place bored me. I wanted to be here, where things are getting hot. Don't you suppose I have my share of curiosity? I want to see these Stars the Cultists are forever speaking about." He rubbed his hands and added in a soberer tone. "It's freezing outside. The wind's enough to hang icicles on your nose. Beta doesn't seem to give any heat at all, at the distance it is."

The white-haired director ground his teeth in sudden exasperation, "Why do you go out of your way to do crazy things. Sheerin? What kind of good are you around here?"

"What kind of good am I around there?" Sheerin spread his palms in comical resignation. "A psychologist isn't worth his salt in the Hideout. They need men of action and strong, healthy women that can breed children. Me? I'm a hundred pounds too heavy for a man of action, and I wouldn't be a success at breeding children. So why bother them with an extra mouth to feed? I feel better over here."

Theremon spoke briskly, "Just what is the Hideout, sir?"

Sheerin seemed to see the columnist for the first time. He frowned and blew his ample cheeks out, "And just who in Lagash are you, redhead?"

Aton compressed his lips and then muttered sullenly, "That's Theremon 762, the newspaper fellow. I suppose you've heard of him."

The columnist offered his hand. "And, of course, you're Sheerin 501 of Saro University. I've heard of you." Then he repeated, "What is this Hideout, sir?"

"Well," said Sheerin, "we have managed to convince a few people of the validity of our prophecy of—er—doom, to be spectacular about it, and those few have taken proper measures. They consist mainly of the immediate members of the families of the Observatory staff, certain of the faculty of Saro University and a few outsiders. Altogether, they number about three hundred, but three quarters are women and children."

"I see! They're supposed to hide where the Darkness and the—er—Stars can't get at them, and then hold out when the rest of the world goes poof."

"If they can. It won't be easy. With all of mankind insane; with the great cities going up in flames—environment will not be conducive to survival. But they have food, water, shelter, and weapons—"

"They've got more," said Aton. "They've got all our records, except for what we will collect today. Those records will mean everything to the next cycle, and *that's* what must survive. The rest can go hang."

Theremon whistled a long, low whistle and sat brooding for several minutes. The men about the table had brought out a multichess board and started a six-member game. Moves were made rapidly and in silence. All eyes bent in furious concentration on the board. Theremon watched them intently and then rose and approached Aton, who sat apart in whispered conversation with Sheerin.

"Listen," he said, "let's go somewhere where we won't bother the rest of the fellows. I want to ask some questions."

The aged astronomer frowned sourly at him, but Sheerin chirped up, "Certainly. It will do me good to talk. It always does. Aton was telling me about your ideas concerning world reaction to a failure of the prediction—and I agree with you.

I read your column pretty regularly, by the way, and as a general thing I like your views."

"Please, Sheerin," growled Aton.

"Eh? Oh, all right. We'll go into the next room. It has softer chairs, anyway."

There *were* softer chairs in the next room. There were also thick red curtains on the windows and a maroon carpet on the floor. With the bricky light of Beta pouring in, the general effect was one of dried blood.

Theremon shuddered, "Say, I'd give ten credits for a decent dose of white light for just a second. I wish Gamma or Delta were in the sky."

"What are your questions?" asked Aton. "Please remember that our time is limited. In a little over an hour and a quarter we're going upstairs, and after that there will be no time for talk."

"Well, here it is." Theremon leaned back and folded his hands on his chest. "You people seem so all-fired serious about this that I'm beginning to believe you. Would you mind explaining what it's all about?"

Aton exploded, "Do you mean to sit there and tell me that you've been bombarding us with ridicule without even finding out what we've been trying to say?"

The columnist grinned sheepishly. "It's not that bad, sir. I've got the general idea. You say that there is going to be a world-wide Darkness in a few hours and that all mankind will go violently insane. What I want now is the science behind it."

"No, you don't. No, you don't," broke in Sheerin. "If you ask Aton for that—supposing him to be in the mood to answer at all—he'll trot out pages of figures and volumes of graphs. You won't make head or tail of it. Now if you were to ask *me,* I could give you the layman's standpoint."

"All right; I ask you."

"Then first I'd like a drink." He rubbed his hands and looked at Aton.

"Water?" grunted Aton.

"Don't be silly!"

"Don't you be silly. No alcohol today. It would be too easy to get my men drunk. I can't afford to tempt them."

The psychologist grumbled wordlessly. He turned to Theremon, impaled him with his sharp eyes, and began.

"You realize, of course, that the history of civilization on Lagash displays a cyclic character—but I mean, *cyclic!*"

"I know," replied Theremon cautiously, "that that is the current archeological theory. Has it been accepted as a fact?"

"Just about. In this last century it's been generally agreed upon. This cyclic character is—or, rather, was—one of *the* great mysteries. We've located series of civilizations, nine of them definitely, and indications of others as well, all of which have reached heights comparable to our own, and all of which, without exception, were destroyed by fire at the very height of their culture.

"And no one could tell why. All centers of culture were thoroughly gutted by fire, with nothing left behind to give a hint as to the cause."

Theremon was following closely. "Wasn't there a Stone Age, too?"

"Probably, but as yet, practically nothing is known of it, except that men of that age were little more than rather intelligent apes. We can forget about that."

"I see. Go on!"

"There have been explanations of these recurrent catastrophes, all of a more or less fantastic nature. Some say that there are periodic rains of fire; some that Lagash passes through a sun every so often; some even wilder things. But there is one theory, quite different from all of these, that has been handed down over a period of centuries."

"I know. You mean this myth of the 'Stars' that the Cultists have in their 'Book of Revelations.'"

"Exactly," rejoined Sheerin with satisfaction. "The Cultists said that every two thousand and fifty years Lagash entered a huge cave, so that all the suns disappeared, and there came *total darkness all over the world!* And then, they say, things called Stars appeared, which robbed men of their souls and left them unreasoning brutes, so that they destroyed the civilization they themselves had built up. Of course, they mix all this up with a lot of religio-mystic notions, but that's the central idea."

There was a short pause in which Sheerin drew a long breath. "And now we come to the Theory of Universal Gravitation." He pronounced the phrase so that the capital letters sounded—and at that point Aton turned from the window, snorted loudly, and stalked out of the room.

The two stared after him, and Theremon said, "What's wrong?"

"Nothing in particular," replied Sheerin. "Two of the men

were due several hours ago and haven't shown up yet. He's
terrifically shorthanded, of course, because all but the really
essential men have gone to the Hideout."

"You don't think the two deserted, do you?"

"Who? Faro and Yimot? Of course not. Still, if they're not
back within the hour, things would be a little sticky." He got
to his feet suddenly, and his eyes twinkled. "Anyway, as long
as Aton is gone——"

Tiptoeing to the nearest window, he squatted, and from the
low window box beneath withdrew a bottle of red liquid that
gurgled suggestively when he shook it.

"I *thought* Aton didn't know about this," he remarked as
he trotted back to the table. "Here! We've only got one glass
so, as the guest, you can have it. I'll keep the bottle." And he
filled the tiny cup with judicious care.

Theremon rose to protest, but Sheerin eyed him sternly.
"Respect your elders, young man."

The newsman seated himself with a look of pain and anguish on his face. "Go ahead, then, you old villain."

The psychologist's Adam's apple wobbled as the bottle
upended, and then, with a satisfied grunt and a smack of the
lips, he began again.

"But what do you know about gravitation?"

"Nothing, except that it is a very recent development, not
too well established, and that the math is so hard that only
twelve men in Lagash are supposed to understand it."

"*Tcha!* Nonsense! Boloney! I can give you all the essential
math in a sentence. The Law of Universal Gravitation states
that there exists a cohesive force among all bodies of the universe, such that the amount of this force between any two
given bodies is proportional to the product of their masses divided by the square of the distance between them."

"Is that all?"

"That's enough! It took four hundred years to develop it."

"Why that long? It sounded simple enough, the way you
said it."

"Because great laws are not divined by flashes of inspiration, whatever you may think. It usually takes the combined
work of a world full of scientists over a period of centuries.
After Genovi 41 discovered that Lagash rotated about the
sun Alpha, rather than vice versa—and that was four
hundred years ago—astronomers have been working. The
complex motions of the six suns were recorded and analyzed
and unwoven. Theory after theory was advanced and checked

and counterchecked and modified and abandoned and revived and converted to something else. It was a devil of a job."

Theremon nodded thoughtfully and held out his glass for more liquor. Sheerin grudgingly allowed a few ruby drops to leave the bottle.

"It was twenty years ago," he continued after remoistening his own throat, "that it was finally demonstrated that the Law of Universal Gravitation accounted exactly for the orbital motions of the six suns. It was a great triumph."

Sheerin stood up and walked to the window, still clutching his bottle, "And now we're getting to the point. In the last decade, the motions of Lagash about Alpha were computed according to gravity, and *it did not account for the orbit observed;* not even when all perturbations due to the other suns were included. Either the law was invalid, or there was another, as yet unknown, factor involved."

Theremon joined Sheerin at the window and gazed out past the wooded slopes to where the spires of Saro City gleamed bloodily on the horizon. The newsman felt the tension of uncertainty grow within him as he cast a short glance at Beta. It glowered redly at Zenith, dwarfed and evil.

"Go ahead, sir," he said softly.

Sheerin replied, "Astronomers stumbled about for years, each proposed theory more untenable than the one before—until Aton had the inspiration of calling in the Cult. The head of the Cult, Sor 5, had access to certain data that simplified the problem considerably. Aton set to work on a new track.

"What if there were another nonluminous planetary body such as Lagash? If there were, you know, it would shine only by reflected light, and if it were composed of bluish rock, as Lagash itself largely is, then, in the redness of the sky, the eternal blaze of the suns would make it invisible—drown it out completely."

Theremon whistled, "What a screwy idea!"

"You think *that's* screwy? Listen to this: Suppose this body rotated about Lagash at such a distance and in such an orbit and had such a mass that its attraction would exactly account for the deviations of Lagash's orbit from theory—do you know what would happen?"

The columnist shook his head.

"Well, sometimes this body would get in the way of a sun." And Sheerin emptied what remained in the bottle at a draft.

"And it does, I suppose," said Theremon flatly.

"Yes! But only one sun lies in its plane of revolutions." He jerked a thumb at the shrunken sun above. "Beta! And it has been shown that the eclipse will occur only when the arrangement of the suns is such that Beta is alone in its hemisphere and at maximum distance, at which time the moon is invariably at minimum distance. The eclipse that results, with the moon seven times the apparent diameter of Beta, covers all of Lagash and lasts well over half a day, so that no spot on the planet escapes the effects. *That eclipse comes once every two thousand and forty-nine years.*"

Theremon's face was drawn into an expressionless mask. "And that's my story?"

The psychologist nodded. "That's all of it. First the eclipse—which will start in three quarters of an hour—then universal Darkness, and, maybe, these mysterious Stars—then madness, and end of the cycle."

He brooded. "We had two months' leeway—we at the Observatory—and that wasn't enough time to persuade Lagash of the danger. Two centuries might not have been enough. But our records are at the Hideout, and today we photograph the eclipse. The next cycle will *start off* with the truth, and when the *next* eclipse comes, mankind will at last be ready for it. Come to think of it, that's part of your story, too."

A thin wind ruffled the curtains at the window as Theremon opened it and leaned out. It played coldly with his hair as he stared at the crimson sunlight on his hand. Then he turned in sudden rebellion.

"What is there in Darkness to drive *me* mad?"

Sheerin smiled to himself as he spun the empty liquor bottle with abstracted motions of his hand. "Have you ever experienced Darkness, young man?"

The newsman leaned against the wall and considered. "No. Can't say I have. But I know what it is. Just—uh—" He made vague motions with his fingers, and then brightened. "Just no light. Like in caves."

"Have you ever been in a cave?"

"In a *cave!* Of course not!"

"I thought not. *I* tried last week—just to see—but I got out in a hurry. I went in until the mouth of the cave was just visible as a blur of light, with black everywhere else. I never thought a person my weight could run that fast."

Theremon's lip curled. "Well, if it comes to that, I guess I wouldn't have run, if I had been there."

The psychologist studied the young man with an annoyed frown.

"My, don't you talk big! I dare you to draw the curtain."

Theremon looked his surprise and said, "What for? If we had four or five suns out there we might want to cut the light down a bit for comfort, but now we haven't enough light as it is."

"That's the point. Just draw the curtain; then come here and sit down."

"All right." Theremon reached for the tasseled string and jerked. The red curtain slid across the wide window, the brass rings hissing their way along the crossbar, and a dusk-red shadow clamped down on the room.

Theremon's footsteps sounded hollowly in the silence as he made his way to the table, and then they stopped halfway. "I can't see you, sir," he whispered.

"Feel your way," ordered Sheerin in a strained voice.

"But I can't see you, sir." The newsman was breathing harshly. "I can't see anything."

"What did you expect?" came the grim reply. "Come here and sit down!"

The footsteps sounded again, waveringly, approaching slowly. There was the sound of someone fumbling with a chair. Theremon's voice came thinly, "Here I am. I feel . . . *ulp* . . . all right."

"You like it, do you?"

"N-no. It's pretty awful. The walls seem to be—" He paused. "They seem to be closing in on me. I keep wanting to push them away. But I'm not going *mad!* In fact, the feeling isn't as bad as it was."

"All right. Draw the curtain back again."

There were cautious footsteps through the dark, the rustle of Theremon's body against the curtain as he felt for the tassel, and then the triumphant *ro-o-o-osh* of the curtain slithering back. Red light flooded the room, and with a cry of joy Theremon looked up at the sun.

Sheerin wiped the moistness off his forehead with the back of a hand and said shakily, "And that was just a dark room."

"It can be stood," said Theremon lightly.

"Yes, a dark room can. But were you at the Jonglor Centennial Exposition two years ago?"

"No, it so happens I never got around to it. Six thousand miles was just a bit too much to travel, even for the exposition."

"Well, I was there. You remember hearing about the 'Tunnel of Mystery' that broke all records in the amusement area—for the first month or so, anyway?"

"Yes. Wasn't there some fuss about it?"

"Very little. It was hushed up. You see, that Tunnel of Mystery was just a mile-long tunnel—with no lights. You got into a little open car and jolted along through Darkness for fifteen minutes. It was very popular—while it lasted."

"Popular?"

"Certainly. There's a fascination in being frightened when *it's part of a game*. A baby is born with three instinctive fears: of loud noises, of falling, and of the absence of light. That's why it's considered so funny to jump at someone and shout 'Boo!' That's why it's such fun to ride a roller coaster. And that's why that Tunnel of Mystery started cleaning up. People came out of that Darkness shaking, breathless, half dead with fear, but they kept on paying to get in."

"Wait a while, I remember now. Some people came out dead, didn't they? There were rumors of that after it shut down."

The psychologist snorted. "Bah! Two or three died. That was nothing! They paid off the families of the dead ones and argued the Jonglor City Council into forgetting it. After all, they said, if people with weak hearts want to go through the tunnel, it was at their own risk—and besides, it wouldn't happen again. So they put a doctor in the front office and had every customer go through a physical examination before getting into the car. That actually *boosted* ticket sales."

"Well, then?"

"But, you see, there was something else. People sometimes came out in perfect order, except that they refused to go into buildings—any buildings; including palaces, mansions, apartment houses, tenements, cottages, huts, shacks, lean-tos, and tents."

Theremon looked shocked. "You mean they refused to come in out of the open. Where'd they sleep?"

"In the open."

"They should have forced them inside."

"Oh, they did, they did. Whereupon these people went into violent hysterics and did their best to bat their brains out against the nearest wall. Once you got them inside, you couldn't keep them there without a strait jacket and a shot of morphine."

"They must have been crazy."

"Which is exactly what they were. One person out of every ten who went into that tunnel came out that way. They called in the psychologists, and we did the only thing possible. We closed down the exhibit." He spread his hands.

"What was the matter with these people?" asked Theremon finally.

"Essentially the same thing that was the matter with you when you thought the walls of the room were crushing in on you in the dark. There is a psychological term for mankind's instinctive fear of the absence of light. We call it 'claustrophobia,' because the lack of light is always tied up with enclosed places, so that fear of one is fear of the other. You see?"

"And those people of the tunnel?"

"Those people of the tunnel consisted of those unfortunates whose mentality did not quite possess the resiliency to overcome the claustrophobia that overtook them in the Darkness. Fifteen minutes without light is a long time; you only had two or three minutes, and I believe you were fairly upset.

"The people of the tunnel had what is called a 'claustrophobic fixation.' Their latent fear of Darkness and enclosed places had crystallized and become active, and, as far as we can tell, permanent. *That's* what fifteen minutes in the dark will do."

There was a long silence, and Theremon's forehead wrinkled slowly into a frown. "I don't believe it's that bad."

"You mean you don't want to believe," snapped Sheerin. "You're afraid to believe. Look out the window!"

Theremon did so, and the psychologist continued without pausing. "Imagine Darkness—everywhere. No light, as far as you can see. The houses, the trees, the fields, the earth, the sky—*black!* And Stars thrown in, for all I know—whatever *they* are. Can you conceive it?"

"Yes, I can," declared Theremon truculently.

And Sheerin slammed his fist down upon the table in sudden passion. "You lie! You can't conceive that. Your brain wasn't built for the conception any more than it was built for the conception of infinity or of eternity. You can only talk about it. A fraction of the reality upsets you, and when the real thing comes, your brain is going to be presented with a phenomenon outside its limits of comprehension. You will go mad, completely and permanently! There is no question of it!"

He added sadly, "And another couple of millennia of painful struggle comes to nothing Tomorrow there won't be a city standing unharmed in all Lagash."

Theremon recovered part of his mental equilibrium. "That doesn't follow. I still don't see that I can go loony just because there isn't a sun in the sky—but even if I did, and everyone else did, how does that harm the cities? Are we going to blow them down?"

But Sheerin was angry, too. "If you were in Darkness, what would you want more than anything else; what would it be that every instinct would call for? Light, damn you, *light!*"

"Well?"

"And how would you get light?"

"I don't know," said Theremon flatly.

"What's the *only* way to get light, short of the sun?"

"How should I know?"

They were standing face to face and nose to nose.

Sheerin said, "You burn something, mister. Ever see a forest fire? Ever go camping and cook a stew over a wood fire? Heat isn't the only thing burning wood gives off, you know. It gives off light, and people know that. And when it's dark they want light, and they're going to *get it.*"

"So they burn wood?"

"So they burn whatever they can get. They've got to have light. They've got to burn something, and wood isn't handy—so they'll burn whatever is nearest. They'll have their light—and every center of habitation goes up in flames!"

Eyes held each other as though the whole matter were a personal affair of respective will powers, and then Theremon broke away wordlessly. His breathing was harsh and ragged, and he scarcely noted the sudden hubbub that came from the adjoining room behind the closed door.

Sheerin spoke, and it was with an effort that he made it sound matter-of-fact. "I think I heard Yimot's voice. He and Faro are probably back. Let's go in and see what kept them."

"Might as well!" muttered Theremon. He drew a long breath and seemed to shake himself. The tension was broken.

The room was in an uproar, with members of the staff clustering about two young men who were removing outer garments even as they parried the miscellany of questions being thrown at them.

Aton bustled through the crowd and faced the newcomers angrily. "Do you realize that it's less than half an hour before deadline? Where have you two been?"

Faro 24 seated himself and rubbed his hands. His cheeks were red with the outdoor chill. "Yimot and I have just finished carrying through a little crazy experiment of our own.

We've been trying to see if we couldn't construct an arrangement by which we could simulate the appearance of Darkness and Stars so as to get an advance notion as to how it looked."

There was a confused murmur from the listeners, and a sudden look of interest entered Aton's eyes. "There wasn't anything said of this before. How did you go about it?"

"Well," said Faro, "the idea came to Yimot and myself long ago, and we've been working it out in our spare time. Yimot knew of a low one-story house down in the city with a domed roof—it had once been used as a museum, I think. Anyway, we bought it—"

"Where did you get the money?" interrupted Aton peremptorily.

"Our bank accounts," grunted Yimot 70. "It cost two thousand credits." Then, defensively, "Well, what of it? Tomorrow, two thousand credits will be two thousand pieces of paper. That's all."

"Sure," agreed Faro. "We bought the place and rigged it up with black velvet from top to bottom so as to get as perfect a Darkness as possible. Then we punched tiny holes in the ceiling and through the roof and covered them with little metal caps, all of which could be shoved aside simultaneously at the close of a switch. At least, we didn't do that part ourselves; we got a carpenter and an electrician and some others—money didn't count. The point was that we could get the light to shine through those holes in the roof, so that we could get a starlike effect."

Not a breath was drawn during the pause that followed. Aton said stiffly:

"You had no right to make a private—"

Faro seemed abashed. "I know, sir—but, frankly, Yimot and I thought the experiment was a little dangerous. If the effect really worked, we half expected to go mad—from what Sheerin says about all this, we thought that would be rather likely. We wanted to take the risk ourselves. Of course, if we found we could retain sanity, it occurred to us that we might develop immunity to the real thing, and then expose the rest of you to the same thing. But things didn't work out at all—"

"Why, what happened?"

It was Yimot who answered. "We shut ourselves in and allowed our eyes to get accustomed to the dark. It's an extremely creepy feeling because the total Darkness makes you feel as if the walls and ceiling are crushing in on you. But we got over that and pulled the switch. The caps fell away and the roof glittered all over with little dots of light—"

"Well?"

"Well—nothing. That was the whacky part of it. Nothing happened. It was just a roof with holes in it, and that's just what it looked like. We tried it over and over again—that's what kept us so late—but there just isn't any effect at all."

There followed a shocked silence, and all eyes turned to Sheerin, who sat motionless, mouth open.

Theremon was the first to speak. "You know what this does to this whole theory you've built up, Sheerin, don't you?" He was grinning with relief.

But Sheerin raised his hand. "Now wait a while. Just let me think this through." And then he snapped his fingers, and when he lifted his head there was neither surprise nor uncertainty in his eyes. "Of course—"

He never finished. From somewhere up above there sounded a sharp clang, and Beenay, starting to his feet, dashed up the stairs with a "What the devil!"

The rest followed after.

Things happened quickly. Once up in the dome, Beenay cast one horrified glance at the shuttered photographic plates and at the man bending over them; and then hurled himself fiercely at the intruder, getting a death grip on his throat. There was a wild threshing, and as others of the staff joined in, the stranger was swallowed up and smothered under the weight of half a dozen angry men.

Aton came up last, breathing heavily. "Let him up!"

There was a reluctant unscrambling and the stranger, panting harshly, with his clothes torn and his forehead bruised, was hauled to his feet. He had a short yellow beard curled elaborately in the style affected by the Cultists.

Beenay shifted his hold to a collar grip and shook the man savagely. "All right, rat, what's the idea? These plates—"

"I wasn't after *them*," retorted the Cultist coldly. "That was an accident."

Beenay followed his glowering stare and snarled, "I see. You were after the cameras themselves. The accident with the plates was a stroke of luck for you, then. If you had touched Snapping Bertha or any of the others, you would have died by slow torture. As it is—" He drew his fist back.

Aton grabbed his sleeve. "Stop that! Let him go!"

The young technician wavered, and his arm dropped reluctantly. Aton pushed him aside and confronted the Cultist. "You're Latimer, aren't you?"

The Cultist bowed stiffly and indicated the symbol upon his hip. "I am Latimer 25, adjutant of the third class to his serenity, Sor 5."

"And"—Aton's white eyebrows lifted—"you were with his serenity when he visited me last week, weren't you?"

Latimer bowed a second time.

"Now, then, what do you want?"

"Nothing that you would give me of your own free will."

"Sor 5 sent you, I suppose—or is this your own idea?"

"I won't answer that question."

"Will there be any further visitors?"

"I won't answer that, either."

Aton glanced at his timepiece and scowled. "Now, man, what is it your master wants of me? I have fulfilled my end of the bargain."

Latimer smiled faintly, but said nothing.

"I asked him," continued Aton angrily, "for data only the Cult could supply, and it was given to me. For that, thank you. In return, I promised to prove the essential truth of the creed of the Cult."

"There was no need to prove that," came the proud retort. "It stands proven by the 'Book of Revelations.'"

"For the handful that constitute the Cult, yes. Don't pretend to mistake my meaning. I offered to present scientific backing for your beliefs. And I did!"

The Cultist's eyes narrowed bitterly. "Yes, you did—with a fox's subtlety, for your pretended explanation backed our beliefs, and at the same time removed all necessity for them. You made of the Darkness and of the Stars a natural phenomenon, and removed all its real significance. That was blasphemy."

"If so, the fault isn't mine. The facts exist. What can I do but state them?"

"Your 'facts' are a fraud and a delusion."

Aton stamped angrily. "How do you know?"

And the answer came with the certainty of absolute faith. "I *know!*"

The director purpled and Beenay whispered urgently. Aton waved him silent. "And what does Sor 5 want us to do? He still thinks, I suppose, that in trying to warn the world to take measures against the menace of madness, we are placing innumerable souls in jeopardy. We aren't succeeding, if that means anything to him."

"The attempt itself has done harm enough, and your vicious effort to gain information by means of your devilish instruments must be stopped. We obey the will of their Stars, and I only regret that my clumsiness prevented me from wrecking your infernal devices."

"It wouldn't have done you too much good," returned Aton. "All our data, except for the direct evidence we intend collecting right now, is already safely cached and well beyond possibility of harm." He smiled grimly. "But that does not affect your present status as an attempted burglar and criminal."

He turned to the men behind him. "Someone call the police at Saro City."

There was a cry of distaste from Sheerin. "Damn it, Aton, what's wrong with you? There's no time for that. Here"—he bustled his way forward—"let me handle this."

Aton stared down his nose at the psychologist. "This is not the time for your monkeyshines, Sheerin. Will you please let me handle this my own way? Right now you are a complete outsider here, and don't forget it."

Sheerin's mouth twisted eloquently. "Now why should we go to the impossible trouble of calling the police—with Beta's eclipse a matter of minutes from now—when this young man here is perfectly willing to pledge his word of honor to remain and cause no trouble whatsoever?"

The Cultist answered promptly, "I will do no such thing. You're free to do what you want, but it's only fair to warn you that just as soon as I get my chance I'm going to finish what I came out here to do. If it's my word of honor you're relying on, you'd better call the police."

Sheerin smiled in a friendly fashion. "You're a determined cuss, aren't you? Well, I'll explain something. Do you see that young man at the window? He's a strong, husky fellow, quite handy with his fists, and he's an outsider besides. Once the eclipse starts there will be nothing for him to do except keep an eye on you. Besides him, there will be myself—a little too stout for active fisticuffs, but still able to help."

"Well, what of it?" demanded Latimer frozenly.

"Listen and I'll tell you," was the reply. "Just as soon as the eclipse starts, we're going to take you, Theremon and I, and deposit you in a little closet with one door, to which is attached one giant lock and no windows. You will remain there for the duration."

"And afterward," breathed Latimer fiercely, "there'll be no

one to let me out. I know as well as you do what the coming of the Stars means—I know it far better than you. With all your minds gone, you are not likely to free me. Suffocation or slow starvation, is it? About what I might have expected from a group of scientists. But I don't give my word. It's a matter of principle, and I won't discuss it further."

Aton seemed perturbed. His faded eyes were troubled. "Really, Sheerin, locking him—"

"Please!" Sheerin motioned him impatiently to silence. "I don't think for a moment things will go that far. Latimer has just tried a clever little bluff, but I'm not a psychologist just because I like the sound of the word." He grinned at the Cultist. "Come now, you don't really think I'm trying anything as crude as slow starvation. My dear Latimer, if I lock you in the closet, you are not going to see the Darkness, and you are not going to see the Stars. It does not take much of a knowledge of the fundamental creed of the Cult to realize that for you to be hidden from the Stars when they appear means the loss of your immortal soul. Now, I believe you to be an honorable man. I'll accept your word of honor to make no further effort to disrupt proceedings if you'll offer it."

A vein throbbed in Latimer's temple, and he seemed to shrink within himself as he said thickly, "You have it!" And then he added with swift fury, "But it is my consolation that you will all be damned for your deeds of today." He turned on his heel and stalked to the high three-legged stool by the door.

Sheerin nodded to the columnist. "Take a seat next to him, Theremon—just as a formality. Hey, Theremon!"

But the newspaperman didn't move. He had gone pale to the lips. "Look at that!" The finger he pointed toward the sky shook, and his voice was dry and cracked.

There was one simultaneous gasp as every eye followed the pointing finger and, for one breathless moment, stared frozenly.

Beta was chipped on one side!

The tiny bit of encroaching blackness was perhaps the width of a fingernail, but to the staring watchers it magnified itself into the crack of doom.

Only for a moment they watched, and after that there was a shrieking confusion that was even shorter of duration and which gave way to an orderly scurry of activity—each man at his prescribed job. At the crucial moment there was no time for emotion. The men were merely scientists with work to do. Even Aton had melted away.

Sheerin said prosaically, "First contact must have been made fifteen minutes ago. A little early, but pretty good considering the uncertainties involved in the calculation." He looked about him and then tiptoed to Theremon, who still remained staring out the window, and dragged him away gently.

"Aton is furious," he whispered, "so stay away. He missed first contact on account of this fuss with Latimer, and if you get in his way he'll have you thrown out the window."

Theremon nodded shortly and sat down. Sheerin stared in surprise at him.

"The devil, man," he exclaimed, "you're shaking."

"Eh?" Theremon licked dry lips and then tried to smile. "I don't feel very well, and that's a fact."

The psychologist's eyes hardened. "You're not losing your nerve?"

"No!" cried Theremon in a flash of indignation. "Give me a chance, will you? I haven't really believed this rigmarole— not way down beneath, anyway—till just this minute. Give me a chance to get used to the idea. You've been preparing yourself for two months or more."

"You're right, at that," replied Sheerin thoughtfully. "Listen! Have you got a family—parents, wife, children?"

Theremon shook his head. "You mean the Hideout, I suppose. No, you don't have to worry about that. I have a sister, but she's two thousand miles away. I don't even know her exact address."

"Well, then, what about yourself? You've got time to get there, and they're one short anyway, since I left. After all, you're not needed here, and you'd make a darned fine addition—"

Theremon looked at the other wearily. "You think I'm scared stiff, don't you? Well, get this, mister, I'm a newspaperman and I've been assigned to cover a story. I intend covering it."

There was a faint smile on the psychologist's face. "I see. Professional honor, is that it?"

"You might call it that. But, man, I'd give my right arm for another bottle of that sockeroo juice even half the size of the one you hogged. If ever a fellow needed a drink, I do."

He broke off. Sheerin was nudging him violently. "Do you hear that? Listen!"

Theremon followed the motion of the other's chin and

stared at the Cultist, who, oblivious to all about him, faced the window, a look of wild elation on his face, droning to himself the while in singsong fashion.

"What's he saying?" whispered the columnist.

"He's quoting 'Book of Revelations,' fifth chapter," replied Sheerin. Then, urgently, "Keep quiet and listen, I tell you."

The Cultist's voice had risen in a sudden increase of fervor:

"'And it came to pass that in those days the sun, Beta, held lone vigil in the sky for ever longer periods as the revolutions passed; until such time as for full half a revolution, it alone, shrunken and cold, shone down upon Lagash.

"'And men did assemble in the public squares and in the highways, there to debate and to marvel at the sight, for a strange depression had seized them. Their minds were troubled and their speech confused, for the souls of men awaited the coming of the Stars.

"'And in the city of Trigon, at high noon, Vendret 2 came forth and said unto the men of Trigon, "Lo, ye sinners! Though ye scorn the ways of righteousness, yet will the time of reckoning come. Even now the Cave approaches to swallow Lagash; yea, and all it contains.

"'And even as he spoke the lip of the Cave of Darkness passed the edge of Beta so that to all Lagash it was hidden from sight. Loud were the cries of men as it vanished, and great the fear of soul that fell upon them.

"'It came to pass that the Darkness of the Cave fell upon Lagash, and there was no light on all the surface of Lagash. Men were even as blinded, nor could one man see his neighbor, though he felt his breath upon his face.

"'And in this blackness there appeared the Stars, in countless numbers, and to the strains of ineffable music of a beauty so wondrous that the very leaves of the trees turned to tongues that cried out in wonder.

"'And in that moment the souls of men departed from them, and their abandoned bodies became even as beasts; yea, even as brutes of the wild; so that through the blackened streets of the cities of Lagash they prowled with wild cries.

"'From the Stars there then reached down the Heavenly Flame, and where it touched, the cities of Lagash flamed to utter destruction, so that of man and of the works of man nought remained.

"'Even then—'"

There was a subtle change in Latimer's tone. His eyes had not shifted, but somehow he had become aware of the absorbed attention of the other two. Easily, without pausing for breath, the timbre of his voice shifted and the syllables became more liquid.

Theremon, caught by surprise, stared. The words seemed on the border of familiarity. There was an elusive shift in the accent, a tiny change in the vowel stress; nothing more—yet Latimer had become thoroughly unintelligible.

Sheerin smiled slyly. "He shifted to some old-cycle tongue, probably their traditional second cycle. That was the language in which the 'Book of Revelations' had originally been written, you know."

"It doesn't matter; I've heard enough." Theremon shoved his chair back and brushed his hair back with hands that no longer shook. "I feel much better now."

"You do?" Sheerin seemed mildly surprised.

"I'll say I do. I had a bad case of jitters just a while back. Listening to you and your gravitation and seeing that eclipse start almost finished me. But this"—he jerked a contemptuous thumb at the yellow-bearded Cultist—"*this* is the sort of thing my nurse used to tell me. I've been laughing at that sort of thing all my life. I'm not going to let it scare me *now*."

He drew a deep breath and said with a hectic gaiety, "But if I expect to keep on the good side of myself, I'm going to turn my chair away from the window."

Sheerin said, "Yes, but you'd better talk lower. Aton just lifted his head out of that box he's got it stuck into and gave you a look that should have killed you."

Theremon made a mouth. "I forgot about the old fellow." With elaborate care he turned the chair from the window, cast one distasteful look over his shoulder and said, "It has occurred to me that there must be considerable immunity against this Star madness."

The psychologist did not answer immediately. Beta was past its zenith now, and the square of bloody sunlight that outlined the window upon the floor had lifted into Sheerin's lap. He stared at its dusky color thoughtfully and then bent and squinted into the sun itself.

The chip in its side had grown to a black encroachment that covered a third of Beta. He shuddered, and when he straightened once more his florid cheeks did not contain quite as much color as they had had previously.

With a smile that was almost apologetic, he reversed his chair also. "There are probably two million people in Saro

City that are all trying to join the Cult at once in one gigantic revival." Then, ironically, "The Cult is in for an hour of unexampled prosperity. I trust they'll make the most of it. Now, what was it you said?"

"Just this. How do the Cultists manage to keep the 'Book of Revelations' going from cycle to cycle, and how on Lagash did it get written in the first place? There must have been some sort of immunity, for if everyone had gone mad, who would be left to write the book?"

Sheerin stared at his questioner ruefully. "Well, now, young man, there isn't any eyewitness answer to that, but we've got a few damned good notions as to what happened. You see, there are three kinds of people who might remain relatively unaffected. First, the very few who don't see the Stars at all; the blind, those who drink themselves into a stupor at the beginning of the eclipse and remain so to the end. We leave them out—because they aren't really witnesses.

"Then there are children below six, to whom the world as a whole is too new and strange for them to be too frightened at Stars and Darkness. They would be just another item in an already surprising world. You see that, don't you?"

The other nodded doubtfully. "I suppose so."

"Lastly, there are those whose minds are too coarsely grained to be entirely toppled. The very insensitive would be scarcely affected—oh, such people as some of our older, work-broken peasants. Well, the children would have fugitive memories, and that, combined with the confused, incoherent babblings of the half-mad morons, formed the basis for the 'Book of Revelations.'

"Naturally, the book was based, in the first place, on the testimony of those least qualified to serve as historians; that is, children and morons; and was probably extensively edited and re-edited through the cycles."

"Do you suppose," broke in Theremon, "that they carried the book through the cycles the way we're planning on handing on the secret of gravitation?"

Sheerin shrugged. "Perhaps, but their exact method is unimportant. They do it, somehow. The point I was getting at was that the book can't help but be a mass of distortion, even if it is based on fact. For instance, do you remember the experiment with the holes in the roof that Faro and Yimot tried—the one that didn't work?"

"Yes."

"You know why it didn't w—" He stopped and rose in

alarm, for Aton was approaching, his face a twisted mask of consternation. *"What's happened?"*

Aton drew him aside and Sheerin could feel the fingers on his elbow twitching.

"Not so loud!" Aton's voice was low and tortured. "I've just gotten word from the Hideout on the private line."

Sheerin broke in anxiously, "They are in trouble?"

"Not *they*." Aton stressed the pronoun significantly. "They sealed themselves off just a while ago, and they're going to stay buried till day after tomorrow. They're safe. But the city, Sheerin—it's a shambles. You have no idea—" He was having difficulty in speaking.

"Well?" snapped Sheerin impatiently. "What of it? It will get worse. What are you shaking about?" Then, suspiciously, "How do you feel?"

Aton's eyes sparkled angrily at the insinuation, and then faded to anxiety once more. "You don't understand. The Cultists are active. They're rousing the people to storm the Observatory—promising them immediate entrance into grace, promising them salvation, promising them anything. What are we to do, Sheerin?"

Sheerin's head bent, and he stared in long abstraction at his toes. He tapped his chin with one knuckle, then looked up and said crisply, "Do? What is there to do? Nothing at all! Do the men know of this?"

"No, of course not!"

"Good! Keep it that way. How long till totality?"

"Not quite an hour."

"There's nothing to do but gamble. It will take time to organize any really formidable mob, and it will take more time to get them out here. We're a good five miles from the city—"

He glared out the window, down the slopes to where the farmed patches gave way to clumps of white houses in the suburbs; down to where the metropolis itself was a blur on the horizon—a mist in the waning blaze of Beta.

He repeated without turning, "It will take time. Keep on working and pray that totality comes first."

Beta was cut in half, the line of division pushing a slight concavity into the still-bright portion of the Sun. It was like a gigantic eyelid shutting slantwise over the light of a world.

The faint clatter of the room in which he stood faded into oblivion, and he sensed only the thick silence of the fields

outside. The very insects seemed frightened mute. And things
were dim.

He jumped at the voice in his ear. Theremon said, "Is
something wrong?"

"Eh? Er—no. Get back to the chair. We're in the way."
They slipped back to their corner, but the psychologist did
not speak for a time. He lifted a finger and loosened his collar. He twisted his neck back and forth but found no relief.
He looked up suddenly.

"Are you having any difficulty in breathing?"

The newspaperman opened his eyes wide and drew two or
three long breaths. "No. Why?"

"I looked out the window too long, I suppose. The dimness
got me. Difficulty in breathing is one of the first symptoms of
a claustrophobic attack."

Theremon drew another long breath. "Well, it hasn't got
me yet. Say, here's another of the fellows."

Beenay had interposed his bulk between the light and the
pair in the corner, and Sheerin squinted up at him anxiously.
"Hello, Beenay."

The astronomer shifted his weight to the other foot and
smiled feebly. "You won't mind if I sit down awhile and join
in on the talk? My cameras are set, and there's nothing to do
till totality." He paused and eyed the Cultist, who fifteen
minutes earlier had drawn a small, skin-bound book from his
sleeve and had been poring intently over it ever since. "That
rat hasn't been making trouble, has he?"

Sheerin shook his head. His shoulders were thrown back
and he frowned his concentration as he forced himself to
breathe regularly. He said, "Have you had any trouble
breathing, Beenay?"

Beenay sniffed the air in his turn. "It doesn't seem stuffy to
me."

"A touch of claustrophobia," explained Sheerin apolo-
getically.

"Oh-h-h! It worked itself differently with me. I get the impression that my eyes are going back on me. Things seem to
blur and—well, nothing is clear. And it's cold, too."

"Oh, it's cold, all right. That's no illusion." Theremon
grimaced. "My toes feel as if I'd been shipping them cross
country in a refrigerating car."

"What we need," put in Sheerin, "is to keep our minds
busy with extraneous affairs. I was telling you a while ago,

Theremon, why Faro's experiments with the holes in the roof came to nothing."

"You were just beginning," replied Theremon. He encircled a knee with both arms and nuzzled his chin against it.

"Well, as I started to say, they were misled by taking the 'Book of Revelations' literally. There probably wasn't any sense in attaching any physical significance to the Stars. It might be, you know, that in the presence of total Darkness, the mind finds it absolutely necessary to create light. This illusion of light might be all the Stars there really are."

"In other words," interposed Theremon, "you mean the Stars are the results of the madness and not one of the causes. Then, what good will Beenay's photographs be?"

"To prove that it is an illusion, maybe; or to prove the opposite, for all I know. Then again——"

But Beenay had drawn his chair closer, and there was an expression of sudden enthusiasm on his face. "Say, I'm glad you two got on to this subject." His eyes narrowed and he lifted one finger. "I've been thinking about these Stars and I've got a really cute notion. Of course, it's strictly ocean foam, and I'm not trying to advance it seriously, but I think it's interesting. Do you want to hear it?"

He seemed half reluctant, but Sheerin leaned back and said, "Go ahead! I'm listening."

"Well, then, supposing there were other suns in the universe." He broke off a little bashfully. "I mean suns that are so far away that they're too dim to see. It sounds as if I've been reading some of that fantastic fiction, I suppose."

"Not necessarily. Still, isn't that possibility eliminated by the fact that, according to the Law of Gravitation, they would make themselves evident by their attractive forces?"

"Not if they were far enough off," rejoined Beenay, "really far off—maybe as much as four light years, or even more. We'd never be able to detect perturbations then, because they'd be too small. Say that there were a lot of suns that far off; a dozen or two, maybe."

Theremon whistled melodiously. "What an idea for a good Sunday supplement article. Two dozen suns in a universe eight light years across. Wow! That would shrink our universe into insignificance. The readers would eat it up."

"Only an idea," said Beenay with a grin, "but you see the point. During eclipse, these dozen suns would become visible, because there'd be no *real* sunlight to drown them out. Since they're so far off, they'd appear small, like so many little marbles. Of course, the Cultists talk of millions of Stars, but that's probably exaggeration. There just isn't any place in the universe you could put a million suns—unless they touch one another."

Sheerin had listened with gradually increasing interest. "You've hit something there, Beenay. And exaggeration is just exactly what would happen. Our minds, as you probably know, can't grasp directly any number higher than five; above that there is only the concept of 'many.' A dozen would become a million just like that. A damn good idea!"

"And I've got another cute little notion," Beenay said. "Have you ever thought what a simple problem gravitation would be if only you had a sufficiently simple system? Supposing you had a universe in which there was a planet with only one sun. The planet would travel in a perfect eclipse and the exact nature of the gravitational force would be so evident it could be accepted as an axiom. Astronomers on such a world would start off with gravity probably before they even invent the telescope. Naked-eye observation would be enough."

"But would such a system be dynamically stable?" questioned Sheerin doubtfully.

"Sure! They call it the 'one-and-one' case. It's been worked out mathematically, but it's the philosophical implications that interest me."

"It's nice to think about," admitted Sheerin, "as a pretty abstraction—like a perfect gas or absolute zero."

"Of course," continued Beenay, "there's the catch that life would be impossible on such a planet. It wouldn't get enough heat and light, and if it rotated there would be total Darkness half of each day. You couldn't expect life—which is fundamentally dependent upon light—to develop under those conditions. Besides—"

Sheerin's chair went over backward as he sprang to his feet in a rude interruption. "Aton's brought out the lights."

Beenay said, "Huh," turned to stare, and then grinned halfway around his head in open relief.

There were half a dozen foot-long, inch-thick rods cradled in Aton's arms. He glared over them at the assembled staff members.

"Get back to work, all of you. Sheerin, come here and help me!"

Sheerin trotted to the older man's side and, one by one, in utter silence, the two adjusted the rods in makeshift metal holders suspended from the walls.

With the air of one carrying through the most sacred item of a religious ritual, Sheerin scraped a large, clumsy match into spluttering life and passed it to Aton, who carried the flame to the upper end of one of the rods.

It hesitated there a while, playing futilely about the tip, until a sudden, crackling flare cast Aton's lined face into yellow highlights. He withdrew the match and a spontaneous cheer rattled the window.

The rod was topped by six inches of wavering flame! Methodically, the other rods were lighted, until six independent fires turned the rear of the room yellow.

The light was dim, dimmer even than the tenuous sunlight. The flames reeled crazily, giving birth to drunken, swaying shadows. The torches smoked devilishly and smelled like a bad day in the kitchen. But they emitted yellow light.

There is something to yellow light—after four hours of somber, dimming Beta. Even Latimer had lifted his eyes from his book and stared in wonder.

Sheerin warmed his hands at the nearest, regardless of the soot that gathered upon them in a fine, gray powder, and muttered ecstatically to himself. "Beautiful! Beautiful! I never realized before what a wonderful color yellow is."

But Theremon regarded the torches suspiciously. He wrinkled his nose at the rancid odor, and said, "What are those things?"

"Wood," said Sheerin shortly.

"Oh, no, they're not. They aren't burning. The top inch is charred and the flame just keeps shooting up out of nothing."

"That's the beauty of it. This is a really efficient artificial-light mechanism. We made a few hundred of them, but most went to the Hideout, of course. You see"—he turned and wiped his blackened hands upon his handkerchief—"you take the pithy core of coarse water reeds, dry them thoroughly and soak them in animal grease. Then you set fire to it and the grease burns, little by little. These torches will burn for almost half an hour without stopping. Ingenious, isn't it? It was developed by one of our own young men at Saro University."

After the momentary sensation, the dome had quieted. Latimer had carried his chair directly beneath a torch and continued reading, lips moving in the monotonous recital of invocations to the Stars. Beenay had drifted away to his cameras once more, and Theremon seized the opportunity to add to his notes on the article he was going to write for the

Saro City *Chronicle* the next day—a procedure he had been following for the last two hours in a perfectly methodical, perfectly conscientious and, as he was well aware, perfectly meaningless fashion.

But, as the gleam of amusement in Sheerin's eyes indicated, careful note taking occupied his mind with something other than the fact that the sky was gradually turning a horrible deep purple-red, as if it were one gigantic, freshly peeled beet; and so it fulfilled its purpose.

The air grew, somehow, denser. Dusk, like a palpable entity, entered the room, and the dancing circle of yellow light about the torches etched itself into ever-sharper distinction against the gathering grayness beyond. There was the odor of smoke and the presence of little chuckling sounds that the torches made as they burned; the soft pad of one of the men circling the table at which he worked, on hesitant tiptoes; the occasional indrawn breath of someone trying to retain composure in a world that was retreating into the shadow.

It was Theremon who first heard the extraneous noise. It was a vague, unorganized *impression* of sound that would have gone unnoticed but for the dead silence that prevailed within the dome.

The newsman sat upright and replaced his notebook. He held his breath and listened; then, with considerable reluctance, threaded his way between the solarscope and one of Beenay's cameras and stood before the window.

The silence ripped to fragments at his startled shout:

"Sheerin!"

Work stopped! The psychologist was at his side in a moment. Aton joined him. Even Yimot 70, high in his little lean-back seat at the eyepiece of the gigantic solarscope, paused and looked downward.

Outside, Beta was a mere smoldering splinter, taking one last desperate look at Lagash. The eastern horizon, in the direction of the city was lost in Darkness, and the road from Saro to the Observatory was a dull-red line bordered on both sides by wooded tracts, the trees of which had somehow lost individuality and merged into a continuous shadowy mass.

But it was the highway itself that held attention, for along it there surged another, and infinitely menacing, shadowy mass.

Aton cried in a cracked voice, "The madmen from the city! They've come!"

"How long to totality?" demanded Sheerin.

"Fifteen minutes, but . . . but they'll be here in five."

"Never mind, keep the men working. We'll hold them off. This place is built like a fortress. Aton, keep an eye on our young Cultist just for luck. Theremon, come with me."

Sheerin was out the door, and Theremon was at his heels. The stairs stretched below them in tight, circular sweeps about the central shaft, fading into a dank and dreary grayness.

The first momentum of their rush had carried them fifty feet down, so that the dim, flickering yellow from the open door of the dome had disappeared and both up above and down below the same dusky shadow crushed in upon them.

Sheerin paused, and his pudgy hand clutched at his chest. His eyes bulged and his voice was a dry cough. "I can't . . . breathe . . . go down . . . yourself. Close all doors—"

Theremon took a few downward steps, then turned. "Wait! Can you hold out a minute?" He was panting himself. The air passed in and out his lungs like so much molasses, and there was a little germ of screeching panic in his mind at the thought of making his way into the mysterious Darkness below by himself.

Theremon, after all, was afraid of the dark!

"Stay here," he said. "I'll be back in a second." He dashed upward two steps at a time, heart pounding—not altogether from the exertion—tumbled into the dome and snatched a torch from its holder. It was foul smelling, and the smoke smarted his eyes almost blind, but he clutched that torch as if he wanted to kiss it for joy, and its flame streamed backward as he hurtled down the stairs again.

Sheerin opened his eyes and moaned as Theremon bent over him. Theremon shook him roughly. "All right, get a hold on yourself. We've got light."

He held the torch at tiptoe height and, propping the tottering psychologist by an elbow, made his way downward in the middle of the protecting circle of illumination.

The offices on the ground floor still possessed what light there was, and Theremon felt the horror about him relax.

"Here," he said brusquely, and passed the torch to Sheerin. "You can hear *them* outside."

And they could. Little scraps of hoarse, wordless shouts.

But Sheerin was right; the Observatory was built like a fortress. Erected in the last century, when the neo-Gavottian style of architecture was at its ugly height, it had been designed for stability and durability, rather than for beauty.

The windows were protected by the grillework of inch-thick iron bars sunk deep into the concrete sills. The walls were solid masonry that an earthquake couldn't have touched, and the main door was a huge oaken slab reinforced with iron at the strategic points. Theremon shot the bolts and they slid shut with a dull clang.

At the other end of the corridor, Sheerin cursed weakly. He pointed to the lock of the back door which had been neatly jimmied into uselessness.

"That must be how Latimer got in," he said.

"Well, don't stand there," cried Theremon impatiently. "Help drag up the furniture—and keep that torch out of my eyes. The smoke's killing me."

He slammed the heavy table up against the door as he spoke, and in two minutes had built a barricade which made up for what it lacked in beauty and symmetry by the sheer inertia of its massiveness.

Somewhere, dimly, far off, they could hear the battering of naked fists upon the door; and the screams and yells from outside had a sort of half reality.

That mob had set off from Saro City with only two things in mind: the attainment of Cultist salvation by the destruction of the Observatory, and a maddening fear that all but paralyzed them. There was no time to think of ground cars, or of weapons, or of leadership, or even of organization. They made for the Observatory on foot and assaulted it with bare hands.

And now that they were there, the last flash of Beta, the last ruby-red drop of flame, flickered feebly over a humanity that had left only stark, universal fear!

Theremon groaned, "Let's get back to the dome!"

In the dome, only Yimot, at the solarscope, had kept his place. The rest were clustered about the cameras, and Beenay was giving his instructions in a hoarse, strained voice.

"Get it straight, all of you. I'm snapping Beta just before totality and changing the plate. That will leave one of you to each camera. You all know about . . . about times of exposure—"

There was a breathless murmur of agreement.

Beenay passed a hand over his eyes. "Are the torches still burning? Never mind, I see them!" He was leaning hard against the back of a chair. "Now remember, don't . . . don't try to look for good shots. Don't waste time trying to get t- two stars at a time in the scope field. One is enough. And

. . . and if you feel yourself going, *get away from the camera.*"

At the door, Sheerin whispered to Theremon, "Take me to Aton. I don't see him."

The newsman did not answer immediately. The vague forms of the astronomers wavered and blurred, and the torches overhead had become only yellow splotches.

"It's dark," he whimpered.

Sheerin held out his hand, "Aton." He stumbled forward. "Aton!"

Theremon stepped after and seized his arm. "Wait, I'll take you." Somehow he made his way across the room. He closed his eyes against the Darkness and his mind against the chaos within it.

No one heard them or paid attention to them. Sheerin stumbled against the wall. "Aton!"

The psychologist felt shaking hands touching him, then withdrawing, and a voice muttering, "Is that you, Sheerin?"

"Aton!" He strove to breathe normally. "Don't worry about the mob. The place will hold them off."

Latimer, the Cultist, rose to his feet, and his face twisted in desperation. His word was pledged, and to break it would mean placing his soul in mortal peril. Yet that word had been forced from him and had not been given freely. The Stars would come soon; he could not stand by and allow— And yet his word was pledged.

Beenay's face was dimly flushed as it looked upward at Beta's last ray, and Latimer, seeing him bend over his camera, made his decision. His nails cut the flesh of his palms as he tensed himself.

He staggered crazily as he started his rush. There was nothing before him but shadows; the very floor beneath his feet lacked substance. And then someone was upon him and he went down with clutching fingers at his throat.

He doubled his knee and drove it hard into his assailant. "Let me up or I'll kill you."

Theremon cried out sharply and muttered through a blinding haze of pain, "You double-crossing rat!"

The newsman seemed conscious of everything at once. He heard Beenay croak, "I've got it. At your cameras, men!" and then there was the strange awareness that the last thread of sunlight had thinned out and snapped.

Simultaneously he heard one last choking gasp from Beenay, and a queer little cry from Sheerin, a hysterical giggle that cut off in a rasp—and a sudden silence, a strange, deadly silence from outside.

And Latimer had gone limp in his loosening grasp. Theremon peered into the Cultist's eyes and saw the blankness of them, staring upward, mirroring the feeble yellow of the torches. He saw the bubble of froth upon Latimer's lips and heard the low animal whimper in Latimer's throat.

With the slow fascination of fear, he lifted himself on one arm and turned his eyes toward the blood-curdling blackness of the window.

Through it shone the Stars!

Not Earth's feeble thirty-six hundred Stars visible to the eye—Lagash was in the center of a giant cluster. Thirty thousand mighty suns shown down in a soul-searing splendor that was more frighteningly cold in its awful indifference than the bitter wind that shivered across the cold, horribly bleak world.

Theremon staggered to his feet, his throat constricting him to breathlessness, all the muscles of his body writhing in a tensity of terror and sheer fear beyond bearing. He was going mad, and knew it, and somewhere deep inside a bit of sanity was screaming, struggling to fight off the hopeless flood of black terror. It was very horrible to go mad and know that you were doing mad—to know that in a little minute you would be here physically and yet all the real essence would be dead and drowned in the black madness. For this was the Dark—the Dark and the Cold and the Doom. The bright walls of the universe were shattered and their awful black fragments were falling down to crush and squeeze and obliterate him.

He jostled someone crawling on hands and knees, but stumbled somehow over him. Hands groping at his tortured throat, he limped toward the flame of the torches that filled all his mad vision.

"Light!" he screamed.

Aton, somewhere, was crying, whimpering horribly like a terribly frightened child. "Stars—all the Stars—we didn't know at all. We didn't know anything. We thought six stars is a universe is something the Stars didn't notice is Darkness forever and ever and ever and the walls are breaking in and we didn't know we couldn't know and anything—"

Someone clawed at the torch, and it fell and snuffed out. In the instant, the awful splendor of the indifferent Stars leaped nearer to them.

On the horizon outside the window, in the direction of Saro City, a crimson glow began growing, strengthening in brightness, that was not the glow of a sun.

The long night had come again.

A GNOME THERE WAS

Unknown
October

by ("Lewis Padgett")
Henry Kuttner (1914-1958)
and C. L. Moore (1911-   ).

*After their marriage in 1940, it was impossible
to tell who wrote what—it didn't matter what name
they used—Kuttner, Moore, "Lewis Padgett," or
"Lawrence O'Donnell." They didn't know themselves, although there were a few exceptions. They
produced some of the most important science fiction and fantasy of the forties, including this wonderful tale from that rich and lamented reservoir of
riches,* Unknown *(a.k.a.* Unknown Worlds*).*

*There is a book on the subject of Gnomes on the
best-seller lists as these words are written, but it is
doubtful if any of them are quite like the creatures
in this delightful story.*

(Henry Kuttner died in February 1958, and Cyril
Kornbluth died a month later, and that double loss rocked
the science fiction world. There hasn't been such a pair of
deaths in successive months since and I hope there never is.
Kuttner was so different from Kornbluth. Kuttner was a
prime example of a man whose personality was *not* like his
stories and Kornbluth a man whose personality *was.* The coincidence of both having names starting with K was striking
and, considering the superstition that deaths come in threes, I
was told that Damon Knight passed an uncomfortable few
months there.—I.A.)

Tim Crockett should never have sneaked into the mine on
Dornsef Mountain. What is winked at in California may have
disastrous results in the coal mines of Pennsylvania. Especially when gnomes are involved.

Not that Tim Crockett knew about the gnomes. He was

298

just investigating conditions among the lower classes, to use his own rather ill-chosen words. He was one of a group of southern Californians who had decided that labor needed them. They were wrong. They needed labor—at least eight hours of it a day.

Crockett, like his colleagues, considered the laborer a combination of a gorilla and The Man with the Hoe, probably numbering the Kallikaks among his ancestors. He spoke fierily of downtrodden minorities, wrote incendiary articles for he group's organ, *Earth,* and deftly maneuvered himself out of entering his father's law office as a clerk. He had, he said, a mission. Unfortunately, he got little sympathy from either the workers or their oppressors.

A psychologist could have analyzed Crockett easily enough. He was a tall, thin, intense-looking young man, with rather beady little eyes, and a nice taste in neckties. All he needed was a vigorous kick in the pants.

But definitely not administered by a gnome!

He was junketing through the country, on his father's money, investigating labor conditions, to the profound annoyance of such laborers as he encountered. It was with this idea in mind that he surreptitiously got into the Ajax coal mine—or, at least, one shaft of it—after disguising himself as a miner and rubbing his face well with black dust. Going down in the lift, he looked singularly untidy in the midst of a group of well-scrubbed faces. Miners look dirty only after a day's work.

Dornsef Mountain is honeycombed, but not with the shafts of the Ajax Company. The gnomes have ways of blocking their tunnels when humans dig too close. The whole place was a complete confusion to Crockett. He let himself drift along with the others, till they began to work. A filled car rumbled past on its tracks. Crockett hesitated, and then sidled over to a husky specimen who seemed to have the marks of a great sorrow stamped on his face.

"Look," he said, "I want to talk to you."

"Inglis?" asked the other inquiringly. "Viskey. Chin. Vine. Hell."

Having thus demonstrated his somewhat incomplete command of English, he bellowed hoarsely with laughter and returned to work, ignoring the baffled Crockett, who turned away to find another victim. But this section of the mine seemed deserted. Another loaded car rumbled past, and Crockett decided to see where it came from. He found out, after banging his head painfully and falling flat at least five times.

It came from a hole in the wall. Crockett entered it, and simultaneously heard a hoarse cry from behind him. The unknown requested Crockett to come back.

"So I can break your slab-sided neck," he promised, adding a stream of sizzling profanity. "Come outa there!"

Crockett cast one glance back, saw a gorillalike shadow lurching after him, and instantly decided that his stratagem had been discovered. The owners of the Ajax mine had sent a strong-arm man to murder him—or, at least, to beat him to a senseless pulp. Terror lent wings to Crockett's flying feet. He rushed on, frantically searching for a side tunnel in which he might lose himself. The bellowing from behind reechoed against the walls. Abruptly Crockett caught a significant sentence clearly.

"—before that dynamite goes off!"

It was at that exact moment that the dynamite went off.

Crockett, however, did not know it. He discovered, quite briefly, that he was flying. Then he was halted, with painful suddenness, by the roof. After that he knew nothing at all, till he recovered to find a head regarding him steadfastly.

It was not a comforting sort of head—not one at which you would instinctively clutch for companionship. It was, in fact, a singularly odd, if not actually revolting, head. Crockett was too much engrossed with staring at it to realize that he was actually seeing in the dark.

How long had he been unconscious? For some obscure reason Crockett felt that it had been quite a while. The explosion had—what?

Buried him here behind a fallen roof of rock? Crockett would have felt little better had he known that he was in a used-up shaft, valueless now, which had been abandoned long since. The miners, blasting to open a new shaft, had realized that the old one would be collapsed, but that didn't matter.

Except to Tim Crockett.

He blinked, and when he reopened his eyes, the head had vanished. This was a relief. Crockett immediately decided the unpleasant thing had been a delusion. Indeed, it was difficult to remember what it had looked like. There was only a vague impression of a turnip-shaped outline, large, luminous eyes, and an incredibly broad slit of a mouth.

Crockett sat up, groaning. Where was this curious silvery radiance coming from? It was like daylight on a foggy afternoon, coming from nowhere in particular, and throwing no shadows. "Radium," thought Crockett, who knew very little of mineralogy.

He was in a shaft that stretched ahead into dimness till it made a sharp turn perhaps fifty feet away. Behind him—behind him the roof had fallen. Instantly Crockett began to experience difficulty in breathing. He flung himself upon the rubbly mound, tossing rocks frantically here and there, gasping and making hoarse, inarticulate noises.

He became aware, presently, of his hands. His movements slowed till he remained perfectly motionless, in a half-crouching posture, glaring at the large, knobbly, and surprising objects that grew from his wrists. Could he, during his period of unconsciousness, have acquired mittens? Even as the thought came to him, Crockett realized that no mittens ever knitted resembled in the slightest degree what he had a right to believe to be his hands. They twitched slightly.

Possibly they were caked with mud—no. It wasn't that. His hands had—altered. They were huge, gnarled, brown objects, like knotted oak roots. Sparse black hairs sprouted on their backs. The nails were definitely in need of a manicure—preferably with a chisel.

Crockett looked down at himself. He made soft cheeping noises, indicative of disbelief. He had squat bow legs, thick and strong, and no more than two feet long—less, if anything. Uncertain with disbelief, Crockett explored his body. It had changed—certainly not for the better.

He was slightly more than four feet high, and about three feet wide, with a barrel chest, enormous splay feet, stubby thick legs, and no neck whatsoever. He was wearing red sandals, blue shorts, and a red tunic which left his lean but sinewy arms bare. His head—

Turnip-shaped. The mouth—*Yipe!* Crockett had inadvertently put his fist clear into it. He withdrew the offending hand instantly, stared around in a dazed fashion, and collapsed on the ground. It couldn't be happening. It was quite impossible. Hallucinations. He was dying of asphyxiation, and delusions were preceding his death.

Crockett shut his eyes, again convinced that his lungs were laboring for breath. "I'm dying," he said. "I c-can't breathe."

A contemptuous voice said, "I hope you don't think you're breathing *air!*"

"I'm n-not—" Crockett didn't finish the sentence. His eyes popped again. He was hearing things.

He heard it again. "You're a singularly lousy specimen of gnome," the voice said. "But under Nid's law we can't pick and choose. Still, you won't be put to digging hard metals, I can see that. Anthracite's about your speed. What're you staring at? You're *very* much uglier than I am."

Crockett, endeavoring to lick his dry lips, was horrified to discover the end of his moist tongue dragging limply over his eyes. He whipped it back, with a loud smacking noise, and managed to sit up. Then he remained perfectly motionless, staring.

The head had reappeared. This time there was a body under it.

"I'm Gru Magru," said the head chattily. "You'll be given a gnomic name, of course, unless your own is guttural enough. What is it?"

"Crockett," the man responded, in a stunned, automatic manner.

"Hey?"

"Crockett."

"Stop making noises like a frog and—oh, I see. Grockett. Fair enough. Now get up and follow me or I'll kick the pants off you."

But Crockett did not immediately rise. He was watching Gru Magru—obviously a gnome. Short, squat, and stunted, the being's figure resembled a bulging little barrel, topped by an inverted turnip. The hair grew up thickly to a peak—the root, as it were. In the turnip face was a loose, immense slit of a mouth, a button of a nose, and two very large eyes.

"Get *up!*" Gru Magru said.

This time Crockett obeyed, but the effort exhausted him completely. If he moved again, he thought, he would go mad. It would be just as well. Gnomes—

Gru Magru planted a large splay foot where it would do the most good, and Crockett described an arc which ended at a jagged boulder fallen from the roof. "Get up," the gnome said, with gratuitous bad temper, "or I'll kick you again. It's bad enough to have an outlying prospect patrol, where I might run into a man any time, without—*Up!* Or—"

Crockett got up. Gru Magru took his arm and impelled him into the depths of the tunnel.

"Well, you're a gnome now," he said. "It's the Nid law. Sometimes I wonder if it's worth the trouble. But I suppose it is—since gnomes can't propagate, and the average population has to be kept up somehow."

"I want to die," Crockett said wildly.

Gru Magru laughed. "Gnomes *can't* die. They're immortal, till the Day. Judgment Day, I mean."

"You're not logical," Crockett pointed out, as though by disproving one factor he could automatically disprove the whole fantastic business. "You're either flesh and blood and have to die eventually, or you're not, and then you're not real."

"Oh, we're flesh and blood, right enough," Gru Magru said. "But we're not mortal. There's a distinction. Not that I've anything against some mortals," he hastened to explain. "Bats, now—and owls—they're fine. But men!" He shuddered. "No gnome can stand the sight of a man."

Crockett clutched at a straw. "I'm a man."

"You were, you mean," Gru said. "Not a very good specimen, either, for my ore. But you're a gnome now. It's the Nid law."

"You keep talking about the Nid law," Crockett complained.

"Of course you don't understand," said Gru Magru, in a patronizing fashion. "It's this way. Back in ancient times, it was decreed that if any humans got lost in underearth, a tithe of them would be transformed into gnomes. The first gnome emperor, Podrang the Third, arranged that. He saw that fairies could kidnap human children and keep them, and spoke to the authorities about it. Said it was unfair. So when miners and such-like are lost underneath, a tithe of them are transformed into gnomes and join us. That's what happened to you. See?"

"No," Crockett said weakly. "Look. You said Podrang was the first gnome emperor. Why was he called Podrang the Third?"

"No time for questions," Gru Magru snapped. "Hurry!"

He was almost running now, dragging the wretched Crockett after him. The new gnome had not yet mastered his rather unusual limbs, and, due to the extreme wideness of his sandals, he was continually stepping on his own feet. Once he trod heavily on his right hand, but after that learned to keep his arms bent and close to his sides. The walls, illuminated with that queer silvery radiance, spun past dizzily.

"W-what's that light?" Crockett managed to gasp. "Where's it coming from?"

"Light?" Gru Magru inquired. "It isn't light."

"Well, it isn't dark—"

"Of course it's dark," the gnome snapped. "How could we see if it wasn't dark?"

There was no possible answer to this, except, Crockett thought wildly, a frantic shriek. And he needed all his breath for running. They were in a labyrinth now, turning and twisting and doubling through innumerable tunnels, and Crockett knew he could never retrace his steps. He regretted having left the scene of the cave-in. But how could he have helped doing so?

"Hurry!" Gru Magru urged. "Hurry!"

"Why?" Crockett got out breathlessly.

"There's a fight going on!" the gnome said.

Just then they rounded a corner and almost blundered into the fight. A seething mass of gnomes filled the tunnel, battling with frantic fury. Red and blue pants and tunics moved in swift patchwork frenzy; turnip heads popped up and down vigorously. It was apparently a free-for-all.

"See!" Gru gloated. "A fight! I could smell it six tunnels away. Oh, a beauty!" He ducked as a malicious-looking little gnome sprang out of the huddle to seize a rock and hurl it with vicious accuracy. The missile missed its mark, and Gru, neglecting his captive, immediately hurled himself upon the little gnome, bore him down on the cave floor, and began to beat his head against it. Both parties shrieked at the tops of their voices, which were lost in the deafening din that resounded through the tunnel.

"Oh—my," Crockett said weakly. He stood staring, which was a mistake. A very large gnome emerged from the pile, seized Crockett by the feet, and threw him away. The terrified inadvertent projectile sailed through the tunnel to crash heavily into something which said, *"Whoo-oof!"* There was a tangle of malformed arms and legs.

Crockett arose to find that he had downed a vicious-looking gnome with flaming red hair and four large diamond buttons on his tunic. This repulsive creature lay motionless, out for the count. Crockett took stock of his injuries—there were none. His new body was hardy, anyway.

"You saved me!" said a new voice. It belonged to a—lady gnome. Crockett decided that if there was anything uglier than a gnome, it was the female of the species. The creature stood crouching just behind him, clutching a large rock in one capable hand.

Crockett ducked.

"I won't hurt you," the other howled above the din that filled the passage. "You saved me! Mugza was trying to pull my ears off—oh! He's waking up!"

The red-haired gnome was indeed recovering consciousness. His first act was to draw up his feet and, without rising,
kick Crockett clear across the tunnel. The feminine gnome
immediately sat on Mugza's chest and pounded his head with
the rock till he subsided.

Then she arose. "You're not hurt? Good! I'm Brockle
Buhn. . . . Oh, look! He'll have his head off in a minute!"

Crockett turned to see that his erstwhile guide, Gru Magru,
was gnomefully tugging at the head of an unidentified opponent, attempting, apparently, to twist it clear off. "What's it
all about?" Crockett howled. "Uh—Brockle Buhn! *Brockle
Buhn!*"

She turned unwillingly. "What?"

"The fight! What started it?"

"I did," she explained. "I said, 'Let's have a fight.' "

"Oh, that was all?"

"Then we started." Brockle Buhn nodded. "What's your
name?"

"Crockett."

"You're new here, aren't you? Oh—I know. You were a
human being!" Suddenly a new light appeared in her bulging
eyes. "Grockett, maybe you can tell me something. What's a
kiss?"

"A—kiss?" Crockett repeated, in a baffled manner.

"Yes. I was listening inside a knoll once, and heard two
human beings talking—male and female, by their voices. I
didn't dare look at them, of course, but the man asked the
woman for a kiss."

"Oh," Crockett said, rather blankly. "He asked for a kiss,
eh?"

"And then there was a smacking noise and the woman said
it was wonderful. I've wondered ever since. Because if any
gnome asked me for a kiss, I wouldn't know what he meant."

"Gnomes don't kiss?" Crockett asked in a perfunctory way.

"Gnomes dig," said Brockle Buhn. "And we eat. I like to
eat. Is a kiss like mud soup?"

"Well, not exactly." Somehow Crockett managed to explain the mechanics of osculation.

The gnome remained silent, pondering deeply. At last she
said, with the air of one bestowing mud soup upon a hungry
applicant, "I'll give you a kiss."

Crockett had a nightmare picture of his whole head being
engulfed in that enormous maw. He backed away. "N-no," he
got out. "I—I'd rather not."

"Then let's fight," said Brockle Buhn, without rancor, and

swung a knotted fist which smacked painfully athwart Crockett's ear. "Oh, no," she said regretfully, turning away. "The fight's over. It wasn't very long, was it?"

Crockett, rubbing his mangled ear, saw that in every direction gnomes were picking themselves up and hurrying off about their business. They seemed to have forgotten all about the recent conflict. The tunnel was once more silent, save for the pad-padding of gnomes' feet on the rock. Gru Magru came over, grinning happily.

"Hello, Brockle Buhn," he greeted. "A good fight. Who's this?" He looked down at the prostrate body of Mugza, the red-haired gnome.

"Mugza," said Brockle Buhn. "He's still out. Let's kick him."

They proceeded to do it with vast enthusiasm, while Crockett watched and decided never to allow himself to be knocked unconscious. It definitely wasn't safe. At last, however, Gru Magru tired of the sport and took Crockett by the arm again. "Come along," he said, and they sauntered along the tunnel, leaving Brockle Buhn jumping up and down on the senseless Mugza's stomach.

"You don't seem to mind hitting people when they're knocked out," Crockett hazarded.

"It's *much* more fun," Gru said happily. "That way you can tell just where you want to hit 'em. Come along. You'll have to be inducted. Another day, another gnome. Keeps the population stable," he explained, and fell to humming a little song.

"Look," Crockett said. "I just thought of something. You say human beings are turned into gnomes to keep the population stable. But if gnomes don't die, doesn't that mean that there are more gnomes now than ever? The population keeps rising, doesn't it?"

"Be still," Gru Magru commanded. "I'm singing."

It was a singularly tuneless song. Crockett, his thoughts veering madly, wondered if the gnomes had a national anthem. Probably "Rock Me to Sleep." Oh, well.

"We're going to see the Emperor," Gru said at last. "He always sees the new gnomes. You'd better make a good impression, or he'll put you to placer-mining lava."

"Uh—" Crockett glanced down at his grimy tunic. "Hadn't I better clean up a bit? That fight made me a mess."

"It wasn't the fight," Gru said insultingly. "What's wrong with you, anyway? I don't see anything amiss."

"My clothes—they're dirty."

"Don't worry about that," said the other. "It's good filthy dirt, isn't it? Here!" He halted, and, stooping, seized a handful of dust, which he rubbed into Crockett's face and hair. "That'll fix you up."

"I—*pffht!* . . . Thanks . . . *pffh!*" said the newest gnome. "I hope I'm dreaming. Because if I'm not—" He didn't finish. Crockett was feeling most unwell.

They went through a labyrinth, far under Dornsef Mountain, and emerged at last in a bare, huge chamber with a throne of rock at one end of it. A small gnome was sitting on the throne paring his toenails. "Bottom of the day to you," Gru said. "Where's the Emperor?"

"Taking a bath," said the other. "I hope he drowns. Mud, mud, mud—morning, noon, and night. First it's too hot. Then it's too cold. Then it's too thick. I work my fingers to the bone mixing his mud baths, and all I get is a kick," the small gnome continued plaintively. "There's such a thing as being *too* dirty. Three mud baths a day—that's carrying it too far. And never a thought for me! Oh, no. I'm a mud puppy, that's what I am. He called me that today. Said there were lumps in the mud. Well, why not? That damned loam we've been getting is enough to turn a worm's stomach. You'll find His Majesty in there," the little gnome finished, jerking his foot toward an archway in the wall.

Crockett was dragged into the next room, where, in a sunken bath filled with steaming, brown mud, a very fat gnome sat, only his eyes discernible through the oozy coating that covered him. He was filling his hands with mud and letting it drip over his head, chuckling in a senile sort of way as he did so.

"Mud," he remarked pleasantly to Gru Magru, in a voice like a lion's bellow. "Nothing like it. Good rich mud. Ah!"

Gru was bumping his head on the floor, his large, capable hand around Crockett's neck forcing the other to follow suit.

"Oh, get up," said the Emperor. "What's this? What's this gnome been up to? Out with it."

"He's new," Gru explained. "I found him topside. The Nid law, you know."

"Yes, of course. Let's have a look at you. Ugh! I'm Podrang the Second, Emperor of the Gnomes. What have you to say to that?"

All Crockett could think of was: "How—how can you be

Podrang the Second? I thought Podrang the Third was the first emperor."

"A chatterbox," said Podrang II, disappearing beneath the surface of the mud and spouting as he rose again. "Take care of him, Gru. Easy work at first. Digging anthracite. Mind you don't eat any while you're on the job," he cautioned the dazed Crockett. "After you've been here a century, you're allowed one mud bath a day. Nothing like 'em," he added, bringing up a gluey handful to smear over his face.

Abruptly he stiffened. His lion's bellow rang out.

"Drook! *Drook!*"

The little gnome Crockett had seen in the throne room scurried in, ringing his hands. "Your Majesty! Isn't the mud warm enough?"

"You crawling blob!" roared Podrang II. "You slobbering offspring of six thousand individual offensive stenches! You mica-eyed, incompetent, draggle-eared, writhing blot on the good name of gnomes! You geological mistake! You—you—"

Drook took advantage of his master's temporary inarticulacy. "It's the best mud, Your Majesty! I refined it myself. Oh, Your Majesty, what's wrong?"

"There's a worm in it!" His Majesty bellowed, and launched into a stream of profanity so horrendous that it practically made the mud boil. Clutching his singed ears, Crockett allowed Gru Magru to drag him away.

"I'd like to get the old boy in a fight," Gru remarked, when they were safely in the depths of a tunnel, "but he'd use magic, of course. That's the way he is. Best emperor we've ever had. Not a scrap of fair play in his bloated body."

"Oh," Crockett said blankly. "Well, what next?"

"You heard Podrang, didn't you? You dig anthracite. And if you eat any, I'll kick your teeth in."

Brooding over the apparent bad tempers of gnomes, Crockett allowed himself to be conducted to a gallery where dozens of gnomes, both male and female, were using picks and mattocks with furious vigor. "This is it," Gru said. "Now! You dig anthracite. You work twenty hours, and then sleep six."

"Then what?"

"Then you start digging again," Gru explained. "You have a brief rest once every ten hours. You mustn't stop digging in between, unless it's for a fight. Now, here's the way you locate coal. Just think of it."

"Eh?"

"How do you think I found you?" Gru asked impatiently. "Gnomes have—certain senses. There's a legend that fairy folk can locate water by using a forked stick. Well, we're attracted to metals. Think of anthracite," he finished, and Crockett obeyed. Instantly he found himself turning to the wall of the tunnel nearest him.

"See how it works?" Gru grinned. "It's a natural evolution, I suppose. Functional. We have to know where the underneath deposits are, so the authorities gave us this sense when we were created. Think of ore—or any deposit in the ground—and you'll be attracted to it. Just as there's a repulsion in all gnomes against daylight."

"Eh?" Crockett started slightly. "What was that?"

"Negative and positive. We need ores, so we're attracted to them. Daylight is harmful to us, so if we think we're getting too close to the surface, we think of light, and it repels us. Try it!"

Crockett obeyed. Something seemed to be pressing down the top of his head.

"Straight up," Gru nodded. "But it's a long way. I saw daylight once. And—a man, too." He stared at the other. "I forgot to explain. Gnomes can't stand the sight of human beings. They—well, there's a limit to how much ugliness a gnome can look at. Now you're one of us, you'll feel the same way. Keep away from daylight, and never look at a man. It's as much as your sanity is worth."

There was a thought stirring in Crockett's mind. He could, then, find his way out of this maze of tunnels, simply by employing his new sense to lead him to daylight. After that—well, at least he would be above ground.

Gru Magru shoved Crockett into a place between two busy gnomes and thrust a pick into his hands. "There. Get to work."

"Thanks for—" Crockett began, when Gru suddenly kicked him and then took his departure, humming happily to himself. Another gnome came up, saw Crockett standing motionless, and told him to get busy, accompanying the command with a blow on his already tender ear. Perforce Crockett seized the pick and began to chop anthracite out of the wall.

"Grockett!" said a familiar voice. "It's you! I thought they'd send you here."

It was Brockle Buhn, the feminine gnome Crockett had already encountered. She was swinging a pick with the others, but dropped it now to grin at her companion.

"You won't be here long," she consoled. "Ten years or so. Unless you run into trouble, and then you'll be put at really hard work."

Crockett's arms were already aching. "*Hard* work! My arms are going to fall off in a minute."

He leaned on his pick. "Is this your regular job?"

"Yes—but I'm seldom here. Usually I'm being punished. I'm a trouble-maker, I am. I eat anthracite."

She demonstrated, and Crockett shuddered at the audible crunching sound. Just then the overseer came up. Brockle Buhn swallowed hastily.

"What's this?" he snarled. "Why aren't you at work?"

"We were just going to fight," Brockle Buhn explained.

"Oh—just the two of you? Or can I join in?"

"Free for all," the unladylike gnome offered, and struck the unsuspecting Crockett over the head with her pick. He went out like a light.

Awakening some time later, he investigated bruised ribs and decided Brockle Buhn must have kicked him after he'd lost consciousness. What a gnome! Crockett sat up, finding himself in the same tunnel, dozens of gnomes busily digging anthracite.

The overseer came toward him. "Awake, eh? Get to work!"

Dazedly Crockett obeyed. Brockle Buhn flashed him a delighted grin. "You missed it. I got an ear—see?" She exhibited it. Crockett hastily lifted an exploring hand. It wasn't his.

Dig . . . dig . . . dig . . . the hours dragged past. Crockett had never worked so hard in his life. But, he noticed, not a gnome complained. Twenty hours of toil, with one brief rest period—he'd slept through that. Dig . . . dig . . . dig . . .

Without ceasing her work, Brockle Buhn said, "I think you'll make a good gnome, Grockett. You're toughening up already. Nobody'd ever believe you were once a man."

"Oh—no?"

"No. What were you, a miner?"

"I was—" Crockett paused suddenly. A curious light came into his eyes.

"I was a labor organizer," he finished.

"What's that?"

"Ever heard of a union?" Crockett asked, his gaze intent.

"Is it an ore?" Brockle Buhn shook her head. "No, I've never heard of it. What's a union?"

Crockett explained. No genuine labor organizer would have accepted that explanation. It was, to say the least, biased.

Brockle Buhn seemed puzzled. "I don't see what you mean, exactly, but I suppose it's all right."

"Try another tack," Crockett said. "Don't you ever get tired of working twenty hours a day?"

"Sure. Who wouldn't?"

"Then why do it?"

"We always have," Brockle Buhn said indulgently. "We can't stop."

"Suppose you did?"

"I'd be punished—beaten with stalactites, or something."

"Suppose you all did," Crockett insisted. "Every damn gnome. Suppose you had a sit-down strike."

"You're crazy," Brockle Buhn said. "Such a thing's never happened. It—it's *human*."

"Kisses never happened underground, either," said Crockett. "No, I don't want one! And I don't want to fight, either. Good heavens, let me get the set-up here. Most of the gnomes work to support the privileged classes."

"No. We just work."

"But why?"

"We always have. And the Emperor wants us to."

"Has the Emperor ever worked?" Crockett demanded, with an air of triumph. "No! He just takes mud baths! Why shouldn't every gnome have the same privilege? Why—"

He talked on, at great length, as he worked. Brockle Buhn listened with increasing interest. And eventually she swallowed the bait—hook, line, and sinker.

An hour later she was nodding agreeably. "I'll pass the word along. Tonight. In the Roaring Cave. Right after work."

"Wait a minute," Crockett objected. "How many gnomes can we get?"

"Well—not very many. Thirty?"

"We'll have to organize first. We'll need a definite plan."

Brockle Buhn went off at a tangent. "Let's fight."

"No! Will you listen? We need a—a council. Who's the worst trouble-maker here?"

"Mugza, I think," she said. "The red-haired gnome you knocked out when he hit me."

Crockett frowned slightly. Would Mugza hold a grudge? Probably not, he decided. Or, rather, he'd be no more ill tempered than other gnomes. Mugza might attempt to throttle Crockett on sight, but he'd no doubt do the same to any other gnome. Besides, as Brockle Buhn went on to explain, Mugza was the gnomic equivalent of a duke. His support would be valuable.

"And Gru Magru," she suggested. "He loves new things, especially if they make trouble."

"Yeah." These were not the two Crockett would have chosen, but at least he could think of no other candidates. "If we could get somebody who's close to the Emperor . . . What about Drook—the guy who gives Podrang his mud baths?"

"Why not? I'll fix it." Brockle Buhn lost interest and surreptitiously began to eat anthracite. Since the overseer was watching, this resulted in a violent quarrel, from which Crockett emerged with a black eye. Whispering profanity under his breath, he went back to digging.

But he had time for a few more words with Brockle Buhn. She'd arrange it. That night there would be a secret meeting of the conspirators.

Crockett had been looking forward to exhausted slumber, but this chance was too good to miss. He had no wish to continue his unpleasant job digging anthracite. His body ached fearfully. Besides, if he could induce the gnomes to strike, he might be able to put the squeeze on Podrang II. Gru Magru had said the Emperor was a magician. Couldn't he, then, transform Crockett back into a man?

"He's never done that," Brockle Buhn said, and Crockett realized he had spoken his thought aloud.

"Couldn't he, though—if he wanted?"

Brockle Buhn merely shuddered, but Crockett had a little gleam of hope. To be human again!

Dig . . . dig . . . dig . . . dig . . . with monotonous, deadening regularity. Crockett sank into a stupor. Unless he got the gnomes to strike, he was faced with an eternity of arduous toil. He was scarcely conscious of knocking off, of feeling Brockle Buhn's gnarled hand under his arm, of being led through passages to a tiny cubicle, which was his new home. The gnome left him there, and he crawled into a stony bunk and went to sleep.

Presently a casual kick aroused him. Blinking, Crockett sat up, instinctively dodging the blow Gru Magru was aiming at his head. He had four guests—Gru, Brockle Buhn, Drook, and the red-haired Mugza.

"Sorry I woke up too soon," Crockett said bitterly. "If I hadn't, you could have got in another kick."

"There's lots of time," Gru said. "Now, what's this all about? I wanted to sleep, but Brockle Buhn here said there was going to be a fight. A *big* one, huh?"

"Eat first," Brockle Buhn said firmly. "I'll fix mud soup for everybody." She bustled away, and presently was busy in a corner, preparing refreshments. The other gnomes squatted on their haunches, and Crockett sat on the edge of his bunk, still dazed with sleep.

But he managed to explain his idea of the union. It was received with interest—chiefly, he felt, because it involved the possibility of a tremendous scrap.

"You mean every Dornsef gnome jumps the Emperor?" Gru asked.

"No, no! Peaceful arbitration. We just refuse to work. All of us."

"*I* can't," Drook said. "Podrang's got to have his mud baths, the bloated old slug. He'd send me to the fumaroles till I was toasted."

"Who'd take you there?" Crockett asked.

"Oh—the guards, I suppose."

"But they'd be on strike, too. *Nobody'd* obey Podrang, till he gave in."

"Then he'd enchant me," Drook said.

"He can't enchant us all," Crockett countered.

"But he could enchant *me*," Drook said with great firmness. "Besides, he *could* put a spell on every gnome in Dornsef. Turn us into stalactites or something."

"Then what? He wouldn't have any gnomes at all. Half a loaf is better than none. We'll just use logic on him. Wouldn't he rather have a little less work done than none at all?"

"Not him," Gru put in. "He'd rather enchant us. Oh, he's a bad one, he is," the gnome finished approvingly.

But Crockett couldn't quite believe this. It was too alien to his understanding of psychology—human psychology, of course. He turned to Mugza, who was glowering furiously.

"What do you think about it?"

"I want to fight," the other said rancorously. "I want to kick somebody."

"Wouldn't you rather have mud baths three times a day?"

Mugza grunted. "Sure. But the Emperor won't let me."

"Why not?"

"Because I want 'em."

"You can't be contented," Crockett said desperately. "There's more to life than—than digging."

"Sure. There's fighting. Podrang lets us fight whenever we want."

Crockett had a sudden inspiration. "But that's just it. He's going to stop all fighting! He's going to pass a new law forbidding fighting except to himself."

It was an effective shot in the dark. Every gnome jumped.

"Stop—*fighting!*" That was Gru, angry and disbelieving. "Why, we've always fought."

"Well, you'll have to stop," Crockett insisted.

"Won't!"

"Exactly! Why should you? Every gnome's entitled to life, liberty, and the pursuit of—of pugilism."

"Let's go and beat up Podrang," Mugza offered, accepting a steaming bowl of mud soup from Brockle Buhn.

"No, that's not the way—no, thanks, Brockle Buhn—not the way at all. A strike's the thing. We'll peaceably force Podrang to give us what we want."

He turned to Drook. "Just what can Podrang do about it if we all sit down and refuse to work?"

The little gnome considered. "He'd swear. And kick me."

"Yeah—and then what?"

"Then he'd go off and enchant everybody, tunnel by tunnel."

"Uh-huh." Crockett nodded. "A good point. Solidarity is what we need. If Podrang finds a few gnomes together, he can scare the hell out of them. But if we're all together— that's it! When the strike's called, we'll all meet in the biggest cave in the joint."

"That's the Council Chamber," Gru said. "Next to Podrang's throne room."

"O.K. We'll meet there. How many gnomes will join us?"

"All of 'em," Mugza grunted, throwing his soup bowl at Drook's head. "The Emperor can't stop us fighting."

"And what weapons can Podrang use, Drook?"

"He might use the Cockatrice Eggs," the other said doubtfully.

"What are those?"

"They're not really eggs," Gru broke in. "They're magic jewels for wholesale enchantments. Different spells in each one. The green ones, I think, are for turning people into earthworms. Podrang just breaks one, and the spell spreads out for twenty feet or so. The red ones are—let's see. Transforming gnomes into human beings—though that's a bit *too* tough. No . . . yes. The blue ones—"

"Into *human beings!*" Crockett's eyes widened. "Where are the eggs kept?"

"Let's fight," Mugza offered, and hurled himself bodily on Drook, who squeaked frantically and beat his attacker over the head with his stone soup bowl, which broke. Brockle Buhn added to the excitement by kicking both battlers impartially, till felled by Gru Magru. Within a few moments the room resounded with the excited screams of gnomic battle. Inevitably Crockett was sucked in. . . .

Of all the perverted, incredible forms of life that had ever existed, gnomes were about the oddest. It was impossible to understand their philosophy. Their minds worked along different paths from human intelligences. Self-preservation and survival of the race—these two vital human instincts were lacking in gnomes. They neither died nor propagated. They just worked and fought. Bad-tempered little monsters, Crockett thought irritably. Yet they had existed for—ages. Since the beginning, maybe. Their social organism was the result of evolution far older than man's. It might be well suited to gnomes. Crockett might be throwing the unnecessary monkey wrench in the machinery.

So what? He wasn't going to spend eternity digging anthracite, even though, in retrospect, he remembered feeling a curious thrill of obscure pleasure as he worked. Digging might be fun for gnomes. Certainly it was their *raison d'être*. In time Crockett himself might lose his human affiliations, and be metamorphosed completely into a gnome. What had happened to other humans who had undergone such an—alteration as he had done? All gnomes looked alike. But maybe Gru Magru had once been human—or Drook—or Brockle Buhn.

They were gnomes now, at any rate, thinking and existing completely as gnomes. And in time he himself would be exactly like them. Already he had acquired the strange tropism that attracted him to metals and repelled him from daylight. But he didn't *like* to dig!

He tried to recall the little he knew about gnomes—miners, metalsmiths, living underground. There was something about the Picts—dwarfish men who hid underground when invaders came to England, centuries ago. That seemed to tie in vaguely with the gnomes' dread of human beings. But the gnomes themselves were certainly not descended from Picts.

Very likely the two separate races and species had become
identified through occupying the same habitat.

Well, that was no help. What about the Emperor? He
wasn't, apparently, a gnome with a high I.Q., but he *was* a
magician. Those jewels—Cockatrice Eggs—were significant.
If he could get hold of the ones that transformed gnomes into
men . . .

But obviously he couldn't, at present. Better wait. Till the
strike had been called. The strike . . .

Crockett went to sleep.

He was roused, painfully, by Brockle Buhn, who seemed to
have adopted him. Very likely it was her curiosity about the
matter of a kiss. From time to time she offered to give
Crockett one, but he steadfastly refused. In lieu of it, she supplied him with breakfast. At least, he thought grimly, he'd get
plenty of iron in his system, even though the rusty chips
rather resembled corn flakes. As a special inducement
Brockle Buhn sprinkled coal dust over the mess.

Well, no doubt his digestive system had also altered.
Crockett wished he could get an X-ray picture of his insides.
Then he decided it would be much too disturbing. Better not
to know. But he could not help wondering. Gears in his stomach? Small millstones? What would happen if he inadvertently swallowed some emery dust? Maybe he could sabotage
the Emperor that way.

Perceiving that his thoughts were beginning to veer wildly,
Crockett gulped the last of his meal and followed Brockle
Buhn to the anthracite tunnel.

"How about the strike? How's it coming?"

"Fine, Grockett." She smiled, and Crockett winced at the
sight. "Tonight all the gnomes will meet in the Roaring Cave.
Just after work."

There was no time for more conversation. The overseer appeared, and the gnomes snatched up their picks. Dig . . . dig
. . . dig . . . It kept up at the same pace. Crockett sweated
and toiled. It wouldn't be for long. His mind slipped a cog, so
that he relapsed into a waking slumber, his muscles responding automatically to the need. Dig, dig, dig. Sometimes a
fight. Once a rest period. Then dig again.

Five centuries later the day ended. It was time to sleep.

But there was something much more important. The union
meeting in the Roaring Cave. Brockle Buhn conducted
Crockett there, a huge cavern hung with glittering green
stalactites. Gnomes came pouring into it. Gnomes and more

gnomes. The turnip heads were everywhere. A dozen fights started. Gru Magru, Mugza, and Drook found places near Crockett. During a lull Brockle Buhn urged him to a platform of rock jutting from the floor.

"Now," she whispered. "They all know about it. Tell them what you want."

Crockett was looking out over the bobbing heads, the red and blue garments, all lit by that eerie silver glow. "Fellow gnomes," he began weakly.

"Fellow gnomes!" The words roared out, magnified by the acoustics of the cavern. That bull bellow gave Crockett courage. He plunged on.

"Why should you work twenty hours a day? Why should you be forbidden to eat the anthracite you dig, while Podrang squats in his bath and laughs at you? Fellow gnomes, the Emperor is only one; you are many! He can't make you work. How would you like mud soup three times a day? The Emperor can't fight you all. If you refuse to work—all of you—he'll have to give in! He'll have to!"

"Tell 'em about the non-fighting edict," Gru Magru called.

Crockett obeyed. That got 'em. Fighting was dear to every gnomic heart. And Crockett kept on talking.

"Podrang will try to back down, you know. He'll pretend he never intended to forbid fighting. That'll show he's afraid of you! We hold the whip hand! We'll strike—and the Emperor can't do a damn thing about it. When he runs out of mud for his baths, he'll capitulate soon enough."

"He'll enchant us all," Drook muttered sadly.

"He won't dare! What good would that do? He knows which side his—uh—which side his mud is buttered on. Podrang is unfair to gnomes! That's our watchword!"

It ended, of course, in a brawl. But Crockett was satisfied. The gnomes would not go to work tomorrow. They would, instead, meet in the Council Chamber, adjoining Podrang's throne room—and sit down.

That night he slept well.

In the morning Crockett went, with Brockle Buhn, to the Council Chamber, a cavern gigantic enough to hold the thousands of gnomes who thronged it. In the silver light their red and blue garments had a curiously elfin quality. Or, perhaps, naturally enough, Crockett thought, were gnomes, strictly speaking, elves?

Drook came up. "I didn't draw Podrang's mud bath," he confided hoarsely. "Oh, but he'll be furious. Listen to him."

And, indeed, a distant crackling of profanity was coming through an archway in one wall of the cavern.

Mugza and Gru Magru joined them. "He'll be along directly," the latter said. "What a fight there'll be!"

"Let's fight now," Mugza suggested. "I want to kick somebody. Hard."

"There's a gnome who's asleep," Crockett said. "If you sneak up on him, you can land a good one right in his face."

Mugza, drooling slightly, departed on his errand, and simultaneously Podrang II, Emperor of the Dornsef Gnomes, stumped into the cavern. It was the first time Crockett had seen the ruler without a coating of mud, and he could not help gulping at the sight. Podrang was *very* ugly. He combined in himself the most repulsive qualities of every gnome Crockett had previously seen. The result was perfectly indescribable.

"Ah," said Podrang, halting and swaying on his short bow legs. "I have guests. Drook! Where in the name of the nine steaming hells is my bath?" But Drook had ducked from sight.

The Emperor nodded. "I see. Well, I won't lose my temper. *I won't lose my temper! I WON'T—*"

He paused as a stalactite was dislodged from the roof and crashed down. In the momentary silence, Crockett stepped forward, cringing slightly.

"W-we're on strike," he announced. "It's a sit-down strike. We won't work till—"

"*Yaaah!*" screamed the infuriated Emperor. "You won't work, eh? Why, you boggle-eyed, flap-tongued, drag-bellied offspring of unmentionable algae! You seething little leprous blotch of bat-nibbled fungus! You cringing parasite on the underside of a dwarfish and ignoble worm! *Yaaah!*"

"Fight!" the irrepressible Mugza yelled, and flung himself on Podrang, only to be felled by a well-placed foul blow.

Crockett's throat felt dry. He raised his voice, trying to keep it steady.

"Your Majesty! If you'll just wait a minute—"

"You mushroom-nosed spawn of degenerate black bats," the enraged Emperor shrieked at the top of his voice. "I'll enchant you all! I'll turn you into naiads! Strike, will you! Stop me from having my mud bath, will you? By Kronos, Nid, Ymir, and Loki, you'll have cause to regret this! *Yaah!*" he finished, inarticulate with fury.

"Quick!" Crockett whispered to Gru and Brockle Buhn.

"Get between him and the door, so he can't get hold of the Cockatrice Eggs."

"They're not in the throne room," Gru Magru explained unhelpfully. "Podrang just grabs them out of the air."

"Oh!" the harassed Crockett groaned. At that strategic moment Brockle Buhn's worst instincts overcame her. With a loud shriek of delight she knocked Crockett down, kicked him twice, and sprang for the Emperor.

She got in one good blow before Podrang hammered her atop the head with one gnarled fist, and instantly her turnip-shaped skull seemed to prolapse into her torso. The Emperor, bright purple with fury, reached out—and a yellow crystal appeared in his hand.

It was one of the Cockatrice Eggs.

Bellowing like a *musth* elephant, Podrang hurled it. A circle of twenty feet was instantly cleared among the massed gnomes. But it wasn't vacant. Dozens of bats rose and fluttered about, adding to the confusion.

Confusion became chaos. With yells of delighted fury, the gnomes rolled forward toward their ruler. "Fight!" the cry thundered out, reverberating from the roof. *"Fight!"*

Podrang snatched another crystal from nothingness—a green one, this time. Thirty-seven gnomes were instantly transformed into earthworms, and were trampled. The Emperor went down under an avalanche of attackers, who abruptly disappeared, turned into mice by another of the Cockatrice Eggs.

Crockett saw one of the crystals sailing toward him, and ran like hell. He found a hiding place behind a stalagmite, and from there watched the carnage. It was definitely a sight worth seeing, though it could not be recommended to a nervous man.

The Cockatrice Eggs exploded in an incessant stream. Whenever that happened, the spell spread out for twenty feet or more before losing its efficacy. Those caught on the fringes of the circle were only partially transformed. Crockett saw one gnome with a mole's head. Another was a worm from the waist down. Another was—*ulp!* Some of the spell-patterns were not, apparently, drawn even from known mythology.

The fury of noise that filled the cavern brought stalactites crashing down incessantly from the roof. Every so often Podrang's battered head would reappear, only to go down again as more gnomes sprang to the attack—to be enchanted. Mice moles, bats, and other things filled the Council Chamber. Crockett shut his eyes and prayed.

He opened them in time to see Podrang snatch a red crystal out of the air, pause, and then deposit it gently behind him. A purple Cockatrice Egg came next. This crashed against the floor, and thirty gnomes turned into tree toads.

Apparently only Podrang was immune to his own magic. The thousands who had filled the cavern were rapidly thinning, for the Cockatrice Eggs seemed to come from an inexhaustible source of supply. How long would it be before Crockett's own turn came? He couldn't hide here forever.

His gaze riveted to the red crystal Podrang had so carefully put down. He was remembering something—the Cockatrice Egg that would transform gnomes into human beings. Of course! Podrang wouldn't use *that,* since the very sight of men was so distressing to gnomes. If Crockett could get his hands on that red crystal . . .

He tried it, sneaking through the confusion, sticking close to the wall of the cavern, till he neared Podrang. The Emperor was swept away by another onrush of gnomes, who abruptly changed into dormice, and Crockett got the red jewel. It felt abnormally cold.

He almost broke it at his feet before a thought stopped and chilled him. He was far under Dornsef Mountain, in a labyrinth of caverns. No human being could find his way out. But a gnome could, with the aid of his strange tropism to daylight.

A bat flew against Crockett's face. He was almost certain it squeaked, "What a fight!" in a parody of Brockle Buhn's voice, but he couldn't be sure. He cast one glance over the cavern before turning to flee.

It was a complete and utter chaos. Bats, moles, worms, ducks, eels, and a dozen other species crawled, flew, ran, bit, shrieked, snarled, grunted, whooped, and croaked all over the place. From all directions the remaining gnomes—only about a thousand now—were converging on a surging mound of gnomes that marked where the Emperor was. As Crockett stared the mound dissolved, and a number of gecko lizards ran to safety.

"Strike, will you!" Podrang bellowed. *"I'll show you!"*

Crockett turned and fled. The throne room was deserted, and he ducked into the first tunnel. There, he concentrated on thinking of daylight. His left ear felt compressed. He sped on till he saw a side passage on the left, slanting up, and turned into it at top speed. The muffled noise of combat died behind him.

He clutched the red Cockatrice Egg tightly. What had gone wrong? Podrang should have stopped to parley. Only—only he hadn't. A singularly bad-tempered and shortsighted gnome. He probably wouldn't stop till he'd depopulated his entire kingdom. At the thought Crockett hurried along faster.

The tropism guided him. Sometimes he took the wrong tunnel, but always, whenever he thought of daylight, he would *feel* the nearest daylight pressing against him. His short, bowed legs were surprisingly hardy.

Then he heard someone running after him.

He didn't turn. The sizzling blast of profanity that curled his ears told him the identity of the pursuer. Podrang had no doubt cleared the Council Chamber, to the last gnome, and was now intending to tear Crockett apart pinch by pinch. That was only one of the things he promised.

Crockett ran. He shot along that tunnel like a bullet. The tropism guided him, but he was terrified lest he reach a dead end. The clamor from behind grew louder. If Crockett hadn't known better, he would have imagined that an army of gnomes pursued him.

Faster! Faster! But now Podrang was in sight. His roars shook the very walls. Crockett sprinted, rounded a corner, and saw a wall of flaming light—a circle of it, in the distance. It was daylight, as it appeared to gnomic eyes.

He could not reach it in time. Podrang was too close. A few more seconds, and those gnarled, terrible hands would close on Crockett's throat. Then Crockett remembered the Cockatrice Egg. If he transformed himself into a man now, Podrang would not dare touch him. And he was almost at the tunnel's mouth.

He stopped, whirling, and lifted the jewel. Simultaneously the Emperor, seeing his intention, reached out with both hands, and snatched six or seven of the crystals out of the air. He threw them directly at Crockett, a fusillade of rainbow colors.

But Crockett had already slammed the red gem down on the rock at his feet. There was an ear-splitting crash. Jewels seemed to burst all around Crockett—but the red one had been broken first.

The roof fell in.

A short while later, Crockett dragged himself painfully from the debris. A glance showed him that the way to the outer world was still open. And—thank heaven!—daylight looked normal again, not that flaming blaze of eye-searing white.

He looked toward the depths of the tunnel, and froze. Podrang was emerging, with some difficulty, from a mound of rubble. His low curses had lost none of their fire.

Crockett turned to run, stumbled over a rock, and fell flat. As he sprang up, he saw that Podrang had seen him.

The gnome stood transfixed for a moment. Then he yelled, spun on his heel, and fled into the darkness. He was gone. The sound of his rapid footfalls died.

Crockett swallowed with difficulty. *Gnomes are afraid of men—whew!* That had been a close squeak. But now . . .

He was more relieved than he had thought. Subconsciously he must have been wondering whether the spell would work, since Podrang had flung six or seven Cockatrice Eggs at him. But he had smashed the red one first. Even the strange, silvery gnome-light was gone. The depths of the cave were utterly black—and silent.

Crockett headed for the entrance. He pulled himself out, luxuriating in the warmth of the afternoon sun. He was near the foot of Dornsef Mountain, in a patch of brambles. A hundred feet away a farmer was plowing one terrace of a field.

Crockett stumbled toward him. As he approached, the man turned.

He stood transfixed for a moment. Then he yelled, spun on his heel, and fled.

His shrieks drifted back up the mountain as Crockett, remembering the Cockatrice Eggs, forced himself to look down at his own body.

Then he screamed, too. But the sound was not one that could ever have emerged from a human throat.

Still, that was natural enough—under the circumstances.

BY HIS BOOTSTRAPS

Astounding Science Fiction
October

by Robert A. Heinlein
(as "Anson MacDonald")

*Heinlein was so prolific that John Campbell
thought it necessary to use a pseudonym for him,
since it might appear strange to have two stories by
the same author in a single issue of the magazine.
Actually, his following was so extensive by 1941
that it probably would not have mattered.*

*The time travel story was a staple in science fic-
tion by the early forties, but here Heinlein gave it a
wonderful twist—and wrote what many believe to
be the ultimate story of its kind.*

(Once again, Bob Heinlein scores. I agree with Marty that
it is probably the best time-travel story in the sub-novel
length ever written. I wish to say, though, that I think that
John Campbell was far too ready to push for pseudonyms. I
guess he felt it was just impossible to have two stories by the
same author—by name—in the same issue, but he should
have tried. Some of the *best* Heinlein stories came out under
the MacDonald name and why should any reader not have
known that? Not only was this story one of them, but "Solution Unsatisfactory" which appeared in the May 1941 *Astounding* along with "Blowups Happen", was another.—Well,
he dominated 1941 and we can't help that.—I.A.)

SNULBUG

Unknown
December

by Anthony Boucher (William Anthony Parker White) (1911-1968)

Anthony Boucher was a sophisticated, witty man who led several lives. Best known as the founding coeditor of The Magazine of Fantasy and Science Fiction *(1949) he was also a talented mystery author, whose novel* Rocket to the Morgue *(1942) used the world of science fiction—fans and writers—as its setting. In addition, as "H. H. Holmes" and as Boucher, he was one of the most influential book reviewers of both mysteries and science fiction from the end of World War II until his death, most notably for the* New York Herald Tribune *and the* New York Times.

As a writer of science fiction and fantasy, he enjoyed a substantial reputation in spite of the fact that he never published a novel. His best stories can be found in the collections Far and Away *(1955) and* The Complete Werewolf *(1969). Especially outstanding are "Barrier" (Astounding, September, 1942), "Nine-Finger Jack" (Esquire, May, 1951) and "Q.U.R." (Astounding, March, 1943).*

"Snulbug" is a delightful fantasy typical of Unknown *in its too-short existence, and it was Tony Boucher's first published work of fantastic fiction.*

(I didn't meet Tony often. He was West Coast and I was East Coast and I didn't travel. We became friends at one stroke, however, as the result of the first letter I ever received from him.

In a story I wrote when I was just about thirty, I referred to the "paler (sexual) passions of the late thirties." That elicited a gentle reproof from Tony almost at once.

"You have a very pleasant surprise ahead of you, Dr. Asi-

mov," he said, and signed it "Anthony Boucher (1911–)."
He was, of course, just turning forty at the time.

We corresponded with reasonable regularity thereafter and
it is only fair to say that I did have the pleasant surprise he
spoke of and have continued to have it as the years continue
to roll by.—I.A.)

"That's a hell of a spell you're using," said the demon, "if
I'm the best you can call up."

He wasn't much, Bill Hitchens had to admit. He looked
lost in the center of that pentacle. His basic design was impressive enough—snakes for hair, curling tusks, a sharptipped
tail, all the works—but he was something under an inch tall.

Bill had chanted the words and lit the powder with the
highest hopes. Even after the feeble flickering flash and the
damp fizzling *zzzt* which had replaced the expected thunder
and lightning, he had still had hopes. He had stared up at the
space above the pentacle waiting to be awe-struck until he
had heard that plaintive little voice from the floor wailing,
"Here I am."

"Nobody's wasted time and power on a misfit like me for
years," the demon went on. "Where'd you get the spell?"

"Just a little something I whipped up," said Bill modestly.

The demon grunted and muttered something about people
that thought they were magicians.

"But I'm not a magician," Bill explained. "I'm a biochemist."

The demon shuddered. "I land the damnedest cases," he
mourned. "Working for a psychiatrist wasn't bad enough, I
should draw a biochemist. Whatever that is."

Bill couldn't check his curiosity. "And what did you do for
a psychiatrist?"

"He showed me to people who were followed by little men
and told them I'd chase the little men away." The demon
pantomimed shooting motions.

"And did they go away?"

"Sure. Only then the people decided they'd sooner have
little men than me. It didn't work so good. Nothing ever
does," he added woefully. "Yours won't either."

Bill sat down and filled his pipe. Calling up demons wasn't
so terrifying after all. Something quiet and homey about it.
"Oh, yes it will," he said. "This is foolproof."

"That's what they all think. People—" The demon wistfully eyed the match as Bill lit his pipe. "But we might as well get it over with. What do you want?"

"I want a laboratory for my embolism experiments. If this method works, it's going to mean that a doctor can spot an embolus in the blood stream long before it's dangerous and remove it safely. My ex-boss, that screwball old occultist Reuben Choatsby, said it wasn't practical—meaning there wasn't a fortune in it for him—and fired me. Everybody else thinks I'm whacky too, and I can't get any backing. So I need ten thousand dollars."

"There!" the demon sighed with satisfaction. "I told you it wouldn't work. That's out for me. They can't start fetching money on demand till three grades higher than me. I told you."

"But you don't," Bill insisted, "appreciate all my fiendish subtlety. Look— Say, what is your name?"

The demon hesitated. "You haven't got another of those things?"

"What things?"

"Matches."

"Sure."

"Light me one, please?"

Bill tossed the burning match into the center of the pentacle. The demon scrambled eagerly out of the now cold ashes of the powder and dived into the flame, rubbing himself with the brisk vigor of a man under a needle-shower. "There!" he gasped joyously. "That's more like it."

"And now what's your name?"

The demon's face fell again. "My name? You really want to know?"

"I've got to call you something."

"Oh, no you don't. I'm going home. No money games for me."

"But I haven't explained yet what you are to do. What's your name?"

"Snulbug." The demon's voice dropped almost too low to be heard.

"Snulbug?" Bill laughed.

"Uh-huh. I've got a cavity in one tusk, my snakes are falling out, I haven't got enough troubles, I should be named Snulbug."

"All right. Now listen, Snulbug, can you travel into the future?"

"A little. I don't like it much, though. It makes you itch in the memory."

"Look, my fine snake-haired friend. It isn't a question of what you like. How would you like to be left there in that pentacle with nobody to throw matches at you?" Snulbug shuddered. "I thought so. Now, you can travel into the future?"

"I said a little."

"And," Bill leaned forward and puffed hard at his corncob as he asked the vital question, "can you bring back material objects?" If the answer was no, all the fine febrile fertility of his spell-making was useless. And if that was useless, heaven alone knew how the Hitchens Embolus Diagnosis would ever succeed in ringing down the halls of history, and incidentally saving a few thousand lives annually.

Snulbug seemed more interested in the warm clouds of pipe smoke than in the question. "Sure," he said. "Within reason I can—" He broke off and stared up piteously. "You don't mean—You can't be going to pull that old gag again?"

"Look, baby. You do what I tell you and leave the worrying to me. You can bring back material objects?"

"Sure. But I warn you—"

Bill cut him off short. "Then as soon as I release you from that pentacle, you're to bring me tomorrow's newspaper."

Snulbug sat down on the burned match and tapped his forehead sorrowfully with his tail tip. "I knew it," he wailed. "I knew it. Three times already this happens to me. I've got limited powers, I'm a runt, I've got a funny name, so I should run foolish errands."

"Foolish errands?" Bill rose and began to pace about the bare attic. "Sir, if I may call you that, I resent such an imputation. I've spent weeks on this idea. Think of the limitless power in knowing the future. Think of what could be done with it: swaying the course of empire, dominating mankind. All I want is to take this stream of unlimited power, turn it into the simple channel of humanitarian research, and get me $10,000; and you call that a foolish errand!"

"That Spaniard," Snulbug moaned. "He was a nice guy, even if his spell was lousy. Had a solid, comfortable brazier where an imp could keep warm. Fine fellow. And he had to ask to see tomorrow's newspaper. I'm warning you—"

"I know," said Bill hastily. "I've been over in my mind all the things that can go wrong. And that's why I'm laying three conditions on you before you get out of that pentacle. I'm not falling for the easy snares."

"All right." Snulbug sounded almost resigned. "Let's hear 'em. Not that they'll do any good."

"First: This newspaper must not contain a notice of my own death or of any other disaster that would frustrate what I can do with it."

"But shucks," Snulbug protested. "I can't guarantee that. If you're slated to die between now and tomorrow, what can I do about it? Not that I guess you're important enough to crash the paper."

"Courtesy, Snulbug. Courtesy to your master. But I tell you what: When you go into the future, you'll know then if I'm going to die? Right. Well, if I am, come back and tell me and we'll work out other plans. This errand will be off."

"People," Snulbug observed, "make such an effort to make trouble for themselves. Go on."

"Second: The newspaper must be of this city and in English. I can just imagine you and your little friends presenting some dope with the Omsk and Tomsk *Daily Vuskutsukt.*"

"We should take so much trouble," said Snulbug.

"And third: The newspaper must belong to this space-time continuum, to this spiral of the serial universe, to this Wheel of If. However you want to put it. It must be a newspaper of the tomorrow that I myself shall experience, not of some other, to me hypothetical, tomorrow."

"Throw me another match," said Snulbug.

"Those three conditions should cover it, I think. There's not a loophole there, and the Hitchens Laboratory is guaranteed."

Snulbug grunted. "You'll find out."

Bill took a sharp blade and duly cut a line of the pentacle with cold steel. But Snulbug simply dived in and out of the flame of his second match, twitching his tail happily, and seemed not to give a rap that the way to freedom was now open.

"Come on!" Bill snapped impatiently. "Or I'll take the match away."

Snulbug got as far as the opening and hesitated. "Twenty-four hours is a long way."

"You can make it."

"I don't know. Look." He shook his head, and a microscopic dead snake fell to the floor. "I'm not at my best. I'm shot to pieces lately, I am. Tap my tail."

"Do what?"

"Go on. Tap it with your fingernail right there where it joins on."

Bill grinned and obeyed. "Nothing happens."

"Sure nothing happens. My reflexes are all haywire. I don't

know as I can make twenty-four hours." He brooded, and his snakes curled up into a concentrated clump. "Look. All you want is tomorrow's newspaper, huh? Just tomorrow's, not the edition that'll be out exactly twenty-four hours from now?"

"It's noon now," Bill reflected. "Sure, I guess tomorrow morning's paper'll do."

"OK. What's the date today?"

"August 21."

"Fine. I'll bring you a paper for August 22. Only I'm warning you: It won't do any good. But here goes nothing. Good-bye now. Hello again. Here you are." There was a string in Snulbug's horny hand, and on the end of the string was a newspaper.

"But hey!" Bill protested. "You haven't been gone."

"People," said Snulbug feelingly, "are dopes. Why should it take any time out of the present to go into the future? I leave this point, I come back to this point. I spent two hours hunting for this damned paper, but that doesn't mean two hours of your time here. People—" he snorted.

Bill scratched his head. "I guess it's all right. Let's see the paper. And I know: You're warning me." He turned quickly to the obituaries to check. No Hitchens. "And I wasn't dead in the time you were in?"

"No," Snulbug admitted. "Not *dead*," he added, with the most pessimistic implications possible.

"What was I, then? Was I—"

"I had salamander blood," Snulbug complained. "They thought I was an undine like my mother and they put me in the cold-water incubator when any dope knows salamandery is a dominant. So I'm a runt and good for nothing but to run errands, and now I should make prophecies! You read your paper and see how much good it does you."

Bill laid down his pipe and folded the paper back from the obituaries to the front page. He had not expected to find anything useful there—what advantage could he gain from knowing who won the next naval engagement or which cities were bombed?—but he was scientifically methodical. And this time method was rewarded. There it was, streaming across the front page in vast black blocks:

MAYOR ASSASSINATED

FIFTH COLUMN KILLS CRUSADER

Bill snapped his fingers. This was it. This was his chance. He jammed his pipe in his mouth, hastily pulled a coat on his shoulders, crammed the priceless paper into a pocket, and started out of the attic. Then he paused and looked around. He'd forgotten Snulbug. Shouldn't there be some sort of formal discharge?

The dismal demon was nowhere in sight. Not in the pentacle or out of it. Not a sign or a trace of him. Bill frowned. This was definitely not methodical. He struck a match and held it over the bowl of his pipe.

A warm sigh of pleasure came from inside the corncob.

Bill took the pipe from his mouth and stared at it. "So that's where you are!" he said musingly.

"I told you salamandry was a dominant," said Snulbug, peering out of the bowl. "I want to go along. I want to see just what kind of a fool you make of yourself." He withdrew his head into the glowing tobacco, muttering about newspapers, spells, and, with a wealth of unhappy scorn, people.

The crusading mayor of Granton was a national figure of splendid proportions. Without hysteria, red baiting, or strikebreaking, he had launched a quietly purposeful and well-directed program against subversive elements which had rapidly converted Granton into the safest and most American city in the country. He was also a persistent advocate of national, state, and municipal subsidy of the arts and sciences—the ideal man to wangle an endowment for the Hitchens Laboratory, if he were not so surrounded by overly skeptical assistants that Bill had never been able to lay the program before him.

This would do it. Rescue him from assassination in the very nick of time—in itself an act worth calling up demons to perform—and then when he asks, "And how, Mr. Hitchens, can I possibly repay you?" come forth with the whole great plan of research. It couldn't miss.

No sound came from the pipe bowl, but Bill clearly heard the words, "Couldn't it just?" ringing in his mind.

He braked his car to a fast stop in the red zone before the city hall, jumped out without even slamming the door, and dashed up the marble steps so rapidly, so purposefully, that pure momentum carried him up three flights and through four suites of offices before anybody had the courage to stop him and say, "What goes?"

The man with the courage was a huge bull-necked plainclothesman, whose bulk made Bill feel relatively about the size of Snulbug. "All right, there," this hulk rumbled. "All right. Where's the fire?"

"In an assassin's gun," said Bill. "And it had better stay there."

Bullneck had not expected a literal answer. He hesitated long enough for Bill to push him to the door marked MAYOR—PRIVATE. But though the husky's brain might move slowly, his muscles made up for the lag. Just as Bill started to shove the door open, a five-pronged mound of flesh lit on his neck and jerked.

Bill crawled from under a desk, ducked Bullneck's left, reached the door, executed a second backward flip, climbed down from the table, ducked a right, reached the door, sailed back in reverse, and lowered himself nimbly from the chandelier.

Bullneck took up a stand in front of the door, spread his legs in ready balance, and drew a service automatic from its holster. "You ain't going in there," he said, to make the situation perfectly clear.

Bill spat out a tooth, wiped the blood from his eyes, picked up the shattered remains of his pipe, and said, "Look. It's now 12:30. At 12:32 a redheaded hunchback is going to come out on that balcony across the street and aim through the open window into the mayor's office. At 12:33 His Honor is going to be slumped over his desk, dead. Unless you help me get him out of range."

"Yeah?" said Bullneck. "And who says so?"

"It says so here. Look. In the paper."

Bullneck guffawed. "How can a paper say what ain't even happened yet? You're nuts, brother, if you ain't something worse. Now go on. Scram. Go peddle your paper."

Bill's glance darted out the window. There was the balcony facing the mayor's office. And there coming out on it—

"Look!" he cried. "If you won't believe me, look out the window. See on that balcony? The redheaded hunchback? Just like I told you. Quick!"

Bullneck stared despite himself. He saw the hunchback peer across into the office. He saw the sudden glint of metal in the hunchback's hand. "Brother," he said to Bill, "I'll tend to you later."

The hunchback had his rifle halfway to his shoulder when Bullneck's automatic spat and Bill braked his car in the red zone, jumped out, and dashed through four suites of offices before anybody had the courage to stop him.

The man with the courage was a huge bull-necked plain-clothesman, who rumbled, "Where's the fire?"

"In an assassin's gun," said Bill, and took advantage of Bullneck's confusion to reach the door marked MAYOR—PRIVATE. But just as he started to push it open, a vast hand lit on his neck and jerked.

As Bill descended from the chandelier after his third try, Bullneck took up a stand in front of the door, with straddled legs and drawn gun. "You ain't going in," he said clarifyingly.

Bill spat out a tooth and outlined the situation. "—12:33," he ended. "His Honor is going to be slumped over the desk dead. Unless you help me get him out of range. See? It says so here. In the paper."

"How can it? Gawn. Go peddle your paper."

Bill's glance darted to the balcony. "Look, if you won't believe me. See the redheaded hunchback? Just like I told you. Quick! We've got to—"

Bullneck stared. He saw the sudden glint of metal in the hunchback's hand. "Brother," he said, "I'll tend to you later."

The hunchback had his rifle halfway to his shoulder when Bullneck's automatic spat and Bill braked his car in the red zone, jumped out, and dashed through four suites before anybody stopped him.

The man who did was a bull-necked plainclothesman, who rumbled—

"Don't you think," said Snulbug, "you've had about enough of this?"

Bill agreed mentally, and there he was sitting in his roadster in front of the city hall. His clothes were unrumpled, his eyes were bloodless, his teeth were all there, and his corncob was still intact. "And just what," he demanded of his pipe bowl, "has been going on?"

Snulbug popped his snaky head out. "Light this again, will you? It's getting cold. Thanks."

"What happened?" Bill insisted.

"People!" Snulbug moaned. "No sense. Don't you see? So long as the newspaper was in the future, it was only a possibility. If you'd had, say, a hunch that the mayor was in danger, maybe you could have saved him. But when I brought it into now, it became a fact. You can't possibly make it untrue."

"But how about man's free will? Can't I do whatever I want to do?"

"Sure. It was your precious free will that brought the paper

into now. You can't undo your own will. And, anyway, your
will's still free. You're free to go getting thrown around chan-
deliers as often as you want. You probably like it. You can
do anything up to the point where it would change what's in
that paper. Then you have to start in again and again and
again until you make up your mind to be sensible."

"But that—" Bill fumbled for words, "that's just as bad as
. . . as fate or predestination. If my soul wills to—"

"Newspapers aren't enough. Time theory isn't enough. So I
should tell him about his soul! People—" and Snulbug withdrew into the bowl.

Bill looked up at the city hall regretfully and shrugged his
resignation. Then he folded his paper to the sports page and
studied it carefully.

Snulbug thrust his head out again as they stopped in the
many-acred parking lot. "Where is it this time?" he wanted to
know. "Not that it matters."

"The racetrack."

"Oh—" Snulbug groaned, "I might have known it. You're
all alike. No sense in the whole caboodle. I suppose you
found a long shot?"

"Darned tooting I did. Alhazred at twenty to one in the
fourth. I've got $500, the only money I've got left on earth.
Plunk on Alhazred's nose it goes, and there's our $10,000."

Snulbug grunted. "I hear his lousy spell, I watch him get
caught on a merry-go-round, it isn't enough, I should see him
lay a bet on a long shot."

"But there isn't a loophole in this. I'm not interfering with
the future; I'm just taking advantage of it. Alhazred'll win
this race whether I bet on him or not. Five pretty hundred-
dollar parimutuel tickets, and behold: The Hitchens Laboratory!" Bill jumped spryly out of his car and strutted along
joyously. Suddenly he paused and addressed his pipe: "Hey!
Why do I feel so good?"

Snulbug sighed dismally. "Why should anybody?"

"No, but I mean: I took a hell of a shellacking from that
plug-ugly in the office. And I haven't got a pain or an ache."

"Of course not. It never happened."

"But I felt it then."

"Sure. In a future that never was. You changed your mind,
didn't you? You decided not to go up there?"

"O.K., but that was after I'd already been beaten up."

"Uh-uh," said Snublug firmly. "It was before you hadn't
been." And he withdrew again into the pipe.

There was a band somewhere in the distance and the raucous burble of an announcer's voice. Crowds clustered around the $2 windows, and the $5 weren't doing bad business. But the $100 window, where the five beautiful pasteboards lived that were to create an embolism laboratory, was almost deserted.

Bill buttonholed a stranger with a purple nose. "What's the next race?"

"Second, Mac."

Swell, Bill thought. Lots of time. And from now on—He hastened to the $100 window and shoved across the five bills that he had drawn from the bank that morning. "Alhazred, on the nose," he said.

The clerk frowned with surprise, but took the money and turned to get the tickets.

Bill buttonholed a stranger with a purple nose. "What's the next race?"

"Second, Mac."

Swell, Bill thought. And then he yelled, "Hey!"

A stranger with a purple nose paused and said, " 'Smatter, Mac?"

"Nothing," Bill groaned. "Just everything."

The stranger hesitated. "Ain't I seen you someplace before?"

"No," said Bill hurriedly. "You were going to, but you haven't. I changed my mind."

The stranger walked away shaking his head and muttering how the ponies could get a guy.

Not till Bill was back in his roadster did he take the corncob from his mouth and glare at it. "All right!" -he barked. "What was wrong this time? Why did I get on a merry-go-round again? I didn't try to change the future!"

Snulbug popped his head out and yawned a tuskful yawn. "I warn him, I explain it, I warn him again, now he wants I should explain it all over."

"But what did I do?"

"What did he do? You changed the odds, you dope. That much folding money on a long shot at a parimutuel track, and the odds change. It wouldn't have paid off at twenty to one, the way it said in the paper."

"Nuts," Bill muttered. "And I suppose that applies to anything? If I study the stock market in this paper and try to invest my $500 according to tomorrow's market—"

"Same thing. The quotations wouldn't be quite the same if you started in playing. I warned you. You're stuck," said

Snulbug. "You're stymied. It's no use." He sounded almost cheerful.

"Isn't it?" Bill mused. "Now look, Snulbug. Me, I'm a great believer in Man. This universe doesn't hold a problem that Man can't eventually solve. And I'm no dumber than the average."

"That's saying a lot, that is," Snulbug sneered. "People—"

"I've got a responsibility now. It's more than just my $10,-000. I've got to redeem the honor of Man. You say this is the insoluble problem. I say there is no insoluble problem."

"I say you talk a lot."

Bill's mind was racing furiously. How can a man take advantage of the future without in any smallest way altering that future? There must be an answer somewhere, and a man who devised the Hitchens Embolus Diagnosis could certainly crack a little nut like this. Man cannot refuse a challenge.

Unthinking, he reached for his tobacco pouch and tapped out his pipe on the sole of his foot. There was a microscopic thud as Snulbug crashed onto the floor of the car.

Bill looked down half-smiling. The tiny demon's tail was lashing madly, and every separate snake stood on end. "This is too much!" Snulbug screamed. "Dumb gags aren't enough, insults aren't enough, I should get thrown around like a damned soul. This is the last straw. Give me my dismissal!"

Bill snapped his fingers gleefully. "Dismissal!" he cried. "I've got it, Snully. We're all set."

Snulbug looked up puzzled and slowly let his snakes droop more amicably. "It won't work," he said, with an omnisciently sad shake of his serpentine head.

It was the dashing act again that carried Bill through the Choatsby Laboratories, where he had been employed so recently, and on up to the very anteroom of old R. C.'s office.

But where you can do battle with a bull-necked guard, there is not a thing you can oppose against the brisk competence of a young lady who says, "I shall find out if Mr. Choatsby will see you." There was nothing to do but wait.

"And what's the brilliant idea this time?" Snulbug obviously feared the worst.

"R. C.'s nuts," said Bill. "He's an astrologer and a pyramidologist and a British Israelite—American Branch Reformed—and Heaven knows what else. He . . . why, he'll even believe in you."

"That's more than I do," said Snulbug. "It's a waste of energy."

"He'll buy this paper. He'll pay anything for it. There's nothing he loves more than futzing around with the occult. He'll never be able to resist a good solid slice of the future with illusions of a fortune thrown in."

"You better hurry, then."

"Why such a rush? It's only 2:30 now. Lots of time. And while the girl's gone there's nothing for us to do but cool our heels."

"You might at least," said Snulbug, "warm the heel of your pipe."

The girl returned at last. "Mr. Choatsby will see you."

Reuben Choatsby overflowed the outsize chair behind his desk. His little face, like a baby's head balanced on a giant suet pudding, beamed as Bill entered. "Changed your mind, eh?" His words came in sudden soft blobs, like the abrupt glugs of pouring syrup. "Good. Need you in K-39. Lab's not the same since you left."

Bill groped for exactly the right words. "That's not it, R.C. I'm on my own now and I'm doing all right."

The baby face soured. "Damned cheek. Competitor of mine, eh? What you want now? Waste my time?"

"Not at all." With a pretty shaky assumption of confidence, Bill perched on the edge of the desk. "R. C.," he said, slowly and impressively, "what would you give for a glimpse into the future?"

Mr. Choatsby glugged vigorously. "Ribbing me? Get out of here! Have you thrown out—Hold on! You're the one—Used to read queer books. Had a grimoire here once." The baby face grew earnest. "What d'you mean?"

"Just what I said, R. C. What would you give for a glimpse into the future?"

Mr. Choatsby hesitated. "How? Time travel? Pyramid? You figured out the King's Chamber?"

"Much simpler than that. I have here"—he took it out of his pocket and folded it so that only the name and the date line were visible—"tomorrow's newspaper."

Mr. Choatsby grabbed. "Let me see."

"Uh-uh. Naughty. You'll see after we discuss terms. But there it is."

"Trick. Had some printer fake it. Don't believe it."

"All right. I never expected you, R. C., to descend to such unenlightened skepticism. But if that's all the faith you have—" Bill stuffed the paper back in his pocket and started for the door.

"Wait!" Mr. Choatsby lowered his voice. "How'd you do it? Sell your soul?"

"That wasn't necessary."

"How? Spells? Cantrips? Incantations? Prove it to me. Show me it's real. Then we'll talk terms."

Bill walked casually to the desk and emptied his pipe into the ash tray.

"I'm underdeveloped. I run errands. I'm named Snulbug. It isn't enough—now I should be a testimonial!"

Mr. Choatsby stared rapt at the furious little demon raging in his ash tray. He watched reverently as Bill held out the pipe for its inmate, filled it with tobacco, and lit it. He listened awe-struck as Snulbug moaned with delight at the flame.

"No more questions," he said. "What terms?"

"Fifteen thousand dollars." Bill was ready for bargaining.

"Don't put it too high," Snulbug warned. "You better hurry."

But Mr. Choatsby had pulled out his checkbook and was scribbling hastily. He blotted the check and handed it over. "It's a deal." He grabbed up the paper. "You're a fool, young man. Fifteen thousand! *Hmf!*" He had it open already at the financial page. "With what I make on the market tomorrow, never notice $15,000. Pennies."

"Hurry up," Snulbug urged.

"Good-bye, sir," Bill began politely, "and thank you for—" But Reuben Choatsby wasn't even listening.

"What's all this hurry?" Bill demanded as he reached the elevator.

"People!" Snulbug sighed. "Never you mind what's the hurry. You get to your bank and deposit that check."

So Bill, with Snulbug's incessant prodding, made a dash to the bank worthy of his descents on the city hall and on the Choatsby Laboratories. He just made it, by stopwatch fractions of a second. The door was already closing as he shoved his way through at three o'clock sharp.

He made his deposit, watched the teller's eyes bug out at the size of the check, and delayed long enough to enjoy the incomparable thrill of changing the account from William Hitchens to The Hitchens Research Laboratory.

Then he climbed once more into his car, where he could talk with his pipe in peace. "Now," he asked as he drove home, "what was the rush?"

"He'd stop payment."

"You mean when he found out about the merry-go-round? But I didn't promise him anything. I just sold him tomorrow's paper. I didn't guarantee he'd make a fortune of it."

"That's all right. But—"

"Sure, you warned me. But where's the hitch? R. C.'s a bandit, but he's honest. He wouldn't stop payment."

"Wouldn't he?"

The car was waiting for a stop signal. The newsboy in the intersection was yelling "Uxtruh!" Bill glanced casually at the headline, did a double take, and instantly thrust out a nickel and seized a paper.

He turned into a side street, stopped the car, and went through this paper. Front page: MAYOR ASSASSINATED. Sports page: Alhazred at twenty to one. Obituaries: The same list he'd read at noon. He turned back to the date line. August 22. Tomorrow.

"I warned you," Snulbug was explaining. "I told you I wasn't strong enough to go far into the future. I'm not a well demon, I'm not. And an itch in the memory is something fierce. I just went far enough ahead to get a paper with tomorrow's date on it. And any dope knows that a Tuesday paper comes out Monday afternoon."

For a moment Bill was dazed. His magic paper, his fifteen-thousand-dollar paper, was being hawked by newsies on every corner. Small wonder R. C. might have stopped payment! And then he saw the other side. He started to laugh. He couldn't stop.

"Look out!" Snulbug shrilled. "You'll drop my pipe. And what's so funny?"

Bill wiped tears from his eyes. "I was right. Don't you see, Snulbug? Man can't be licked. My magic was lousy. All it could call up was you. You brought me what was practically a fake, and I got caught on the merry-go-round of time trying to use it. You were right enough there; no good could come of that magic.

"But without the magic, just using human psychology, knowing a man's weaknesses, playing on them, I made a syrup-voiced old bandit endow the very research he'd tabooed, and do more good for humanity than he's done in all the rest of his life. I was right, Snulbug. You can't lick Man."

Snulbug's snakes writhed into knots of scorn. "People!" he snorted. "You'll find out." And he shook his head with dismal satisfaction.

HEREAFTER, INC.

Unknown
December

by Lester del Rey (1915-   )

*Although generally thought of as a leading science
fiction writer, Lester Del Rey is equally at home with
fantasy. He had a number of outstanding fantasies in*
Unknown *during the too-short life of that great
magazine, including "The Pipes of Pan" (May,
1940), "Forsaking All Others" (August, 1939),
"Anything" (October, 1939), "Doubled in Brass"
(January, 1940) and the wonderful "The Cop-
persmith" (September, 1939). A fantasy novel of note
is* Day of the Giants *(1959). In addition, he edited
the outstanding magazine* Fantasy Fiction *during its
short run in the early 1950s, and presently edits the
fantasy line at Del Rey Books.*

*"Hereafter, Inc." is a remarkable story, one of the
very best fantasies that examines the possible nature
of one man's Heaven (or is it one man's Hell?).*

(Lester and I have been friends for forty years, which is
not in the least surprising in his case for he is an old man,
but I don't quite see how that could be possible for me.

When I first met him, he weighed about 85 pounds and it
was the general feeling that the reason he could write such
convincing fantasy was that he was a leprechaun.

He is now gray and bearded but he has lost none of his
volubility, none of his feistiness, none of his know-it-all characteristics (which would be unbearable except that he *does*
know it all). He is no longer a leprechaun, however. It is my
private theory (for those of you who have read *Lord of the
Rings*) that he is Gandalf.—I.A.)

Phineas Theophilus Potts, who would have been the last to
admit and the first to believe he was a godly man, creaked
over in bed and stuck out one scrawny arm wrathfully. The
raucous jangling of the alarm was an unusually painful

cancer in his soul that morning. Then his waking mind took over and he checked his hand, bringing it down on the alarm button with precise, but gentle, firmness. Would he never learn to control these little angers? In this world one should bear all troubles with uncomplaining meekness, not rebel against them; otherwise— But it was too early in the morning to think of that.

He wriggled out of bed and gave his thoughts over to the ritual of remembering yesterday's sins, checking to make sure all had been covered and wiped out the night before. That's when he got his first shock; he couldn't remember anything about the day before—bad, very bad. Well, no doubt it was another trap of the forces conspiring to secure Potts' soul. Tch, tch. Terrible, but he could circumvent even that snare.

There was no mere mumbling by habit to his confession; word after word rolled off his tongue carefully with full knowledge and unctuous shame until he reached the concluding lines. "For the manifold sins which I have committed and for this greater sin which now afflicts me, forgive and guide me to sin no more, but preserve me in righteousness all the days of my life. Amen." Thus having avoided the pitfall and saved himself again from eternal combustion, he scrubbed hands with himself and began climbing into his scratchy underclothes and cheap black suit. Then he indulged in a breakfast of dry toast and buttermilk flavored with self-denial and was ready to fare forth into the world of temptation around him.

The telephone jangled against his nerves and he jumped, grabbing for it impatiently before he remembered; he addressed the mouthpiece contritely. "Phineas Potts speaking."

It was Mr. Sloane, his lusty animal voice barking out from the receiver. " 'Lo, Phin, they told me you're ready to come down to work today. Business is booming and we can use you. How about it?"

"Certainly, Mr. Sloane. I'm not one to shirk my duty." There was no reason for the call that Potts could see; he hadn't missed a day in twelve years. "You know—"

"Sure, okay. That's fine. Just wanted to warn you that we've moved. You'll see the name plate right across the street when you come out—swell place, too. Sure you can make it all right?"

"I shall be there in ten minutes, Mr. Sloane," Phineas assured him, and remembered in time to hang up without displaying distaste. Tch, poor Sloane, wallowing in sin and

ignorant of the doom that awaited him. Why, the last time
Phineas had chided his employer—mildly, too—Sloane had
actually laughed at him! Dear. Well, no doubt he incurred
grace by trying to save the poor lost soul, even though his efforts seemed futile. Of course, there was danger in consorting
with such people, but no doubt his sacrifices would be duly
recorded.

There was a new elevator boy, apparently, when he came
out of his room. He sniffed pointedly at the smoke from the
boy's cigarette; the boy twitched his lips, but did not throw it
away.

"Okay, bub," he grunted as the doors clanked shut, grating
across Phineas' nerves, "I don't like it no better'n you will,
but here we are."

Bub! Phineas glared at the shoulders turned to him and
shuddered. He'd see Mrs. Biddle about this later.

Suppressing his feelings with some effort, he headed across
the lobby, scarcely noting it, and stepped out onto the street.
Then he stopped. That was the second jolt. He swallowed
twice, opened his eyes and lifted them for the first time in
weeks, and looked again. It hadn't changed. Where there
should have been a little twisted side street near the tenements, he saw instead a broad gleaming thoroughfare, busy
with people and bright in warm golden sunshine. Opposite,
the ugly stores were replaced with bright, new office buildings, and the elevated tracks were completely missing. He
swung slowly about, clutching his umbrella for support as he
faced the hotel; it was still a hotel—but not his—definitely
not his. Nor was the lobby the same. He fumbled back into
it, shaken and bewildered.

The girl at the desk smiled up at him out of dancing eyes,
and she certainly wasn't the manager. Nor would prim Mrs.
Biddle, who went to his church, have hired this brazen little
thing; both her lips and fingernails were bright crimson, to
begin with, and beyond that he preferred not to go.

The brazen little thing smiled again, as if glorying in her
obvious idolatry. "Forget something, Mr. Potts?"

"I . . . uh . . . no. That is . . . you know who I am?"

She nodded brightly. "Yes indeed, Mr. Potts. You moved
in yesterday. Room 408. Is everything satisfactory?"

Phineas half nodded, gulped, and stumbled out again.
Moved in? He couldn't recall it. Why should he leave Mrs.
Biddle's? And 408 was his old room number; the room was
identical with the one he had lived in, even to the gray streak
on the wallpaper that had bothered his eyes for years. Some-

thing was horribly wrong—first the lack of memory, then Sloane's peculiar call, now this. He was too upset even to realize that this was probably another temptation set before him.

Mechanically, Phineas spied Sloane's name plate on one of the new buildings, and crossed over into it. "Morning, Mr. Potts," said the elevator boy, and Phineas jumped. He'd never seen this person before, either. "Fourth floor, Mr. Potts. Mr. Sloane's office is just two doors down."

Phineas followed the directions automatically, found the door marked G. R. SLOANE—ARCHITECT, and pushed into a huge room filled with the almost unbearable clatter of typewriters and Comptometers, the buzz of voices, and the jarring thump of an addressing machine. But this morning the familiarity of the sound seemed like a haven out of the wilderness until he looked around. Not only had Sloane moved, but he'd apparently also expanded and changed most of his office force. Only old Callahan was left, and Callahan— Strange, he felt sure Callahan had retired or something the year before, Oh, well, that was the least of his puzzles.

Callahan seemed to sense his stare, for he jumped up and brought a hamlike fist down on Phineas' back, almost knocking out the ill-fitting false teeth. "Phin Potts, you old doommonger! Welcome back!" He thumped again and Potts coughed, trying to reach the spot and rub out the sting. Not only did Callahan have to be an atheist—an argumentative one—but he had to indulge in this gross horseplay. Why hadn't the man stayed properly retired?

"Mr. Sloane?" he managed to gurgle.

Sloane himself answered, his rugged face split in a grin. "Hi, Phin. Let him alone, Callahan. Another thump like that and I'll have to hire a new draftsman. Come on Phin, there's the devil's own amount of work piled up for you now that you're back from your little illness." He led him around a bunch of tables where bright-painted hussies were busily typing, down a hall, and into the drafting room, exchanging words with others that made Phineas wince. Really, his language seemed to grow worse each day.

"Mr. Sloane, would you please—"

"Mind not using such language," Sloane finished, and grinned. "Phin, I can't help it. I feel too good. Business is terrific and I've got the world by the tail. How do you feel?"

"Very well, thank you." Phinease fumbled and caught the thread of former conversation that had been bothering him. "You said something about—illness?"

"Think nothing of it. After working for me twelve years, I'm not going to dock your pay for a mere month's absence. Kind of a shame you had to be off just when I needed you, but such things will happen, so we'll just forget it, eh?" He brushed aside the other's muttered attempt at questioning and dug into the plans. "Here, better start on this—you'll notice some changes, but it's a lot like what we used to do; something like the Oswego we built in '37. Only thing that'll give you trouble is the new steel they put out now, but you can follow specifications on that."

Phineas picked up the specifications, ran them over, and blinked. This would never do; much as he loathed the work, he was an excellent draftsman, and he knew enough of general structural design to know this would never do. "But, two-inch I-beams here—"

" 'Sall right, Phin, structural strength is about twelve times what you're used to. Makes some really nice designing possible, too. Just follow the things like I said, and I'll go over it all later. Things changed a little while you were delirious. But I'm in a devil of a rush right now. See you." He stuck his body through the door, thrust his head back inside and cocked an eyebrow. "Lunch? Need somebody to show you around, I guess."

"As you wish, Mr. Sloane," agreed Phineas. "But would you please mind—"

"Not swearing. Sure, okay. And no religious arguments this time; if I'm damned, I like it." Then he was gone, leaving Phineas alone—he couldn't work with the distraction of others, and always had a room to himself.

So he'd been sick had he, even delirious? Well, that might explain things. Phineas had heard that such things sometimes produced a hiatus in the memory, and it was a better explanation than nothing. With some relief, he put it out of his mind, remembering only to confess how sinfully he'd lost his trust in divine guidance this morning, shook his head mournfully, and began work with dutiful resignation. Since it had obviously been ordained that he should make his simple living at drafting, draft he would, with no complaints, and there would be no fault to be found with him there.

Then the pen began to scratch. He cleaned and adjusted it, finding nothing wrong, but still it made little grating sounds on the paper, lifting up the raw edges of his nerves. Had Phineas believed in evolution, he'd have said the hair his ancestors had once grown was trying to stand on end, but he had no use for such heretical ideas. Well, he was not one to complain. He unclenched his teeth and sought forbearance and peace within.

Then, outside, the addressograph began to thump again, and he had to force himself not to ruin the lines as his body tried to flinch. Be patient, all these trials would be rewarded. Finally, he turned to the only anodyne he knew, contemplation of the fate of heretics and sinners. Of course, he was sorry for them roasting eternally and crying for water which they would never get—very sorry for the poor deluded creatures, as any righteous man should be. Yet still they had been given their chance and not made proper use of it, so it was only just. Picturing morbidly the hell of his most dour Puritan ancestors—something very real to him—he almost failed to notice the ache of his bunion where the cheap shoes pinched. But not quite.

Callahan was humming out in the office, and Phineas could just recognize the tune. Once the atheist had come in roaring drunk, and before they'd sent him home, he'd cornered Phineas and sung it through, unexpurgated. Now, in time with the humming, the words insisted on trickling through the suffering little man's mind, and try as he would, they refused to leave. Prayer did no good. Then he added Callahan to the tortured sinners, and that worked better.

"Pencils, shoestrings, razor blades?" The words behind him startled him, and he regained his balance on the stool with difficulty. Standing just inside the door was a one-legged hunchback with a handful of cheap articles. "Pencils?" he repeated. "Only a nickel. Help a poor cripple?" But the grin on his face belied the words.

"Indeed no, no pencils." Phineas shuddered as the fellow hobbled over to a window and rid himself of a chew of tobacco. "Why don't you try the charities? Furthermore, we don't allow beggars here."

"Ain't none," the fellow answered with ambiguous cheerfulness, stuffing in a new bite.

"Then have faith in the Lord and He will provide." Naturally, man had been destined to toil through the days of his life in this mortal sphere, and toil he must to achieve salvation. He had no intention of ruining this uncouth person's small chance to be saved by keeping him in idleness.

The beggar nodded and touched his cap. "One of them, eh? Too bad. Well, keep your chin up, maybe it'll be better later." Then he went off down the hall, whistling, leaving Phineas to puzzle over his words and give it up as a bad job.

Potts rubbed his bunion tenderly, then desisted, realizing that pain was only a test, and should be borne meekly. The pen still scratched, the addressing machine thumped, and a bee had buzzed in somehow and went zipping about. It was a large and active bee.

Phineas cowered down and made himself work, sweating a little as the bee lighted on his drafting board. Then, mercifully, it flew away and for a few minutes he couldn't hear it. When it began again, it was behind him. He started to turn his head, then decided against it; the bee might take the motion as an act of aggression, and declare war. His hands on the pen were moist and clammy, and his fingers ached from gripping it too tightly, but somehow, he forced himself to go on working.

The bee was evidently in no hurry to leave. It flashed by his nose, buzzing, making him jerk back and spatter a blob of ink into the plans, then went zooming around his head and settled on his bald spot. Phineas held his breath and the bee stood pat. Ten, twenty, thirty seconds. His breath went out suddenly with a rush. The insect gave a brief buzz, evidently deciding the noise was harmless, and began strolling down over his forehead and out onto his nose. It tickled; the inside of his nose tickled, sympathetically.

"No, no," Phineas whispered desperately. "N—*Achee*OO! EEOW!" He grabbed for his nose and jerked violently, bumping his shins against the desk and splashing more ink on the plans. "Damn, oh, da—"

It was unbelievable; it couldn't be true! His own mouth had betrayed him! With shocked and leaden fingers he released the pen and bowed his head, but no sense of saving grace would come. Too well he could remember that even the smallest sin deserves just damnation. Now he was really sweating, and the visions of eternal torment came trooping back; but this time he was in Callahan's place, and try as he would, he couldn't switch. He was doomed!

Callahan found him in that position a minute later, and his rough, mocking laugh cut into Phineas' wounded soul. "Sure, an angel as I live and breathe." He dumped some papers onto the desk and gave another backbreaking thump. "Got the first sheets done, Phin?"

Miserably, Phineas shook his head, glancing at the clock. They should have been ready an hour ago. Another sin was piled upon his burden, beyond all hope of redemption, and of all people, Callahan had caught him not working when he was already behind. But the old Irishman didn't seem to be gloating.

"There now, don't take it so hard, Phin. Nobody expects you to work like a horse when you've been sick. Mr. Sloane wants you to come out to lunch with him now."

"I—uh—" Words wouldn't come.

Callahan thumped him on the back again, this time lightly enough to rattle only two ribs. "Go along with you. What's left is beginner's stuff and I'll finish it while you're eating. I'm ahead and got nothing to do, anyhow. Go on." He practically picked the smaller man off the stool and shoved him through the door. "Sloane's waiting. Heck, I'll be glad to do it. Feel so good I can't find enough to keep me busy."

Sloane was flirting with one of the typists as Phineas plodded up, but he wound up that business with a wink and grabbed for his hat. " 'Smatter, Phin? You look all in. Bad bruise on your nose, too. Well, a good lunch'll fix up the first part, at least. Best damned food you ever ate, and right around the corner."

"Yes, Mr. Sloane, but would you . . . uh!" He couldn't ask that now. He himself was a sinner, given to violent language. Glumly he followed the other out and into the corner restaurant. Then, as he settled into the seat, he realized he couldn't eat; first among his penances should be giving up lunches.

"I . . . uh . . . don't feel very hungry, Mr. Sloane. I'll just have a cup of tea, I think." The odors of the food in the clean little restaurant that brought twinges to his stomach would only make his penance that much greater.

But Sloane was ordering for two. "Same as usual, honey, and you might as well bring a second for my friend here." He turned to Phineas. "Trouble with you, Phin, is that you don't eat enough. Wait'll you get a whiff of the ham they serve here—and the pie! Starting now, you're eating right if I have to stuff it down you. Ah!"

Service was prompt, and the plates began to appear before the little man's eyes. He could feel his mouth watering, and had to swallow to protest. Then the look in Sloane's eyes made him decide not to. Well, at least he could fast morning and night instead. He nodded to himself glumly, wishing his craven appetite wouldn't insist on deriving so much pleasure from the food.

"And so," Sloane's voice broke in on his consciousness again, "after this, you're either going to promise me you'll eat three good meals a day or I'll come around and stuff it down you. Hear?"

"Yes, Mr. Sloane, but—"

"Good. I'm taking that as a promise."

Phineas cringed. He hadn't meant it that way; it couldn't go through as a promise. "But—"

"No buts about it. Down there I figured you had as good a chance of being right as I did, so I didn't open my mouth on the subject. But up here, that's done with. No reason why you can't enjoy life now."

That was too much. "Life," said Phineas, laying down his knife and preparing for siege, "was meant to give us a chance to prepare for the life to come, not to be squandered in wanton pleasure. Surely it's better to suffer through a few brief years, resisting temptations, than to be forever damned to perdition. And would you sacrifice heaven for mere mundane cravings, transient and worthless?"

"Stow it, Phin. Doesn't seem to me I sacrificed much to get here." Then, at Phineas' bewildered look, "Don't tell me you don't realize where you are? They told me they were sending a boy with the message; well, I guess he just missed you. You're dead, Phin! *This* is Heaven! We don't talk much about it, but that's the way it is!"

"No!" The world was rolling in circles under Phineas' seat. He stared uncomprehendingly at Sloane, finding no slightest sign of mockery on the man's face. And there was the hole in the memory of sins, and the changes, and—Callahan! Why, Callahan had died and been buried the year before; and here he was, looking ten years younger, and hearty as ever. But it was all illusion; of course, it was all illusion. Callahan wouldn't be in heaven. "No, it can't be."

"But it is, Phin. Remember? I was down your way to get you for overtime work, and yelled at you just as you came out of your house. Then you started to cross, I yelled again—Come back now?"

There'd been a screeching of tires, Sloane running toward him suddenly waving frantically, and—blackout! "Then it hit? And this . . . is—"

"Uh-huh. Seems they picked me up with a shovel, but it took a month to finish you off." Sloane dug into the pie, rolling it on his tongue and grinning. "And this is Hereafter. A darned good one, too, even if nobody meets you at the gate to say 'Welcome to Heaven.' "

Phineas clutched at the straw. "They didn't tell you it was Heaven, then? Oh." That explained everything. Of course, he

should have known. This wasn't heaven after all; it couldn't
be. And though it differed from his conceptions, it most certainly could be the other place; there'd been that bee! Tch, it
was just like Callahan and Sloane to enjoy perdition,
midguided sinners, glorying in their unholiness.

Slowly the world righted itself, and Phineas Potts regained
his normal state. To be sure, he'd used an ugly word, but
what could be expected of him in this vile place? They'd
never hold it against him under the circumstances. He lowered his eyes thankfully, paying no attention to Sloane's idle
remarks about unfortunates. Now if he could just find the authorities of this place and get the mistake straightened out, all
might yet be well. He had always done his best to be righteous. Perhaps a slight delay, but not long; and then—no Callahan, no Sloane, no drafting, or bees, or grating noises!

He drew himself up and looked across at Sloane, sadly, but
justly doomed to this strange gehenna. "Mr. Sloane," he
asked firmly, "is there some place here where I can find . . .
uh . . . authorities to . . . umm—"

"You mean you want to register a complaint? Why sure, a
big white building about six blocks down; Adjustment and
Appointment office." Sloane studied him thoroughly. "Darned
if you don't look like you had a raw deal about something, at
that. Look, Phin, they made mistakes sometimes, of course,
but if they've handed you the little end, we'll go right down
there and get it put right."

Phineas shook his head quickly. The proper attitude, no
doubt was to leave Sloane in ignorance of the truth as long as
possible, and that meant he'd have to go alone. "Thank you,
Mr. Sloane, but I'll go by myself, if you don't mind. And
. . . uh . . . if I don't come back . . . uh—"

"Sure, take the whole afternoon off. Hey, wait, aren't you
gonna finish lunch?"

But Phineas Potts was gone, his creaking legs carrying him
out into the mellow noon sunlight and toward the towering
white building that must be his destination. The fate of a
man's soul is nothing to dally over, and he wasn't dallying.
He tucked his umbrella close under his arm to avoid contact
with the host of the damned, shuddering at the thought of
mingling with them. Still, undoubtedly this torture would be
added to the list of others, and his reward be made that much
greater. Then he was at the Office of Administration, Ap-
pointments, and Adjustments.

There was another painted Jezebel at the desk marked IN-
FORMATION, and he headed there, barely collecting his

thoughts in time to avoid disgraceful excitement. She grinned
at him and actually winked! "Mr. Potts, isn't it? Oh, I'm so
sorry you left before our messenger arrived. But if there's
something we can do now—"

"There is," he told her firmly, though not too unkindly; after all, her punishment was ample without his anger. "I wish
to see an authority here. I have a complaint; a most grievous
complaint."

"Oh, that's too bad, Mr. Potts. But if you'll see Mr.
Alexander, down the hall, third door left, I'm sure he can adjust it."

He waited no longer, but hurried where she pointed. As he
approached, the third door opened and a dignified-looking
man in a gray business suit stepped to it. The man held out a
hand instantly. "I'm Mr. Alexander. Come in, won't you?
Katy said you had a complaint. Sit right over there, Mr.
Potts. Ah, so. Now, if you'll tell me about it, I think we can
straighten it all out."

Phineas told him—in detail. "And so," he concluded
firmly—quite firmly, "I feel I've been done a grave injustice,
Mr. Alexander. I'm positive my destination should have been
the other place."

"The other place?" Alexander seemed surprised.

"Exactly so. Heaven, to be more precise."

Alexander nodded thoughtfully. "Quite so, Mr. Potts. Only
I'm afraid there's been a little misunderstanding. You see
. . . ah . . . this is Heaven. Still, I can see you don't believe
me yet, so we've failed to place you properly. We really want
to make people happy here, you know. So, if you'll just tell
me what you find wrong, we'll do what we can to rectify it."

"Oh." Phineas considered. This might be a trick, of course,
but still, if they could make him happy here, give him his due
reward for the years filled with temptation resisted and noble
suffering in meekness and humility, there seemed nothing
wrong with it. Possibly, it came to him, there were varying
degrees of blessedness, and even such creatures as Callahan
and his ilk were granted the lower ones—though it didn't
seem quite just. But certainly his level wasn't Callahan's.

"Very well," he decided. "First, I find myself living in that
room with the gray streak on the wallpaper, sir, and for years
I've loathed it; and the alarm and telephone; and—"

Alexander smiled. "One at a time please. Now, about the
room. I really felt we'd done a masterly job on that, you
know. Isn't it exactly like your room on the former level of

life? Ah, I see it is. And didn't you choose and furnish that room yourself?"

"Yes, but—"

"Ah, then we were right. Naturally, Mr. Potts, we assumed that since it was of your own former creation, it was best suited to you. And besides, you need the alarm and telephone to keep you on time and in contact with your work, you know."

"But I loathe drafting!" Phineas glanced at this demon who was trying to trap him, expecting it to wilt to its true form. It didn't. Instead, the thing that was Mr. Alexander shook his head slowly and sighed.

"Now that is a pity; and we were so pleased to find we could even give you the same employer as before. Really, we felt you'd be happier under him than a stranger. However, if you don't like it, I suppose we could change. What other kind of work would you like?"

Now that was more like it, and perhaps he had even misjudged Alexander. Work was something Phineas hadn't expected, but—yes, that would be nice, if it could be arranged here. "I felt once I was *called,*" he suggested.

"Minister, you mean? Now that's fine. Never get too many of them, Mr. Potts. Wonderful men, do wonderful work here. They really add enormously to the happiness of our Hereafter, you know. Let me see, what experience have you had?" He beamed at Potts, who thawed under it; then he turned to a bookshelf, selected a heavy volume and consulted it. Slowly the beam vanished, and worry took its place.

"Ah, yes, Phineas Theophilus Potts. Yes, entered training 1903. Hmmm. Dismissed after two years of study, due to a feeling he might . . . might not be quite temperamentally suited to the work and that he was somewhat too fana . . . ahem! . . . overly zealous in his criticism of others. Then transferred to his uncle's shop and took up drafting, which was thereafter his life's work. Umm. Really, that's too bad." Alexander turned back to Phineas. "Then, Mr. Potts, I take it you never had any actual experience at this sort of work?"

Phineas squirmed. "No, but—"

"Too bad." Alexander sighed. "Really, I'd like to make things more to your satisfaction, but after all, no experience—afraid it wouldn't do. Tell you what, we don't like to be hasty in our judgments; if you'll just picture exactly the life you want—no need to describe it, I'll get it if you merely think it—maybe we can adjust things. Try hard now."

With faint hope, Phineas tried. Alexander's voice droned

out at him. "A little harder. No, that's only a negative picture
of what you'd like not to do. Ah . . . um, no. I thought for a
minute you had something, but it's gone. I think you're trying
to picture abstractions, Mr. Potts, and you know one can't do
that; I get something very vague, but it makes no sense.
There! That's better."

He seemed to listen for a few seconds longer, and Phineas
was convinced now it was all sham; he'd given up trying.
What was the use? Vague jumbled thoughts were all he had
left, and now Alexander's voice broke in on them.

"Really, Mr. Potts, I'm afraid there's nothing we can do
for you. I get a very clear picture now, but it's exactly the
life we'd arranged for you, you see. Same room, same work.
Apparently that's the only life you know. Of course, if you
want to improve we have a great many very fine schools located throughout the city."

Phineas jerked upright, the control over his temper barely
on. "You mean—you mean, I've got to go on like that?"

"Afraid so."

"But you distinctly said this was Heaven."

"It is."

"And I tell you," Phineas cried, forgetting all about controlling his temper, "that this is Hell!"

"Quite so, I never denied it. Now, Mr. Potts, I'd like to
discuss this further, but others are waiting, so I'm afraid I'll
have to ask you to leave."

Alexander looked up from his papers, and as he looked,
Phineas found himself outside the door, shaken and sick.
The door remained open as the girl called Katy came up,
looked at him in surprise, and went in. Then it closed, but
still he stood there, unable to move, leaning against the
wooden frame for support.

There was a mutter of voices within, and his whirling
thoughts seized on them for anchor. Katy's voice first. "—
seems to take it terribly hard, Mr. Alexander. Isn't there
something we can do?"

Then the low voice of Alexander. "Nothing, Katy. It's up
to him now. I suggested the schools, but I'm afraid he's another unfortunate. Probably even now he's out there convincing himself that all this is merely illusion, made to try his soul
and test his ability to remain unchanged. If that's the case,
well, poor devil, there isn't much we can do, you know."

But Phineas wasn't listening then. He clutched the words
he'd heard savagely to his bosom and went stiffly out and
back toward the office of G. R. Sloane across from the little

room, No. 408. Of course he should have known. All this was merely illusion, made to try his soul. Illusion and test, no more.

Let them try him, they would find him humble in his sufferings as always, not complaining, resisting firmly their temptations. Even though Sloane denied him the right to fast, still he would find some other way to do proper penance for his sins; though Callahan broke his back, though a thousand bees attacked him at once, still he would prevail.

"Forgive and guide me to sin no more, but preserve me in righteousness all the days of my life," he repeated, and turned into the building where there was more work and misery waiting for him. Sometime he'd be rewarded. Sometime.

Back in his head a small shred of doubt sniggered gleefully.

THE STAR MOUSE

Planet Stories,

February

by Fredric Brown

Although the late Fredric Brown built his reputation on the wit and humor that characterized his stories, he also brought a strong dose of cynicism to his work. He specialized in the short-short, and science fiction has yet to see his equal in this possibly most difficult of formats. His novels include the hilarious What Mad Universe *(1949), the sober and moving* The Lights in the Sky Are Stars *(1953) and* Martians Go Home, *(1955), but the finest sf book that carries his name is* The Best of Fredric Brown *(1977). A fine craftsman in several* genres, *his mystery and suspense fiction is even better than his sf.*

"The Star Mouse" is a fable for all ages, featuring one of the most endearing protaganists in the history of science fiction.

(It wasn't till December 1948 that I first met Fred Brown at a meeting of the Hydra Club at the home of Fletcher Pratt. Fred was short and thin and looked like a bookkeeper, but he was the classic example of a man who didn't look like the books he wrote. His book *Screaming Mimi* was a classic and my personal favorite of his works. He insisted on playing chess with me but was five times as good as I was. However, he talked as he played (perhaps without knowing it) and constantly reasoned out what he thought I was doing. I caught on and started doing what he thought I was doing and in the end I managed to elicit a draw then quit while I was ahead. When someone asks me, by the way, if it is possible to write good science fiction without knowing any science, I always say "yes" and as examples cite several writers, of whom Fred Brown is one. —I.A.)

Mitkey, the Mouse, wasn't Mitkey then.

He was just another mouse, who lived behind the floor-boards and plaster of the house of the great Herr Professor Oberburger, formerly of Vienna and Heidelberg; then a refugee from the excessive admiration of the more powerful of his fellow-countrymen. The excessive admiration had concerned, not Herr Oberburger himself, but a certain gas which had been a by-product of an unsuccessful rocket fuel—which might have been a highly successful something else.

If, of course, the Professor had given them the correct formula. Which he—Well, anyway, the Professor had made good his escape and now lived in a house in Conneticut. And so did Mitkey.

A small grey mouse, and a small gray man. Nothing unusual about either of them. Particularly there was nothing unusual about Mitkey; he had a family and he liked cheese and if there were Rotarians among mice, he would have been a Rotarian.

The Herr Professor, of course, had his mild eccentricities. A confirmed bachelor, he had no one to talk to except himself, but he considered himself an excellent conversationalist and held constant verbal communion with himself while he worked. That fact, it turned out later, was important, because Mitkey had excellent ears and heard those night-long soliloquies. He didn't understand them, of course. If he thought about them at all, he merely thought of the Professor as a large and noisy super-mouse who squeaked overmuch.

"Und now," he would say to himself, "ve vill see vether this eggshaust tube vas broberly machined. It should fidt vithin vun vun-hundredth thousandth uf an indtch. Ahhh, it iss berfect. Und now—"

Night after night, day after day, month after month. The gleaming thing grew, and the gleam in Herr Oberburger's eyes grew apace.

It was about three and a half feet long, with weirdly shaped vanes, and it rested on a temporary framework on a table in the center of the room that served the Herr Professor for all purposes. The house in which he and Mitkey lived was a four-room structure, but the Professor hadn't yet found it out, seemingly. Originally, he had planned to use the big room as a laboratory only, but he found it more convenient to sleep on a cot in one corner of it, when he slept at all, and to do the little cooking he did over the same gas burner over which he melted down golden grains of TNT into a dangerous soup which he salted and peppered with strange condiments, but did not eat.

"Und now I shall bour it into tubes, und see vether vun tube adjacent to another eggsplodes der second tube vhen der virst tube iss—"

That was the night Mitkey almost decided to move himself and his family to a more stable abode, one that did not rock and sway and try to turn handsprings on its foundations. But Mitkey didn't move after all, because there were compensations. New mouseholes all over, and—joy of joy!—a big crack in the back of the refrigerator where the Professor kept, among other things, food.

Of course the tubes had been not larger than capillary size, or the house would not have remained around the mouseholes. And of course Mitkey could not guess what was coming or understand the Herr Professor's brand of English (nor any other brand of English, for that matter) or he would not have let even a crack in the refrigerator tempt him.

The Professor was jubilant that morning.

"Der fuel, it vorks! Der second tube, it did not eggsplode. Und Der virst, in *seggtions,* as I had eggspectedt! Und it is more bowerful; there will be blenty of room for der combartment—"

Ah, yes, the compartment. That was where Mitkey came in, although even the Professor didn't know it yet. In fact the Professor didn't even know that Mitkey existed.

"Und now," he was saying to his favorite listener, "it is but a matter of combining der fuel tubes so they work in obbosite bairs. Und then—"

That was the moment when the Herr Professor's eyes first fell on Mitkey. Rather, they fell upon a pair of gray whiskers and a black, shiny little nose protruding from a hole in the baseboards.

"Vell!" he said, "vot haff ve here! Mitkey Mouse himself! Mitkey, how would you like to go for a ride, negst veek? Ve shall see."

That is how it came about that the next time the Professor sent into town for supplies, his order included a mousetrap—not one of the vicious kind that kills but one of the wire-cage kind. And it had not been set, with cheese, for more than ten minutes before Mitkey's sharp little nose had smelled out that cheese and he had followed his nose into captivity.

Not, however, an unpleasant captivity. Mitkey was an honored guest. The cage reposed now on the table at which the Professor did most of his work, and cheese in indigestion-giving abundance was pushed through the bars, and the Professor didn't talk to himself any more.

"You see, Mitkey, I vas going to send to der laboratory in Hartford for a vhite mouse, budt vhy should I, mit you here? I am sure you are more sound und healthy und able to vithstand a long chourney than those laboratory mices. No? Ah, you viggle your viskers und that means yes, no? Und being used to living in dark holes, you should suffer less than they from glaustrophobia, no?"

And Mitkey grew fat and happy and forgot all about trying to get out of the cage. I fear that he even forgot about the family he had abandoned, but he knew, if he knew anything, that he need not worry about them in the slightest. At least not until and unless the Professor discovered and repaired the hole in the refrigerator. And the Professor's mind was most emphatically not on refrigeration.

"Und so, Mitkey, ve shall place this vane so—it iss only of assistance in der landing, in an atmosphere. It und these vill bring you down safely und slowly enough that der shock-absorbers in der movable combartment vill keep you from bumping your head too hard, I think." Of course, Mitkey missed the ominous note to that "I think" qualification because he missed all the rest of it. He did not, as has been explained, speak English. Not then.

But Herr Oberburger talked to him just the same. He showed him pictures. "Did you effer see der Mouse you vas named after, Mitkey? Vhat? No? Loogk, this is der original Mitkey Mouse, by Valt Dissney. But I think you are cuter, Mitkey."

Probably the Professor was a bit crazy to talk that way to a little gray mouse. In fact, he must have been crazy to make a rocket that worked. For the odd thing was that the Herr Professor was not really an inventor. There was, as he carefully explained to Mitkey, not one single thing about that rocket that was new. The Herr Professor was a technician; he could take other people's ideas and make then work. His only real invention—the rocket fuel that wasn't one—had been turned over to the United States Government and had proved to be something already known and discarded because it was too expensive for practical use.

As he explained very carefully to Mitkey, "It iss burely a matter of absolute accuracy and mathematical correctness Mitkey. Idt iss all here—ve merely combine—und ve achieff vhat, Mitkey?

"Eggscape velocity, Mitkey! Chust barely, it adds up to eggscape velocity. Maybe. There are yet unknown factors, Mitkey, in der ubper atmosphere, der troposphere, der stratosphere. Ve think ve know eggsactly how much air there iss to calculate resistance against, but are ve absolutely sure? No, Mitkey, ve are not. Ve haff not been there. Und der marchin iss so narrow that so much as an air current might affect it."

But Mitkey cared not a whit. In the shadow of the tapering aluminum-alloy cylinder he waxed fat and happy.

"Der tag, Mitkey, der tag! Und I shall not lie to you, Mitkey. I shall not giff you valse assurances. You go on a dancherous chourney, mein little friend.

"A vifty-vifty chance ve giff you, Mitkey. Not der moon or bust, but der moon und bust, or else maybe safely back to earth. You see, my boor little Mitkey, der moon iss not made of green cheese und if it were, you vould not live to eat it because there iss not enough atmosphere to bring you down safely und vith your viskers still on.

"Und vhy then, you may vell ask, do I send you? Because der rocket may *not* attain eggscape velocity. Und in that case it iss still an eggsperiment, but a different vun. Der rocket, if it goes not to der moon, falls back on der earth, no? Und in that case certain instruments shall giff us further information than ve haff yet about things up there in space. Und you shall giff us information, by vether or not you are yet alife, vether der shock absorbers und vanes are sufficient in an earth-equivalent atmosphere. You see?

"Then later, vhen ve send rockets to Venus maybe vhere an atmosphere eggsists, ve shall haff data to calculate the needed size of vanes und shock absorbers, no? Und in either case, und vether nor not you return, Mitkey, you shall be vamous! You shall be der virst liffing greature to go out beyond der stratosphere of der earth, out into space.

"Mitkey, you shall be der Star-Mouse! I enfy you, Mitkey, und I only vish I vere your size, so I could go, too."

Der tag, and the door to the compartment. "Gootbye, little Mitkey Mouse." Darkness. Silence. Noise!

"Der rocket—if it goes not to der moon—falls back on der earth, no?" That was what the Herr Professor thought. But the best-laid plans of mice and men gang aft agley. Even star-mice.

All because of Prxl.

The Herr Professor found himself very lonely. After having had Mitkey to talk to, soliloquies were somehow empty and inadequate.

There may be some who say that the company of a small gray mouse is a poor substitute for a wife; but others may disagree. And, anyway, the Professor had never had a wife, and he *had* a mouse to talk to, so he missed one and, if he missed the other, he didn't know it.

During the long night after the launching of the rocket, he had been very busy with his telescope, a sweet little eight-inch reflector, checking its course as it gathered momentum. The exhaust explosions made a tiny fluctuating point of light that was possible to follow, if one knew where to look.

But the following day there seemed to be nothing to do, and he was too excited to sleep, although he tried. So he compromised by doing a spot of housekeeping, cleaning the pots and pans. It was while he was so engaged that he heard a series of frantic little squeaks and discovered that another small gray mouse, with shorter whiskers and a shorter tail than Mitkey, had walked into the wire-cage mousetrap.

"Vell, vell," said the Professor, "vot haff ve here? Minnie? Iss it Minnie come to look for her Mitkey?"

The Professor was not a biologist, but he happened to be right. It *was* Minnie. Rather, it was Mitkey's mate, so the name was appropriate. What strange vagary of mind had induced her to walk into an unbaited trap, the Professor neither knew nor cared, but he was delighted. He promptly remedied the lack of bait by pushing a sizable piece of cheese through the bars.

Thus it was that Minnie came to fill the place of her far-traveling spouse as repository for the Professor's confidences. Whether she worried about her family or not there is no way of knowing, but she need not have done so. they were now large enough to fend for themselves, particularly in a house that offered abundant cover and easy access to the refrigerator.

"Ah, und now it iss dargk enough, Minnie, that ve can look for that husband of yours. His viery trail across the sky. True, Minnie, it iss a very small viery trail und der astronomers vill not notice it, because they do not know vhere to look. But ve do.

"He iss going to be a very vamous mouse, Minnie, this Mitkey of ours, vhen ve tell der vorld about him und about mein rocket. You see, Minnie ve haff not told them yet. Ve shall vait und giff der gomplete story all at vunce. By dawn of tomorrow ve'll—

"Ah, there he iss, Minnie! Vaint, but there. I'd hold you up to der scope und let you look, but it vould not be vocused, right for your eyes, und I do not know how to—

"Almost vun hundred thousand miles, Minnie, und still agcelerating, but not for much longer. Our Mitkey iss on schedule; in fagt he iss going vaster than ve had vigured, no? It iss sure now that he vill eggscape the gravitation of der earth, und fall upon der moon!"

Of course, it was purely coincidental that Minnie squeaked.

"Ah, yess, Minnie, little Minnie. I know, I know. Ve shall neffer see our Mitkey again, und I almost vish our eggsperiment had vailed. But there are gompensations, Minnie. He shall be der most vamous of all mices. Der Star-Mouse! Virst liffing greature effer to go beyond der gravitational pull of earth!"

The night was long. Occasionally high clouds obscured vision.

"Minnie, I shall make you more gomfortable than in that so-small vire cage. You vould like to seem to be vree, vould you not, vithout bars, like der animals at modern zoos, vith moats instead?"

And so, to fill in an hour when a cloud obscured the sky, the Herr Professor made Minnie her new home. It was the end of a wooden crate, about half an inch thick and a foot square, laid flat on the table, and with no visible barrier around it.

But he covered the top with metal foil at the edges, and he placed the board on another larger board which also had a strip of metal foil surrounding the island of Minnie's home. And wires from the two areas of metal foil to opposite terminals of a small transformer which he placed nearby.

"Und now, Minnie, I shall blace you on your island, vhich shall be liberally supplied mitt cheese and vater, und you shall vind it iss an eggcelent blace to liff. But you vill get a mild shock or two vhen you try to step off der edge of der island. It vill not hurt much, but you vill not like it, und after a few tries you vill learn not to try again, no? Und—"

And night again.

Minnie happy on her island, her lesson well learned. She would no longer so much as step on the inner strip of metal foil. It was a mouse paradise of an island, though. There was a cliff of cheese bigger than Minnie herself. It kept her busy. Mouse and cheese; soon one would be a transmutation of the other.

But Professor Oberburger wasn't thinking about that. The Professor was worried. When he had calculated and recalculated and aimed his eight-inch reflector through the hole in the roof and turned out the lights—

Yes, there are advantages to being a bachelor after all. If one wants a hole in the roof, one simply knocks a hole in the roof and there is nobody to tell one that one is crazy. If winter comes, or if it rains, one can always call a carpenter or use a tarpaulin.

But the faint trail of light wasn't there. The Professor frowned and re-calculated and re-re-calculated and shifted his telescope three-tenths of a minute and still the rocket wasn't there.

"Minnie, something iss wrong. Either der tubes haff stopped viring, or—"

Or the rocket was no longer traversing a straight line relative to its point of departure. By straight, of course, is meant parabolically curved relative to everything other than velocity.

So the Herr Professor did the only thing remaining for him to do and began to search, with the telescope, in widening circles. It was two hours before he found it, five degrees off course already and veering more and more into a— Well, there was only one thing you could call it. A tailspin.

The darned thing was going in circles, circles which appeared to constitute an orbit about something that couldn't possibly be there. Then narrowing into a concentric spiral.

Then—out. Gone. Darkness. No rocket flares.

The Professor's face was pale as he turned to Minnie.

"It *iss imbossible*, Minnie. Mein own eyes, but it could not be. Even if vun side stopped viring, it could not haff gone into such sudden circles." His pencil verified a suspicion. "Und, Minnie, it decelerated vaster than bossible. Even mitt *no* tubes viring, its momentum vould haff been more—"

The rest of the night—telescope and calculus—yielded no clue. That is, no believable clue. Some force not inherent in the rocket itself, and not accountable by gravitation—even of a hypothetical body—had acted.

"Mein poor Mitkey."

The gray, inscrutable dawn. "Mein Minnie, it vill haff to be a secret. Ve dare not publish vhat ve saw, for it vould not be believed. I am not sure I believe it myself, Minnie. Berhaps because I vas offertired vrom not sleeping, I chust imachined that I saw—"

Later. "But, Minnie, ve shall hope. Vun hundred vifty thousand miles out, it vas. It vill fall back upon der earth. But I gannot tell vhere! I thought that if it did, I vould be able to galculate its course, und— But after those goncentric cirgles—Minnie, not even *Einstein* could galculate vhere it vill land. Not effen me. All ve can do iss hope that ve shall hear of vhere it falls."

Cloudy day. Black night jealous of its mysteries.

"Minnie, our poor Mitkey. There is *nothing* could have cauzed—"

But something had.

Prxl.

Prxl is an asteroid. It isn't called that by earthly astronomers, because—for excellent reasons—they have not discovered it. So we will call it by the nearest possible transliteration of the name its inhabitants use. Yes, it's inhabited.

Come to think of it, Professor Oberburger's attempt to send a rocket to the moon had some strange results. Or rather, Prxl did.

You wouldn't think that an asteroid could reform a drunk, would you? But one Charles Winslow, a besotted citizen of Bridgeport, Connecticut, never took a drink when—right on Grove Street—a mouse asked him the road to Hartford. The mouse was wearing bright red pants and vivid yellow gloves—

But that was fifteen months after the Professor lost his rocket. We'd better start over again.

Prxl is an asteroid. One of those despised celestial bodies which terrestrial astronomers call vermin of the sky, because the darned things leave trails across the plates that clutter up the more important observations of novae and nebulae. Fifty thousand fleas on the dark dog of night.

Tiny things, most of them. Astronomers have been discovering recently that some of them come close to Earth. Amazingly close. There was excitement in 1932 when Amor came within ten million miles; astronomically, a mere mashie shot. Then Apollo cut that almost in half, and in 1936 Adonis came within less than one and a half million miles.

In 1937, Hermes, less than half a million but the astronomers got really excited when they calculated its orbit and found that the little mile-long asteroid can come within a mere 220,000 miles, closer than Earth's own moon.

Some day they may be still more excited, if and when they spot the ⅜-mile asteroid Prxl, that obstacle of space, making a transit across the moon and discover that it frequently comes within a mere hundred thousand miles of our rapidly whirling world.

Only in event of a transit will they ever discover it, though, for Prxl does not reflect light. It hasn't, anyway, for several million years since its inhabitants coated it with a black, light-absorbing pigment derived from its interior. Monumental task, painting a world, for creatures half an inch tall. But worth it, at the time. When they'd shifted its orbit, they were safe from their enemies. There were giants in those days— eight-inch-tall marauding pirates from Diemos. Got to Earth a couple of times too, before they faded out of the picture. Pleasant little giants who killed because they enjoyed it. Records in now-buried cities on Diemos might explain what happened to the dinosaurs. And why the promising Cro-Magnons disappeared at the height of their promise only a cosmic few minutes after the dinosaurs went west.

But Prxl survived. Tiny world no longer reflecting the sun's rays, lost to the cosmic killers when its orbit was shifted.

Prxl. Still civilized, with a civilization millions of years old. Its coat of blackness preserved and renewed regularly, more through tradition than fear of enemies in these later degenerate days. Mighty but stagnant civilization, standing still on a world that whizzes like a bullet.

And Mitkey Mouse.

Klarloth, head scientist of a race of scientists, tapped his assistant Bemj on what would have been Bemj's shoulder if he had had one. "Look," he said, "what approaches Prxl. Obviously artificial propulsion."

Bemj looked into the wall plate and then directed a thought wave at the mechanism that jumped the magnification of a thousand-fold through an alteration of the electronic field.

The image leaped, blurred, then steadied. "Fabricated," said Bemj. "Extremely crude, I must say. Primitive explosive-powered rocket. Wait, I'll check where it came from.

He took the readings from the dials about the viewplate and hurled them as thoughts against the psychocoil of the computer, then waited while that most complicated of machines digested all the factors and prepared the answer. Then, eagerly, he slid his mind into rapport with its projector. Klarloth likewise listened in to the silent broadcast.

Exact point on Earth and exact time of departure. Untranslatable expression of curve of trajectory, and point on that curve where deflected by gravitational pull of Prxl. The destination—or rather the original intended destination—of the rocket was obvious, Earth's moon. Time and place of arrival on Prxl if present course of rocket were unchanged.

"Earth," said Klarloth meditatively. "They were a long way from rocket travel the last time we checked them. Some sort of a crusade, or battle of beliefs, going on, wasn't there?"

Bemj nodded. "Catapults. Bows and arrows. They've taken a long stride since, even if this is only an early experimental thing of a rocket. Shall we destroy it before it gets here?"

Klarloth shook his head thoughtfully. "Let's look it over. May save us a trip to Earth; we can judge their present state of development pretty well from the rocket itself."

"But then we'll have to—"

"Of course. Call the Station. Tell them to train their attracto-repulsors on it and to swing it into a temporary orbit until they prepare a landing-cradle. And not to forget to damp out the explosive before they bring it down."

"Temporary force-field around point of landing—in case?"

"Naturally."

So despite the almost complete absence of atmosphere in which the vanes could have functioned, the rocket came down safely and so softly that Mitkey, in the dark compartment, knew only that the awful noise had stopped.

Mitkey felt better. He ate some more of the cheese with which the compartment was liberally provided. Then he resumed trying to gnaw a hole in the inch-thick wood with which the compartment was lined. That wooden lining was a kind of thought of the Herr Professor for Mitkey's mental well-being. He knew that trying to gnaw his way out would give Mitkey something to do en route which would keep him

from getting the screaming meemies. The idea had worked;
being busy, Mitkey hadn't suffered mentally from his dark
confinement. And now that things were quiet, he chewed
away more industriously and more happily than ever, sub-
limely unaware that when he got through the wood, he'd find
only metal which he couldn't chew. But better people than
Mitkey have found things they couldn't chew.

Meanwhile, Klarloth and Bemj and several thousand other
Prxlians stood gazing up at the huge rocket which, even lying
on its side, towered high over their heads. Some of the
younger ones, forgetting the invisible field of force, walked
too close and came back, ruefully rubbing bumped heads.

Klarloth himself was at the psychograph.

"There *is* life inside the rocket," he told Bemj. "But the impressions are confused. One creature, but I cannot follow its
thought processes. At the moment it seems to be doing something with its teeth."

"It could not be an Earthling, one of the dominant race.
One of them is much larger than this huge rocket. Gigantic
creatures. Perhaps, unable to construct a rocket large enough
to hold one of themselves, they sent an experimental creature,
such as our wooraths."

"I believe you've guessed right, Bemj. Well, when we have
explored its mind thoroughly, we may still learn enough to
save us a checkup trip to Earth. I am going to open the
door."

"But air—creatures of Earth would need a heavy, almost a
dense atmosphere. It could not live."

"We retain the force-field, of course. It will keep the air in.
Obviously there is a source of supply of air within the rocket
or the creature would not have survived the trip."

Klarloth operated controls, and the force-field itself put
forth invisible pseudo-pods and turned the outer screw-door,
then reached within and unlatched the inner door to the compartment itself.

All Prxl watched breathlessly as a monstrous gray head
pushed out of the huge aperture yawning overhead. Thick
whiskers, each as long as the body of a Prxlian—

Mitkey jumped down, and took a forward step that
bumped his black nose hard—into something that wasn't
there. He squeaked, and jumped backward against the rocket.

There was disgust in Bemj's face as he looked up at the

monster. "Obviously much less intelligent than a woorath. Might just as well turn on the ray."

"Not at all," interrupted Klarloth. "You forget certain very obvious facts. The creature is unintelligent, of course, but the subconscious of every animal holds in itself every memory, every impression, every sense image, to which it has ever been subjected. If this creature has ever heard the speech of the Earthlings, or seen any of their works—besides this rocket—every word and every picture is indelibly graven. You see now what I mean?"

"Naturally. How stupid of me, Klarloth. Well, one thing is obvious from the rocket itself: we have nothing to fear from the science of Earth for at least a few millennia. So there is no hurry, which is fortunate. For to send back the creature's memory to the time of its birth, and to follow each sensory impression in the psychograph will require—well, a time at least equivalent to the age of the creature, whatever that is, plus the time necessary for us to interpret and assimilate each."

"But that will not be necessary, Bemj."

"No? Oh, you mean the X-19 waves?"

"Exactly. Focused upon this creature's brain center, they can, without disturbing his memories, be so delicately adjusted as to increase his intelligence—now probably about .0001 in the scale—to the point where he is a reasoning creature. Almost automatically, during the process, he will assimilate his own memories, and understand them just as he would if he had been intelligent at the time he received those impressions.

"See, Bemj? He will automatically sort out irrelevant data and will be able to answer our questions."

"But would you make him as intelligent as—?"

"As we? No, the X-19 waves would not work so far. I would say to about .2 on the scale. That, judging from the rocket, coupled with what we remember of Earthlings from our last trip there, is about their present place on the intelligence scale."

"Ummm, yes. At that level, he would comprehend his experiences on Earth just sufficiently that he would not be dangerous to us, too. Equal to an intelligent Earthling. Just about right for our purpose. Then, shall we teach him our language?"

"Wait," said Klarloth. He studied the psychograph closely for a while. "No, I do not think so. He will have a language of his own. I see in his subconscious, memories of many long conversations. Strangely, they all seem to be monologues by one person. But he will have a language—a simple one. It would take him a long time, even under treatment, to grasp the concepts of our own method of communication. But we can learn his, while he is under the X-19 machine, in a few minutes."

"Does he understand, now, any of that language?"

Klarloth studied the psychograph again. "No, I do not believe he— Wait, there is one word that seems to mean something to him. The word 'Mitkey.' It seems to be his name, and I believe that, from hearing it many times, he vaguely associates it with himself."

"And quarters for him—with air-locks and such?"

"Of course. Order them built."

To say it was a strange experience for Mitkey is understatement. Knowledge is a strange thing, even when it is acquired gradually. To have it thrust upon me—

And there were little things that had to be straightened out. Like the matter of vocal chords. His weren't adapted to the language he now found he knew. Bemj fixed that; you would hardly call it an operation because Mitkey—even with his new awareness—didn't know what was going on, and he was wide awake at the time. And they didn't explain to Mitkey about the J-dimension with which one can get at the inwardness of things without penetrating the outside.

They figured things like that weren't in Mitkey's line, and anyway they were more interested in learning from him than teaching him. Bemj and Klarloth and a dozen others deemed worthy of the privilege. If one of them wasn't talking to him, another was.

Their questioning helped his own growing understanding. He would not, usually, know that he knew the answer to a question until it was asked. Then he'd piece together, without knowing just how he did it (any more than you or I know *how* we know things) and give them the answer.

Bemj: "Iss this language vhich you sbeak a universal vun?"

And Mitkey, even though he'd never thought about it before, had the answer ready: "No, it iss not. It iss Englitch, but I remember der Herr Brofessor sbeaking of other tongues. I belief he sboke another himself originally, but in America he always sboke Englitch to become more vamiliar mitt it. It iss a beaudiful sbeech, is it not?"

"Hmmmm," said Bemj.

Klarloth? "Und your race, the mices. Are they treated vell?"

"Nobt by most people," Mitkey told him. And explained.

"I vould like to do something for them," he added. "Look, could I not take back mitt me this brocess vhich you used upon me? Abbly it to other mices, und greate a race of super-mices?"

"Vhy not?" asked Bemj.

He saw Klarloth looking at him strangely, and threw his mind into rapport with the chief scientist's, with Mitkey left out of the silent communion.

"Yes, of course," Bemj told Klarloth, "it will lead to trouble on Earth, grave trouble. Two equal classes of beings so dissimilar as mice and men cannot live together in amity. But why should that concern us, other than favorably? The resultant mess will slow down progress on Earth—give us a few more millennia of peace before Earthlings discover we are here, and trouble starts. You know these Earthlings."

"But you would give them the X-19 waves? They might—"

"No, of course not. But we can explain to Mitkey here how to make a very crude and limited machine for them. A primitive one which would suffice for nothing more than the specific task of converting mouse mentality from .0001 to .2, Mitkey's own level and that of the bifurcated Earthlings."

"It is possible," communicated Klarloth. "It is certain that for eons to come they will be incapable of understanding its basic principle."

"But could they not use even a crude machine to raise their own level of intelligence?"

"You forget, Bemj, the basic limitation of the X-19 rays; that no one can possibly design a projector capable of raising any mentality to a point on the scale higher than his own. Not even we."

All this, of course, over Mitkey's head, in silent Prxlian.

More interviews, and more.

Klarloth again: "Mitkey, ve varn you of vun thing. Avoid carelessness vith electricity. Der new molecular rearranchement of your brain center—it iss unstable, und—"

Bemj: "Mitkey, are you sure your Herr Brofessor iss der most advanced of all who eggsperiment vith der rockets?"

"In cheneral, yess, Bemj. There are others who on vun specific boint, such as eggsplosives, mathematics, astrovisics, may know more, but not much more. Und for combining these knowledges, he iss ahead."

"It iss vell," said Bemj.

Small gray mouse towering like a dinosaur over tinier half-inch Prxlians. Meek, herbivorous creature though he was, Mitkey could have killed any one of them with a single bite. But, of course, it never occurred to him to do so, nor to them to fear that he might.

They turned him inside out mentally. They did a pretty good job of study on him physically, too, but that was through the J-dimension, and Mitkey didn't even know about it.

They found out what made him tick, and they found out everything he knew and some things he didn't even know he knew. And they grew quite fond of him.

"Mitkey," said Klarloth one day, "all der civilized races on Earth vear glothing, do they not? Vell, if you are to raise der level of mices to men, vould it not be vitting that you vear glothes, too?"

"An eggcelent idea, Herr Klarloth. Und I know chust vhat kind I should like. Der Herr Brofessor vunce showed me a bicture of a mouse bainted by der artist Dissney, und der mouse vore glothing. Der mouse vas not a real-life vun, but an imachinary mouse in a barable, und der Brofessor named me after der Dissney mouse."

"Vot kind of glothing vas it, Mitkey?"

"Bright red bants mitt two big yellow buttons in frondt und two in back, und yellow shoes for der back feet und a pair of yellow gloves for der front. A hole in der seat of der bants to aggomodate der tail."

"Ogay, Mitkey. Such shall be ready for you in fife minutes."

That was on the eve of Mitkey's departure. Originally Bemj had suggested awaiting the moment when Prxl's eccentric orbit would again take it within a hundred and fifty thousand miles of Earth. But, as Klarloth pointed out, that would be fifty-five Earth years ahead, and Mitkey wouldn't last that long. Not unless they—And Bemj agreed that they had better not risk sending a secret like that back to Earth.

So they compromised by refueling Mitkey's rocket with something that would cancel out the million and a quarter odd miles he would have to travel. That secret they didn't have to worry about, because the fuel would be gone by the time the rocket landed.

Day of departure.

"Ve haff done our best, Mitkey, to set und time der rocket so it vill land on or near der spot from vhich you left Earth. But you gannot eggspect agguracy in a voyach so long as this. But you vill land near. The rest iss up to you. Ve haff equivipped the rocket ship for effery contingency."

"Thank you, Herr Klarloth, Herr Bemj. Gootbye."

"Gootbye, Mitkey. Ve hate to loose you.

"Gootbye, Mitkey."

"Gootbye, gootbye . . ."

For a million and a quarter miles, the aim was really excellent. The rocket landed in Long Island Sound, ten miles out from Bridgeport, about sixty miles from the house of Professor Oberburger near Hartford.

They had prepared for a water landing, of course. The rocket went down to the bottom, but before it was more than a few dozen feet under the surface, Mitkey opened the door—especially reequipped to open from the inside—and stepped out.

Over his regular clothes he wore a neat little diving suit that would have protected him at any reasonable depth, and which, being lighter than water, brought him to the surface quickly where he was able to open his helmet.

He had enough synthetic food to last him for a week, but it wasn't necessary, as things turned out. The night boat from Boston carried him in to Bridgeport on its anchor chain, and once in sight of land he was able to divest himself of the diving suit and let it sink to the bottom after he'd punctured the tiny compartments that made it float, as he'd promised Klarloth he would do.

Almost instinctively, Mitkey knew that he'd do well to avoid human beings until he'd reached Professor Oberburger and told his story. His worst danger proved to be the rats at the wharf where he swam ashore. They were ten times Mitkey's size and had teeth that could have taken him apart in two bites.

But mind has always triumphed over matter. Mitkey pointed an imperious yellow glove and said, "Scram," and the rats scrammed. They'd never seen anything like Mitkey before, and they were impressed.

So for that matter, was the drunk of whom Mitkey inquired the way to Hartford. We mentioned that episode before. That was the only time Mitkey tried direct communication with strange human beings. He took, of course, every precaution. He addressed his remarks from a strategic position only inches away from a hole into which he could have popped. But it was the drunk who did the popping, without even waiting to answer Mitkey's question.

But he got there, finally. He made his way afoot to the north side of town and hid out behind a gas station until he heard a motorist who had pulled in for gasoline inquire the way to Hartford. And Mitkey was a stowaway when the car started up.

The rest wasn't hard. The calculations of the Prxlians showed that the starting point of the rocket was five Earth miles northwest of what showed on their telescopomaps as a city, and which from the Professor's conversation Mitkey knew would be Hartford.

He got there.

"Hello, Brofessor."

The Herr Professor Oberburger looked up, startled. There was no one in sight. "Vot?" he asked, of the air. "Who iss?"

"It iss I, Brofessor. Mitkey, der mouse whom you sent to der moon. But I vas not there. Insteadt, I—"

"Vot?? It iss imbossible. Somebody blays der choke. But— but nobody *knows* about that rocket. Vhen it vailed, I didn't told nobody. Nobody but me knows—"

"And me, Brofessor."

The Herr Professor sighed heavily. "Offervork. I am going vhat they call battly in der bel—"

"No, Brofessor. This is really me, Mitkey. I can talk now. Chust like you."

"You say you can—I do not belief it. Vhy can I not see you, then. Vhere are you? Vhy don't you—"

"I am hiding, Brofessor, in der vall chust behind der big hole. I vanted to be sure efferything vas ogay before I showed myself Then you would not get eggcited und throw something at me maybe."

"Vot? Vhy, Mitkey, if it iss really you and I am not asleep or going— Vhy, Mitkey, you know better than to think I might do something like that!"

"Ogay, Brofessor."

Mitkey stepped out of the hole in the wall, and the Professor looked at him and rubbed his eyes and looked again and rubbed his eyes and—

"I am grazy," he said finally. "Red bants he vears yet, und yellow— It gannot be. I am grazy."

"No, Brofessor. Listen, I'll tell you all about."

And Mitkey told him.

Gray dawn, and a small gray mouse still talking earnestly.

"Yes, Brofessor. I see your boint, that you think an intelligent race of mices und an intelligent race of men could not get along side by sides. But it vould not be side by sides; as I said, there are only a ferry few beople in the smallest continent of Australia. Und it vould cost little to bring them back und turn offer that continent to us mices. Ve vould call it Moustralia instead Australia, und ve vould instead of Sydney call der capital Dissney, in honor of—"

"But, Mitkey—"

"But, Brofessor, look vot ve offer for that continent. *All* mices vould go there. Ve civilize a few und the few help us catch others und bring them in to put them under red ray machine, und the others help catch more und build more machines und it grows like a snowball rolling down hill. Und ve sign a nonaggression pact mitt humans und stay on Moustralia und raise our own food und—"

"But, Mitkey—"

"Und look vot ve offer you in eggschange, Herr Brofessor! Ve vill eggsterminate your vorst enemy—der rats. Ve do not like them either. Und vun battalion of vun thousand mices, armed mitt gas masks und small gas bombs, could go right in effery hole after der rats und could eggsterminate effery rat in a city in vun day or two. In der whole vorld ve could eggsterminate effery last rat in a year, und at the same time catch und civilize effery mouse und ship him to Moustralia, und—"

"But, Mitkey—"

"Vot, Brofessor?"

"It vould vork, but it would not vork. You could eggsterminate der rats, yess. But how long vould it be before conflicts of interests vould lead to der mices trying to eggsterminate de people or der people trying to eggsterminate der—"

"They vould not dare, Brofessor! Ve could make weapons that vould—"

"You see, Mitkey?"

"But it vould not habben. If men vill honor our rights, ve vill honor—"

The Herr Professor sighed.

"I—I vill act as your intermediary, Mitkey, und offer your

broposition, und— Vell, it iss true that getting rid of rats vould be a great boon to der human race. But—"

"Thank you, Brofessor."

"By der vay, Mitkey. I haff Minnie. Your vife, I guess it iss, unless there vas other mices around. She iss in der other room; I put her there chust before you ariffed, so she vould be in der dark und could sleep. You vant to see her?"

"Vife?" said Mitkey. It had been so long that he had really forgotten the family he had perforce abandoned. The memory returned slowly.

"Vell," he said."—ummm, yess. Ve vill get her and I shall construct quvick a small X-19 prochector und—Yess, it vill help you in your negotiations mitt der governments if there are sefferal of us already so they can see I am not chust a freak like they might otherwise suspegt."

It wasn't deliberate. It couldn't have been, because the Professor didn't know about Klarloth's warning to Mitkey about carelessness with electricity—"Der new molecular rearranchement of your brain center—it iss unstable, und—"

And the Professor was still back in the lighted room when Mitkey ran into the room where Minnie was in her barless cage. She was alseep, and the sight of her— Memory of his earlier days came back like a flash and suddenly Mitkey knew how lonesome he had been.

"Minnie!" he called, forgetting that she could not understand.

And stepped up on the board where she lay. "Squeak!" The mild electrical current between the two strips of tinfoil got him.

There was silence for a while.

Then: "Mitkey," called the Herr Professor. "Come on back und ve vill discuss this—"

He stepped through the doorway and saw them, there in the gray light of dawn, two small gray mice cuddled happily together. He couldn't tell which was which, because Mitkey's teeth had torn off the red and yellow garments which had suddenly been strange, confining and obnoxious things.

"Vot on earth?" asked Professor Oberburger. Then he remembered the current, and guessed.

"Mitkey! Can you no longer talk? Iss der—"

Silence.

Then the Professor smiled. "Mitkey," he said, "my little star-mouse. I think you are more happier now."

He watched them a moment, fondly, then reached down and flipped the switch that broke the electrical barrier. Of course they didn't know they were free, but when the Professor picked them up and placed them carefully on the floor, one ran immediately for the hole in the wall. The other followed, but turned around and looked back—still a trace of puzzlement in the little black eyes, a puzzlement that faded.

"Gootbye, Mitkey. You vill be happier this vay. Und there vill always be cheese."

"Squeak," said the little gray mouse, and it popped into the hole.

"Gootbye—" it might, or might not, have meant.

THE WINGS OF NIGHT

Astounding,

March

by Lester Del Rey

Lester Del Rey continued to produce outstanding science fiction through the early 1940s, and 1942 was highlighted by the remarkable and classic "Nerves" (see page 497). The latter story over-shadowed his other work in 1942 but "The Wings of Night" deserves wider attention and reprinting than it had received—it contains all of the idealism and tolerance of the then-new best science fiction of the period, and is a very exciting story besides. If he had published only this story in 1942, it would still have been a memorable year for him.

(Lester and I play a conversational game that has been in progress, more or less, for forty years. The rules are simple. If one of us makes a statement, the other contradicts it. To any contradiction, the proper answer is a slur, which must be topped with a minimum of delay. This sounds as though it will escalate itself in a matter of seconds to a nuclear explosion, but it never does. There is a rigid agreement to the effect that the game can only be played in the presence of other people (especially our wives) who stop us by the fifth exchange. Lately, I notice, they have begun to stop us as soon as one of us says something and the other opens his mouth. We have a great deal of difficulty in persuading people that we are actually the best of friends and that our conservation is always gentle and loving (when we are alone).—IA)

"DAMN ALL MARTIANS!" Fats Welch's thin mouth bit out the words with all the malice of an offended member of a superior race. "Here we are, loaded down with as sweet a high-rate cargo of iridium as ever came out of the asteroids, just barely over the moon, and that injector starts mis-metering again. If I ever see that bulbous Marshy—"

"Yeah." Slim Lane groped back with his right hand for the flexible-shaft wrench, found it, and began wriggling and grunting forward into the mess of machinery again. "Yeah. I know. You'll make mincemeat out of him. Did you ever figure that maybe you were making your own trouble? That maybe Martians are people after all? Lyro Bmachis told you it would take two days to make the overhaul of the injector control hookup, so you knocked him across the field, called his ancestors dirty dogs and gave him just eight hours to finish repairs. Now you expect his rush job to be a labor of love for you— Oh, skip it, Fats, and give me the screwdriver."

What was the use? He'd been over it all with Fats a dozen times before, and it never got him anywhere. Fats was a good rocket man, but he couldn't stretch his imagination far enough to forget the hogwash the Reconstruction Empire was dishing out about the Destiny of Man and the Divine Plan whereby humans were created to exploit all other races. Not that it would do Fats much good if he did. Slim knew the value of idealism—none better.

He'd come out of college with a bad dose of it and an inherited fortune big enough for three men, filled with the old crusading spirit. He'd written and published books, made speeches, interviewed administrators, lobbied, joined and organized societies, and been called things that weren't complimentary. Now he was pushing freight from Mars to Earth for a living, quarter owner of a space-worn freighter. And Fats, who'd come up from a tube cleaner without the help of ideals; owned the other three-quarters.

Fats watched him climb out of the hold. "Well?"

"Nothing. I can't fix it—don't know enough about electronics. There's something wrong with the relays that control the time interval, but the indicators don't show where, and I'd hate to experiment out here."

"Make it to Earth—maybe?"

Slim shook his head. "I doubt it, Fats. Better set us down on Luna somewhere, if you can handle her that far. Then maybe we can find out what's wrong before we run out of air."

Fats had figured as much and was already braking the ship down working against the spasmodic flutter of the blasts and swearing at the effects of even the moon's weak gravity. But

the screens showed that he was making progress toward the
spot he'd chosen—a small flat plain with an area in the center that seemed unusually clear of debris and pockmarks.

"Wish they'd at least put up an emergency station out
here," he muttered.

"They had one once," Slim said. "But nobody ever goes to
Luna, and there's no reason for passenger ships to land there.
Takes less fuel for them to coast down on their fins through
Earth's atmosphere than to jet down here. Freighters like us
don't count, anyway. Funny how regular and flat that place
is; we can't be over a mile up and I don't see even a meteor
scar." .

"Luck's with us, then. I'd hate to hit a baby crater and rip
off a tube or poke a hole in the shell." Fats glanced at the radio altimeter and fall indicator. "We're gonna hit plenty hard.
If— Hey, what the deuce?"

Slim's eyes flicked to the screen just in time to see the flat
plain split into two halves and slide smoothly out from under
them as they seemed about to touch it; then they were dropping slowly into a crater of some sort, seemingly bottomless
and widening out rapidly; the roar of the tubes picked up
suddenly. Above them, the overscreens showed a pair of
translucent slides closing together again. His eyes stared at
the height indicator, neither believing nor doubting.

"Hundred and sixty miles down and trapped in! Tube
sounds show air in some amount, at least, even up here. This
crazy trap can't be here; there's no reason for it."

"Right now, who cares? We can't go through that slide up
there again, so we go down and find out, I guess. Damn, no
telling what kind of landing field we'll find when we reach
bottom." Fats' lack of excess imagination came in handy in
cases like this. He went about the business of jockeying down
the enormous crater as if he were docking at York port, too
busy with the uncertain blast to worry about what he might
find at the bottom. Slim gazed at him in wonder, then fell
back to staring at the screens for some indication of the reason behind this obviously artificial trap.

Lhin scratched idly through the pile of dirt and rotten
shale, pried out a thin scrap of reddened stone his eyes had
missed the first time and rose slowly to his feet. The Great
Ones had been good to him, sending a rockslide just when the
old beds were wearing thin and poor from repeated digging.
His sensitive nostrils told him there was magnesium, ferrous

matter and sulphur in abundance, all more than welcome. Of course, he'd hoped there might be copper, even as little as the end of his finger, but of that there seemed no sign. And without copper—

He shrugged the thought aside as he had done a thousand times before, and picked up his crude basket, now filled half with broken rock and half with the lichen-like growth that filled this end of the crater. One of his hands ground a bit of rotten stone together with shreds of lichen and he popped the mixture into his mouth. Grace to the Great Ones who had sent the slide; the pleasant flavor of magnesium tickled his tongue, and the lichens were full-flavored from the new richness of the soil around them. Now, with a trace of copper, there would have been nothing left to wish for.

With a rueful twitch of his supple tail, Lhin grunted and turned back toward his cave, casting a cursory glance up at the roof of the cavern. Up there, long miles away, a bright glare lanced down, diffusing out as it pierced through the layers of air, showing that the long lunar day was nearing noon, when the sun would lance down directly through the small guarding gate. It was too high to see, but he knew of the covered opening where the sloping walls of the huge valley ended and the roof began. Through all the millennia of his race's slow defeat, that great roof had stood, unsupported except for the walls that stretched out in a circle of perhaps fifty miles diameter, strong and more lasting than even the crater itself; the one abiding monument to the greatness that had been his people's.

He knew without having to think of it that the roof was artificial, built when the last thin air was deserting the moon, and the race had sought a final refuge here in the deepest crater, where oxygen could be trapped and kept from leaking away. In a vague way, he could sense the ages that had passed since then and wonder at the permanence of the domed roof, proof against all time.

Once, as the whole space about him testified, his had been a mighty race. But time had worked on them, aging the race as it had individuals, removing the vigor of their youth and sending in the slow creepers of hopelessness. What good was existence here, cooped up in one small colony, away from their world? Their numbers had diminished and some of their skill had gone from them. Their machines had crumbled and vanished, unreplaced, and they had fallen back to the primitive, digging out the rocks of the crater walls and the lichens they had cultured to draw energy from the heat and radioactive phosphorescence of the valley instead of sunlight. Fewer young were planted each year, and of the few, a smaller percentage proved fertile, so that their original million fell to thousands, then to hundreds, and finally to a few grubbing individuals.

Only then had they awakened to the danger of extinction, to find it too late. There had been three elders when Lhin was grown, his seed being the only fertile one. Now the elders were gone long years since, and Lhin had the entire length and breadth of the crater to himself. And life was a long series of sleeps and food forages, relieved only by the same thoughts that had been in his mind while his dead world turned to the light and away more than a thousand times. Monotony had slowly killed off his race, but now that its work was nearly done, it had ended. Lhin was content with his type of life; he was habituated and immune to boredom.

His feet had been moving slowly along with the turning of his thoughts, and he was out of the valley proper, near the door of the shelter carved into the rocky walls which he had chosen from the many as his home. He munched another mouthful of rock and lichen and let the diffused sunlight shine on him for a few minutes more, then turned into the cave. He needed no light, since the rock walls about had all been rendered radioactive in the dim youth of his race, and his eyes were adapted to wide ranges of light conditions. He passed quickly through the outer room containing his woven lichen bed and few simple furnishings and back into the combination nursery and workshop, an illogical but ever-present hope drawing him back to the far corner.

But, as always, it was reasonless. The box of rich earth, pulped to a fine loam and watered carefully, was barren of life. There was not even the beginnings of a small red shoot to awaken him to hope for the future. His seed was infertile, and the time when all life would be extinct was growing near. Bitterly he turned his back on the nursery bed.

So little lacking, yet so much! A few hundred molecules of copper salt to eat, and the seeds he grew would be fertile; or those same copper molecules added to the water would render the present seeds capable of growing into vigorous manhood—or womanhood; Lhin's people carried both male and female elements within each member, and could grow the seeds that became their children either alone or with another. So long as one member of the race lived, as many as a hundred young a year could be reared in the carefully tended incubating soil—if the vital hormone containing copper could be made.

But that, it seemed, was not to be. Lhin went over his laboriously constructed apparatus of hand-cut rock bowls and slender rods bound together into tubes, and his hearts were heavy within him. The slow fire of dried lichen and gummy tar burned still, and slow, drop by drop, liquid oozed from the last tube into a bowl. But even in that there was no slightest odor of copper salts. Well, he had tried that and failed. The accumulation of years of refining had gone into the water that kept the nursery soil damp, and in it there had been too little of the needed mineral for life. Almost dispassionately he threw the permanent metal rolls of his race's science back into their cylinders and began disassembling the chemical part of his workshop.

That meant the other solution, harder, and filled with risks, but necessary now. Somewhere up near the roof, the records indicated, there was copper in small amounts, but well past the breathable concentration of air. That meant a helmet and tanks for compressed air, along with hooks and grapples to bridge the eroded sections of the old trail and steps leading up, instruments to detect the copper and a pump to fill the tanks. Then he must carry many tanks forward, cache them and go up to make another cache, step by step, until his supply line would reach the top and—perhaps—he could find copper for a new beginning.

He deliberately avoided thinking of the time required and the chances of failure. His foot came down on the little bellows and blue flames licked up from his crude forge as he drew out the hunks of refined metal and began heating them to malleability. Even the shaping of it by hand to the patterns of the ancient records was almost impossible, and yet, somehow, he must accomplish it correctly. His race must not die!

He was still working doggedly hours later when a high-pitched note shot through the cave. A meteor, coming into the fields around the sealing slides of the roof, and a large one! In all Lhin's life there had been none big enough to activate the warning screens, and he had doubted that the mechanism, though meant to be ageless and draw sun power until the sun died, was still functioning. As he stood staring at the door senselessly the whistling note came again.

Now, unless he pressed his hand over the inductance grid, the automatic forces would come into play, twisting the me-

teor aside and beyond the roof. But he gave no thought to
that as he dashed forward and slapped his fingers against the
grilled panel. It was for that he had chosen this rock house,
once the quarters of the Watchers who let the few scouting
rockets of dim past ages in and out. A small glow from the
girl indicated the meteor was through, and he dropped his
hand, letting the slides close again.

Then he waited impatiently for it to strike, moving out to
the entrance. Perhaps the Great Ones were kind and were answering his prayers at last. Since he could find no copper
here, they were sending a token from outer space to him, and
who knew what fabulous amounts it might contain—perhaps
even as much as he could hold in one hand! But why hadn't
it struck? He scanned the roof anxiously, numb with a fear
that he had been too late and the forces had thrown it aside.

No, there was a flare above—but surely not such as a meteor that size should make as it sliced down through the resisting air! A sharp stinging whine hit his ears finally, flickering off and on; and that was not the sound a meteor would
logically make. He stared harder, wondering, and saw that it
was settling downward slowly, not in a sudden rush, and that
the flare struck down instead of fading out behind. That
meant—could only mean—intelligent control! A rocket!

Lhin's mind spun under the shock, and crazy ideas of his
ancestors' return, of another unknown refuge, of the Great
Ones' personal visit slid into his thoughts. Basically, though,
he was severely logical, and one by one he rejected them.
This machine could not come from the barren moon, and
that left only the fabled planet lying under the bottom of his
world, or those that wandered around the sun in other orbits.
Intelligence there?

His mind slid over the records he had read, made when his
ancestors had crossed space to those worlds, long before the
refuge was built. They had been unable to colonize, due to
the oppressive pull of gravity, but they had observed in detail.
On the second planet were only squamous things that slid
through the water and curious fronds on the little dry land;
on his own primary, gigantic beasts covered the globe, along
with growth rooted to the ground. No intelligence on those
worlds. The fourth, though, was peopled by more familiar
life, and like his own evolutionary forerunners, there was no
division into animal and vegetable, but both were present in
all. Ball-shaped blobs of life had already formed into packs,
guided by instinct, with no means of communication. Yet, of

the other worlds known, that seemed the most probable source of intelligence. If, by some miracle, they came from the third, he abandoned hope; the blood lust of that world was too plainly written in the records, where living mountain-like beasts tore at others through all the rolls of etched pictures. Half filled with dread, half with anticipation, he heard the ship land somewhere near and started toward it, his tail curved tightly behind him.

He knew, as he caught sight of the two creatures outside the opened lock of the vessel, that his guess had been wrong. The creatures were bifurcate, like himself, though massive and much larger, and that meant the third world. He hesitated, watching carefully as they stared about, apparently keenly enjoying the air around them. Then one spoke to the other, and his mind shook under a new shock.

The articulation and intonation were intelligent, but the sounds were a meaningless babble. Speech—that! It must be, though the words held no meaning. Wait—in the old records. Slha the Freethinker had touched on some such thought; he had written of remote days when the Lunarites had had no speech and postulated that they had invented the sounds and given them arbitrary meaning, and that only by slow ages of use had they become instinctive in the new-grown infants—had even dared to question that the Great Ones had ordered speech and sound meanings as the inevitable complement of intelligence. And now, it seemed, he was right. Lhin groped up through the fog of his discovery and tightened his thoughts into a beam.

Again, shock struck at him. Their minds were hard to reach, and once he did find the key and grope forward into their thoughts, it was apparent that they could not read his! Yet·they were intelligent. But the one on whom his thoughts centered noticed him finally, and grabbed at the other. The words were still harsh and senseless, but the general meaning reached the moon man. "Fats, what's that?"

The other turned and stared at Lhin's approach. "Dunno. Looks like a scrawny three-foot monkey. Reckon it's harmless?"

"Probably, maybe even intelligent. It's a cinch no band of political refugees built this place—nonhuman construction. Hi there!" The one who thought of himself as Slim—massive though he appeared—turned to the approaching Lunarite. "What and who are you?"

"Lhin," he answered, noting surprised pleasure in Slim's mind. "Lhin—me Lhin."

Fats grunted. "Guess you're right, Slim. Seems to savvy you. Wonder who came here and taught him English."

Lhin fumbled clumsily, trying to pin down the individual sounds to their meanings and remember them. "No sahffy Enlhish. No who came here. You—" He ran out of words and drew nearer, making motions toward Slim's head, then his own. Surprisingly, Slim got it.

"He means he knows what we're thinking, I guess. Telepathy."

"Yeah? Marshies claim they can do it among themselves, but I never saw one read a human mind. They claim we don't open up right. Maybe this Ream monkey's lying to you."

"I doubt it. Take another look at the radioactivity meter in the viability tester—men wouldn't come here and go home without spreading the good word. Anyway, his name isn't Ream—Lean comes closer to the sound he made, though we'll never get it right." He half sent a thought to Lhin, who dutifully pronounced his name again. "See? His liquid isn't . . . it's a glottal stop. And he makes the final consonant a labial, though it sounds something like our dental. We can't make sounds like that. Wonder how intelligent he is."

He turned back into the ship before Lhin could puzzle out some kind of answer, and was out a moment later with a small bundle under his arm. "Space English code book," he explained to Fats. "Same as they used to teach the Martians English a century ago."

Then to Lhin: "Here are the six hundred most useful words of our language, organized, so it'll beat waiting for you to pick them up bit by bit. You look at the diagramed pictures while I say and think the word. Now. One—w-uh-nn; two—t-ooo. Getting it?"

Fats watched them for a while, half amused, then grew tired of it. "Okay Slim, you molly-coddle the native awhile and see what you learn. I'm going over to the walls and investigate that radioactive stuff until you're ready to start repairs. Wish radios weren't so darned limited in these freighters and we could get a call through."

He wandered off, but Lhin and Slim were hardly aware of it. They were going through the difficult task of organizing a means of communication, with almost no common background, which should have been worse than impossible in terms of hours. Yet, strange as the word associations and sounds were, and odd as their organization into meaningful groups they were still only speech, after all. And Lhin had grown into life with a highly complex speech as natural to him as breathing. He twisted his lips over the sounds and nailed the meanings down in his mind, one by one, indelibly.

Fats finally found them in Lhin's cave, tracing them by the sound of their voices, and sat down to watch, as an adult might watch a child playing with a dog. He bore Lhin no ill will, but neither could he regard the moon man as anything but some clever animal, like the Martians or the primitives of Venus; if Slim enjoyed treating them as equals, let him have his way for the time.

Lhin was vaguely conscious of those thoughts and others more disturbing, but he was too wrapped up in the new experience of having some living mind to communicate with, after nearly a century of being alone with himself. And there were more important things. He wriggled his tail, spread his arms, and fought over the Earth sounds while Slim followed as best he could.

Finally the Earth man nodded. "I think I get it. All of them have died off except you, and you don't like the idea of coming to a dead end. Um-m-m. I wouldn't either. So now you hope these Great Ones of yours—we call 'em God—have sent us down here to fix things up. How?"

Lhin beamed, his face contorting into a furrowed grimace of pleasure before he realized Slim misinterpreted the gesture. Slim meant well. Once he knew what was needed, perhaps he would even give the copper gladly, since the old records showed that the third world was richest of all in minerals.

"Nra is needed. Life comes from making many simple things one not-simple thing—air, drink, stuff, eat stuff, all that I have, so I live. But to begin the new life, Nra is needed. It makes things begin. The seed has no life—with Nra it lives. But I had no word."

He waited impatiently while Slim digested that. "Sort of a vitamin or hormone, something like Vitamin E_6, eh? Maybe we could make it, but—"

Lhin nodded. Surely the Great Ones were kind. His hearts were warm as he thought of the many seeds carefully wrapped and stored that could be made to grow with the needed copper. And now the Earth man was willing to help. A little longer and all would be well.

"No need to make," he piped happily. "Simple stuff. The

seed or I can make, in us. But we need Nra to make it. See."
He pulled a handful of rock from the basket lying near,
chewed it carefully, and indicated that it was being changed
inside him.

Fats awoke to greater attention. "Do that again, monkey!"
Lhin obliged, curious to note that they apparently ate nothing
other life had not prepared for them. "Darn. Rocks—just
plain rocks—and he eats them. Has he got a craw like a bird,
Slim?"

"He digests them. If you've read of those half-plant, half-
animal things the Martians came from, you'll know what his
metabolism's like. Look, Lhin, I take it you mean an element.
Sodium calcium, chlorine? No, I guess you have all those,
Iodine, maybe? Hm-m-m." He went over a couple of dozen
he could imagine having anything to do with life, but copper
was not among them, by accident, and a slow fear crept up
into the Lunarite's thoughts. This strange barrier to communication—would it ruin all?

He groped for the answer—and relaxed. Of course, though
no common word existed, the element itself was common in
structure. Hurriedly he slipped the pages of the code book to
a blank one and reached for the Earth man's pencil. Then, as
Slim and Fats stared curiously, he began sketching in the
atomic structure of copper, particle by particle, from the center out, as the master physicists of his race had discovered it
to be.

It meant nothing to them! Slim handed the paper back,
shaking his head. "Fella, if I'm right in thinking that's a picture of some atom, we've got a lot to learn back on Earth.
Wheoo!"

Fats twisted his lips. "If that's an atom, I'm a fried egg.
Come on, Slim, it's sleepy time and you've fooled away half a
day. Anyhow, I want to talk that radioactive business over
with you. It's so strong it'd cook us in half an hour if we
weren't wearing these portable nullifiers—yet the monkey
seems to thrive on it. I got an idea."

Slim came back from his brown study and stared at his
watch. "Darn it! Look, Lhin, don't give up yet; we'll talk all
this over tomorrow again. But Fats is right; it's time for us to
sleep. So long, fella."

Lhin nodded a temporary farewell in his own tongue and
slumped back on his rough bed. Outside, he heard Fats ex-
tolling a scheme of some kind for getting out the radioactives with Lhin's help, somehow, and Slim's protesting voice.

But he paid no attention. The atomic structure had been right, he knew, but they were only groping toward it in their science, and their minds knew too little of the subject to enable them to grasp his pictures.

Chemical formulas? Reactions that would eliminate others, one by one? If they were chemists, perhaps, but even Slim knew too little for that. Yet, obviously, unless there was no copper on Earth, there was an answer somewhere. Surely the Great Ones whom they called God would never answer generations of faithful prayer with a mockery! There was an answer, and while they slept, he would find it, though he had to search through every record roll for clues.

Hours later he was trudging across the plain toward the ship, hope again high. The answer, once found, was simple. All elements formed themselves into families and classes. Slim had mentioned sodium, and copper was related in the more primitive tables, such as Earth might use. More important, its atomic number was twenty-nine by theory elementary enough for any race that could build rockets.

The locks were open, and he slipped through both, the wavering half-formed thoughts of the men leading him to them unerringly. Once in their presence, he stopped, wondering about their habits. Already he had learned that what held true for his people was not necessarily the rule with them, and they might not approve of his arousing a sleeper. Finally, torn between politeness and impatience, he squatted on the metal floor, clutching the record roll, his nostrils sampling the metals around him. Copper was not there; but he hadn't expected so rare an element, though there were others here that he failed completely to recognize and guessed were among the heavy ones almost lacking on the moon.

Fats gurgled and scrimmaged around with his arms, yawned, sat up, still half asleep. His thoughts were full of some Earth person of the female element which Lhin had noted was missing in these two, and what he'd do "when he got rich." Lhin was highly interested in the thought pictures until he realized that it would be best not to intrude on these obviously secret things. He withdrew his mind just as the man noted him.

Fats was never at his best while waking up. He came to his feet with a bellow and grabbed for something. "Why, you sneaking little monkey! Trying to sneak up and cut our—"

Lhin squealed and avoided the blow that would have left him a shapeless blob, uncertain of how he had offended, but warned by caution to leave. Physical fear was impossible for him—too many generations had grown and died with no need of it. But it came as a numbing shock that these beings would actually kill another intelligent person. Was life so cheap on Earth?

"Hey! Hey, Fats, stop it!" Slim had awakened at the sound of the commotion, and a hasty glance showed Lhin that he was holding the other's arms. "Lay off, will you? What's going on?"

But now Fats was fully awake and calming down. He dropped the metal bar and grinned wryly. "I dunno. I guess he meant all right, but he was sitting there with that metal thing in his hands, staring at me, and I figured he meant to cut my throat or something. I'm all right now. Come on back, monkey; it's all right."

Slim let his partner go and nodded at Lhin. "Sure, come back, fella. Fats has some funny ideas about nonhumans, but he's a good-hearted sort, on the whole. Be a good doggie and he won't kick you—he might even scratch your ears."

"Nuts." Fats was grinning, good nature restored. He knew Slim meant it as a crack, but it didn't bother him; what was wrong with treating Marshies and monkeys like what they were? "Whatcha got there, monkey? More pictures that mean nothing?"

Lhin nodded in imitation of their assent gesture and held out the roll to Slim; Fats' attitude was no longer unfriendly, but he was an unknown quantity, and Slim seemed the more interested. "Pictures that mean much, I hope. Here is Nra, twenty-nine, under sodium."

"Periodic table," Slim told Fats. "At least, it looks like one. Get me the handbook, will you? Hm-m-m. Under sodium, No. 29. Sodium, potassium, copper. And it's No. 29, all right. That it, Lhin?"

Lhin's eyes were blazing with triumph. Grace to the Great Ones. "Yes, it is copper. Perhaps you have some? Even a gram, perhaps?"

"A thousand grams, if you like. According to your notions, we're lousy with the stuff. Help yourself."

Fats cut in. "Sure, monkey, we got copper, if that's the stuff you've been yelling about. What'll you pay for it?"

"Pay?"

"Sure, give in return. We help you; you help us. That's fair, isn't it?"

It hadn't occurred to Lhin, but it did seem fair. But what

had he to give? And then, he realized what was in the man's mind. For the copper, he was to work, digging out and purifying the radioactives that gave warmth and light and life to the crater, so painfully brought into being when the place was first constructed, transmuted to meet the special needs of the people who were to live there. And after him, his sons and their sons, mining and sweating for Earth, and being paid in barely enough copper to keep Earth supplied with laborers. Fat's mind filled again with dreams of the other Earth creature. For that, he would doom a race to life without pride or hope or accomplishments. Lhin found no understanding in it. There were so many of those creatures on Earth—why should his enslavement be necessary?

Nor was enslavement all. Eventually, doom was as certain that way as the other, once Earth was glutted with the radioactives, or when the supply here dropped below the vital point, great as the reserve was. He shuddered under the decision forced upon him.

Slim's hand fell on his shoulder. "Fats has things slightly wrong, Lhin. Haven't you, Fats?"

There was something in Slim's hand, something Lhin knew dimly was a weapon. The other man squirmed, but his grin remained.

"You're touched, Slim, soft. Maybe you believe all this junk about other races' equality, but you won't kill me for it. I'm standing pat—I'm not giving away my copper."

And suddenly Slim was grinning, too, and putting the weapon back. "Okay, don't. Lhin can have my share. There's plenty on the ship in forms we can spare, and don't forget I own a quarter of it."

Fats' thoughts contained no answer to that. He mulled it over slowly, then shrugged. Slim was right enough about it, and could do as he wanted with his share. Anyhow— "Okay. Have it your way. I'll help you pry it off wherever it is, or dig it out. How about that wire down in the engine locker?"

Lhin stood silently watching them as they opened a small locker and rummaged through it, studying the engines and controls with half his mind, the other half quivering with ecstasy at the thought of copper—not just a handful, but all he could carry, in pure form, easily turned into digestible sulphate with acids he had already prepared for his former attempt at collecting it. In a year, the crater would be populated again, teeming with life. Perhaps three or four hundred sons left, and as they multiplied, more and yet more.

A detail of the hookup he was studying brought that part of his mind uppermost, and he tugged at Slim's trouser leg. "That ... that ... is not good, is it?"

"Huh? No, it isn't, fella. That's what brought us here. Why?"

"Then, without radioactives, I can pay. I will fix it." A momentary doubt struck him. "That is to pay, is it not?"

Fats heaved a coil of wonderful-smelling wire out of the locker, wiped off sweat, and nodded. "That's to pay, all right, but you let those things alone. They're bad enough, already, and maybe even Slim can't fix it."

"I can fix."

"Yeah. What school did you get your degree in electronics from? Two hundred feet in this coil, makes fifty for him. You gonna give it all to him, Slim?"

"Guess so." Slim was looking at Lhin doubtfully, only half watching as the other measured and cut the wire. "Ever touched anything like that before, Lhin? Controls for the ion feed and injectors are pretty complicated in these ships. What makes you think you can do it—unless your people had things like this and you studied the records."

Lhin fought for words as he tried to explain. His people had had nothing like that—their atomics had worked from a different angle, since uranium was almost nonexistent on the moon, and they had used a direct application of it. But the principles were plain to him, even from what he could see outside; he could feel the way it worked in his head.

"I feel. When I first grew, I could fix that. It is the way I think, not the way I learn, though I have read all the records. For three hundred million years, my people have learned it—now I feel it."

"Three hundred million years! I knew your race was old when you told me you were born talking and reading, but—galloping dinosaurs!"

"My people saw those things on your world, yes," Lhin assured him solemnly. "Then I shall fix?"

Slim shook his head in confusion and handed over a tool kit without another word. "Three hundred million years, Fats, and during almost all that time they were farther ahead than we are now. Figure that one out. When we were little crawling things living off dinosaur eggs, they were flitting from planet to planet—only I don't suppose they could stay very long; six times normal gravity for them. And now, just because they had to stay on a light world and their air losses made them gather here where things weren't normal, Lhin's all that's left."

"Yeah, and how does that make him a mechanic?"

"Instinct. In the same amount of time, look at the instincts the animals picked up. He has an instinct for machinery; he doesn't know all about it, probably, but he can instinctively feel how a thing should work. Add to that the collection of science records he was showing me and the amount of reading he's probably done, and there should be almost nothing he couldn't do to a machine."

There wasn't much use in arguing, Fats decided, as he watched what was happening. The monkey either fixed things or they never would leave. Lhin had taken snips and disconnected the control box completely; now he was taking that to pieces, one thing at a time. With a curious deftness, he unhooked wires, lifted out tubes, uncoupled transformers.

It seemed simple enough to him. They had converted energy from the atomic fuel, and they used certain forces to ionize matter, control the rate of ionization, feed the ions to the rocket tubes, and force them outward at high speed through helices. An elementary problem in applied electronics to govern the rate and control the ionization forces.

With small quick hands he bent wires into coils, placed other coils in relation, and coupled a tube to the combination. Around the whole, other coils and tubes took shape, then a long feeder connected to the pipe that carried the compound to be ionized, and bus bars to the energy intake. The injectors that handled the feeding of ions were needlessly complicated, but he let them alone, since they were workable as they were. It had taken him less than fifteen minutes.

"It will now work. But use care when you first try it. Now it makes all work, not a little as it did before."

Slim inspected it. "That all? What about this pile of stuff you didn't use?"

"There was no need. It was very poor. Now it is good." As best he could, he explained to Slim what happened when it was used now; before, it would have taken a well-trained technician to describe, even with the complicated words at his command. But what was there now was the product of a science that had gone beyond the stumbling complications of first attempts. Something was to be done, and was done, as simply as possible. Slim's only puzzle was that it hadn't been done that way in the first place—a normal reaction, once the final simplification is reached. He nodded.

"Good. Fats, this is the business. You'll get about 99.99%
efficiency now, instead of the 20% maximum before. You're
all right, Lhin."

Fats knew nothing of electronics, but it had sounded right
as Lhin explained, and he made no comment. Instead, he
headed for the control room. "Okay, we'll leave here, then.
So long, monkey."

Slim gathered up the wire and handed it to Lhin, accompanying him to the air lock. On the ground as the locks closed,
the moon man looked up and managed an Earth smile. "I
shall open the doors above for you to go through. And you
are paid, and all is fair, not so? Then—so long, Slim. The
Great Ones love you that you have given my people back to
me."

" 'Dios," Slim answered, and waved, just before the doors
came shut. "Maybe we'll be back sometime and see how you
make out."

Back at the cave, Lhin fondled the copper and waited for
the sounds the rockets would make, filled with mixed emotions and uncertainties. The copper was pure ecstasy to him,
but there were thoughts in Fats' mind which were not all
clear. Well, he had the copper for generations to come; what
happened to his people now rested on the laps of the Great
Ones.

He stood outside the entrance, watching, the now-steady
rocket blast upward and away, carrying with it the fate of his
race. If they told of the radioactives, slavery and extinction.
If they remained silent, perhaps a return to former greatness,
and passage might be resumed to other planets, long deserted
even at the height of their progress; but now planets bearing
life and intelligence instead of mere jungles. Perhaps, in time,
and with materials bought from other worlds with ancient
knowledge, even a solution that would let them restore their
world to its ancient glory, as they had dreamed before
hopelessness and the dark wings of a race's night had settled
over them.

As he watched, the rocket spiraled directly above him, cutting the light off and on with a shadow like the beat of wings
from the mists of antiquity, when winged life had filled the
air of the moon. An omen, perhaps, those sable wings that
reached up and passed through the roof as he released the
slides, then went skimming out, leaving all clear behind. But
whether a good omen or ill, he had not decided.

He carried the copper wire back to the nursery.

And on the ship, Slim watched Fats wiggle and try to think, and there was amusement on his face. "Well, was he good? As good as any human, perhaps?"

"Yeah. All right, better. I'll admit anything you want. He's as good as I am—maybe he's better. That satisfy you?"

"No." Slim was beating the iron while it was hot. "What about those radioactives?"

Fats threw more power into the tubes, and gasped as the new force behind the rockets pushed him back into his seat. He eased up gently, staring straight ahead. Finally he shrugged and turned back to Slim.

"Okay, you win. The monkey keeps his freedom and I keep my lip buttoned. Satisfied?"

"Yeah." Slim was more than satisfied. To him, also, things seemed an omen of the future, and proof that idealism was not altogether folly. Some day the wings of dark prejudice and contempt for others might lift from all Earth's Empire, as they were lifting from Fats' mind. Perhaps not in his time, but eventually; and intelligence, not race, would rule.

"Well satisfied, Fats," he said. "And you don't need to worry about losing too much. We'll make all the money we can ever spend from the new principles of Lhin's hookup; I've thought of a dozen applications already. What do you figure on doing with your share?"

Fats grinned. "Be a damned fool. Help you start your propaganda again and go around kissing Marshies and monkeys. Wonder what our little monkey's thinking."

Lhin wasn't thinking, then; he'd solved the riddle of the factors in Fats' mind, and he knew what the decision would be. Now he was making copper sulphate, and seeing dawn come up where night had been. There's something beautiful about any dawn, and this was very lovely to him.

FOUNDATION

Astounding,

May

by Isaac Asimov

*(I suppose that of all the fiction I have written
The Foundation Trilogy is far and away the most
successful. It received a Hugo for the "best all-time
novel series in 1966 and it has been selling steadily in both hard and soft covers for thirty years
with no signs of any letup.*

*Yet before the books appeared (1951–1953), it
was a series of nine interconnected stories that appeared in* Astounding *between 1942 and 1950.
The first was this one, "Foundation."*

Naturally, I had no idea when I wrote the story what the
future would hold for it. It began on August 1, 1941, when I
presented John Campbell with the idea for a story involving
the fall of the Galactic Empire written as a historical novel.

Campbell loved the idea so much that he wouldn't dream
of letting me write a single story about it. He insisted on an
open-ended series after the fashion of Heinlein's "Future History" series.

Campbell dazzled me into agreeing (I was always being
dazzled by him) and on August 11, I began the story. It took
me three weeks to write (I only wrote in my spare time for I
was working toward my doctorate at Columbia at the time)
and, uncertain whether Campbell might not change his mind
about letting me do more stories in the series, I deliberately
didn't reveal the ending but let it hang. This made it certain
that Campbell would either reject the story or demand a
sequel.

He demanded a sequel.—I.A.)

Hari Seldon was old and tired. His voice, roared out though it was, by the amplifying system, was old and tired as well.

There were few in that small assemblage that did not realize that Hari Seldon would be dead before the next spring. And they listened in respectful silence to the last official words of the Galaxy's greatest mind.

"This is the final meeting," that tired voice said, "of the group I had called together over twenty years ago." Seldon's eyes swept the seated scientists. He was alone on the platform, alone in the wheelchair to which a stroke had confined him two years before, and on his lap was the last volume— the fifty-second—of the minutes of previous meetings. It was opened to the last page.

He continued: "The group I called together represented the best the Galactic Empire could offer of its philosophers, its psychologists, its historians and its physical scientists. And in the twenty years since, we have considered the greatest problem ever to confront any group of fifty men—perhaps the greatest ever to confront any number of men.

"We have not always agreed on methods or on procedure. We have spent months and, doubtless, years on futile debates over relatively minor issues. On more than one occasion, sizable sections of our group threatened to break away altogether.

"And yet"—his old face lit in a gentle smile—"we solved the problem. Many of the original members died and were replaced by others. Schemes were abandoned; plans voted down; procedures proven faulty.

"Yet we solved the problem; and not one member, while yet alive, left our group. I am glad of that."

He paused, and allowed the subdued applause to die.

"We have done; and our work is over. The Galactic Empire is falling, but its culture shall not die, and provision has been made for a new and greater culture to develop therefrom. The two Scientific Refuges we planned have been established: one at each end of the Galaxy, at Terminus and at Star's End. They are in operation and already moving along the inevitable lines we have drawn for them.

"For us is left only one last item, and that fifty years in the future. That item, already worked out in detail, will be the instigation of revolts in the key sectors of Anacreon and Loris. It will set that final machinery in motion to work itself out in the millennium that follows."

Hari Seldon's tired head dropped. "Gentlemen, the last meeting of our group is hereby adjourned. We began in secret; we have worked throughout in secret; and now end in secret—to wait for our reward a thousand years hence with the establishment of the Second Galactic Empire."

The last volume of minutes closed, and Hari Seldon's thin hand fell away from it.

"I am finished!" he whispered.

Lewis Pirenne was busily engaged at his desk in the one well-lit corner of the room. Work had to be coordinated. Effort had to be organized. Threads had to be woven into a pattern.

Fifty years now; fifty years to establish themselves and set up Encyclopedia Foundation Number One into a smoothly working unit. Fifty years to gather the raw material. Fifty years to prepare.

It had been done. Five more years would see the publication of the first volume of the most monumental work the Galaxy had ever conceived. And then at ten-year intervals— regularly—like clockwork—volume after volume after volume. And with them there would be supplements; special articles on events of current interest, until—

Pirenne stirred uneasily, as the muted buzzer upon his desk muttered peevishly. He had almost forgotten the appointment. He shoved the door release and out of an abstracted corner of one eye saw the door open and the broad figure of Salvor Hardin enter. Pirenne did not look up.

Hardin smiled to himself. He was in a hurry, but he knew better than to take offense at Pirenne's cavalier treatment of anything or anyone that disturbed him at his work. He buried himself in the chair on the other side of the desk and waited.

Pirenne's stylus made the faintest scraping sound as it raced across paper. Otherwise, neither motion nor sound. And then Hardin withdrew a two-credit coin from his vest pocket. He flipped it and its stainless-steel surface caught glitters of light as it tumbled through the air. He caught it and flipped it again, watching the flashing reflections lazily. Stainless steel made good medium of exchange on a planet where all metal had to be imported.

Pirenne looked up and blinked. "Stop that!" he said querulously.

"Eh?"

"That infernal coin tossing. Stop it!"

"Oh." Hardin pocketed the metal disk. "Tell me when you're ready, will you? I promised to be back at the City Council meeting before the new aqueduct project is put to a vote."

Pirenne sighed and shoved himself away from the desk. "I'm ready. But I hope you aren't going to bother me with city affairs. Take care of that yourself, please. The Encyclopedia takes up all my time."

"Have you heard the news?" questioned Hardin, phlegmatically.

"What news?"

"The news that the Terminus City ultra-wave set received two hours ago. The Royal Governor of the Prefect of Anacreon has assumed the title of king."

"Well? What *of* it?"

"It means," responded Hardin, "that we're cut off from the inner regions of the Empire. Do you realize that Anacreon stands square across what was our last remaining trade route to Santanni and to Trantor and to Vega itself? Where is our metal to come from? We haven't managed to get a steel or aluminum shipment through in six months and now we won't be able to get any at all, except by grace of the King of Anacreon."

Pirenne *tch-tched* impatiently. "Get them through him, then."

"But can we? Listen, Pirenne, according to the charter which established this Foundation, the Board of Trustees of the Encyclopedia Committee has been given full administrative powers. I, as Mayor of Terminus City, have just enough power to blow my own nose and perhaps to sneeze if you countersign an order giving me permission. It's up to you and your Board then. I'm asking you in the name of the City, whose prosperity depends upon uninterrupted commerce with the Galaxy, to call an emergency meeting—"

"Stop! A campaign speech is out of order. Now, Hardin, the Board of Trustees has not barred the establishment of a municipal government on Terminus. We understand one to be necessary because of the increase in population since the Foundation was established fifty years ago, and because of the increasing number of people involved in non-Encyclopedia affairs. *But* that does not mean that the first and *only* aim of the Foundation is no longer to publish the definitive Encyclopedia of all human knowledge. We are a State-supported, scientific institution, Hardin. We cannot—must not—*will* not interfere in local politics."

"Local politics! By the Emperor's left big toe, Pirenne, this is a matter of life and death. The planet, Terminus, by itself cannot support a mechanized civilization. It lacks metals. You know that. It hasn't a trace of iron, copper, or aluminum in the surface rocks, and precious little of anything else. What do you think will happen to the Encyclopedia if this watchamacallum King of Anacreon clamps down on us?"

"On *us*? Are you forgetting that we are under the direct control of the Emperor himself? We are not part of the Prefect of Anacreon or of any other prefect. Memorize that! We are part of the Emperor's personal domain and no one touches us. The Empire can protect its own."

"Then why didn't it prevent the Royal Governor of Anacreon from kicking over the traces? And only Anacreon? At least twenty of the outermost prefects of the Galaxy, the entire Periphery as a matter of fact, have begun steering things their own way. I tell you I feel darned uncertain of the Empire and its ability to protect us."

"Hokum! Royal Governors, Kings—what's the difference? The Empire is always shot through with a certain amount of politics and with different men pulling this way and that. Governors have rebelled, and, for that matter, Emperors have been deposed or assassinated before this. But what has that to do with the Empire itself? Forget it, Hardin. It's none of our business. We are first of all and last of all—scientists. And our concern is the Encyclopedia. Oh, yes, I'd almost forgotten. Hardin!"

"Well?"

"Do something about that paper of yours!" Pirenne's voice was angry.

"The Terminus City *Journal?* It isn't mine; it's privately owned. What's it been doing?"

"For weeks now it has been recommending that the fiftieth anniversary of the establishment of the Foundation be made the occasion for public holidays and quite inappropriate celebrations."

"And why not? The radium clock will open the First Vault

in three months. I would call that a big occasion, wouldn't you?"

"Not for silly pageantry, Hardin. The First Vault and its opening concern the Board of Trustees alone. Anything of importance will be communicated to the people. That is final and please make it plain to the *Journal*."

"I'm sorry, Pirenne, but the City Charter guarantees a certain minor matter known as freedom of the press."

"It may. But the Board of Trustees does not. I am the Emperor's representative on Terminus, Hardin, and have full powers in this respect."

Hardin's expression became that of a man counting to ten, mentally. He said grimly, "In connection with your status as Emperor's representative, then, I have a final piece of news to give you."

"About Anacreon?" Pirenne's lips tightened. He felt annoyed.

"Yes. A special envoy will be sent to us from Anacreon. In two weeks."

"An envoy? Here? From Anacreon?" Pirenne chewed that. "What for?"

"Hardin stood up, and shoved his chair back up against the desk. "I give you one guess."

And he left—quite unceremoniously.

Anselm haut Rodric—"haut" itself signifying noble blood—Sub-prefect of Pluema and Envoy Extraordinary of his Highness of Anacreon—plus half a dozen other titles— was met by Salvor Hardin at the spaceport with all the imposing ritual of a state occasion.

With a tight smile and a low bow, the sub-prefect had flipped his blaster from its holster and presented it to Hardin butt first. Hardin returned the compliment with a blaster specifically borrowed for the occasion. Friendship and good will were thus established, and if Hardin noted the barest bulge at Haut Rodric's shoulder, he prudently said nothing.

The ground car that received them then—preceded, flanked and followed by the suitable cloud of minor functionaries—proceeded in a slow, ceremonious manner to Cyclopedia Square, cheered on its way by a properly enthusiastic crowd.

Sub-prefect Anselm received the cheers with the complaisant indifference of a soldier and nobleman.

He said to Hardin, "And this city is all your world?"

Hardin raised his voice to be heard above the clamor. "We are a young world, your eminence. In our short history we have had but few members of the higher nobility visiting our poor planet. Hence, our enthusiasm."

It is certain that "higher nobility" did not recognize irony when he heard it.

He said thoughtfully, "Founded fifty years ago. Hm-m-m! You have a great deal of unexploited land here, mayor. You have never considered dividing it into estates?"

"There is no necessity as yet. We're extremely centralized; we have to be, because of the Encyclopedia. Some day, perhaps, when our population has grown——"

"A strange world! You have no peasantry?"

Hardin reflected that it didn't require a great deal of acumen to tell that his eminence was indulging in a bit of fairly clumsy pumping. He replied casually, "No—nor nobility."

Haut Rodric's eyebrows lifted. "And your leader—the man I am to meet?"

"You mean Dr Pirenne? Yes! He is the Chairman of the Board of Trustees—and a personal representative of the Emperor."

"*Doctor?* No other title? A *scholar?* and he rates above the civil authority?"

"Why, certainly," replied Hardin amiably. "We're all scholars more or less. After all, we're not so much a world as a scientific foundation—under the direct control of the Emperor."

There was a faint emphasis upon the last phrase that seemed to disconcert the sub-prefect. He remained thoughtfully silent during the rest of the slow way to Cyclopedia Square.

If Hardin found himself bored by the afternoon and evening that followed, he had at least the satisfaction of realizing that Pirenne and Haut Rodric—having met with loud and mutual protestations of esteem and regard—were detesting each other's company a good deal more.

Haut Rodric had attended with glazed eye to Pirenne's lecture during the "inspection tour" of the Encyclopedia Building. With polite and vacant smile, he had listened to the latter's rapid patter as they passed through the vast storehouses of reference films and the numerous projection rooms.

It was only after he had gone down level by level into and

through the composing departments, editing departments, publishing departments, and filming departments that he made his first comprehensive statement.

"This is all very interesting," he said, "but it seems a strange occupation for grown men. What good is it?"

It was a remark, Hardin noted, for which Pirenne found no answer, though the expression of his face was most eloquent.

The dinner that evening was much the mirror image of the events of that afternoon, for Haut Rodric monopolized the conversation by describing—in minute technical detail and with incredible zest—his own exploits as battalion head during the recent war between Anacreon and the neighboring newly proclaimed Kingdom of Smyrno.

The details of the sub-prefect's account were not completed until dinner was over and one by one the minor officials had drifted away. The last bit of triumphant description of mangled spaceships came when he had accompanied Pirenne and Hardin onto the balcony and relaxed in the warm air of the summer evening.

"And now," he said, with a heavy joviality, "to serious matters."

"By all means," murmured Hardin, lighting a long cigar of Vegan tobacco—not many left, he reflected—and teetering his chair back on two legs.

The Galaxy was high in the sky and its misty lens shape stretched lazily from horizon to horizon. The few stars here at the very edge of the universe were insignificant twinkles in comparison.

"Of course," said the sub-prefect, "all the formal discussions—the paper signing and such dull technicalities, that is—will take place before the—what is it you call your council?"

"The Board of Trustees," replied Pirenne coldly.

"Queer name! Anyway, that's for tomorrow. We might as well clear away some of the underbrush, man to man, right now, though. Hey?"

"And this means—" prodded Hardin.

"Just this. There's been a certain change in the situation out here in the Periphery and the status of your planet has become a trifle uncertain. It would be very convenient if we succeeded in coming to an undestanding as to how the matter stands. By the way, mayor, have you another one of those cigars?"

Hardin started and produced one reluctantly.

Anselm haut Rodric sniffed at it and emitted a clucking sound of pleasure. "Vegan tobacco! Where did you get it?"

"We received some last shipment. There's hardly any left. Space knows when we'll get more—if ever."

Pirenne scowled. He didn't smoke—and, for that matter, detested the odor. "Let me understand this, your eminence. Your mission is merely one of clarification?"

Haut Rodric nodded through the smoke of his first lusty puffs.

"In that case, it is soon over. The situation with respect to Encyclopedia Foundation Number One is what it always has been."

"Ah! And what is it that it always has been?"

"Just this: A State-supported scientific institution and part of the personal domain of his august majesty, the Emperor."

The sub-prefect seemed unimpressed. He blew smoke rings. "That's a nice theory, Dr Pirenne. I imagine you've got charters with the Imperial Seal upon it—but what's the actual situation? How do you stand with respect to Smyrno? You're not fifty parsecs from Smyrno's capital, you know. And what about Konom and Daribow?"

Pirenne said: "We have nothing to do with any prefect. As part of the Emperor's—"

"They're not prefects," reminded Haut Rodric, "they're kingdoms now."

"Kingdoms then. We have nothing to do with them. As a scientific institution—"

"Science be dashed!" swore the other, via a bouncing soldiery oath that ionized the atmosphere. "What the devil has that got to do with the fact that we're liable to see Terminus taken over by Smyrno at any time?"

"And the Emperor? He would just sit by?"

Haut Rodric calmed down and said: "Well, now, Dr Pirenne, you respect the Emperor's property and so does Anacreon, but Smyrno might not. Remember, we've just signed a treaty with the Emperor—I'll present a copy to that Board of yours tomorrow—which places upon us the responsibility of maintaining order within the borders of the Old Prefect of Anacreon on behalf of the Emperor. Our duty is clear, then, isn't it?"

"Certainly. But Terminus is not part of the Prefect of Anacreon."

"And Smyrno—"

"Nor is it part of the Prefect of Smyrno. It's not part of any prefect."

"Does Smyrno know that?"

"I don't care what it knows."

"*We* do. We've just finished a war with her and she still holds two stellar systems that are ours. Terminus occupies an extremely strategic spot, between the two nations."

Hardin felt weary. He broke in: "What is your proposition, your eminence?"

The sub-prefect seemed quite ready to stop fencing in favor of more direct statements. He said briskly, "It seems perfectly obvious that, since Terminus cannot defend itself, Anacreon must take over the job for its own sake. You understand we have no desire to interfere with internal administration—"

"Uh-huh," grunted Hardin dryly.

"—but we believe that it would be best for all concerned to have Anacreon establish a military base upon the planet."

"And that is all you would want—a military base in some of the vast unoccupied territory—and let it go at that."

"Well, of course, there would be the matter of supporting the protecting forces."

Hardin's chair came down on all fours, and his elbows went forward on his knees. "Now we're getting to the nub. Let's put it into language. Terminus is to be a protectorate and to pay tribute."

"Not tribute. Taxes. We're protecting you. You pay for it."

Pirenne banged his hand on the chair with sudden violence. "Let me speak, Hardin. Your eminence, I don't care a rusty half-credit coin for Anacreon, Smyrno, or all your local politics and petty wars. I tell you this is a State-supported tax-free institution."

"State-supported? But *we* are the State, Dr Pirenne, and we're not supporting."

Pirenne rose angrily. "Your eminence, I am the direct representative of—"

"—his august majesty, the Emperor," chorused Anselm haut Rodric sourly. "And I am the direct representative of the King of Anacreon. Anacreon is a lot nearer, Dr Pirenne."

"Let's get back to business," urged Hardin. "How would you take these so-called taxes, your eminence? Would you take them in kind: wheat, potatoes, vegetables, cattle?"

The sub-prefect stared. "What the devil? What do we need

with those? We've got hefty surpluses. Gold, of course. Chromium or vanadium would be even better, incidentally, if you have it in quantity."

Hardin laughed. "Quantity! We haven't even got iron in quantity. Gold! Here, take a look at our currency." He tossed a coin to the envoy.

Haut Rodric bounced it and stared. "What is it? Steel?"

"That's right."

"I don't understand."

"Terminus is a planet practically without metals. We import it all. Consequently, we have no gold, and nothing to pay unless you want a few thousand bushels of potatoes."

"Well—manufactured goods."

"Without metal? What do we make our machines out of?"

There was a pause and Pirenne tried again. "This whole discussion is wide of the point. Terminus is not a planet, but a scientific foundation preparing a great encyclopedia. Space, man, have you no respect for science?"

"Encyclopedias don't win wars." Haut Rodric's brows furrowed. "A completely unproductive world, then—and practically unoccupied at that. Well, you might pay with land."

"What do you mean?" asked Pirenne.

"This world is just about empty and the unoccupied land is probably fertile. There are many of the nobility on Anacreon that would like an addition to their estates."

"You can't propose any such—"

"There's no necessity of looking so alarmed, Dr Pirenne. There's plenty for all of us. If it comes to what it comes, and you cooperate, we could probably arrange it so that you lose nothing. Titles can be conferred and estates granted. You understand me, I think."

Pirenne sneered. "Thanks!"

And then Hardin said ingenuously: "Could Anacreon supply us with adequate quantities of praseodymium for our atomic-power plant? We've only a few years' supply left."

There was a gasp from Pirenne and then a dead silence for minutes. When Haut Rodric spoke it was in a voice quite different from what it had been till then:

"You have atomic power?"

"Certainly. What's unusual in that? I imagine atomic power is fifty thousand years old now. Why shouldn't we have it? Except that it's a little difficult to get praseodymium."

"Yes . . . yes." The envoy paused and added uncomfortably: "Well, gentlemen, we'll pursue the subject tomorrow. You'll excuse me—"

Pirenne looked after him and gritted through his teeth: "That insufferable, dull-witted donkey! That—"

Hardin broke in: "Not at all. He's merely the product of his environment. He doesn't understand much except that 'I got a gun and you ain't.' "

Pirenne whirled on him in exasperation. "What in space did you mean by the talk about military bases and tribute? Are you crazy?"

"No. I merely gave him rope and let him talk. You'll notice that he managed to stumble out with Anacreon's real intentions—that is, the parceling up of Terminus into landed estates. Of course, I don't intend to let that happen."

"*You* don't intend. *You* don't. And who are you? And may I ask what you meant by blowing off your mouth about our atomic-power plant? Why, it's just the thing that would make us a military target."

"Yes," grinned Hardin. "A military target to stay away from. Isn't it obvious why I brought the subject up? It happened to confirm a very strong suspicion I had had."

"And that was what?"

"That Anacreon no longer has an atomic-power company—and that, therefore, the rest of the Periphery no longer has one as well. Interesting, wouldn't you say?"

"Bah!" Pirenne left in fiendish humor, and Hardin smiled gently.

He threw his cigar away and looked up at the outstretched Galaxy. "Back to oil and coal, are they?" he murmured—and what the rest of his thoughts were he kept to himself.

When Hardin denied owning the *Journal,* he was perhaps technically correct, but no more. Hardin had been the leading spirit in the drive to incorporate Terminus into an autonomous municipality—he had been elected its first mayor—so it was not surprising that, though not a single share of *Journal* stock was in his name, some sixty percent was controlled by him in more devious fashions.

There were ways.

Consequently, when Hardin began suggesting to Pirenne that he be allowed to attend meetings of the Board of Trustees, it was not quite coincidence that the *Journal* began a similar campaign. And the first mass meeting in the history of the Foundation was held, demanding representation of the City in the "national" government.

And, eventually, Pirenne capitulated with ill grace.

Hardin, as he sat at the foot of the table, speculated idly as to just what it was that made physical scientists such poor administrators. It might be merely that they were too used to inflexible fact and far too unused to pliable people.

In any case, there was Tomaz Sutt and Jord Fara on his left; Lundin Crast and Yate Fulham on his right; with Pirenne, himself, presiding. He knew them all, of course, but they seemed to have put on an extra-special bit of pomposity for the occasion.

Hardin half dozed through the initial formalities and then perked up when Pirenne sipped at the glass of water before him by way of preparation and said:

"I find it very gratifying to be able to inform the Board that, since our last meeting, I have received word that Lord Dorwin, Chancellor of the Empire, will arrive at Terminus in two weeks. It may be taken for granted that our relations with Anacreon will be smoothed out to our complete satisfaction as soon as the Emperor is informed of the situation."

He smiled and addressed Hardin across the length of the table. "Information to this effect has been given to the *Journal.*"

Hardin snickered below his breath. It seemed evident that Pirenne's desire to strut this information before him had been one reason for his admission into the sacro-sanctum.

He said evenly, "Leaving vague expressions out of account, what do you expect Lord Dorwin to do?"

Tomaz Sutt replied. He had a bad habit of addressing one in the third person when in his more stately moods.

"It is quite evident," he observed, "that Mayor Hardin is a professional cynic. He can scarcely fail to realize that the Emperor would be most unlikely to allow his personal rights to be infringed."

"Why? What would he do in case they were?"

There was an annoyed stir. Pirenne said, "You are out of order," and, as an after-thought, "and are making what are near-treasonable statements, besides."

"Am I to consider myself answered?"

"Yes! If you have nothing further to say—"

"Don't jump to conclusions. I'd like to ask a question. Besides this stroke of diplomacy—which may or may not prove to mean anything—has anything concrete been done to meet the Anacreonic menace?"

Yate Fulham drew one hand along his ferocious red moustache. "You see a menace there, do you?"

"Don't you?"

"Scarcely"—this with indulgence. "The Emperor—"

"Great Space!" Hardin felt annoyed. "What is this? Every once in a while someone mentions 'Emperor' or 'Empire' as if it were a magic word. The Emperor is fifty thousand parsecs away, and I doubt whether he gives a damn about us. And if he does, what can he do? What there was of the imperial navy in these regions is in the hands of the four kingdoms now and Anacreon has its share. Listen, we have to fight with guns, not with words.

"Now, get this. We've had two months of grace so far, mainly because we've given Anacreon the idea that we've got atomic weapons. Well, we all know that that's a little white lie. We've got atomic power, but only for commercial uses, and darn little at that. They're going to find that out soon, and if you think they're going to enjoy being jollied along, you're mistaken."

"My dear sir—"

"Hold on; I'm not finished." Hardin was warming up. He liked this. "It's all very well to drag chancellors into this, but it would be much nicer to drag a few great big siege guns fitted for beautiful atomic bombs into it. We've lost two months, gentlemen, and we may not have another two months to lose. What do you propose to do?"

Said Lundin Crast, his long nose wrinkling angrily, "If you're proposing the militarization of the Foundation, I won't hear a word of it. It would mark our open entrance into the field of politics. We, Mr Mayor, are a scientific foundation and nothing else."

Added Sutt, "He does not realize, moreover, that building armaments would mean withdrawing men—valuable men—from the Encyclopedia. That cannot be done, come what may."

"Very true," agreed Pirenne. "The Encyclopedia first—always."

Hardin groaned in spirit. The Board seemed to suffer violently from Encyclopedia on the brain.

He said icily, "Has it ever occurred to the Board that it is barely possible that Terminus may have interests other than the Encyclopedia?"

Pirenne replied, "I do not conceive, Hardin, that the Foundation can have any interest other than the Encyclopedia."

"I didn't say the Foundation; I said *Terminus*. I'm afraid you don't understand the situation. There's a good million of us here on Terminus, and not more than a hundred and fifty thousand are working directly on the Encyclopedia. To the rest of us, this is *home*. We were born here. We're living here. Compared with our farms and our homes and our factories, the Encyclopedia means little to us. We want them protected—"

He was shouted down.

"The Encyclopedia first," ground out Crast. "We have a mission to fulfill."

"Mission, hell," shouted Hardin. "That might have been true fifty years ago. But this is a new generation."

"That has nothing to do with it," replied Pirenne. "We are scientists."

And Hardin leaped through the opening. "Are you, though? That's a nice hallucination, isn't it? Your bunch here is a perfect example of what's been wrong with the entire Galaxy for thousands of years. What kind of science is it to be stuck out here for centuries classifying the work of scientists of the last millennium? Have you ever thought of working onward, *extending* their knowledge and improving upon it? No! You're quite happy to stagnate. The whole Galaxy is, and has been for space knows how long. That's why the Periphery is revolting; that's why communications are breaking down; that's why petty wars are becoming eternal; that's why whole systems are losing atomic power and going back to barbarous techniques of a chemical power.

"If you ask me," he cried, *"the Galaxy is going to pot!"*

He paused and dropped into his chair to catch his breath, paying no attention to the two or three that were attempting simultaneously to answer him.

Crast got the floor. "I don't know what you're trying to gain by your hysterical statements, Mr Mayor. Certainly, you are adding nothing constructive to the discussion. I move, Mr Chairman, that the last speaker's remarks be placed out of order and the discussion be resumed from the point where it was interrupted."

Jord Fara bestirred himself for the first time. Up to this point Fara had taken no part in the argument even at its hottest. But now his ponderous voice, every bit as ponderous as his three-hundred-pound body, burst its bass way out.

"Haven't we forgotten something, gentlemen?"

"What?" asked Pirenne, peevishly.

"That in a month we celebrate our fiftieth anniversary." Fara had a trick of uttering the most obvious platitudes with great profundity.

"What of it?"

"And on that anniversary," continued Fara, placidly, "Hari Seldon's First Vault will open. Have you ever considered what might be in the First Vault?"

"I don't know. Routine matters. A stock speech of congratulations, perhaps. I don't think any significance need be placed on the First Vault—though the *Journal*"—and he glanced at Hardin, who grinned back—"did try to make an issue of it. I put a stop to that."

"Ah," said Fara, "but perhaps you are wrong. Doesn't it strike you"—he paused and put a finger to his round little nose—"that the Vault is opening at a very convenient time?"

"Very *in*convenient time, you mean," muttered Fulham. "We've got some other things to worry about."

"Other things are more important than a message from Hari Seldon? I think not." Fara was growing more pontifical than ever, and Hardin eyed him thoughtfully. What was he getting at?

"In fact," said Fara happily, "you all seem to forget that Seldon was the greatest psychologist of our time and that he was the founder of our Foundation. It seems reasonable to assume that he used his science to determine the probable course of the history of the immediate future. If he did, as seems likely, I repeat, he would certainly have managed to find a way to warn us of danger and, perhaps, to point out a solution. The Encyclopedia was very dear to his heart, you know."

An aura of puzzled doubt prevailed. Pirenne hemmed. "Well, now, I don't know. Psychology is a great science, but—there are no psychologists among us at the moment, I believe. It seems to me we're on uncertain ground."

Fara turned to Hardin. "Didn't you study psychology under Alurin?"

Hardin answered, half in reverie, "Yes. I never completed my studies, though. I got tired of theory. I wanted to be a

psychological engineer, but we lacked the facilities, so I did
the next best thing—I went into politics. It's practically the
same thing."

"Well, what do you think of the First Vault?"

And Hardin replied cautiously, "I don't know."

He did not say a word for the remainder of the meeting—
even though it got back to the subject of the Chancellor of
the Empire.

In fact, he didn't even listen. He'd been put on a new track
and things were falling into place—just a little. Little angles
were fitting together—one or two.

And psychology was the key. He was sure of that.

He was trying desperately to remember the psychological
theory he had once learned—and from it he got one thing
right at the start.

A great psychologist such as Seldon could unravel human
emotions and human reactions sufficiently to be able to
predict broadly the historical sweep of the future.

And that meant—hm-m-m!

Lord Dorwin took snuff. He also had long hair, curled in-
tricately and, quite obviously, artifically; to which were added
a pair of fluffy, blond sideburns, which he fondled affec-
tionately. Then, too, he spoke in over-precise statements and
left out all the *r*'s.

At the moment, Hardin had no time to think of more of
the reasons for the instant detestation in which he had held
the noble chancellor. Oh, yes, the elegant gestures of one
hand with which he accompanied his remarks and the studied
condescension with which he accompanied even a simple affirmative.

But, at any rate, the problem now was to locate him. He
had disappeared with Pirenne half an hour before—passed
clean out of sight, blast him.

Hardin was quite sure that his own absence during the preliminary discussions would quite suit Pirenne.

But Pirenne had been seen in this wing and on this floor. It
was simply a matter of trying every door. Halfway down, he
said, "Ah!" and stepped into the darkened room. The profile
of Lord Dorwin's intricate hairdo was unmistakable against
the lighted screen.

Lord Dorwin looked up and said, "Ah, Hahdin. You ah
looking foah us, no doubt?" He held out his snuffbox—over-
adorned and poor workmanship at that, noted Hardin—and

was politely refused, whereat he helped himself to a pinch and smiled graciously.

Pirenne scowled and Hardin met that with an expression of blank indifference.

The only sound to break the short silence that followed was the clicking of the lid of Lord Dorwin's snuffbox. And then he put it away and said:

"A gweat achievement, this Encyclopedia of yoahs, Hahdin. A feat, indeed, to rank with the most majestic accomplishments of all time."

"Most of us think so, milord. It's an accomplishment not quite accomplished as yet, however."

"Fwom the little I have seen of the efficiency of yoah Foundation, I have no feahs on that scoah." And he nodded to Pirenne, who responded with a delighted bow.

Quite a love feast, thought Hardin. "I wasn't complaining about the lack of efficiency, milord, as much as of the definite excess of efficiency on the part of the Anacreonians—though in another and more destructive direction."

"Ah, yes, Anacweon." A negligent wave of the hand. "I have just come from theah. Most bahbawous planet. It is thowoughly inconceivable that human beings could live heah in the Pewiphewy. The lack of the most elementawy wequiahments of a cultuahed gentleman; the absence of the most fundamental necessities foah comfoht and convenience—the uttah disuetude into which they—"

Hardin interrupted dryly: "The Anacreonians, unfortunately, have all the elementary requirements for warfare and all the fundamental necessities for destruction."

"Quite, quite." Lord Dorwin seemed annoyed, perhaps at being stopped midway in his sentence. "But we ahn't to discuss business now, y'know. Weally, I'm othah-wise concehnued. Doctah Piwenne, ahn't you going to show me the second volume? Do, please."

The lights clicked out and for the next half-hour Hardin might as well have been on Anacreon for all the attention they paid him. The book upon the screen made little sense to him, nor did he trouble to make the attempt to follow, but Lord Dorwin became quite humanly excited at times. Hardin noticed that during these moments of excitement the chancellor pronounced his *r*'s.

When the lights went on again, Lord Dorwin said,

"Mahvelous. Twuly mahvelous. You ah not, by chance, intewested in ahchaeology, ah you, Hahdin?"

"Eh?" Hardin shook himself out of an abstracted reverie. "No, milord, can't say I am. I'm a psychologist by original intention and a politician by final decision."

"Ah! No doubt intewesting studies. I, myself, y'know'—he helped himself to a giant pinch of snuff—"dabble in ahchaeology."

"Indeed?"

"His lordship," interrupted Pirenne, "is most thoroughly acquainted with the field."

"Well, p'haps I am, p'haps I am," said his lordship complacently. "I *have* done an awful amount of wuhk in the science. Extwemely well-read, in fact. I've gone thwough all of Jawdun, Obijasi, Kwomwill . . . oh, all of them, y'know."

"I've heard of them, of course," said Hardin, "but I've never read them."

"You should some day, my deah fellow. It would amply repay you. Why, I cetainly considah it well wuhth the twip heah to the Pewiphewy to see this copy of Lameth. Would you believe it, my libwawy totally lacks a copy. By the way, Doctah Piwenne, you have not fohgotten yoah pwomise to twansdevelop a copy foah me befoah I leave?"

"Only too pleased."

"Lameth, you must know," continued the chancellor, pontifically, "pwesents a new and most intewesting addition to my pwevious knowledge of the 'Owigin Question.' "

"Which question?" asked Hardin.

"The 'Owigin Question.' The place of the owigin of the human species, y'know. Shahly you must know that it is thought that owiginally the human wace occupied only one planetawy system."

"Well, yes, I know that."

"Of course, no one knows exactly which system it is—lost in the mists of antiquity. Theah ah theawies, howevah. Siwius, some say. Othahs insist on Alpha Centauwi, oah on Sol, oah on 61 Cygni—all in the Siwius sectah, you see."

"And what does Lameth say?"

"Well, he goes off along a new twail completely. He twies to show the ahchaeological wemains on the thuhd planet of the Ahctuwian System show that humanity existed theah befoah theah wah any indications of space-twavel."

"And that means it was humanity's birth planet?"

"P'haps. I must wead it closely and weigh the evidence befoah I can say foah cuhtain. One must see just how weliable his obsuhvations ah."

Hardin remained silent for a short while. Then he said, "When did Lameth write this book?"

"Oh—I should say about eight hundwed yeahs ago. Of cohse, he has based it lahgely on the pwevious wuhk of Gleen."

"Then why rely on him? Why not go to Arcturus and study the remains for yourself?"

Lord Dorwin raised his eyebrows and took a pinch of snuff hurriedly. "Why, whatevah foah, my deah fellow."

"To get the information firsthand, of course."

"But wheah's the necessity? It seems an uncommonly woundabout and hopelessly wigmawolish method of getting anywheahs. Look heah, now, I've got the wuhks of all the old mastahs—the gweat ahchaeologists of the past. I weigh them against each othah—balance the disagweements—analyze the conflicting statements—decide which is pwobably cowwect—and come to a conclusion. That is the scientific method. At least"—patronizingly—"as I see it. How insuffewably cwude it would be to go to Ahctuwus, oah to Sol, foah instance, and blundah about, when the old mastahs have covahed the gwound so much moah effectually than we could possibly hope to do."

Hardin murmured politely, "I see."

Scientific method, hell! No wonder the Galaxy was going to pot.

"Come, milord," said Pirenne, "I think we had better be returning."

"Ah, yes. P'haps we had."

As they left the room, Hardin said suddenly, "Milord, may I ask a question?"

Lord Dorwin smiled blandly and emphasized his answer with a gracious flutter of the hand. "Cehtainly, my deah fellow. Only too happy to be of service. If I can help you in any way fwom my pooah stoah of knowledge—"

"It isn't exactly about archaeology, milord."

"No?"

"No. It's this: Last year we received news here in Terminus about the explosion of a power plant on Planet V of Gamma Andromeda. We got the barest outline of the accident—no details at all. I wonder if you could tell me exactly what happened."

12 *Isaac Asimov*

Pirenne's mouth twisted. "I wonder you annoy his lordship
with questions on totally irrelevant subjects."

"Not at all, Doctah Piwenne," interceded the chancellor.
"It is quite all wight. Theah isn't much to say concehning it
in any case. The powah plant did explode and it was quite a
catastwophe, y'know. I believe sevewal million people wah
killed and at least half the planet was simply laid in wuins.
Weally, the govuhment is sewiously considewing placing
seveah westwictions upon the indiscwiminate use of atomic
powah—though that is not a thing for genewal publication,
y'know."

"I understand," said Hardin. "But what was wrong with
the plant?"

"Well, weally," replied Lord Dorwin indifferently, "who
knows? It had bwoken down some yeahs pweviously and it is
thought that the weplacements and wepaiah wuhk was most
infewiah. It is *so* diffcult these days to find men who *weally*
undahstand the moah technical details of ouah powah systems." And he took a sorrowful pinch of snuff.

"You realize," said Hardin, "that the independent
kingdoms of the Periphery have lost atomic power altogether?"

"Have they? I'm not at all suhpwised. Barbawous
planets—Oh, but my deah fellow, don't call them independent. They ahn't, y'know. The tweaties we've made with them
ah pwoof of that. They acknowledge the soveweignty of the
Empewah. They'd have to, of cohse, oah we wouldn't tweat
with them."

"That may be so, but they have considerable freedom of
action."

"Yes, I suppose so. Considewable. But that scahcely mat-
tahs. The Empiah is fah bettah off, with the Piwiphewy
thwown upon its own wesoahces—as it is, moah oah less.
They ahn't any good to us, y'know. Most bahbawous planets.
Scahcely civilized."

"They were civilized in the past. Anacreon was one of the
richest of the outlying provinces. I understand it compared
favorably with Vega itself."

"Oh, but, Hahdin, that was centuwies ago. You can
scahcely dwaw conclusion fwom that. Things wah diffewent
in the old gweat days. We ahn't the men we used to be,
y'know. But, Hahdin, come, you ah a most puhsistent chap.
I've told you I simply won't discuss business today. Doctah
Piwenne did pwepayah me foah you. He told me you would

twy to badgah me, but I'm fah too old a hand foah that. Leave it foah next day."

And that was that.

This was the second meeting of the Board that Hardin had attended, if one were to exclude the informal talks the Board members had had with the now-departed Lord Dorwin. Yet the mayor had a perfectly definite idea that at least one other, and possibly two or three, had been held, to which he had somehow never received an invitation.

Nor, it seemed to him, would he have received notification of this one had it not been for the ultimatum.

At least, it amounted to an ultimatum, though a superficial reading of the visigraphed document would lead one to suppose that it was a friendly interchange of greetings between two potentates.

Hardin fingered it gingerly. It started off floridly with a salutation from "His Puissant Majesty, the King of Anacreon, to his friend and brother, Dr. Lewis Pirenne, Chairman of the Board of Trustees, of the Encyclopedia Foundation Number One," and it ended even more lavishly with a gigantic, multicolored seal of the most involved symbolism.

But it was an ultimatum just the same.

Hardin said, "It turned out that we didn't have much time after all—only three months. But little as it was, we threw it away unused. This thing here gives us a week. What do we do now?"

Pirenne frowned worriedly. "There must be a loophole. It is absolutely unbelievable that they would push matters to extremities in the face of what Lord Dorwin has assured us regarding the attitude of the Emperor and the Empire."

Hardin perked up. "I see. You have informed the King of Anacreon of this alleged attitude?"

"I did—after having placed the proposal to the Board for a vote and having received unanimous consent."

"And when did this vote take place?"

Pirenne climbed onto his dignity. "I do not believe I am answerable to you in any way, Mayor Hardin."

"All right. I'm not that vitally interested. It's just my opinion that it was your diplomatic transmission of Lord Dorwin's valuable contribution to the situation"—he lifted the corner of his mouth in a sour half-smile—"that was the direct cause of this friendly little note. They might have delayed longer otherwise—though I don't think the additional time

would have helped Terminus any, considering the attitude of
the Board."

Said Yate Fulham: "And just how do you arrive at that remarkable conclusion, Mr Mayor?"

"In a rather simple way. It merely required the use of that
much-neglected commodity—common sense. You see, there
is a branch of human knowledge known as symbolic logic,
which can be used to prune away all sorts of clogging dead-
wood that clutters up human language."

"What about it?" said Fulham.

"I applied it. Among other things, I applied it to this
document here. I didn't really need to for myself because I
knew what it was all about, but I think I can explain it more
easily to five physical scientists by symbols rather than by
words."

Hardin removed a few sheets of paper from the pad under
his arm and spread them out. "I didn't do this myself, by the
way," he said. "Muller Holk of the Division of Logic has his
name signed to the analyses, as you can see."

Pirenne leaned over the table to get a better view and
Hardin continued: "The message from Anacreon was a
simple problem, naturally, for the men who wrote it were
men of action rather than men of words. It boils down easily
and straightforwardly to the unqualified statement, which in
symbols is what you see, and which in words, roughly translated, is, 'You give us what we want in a week, or we beat
the hell out of you and take it anyway.' "

There was silence as the five members of the Board ran
down the line of symbols, and then Pirenne sat down and
coughed uneasily.

Hardin said, "No loophole, is there, Dr Pirenne?"

"Doesn't seem to be."

"All right." Hardin replaced the sheets. "Before you now
you see a copy of the treaty between the Empire and Anacreon—a treaty, incidentally, which is signed on the Emperor's behalf by the same Lord Dorwin who was here last
week—and with it a symbolic analysis."

The treaty ran through five pages of fine print and the
analysis was scrawled out in just under half a page.

"As you see, gentlemen, something like ninety percent of
the treaty boiled right out of the analysis as being meaningless, and what we end up with can be described in the following interesting manner:

"Obligations of Anacreon to the Empire: *None!*

"Powers of the Empire over Anacreon: *None!*"

Again the five followed the reasoning anxiously, checking carefully back to the treaty, and when they were finished, Pirenne said in a worried fashion, "That seems to be correct."

"You admit, then, that the treaty is nothing but a declaration of total independence on the part of Anacreon and a recognition of that status by the Empire?"

"It seems so."

"And do you suppose that Anacreon doesn't realize that, and is not anxious to emphasize the position of independence—so that it would naturally tend to resent any appearance of threats from the Empire? Particularly when it is evident that the Empire is powerless to fulfill any such threats, or it would never have allowed independence."

"But then," interposed Sutt, "how would Mayor Hardin account for Lord Dorwin's assurances of Empire support? They seemed—" He shrugged. "Well, they seemed satisfactory."

Hardin threw himself back in the chair. "You know, that's the most interesting part of the whole business. I'll admit I had thought his lordship a most consummate donkey when I first met him—but it turned out that he was actually an accomplished diplomat and a most clever man. I took the liberty of recording all his statements."

There was a flurry, and Pirenne opened his mouth in horror.

"What of it?" demanded Hardin. "I realize it was a gross breach of hospitality and a thing no so-called gentleman would do. Also, that if his lordship had caught on, things might have been unpleasant; but he didn't, and I have the record, and that's that. I took that record, had it copied out and sent that to Holk for analysis, also."

Lundin Crast said, "And where is the analysis?"

"That," replied Hardin, "is the interesting thing. The analysis was the most difficult of the three by all odds. When Holk, after two days of steady work, suceeded in eliminating meaningless statements, vague gibberish, useless qualifications—in short, all the goo and dribble—he found he had nothing left. Everything cancelled out.

"Lord Dorwin, gentlemen, in five days of discussion *didn't say one damned thing,* and said it so you never noticed. *There* are the assurances you had from your precious Empire."

Hardin might have placed an actively working stench bomb upon the table and created no more confusion than existed after his last statement. He waited, with weary patience, for it to die down.

"So," he concluded, "when you sent threats—and that's what they were—concerning Empire action to Anacreon, you merely irritated a monarch who knew better. Naturally, his ego would demand immediate action, and the ultimatum is the result—which brings me to my original statement. We have one week left and what do we do now?"

"It seems," said Sutt, "that we have no choice but to allow Anacreon to establish military bases on Terminus."

"I agree with you there," replied Hardin, "but what do we do toward kicking them off again at the first opportunity?"

Yate Fulham's mustache twitched. "That sounds as if you have made up your mind that violence must be used against them."

"Violence," came the retort, "is the last refuge of the incompetent. But I certainly don't intend to lay down the welcome mat and brush off the best furniture for their use."

"I still don't like the way you put that," insisted Fulham. "It is a dangerous attitude; the more dangerous because we have noticed lately that a sizable section of the populace seems to respond to all your suggestions just so. I might as well tell you, Mayor Hardin, that the Board is not quite blind to your recent activities."

He paused and there was general agreement. Hardin shrugged.

Fulham went on: "If you were to inflame the City into an act of violence, you would achieve elaborate suicide—and we don't intend to allow that. Our policy has but one cardinal principle, and that is the Encyclopedia. Whatever we decide to do or not to do will be so decided because it will be the measure required to keep that Encyclopedia safe."

"Then," said Hardin, "you come to the conclusion that we must continue our intensive campaign of doing nothing."

Pirenne said bitterly, "You have yourself demonstrated that the Empire cannot help us; though how and why it can be so, I don't understand. If compromise is necessary—"

Hardin had the nightmare-like sensation of running at top speed and getting nowhere. "There *is* no compromise? Don't you realize that this bosh about military bases is a particularly inferior grade of drivel? Haut Rodric told us what Anacreon was after—outright annexation and imposition of its own feudal system of landed estates and peasant-aristocracy economy upon us. What is left of our bluff of atomic power, may force them to move slowly, but they will move nonetheless."

He had risen indignantly, and the rest rose with him—except for Jord Fara.

And then Jord Fara spoke. "Everyone will please sit down. We've gone quite far enough, I think. Come, there's no use looking so furious, Mayor Hardin; none of us has been committing treason."

"You'll have to convince me of that!"

Fara smiled gently. "You know you don't mean that. Let me speak!"

His little shrewd eyes were half closed, and the perspiration gleamed on the smooth expanse of his chin. "There seems no point in concealing that the Board has come to the decision that the real solution to the Anacreonian problem lies in what is to be revealed to us when the First Vault opens six days from now."

"Is that your contribution to the matter?"

"Yes."

"We are to do nothing, is that right, except to wait in quiet serenity and utter faith for the *deus ex machina* to pop out of the First Vault?"

"Stripped of your emotional phraseology, that's the idea."

"Such unsubtle escapism! Really, Dr Fara, such folly smacks of genius. A lesser mind would be incapable of it."

Fara smiled indulgently. "Your taste in epigrams is amusing, Hardin, but out of place. As a matter of fact, I think you remember my line of argument concerning the First Vault about three weeks ago."

"Yes, I remember it. I don't deny that it was anything but a stupid idea from the standpoint of deductive logic alone. You said—stop me when I make a mistake—that Hari Seldon was the greatest psychologist in the System; that, hence, he could forsee the tight and uncomfortable spot we're in now; that, hence, he established the First Vault as a method of telling us the way out."

"You've got the essence of the idea."

"Would it surprise you to hear that I've given considerable thought to the matter these last weeks?"

"Very flattering. With what result?"

"With the result that pure deduction is found wanting.

Again what is needed is a little sprinkling of common sense."

"For instance?"

"For instance, if he foresaw the Anacreonian mess, why not have placed us on some other planet nearer the Galactic centers? Why put us out here at all if he could see in advance the break in communicttion lines, our isolation from the Galaxy, the threat of our neighbors—and our helplessness because of the lack of metals on Terminus? That above all! Or if he foresaw all this, why not have warned the original settlers in advance so that they might have had time to prepare, rather than wait, as he is doing, until one foot is over the cliff, before doing so?

"And don't forget this. Even though he could foresee the problem *then,* we can see it equally well *now.* Therefore, if he could foresee the solution then, we should be able to see the solution now. After all, Seldon was not a magician. There are no trick methods of escaping from a dilemma that he can see and we can't."

"But, Hardin," reminded Fara, "we can't!"

"But you haven't *tried.* You haven't tried once. First, you refused to admit that there was a menace at all! Then you reposed an absolutely blind faith in the Emperor! Now you've shifted it to Hari Seldon. Throughout you have invariably relied on authority or on the past—never on yourselves."

His fists balled spasmodically. "It amounts to a diseased attitude—a conditioned reflex that shunts aside the independence of your minds whenever it is a question of opposing authority. There seems no doubt ever in your minds that the Emperor is more powerful than you are, or Hari Seldon wiser. And that's wrong, don't you see?"

For some reason, no one cared to answer him.

Hardin continued: "It isn't just you. It's the whole Galaxy. Pirenne heard Lord Dorwin's idea of scientific research. Lord Dorwin thought the way to be a good archaeologist was to read all the books on the subject—written by men who were dead for centuries. He thought that the way to solve archaeological puzzles was to weigh opposing authorities. And Pirenne listened and made no objections. Don't you see that there's something wrong with that?"

Again the note of near-pleading in his voice. Again no answer.

He went on: "And you men and half of Terminus as well are just as bad. We sit here, considering the Encyclopedia the all-in-all. We consider the greatest end of science to be the classification of past data. It *is* important, but is there no further work to be done? We're receding and forgetting, don't you see? Here in the Periphery they've lost atomic power. In Gamma Andromeda, a power plant has blown up because of poor repairs, and the Chancellor of the Empire complains that atomic technicians are scarce. And the solution? To train new ones? Never! Instead, they're to restrict atomic power."

And for the third time: "Don't you *see?* It's Galaxy-wide. It's a worship of the past. It's a deterioration—*a stagnation!*"

He stared from one to the other and they gazed fixedly at him.

Fara was the first to recover. "Well, mystical philosophy isn't going to help us here. Let us be concrete. Do you deny that Hari Seldon could easily have worked out historical trends of the future by simple psychological technique?"

"No, of course not," cried Hardin. "But we can't rely on him for a solution. At best, he might indicate the problem, but if ever there is to be a solution, we must work it out ourselves. He can't do it for us."

Fulham spoke suddenly. "What do you mean—'indicate the problem'? We *know* the problem."

Hardin whirled on him. "You think you do? You think Anacreon is all Hardi Seldon is likely to be worried about. I disagree! I tell you, gentlemen, that as yet none of you has the faintest conception of what is really going on."

"And you do?" questioned Pirenne, hostilely.

"I think so!" Hardin jumped up and pushed his chair away. His eyes were cold and hard. "If there's one thing that's definite, it is that there's something smelly about the whole situation; something that is bigger than anything we've talked about yet. Just ask yourself this question; Why was it that among the original population of the Foundation not one first-class psychologist was included, except Bor Alurin? And *he* carefully refrained from training his pupils in more than the fundamentals."

A short silence and Fara said, "All right. Why?"

"Perhaps because a psychologist might have caught on to what this was all about—and too soon to suit Hari Seldon. As it is, we've been stumbling about, getting misty glimpses of the truth and no more. And that is what Hari Seldon wanted."

He laughed harshly. "Good day, gentlemen!"

He stalked out of the room.

Mayor Hardin chewed at the end of his cigar. It had gone
out but he was past noticing that. He hadn't slept the night
before and he had a good idea that he wouldn't sleep this
coming night. His eyes showed it.

He said wearily, "And that covers it?"

"I think so." Yohan Lee put a hand to his chin. "How does
it sound?"

"Not too bad. It's got to be done, you understand, with impudence. That is, there is to be no hesitation; no time to allow them to grasp the situation. Once we are in position to
give orders, why, give them as though you were born to do
so, and they'll obey out of habit. That's the essence of a
coup."

"If the Board remains irresolute for even—"

"The Board? Count them out. After tomorrow, their importance as a factor in Terminus affairs won't matter a rusty
half-credit."

Lee nodded slowly. "Yet it is strange that they've done
nothing to stop us so far. You say they weren't entirely in the
dark."

"Fara indicated as much. And Pirenne's been suspicious
of me since I was elected. But, you see, they never had the capacity of really understanding what was up. Their whole
training has been authoritarian. They are sure that the Emperor, just because he is the Emperor, is all-powerful. And
they are sure that the Board of Trustees, simply because it is
the Board of Trustees acting in the name of the Emperor,
cannot be in a position where it does not give the orders.
That incapacity to recognize the possibility of revolt is our
best ally."

He heaved out of his chair and went to the water cooler.
"They're not bad fellows, Lee, when they stick to their Encyclopedia—and we'll see that that's where they stick in the future. They're hopelessly incompetent when it comes to ruling
Terminus. Go away, now, and start things rolling. I want to
be alone."

He sat down on the corner of his desk and stared at the
cup of water.

Space! If only he were as confident as he pretended! The
Anacreonians were landing in two days and what had he to
go on but a set of notions and half-guesses as to what Hari
Seldon had been driving at these past fifty years? He wasn't
even a real, honest-to-goodness psychologist—just a fumbler

with a little training trying to outguess the greatest mind of the age.

If Fara were right; if Anacreon were all the problem Hari Seldon had foreseen; if the Encyclopedia were all he was interested in preserving—then what price *coup d'état?*

He shrugged and drank his water.

The First Vault was furnished with considerably more than six chairs, as though a larger company had been expected. Hardin noted that thoughtfully and seated himself wearily in a corner just as far from the other five as possible.

The Board members did not seem to object to that arrangement. They spoke among themselves in whispers, which fell off into sibilant monosyllables, and then into nothing at all. Of them all, only Jord Fara seemed even reasonably calm. He had produced a watch and was staring at it somberly.

Hardin glanced at his own watch and then at the glass cubicle—absolutely empty—that dominated half the room. It was the only unusual feature of the room, for aside from that there was no indication that somewhere a speck of radium was wasting away toward that precise moment when a tumbler would fall, a connection be made and—

The lights went dim!

They didn't go out, but merely yellowed and sank with a suddenness that made Hardin jump. He had lifted his eyes to the ceiling lights in startled fashion, and when he brought them down the glass cubicle was no longer empty.

A figure occupied it—a figure in a wheelchair!

It said nothing for a few moments, but it closed the book upon its lap and fingered it idly. And then it smiled, and the face seemed all alive.

It said, "I am Hari Seldon." The voice was old and soft.

Hardin almost rose to acknowledge the introduction and stopped himself in the act.

The voice continued conversationally: "I can't see you, you know, so I can't greet you properly. I don't even know how many of you there are, so all this must be conducted informally. If any of you are standing, please sit down; and if you care to smoke, I wouldn't mind." There was a light chuckle. "Why should I? I'm not really here."

Hardin fumbled for a cigar almost automatically, but thought better of it.

Hari Seldon put away his book—as if laying it upon a desk at his side—and when his fingers let go, it disappeared.

He said, "It is fifty years now since this Foundation was established—fifty years in which the members of the Foundation have been ignorant of what it was they were working toward. It was necessary that they be ignorant, but now the necessity is gone.

"The Encyclopedia Foundation, to begin with, is a fraud, and always has been!"

There was the sound of a scramble behind Hardin and one or two muffled exclamations, but he did not turn around.

Hari Seldon was, of course, undisturbed. He went on, "It is a fraud in the sense that neither I nor my colleagues care at all whether a single volume of the Encyclopedia is ever published. It has served its purpose, since by it we extracted an imperial charter from the Emperor, by it we attracted the hundred thousand scientists necessary for our scheme, and by it we managed to keep them preoccupied while events shaped themselves, until it was too late for any of them to draw back.

"In the fifty years that you have worked on this fraudulent project—there is no use in softening phrases—your retreat has been cut off, and you have now no choice but to proceed on the infinitely more important project that was, and is, our real plan.

"To that end we have placed you on such a planet and at such a time that in fifty years you were maneuvered to the point where you no longer have freedom of action. From now on, and into the centuries, the path you must take is inevitable. You will be faced with a series of crises, as you are now faced with the first, and in each case your freedom of action will become similarly circumscribed so that you will be forced along one, and only one, path.

"It is that path which our psychology has worked out—and for a reason.

"For centuries Galactic civilization has stagnated and declined, though only a few ever realized that. But now, at least, the Periphery is breaking away and the political unity of the Empire is shattered. Somewhere in the fifty years just past is where the historians of the future will place an arbitrary line and say, 'This marks the Fall of the Galactic Empire.'

"And they will be right, though scarcely any will recognize that Fall for additional centuries.

"And after the Fall will come inevitable barbarism, a period which, our psychohistory tells us, shall, under ordinary circumstances, last from thirty to fifty thousand years. We cannot stop the Fall. We do not wish to; for Empire culture has lost whatever virility and worth it once had. But we can shorten the period of barbarism that must follow—down to a single thousand years.

"The ins and outs of that shortening, we cannot tell you; just as we could not tell you the truth about the Foundation fifty years ago. Were you to discover those ins and outs, our plan might fail; as it would have had you penetrated the fraud of the Encyclopedia earlier; for then, by knowledge, your freedom of action would be expanded and the number of additional variables introduced would become greater than our psychology could handle.

"But you won't, for there are no psychologists on Terminus, and never were, but for Alurin—and he was one of us.

"But this I can tell you: Terminus and its companion Foundation at the other end of the Galaxy are the seeds of the Renascence and the future founders of the Second Galactic Empire. And it is the present crisis that is starting Terminus off to that climax.

"This, by the way, is a rather straightforward crisis, much simpler than many of those that are ahead. To reduce it to its fundamentals, it is this: You are a planet suddenly cut off from the still-civilized centers of the Galaxy, and threatened by your stronger neighbors. You are a small world of scientists surrounded by vast and rapidly expanding reaches of barbarism. You are an island of atomic power in a growing ocean of more primitive energy, but are helpless despite that, because of your lack of metals.

"You see, then, that you are faced by hard necessity, and that action is forced on you. The nature of that action—that is, the solution to your dilemma—is, of course, obvious!"

The image of Hari Seldon reached into open air and the book once more appeared in his hand. He opened it and said:

"But whatever devious course your future history may take, impress it always upon your descendants that the path has been marked out, and that at its end is a new and greater Empire!"

And as his eyes bent to his book, he flicked into nothingness, and the lights brightened once more.

Hardin looked up to see Pirenne facing him, eyes tragic
and lips trembling.

The chairman's voice was firm but toneless. "You were
right, it seems. If you will see us tonight at six, the Board will
consult with you as to the next move."

They shook his hand, each one, and left; and Hardin
smiled to himself. They were fundamentally sound at that;
for they were scientists enough to admit that they were
wrong—but for them, it was too late.

He looked at his watch. By this time, it was all over. Lee's
men were in control and the Board was giving orders no
longer.

The Anacreonians were landing their first spaceships tomorrow, but that was all right, too. In six months, *they* would
be giving orders no longer.

In fact, as Hari Seldon had said, and as Salvor Hardin had
guessed since the day that Anselm haut Rodric had first revealed to him Anacreon's lack of atomic power—the solution
to this first crisis was obvious.

Obvious as all hell!

ASYLUM

Astounding,

May

by A. E. van Vogt

*One of the most interesting continuing themes in
modern science fiction involves guardianship—the
concept that the human species needs to be
watched, observed, controlled and/or prepared until
such time as we are "fit" for contact with other life
forms or until other life forms are "fit" to meet us.
"Asylum" is one of the finest early examples of this
kind of story, this time combining the theme with
vampirism, and for good measure, throwing in
some very interesting observations on the nature of
comparative intelligence.*

(I have always found it interesting that in science fiction
tales, organisms of super-human intelligence are so often por-
trayed as cold and cruel. It is, I suppose, an offshoot of the
"mad scientist" theme and the feeling that intelligence, *per se*,
is evil. I'm not really astonished that such a feeling should
arise. If you were to observe someone know something you
did not and use that knowledge to do something you could
not—fix an automobile, for instance—you might not enjoy
the feeling of inferiority it engendered, or the feeling of
helpless dependence. You might hug to your chest the feeling
that ignorance is really better and that uniformed people
make up for it by being nicer. But why do science fiction
writers so often spread that idea when they themselves are
generally so intelligent? I wonder.—I.A.)

I

Indecision was dark in the man's thoughts as he walked
across the spaceship control room to the cot where the
woman lay so taut and so still. He bent over her; he said in
his deep voice, "We're slowing down, Merla."

425

No answer, no movement, not a quiver in her delicate, abnormally blanched cheeks. Her fine nostrils dilated ever so slightly with each measured breath. That was all.

The Dreegh lifted her arm, then let it go. It dropped to her lap like a piece of lifeless wood, and her body remained rigid and unnatural. Carefully, he put his fingers to one eye, raised the lid, peered into it. It stared back at him, a clouded, sightless blue.

He straightened, and stood very still there in the utter silence of the hurtling ship. For a moment, then, in the intensity of his posture and in the dark ruthlessness of his lean, hard features, he seemed the veritable embodiment of grim, icy calculation.

He thought grayly, *If I revived her now, she'd have more time to attack me, and more strength. If I waited, she'd be weaker—*

Slowly, he relaxed. Some of the weariness of the years he and this woman had spent together in the dark vastness of space came to shatter her abnormal logic. Bleak sympathy touched him—and the decision was made.

He prepared an injection, and fed it into her arm. His gray eyes held a steely brightness as he put his lips near the woman's ear; in a ringing, resonant voice he said, "We're near a star system. There'll be blood, Merla! And life!"

The woman stirred; momentarily, she seemed like a golden-haired doll come alive. No color touched her perfectly formed cheeks, but alertness crept into her eyes. She stared up at him with a hardening hostility, half questioning.

"I've been chemical," she said—and abruptly the doll-like effect was gone. Her gaze tightened on him, and some of the prettiness vanished from her face. Her lips twisted into words: "It's damned funny, Jeel, that you're still O.K. If I thought—"

He was cold, watchful. "Forget it," he said curtly. "You're an energy waster, and you know it. Anyway, we're going to land."

The flame-like tenseness of her faded. She sat up painfully, but there was a thoughtful look on her face as she said, "I'm interested in the risks. This is not a Galactic planet, is it?"

"There are no Galactics out here. But there is an Observer. I've been catching the secret *ultra* signals for the last two hours"—a sardonic note entered his voice—"warning all ships to stay clear because the system isn't ready for any kind of contact with Galactic planets."

Some of the diabolic glee that was in his thoughts must have communicated through his tone. The woman stared at him, and slowly her eyes widened. She half whispered, "You mean—"

He shrugged. "The signals ought to be registering full blast now. We'll see what degree system this is. But you can start hoping hard right now."

At the control board, he cautiously manipulated the room into darkness and set the automatics—a picture took form on a screen on the opposite wall.

At first there was only a point of light in the middle of a starry sky, then a planet floating brightly in the dark space, continents and oceans plainly visible. A voice came out of the screen:

"This star system contains one inhabited planet, the third from the sun, called Earth by its inhabitants. It was colonized by Galactics about seven thousand years ago in the usual manner. It is now in the third degree of development, having attained a limited form of space travel little more than a hundred years ago. It—"

With a swift movement, the man cut off the picture and turned on the light, then looked across at the woman in a blank, triumphant silence.

"Third degree!" he said softly, and there was an almost incredulous note in his voice. "Only third degree. Merla, do you realize what this means? This is the opportunity of the ages. I'm going to call the Dreegh tribe. If we can't get away with several tankers of blood and a whole battery of 'life,' we don't deserve to be immortal. We—"

He turned toward the communicator, and for that exultant moment caution was a dim thing in the back of his mind. From the corner of his eye, he saw the woman flow from the edge of the cot. Too late he twisted aside. The frantic jerk saved him only partially; it was their cheeks, not their lips that met.

Blue flame flashed from him to her. The burning energy seared his cheek to instant, bleeding rawness. He half fell to the floor from the shock; and then, furious with the intense agony, he fought free.

"I'll break your bones!" he raged.

Her laughter, unlovely with her own suppressed fury, floated up at him from the floor, where he had flung her. She snarled, "So you did have a secret supply of 'life' for yourself. You damned double-crosser!"

His black mortification dimmed before the stark realization that anger was useless. Tense with the weakness that was already a weight on his muscles, he whirled toward the control board, and began feverishly to make the adjustments that would pull the ship back into normal space and time.

The body urge grew in him swiftly, a dark, remorseless need. Twice, black nausea sent him reeling to the cot; but each time he fought back to the control board. He sat there finally at the controls, head drooping, conscious of the numbing tautness that crept deeper, deeper—

Almost, he drove the ship too fast. It turned a blazing white when at last it struck the atmosphere of the third planet. But those hard metals held their shape; and the terrible speeds yielded to the fury of the reversers and to the pressure of the air that thickened with every receding mile.

It was the woman who helped his faltering form into the tiny lifeboat. He lay there, gathering strength, staring with tense eagerness down at the blazing sea of lights that was the first city he had seen on the night side of this strange world.

Dully, he watched as the woman carefully eased the small ship into the darkness behind a shed in a little back alley; and, because succor seemed suddenly near, sheer hope enabled him to walk beside her to the dimly lighted residential street nearby.

He would have walked on blankly into the street, but the woman's fingers held him back into the shadows of the alleyway.

"Are you mad?" she whispered. "Lie down. We'll stay right here till someone comes."

The cement was hard beneath his body, but after a moment of the painful rest it brought, he felt a faint surge of energy; and he was able to voice his bitter thought: "If you hadn't stolen most of my carefully saved 'life,' we wouldn't be in this desperate position. You know well that it's more important that I remain at full power."

In the dark beside him, the woman lay quiet for a while; then her defiant whisper came: "We both need a change of blood and a new charge of 'life.' Perhaps I did take a little too much out of you, but that was because I had to steal it. You wouldn't have given it to me of your own free will, and you know it."

For a time, the futility of argument held him silent, but, as the minutes dragged, that dreadful physical urgency once more tainted his thoughts, he said heavily, "You realize of course that we've revealed our presence. We should have waited for the others to come. There's no doubt at all that our ship was spotted by the Galactic Observer in this system before we reached the outer planets. They'll have tracers on us wherever we go, and, no matter where we bury our machine, they'll know its exact location. It is impossible to hide the interstellar drive energies; and, since they wouldn't make the mistake of bringing such energies to a third-degree planet, we can't hope to locate them in that fashion.

"But we must expect an attack of some kind. I only hope one of the great Galactics doesn't take part in it."

"One of *them!*" Her whisper was a gasp, then she snapped irritably, "Don't try to scare me. You've told me time and again that—"

"All right, all right!" He spoke grudgingly, wearily. "A million years have proven that they consider us beneath their personal attention. And"—in spite of his appalling weakness, scorn came—"let any of the kind of agents they have in these lower category planets try to stop us."

"Hush!" Her whisper was tense. "Footsteps! Quick, get to your feet!"

He was aware of the shadowed form of her rising; then her hands were tugging at him. Dizzily, he stood up.

"I don't think," he began wanly, "that I can—"

"Jeel!" Her whisper beat at him; her hands shook him. "It's a man and a woman. They're 'life,' Jeel, 'life'!"

Life!

He straightened with a terrible effort. A spark of the unquenchable will to live that had brought him across the black miles and the blacker years burst into flames inside him. Lightly, swiftly, he fell into step beside Merla, and strode beside her into the open. He saw the shapes of the man and the woman.

In the half-night under the trees of that street, the couple came toward them, drawing aside to let them pass; first the woman came, then the man—and it was as simple as if all his strength had been there in his muscles.

He saw Merla launch herself at the man; and then he was grabbing the woman, his head bending instantly for that abnormal kiss—

Afterward—after they had taken the blood, too—grimness came to the man, a hard fabric of thought and counter-thought, that slowly formed into purpose; he said: "We'll leave the bodies here."

Her startled whisper rose in objection, but he cut her short harshly: "Let me handle this. These dead bodies will draw to this city news gatherers, news reporters or whatever their breed are called on this planet; and we need such a person now. Somewhere in the reservoir of facts possessed by a person of this type must be clues, meaningless to him, but by which we can discover the secret base of the Galactic Observer in this system. We must find that base, discover its strength and destroy it if necessary when the tribe comes."

His voice took on a steely note: "And now we've got to explore this city, find a much frequented building, under which we can bury our ship, learn the language, replenish our own vital supplies—and capture that reporter.

"After I'm through with him"—his tone became silk smooth—"he will undoubtedly provide you with that physical diversion which you apparently crave when you have been particularly chemical."

He laughed gently, as her fingers gripped his arm in the darkness, a convulsive gesture; her voice came: "Thank you, Jeel, you do understand, don't you?"

II

Behind Leigh, a door opened. Instantly the clatter of voices in the room faded to a murmur. He turned alertly, tossing his cigarette onto the marble floor, and stepping on it, all in one motion.

Overhead, the lights brightened to daylight intensity; and in that blaze he saw what the other eyes were already staring at: the two bodies, the man's and the woman's, as they were wheeled in.

The dead couple lay side by side on the flat, gleaming top of the carrier. Their bodies were rigid, their eyes closed; they looked as dead as they were, and not at all, Leigh thought, as if they were sleeping.

He caught himself making a mental note of that fact—and felt abruptly shocked.

The first murders on the North American continent in

twenty-seven years. And it was only another job. By Heaven, he was tougher than he'd ever believed.

He grew aware that the voices had stopped completely. The only sound was the hoarse breathing of the man nearest him—and then the scrape of his own shoes as he went forward.

His movement acted like a signal on that tense group of men. There was a general pressing forward. Leigh had a moment of hard anxiety; and then his bigger, harder muscles brought him where he wanted to be, opposite the two heads.

He leaned forward in dark absorption. His fingers probed gingerly the neck of the woman, where the incisions showed. He did not look up at the attendant, as he said softly, "This is where the blood was drained?"

"Yes."

Before he could speak again, another reporter interjected: "Any special comment from the police scientists? The murders are more than a day old now. There ought to be something new."

Leigh scarcely heard. The woman's body, electrically warmed for embalming, felt eerily lifelike to his touch. It was only after a long moment that he noticed her lips were badly, almost brutally bruised.

His gaze flicked to the man; and there were the same neck cuts, the same torn lips. He looked up, questions quivered on his tongue—and remained unspoken as realization came that the calm-voiced attendant was still talking. The man was saying, "—normally, when the electric embalmers are applied, there is resistance from the static electricity of the body. Curiously, that resistance was not present in either body."

Somebody said, "Just what does that mean?"

"This static force is actually a form of life force, which usually trickles out of a corpse over a period of a month. We know of no way to hasten the process, but the bruises on the lips show distinct burns, which are suggestive."

There was a craning of necks, a crowding forward; and Leigh allowed himself to be pushed aside. He stopped attentively, as the attendant said, "Presumably, a pervert could have kissed with such violence."

"I thought," Leigh called distinctly, "there were no more perverts since Professor Ungarn persuaded the government to institute his brand of mechanical psychology in all schools, thus ending murder, theft, war and all unsocial perversions."

The attendant in his black frock coat hesitated; then: "A very bad one seems to have been missed."

He finished: "That's all, gentlemen. No clues, no promise of an early capture and only this final fact: We've wirelessed Professor Ungarn and, by great good fortune, we caught him on his way to Earth from his meteorite retreat near Jupiter. He'll be landing shortly after dark, in a few hours now."

The lights dimmed. As Leigh stood frowning, watching the bodies being wheeled out, a phrase floated out of the gathering chorus of voices:

"—The kiss of death—"

"I tell you," another voice said, "the captain of this space liner swears it happened—the spaceship came past him at a million miles an hour, and it was slowing down, get that, slowing down—two days ago."

"—The vampire case! That's what I'm going to call it—"

That's what Leigh called it, too, as he talked briefly into his wrist communicator. He finished: "I'm going to supper now, Jim."

"Okay, Bill." The local editor's voice came metallically. "And say, I'm supposed to commend you. Nine thousand papers took the Planetarian Service on this story, as compared with about forty-seven hundred who bought from Universal, who got the second largest coverage.

"And I think you've got the right angle for today also. Husband and wife, ordinary young couple, taking an evening's walk. Some devil hauls up alongside them, drains their blood into a tank, their life energy onto a wire or something—people will believe that, I guess. Anyway, you suggest it could happen to anybody; so be careful, folks. And you warn that, in these days of interplanetary speeds, he could be anywhere tonight for his next murder.

"As I said before, good stuff. That'll keep the story frying hard for tonight. Oh, by the way—"

"Shoot!"

"A kid called half an hour ago to see you. Said you expected him."

"A kid?" Leigh frowned.

"Name of Patrick. High school age, about sixteen. No, come to think of it, that was only my first impression. Eighteen, maybe twenty, very bright, confident, proud."

"I remember now," said Leigh. "College student. Interview for a college paper. Called me up this afternoon. One of those damned persuasive talkers. Before I knew it, I was signed up for supper at Constantine's."

"That's right. I was supposed to remind you. O.K.?"

Leigh shrugged. "I promised," he said.

Actually, as he went out into the blaze of late afternoon, sunlit street, there was not a thought in his head. Nor a premonition.

Around him, the swarm of humankind began to thicken. Vast buildings discharged the first surge of the five o'clock tidal wave—and twice Leigh felt the tug at his arm before it struck him that someone was not just bumping him.

He turned, and stared down at a pair of dark, eager eyes set in a brown, wizened face. The little man waved a sheaf of papers at him. Leigh caught a glimpse of writing in longhand on the papers. Then the fellow was babbling:

"Mr. Leigh, hundred dollars for these . . . biggest story—"

"Oh," said Leigh. His interest collapsed; then his mind roused itself from its almost blank state, and pure politeness made him say, "Take it up to the Planetarian office. Jim Brian will pay you what the story is worth."

He walked on, the vague conviction in his mind that the matter was settled. Then, abruptly, there was the tugging at his arm again.

"Scoop!" the little man was muttering. "Professor Ungarn's log, all about a spaceship that came from the stars. Devils in it who drink blood and kiss people to death!"

"See here!" Leigh began, irritated; and then he stopped physically and mentally. A strange ugly chill swept through him. He stood there, swaying a little from the shock of the thought that was frozen in his brain:

The newspapers with those details of "blood" and "kiss" were not on the street yet, wouldn't be for another five minutes. . . . .

The man was saying, "Look, it's got Professor Ungarn's name printed in gold on the top of each sheet, and it's all about how he first spotted the ship eighteen light years out, and how it came all that distance in a few hours . . . and he knows where it is now and—"

Leigh heard, but that was all. His reporter's brain, that special, highly developed department, was whirling with a little swarm of thoughts that suddenly straightened into a hard, bright pattern; and in that tightly built design, there

was no room for any such brazen coincidence as this man
coming to him here in this crowded street.

He said, "Let me see those!" And reached as he spoke.

The papers came free from the other's fingers into his
hands, but Leigh did not even glance at them. His brain was
crystal-clear, his eyes cold; he snapped: "I don't know what
game you're trying to pull. I want to know three things, and
make your answers damned fast! One: How did you pick me
out, name and job and all, here in this packed street of a city
I haven't been in for a year?"

He was vaguely aware of the little man trying to speak,
stammering incomprehensible words. But he paid no attention. Remorselessly, he pounded on:

"Two: Professor Ungarn is arriving from Jupiter in three
hours. How do you explain your possession of papers he must
have written, less than two days ago?"

"Look, boss," the man chattered, "you've got me all
wrong—"

"My third question," Leigh said grimly, "is how are you
going to explain to the police your pre-knowledge of the details of—murder?"

"Huh!" The little man's eyes were glassy, and for the first
time pity came to Leigh. He said almost softly, "All right,
fellah, start talking."

The words came swiftly, and at first they were simply
senseless sounds; only gradually did coherence come.

"—And that's the way it was, boss. I'm standing there, and
this kid comes up to me and points you out, and gives me
five bucks and those papers you've got, and tells me what I'm
supposed to say to you and—"

"Kid!" said Leigh; and the first shock was already in him.

"Yeah, kid about sixteen; no, more like eighteen or twenty
. . . and he gives me the papers and—"

"This kid," said Leigh, "would you say he was of college
age?"

"That's it, boss; you've got it. That's just what he was. You
know him, eh? O.K., that leaves me in the clear, and I'll be
going—"

"Wait!" Leigh called, but the little man seemed suddenly
to realize that he need only run, for he jerked into a mad
pace; and people stared, and that was all. He vanished
around a corner, and was gone forever.

Leigh stood, frowning, reading the thin sheaf of papers.

And there was nothing beyond what the little man had already conveyed by his incoherent word of mouth, simply a vague series of entries on sheets from a loose-leaf notebook.

Written down, the tale about the spaceship and its occupants lacked depth, and seemed more unconvincing each passing second. True, there was the single word "Ungarn" inscribed in gold on the top of each sheet but—

Leigh shook himself. The sense of silly hoax grew so violently that he thought with abrupt anger: *If that damned fool college kid really pulled a stunt like*—

The thought ended; for the idea was as senseless as everything that had happened.

And still there was no real tension in him. He was only going to a restaurant.

He turned into the splendid foyer that was the beginning of the vast and wonderful Constantine's. In the great doorway, he paused for a moment to survey the expansive glitter of tables, the hanging garden tearooms; and it was all there.

Brilliant Constantine's famous the world over—but not much changed from his last visit.

Leigh gave his name, and began: "A Mr. Patrick made reservations, I understand—"

The girl cut him short. "Oh, yes, Mr. Leigh. Mr. Patrick reserved Private 3 for you. He just now phoned to say he'd be along in a few minutes. Our premier will escort you."

Leigh was turning away, a vague puzzled thought in his mind at the way the girl had gushed, when a flamelike thought struck him: "Just a minute, did you say *Private 3*? Who's paying for this?"

The girl glowed at him: "It was paid by phone. Forty-five hundred dollars!"

Leigh stood very still. In a single, flashing moment, this meeting that, even after what had happened on the street, had seemed scarcely more than an irritation to be gotten over with, was become a fantastic, abnormal thing.

Forty-five—hundred—dollars! Could it be some damned fool rich kid sent by a college paper, but who had pulled this whole affair because he was determined to make a strong, personal impression?

Coldly, alertly, his brain rejected the solution. Humanity produced egoists on an elephantiastic scale, but not one who would order a feast like that to impress a reporter.

His eyes narrowed on an idea. "Where's your registered phone?" he asked curtly.

A minute later, he was saying into the mouthpiece: "Is that the Amalgamated Universities Secretariat? . . . I want to find out if there is a Mr. Patrick registered at any of your local colleges, and, if there is, whether or not he has been authorized by any college paper to interview William Leigh of the Planetarian News Service. This is Leigh calling."

It took six minutes, and then the answer came, brisk, tremendous and final: "There are three Mr. Patricks in our seventeen units. All are at present having supper at their various official residences. There are four Miss Patricks similarly accounted for by our staff of secretaries. None of these seven is in any way connected with a university paper. Do you wish any assistance in dealing with the impostor?"

Leigh hesitated; and when he finally spoke, it was with the queer, dark realization that he was committing himself. "No," he said, and hung up.

He came out of the phone box, shaken by his own thoughts. There was only one reason why he was in this city at this time. Murder! And he knew scarcely a soul. Therefore—

It was absolutely incredible that any stranger would want to see him for a reason not connected with his own purpose. He shook the ugly thrill out of his system; he said, "To Private 3, please—"

Tensed but cool, he examined the apartment that was Private 3. Actually that was all it was, a splendidly furnished apartment with a palacelike dining salon dominating the five rooms, and one entire wall of the salon was lined with decorated mirror facings, behind which glittered hundreds of bottles of liquors.

The brands were strange to his inexpensive tastes, the scent of several that he opened heady and—quite uninviting. In the ladies' dressing room was a long showcase displaying a gleaming array of jewelry—several hundred thousand dollars' worth, if it was genuine, he estimated swiftly.

Leigh whistled softly to himself. On the surface, Constantine's appeared to supply good rental value for the money they charged.

"I'm glad you're physically big," said a cool voice behind him. "So many reporters are thin and small."

It was the voice that did it, subtly, differently toned than it had been over the phone in the early afternoon. Deliberately different.

The difference, he noted as he turned, was in the body, too, the difference in the shape of a woman from a boy, skillfully but not perfectly concealed under the well-tailored man's suit—actually, of course, she was quite boyish in build, young, finely molded.

And, actually, he would never have suspected if she had not allowed her voice to be so purposefully womanish. She echoed his thought coolly: "Yes, I wanted you to know. But now, there's no use wasting words. You know as much as you need to know. Here's a gun. The spaceship is buried below this building."

Leigh made no effort to take the weapon, nor did he even glance at it. Instead, cool now that the first shock was over, he seated himself on the silk-yielding chair of the vanity dresser in one corner, leaned heavily back against the vanity itself, raised his eyebrows and said, "Consider me a slow-witted lunk who's got to know what it's all about. Why so much preliminary hocus-pocus?"

He thought deliberately: He had never in his adult life allowed himself to be rushed into anything. He was not going to start now.

III

The girl, he saw after a moment, was small of build. Which was odd, he decided carefully. Because his first impression had been of reasonable length of body. Or perhaps—he considered the possibility unhurriedly—this second effect was a more considered result of her male disguise.

He dismissed that particular problem as temporarily insoluble, and because actually—it struck him abruptly—this girl's size was unimportant. She had long, black lashes and dark eyes that glowed at him from a proud, almost haughty face. And that was it; quite definitely that was the essence of her blazing, powerful personality.

Pride was in the way she held her head. It was in the poised easiness of every movement, the natural shift from grace to grace as she walked slowly toward him. Not conscious pride here, but an awareness of superiority that affected every movement of her muscles, and came vibrantly into her voice, as she said scathingly, "I picked you because every newspaper I've read today carried your account of the murders, and because it seemed to me that somebody who already was actively working on the case would be reasonably quick at grasping essentials. As for the dramatic preparation, I considered that would be more convincing than drab explanation. I see I was mistaken in all these assumptions."

She was quite close to him now. She leaned over, laid her revolver on the vanity beside his arm, and finished almost indifferently: "Here's an effective weapon. It doesn't shoot bullets, but it has a trigger and you aim it like any gun. In the event you develop the beginning of courage, come down the tunnel after me as quickly as possible, but don't blunder in on me and the people I shall be talking to. Stay hidden! Act only if I'm threatened."

Tunnel, Leigh thought stolidly, as she walked with a free, swift stride out of the room—tunnel here in this apartment called Private 3. Either he was crazy, or she was.

Quite suddenly, realization came that he ought to be offended at the way she had spoken. And that insultingly simple come-on trick of hers, leaving the room. Leaving him to develop curiosity—he smiled ruefully; if he hadn't been a reporter, he'd show her that such a second-rate psychology didn't work on him.

Still annoyed, he climbed to his feet, took the gun, and then paused briefly as the odd, muffled sound came of a door opening reluctantly—

He found her in the bedroom to the left of the dining salon; and because his mind was still in that state of pure receptiveness, which, for him, replaced indecisiveness, he felt only the vaguest surprise to see that she had the end of a lush green rug rolled back, and that there was a hole in the floor at her feet.

The gleaming square of floor that must have covered the opening, lay back neatly, pinned to position by a single, glitteringly complicated hinge. But Leigh scarcely noticed that.

His gaze reached beyond that—tunnel—to the girl; and, in that moment, just before she became aware of him, there was the barest suggestion of uncertainty about her. And her right profile, half turned away from him, showed pursed lips, a strained whiteness, as if—

The impression he received was of indecisiveness. He had the subtle sense of observing a young woman who, briefly, had lost her superb confidence. Then she saw him; and his whole emotion picture twisted.

She didn't seem to stiffen in any way. Paying no attention to him at all, she stepped down to the first stair of the little stairway that led down into the hole, and began to descend without a quiver of hesitation. And yet—

Yet his first conviction that she had faltered brought him forward with narrowed eyes. And, suddenly, that certainty of her brief fear made this whole madness real. He plunged forward, down the steep stairway, and pulled up only when he saw that he was actually in a smooth, dimly lighted tunnel; and that the girl had paused, one finger to her lips.

"*Sssshh!*" she said. "The door of the ship may be open."

Irritation struck Leigh, a hard trickle of anger. Now that he had committed himself, he felt automatically the leader of this fantastic expedition; and that girl's pretensions, the devastating haughtiness of her merely produced his first real impatience.

"Don't *ssshh* me!" he whispered sharply. "Just give me the facts, and I'll do the rest."

He stopped. For the first time the meaning of all the words she had spoken penetrated. His anger collapsed like a plane in a crash landing.

"Ship!" he said incredulously. "Are you trying to tell me there's actually a spaceship buried here under Constantine's?"

The girl seemed not to hear; and Leigh saw that they were at the end of a short passageway. Metal gleamed dully just ahead. Then the girl was saying:

"Here's the door. Now, remember, you act as guard. Stay hidden, ready to shoot. And if I yell 'Shoot,' you shoot!"

She bent forward. There was the tiniest scarlet flash. The door opened, revealing a second door just beyond. Again that minute, intense blaze of red; and that door too swung open.

It was swiftly done, too swiftly. Before Leigh could more than grasp that the crisis was come, the girl stepped coolly into the brilliantly lighted room beyond the second door.

There was shadow where Leigh stood half-paralyzed by the girl's action. There was deeper shadow against the metal wall toward which he pressed himself in one instinctive move. He froze there, cursing silently at a stupid young woman who actually walked into a den of enemies of unknown numbers without a genuine plan of self-protection.

Or did she knew how many there were? And who?

The questions made twisting paths in his mind down, down to a thrall of blankness—that ended only when an entirely different thought replaced it:

At least he was out here with a gun, unnoticed—or was he?

He waited tensely. But the door remained open; and there was no apparent movement towards it. Slowly, Leigh let himself relax, and allowed his straining mind to absorb its first considered impressions.

The portion of underground room that he could see showed one end of what seemed to be a control board, a metal wall that blinked with tiny lights, the edge of a rather sumptuous cot—and the whole was actually so suggestive of a spaceship that Leigh's logic resistance collapsed.

Incredibly, here under the ground, actually *under* Constantine's was a small spaceship and—

That thought ended, too, as the silence beyond the open door, the curiously long silence, was broken by a man's cool voice:

"I wouldn't even try to raise that gun if I were you. The fact that you have said nothing since entering shows how enormously different we are from what you expected."

He laughed gently, an unhurried, deep-throated derisive laughter that came clearly to Leigh. The man said:

"Merla, what would you say is the psychology behind this young lady's action? You have of course noticed that she is a young lady, and not a boy."

A richly toned woman's voice replied: "She was born here, Jeel. She has none of the normal characteristics of a Klugg, but she is a Galactic, though definitely not the Galactic Observer. Probably, she's not alone. Shall I investigate?"

"No!" The man sounded indifferent to the tensing Leigh. "We don't have to worry about a Klugg's assistant."

Leigh relaxed slowly, but there was a vast uneasiness in his solar nerves, a sense of emptiness, the first realization of how great a part the calm assurance of the young woman had played in the fabricating of his own basic confidence.

Shattered now! Before the enormous certainties of these two, and in the face of their instant penetration of her male disguise, the effects of the girl's rather wonderful personality seemed a remote pattern, secondary, definitely overwhelmed.

He forced the fear from him, as the girl spoke; forced his

courage to grow with each word she uttered, feeding on the haughty and immense confidence that was there. It didn't matter whether she was simulating or not, because they were in this now, he as deep as she; and only the utmost boldness could hope to draw a fraction of victory from the defeat that loomed so starkly.

With genuine admiration, he noted the glowing intensity of her speech, as she said, "My silence had its origin in the fact that you are the first Dreeghs I have ever seen. Naturally, I studied you with some curiosity, but I can assure you I am not impressed.

"However, in view of your extraordinary opinions on the matter, I shall come to the point at once: I have been instructed by the Galactic Observer of this system to inform you to be gone by morning. Our sole reason for giving you that much leeway is that we don't wish to bring the truth of all this into the open.

"But don't count on that. Earth is on the verge of being given fourth-degree rating; and, as you probably know, in emergencies fourths are given Galactic knowledge. That emergency we will consider to have arrived tomorrow at dawn."

"Well, well"—the man was laughing gently, satirically—"a pretty speech, powerfully spoken, but meaningless for us who can analyze its pretensions, however sincere, back to the Klugg origin."

"What do you intend with her, Jeel?"

The man was cold, deadly, utterly sure. "There's no reason why she should escape. She had blood and more than normal life. It will convey to the Observer with clarity our contempt for his ultimatum."

He finished with a slow, surprisingly rich laughter: "We shall now enact a simple drama. The young lady will attempt to jerk up her gun and shoot me with it. Before she can even begin to succeed, I shall have my own weapon out and firing. The whole thing, as she will discover, is a matter of nervous coordination. And Kluggs are chronically almost as slow-moving as human beings."

Silence.

His voice stopped. His laughter trickled away.

In all his alert years, Leigh had never felt more indecisive. His emotions said—*now*; surely, she'd call now. And even if she didn't, he must act on his own. Rush in! Shoot!

But his mind was cold with an awful dread. There was something about the man's voice, a surging power, a blazing, incredible certainty. Abnormal, savage strength was here; and if this was really a spaceship from the stars—

His brain wouldn't follow that flashing, terrible thought. He crouched, fingering the gun she had given him, dimly conscious for the first time that it felt queer, unlike any revolver he'd ever had.

He crouched stiffy, waiting—and the silence from the spaceship control room, from the tensed figures that must be there just beyond his line of vision, continued. The same curious silence that had followed the girl's entrance short minutes before. Only this time it was the girl who broke it, her voice faintly breathless but withal cool, vibrant, unafraid: "I'm here to warn, not to force issues. And unless you're charged with the life energy of fifteen men, I wouldn't advise you to try anything either. After all, I came here knowing what you were."

"What do you think, Merla? Can we be sure she's a Klugg? Could she possibly be of the higher Lennel type?"

It was the man, his tone conceding her point, but the decision was still there, the implacable purpose, the high, tremendous confidence.

And yet, in spite of that unrelenting sense of imminent violence, Leigh felt himself torn from the thought of her danger—and his. His reporter's brain twisted irresistibly to the fantastic meaning of what was taking place:

—*Life energy of fifteen men*—

It was all there; in a monstrous way it all fitted. The two dead bodies he had seen drained of blood and *life energy*, the repeated reference to a Galactic Observer, with whom the girl was connected.

Leigh thought almost blankly: Galactic meant—well— Galactic; and that was so terrific that— He grew aware that the woman was speaking.

"Klugg!" she said positively. "Pay no attention to her protestations, Jeel. You know, I'm sensitive when it comes to women. She's lying. She's just a little fool who walked in here expecting us to be frightened of her. Destroy her at your pleasure."

"I'm not given to waiting," said the man. "So—"

Quite automatically, Leigh leaped for the open doorway. He had a flashing glimpse of a man and woman, dressed in

evening clothes, the man standing, the woman seated. There
was awareness of a gleaming, metallic background, the control board, part of which he had already seen, now revealed
as a massive thing of glowing instruments; and then all that
blotted out as he snapped, "That will do. Put up your hands."

For a long, dazzling moment he had the impression that
his entry was a complete surprise; and that he dominated the
situation. None of the three people in the room was turned
toward him. The man, Jeel and the girl were standing, facing
each other; the woman, Merla, sat in a deep chair, her fine
profile to him, her golden head flung back.

It was she who, still without looking at him, sneered visibly—and spoke the words that ended his brief conviction of
triumph. She said to the disguised girl, "You certainly travel
in low company, a stupid human being. Tell him to go away
before he's damaged."

The girl said, "Leigh, I'm sorry I brought you into this. Every move you made in entering was heard, observed and dismissed before you could even adjust your mind to the scene."

"Is his name Leigh?" said the woman sharply. "I thought I
recognized him as he entered. He's very like his photograph
over his newspaper column." Her voice grew strangely tense:
"Jeel, a newspaper reporter!"

"We don't need him now," the man said. "We know who
the Galactic Observer is."

"Eh?" said Leigh; his mind fastened hard on those amazing
words. "Who? How did you find out? What—"

"The information," said the woman; and it struck him suddenly that the strange quality in her voice was eagerness,
"will be of no use to you. Regardless of what happens to the
girl, you're staying."

She glanced swiftly at the man, as if seeking his sanction.
"Remember, Jeel, you promised."

It was all quite senseless, so meaningless that Leigh had no
sense of personal danger. His mind scarcely more than passed
the words; his eyes concentrated tautly on a reality that had,
until that moment escaped his awareness. He said softly,
"Just now you used the phrase, 'Regardless of what happens
to the girl.' When I came in, you said, 'Tell him to go away
before he's damaged.' "

Leigh smiled grimly: "I need hardly say this is a far cry
from the threat of immediate death that hung over us a few
seconds ago. And I have just now noticed the reason.

"A little while ago, I heard our pal, Jeel, dare my little girl friend here to raise her gun. I notice now that *she has it raised.* My entrance did have an effect." He addressed himself to the girl, finished swiftly: "Shall we shoot—or withdraw?"

It was the man who answered: "I would advise withdrawal. I could still win, but I am not the heroic type who takes the risk of what might well be a close call."

He added, in an aside to the woman: "Merla, we can always catch this man, Leigh, now that we know who he is."

The girl said, "You first, Mr. Leigh." And Leigh did not stop to argue.

Metal doors clanged behind him, as he charged along the tunnel. After a moment, he was aware of the girl running lightly beside him.

The strangely unreal, the unbelievable murderous little drama was over, finished as fantastically as it had begun.

IV

Outside Constantine's a gray light gathered around them. A twilight side street it was, and people hurried past them with the strange, anxious look of the late for supper. Night was falling.

Leigh stared at his companion; in the dimness of the deep dusk, she seemed all boy, slightly, lithely built, striding along boldly. He laughed a little, huskily, then more grimly.

"Just what was all that? Did we escape by the skin of our teeth? Or did we win? What made you think you could act like God, and give those tough eggs twelve hours to get out of the Solar System?"

The girl was silent after he had spoken. She walked just ahead of him, head bent into the gloom. Abruptly, she turned, and said, "I hope you will have no nonsensical idea of telling what you've seen or heard."

Leigh said: "This is the biggest story since—"

"Look"—the girl's voice was pitying—"you're not going to print a word because in about ten seconds you'll see that no one in the world would believe the first paragraph."

In the darkness, Leigh smiled tightly: "The mechanical psychologist will verify every syllable."

"I came prepared for that, too!" said the vibrant voice. Her hand swung up, toward his face. Too late, he jerked back.

Light flared in his eyes, a dazzling, blinding force that exploded into his sensitive optic nerves with all the agonizing power of intolerable brightness. Leigh cursed aloud, wildly, and snatched forward toward his tormentor. His right hand grazed a shoulder. He lashed out violently with his left, and tantalizingly caught only the edge of a sleeve that instantly jerked away.

"You little devil!" he raged futilely. "You've blinded me."

"You'll be all right," came the cool answer, "but you'll find that the mechanical psychologist will report anything you say as the purest imagination. In view of your threat to publish, I had to do that. Now, give me my gun."

The first glimmer of sight was returning. Leigh could see her body a dim, wavering shape in the night. In spite of the continuing pain, Leigh smiled grimly. He said softly, "I've just now remembered you said this gun didn't shoot bullets. Even the *feel* of it suggests that it'll make an interesting proof of anything I say. So—"

His smile faded abruptly. For the girl stepped forward. The metal that jabbed into his ribs was so hardly thrust, it made him grunt.

"Give me that gun!"

"Like fun I will," Leigh snapped. "You ungrateful little ruffian, how dare you treat me so shoddily after I saved your life? I ought to knock you one right on the jaw for—"

He stopped—stopped because with staggering suddenness the hard, hard realization struck that she meant it. This was no girl raised in a refined school, who wouldn't dare to shoot, but a cold-blooded young creature, who had already proved the metalliclike fabric of which her courage was made.

He had never had any notions about the superiority of man over woman; and he felt none now. Without a single word, almost hastily, he handed the weapon over. The girl took it, and said coldly:

"You seem to be laboring under the illusion that your entry into the spaceship enabled me to raise my weapon. You're quite mistaken. What you did do was to provide me with the opportunity to let them think that that was the situation, and that they dominated it. But I assure you, that is the extent of your assistance, almost valueless."

Leigh laughed out loud, a pitying, ridiculing laugh.

"In my admittedly short life," he said laconically, "I've learned to recognize a quality of personality and magnetism in human beings. You've got it, a lot of it, but not a fraction of what either of those two had, particularly the man. He was terrible. He was absolutely the most abnormally magnetic human being I've ever run across. Lady, I can only guess what all this is about, but I'd advise you"—Leigh paused, then finished slashingly—"you and all the other Kluggs to stay away from that couple.

"Personally, I'm going to get the police in on this, and there's going to be a raid on Private 3. I didn't like that odd threat that they could capture me any time. Why me—"

He broke off hastily: "Hey, where are you going? I want to know your name. I want to know what made you think you could order those two around. *Who did you think you were?*"

He said no more, his whole effort concentrated on running. He could see her for a moment, a hazy, boyish figure against a dim corner light. Then she was around the corner.

His only point of contact with all this; and if she got away—

Sweating, he rounded the corner; and at first the street seemed dark and empty of life. Then he saw the car.

A normal-looking, high-hooded coupe, long, low-built, that began to move forward noiselessly and—quite normally.

It became abnormal. It lifted. Amazingly, it lifted from the ground. He had a swift glimpse of white rubber wheels folding out of sight. Streamlined, almost cigar-shaped now, the spaceship that had been a car darted at a steep angle into the sky.

Instantly it was gone.

Above Leigh, the gathering night towered, a strange, bright blue. In spite of the brilliant lights of the city glaring into the sky, one or two stars showed. He stared up at them, empty inside, thinking: *It was like a dream. Those—Dreeghs—coming out of space—bloodsuckers, vampires.*

Suddenly hungry, he bought a chocolate from a sidewalk stand, and stood munching it.

He began to feel better. He walked over to a nearby wall socket, and plugged in his wrist radio.

"Jim," he said, "I've got some stuff, not for publication, but maybe we can get some police action on it. Then I want you to have a mechanical psychologist sent to my hotel room. There must be some memory that can be salvaged from my brain—"

He went on briskly. His sense of inadequacy waned notably. Reporter Leigh was himself again.

V

The little glistening balls of the mechanical psychologist were whirring faster, faster. They became a single, glowing circle in the darkness. And not till then did the first, delicious whiff of psycho-gas touch his nostrils. He felt himself drifting, slipping—

A voice began to speak in the dim distance, so far away that not a word came through. There was only the sound, the faint, curious sound, and the feeling, stronger every instant, that he would soon be able to hear the fascinating things it seemed to be saying.

The longing to hear, to become a part of the swelling, murmuring sound drew his whole being in little rhythmical, wave-like surges. And still the promise of meaning was unfulfilled.

Other, private thoughts ended utterly. Only the mindless chant remained, and the pleasing gas holding him so close to sleep, its flow nevertheless so delicately adjusted that his mind hovered minute after minute on the ultimate abyss of consciousness.

He lay, finally, still partially awake, but even the voice was merging now into blackness. It clung for a while, a gentle, friendly, melodious sound in the remote background of his brain, becoming more remote with each passing instant. He slept, a deep, hypnotic sleep, as the machine purred on—

When Leigh opened his eyes, the bedroom was dark except for the floor lamp beside a corner chair. It illuminated the darkly dressed woman who sat there, all except her face, which was in shadow above the circle of light.

He must have moved, for the shadowed head suddenly looked up from some sheets of typewriter-size paper. The voice of Merla, the Dreegh, said:

"The girl did a very good job of erasing your subconscious memories. There's only one possible clue to her identity and—"

Her words went on, but his brain jangled them to senseless-ness in that first horrible shock of recognition. It was too much, too much fear in too short a time. For a brief, terrible moment, he was like a child, and strange, cunning, *intense* thoughts of escape came:

If he could slide to the side of the bed, away from where she was sitting, and run for the bathroom door—

"Surely, Mr. Leigh," the woman's voice reached toward him, "you know better than to try anything foolish. And, surely, if I had intended to kill you, I would have done it much more easily while you were asleep."

Leigh lay very still, gathering his mind back into his head, licking dry lips. Her words were utterly unreassuring. "What—do—you—want?" he managed finally.

"Information!" Laconically. "What was that girl?"

"I don't know." He stared into the half gloom, where her face was. His eyes were more accustomed to the light now, and he could catch the faint, golden glint of her hair. "I thought—you knew."

He went on more swiftly: "I thought you knew the Galactic Observer; and that implied the girl could be identified any time."

He had the impression she was smiling. She said, "Our statement to that effect was designed to throw both you and the girl off guard, and constituted the partial victory we snatched from what had become an impossible situation."

The body sickness was still upon Leigh, but the desperate fear that had produced it was fading before the implications of her confession of weakness, the realization that these Dreeghs were not so superhuman as he had thought. Relief was followed by caution. Careful, he warned himself, it wouldn't be wise to underestimate. But he couldn't help saying, "So you weren't so smart. And I'd like to point out that even your so-called snatching of victory from defeat was not so well done. Your husband's statement that you could pick me up any time could easily have spoiled the picking."

The woman's voice was cool, faintly contemptuous. "If you knew anything of psychology, you would realize that the vague phrasing of the threat actually lulled you. Certainly, you failed to take even minimum precautions. And the girl has definitely not made any effort to protect you."

The suggestion of deliberately subtle tactics brought to Leigh a twinge of returning alarm. Deep, deep inside him was the thought: What ending did the Dreegh woman plan for this strange meeting?

"You realize, of course," the Dreegh said softly, "that you will either be of value to us alive—or dead. There are no easy alternatives. I would advise alertness and utmost sincerity in your cooperation. You are in this affair without limit."

So that was the plan. A thin bead of perspiration trickled

down Leigh's cheek. And his fingers trembled as he reached for a cigarette on the table beside the bed.

He was shakily lighting the cigarette when his gaze fastened on the window. That brought a faint shock, for it was raining, a furious rain that hammered soundlessly against the noise-proof glass.

. . He pictured the bleak, empty streets, their brilliance dulled by the black, rain-filled night; and, strangely, the mind picture unnerved him.

Deserted streets—deserted Leigh. For he was deserted here; all the friends he had, scattered over the great reaches of the earth, couldn't add one ounce of strength, or bring one real ray of hope to him in this darkened room, against this woman who sat so calmly under the light, studying him from shadowed eyes.

With a sharp effort, Leigh steadied himself. He said, "I gather that's my psychograph report you have in your hand. What does it say?"

"Very disappointing." Her voice seemed far away. "There's a warning in it about your diet. It seems your meals are irregular."

She was playing with him. The heavy attempt at humor made her seem more inhuman, not less; for, somehow, the words clashed unbearably with the reality of her; the dark immensity of space across which she had come, the unnatural lusts that had brought her and the man to this literally unprotected Earth.

Leigh shivered. Then he thought fiercely: "Damn it, I'm scaring myself. So long as she stays in her chair, she can't pull the vampire on me."

The harder thought came that it was no use being frightened. He'd better simply be himself, and await events. Aloud, he said, "If there's nothing in the psychograph, then I'm afraid I can't help you. You might as well leave. Your presence isn't making me any happier."

In a dim way, he hoped she'd laugh. But she didn't. She sat there, her eyes glinting dully out of the gloom. At last, she said, "We'll go through this report together. I think we can safely omit the references to your health as being irrelevant. But there are a number of factors that I want developed. Who is Professor Ungarn?"

"A scientist." Leigh spoke frankly. "He invented this system of mechanical hypnosis, and he was called in when the

dead bodies were found because the killings seemed to have
been done by perverts."

"Have you any knowledge of his physical appearance?"

"I've never seen him," Leigh said more slowly. "He never
gives interviews, and his photograph is not available now. I've
heard stories, but—"

He hesitated. It wasn't, he thought frowning, as if he was
giving what was not general knowledge. What was the
woman getting at, anyway? Ungarn—

"These stories," she said, "do they give the impression that
he's a man of inordinate magnetic force, but with lines of
mental suffering etched in his face, and a sort of resignation?"

"Resignation to what?" Leigh exclaimed sharply. "I haven't
the faintest idea what you're talking about. I've only seen
photographs, and they show a fine, rather sensitive, tired
face."

She said, "There would be more information in any library?"

"Or in the Planetarian Service morgue," Leigh said, and
could have bitten off his tongue for that bit of gratuitous information.

"Morgue?" said the woman.

Leigh explained, but his voice was trembling with self-rage.
For seconds now the feeling had been growing on him: Was
it possible this devilish woman was on the right track? And
getting damaging answers out of him because he dared not
stop and organize for lying.

Even as savage anxiety came, he had an incongruous sense
of the unfairness of the abnormally swift way she had solved
the Observer's identity because, damn it, damn it, it could be
Professor Ungarn.

Ungarn, the mystery scientist, great inventor in a dozen
highly complicated, widely separated fields; and there was
that mysterious meteorite home near one of Jupiter's moons
and he had a daughter, named Patricia. Good heavens, Patrick—Patricia—

His shaky stream of thoughts ended, as the woman said:

"Can you have your office send the information to your recorder here?"

"Y-yes!" His reluctance was so obvious that the woman
bent into the light. For a moment, her golden hair glittered;
her pale-blue eyes glowed at him in a strangely humorless, satanic amusement.

"Ah!" she said, "you think so, too?"

She laughed, an odd, musical laugh—odd in that it was at once so curt and so pleasant. The laugh ended abruptly, unnaturally, on a high note. And then—although he had not seen her move—there was a metal thing in her hand, pointing at him. Her voice came at him, with a brittle, jarring command:

"You will climb out of the bed, operate the recorder and naturally you will do nothing, say nothing but what is necessary."

Leigh felt genuinely dizzy. The room swayed, and he thought sickly: If he could only faint.

But he recognized dismally that that was beyond the power of his tough body. It was sheer mental dismay that made his nerves so shivery. And even that faded like fog in strong sunlight, as he walked to the recorder. For the first time in his life, he hated the resilience of strength that made his voice steady as a rock, as, after setting the machine, he said, "This is William Leigh. Give me all the dope you've got on Professor Garret Ungarn."

There was a pause, during which he thought hopelessly: "It wasn't as if he were giving information not otherwise accessible. Only—"

There was a click in the machine, then a brisk voice: "You've got it. Sign the form."

Leigh signed, and watched the signature dissolve into the machine. It was then, as he was straightening, that the woman said:

"Shall I read it here, Jeel, or shall we take the machine along?"

That was mind-wrecking. Like a man possessed, Leigh whirled; and then, very carefully, he sat down on the bed.

The Dreegh, Jeel, was leaning idly against the jamb of the bathroom door, a dark, malignantly handsome man, with a faint, unpleasant smile on his lips. Behind him—incredibly, behind him, through the open bathroom door was, not the gleaming bath, but another door; and beyond that door still another door, and beyond that—

The control room of the Dreegh spaceship!

There it was, exactly as he had seen it in the solid ground under Constantine's. He had the same partial view of the sumptuous cot the imposing section of instrument board, the tastefully padded floor—

In his bathroom!

The insane thought came to Leigh: "Oh, yes, I keep my spaceship in my bathroom and—" It was the Dreegh's voice that drew his brain from its dizzy contemplation; the Dreegh saying, "I think we'd better leave. I'm having difficulty—holding the ship on the alternation of space-time planes. Bring the man and the machine and—"

Leigh didn't hear the last word. He jerked his mind all the way out of the—bathroom. "You're—taking—me?"

"Why, of course." It was the woman who spoke. "You've been promised to me, and, besides, we'll need your help in finding Ungarn's meteorite."

Leigh sat very still. The unnatural thought came: He was glad that he had in the past proven to himself that he was not a coward.

For here was certainty of death.

He saw after a moment that the rain was still beating against the glass, great, sparkling drops that washed murkily down the broad panes. And he saw that the night was dark.

Dark night, dark rain, dark destiny—they fitted his dark, grim thoughts. With an effort he forced his body, his mind, into greater stiffness. Automatically, he shifted his position, so that the weight of muscles would draw a tight band over the hollowness that he felt in his stomach. When at last he faced his alien captors again, Reporter Leigh was cold with acceptance of his fate—and prepared to fight for his life.

"I can't think of a single reason," he said, "why I should go with you. And if you think I'm going to help you destroy the Observer, you're crazy."

The woman said matter-of-factly: "There was a passing reference in your psychograph to a Mrs. Henry Leigh, who lives in a village called Relton, on the Pacific coast. We could be there in half an hour, your mother and her home destroyed within a minute after that. Or, perhaps, we could add her blood to our reserves."

"She would be too old," the man said in a chill tone. "We do not want the blood of old people."

It was the icy objection that brought horror to Leigh. He had a brief, terrible picture of a silent, immensely swift ship sweeping out of the Eastern night, over the peaceful hamlet; and then unearthly energies would reach down in a blaze of fury.

One second of slashing fire, and the ship would sweep on over the long, dark waters to the west.

The deadly picture faded. The woman was saying, gently:

"Jeel and I have evolved an interesting little system of interviewing human beings of the lower order. For some reason, he frightens people merely by his presence. Similarly, people develop an unnatural fear of me when they see me clearly in a strong light. So we have always tried to arrange our meetings with human beings with me sitting in semidarkness and Jeel very much in the background. It has proved very effective."

She stood up, a tall, lithely built, shadowed figure in a rather tight-fitting skirt and a dark blouse. She finished: "But now, shall we go? You bring the machine, Mr. Leigh."

"I'll take it," said the Dreegh.

Leigh glanced sharply at the lean, sinewed face of the terrible man, startled at the instant, accurate suspicion of the desperate intention that had formed in his mind.

The Dreegh loomed over the small machine, where it stood on a corner desk. "How does it work?" he asked almost mildly.

Trembling, Leigh stepped forward. There was still a chance that he could manage this without additional danger to anyone. Not that it would be more than a vexation, unless—as their suggestion about funding the Ungarn meteorite indicated—they headed straight out to space. Then, why, it might actually cause real delay. He began swiftly:

"Press the key marked 'Titles,' and the machine will type all the main headings."

"That sounds reasonable." The long, grim-faced head nodded. The Dreegh reached forward, pressed the button. The recorder hummed softly, and a section of it lit up, showing typed lines under a transparent covering. There were several headings.

"—'His Meteorite Home,'" the Dreegh read. "That's what I want. What is the next step?"

"Press the key marked 'Subheads.'"

Leigh was suddenly shaky. He groaned inwardly. Was it possible this creature-man was going to obtain the information he wanted? Certainly, such a tremendous intelligence would not easily be led away from logical sequence.

He forced himself to grimness. He'd have to take a chance.

"The subhead I desire," said the Dreegh, "is marked 'Location.' And there is a number, one, in front of it. What next?"

"Press Key No. 1," Leigh said, "then press the key lettered 'General Release.' "

The moment he had spoken, he grew taut. If this worked—and it should. There was no reason why it shouldn't.

Key No. 1 would impart all the information under that heading. And surely the man would not want more until later. After all, this was only a test. They were in a hurry.

And later, when the Dreegh discovered that the "General Release" key had dissolved all the other information—it would be too late.

The thought dimmed. Leigh started. The Dreegh was staring at him with a bleak sardonicism. The man said, "Your voice has been like an organ; each word uttered full of subtle shadings that mean much to the sensitive ear. Accordingly"—a steely, ferocious smile twisted that lean and deadly face—"I shall press Key No. 1. But not 'General Release.' And as soon as I've examined the little story on the recorder, I shall attend to you for that attempted trick. The sentence is—death."

"Jeel!"

"Death!" reiterated the man flatly. And the woman was silent.

There was silence, then, except for the subdued humming of the recorder. Leigh's mind was almost without thought. He felt fleshless, a strange, disembodied soul; and only gradually did a curious realization grow that he was waiting here on the brink of a night darker than the black wastes of space from which these monster humans had come.

Consciousness came of kinship with the black rain that poured with such solid, noiseless power against the glinting panes. For soon he would be part of the inorganic darkness—a shadowed figure sprawling sightlessly in this dim room.

His aimless gaze returned to the recorder machine, and to the grim man who stood so thoughtfully, staring down at the words it was unfolding.

His thought quickened. His life, that had been pressed so shockingly out of his system by the sentence of death, quivered forth. He straightened, physically and mentally. And, suddenly, there was purpose in him.

If death was inescapable, at least he could try again, somehow, to knock down that "General Release" key. He stared at the key, measuring the distance; and the gray thought came: What incredible irony that he should die, that he should waste his effort, to prevent the Dreeghs from having *this minute* information that was available from ten thousand sources. And yet—

The purpose remained. Three feet, he thought carefully, perhaps four. If he should fling himself toward it, how could even a Dreegh prevent the dead weight of his body and his extended fingers from accomplishing such a simple, straightforward mission?

After all, his sudden action had once before frustrated the Dreeghs, permitting the Ungarn girl—in spite of her denials—to get her gun into position for firing. And—

He grew rigid as he saw that the Dreegh was turning away from the machine. The man pursed his lips, but it was the woman, Merla, who spoke from where she stood in the gloom: "Well?"

The man frowned. "The exact location is nowhere on record. Apparently, there has been no development of meteorites in this system. I suspected as much. After all, space travel has only existed a hundred years; and the new planets and the moons of Jupiter have absorbed all the energies of exploring, exploiting man."

"I could have told you that," said Leigh.

If he could move a little to one side of the recorder, so that the Dreegh would have to do more than simply put his arm out—

The man was saying, "There is, however, a reference to some man who transports food and merchandise from the moon Europa to the Ungarns. We will . . . er . . . persuade this man to show us the way."

"One of these days," said Leigh, "you're going to discover that all human beings cannot be persuaded. What pressure are you going to put on this chap? Suppose he hasn't got a mother."

"He has—life!" said the woman softly.

"One look at you," Leigh snapped, "and he'd know that he'd lose that, anyway."

As he spoke, he stepped with enormous casualness to the left, one short step. He had a violent impulse to say something, anything to cover the action. But his voice had betrayed him once. And actually it might already have done so again. The cold face of the man was almost too enigmatic.

"We could," said the woman, "use William Leigh to persuade him."

The words were softly spoken, but they shocked Leigh to his bones. For they offered a distorted hope. And that shattered his will to action. His purpose faded into remoteness. Almost grimly, he fought to draw that hard determination back into his consciousness. He concentrated his gaze on the recorder machine, but the woman was speaking again; and his mind wouldn't hold anything except the urgent meaning of her words:

"He is too valuable a slave to destroy. We can always take his blood and energy, but now we must send him to Europa, there to find the freighter pilot of the Ungarns, and actually accompany him to the Ungarn meteorite. If he could investigate the interior, our attack might conceivably be simplified, and there is just a possibility that there might be new weapons, of which we should be informed. We must not underestimate the science of the great Galactics.

"Naturally, before we allowed Leigh his freedom, we would do a little tampering with his mind, and so blot out from his conscious mind all that has happened in this hotel room.

"The identification of Professor Ungarn as the Galactic Observer we would make plausible for Leigh by a little rewriting of his psychograph report; and tomorrow he will waken in his bed with a new purpose, based on some simple human impulse such as love of the girl."

The very fact that the Dreegh, Jeel, was allowing her to go on, brought the first, faint color to Leigh's cheeks, a thin flush at the enormous series of betrayals she was so passionately expecting of him. Nevertheless, so weak was his resistance to the idea of continued life, that he could only snap:

"If you think I'm going to fall in love with a dame who's got twice my I. Q., you're—"

The woman cut him off. "Shut up, you fool! Can't you see I've saved your life?"

The man was cold, ice-cold. "Yes, we shall use him, not because he is essential, but because we have time to search for easier victories. The first members of the Dreegh tribe will not arrive for a month and a half, and it will take Mr. Leigh a month of that to get to the moon, Europa, by one of Earth's primitive passenger liners. Fortunately, the nearest

Galactic military base is well over three months distant—by
Galactic ship speeds.

"Finally"—with a disconcerting, tigerish swiftness, the
Dreegh whirled full upon Leigh; eyes that were like pools of
black fire measured his own startled stare—"finally, as a notable reminder to your subconscious of the error of trickery,
and as complete punishment for past and—intended—
offenses, *this!*

Despairingly, Leigh twisted away from the metal that
glowed at him. His muscles tried horribly to carry out the
purpose that had been working to a crisis inside him. He
lunged for the recorder—but *something* caught his body.
Something—not physical. But the very pain seemed mortal.

There was no visible flame of energy, only that glow at the
metal source. But his nerves writhed; enormous forces contorted his throat muscles, froze the scream that quivered
there, hideously.

His whole being welcomed the blackness that came mercifully to blot out the hellish pain.

VI

On the third day, Europa began to give up some of the sky
to the vast mass of Jupiter behind it. The engines that so im-
perfectly transformed magnetic attraction to a half-hearted
repulsion functioned more and more smoothly as the infinite
complication of pull and counterpull yielded to distance.

The old, slow, small freighter scurried on into the immense, enveloping night; and the days dragged into weeks,
the weeks crawled their drab course toward the full month.

On the thirty-seventh day, the sense of slowing up was so
distinct that Leigh crept dully out of his bunk, and croaked,
"How much farther?"

He was aware of the stolid-faced space trucker grinning at
him. The man's name was Hanardy, and he said now matter-
of-factly, "We're just pulling in. See that spot of light over to
the left? It's moving this way."

He ended with a rough sympathy. "Been a tough trip, eh?
Tougher'n you figgered when you offered to write up my little
route for your big syndicate."

Leigh scarcely heard. He was clawing at the porthole,
straining to penetrate the blackness. At first his eyes kept

blinking and nothing came. Stars were out there, but it was long seconds before his bleary gaze made out moving lights. He counted them with sluggish puzzlement:

"One, two, three—seven—" he counted. "And all traveling together."

"What's that?" Hanardy bent beside him. "Seven?"

There was a brief silence between them, as the lights grew visibly dim with distance, and winked out.

"Too bad," Leigh ventured, "that Jupiter's behind us. They mightn't fade out like that in silhouette. Which one was Ungarn's meteorite?"

With a shock, he grew aware that Hanardy was standing. The man's heavy face was dark with frown. Hanardy said slowly:

"Those were ships. I never saw ships go so fast before. They were out of sight in less than a minute."

The frown faded from his stolid face. He shrugged. "Some of those new police ships, I guess. And we must have seen them from a funny angle for them to disappear so fast."

Leigh half sat, half knelt, frozen into immobility. And after that one swift glance at the pilot's rough face, he averted his own. For a moment, the black fear was in him that his wild thoughts would blaze from his eyes.

Dreeghs! Two and a half months had wound their appallingly slow course since the murders. More than a month to get from Earth to Europa, and now this miserable, lonely journey with Hanardy, the man who trucked for the Ungarns.

Every day of that time, he had known with an inner certainty that none of this incredible business had gone backward. That it could only have assumed a hidden, more dangerous form. The one fortunate reality in the whole mad affair was that he had wakened on the morning after the mechanical psychologist test from a dreamless sleep; and there in the psychograph report was the identification of Ungarn as the Observer, and the statement, borne out by an all too familiar emotional tension, that he was in love with the girl.

Now this! His mind flared. Dreeghs in seven ships. That meant the first had been reinforced by—many. And perhaps the seven were only a reconnaissance group, withdrawing at Hanardy's approach.

Or perhaps those fantastic murderers had already attacked the Observer's base. Perhaps the girl—

He fought the desperate thought out of his consciousness, and watched, frowning, as the Ungarn meteorite made a dark, glinting path in the blackness to one side. The two objects, the ship and the bleak, rough-shaped mass of metallic stone drew together in the night, the ship slightly behind.

A great steel door slid open in the rock. Skillfully, the ship glided into the chasm. There was a noisy clicking. Hanardy came out of the control room, his face dark with puzzlement.

"Those damn ships are out there again," he said. "I've closed the big steel locks, but I'd better tell the professor and—"

Crash! The world jiggled. The floor came up and hit Leigh a violent blow. He lay there, cold in spite of the thoughts that burned at fire heat in his mind:

For some reason, the vampires had waited until the freighter was inside. Then instantly, ferociously, attacked.

In packs!

"Hanardy!" A vibrant girl's voice blared from one of the loudspeakers.

The pilot sat up shakily on the floor, where he had fallen, near Leigh. "Yes, Miss Patricia."

"You dared to bring a stranger with you!"

"It's only a reporter, miss; he's writing up my route for me."

"You conceited fool! That's William Leigh. He's a hypnotized spy of those devils who are attacking us. Bring him immediately to my apartment. He must be killed at once."

"Huh!" Leigh began; and then slowly he began to stiffen. For the pilot was staring at him from narrowing eyes, all the friendliness gone from his rough, heavy face. Finally, Leigh laughed curtly.

"Don't you be a fool, too, Hanardy. I made the mistake once of saving that young lady's life, and she's hated me ever since."

The heavy face scowled at him. "So you knew her before, eh? You didn't tell me that. You'd better come along before I sock you one."

Almost awkwardly, he drew the gun from his side holster, and pointed its ugly snout at Leigh.

"Get along!" he said.

Hanardy reached toward a tiny arrangement of lights

beside the paneled door of Patricia Ungarn's apartment—and Leigh gave one leap, one blow. He caught the short, heavy body as it fell, grabbed at the sagging gun, lowered the dead weight to the floor of the corridor; and then, for a grim, tense moment, he stood like a great animal, straining for sound.

Silence! He studied the bland panels of the doorway to the apartment, as if by sheer, savage intentness he would penetrate their golden, beautiful grained opaqueness.

It was the silence that struck him again after a moment, the emptiness of the long, tunnel-like corridors. He thought, amazed: Was it possible father and daughter actually lived here without companions or servants or any human association? And that they had some idea that they could withstand the attack of the mighty and terrible Dreeghs?

They had a lot of stuff here, of course: Earthlike gravity and—and, by heaven, he'd better get going before the girl acquired impatience and came out with one of her fancy weapons. What he must do was quite simple, unconnected with any nonsense of spring, hynotic or otherwise.

He must find the combination automobile-spaceship in which—*Mr.* Patrick—had escaped him that night after they left Constantine's. And with that tiny ship, he must try to slip out of Ungarn's meteorite, sneak through the Dreegh line, and so head back for Earth.

What a fool he had been, a mediocre human being, mixing in such fast, brainy company. The world was full of more normal, thoroughly dumb girls. Why in hell wasn't he safely married to one of them and—and damn it, it was time he got busy.

He began laboriously to drag Hanardy along the smooth flooring. Halfway to the nearest corner, the man stirred. Instantly, quite coolly, Leigh struck him with the revolver butt, hard. This was not time for squeamishness.

The pilot dropped; and the rest was simple. He deserted the body as soon as he had pulled it out of sight behind the corner, and raced along the hallway, trying doors. The first four wouldn't open. At the fifth, he pulled up in a dark consideration.

It was impossible that the whole place was locked up. Two people in an isolated meteorite wouldn't go around perpetually locking and unlocking doors. There must be a trick catch.

There was. The fifth door yielded to a simple pressure on a tiny, half-hidden push button, that had seemed an integral part of the design of the latch. He stepped through the entrance, then started back in brief, terrible shock.

The room had no ceiling. Above him was—space. An ice-cold blast of air swept at him.

He had a flashing glimpse of gigantic machines in the room, machines that dimly resembled the ultramodern astronomical observatory on the moon that he had visited on opening day two days before. That one, swift look was all Leigh allowed himself. Then he stepped back into the hallway. The door of the observatory closed automatically in his face.

He stood there, chagrined. Silly fool! The very fact that cold air had blown at him showed that the open effect of the ceiling was only an illusion of invisible glass. Good Lord, in that room might be wizard telescopes that could see to the stars. Or—an ugly thrill raced along his spine—he might have seen the Dreeghs attacking.

He shook out of his system the brief, abnormal desire to look again. This was no time for distractions. For, by now, the girl must know that something was wrong.

At top speed, Leigh ran to the sixth door. It opened into a little cubbyhole. A blank moment passed before he recognized what it was.

An elevator!

He scrambled in. The farther he got away from the residential floor, the less the likelihood of quick discovery.

He turned to close the door, and saw that it was shutting automatically. It clicked softly; the elevator immediately began to go up. Piercingly sharp doubt came to Leigh. The machine was apparently geared to go to some definite point. And that could be very bad.

His eyes searched hastily for controls. But nothing was visible. Gun poised, he stood grim and alert as the elevator stopped. The door slid open.

Leigh stared. There was no room. The door opened—onto blackness.

Not the blackness of space with its stars. Or a dark room, half revealed by the light from the elevator. But—blackness! Impenetrable.

Leigh put a tentative hand forward, half expecting to feel a solid object. But as his hand entered the black area, it vanished. He jerked it back, and stared at it, dismayed. It shone with a light of its own, all the bones plainly visible.

Swiftly, the light faded, the skin became opaque, but his whole arm pulsed with a pattern of pain.

The stark, terrible thought came that this could be a death chamber. After all, the elevator had deliberately brought him here; it might not have been automatic. Outside forces could have directed it. True, he had stepped in of his own free will, but—

Fool, fool!

He laughed bitterly, braced himself—and then it happened.

There was a flash out of the blackness. Something that sparkled vividly, something material that blazed a brilliant path to his forehead—and drew itself inside his head. And then—

He was no longer in the elevator. On either side of him stretched a long corridor. The stocky Hanardy was just reaching for some tiny lights beside the door of Patricia Ungarn's apartment.

The man's fingers touched one of the lights. It dimmed. Softly, the door opened. A young woman with proud, insolent eyes and a queenlike bearing stood there.

"Father wants you down on Level 4," she said to Hanardy. "One of the energy screens has gone down; and he needs some machine work before he can put up another."

She turned to Leigh; her voice took on metallic overtones as she said: *"Mr. Leigh, you can come in!"*

The crazy part of it was that he walked in with scarcely a physical tremor. A cool breeze caressed his cheeks; and there was the liltingly sweet sound of birds singing in the distance. Leigh stood stockstill for a moment after he had entered, dazed partly by the wonders of the room and the unbelievable sunlit garden beyond the French windows, partly, by—what?

What had happened to him?

Gingerly, he put his hands to his head, and felt his forehead, then his whole head. But nothing was wrong, not a contusion, not a pain. He grew aware of the girl staring at him, and realization came that his actions must seem unutterably queer.

"What is the matter with you?" the girl asked.

Leigh looked at her with abrupt, grim suspicion. He snapped harshly: "Don't pull that innocent stuff. I've been up in the blackness room, and all I've got to say is, if you're going to kill me, don't skulk behind artificial night and other trickery."

The girl's eyes, he saw, were narrowed, unpleasantly cold. "I don't know what you're trying to pretend," she said icily. "I assure you it will not postpone the death we have to deal you."

She hesitated, then finished sharply: "The *what* room?"

Leigh explained grimly, puzzled by her puzzlement, then annoyed by the contemptuous smile that grew into her face. She cut him off curtly: "I've never heard a less balanced story. If your intention was to astound me and delay your death with that improbable tale, it has failed. You must be mad. You didn't knock out Hanardy, because when I opened the door, Hanardy was there, and I sent him down to Father."

"See here!" Leigh began. He stopped wildly. By heaven, Hanardy had been there as she opened the door!

And yet earlier—

WHEN?

Doggedly, Leigh pushed the thought on: Earlier, he had attacked Hanardy. And then he—Leigh—had gone up in an elevator; and then, somehow, back and—

Shakily, he felt his head again. And it was absolutely normal. Only, he thought, there was something inside it that sparkled.

Something—

With a start, he grew aware that the girl was quite deliberately drawing a gun from a pocket of her simple white dress. He stared at the weapon, and before its gleaming menace, his thoughts faded, all except the deadly consciousness that what he had said had delayed her several minutes now. It was the only thing that could delay her further until, somehow—

The vague hope wouldn't finish. Urgently, he said, "I'm going to assume you're genuinely puzzled by my words. Let's begin at the beginning. There is such a room, is there not?"

"Please," said the girl wearily, "let us not have any of your logic. My I. Q. is 243, yours is 112. So I assure you I am quite capable of reasoning from any beginning you can think of."

She went on, her low voice as curt as the sound of struck steel: "There is no 'blackness' room, as you call it, no sparkling thing that crawls inside a human head. There is but one fact: The Dreeghs in their visit to your hotel room, hypnotized you; and this curious mind illusion can only be a result of that hypnotism—don't argue with me—"

With a savage gesture of her gun, she cut off his attempt to speak. "There's no time. For some reason, the Dreeghs did something to you. Why? What did you see in those rooms?"

Even as he explained and described, Leigh was thinking that he'd have to catch hold of himself, get a plan, however risky, and carry it through. The purpose was tight and cold in his mind as he obeyed her motion, and went ahead of her into the corridor. It was there, an icy determination, as he counted the doors from the corner where he had left the unconscious Hanardy.

"One, two, three, four, *five*. This door!" he said.

"Open it!" The girl gestured.

He did so; and his lower jaw sagged. He was staring into a fine, cozy room filled with shelf on shelf of beautifully bound books. There were comfortable chairs, a magnificent rag rug and—

It was the girl who closed the door firmly and—he trembled with the tremendousness of the opportunity—she walked ahead of him to the sixth door.

"And this is your elevator?"

Leigh nodded mutely; and because his whole body was shaking, he was only dimly surprised that there was no elevator, but a long, empty, silent corridor.

The girl was standing with her back partly to him; and if he hit her, it would knock her hard against the door jamb and—

The sheer brutality of the thought was what stopped him, held him for the barest second—as the girl whirled, and looked straight into his eyes.

Her gun was up, pointing steadily. "Not that way," she said quietly. "For a moment I was wishing you would have the nerve to try it. But, after all, that would be the weak way for me."

Her eyes glowed with a fierce pride. "After all, I've killed before through necessity, and hated it. You can see yourself that, because of what the Dreeghs have done to you, it is necessary. So—"

Her voice took on a whiplash quality. "So back to my rooms. I have a space lock there to get rid of your body. Get going!"

It was the emptiness, the silence except for the faint click of their shoes that caught at Leigh's nerves, as he walked hopelessly back to the apartment. This meteorite hurtling darkly through the remote wastes of the Solar System, pursued and attacked by deadly ships from the fixed stars, and himself inside it, under sentence of death, the executioner to be a girl—

And that was the devastating part. He couldn't begin to argue with this damnable young woman, for every word would sound like pleading. The very thought of mentally getting down on his knees to any woman was paralyzing.

The singing of the birds, as he entered the apartment, perked him violently out of his black passion. Abruptly marveling, he walked to the stately French windows and stared at the glorious summery garden.

At least two acres of green wonder spread before him, a blaze of flowers, trees where gorgeously colored birds fluttered and trilled, a wide, deep pool of green, green water, and over all, the glory of brilliant sunshine.

It was the sunshine that held Leigh finally; and he stood almost breathless for a long minute before it seemed that he had the solution. He said in a hushed voice, without turning:

"The roof—is an arrangement—of magnifying glass. It makes the Sun as big as on Earth. Is that the—"

"You'd better turn around," came the hostile, vibrant voice from behind him. "I don't shoot people in the back. And I want to get this over with."

It was the moralistic smugness of her words that shook every muscle in Leigh's body. He whirled, and raged: "You damned little Klugg. You can't shoot me in the back, eh? Oh, no! And you couldn't possibly shoot me while I was attacking you because that would be the weak way. It's all got to be made tight with your conscience."

He stopped so short that, if he had been running instead of talking, he would have stumbled. Figuratively, almost literally, he saw Patricia Ungarn for the first time since his arrival. His mind had been so concentrated, so absorbed by deadly things that—

—For the first time as a woman.

Leigh drew a long breath. Dressed as a man, she had been darkly handsome in an extremely youthful fashion. Now she wore a simple, snow-white sports dress. It was scarcely more than a tunic, and came well above her knees.

Her hair shone with a brilliant brownness, and cascaded down to her shoulders. Her bare arms and legs gleamed a deep, healthy tan. Sandals pure white graced her feet. Her face—

The impression of extraordinary beauty yielded to the amazing fact that her perfect cheeks were flushing vividly. The girl snapped: "Don't you dare use that word to me."

She must have been utterly beside herself. Her fury was such an enormous fact that Leigh gasped; and he couldn't have stopped himself from saying what he did, if the salvation of his soul had depended on it.

"Klugg!" he said, "Klugg, Klugg, Klugg! So you realize now that the Dreeghs had you down pat, that all your mighty pretension was simply your Klugg mind demanding pretentious compensation for a dreary, lonely life. You had to think you were somebody, and yet all the time you must have known they'd only ship the tenth-raters to these remote posts. Klugg, not even Lennel; the Dreegh woman wouldn't even grant you Lennel status, whatever that is. And she'd know. Because if you're I. Q. 243, the Dreeghs were 400. You've realized that, too, haven't you?"

"Shut up! Or I'll kill you by inches!" said Patricia Ungarn; and Leigh was amazed to see that she was as white as a sheet. The astounded realization came that he had struck, not only the emotional Achilles heel of this strange and terrible young woman, but the very vital roots of her mental existence.

"So," he said deliberately, "the high morality is growing dim. Now you can torture me to death without a qualm. And to think that I came here to ask you to marry me because I thought a Klugg and a human being might get along."

"You what?" said the girl. Then she sneered. "So that was the form of their hypnotism. They would use some simple impulse for a simple human mind.

"But now I think we've had just about enough. I know just the type of thoughts that come to a male human in love; and even the realization that you're not responsible makes the very idea none the less bearable. I feel sickened, utterly insulted. Know, please, that my future husband is arriving with the reinforcements three weeks from now. He will be trained to take over Father's work—"

"Another Klugg!" said Leigh, and the girl turned shades whiter.

Leigh stood utterly thunderstruck. In all his life, he had never gotten anybody going the way he had this young girl. The intellectual mask was off, and underneath was a seething mass of emotions bitter beyond the power of words to express. Here was evidence of a life so lonely that it strained his imagination. Her every word showed an incredible pent-up masochism as well as sadism, for she was torturing herself as well as him.

And he couldn't stop now to feel sorry for her. His life was at stake, and only more words could postpone death—or bring the swift and bearable surcease of a gun fired in sudden passion. He hammered on grimly: "I'd like to ask one question. How did you find out my I. Q. was 112? What special interest made you inquire about that? Is it possible that, all by yourself here, you, too, had a special type of thought, and that, though your intellect rejected the very idea of such lowly love, its existence is the mainspring behind your fantastic determination to kill, rather than cure me? I—"

"That will do," interrupted Patricia Ungarn.

It required one lengthy moment for Leigh to realize that in those few short seconds she had pulled herself completely together.

He stared in gathering alarm, as her gun motioned toward a door he had not seen before.

She said curtly, "I suppose there is a solution other than death. That is, immediate death. And I have decided to accept the resultant loss of my spaceship."

She nodded at the door. "It's there in the air lock. It works very simply. The steering wheel pulls up or down or sideways, and that's the way the ship will go. Just step on the accelerator, and the machine will go forward. The decelerator is the left pedal. The automobile wheels fold in automatically as soon as they lift from the floor.

"Now, get going. I need hardly tell you that the Dreeghs will probably catch you. But you can't stay here. That's obvious."

"Thanks!" That was all Leigh allowed himself to say. He had exploded an emotional powder keg, and he dared not tamper even a single word further. There was a tremendous psychological mystery here, but it was not for him to solve.

Suddenly shaky from realization of what was still ahead of him, he walked gingerly toward the air lock. And then—

It happened!

He had a sense of unutterable nausea. There was a wild swaying through blackness and—

He was standing at the paneled doorway leading from the corridor to Patricia Ungarn's apartment. Beside him stood Hanardy. The door opened. The young woman who stood

there said strangely familiar words to Hanardy, about going
down to the fourth level to fix an energy screen. Then she
turned to Leigh, and in a voice hard and metallic said, "*Mr.
Leigh, you can come in.*"

VII

The crazy part of it was that he walked in with scarcely a
physical tremor. A cool breeze caressed his cheeks; and there
was the liltingly sweet sound of birds singing in the distance.
Leigh stood stockstill for a moment after he had entered; by
sheer will power he emptied the terrible daze out of his mind,
and bent, mentally, into the cyclone path of complete
memory. Everything was there suddenly, the way the Dreeghs
had come to his hotel apartment and ruthlessly forced him to
their will, the way the "blackness" room had affected him,
and how the girl had spared his life.

For some reason, the whole scene with the girl had been
unsatisfactory to—Jeel; and it was now, fantastically, to be
repeated.

That thought ended. The entire tremendous reality of what
had happened yielded to a vastly greater fact:

There was—something—inside his head, a distinctly physical something; and in a queer, horrible, inexperienced way,
his mind was instinctively fighting—it. The result was ghastly
confusion. Which hurt him, not the thing.

Whatever it was, rested inside his head, unaffected by his
brain's feverish contortions, cold, aloof, watching.

Watching.

Madly, then, he realized what it was. Another mind. Leigh
shrank from the thought as from the purest destroying fire.
He tensed his brain. For a moment the frenzy of his horror
was so great that his face twisted with the anguish of his efforts. And everything blurred.

Exhausted finally, he simply stood there. And the thing-
mind was still inside his head.

Untouched.

What had happened to him?

Shakily, Leigh put his hands up to his forehead; then he
felt his whole head; there was a vague idea in him that if he
pressed—

He jerked his hands down with an unspoken curse. Damnation on damnation, he was even repeating the actions of

this scene. He grew aware of the girl staring at him. He heard her say, "What is the matter with you?"

It was the sound of the words, exactly the same words, that did it. He smiled wryly. His mind drew back from the abyss, where it had teetered.

He was sane again.

Gloomy recognition came then that his brain was still a long way down; sane yes, but dispirited. It was only too obvious that the girl had no memory of the previous scene, or she wouldn't be parroting. She'd—

That thought stopped, too. Because a strange thing was happening. The mind inside him stirred, and looked through his—Leigh's—eyes. Looked intently.

Intently.

The room and the girl in it changed, not physically, but subjectively, in what he saw, in the—details.

Details burned at him; furniture and design that a moment before had seemed a flowing, artistic whole, abruptly showed flaws, hideous errors in taste and arrangement and structure.

His gaze flashed out to the garden, and in instants tore it to mental shreds. Never in all his existence had he seen or felt criticism on such a high, devastating scale. Only—

Only it wasn't criticism. Actually. The mind was indifferent. It saw things. Automatically, it saw some of the possibilities; and by comparison the reality suffered.

It was not a matter of anything being hopelessly bad. The wrongness was frequently a subtle thing. Birds not suited, for a dozen reasons, to their environment. Shrubs that added infinitesimal discord not harmony to the superb garden.

The mind flashed back from the garden; and this time, for the first time, studied the girl.

On all Earth, no woman had ever been so piercingly examined. The structure of her body and her face, to Leigh so finely, proudly shaped, so gloriously patrician—found low grade now.

An excellent example of low-grade development in isolation.

That was the thought, not contemptuous, not derogatory, simply an impression by an appallingly direct mind that saw—overtones, realities behind realities, a thousand facts where one showed.

There followed crystal-clear awareness of the girl's psychology, objective admiration for the system of isolated upbringing that made Klugg girls such fine breeders; and then—

Purpose!

Instantly carried out. Leigh took three swift steps toward
the girl. He was aware of her snatching at the gun in her
pocket, and there was the sheerest startled amazement on her
face. Then he had her.

Her muscles writhed like steel springs. But they were
hopeless against his superstrength, his superspeed. He tied her
with some wire he had noticed in a half-opened clothes
closet.

Then he stepped back, and to Leigh came the shocked personal thought of the incredible thing that had happened, comprehension that all this, which seemed so normal, was
actually so devastatingly superhuman, so swift that—seconds
only had passed since he came into the room.

Private thought ended. He grew aware of the mind, contemplating what it had done, and what it must do before the
meteorite would be completely under control.

Vampire victory was near.

There was a phase of walking along empty corridors, down
several flights of stairs. The vague, dull thought came to
Leigh, his own personal thought, that the Dreegh seemed to
know completely the interior of the meteorite.

Somehow, during the periods of—transition, of time
manipulation, the creature-mind must have used his, Leigh's,
body to explore the vast tomb of a place *thoroughly*. And
now, with utter simplicity of purpose—*he* was heading for
the machine shops on the fourth level, where Professor Ungarn and Hanardy labored to put up another energy defense
screen.

He found Hanardy alone, working at a lathe that
throbbed—and the sound made it easy to sneak up—

The professor was in a vast room, where great engines
hummed a strange, deep tune of titanic power. He was a tall
man, and his back was turned to the door as Leigh entered.

But he was immeasurably quicker than Hanardy, quicker
even than the girl. He sensed danger. He whirled with a catlike agility. Literally. And succumbed instantly to muscles
that could have torn him limb from limb. It was during the
binding of the man's hands that Leigh had time for an impression.

In the photographs that Leigh had seen, as he had told the

Dreegh, Merla, in the hotel, the professor's face had been sensitive, tired-looking, withal noble. He was more than that, tremendously more.

The man radiated power, as no photograph could show it, good power in contrast to the savage, malignant, immensely great power of the Dreegh.

The sense of power faded before the aura of—weariness. Cosmic weariness. It was a lined, an amazingly lined face. In a flash, Leigh remembered what the Dreegh woman had said; and it was all there: deep-graven lines of tragedy and untold mental suffering, interlaced with a curious peacefulness, like—resignation.

On that night months ago, he had asked the Dreegh woman: Resignation to what? And now, here in this tortured, kindly face was the answer:

Resignation to hell.

Queerly, an unexpected second answer trickled in his mind: Morons; they're Galactic morons. Kluggs.

The thought seemed to have no source; but it gathered with all the fury of a storm. Professor Ungarn and his daughter were Kluggs, *morons* in the incredible Galactic sense. No wonder the girl had reacted like a crazy person. Obviously born here, she must have only guessed the truth in the last two months.

The I. Q. of human morons wavered between seventy-five and ninety, of Kluggs possibly between two hundred twenty-five and, say, two hundred forty-three.

Two hundred forty-three. What kind of civilization was this Galactic—if Dreeghs were four hundred and—

Somebody, of course, had to do the dreary, routine work of civilization; and Kluggs and Lennels and their kind were obviously elected. No wonder they looked like morons with that weight of inferiority to influence their very nerve and muscle structure. No wonder whole planets were kept in ignorance—

Leigh left the professor tied hand and foot, and began to turn off power switches. Some of the great motors were slowing noticeably as he went out of that mighty engine room; the potent hum of power dimmed.

Back in the girl's room, he entered the air lock, climbed into the small automobile spaceship—and launched into the night.

Instantly, the gleaming mass of meteorite receded into the

darkness behind him. Instantly, magnetic force rays caught his tiny craft, and drew it remorselessly toward the hundred and fifty foot, cigar-shaped machine that flashed out of the darkness.

He felt the spy rays; and he must have been recognized. For another ship flashed up to claim him.

Air locks opened noiselessly—and shut. Sickly, Leigh stared at the two Dreeghs, the tall man and the tall woman; and, as from a great distance, heard himself explaining what he had done.

Dimly, hopelessly, he wondered why he should have to explain. Then he heard Jeel say:

"Merla, this is the most astoundingly successful case of hypnotism in our existence. He'd done—everything. Even the tiniest thoughts we put into his mind have been carried out to the letter. And the proof is, the screens are going down. With the control of this station, we can hold out even after the Galactic warships arrive—and fill our tankers and our energy reservoirs for ten thousand years. Do you hear, *ten thousand years?*"

His excitement died. He smiled with sudden, dry understanding as he looked at the woman. Then he said laconically:

"My dear, the reward is all yours. We could have broken down those screens in another twelve hours, but it would have meant the destruction of the meteorite. This victory is so much greater. Take your reporter. Satisfy your craving—while the rest of us prepare for the occupation. Meanwhile, I'll tie him up for you."

Leigh thought, a cold, remote thought: The kiss of death—

He shivered in sudden, appalled realization of what he had done—

He lay on the couch, where Jeel had tied him. He was surprised, after a moment, to notice that, though the mind had withdrawn into the background of his brain—it was still there, cold, steely, abnormally conscious.

The wonder came: what possible satisfaction could Jeel obtain from experiencing the mortal thrill of death with him? These people were utterly abnormal, of course, but—

The wonder died like dry grass under a heat ray, as the woman came into the room, and glided toward him. She smiled; she sat down on the edge of the couch.

"So here you are," she said.

She was, Leigh thought, like a tigress. There was purpose in every cunning muscle of her long body. In surprise he saw that she had changed her dress. She wore a sleek, flimsy, sheeny, tight-fitting gown that set off in startling fashion her golden hair and starkly white face. Utterly fascinated, he watched her. Almost automatically, he said, "Yes, I'm here."

Silly words. But he didn't feel silly. Tenseness came the moment he had spoken. It was her eyes that did it. For the first time since he had first seen her, her eyes struck him like a blow. Blue eyes, and steady. So steady. Not the steady frankness of honesty. But steady—like dead eyes.

A chill grew on Leigh, a special, extra chill, adding to the ice that was already there inside him; and the unholy thought came that this was a dead woman—artificially kept alive by the blood and *life* of dead men and women.

She smiled, but the bleakness remained in those cold fish eyes. No smile, no warmth could ever bring light to that chill, beautiful countenance. But she smiled the form of a smile, and she said, "We Dreeghs live a hard, lonely life. So lonely that sometimes I cannot help thinking our struggle to remain alive is a blind, mad thing. We're what we are through no fault of our own. It happened during an interstellar flight that took place a million years ago—"

She stopped, almost hopelessly. "It seems longer. It must be longer. I've really lost track."

She went on, suddenly grim, as if the memory, the very telling, brought a return of horror: "We were among several thousand holidayers who were caught in the gravitational pull of a sun, afterward called the Dreegh sun.

"Its rays, immensely dangerous to human life, infected us all. It was discovered that only continuous blood transfusions, and the life force of other human beings, could save us. For a while we received donations; then the government decided to have us destroyed as hopeless incurables.

"We were all young, terribly young and in love with life; some hundreds of us had been expecting the sentence, and we still had friends in the beginning. We escaped, and we've been fighting ever since to stay alive."

And still he could feel no sympathy. It was odd, for all the thoughts she undoubtedly wanted him to have, came. Picture of a bleak, endless existence in spaceships, staring out into the perpetual night; all life circumscribed by the tireless, abnormal needs of bodies gone mad from ravenous disease.

It was all there, all the emotional pictures. But no emotions came. She was too cold; the years and the devil's hunt had stamped her soul and her eyes and her face.

And besides, her body seemed tenser now, leaning toward him, bending forward closer, closer, till he could hear her slow, measured breathing. Even her eyes suddenly held the vaguest inner light—her whole being quivered with the chill tensity of her purpose; when she spoke, she almost breathed the words:

"I want you to kiss me, and don't be afraid. I shall keep you alive for days, but I must have response, not passivity. You're a bachelor, at least thirty. You won't have any more morals about that matter than I. But you must let your whole body yield."

He didn't believe it. Her face hovered six inches above his; and there was such a ferocity of suppressed eagerness in her that it could only mean death.

Her lips were pursed, as if to suck, and they quivered with a strange, tense, trembling desire, utterly unnatural, almost obscene. Her nostrils dilated at every breath—and no normal woman who had kissed as often as she must have in all her years could feel like that, if that was all she expected to get.

"Quick!" she said breathlessly. "Yield, yield!"

Leigh scarcely heard; for that other mind that had been lingering in his brain, surged forward in its incredible way. He heard himself say, "I'll trust your promise because I can't resist such an appeal. You can kiss your head off. I guess I can stand it—"

There was a blue flash, an agonizing burning sensation that spread suddenly to every nerve of his body.

The anguish became a series of tiny pains, like small needles piercing a thousand bits of his flesh. Tingling, writhing a little, amazed that he was still alive, Leigh opened his eyes.

He felt a wave of purely personal surprise.

The woman lay slumped, lips half twisted off of his, body collapsed hard across his chest. And the mind, that blazing mind was there, watching—as the tall figure of the Dreegh man sauntered into the room, stiffened, and then darted forward.

He jerked her limp form into his arms. There was the same kind of blue flash as their lips met, from the man to the woman. She stirred finally, moaning. He shook her brutally.

"You wretched fool!" he raged. "How did you let a thing like that happen? You would have been dead in another minute, if I hadn't come along."

"I—don't—know." Her voice was thin and old. She sank down to the floor at his feet, and slumped there like a tired old woman. Her blonde hair straggled, and looked curiously faded. "I don't know, Jeel. I tried to get his life force, and he got mine instead. He—"

She stopped. Her blue eyes widened. She staggered to her feet. "Jeel, he must be a spy. No human being could do a thing like that to me.

"Jeel"—there was sudden terror in her voice—"Jeel, get out of this room. Don't you realize? He's got my energy in him. He's lying there now, and whatever has control of him has my energy to work with—"

"All right, all right." He patted her fingers. "I assure you he's only a human being. And he's got your energy. You made a mistake, and the flow went the wrong way. But it would take much more than that for *anyone* to use a human body successfully against us. So—"

"You don't understand!"

Her voice shook. "Jeel, I've been cheating. I don't know what got into me, but I couldn't get enough life force. Every time I was able, during the four times we stayed on Earth, I sneaked out.

"I caught men on the street. I don't know exactly how many because I dissolved their bodies after I was through with them. But there were dozens. And he's got all the energy I collected, enough for scores of years, enough for—don't you see?—enough for *them*."

"My dear!" The Dreegh shook her violently, as a doctor would an hysterical woman. "For a million years, the great ones of Galactic have ignored us and—"

He paused. A black frown twisted his long face. He whirled like the tiger man he was, snatching at his gun—as Leigh stood up.

The man Leigh was no longer surprised at—anything. At the way the hard cords fell rotted from his wrists and legs. At the way the Dreegh froze rigid after one look into his eyes. For the first shock of the tremendous, the almost cataclysmic, truth was already in him.

"There is only one difference," said Leigh in a voice so vibrant that the top of his head shivered from the unaccustomed violence of sound. "This time there are two hundred twenty-seven Dreegh ships gathered in one concentrated area. The rest—and our records show only a dozen others—we can safely leave to our police patrols."

The Great Galactic, who had been William Leigh, smiled darkly and walked toward his captives. "It has been a most interesting experiment in deliberate splitting of personality. Three years ago, our time manipulators showed this opportunity of destroying the Dreeghs, who hitherto had escaped by reason of the vastness of our galaxy.

"And so I came to Earth, and here built up the character of William Leigh, reporter, complete with family and past history. It was necessary to withdraw into a special compartment of the brain some nine-tenths of my mind, and to drain completely an equal percentage of life energy.

"That was the difficulty. How to replace that energy in sufficient degree at the proper time, without playing the role of vampire. I constructed a number of energy caches, but naturally at no time had we been able to see all the future. We could not see the details of what was to transpire aboard this ship, or in my hotel room that night you came, or under Constantine's restaurant.

"Besides, if I had possessed full energy as I approached this ship, your spy ray would have registered it; and you would instantly have destroyed my small automobile-spaceship.

"My first necessity, accordingly, was to come to the meteorite, and obtain an initial control over my own body through the medium of what my Earth personality called the 'blackness' room.

"That Earth personality offered unexpected difficulties. In three years it had gathered momentum as a personality, and that impetus made it necessary to repeat a scene with Patricia Ungarn, and to appear directly as another conscious mind, in order to convince Leigh that he must yield. The rest of course was a matter of gaining additional life energy after boarding your ship, which"—he bowed slightly at the muscularly congealed body of the woman—"which she supplied me.

"I have explained all this because of the fact that a mind will accept complete control only if full understanding of— defeat—is present. I must finally inform you, therefore, that you are to remain alive for the next few days, during which time you will assist me in making personal contact with your friends."

He made a gesture of dismissal: "Return to your normal existence. I have still to coordinate my two personalities completely, and that does not require your presence."

The Dreeghs went out blank-eyed, almost briskly; and the two minds in one body were—alone!

For Leigh, the Leigh of Earth, the first desperate shock was past. The room was curiously dim, as if he was staring out through eyes that were no longer—his!

He thought, with a horrible effort at self-control: "I've got to fight. Some *thing* is trying to possess my body. All the rest is lie."

A soothing mind-pulsation stole into the shadowed chamber where his—self—was cornered:

"No lie, but wondrous truth. You have not seen what the Dreeghs saw and felt, for you are inside this body, and know not that it has come marvelously *alive*, unlike anything that your petty dreams on Earth could begin to conceive. You must accept your high destiny, else the sight of your own body will be a terrible thing to you. Be calm, be braver than you've ever been, and pain will turn to joy."

Calm came out. His mind quivered in its dark corner, abnormally conscious of strange and unnatural pressures that pushed in at it like winds out of unearthly night. For a moment of terrible fear, it funked that pressing night, then forced back to sanity, and had another thought of its own, a grimly cunning thought:

The devilish interloper was arguing. Could that mean—his mind rocked with hope—that coordination was impossible without *his* yielding to clever persuasion?

Never would he yield.

"Think," whispered the alien mind, "think of being one valuable facet of a mind with an I. Q. 1200, think of yourself as having played a role; and now you are returning to normalcy, a normalcy of unlimited power. You have been an actor completely absorbed in your role, but the play is over; you are alone in your dressing room removing the grease paint; your mood of the play is fading, fading, fading—"

"Go to hell!" said William Leigh, loudly. "I'm William Leigh, I. Q. 112, satisfied to be just what I am. I don't give a damn whether you built me up from the component elements of your brain, or whether I was born normally. I can just see what you're trying to do with that hypnotic suggestion stuff, but it isn't working. I'm here, I'm myself, and I stay myself. Go find yourself another body, if you're so smart."

Silence settled where his voice had been; and the emptiness, the utter lack of sound brought a sharp twinge of fear greater than that which he had had before he spoke.

He was so intent on that inner struggle that he was not aware of outer movement until—

With a start he grew aware that he was staring out of a port window. Night spread there, the living night of space.

A trick, he thought in an agony of fear; a trick somehow designed to add to the corroding power of hypnotism.

A trick! He tried to jerk back—and, terrifyingly, couldn't. His body wouldn't move. Instantly, then, he tried to speak, to crash through that enveloping blanket of unholy silence. But no sound came.

Not a muscle, nor a finger stirred; not a single nerve so much as trembled.

He was alone.

Cut off in his little corner of brain.

Lost.

Yes, lost, came a strangely pitying sibilation of thought, lost to a cheap, sordid existence, lost to a life whose end is visible from the hour of birth, lost to a civilization that has already had to be saved from itself a thousand times. Even you, I think, can see that all this is lost to you forever—

Leigh thought starkly: The *thing* was trying by a repetition of ideas, by showing evidence of defeat, to lay the foundations of further defeat. It was the oldest trick of simple hypnotism for simple people. And he couldn't let it work—

You have, urged the mind inexorably, accepted the fact that you were playing a role; and now you have recognized our oneness, and are giving up the role. The proof of this recognition on your part is that you have yielded control of—our—body.

—Our body, *our* body, OUR body—

The words re-echoed like some Gargantuan sound through his brain, then merged swiftly into that calm, other-mind pulsation.

—Concentration. All intellect derives from capacity to concentrate; and, progressively, the body itself shows *life*, reflects and focuses that gathering, vaulting power.

—One more step remains: You must see—

..Amazingly, then, he was staring into a mirror. Where it had come from, he had no memory. It was there in front of

him, where, an instant before, had been a black porthole—
and there was an image in the mirror, shapeless at first to his
blurred vision.

Deliberately—he felt the enormous deliberateness—the
vision was cleared for him. He *saw*—and then he didn't.

His brain wouldn't look. It twisted in a mad desperation,
like a body buried alive, and briefly, horrendously conscious
of its fate. Insanely, it fought away from the blazing thing in
the mirror. So awful was the effort, so titanic the fear, that it
began to gibber mentally, its consciousness to whirl dizzily,
like a wheel spinning faster, faster—

The wheel shattered into ten thousand aching fragments.
Darkness came, blacker than Galactic night. And there was—
Oneness!

PROOF

Astounding,

June

by Hal Clement (1922-   )

Hal Clement (Harry Clement Stubbs) has taught science at the secondary school level all of his adult life and he knows his subject thoroughly. The percentage of science fiction writers who write convincingly about the technical details of scientific extrapolation is small indeed—the so-called "hard" sf writers are a tiny and rather exclusive club, and Hal Clement would certainly have to be considered one of the pioneering founders of this organization. His reputation rests on his novels, especially Mission of Gravity *(1954),* Cycle of Fire *(1957), and* Iceworld *(1953) His 1950 novel,* Needle, *was one of the first successful fusions of the sf and mystery genres.*

"Proof" is one of very rare stories that portray intelligent life on the Sun, *and it was Hal Clement's first published fiction.*

(I'm always afraid to describe Harry because I have the distinct feeling nobody will believe me. To begin with, he's highly intelligent, but we expect that of a science fiction writer. He knows his science thoroughly, at least as well as anyone in the field. He doesn't smoke, he doesn't drink, I've never heard him use bad language, or raise his voice, or say anything unkind. He's quiet, honest, helpful. Oh, heck, go through the list of virtues a boy scout is supposed to have, and he has them all. And here's the most unbelievable thing—with all that virtue, he manages to be so unobtrusive about it that I don't think he has an enemy in the world. —I. A.

Kron held his huge freighter motionless, feeling forward for outside contact. The tremendous interplay of magnetic and electrostatic fields just beyond the city's edge was as clearly perceptible to his senses as the city itself—a mile-wide disk ringed with conical field towers, stretching away behind and to each side. The ship was poised between two of the towers; immediately behind it was the field from which Kron had just taken off. The area was covered with cradles of various forms—cup-shaped receptacles which held city craft like Kron's own; long, boat-shaped hollows wherein reposed the cigarlike vessels which plied between the cities; and towering skeleton frameworks which held upright the slender double cones that hurtled across the dark, lifeless regions between stars.

Beyond the landing field was the city proper; the surface of the disk was covered with geometrically shaped buildings—cones, cylinders, prisms and hemispheres—jumbled together.

Kron could "see" all this as easily as a human being in an airplane can see New York; but no human eyes could have perceived this city, even if a man could have existed anywhere near it. The city, buildings and all, glowed a savage, white heat; and about and beyond it—a part of it, to human eyes—raged the equally dazzling incandescent gases of the solar photosphere.

The freighter was preparing to launch itself into that fiery ocean; Kron was watching the play of the artificial reaction fields that supported the city, preparatory to plunging through them at a safe moment.

There was considerable risk of being flattened against the edge of the disk if an inauspicous choice was made, but Kron was an experienced flier, and slipped past the barrier with a sudden, hurtling acceleration that would have pulped any body of flesh and bone. The outer fringe of the field flung the globe sharply downward; then it was free, and the city was dwindling above them.

Kron and four others remained at their posts; the rest of the crew of thirty relaxed, their spherical bodies lying passive in the cuplike rests distributed through the ship, bathing in the fierce radiance on which those bodies fed, and which was continually streaming from a three-inch spheroid at the cen-

ter of the craft. That an artificial source of energy should be
needed in such an environment may seem strange, but to
these creatures the outer layers of the sun were far more inhospitable to life than is the stratosphere of Earth to human
beings.

They had evolved far down near the solar core, where
pressures and temperatures were such that matter existed in
the "collapsed" state characteristic of the entire mass of white
dwarf stars. Their bodies were simply constructed: a matrix
of close-packed electrons—really an unimaginably dense electrostatic field, possessing quasi-solid properties—surrounded a
core of neutrons, compacted to the ultimate degree. Radiation of sufficient energy, falling on the "skin," was stabilized,
altered to the pattern and structure of neutrons; the tiny particles of neutronium which resulted were borne along a circu-
latory system—of magnetic fields, instead of blood—to the
nucleus, where it was stored.

The face had evolved to the point where no material ap-
pendages were needed. Projected beams and fields of force
were their limbs, powered by the annihilation of some of
their own neutron substance. Their strange senses gave them
awareness not only of electromagnetic rediation, permitting
them to "see" in a more or less normal fashion, but also of
energies still undreamed of by human scientists. Kron, now
hundreds of miles below the city, was still dimly aware of its
location, though radio waves, light, and gamma rays were all
hopelessly fogged in the clouds of free electrons. At his goal,
far down in the solar interior, "seeing" conditions would be
worse—anything more than a few hundred yards distant
would be quite undetectable even to him.

Poised beside Kron, near the center of the spheroidal Sunship, was another being. Its body was ovoid in shape, like
that of the Solarian, but longer and narrower, while the ends
were tipped with pyramidal structures of neutronium, which
projected through the "skin." A second, fainter static aura
outside the principal surface enveloped the creature; and as
the crew relaxed in their cups, a beam of energy from this
envelope impinged on Kron's body. It carried a meaning,
transmitting a clear thought from one being to the other.

"I still find difficulty in believing my senses," stated the
stranger. "My own worlds revolve about another which is
somewhat similar to this; but such a vast and tenuous atmosphere is most unlike conditions at home. Have you ever been
away from Sol?"

"Yes," replied Kron, "I was once on the crew of an inter-stellar projectile. I have never seen your star, however; my acquaintance with it is entirely through hearsay. I am told it consists almost entirely of collapsed matter, like the core of our own; but there is practically no atmosphere. Can this be so? I should think, at the temperature necessary for life, gases would break free of the core and form an envelope."

"They tend to do so, of course," returned the other, "but our surface gravity is immeasurably greater than anything you have here; even your core pull is less, since it is much less dense than our star. Only the fact that our worlds are small, thus causing a rapid diminution of gravity as one leaves them, makes it possible to get a ship away from them at all; atoms, with only their original velocities, remain within a few miles of the surface.

"But you remind me of my purpose on this world—to check certain points of a new theory concerning the possible behavior of aggregations of normal atoms. That was why I arranged a trip on your flier; I have to make density, pressure, temperature, and a dozen other kinds of measure-ments at a couple of thousand different levels, in your atmo-sphere. While I'm doing it, would you mind telling me why you make these regular trips—and why, for that matter, you live so far above your natural level? I should think you would find life easier below, since there would be no need to remain in sealed buildings or to expend such a terrific amount of power in supporting your cities."

Kron's answer was slow.

"We make the journeys to obtain neutronium. It is impos-sible to convert enough power from the immediate neighbor-hood of the cities to support them; we must descend periodically for more, even though our converters take so much as to lower the solar temperature considerably for thousands of miles around each city.

"The trips are dangerous—you should have been told that. We carry a crew of thirty, when two would be enough to man this ship, for we must fight, as well as fly. You spoke truly when you said that the lower regions of Sol are our natural home; but for aeons we have not dared to make more than fleeting visits, to steal the power which is life to us.

"Your little worlds have been almost completely subju-gated by your people, Sirian; they never had life forms suffi-ciently powerful to threaten seriously your domination. But Sol, whose core alone is far larger than the Sirius B pair, did develop such creatures. Some are vast, stupid, slow-moving or immobile; others are semi-intelligent and rapid movers; all are more than willing to ingest the ready-compacted neutronium of another living being."

Kron's tale was interrupted for a moment, as the Sirian sent a ray probing out through the ship's wall, testing the physical state of the inferno beyond. A record was made, and the Solarian resumed.

"We, according to logical theory, were once just such a race—of small intelligence, seeking the needs of life among a horde of competing organisms. Our greatest enemy was a being much like ourselves in size and power—just slightly superior in both ways. We were somewhat ahead in intelligence, and I suppose we owe them some thanks—without the competition they provided, we should not have been forced to develop our minds to their present level. We learned to cooperate in fighting them, and from that came the discovery that many of us together could handle natural forces that a single individual could not even approach, and survive. The creation of force effects that had no counterpart in nature was the next step; and, with the understanding of them, our science grew.

"The first cities were of neutronium, like those of today, but it was necessary to stabilize the neutrons with fields of energy; at core temperature, as you know, neutronium is a gas. The cities were spherical and much smaller than our present ones. For a long time, we managed to defend them.

"But our enemies evolved, too; not in intelligence, but in power and fecundity. With overspecialization of their physical powers, their mentalities actually degenerated; they became little more than highly organized machines, driven, by an age-old enmity toward our race, to seek us out and destroy us. Their new powers at last enabled them to neutralize, by brute force, the fields which held our cities in shape; and then it was that, from necessity, we fled to the wild, inhospitable upper regions of Sol's atmosphere. Many cities were destroyed by the enemy before a means of supporting them was devised; many more fell victims to forces which we generated, without being able to control, in the effort. The dangers of our present-day trips seem trivial beside those our ancestors braved, in spite of the fact that ships not infrequently fail to return from their flights. Does that answer your question?"

The Sirian's reply was hesitant. "I guess it does. You of Sol must have developed far more rapidly than we, under that drive; your science, I know, is superior to ours in certain ways, although it was my race which first developed space flight."

"You had greater opportunities in that line," returned Kron. "Two small stars, less than a diameter apart, circling a larger one at a distance incomparably smaller than the usual interstellar interval, provided perfect ground for experimental flights; between your world and mine, even radiation requires some hundred and thirty rotations to make the journey, and even the nearest other star is almost half as far.

"But enough of this—history is considered by too many to be a dry subject. What brings you on a trip with a power flier? You certainly have not learned anything yet which you could not have been told in the city."

During the conversation, the Sirian had periodically tested the atmosphere beyond the hull. He spoke rather absently, as though concentrating on something other than his words.

"I would not be too sure of that, Solarian. My measurements are of greater delicacy than we have ever before achieved. I am looking for a very special effect, to substantiate or disprove an hypothesis which I have recently advanced—much to the detriment of my prestige. If you are interested, I might explain: laugh afterward if you care to— you will not be the first.

"The theory is simplicity itself. It has occurred to me that matter—ordinary substances like iron and calcium—might actually take on solid form, like neutronium, under the proper conditions. The normal gas, you know, consists of minute particles traveling with considerable speed in all directions. There seems to be no way of telling whether or not these atoms exert appreciable forces on one another; but it seems to me that if they were brought closely enough together, or slowed down sufficiently, some such effects might be detected."

"How, and why?" asked Kron. "If the forces are there, why should they not be detectable under ordinary conditions?"

"Tiny changes in velocity due to mutual attraction or repulsion would scarcely be noticed when the atomic speeds are of the order of hundreds of kilometers per second," returned the Sirian. "The effects I seek to detect are of a different nature. Consider, please. We know the sizes of the various atoms, from their radiations. We also know that under normal conditions, a given mass of any particular gas fills a certain volume. If, however, we surround this gas with an impenetrable container and exert pressure, that volume decreases. We would expect that decrease to be proportional to the pressure, except for an easily determined constant due to the size of the atoms, if no interatomic forces existed; to detect such forces, I am making a complete series of pressure-density tests, more delicate than any heretofore, from the level of your cities down to the neutron core of your world.

"If we could reduce the kinetic energy of the atoms—slow down their motions of translation—the task would probably be simpler; but I see no way to accomplish that. Perhaps, if we could negate nearly all of that energy, the interatomic forces would actually hold the atoms in definite relative positions, approximating the solid state. It was that somewhat injudicious and perhaps too imaginative suggestion which caused my whole idea to be ridiculed on Sirius."

The ship dropped several hundred miles in the few seconds after Kron answered; since gaseous friction is independent of change in density, the high pressures of the regions being penetrated would be no bar to high speed of flight. Unfortunately, the viscosity of a gas does increase directly as the square root of its temperature; and at the lower levels of the sun, travel would be slow.

"Whether or not our scientists will listen to you, I cannot say," said Kron finally. "Some of them are a rather imaginative crowd, I guess and none of them will ignore any data you may produce.

"I do not laugh, either. My reason will certainly interest you, as your theory intrigues me. It is the first time anyone has accounted even partly for the things that happened to us on one of my flights."

The other members of the crew shifted slightly on their cradles; a ripple of interest passed through them, for all had heard rumors and vague tales of Kron's time in the space carrier fleets. The Sirian settled himself more comfortably; Kron dimmed the central globe of radiance a trifle, for the outside temperature was now considerably higher, and began the tale.

"This happened toward the end of my career in space. I had made many voyages with the merchant and passenger vessels, had been promoted from the lowest ranks, through many rotations, to the post of independent captain. I had my own cruiser—a special long-period explorer, owned by the

Solarian government. She was shaped like our modern interstellar carriers, consisting of two cones, bases together, with the field ring just forward of their meeting point. She was larger than most, being designed to carry fuel for exceptionally long flights.

"Another cruiser, similar in every respect, was under the command of a comrade of mine, named Akro; and the two of us were commissioned to transport a party of scientists and explorers to the then newly discovered Fourth System, which lies, as you know, nearly in the plane of the solar equator, but about half again as distant as Sirius.

"We made good time, averaging nearly half the speed of radiation, and reached the star with a good portion of our hulls still unconsumed. We need not have worried about that, in any case; the star was denser even than the Sirius B twins, and neutronium was very plentiful. I restocked at once, plating my inner walls with the stuff until they had reached their original thickness, although experience indicated that the original supply was ample to carry us back to Sol, to Sirius, or to Procyon B.

"Akro, at the request of the scientists, did not refuel. Life was present on the star, as it seems to be on all stars where the atomic velocities and the density are high enough; and the biologists wanted to bring back specimens. That meant that room would be needed, and if Akro replated his walls to normal thickness, that room would be lacking—as I have mentioned, these were special long-range craft, and a large portion of their volume consisted of available neutronium.

"So it happened that the other ship left the Fourth System with a low, but theoretically sufficient, stock of fuel, and half a dozen compartments filled with specimens of alien life. I kept within detection distance at all times, in case of trouble, for some of those life forms were as dangerous as those of Sol, and, like them, all consumed neutronium. They had to be kept well under control to safeguard the very walls of the ship, and it is surprisingly difficult to make a wild beast, surrounded by food, stay on short rations.

"Some of the creatures proved absolutely unmanageable; they had to be destroyed. Others were calmed by lowering the atomic excitation of their compartments, sending them into a stupor; but the scientists were reluctant to try that in most cases, since not all of the beings could stand such treatment.

"So, for nearly four hundred solar rotations, Akro practically fought his vessel across space—fought successfully. He managed on his own power until we were within a few hundred diameters of Sol; but I had to help him with the landing—or try to, for the landing was never made.

"It may seem strange, but there is a large volume of space in the neighborhood of this sun which is hardly ever traversed. The normal landing orbit arches high over one of the poles of rotation, enters atmosphere almost tangentially somewhere between that pole and the equator and kills as much as remains of the ship's velocity in the outer atmospheric layers. There is a minimum of magnetic interference that way, since the flier practically coasts along the lines of force of the solar magnetic field.

"As a result, few ships pass through the space near the plane of the solar equator. One or two may have done so before us, and I know of several that searched the region later; but none encountered the thing which we found.

"About the time we would normally have started correcting our orbits for a tangential landing, Akro radiated me the information that he could not possibly control his ship any farther with the power still available to him. His walls were already so thin that radiation loss, ordinarily negligible, was becoming a definite menace to his vessel. All his remaining energy would have to be employed in keeping the interior of his ship habitable.

"The only thing I could do was to attach our ships together with an attractor beam, and make a nearly perpendicular drop to Sol. We would have to take our chances, with magnetic and electrostatic disturbances in the city-supporting fields which cover so much of the near-equatorial zones, and try to graze the nucleus of the Sun instead of its outer atmosphere, so that Akro could replenish his rapidly failing power.

"Akro's hull was radiating quite perceptibly now; it made an easy target for an attractor. We connected without difficulty, and our slightly different linear velocities caused us to revolve slowly about each other, pivoting on the center of mass of our two ships. I cut off my driving fields, and we fell spinning toward Sol.

"I was becoming seriously worried about Akro's chances of survival. The now-alarming energy loss through his almost consumed hull threatened to exhaust his supply long before we reached the core; and we were still more than a hundred diameters out. I could not give him any power; we were revolving about each other at a distance of about one-tenth of a solar diameter. To lessen that distance materially would increase our speed of revolution to a point where the attractor could not overcome centrifugal force; and I had neither power nor time to perform the delicate job of exactly neutralizing our rotary momentum without throwing us entirely off course. All we could do was hope.

"We were somewhere between one hundred and one hundred fifty diameters out when there occurred the most peculiar phenomenon I have ever encountered. The plane of revolution of our two ships passed near Sol, but was nearly perpendicular to the solar equator; at the time of which I speak, Akro's ship was almost directly between my flier and the sun. Observations had just shown that we were accelerating sunward at an unexpectedly high pace, when a call came from Akro.

" 'Kron! I am being pulled away from your attractor! There is a large mass somewhere near, for the pull is gravitational, but it emits no radiation that I can detect. Increase your pull, if you can; I cannot possibly free myself alone.'

"I did what I could, which was very little. Since we did not know the location of the disturbing dark body, it was impossible to tell just what I should do to avoid bringing my own or Akro's vessel too close. I think now that if I had released him immediately he would have swung clear, for the body was not large, I believe. Unfortunately, I did the opposite, and nearly lost my own ship as well. Two of my crew were throwing as much power as they could convert and handle into the attractor, and trying to hold it on the still easily visible hull of Akro's ship; but the motions of the latter were so peculiar that aiming was a difficult task. They held the ship as long as we could see it; but quite suddenly the radiations by means of which we perceived the vessel faded out, and before we could find a band which would get through, the sudden cessation of our centripetal acceleration told us that the beam had slipped from its target.

"We found that electromagnetic radiations of wavelengths in the octave above H-alpha would penetrate the interference, and Akro's hull was leaking energy enough to radiate in that band. When we found him, however, we could scarcely believe our senses; his velocity was now nearly at right angles to his former course, and his hull radiation had become far weaker. What terrific force had caused this acceleration, and what strange field was blanketing the radiation, were questions none of us could answer.

"Strain as we might, not one of us could pick up an erg of

radiant energy that might emanate from the thing that had trapped Akro. We could only watch, and endeavor to plot his course relative to our own, at first. Our ships were nearing each other rapidly, and we were attempting to determine the time and distance of closest approach, when we were startled by the impact of a communicator beam. Akro was alive! The beam was weak, very weak, showing what an infinitesimal amount of power he felt he could spare. His words were not encouraging.

" 'Kron! You may as well cut your attractor, if you are still trying to catch me. No power that I dare supply seems to move me perceptibly in any direction from this course. We are badly shocked, for we hit something that felt almost solid. The walls, even, are strained, and may go at any time.'

" 'Can you perceive anything around you?' I returned. 'You seem to us to be alone in space, though something is absorbing most of your radiated energy. There must be energies in the cosmos of which we have never dreamed, simply because they did not affect our senses. What do your scientists say?'

" 'Very little,' was the answer. 'They have made a few tests, but they say that anything they project is absorbed without reradiating anything useful. We seem to be in a sort of energy vacuum—it takes everything and returns nothing.'

"This was the most alarming item yet. Even in free space, we had been doubtful of Akro's chances of survival; now they seemed reduced to the ultimate zero.

"Meanwhile, our ships were rapidly approaching each other. As nearly as my navigators could tell, both vessels were pursuing almost straight lines in space. The lines were nearly perpendicular but did not lie in a common plane; their minimum distance apart was about one one-thousandth of a solar diameter. His velocity seemed nearly constant, while I was accelerating sunward. It seemed that we would reach the near-intersection point almost simultaneously, which meant that my ship was certain to approach the energy vacuum much too closely. I did not dare to try to pull Akro free with an attractor; it was only too obvious that such an attempt could only end in disaster for both vessels. If he could not free himself, he was lost.

"We could only watch helplessly as the point of light marking the position of Akro's flier swept closer and closer. At first, as I have said, it seemed perfectly free in space; but as we looked, the region around it began to radiate feebly.

There was nothing recognizable about the vibrations, simply a continuous spectrum, cut off by some interference just below the H-alpha wavelength and, at the other end, some three octaves higher. As the emission grew stronger, the visible region around the stranded ship grew larger, fading into nothingness at the edges. Brighter and broader the patch of radiance grew, as we swept toward it."

That same radiance was seriously inconveniencing Gordon Aller, who was supposed to be surveying for a geological map of northern Australia. He was camped by the only water hole in many miles, and had stayed up long after dark preparing his cameras, barometer, soil kit, and other equipment for the morrow's work.

The arrangement of instruments completed, he did not at once retire to his blankets. With his back against a smooth rock, and a short, blackened pipe clenched in his teeth, he sat for some time, pondering. The object of his musing does not matter to us; though his eyes were directed heavenward, he was sufficiently accustomed to the southern sky to render it improbable that he was paying much attention to its beauties.

However that may be, his gaze was suddenly attracted to the zenith. He had often seen stars which appeared to move when near the edge of his field of vision—it is a common illusion; but this one continued to shift as he turned his eyes upward.

Not far from Achernar was a brilliant white point, which brightened as Aller watched it. It was moving slowly northward, it seemed; but only a moment was needed for the man to realize that the slowness was illusory. The thing was slashing almost vertically downward at an enormous speed, and must strike Earth not far from his camp.

Aller was not an astronomer and had no idea of astronomical distances or speeds. He may be forgiven for thinking of the object as traveling perhaps as fast as a modern fighting plane, and first appearing at a height of two or three miles. The natural conclusion from this belief was that the crash would occur within a few hundred feet of the camp. Aller paled; he had seen pictures of the Devil's Pit in Arizona.

Actually, of course, the meteor first presented itself to his gaze at a height of some eighty miles, and was then traveling at a rate of many miles per second relative to Earth. At that speed, the air presented a practically solid obstacle to its flight, and the object was forced to a fairly constant velocity of ten or twelve hundred yards a second while still nearly ten miles from Earth's surface. It was at that point that Aller's eyes caught up with, and succeeded in focusing upon, the celestial visitor.

That first burst of light had been radiated by the frightfully compressed and heated air in front of the thing; as the original velocity departed, so did the dazzling light. Aller got a clear view of the meteor at a range of less than five miles, for perhaps ten seconds before the impact. It was still incandescent, radiating a bright cherry red; this must have been due to the loss from within, for so brief a contact even with such highly heated air could not have warmed the Sunship's neutronium walls a measurable fraction of a degree.

Aller felt the ground tremble as the vessel struck. A geyser of earth, barely visible in the reddish light of the hull, spouted skyward, to fall back seconds later with a long-drawn-out rumble. The man stared at the spot, two miles away, which was still giving off a faint glow. Were "shooting stars" as regularly shaped as that? He had seen a smooth, slender body, more than a hundred feet in length, apparently composed of two cones of unequal length, joined together at the bases. Around the longer cone, not far from the point of juncture, was a thick bulging ring; no further details were visible at the distance from which he had observed. Aller's vague recollections of meteorites, seen in various museums, brought images of irregular, clinkerlike objects before his mind's eye. What, then, could this thing be?

He was not imaginative enough to think for a moment of any possible extraterrestrial source for an aircraft; when it did occur to him that the object was of artificial origin, he thought more of some experimental machine produced by one of the more progressive Earth nations.

At the thought, Aller strapped a first-aid kit to his side and set out toward the crater, in the face of the obvious fact that nothing human could possibly have survived such a crash. He stumbled over the uneven terrain for a quarter of a mile and then stopped on a small rise of ground to examine more closely the site of the wreck.

The glow should have died by this time, for Aller had taken all of ten minutes to pick his way those few hundred yards; but the dull-red light ahead had changed to a brilliant orange radiance against which the serrated edges of the pit were clearly silhouetted. No flames were visible; whence came the increasing heat? Aller attempted to get closer, but a wave of frightfully hot air blistered his face and hands and drove him back. He took up a station near his former camp and watched.

If the hull of the flier had been anywhere near its normal thickness, the tremendous mass of neutronium would have sunk through the hardest of rocks as though they were liquid. There was, however, scarcely more than a paper thickness of the substance at any part of the walls; and an upthrust of adamantine volcanic rock not far beneath the surface of the desert proved thick enough to absorb the Sunship's momentum and to support its still enormous weight. Consequently, the ship was covered only by a thin layer of powdered rock which had fallen back into the crater. The disturbances arising from the now extremely rapid loss of energy from Akro's ship were, as a result, decidedly visible from the surface.

The hull, though thin, was still intact; but its temperature was now far above the melting point of the surrounding rocks. The thin layer of pulverized material above the ship melted and flowed away almost instantly, permitting free radiation to the air above; and so enormous is the specific heat of neutronium that no perceptible lowering of hull temperature occurred.

Aller, from his point of observation, saw the brilliant fan of light that sprang from the pit as the flier's hull was exposed—the vessel itself was invisible to him, since he was only slightly above the level of the crater's mouth. He wondered if the impact of the "meteor" had released some pent-up volcanic energy, and began to doubt, quite justifiably, if he was at a safe distance. His doubts vanished and were replaced by certainty as the edges of the crater began to glow dull red, then bright orange, and slowly subsided out of sight. He began packing the most valuable items of his equipment, while a muted, continuous roaring and occasional heavy thuds from the direction of the pit admonished him to hasten.

When he straightened up, with the seventy-pound pack settled on his shoulders, there was simply a lake of lava where the crater had been. The fiery area spread even as he watched; and without further delay he set off on his own back trail. He could see easily by the light diffused from the inferno behind him; and he made fairly good time, considering his burden and the fact that he had not slept since the preceding night.

The rock beneath Akro's craft was, as we have said, extremely hard. Since there was relatively free escape upward for the constantly liberated energy, this stratum melted very slowly, gradually letting the vessel sink deeper into the earth. What would have happened if Akro's power supply had been greater is problematical; Aller can tell us only that some five hours after the landing, as he was resting for a few moments near the top of a rocky hillock, the phenomenon came to a cataclysmic end.

A quivering of the earth beneath him caused the surveyor to look back toward his erstwhile camp. The lake of lava, which by this time was the better part of a mile in breadth, seemed curiously agitated. Aller, from his rather poor vantage point, could see huge bubbles of pasty lava hump themselves up and burst, releasing brilliant clouds of vapor. Each cloud illuminated earth and sky before cooling to invisibility, so that the effect was somewhat similar to a series of lightning flashes.

For a short time—certainly no longer than a quarter of a minute—Aller was able to watch as the activity increased. Then a particularly violent shock almost flung him from the hilltop, and at nearly the same instant the entire volume of molten rock fountained skyward. For an instant it seemed to hang there, a white, raging pillar of liquid and gas; then it dissolved, giving way before the savage thrust of the suddenly released energy below. A tongue of radiance, of an intensity indescribable in mere words, stabbed upward, into and through the lava, volatilizing instantly. A dozen square miles of desert glowed white, then an almost invisible violet, and disappeared in superheated gas. Around the edges of this region, great gouts of lava and immense fragments of solid rock were hurled to all points of the compass.

Radiation exerts pressure; at the temperature found in the cores of stars, that pressure must be measured in thousands of tons per square inch. It was this thrust, rather than the by no means negligible gas pressure of the boiling lava, which wrought most of the destruction.

Aller saw little of what occurred. When the lava was hurled upward, he had flung an arm across his face to protect his eyes from the glare. That act unquestionably saved his eyesight as the real flash followed; as it was, his body was seared and blistered through his clothing. The second, heavier, shock knocked his feet from under him, and he half crawled, half rolled down to the comparative shelter of the little hill. Even here, gusts of hot air almost cooked him; only the speed with which the phenomenon ended saved his life.

Within minutes, both the temblors and hot winds had ceased; and he crawled painfully to the hilltop again to gaze wonderingly at the five-mile crater, ringed by a pile of tumbled, still-glowing rock fragments.

Far beneath that pit, shards of neutronium, no more able to remain near the surface than the steel pieces of a wrecked ocean vessel can float on water, were sinking through rock and metal to a final resting place at Earth's heart.

"The glow spread as we watched, still giving no clue to the nature of the substance radiating it," continued Kron. "Most of it seemed to originate between us and Akro's ship; Akro himself said that but little energy was being lost on the far side. His messages, during that last brief period as we swept by our point of closest approach, were clear—so clear that we could almost see, as he did, the tenuous light beyond the ever-thinning walls of his ship; the light that represented but a tiny percentage of the energy being sucked from the hull surface.

"We saw, as though with his own senses, the tiny perforation appear near one end of the ship; saw it extend, with the speed of thought, from one end of the hull to the other, permitted the free escape of all the energy in a single instant; and, from our point of vantage, saw the glowing area where the ship had been suddenly brightened, blazing for a moment almost as brightly as a piece of sun matter.

"In that moment, every one of us saw the identifying frequencies as the heat from Akro's disrupted ship raised the substance which had trapped him to an energy level which permitted atomic radiation. Every one of us recognized the spectra of iron, of calcium, of carbon, and of silicon and a score of the other elements—Sirian, I tell you that that 'trapping field' was *matter*—matter in such a state that it could not radiate, and could offer resistance to other bodies in exactly the fashion of a solid. I thought, and have always thought, that some strange field of force held the atoms in their 'solid' positions; you have convinced me that I was wrong. The 'field' was the sum of the interacting atomic forces which you are trying to detect. The energy level of that material body was so low that those forces were able to act without interference. The condition you could not conceive of reaching artificially actually exists in nature!"

"You go too fast, Kron," responded the Sirian. "Your first idea is far more likely to be the true one. The idea of unknown radiant or static force fields is easy to grasp; the one you propose in its place defies common sense. My theories called for some such conditions as you described, granted the one premise of a sufficiently low energy level; but a place in the real Universe so devoid of energy as to absorb that of a well-insulated interstellar flier is utterly inconceivable. I have assumed your tale to be true as to details, though you offer neither witnesses nor records to support it; but I seem to have heard that you have somewhat of a reputation as an entertainer, and you seem quick-witted enough to have woven such a tale on the spot, purely from the ideas I suggested. I compliment you on the tale, Kron; it was entrancing; but I seriously advise you not to make anything more out of it. Shall we leave it at that, my friend?"

"As you will," replied Kron.

NERVES

Astounding,

September

by Lester Del Rey

The word "classic" is used to describe everything from old cars to basketball tournaments, and is severely abused and overused in the science fiction field. However, "Nerves" deserves the appellation because it is a terrific story and because it vividly portrays the impact of science and technology on people and society, one of the hall marks of quality science fiction. It is also a gripping story with powerful characterizations—little wonder that it had readers shaking their heads and saying, "It will be something like this." Written at the height of the secret Manhattan Project, any resemblance to what might have happened at Three-Mile Island is strictly coincidental and a figment of your imagination. Del Rey expanded the story to novel length in 1956.

(Lester is great on one-liners. I always listen to him very carefully—when we're not playing our game—for whatever I can appropriate. He said once, "The trouble with Indian philosophy is that it produced India." When someone asked him his birthday, so he could work out his astrological personality, he answered, "Observe my personality and deduce my birthday." He's one of those people who is absolutely immune to the lure of the fringe-crackpottery in science. That's why, perhaps, he is so prescient.—I.A.)

The graveled walks between the sprawling, utilitarian structures of the National Atomic Products Co., Inc., were crowded with the usual five o'clock mass of young huskies just off work or going on the extra shift, and the company cafeteria was jammed to capacity and overflowing. But they

made good-natured way for Doc Ferrel as he came out, not
bothering to stop their horseplay as they would have done
with any of the other half hundred officials of the company.
He'd been just Doc to them too long for any need of formality.

He nodded back at them easily, pushed through, and went
down the walk toward the Infirmary Building, taking his own
time. When a man has turned fifty, with gray hairs and enlarged waistline to show for it, he begins to realize that comfort and relaxation are worth cultivating. Besides, Doc could
see no good reason for filling his stomach with food and then
rushing around in a flurry that gave him no chance to digest
it. He let himself in the side entrance, palming his cigar out
of long habit, and passed through the surgery to the door
marked:

PRIVATE
ROGER T. FERREL
PHYSICIAN IN CHARGE

As always, the little room was heavy with the odor of stale
smoke and littered with scraps of this and that. His assistant
was already there, rummaging busily through the desk with
the brass nerve that was typical of him; Ferrel had no objections to it, though, since Blake's rock-steady hands and unruf-
fled brain were always dependable in a pinch of any sort.

Blake looked up and grinned confidently. "Hi, Doc. Where
the deuce do you keep your cigarettes, anyway? Never mind,
got 'em. . . . Ah, that's better! Good thing there's one room
in this darned building where the 'No Smoking' signs don't
count. You and the wife coming out this evening?"

"Not a chance, Blake." Ferrel stuck the cigar back in his
mouth and settled down into the old leather chair, shaking his
head. "Palmer phoned down half an hour ago to ask me if
I'd stick through the graveyard shift. Seems the plant's got a
rush order for some particular batch of dust that takes about
twelve hours to cook, so they'll be running No. 3 and 4 till
midnight or later."

"Hm-m-m. So you're hooked again. I don't see why any of
us has to stick here—nothing serious ever pops up now. Look
what I had today; three cases of athlete's foot—better send a
memo down to the showers for extra disinfection—a guy
with dandruff, four running noses, and the office boy with a
sliver in his thumb! They bring everything to us except their

babies—and they'd have them here if they could—but nothing that couldn't wait a week or a month. Anne's been counting on you and the missus, Doc; she'll be disappointed if you aren't there to celebrate her sticking ten years with me. Why don't you let the kid stick it out alone tonight?"

"I wish I could, but this happens to be my job. As a matter of fact, though, Jenkins worked up an acute case of duty and decided to stay on with me tonight." Ferrel twitched his lips in a stiff smile, remembering back to the time when his waistline had been smaller than his chest and he'd gone through the same feeling that destiny had singled him out to save the world. "The kid had his first real case today, and he's all puffed up. Handled it all by himself, so he's now Dr. Jenkins, if you please."

Blake had his own memories. "Yeah? Wonder when he'll realize that everything he did by himself came from your hints? What was it, anyway?"

"Same old story—simple radiation burns. No matter how much we tell the men when they first come in, most of them can't see why they should wear three ninety-five percent efficient shields when the main converter shield cuts off all but one-tenth percent of the radiation. Somehow, this fellow managed to leave off his two inner shields and pick up a year's burn in six hours. Now he's probably back on No. 1, still running through the hundred liturgies I gave him to say and hoping we won't get him sacked."

No. 1 was the first converter around which National Atomic had built its present monopoly in artificial radioactives, back in the days when shields were still inefficient to one part in a thousand and the materials handled were milder than the modern ones. They still used it for the gentler reactions, prices of converters being what they were; anyhow, if reasonable precautions were taken, there was no serious danger.

"A tenth percent will kill; five percent thereof is one two-hundredth; five percent of that is one four-thousandth; and five percent again leaves one eighty-thousandth, safe for all but fools." Blake sing-songed the liturgy solemnly, then chuckled. "You're getting old, Doc; you used to give them a thousand times. Well, if you get the chance, you and Mrs. Ferrel drop out and say hello, even if it's after midnight. Anne's gonna be disappointed, but she ought to know how it goes. So long."

" 'Night." Ferrel watched him leave, still smiling faintly.

Some day his own son would be out of medical school, and
Blake would make a good man for him to start under and begin the same old grind upward. First, like young Jenkins, he'd
be filled with his mission to humanity, tense and uncertain,
but somehow things would roll along through Blake's stage
and up, probably to Doc's own level, where the same old
problems were solved in the same old way, and life settled
down into a comfortable, mellow dullness.

There were worse lives, certainly, even though it wasn't
like the mass of murders, kidnapings and applied miracles
played up in the current movie series about Dr. Hoozis.
Come to think of it, Hoozis was supposed to be working in
an atomic products plant right now—but one where chrome-
plated converters covered with pretty neon tubes were mys-
teriously blowing up every second day, and men were
brought in with blue flames all over them to be cured instantly in time to utter the magic words so the hero could
dash in and put out the atomic flame barehanded. Ferrel
grunted and reached back for his old copy of the "Decameron."

Then he heard Jenkins out in the surgery, puttering around
with quick, nervous little sounds. Never do to let the boy find
him loafing back here, when the possible fate of the world so
obviously hung on his alertness. Young doctors had to be
disillusioned slowly, or they became bitter and their work suffered. Yet, in spite of his amusement at Jenkins' nervousness,
he couldn't help envying the thin-faced young man's erect
shoulders and flat stomach. Years crept by, it seemed.

Jenkins straightened out a wrinkle in his white jacket fuss-
ily and looked up. "I've been getting the surgery ready for instant use, Dr. Ferrel. Do you think it's safe to keep only Miss
Dodd and one male attendant here—shouldn't we have more
than the bare legally sanctioned staff?"

"Dodd's a one-man staff," Ferrel assured him. "Expecting
accidents tonight?"

"No, sir, not exactly. But do you know what they're running off?"

"No." Ferrel hadn't asked Palmer; he'd learned long before
that he couldn't keep up with the atomic engineering developments, and had stopped trying. "Some new type of atomic
tank fuel for the army to use in its war games?"

"Worse than that, sir. They're making their first commercial run of Natomic I-713 in both No. 3 and 4 converters at once."

"So? Seems to me I did hear something about that. Had to do with killing off boll weevils, didn't it?" Ferrel was vaguely familiar with the process of sowing radioactive dust in a circle outside the weevil area, to isolate the pest, then gradually moving inward from the border. Used with proper precautions, it had slowly killed off the weevil and driven it back into half the territory once occupied.

Jenkins managed to look disappointed, surprised and slightly superior without a visible change of expression. "There was an article on it in the *Natomic Weekly Ray* of last issue, Dr. Ferrel. You probably know that the trouble with Natomic I-344, which they've been using, was its half life of over four months; that made the land sowed useless for planting the next year, so they had to move very slowly. I-713 has a half life of less than a week and reached safe limits in about two months, so they'll be able to isolate whole strips of hundreds of miles during the winter and still have the land usable by spring. Field tests have been highly successful, and we've just gotten a huge order from two States that want immediate delivery."

"After their legislatures waited six months debating whether to use it or not," Ferrel hazarded out of long experience. "Hm-m-m, sounds good if they can sow enough earthworms after them to keep the ground in good condition. But what's the worry?"

Jenkins shook his head indignantly. "I'm not worried. I simply think we should take every possible precaution and be ready for any accident; after all, they're working on something new, and a half life of a week is rather strong, don't you think? Besides, I looked over some of the reaction charts in the article, and—What was that?"

From somewhere to the left of the infirmary, a muffled growl was being accompanied by ground tremors; then it gave place to a steady hissing, barely audible through the insulated walls of the building. Ferrel listened a moment and shrugged. "Nothing to worry about, Jenkins. You'll hear it a dozen times a year. Ever since the Great War when he tried to commit hara-kiri over the treachery of his people, Hokusai's been bugs about getting an atomic explosive bomb which will let us wipe out the rest of the world. Some day you'll probably see the little guy brought in here minus his head, but so far he hasn't found anything with short enough a half life that can be controlled until needed. What about the reaction charts on I-713?"

"Nothing definite, I suppose." Jenkins turned reluctantly away from the sound, still frowning. "I know it worked in small lots, but there's something about one of the intermediate steps I distrust, sir. I thought I recognized . . . I tried to ask one of the engineers about it. He practically told me to shut up until I'd studied atomic engineering myself."

Seeing the boy's face whiten over tensed jaw muscles, Ferrel held back his smile and nodded slowly. Something funny there; of course. Jenkins' pride had been wounded, but hardly that much. Some day, he'd have to find out what was behind it. Little things like that could ruin a man's steadiness with the instruments, if he kept it to himself. Meantime, the subject was best dropped.

The telephone girl's heavily syllabized voice cut into his thoughts from the annunciator. "Dr. Ferrel. Dr. Ferrel wanted on the telephone. Dr. Ferrel, please!"

Jenkins' face blanched still further, and his eyes darted to his superior sharply. Doc grunted casually. "Probably Palmer's bored and wants to tell me all about his grandson again. He thinks that child's an all-time genius because it says two words at eighteen months."

But inside the office, he stopped to wipe his hands free of perspiration before answering; there was something contagious about Jenkins' suppressed fears. And Palmer's face on the little television screen didn't help any, though the director was wearing his usual set smile. Ferrel knew it wasn't about the baby this time, and he was right.

" 'Lo, Ferrel." Palmer's heartily confident voice was quite normal, but the use of the last name was a clear sign of some trouble. "There's been a little accident in the plant, they tell me. They're bringing a few men over to the infirmary for treatment—probably not right away, though. Has Blake gone yet?"

"He's been gone fifteen minutes or more. Think it's serious enough to call him back, or are Jenkins and myself enough?"

Jenkins? Oh, the new doctor." Palmer hesitated, and his arms showed quite clearly the doodling operations of his hands, out of sight of the vision cell. "No, of course, no need to call Blake back, I suppose—not yet, anyhow. Just worry anyone who saw him coming in. Probably nothing serious."

"What is it—radiation burns, or straight accident?"

"Oh—radiation mostly—maybe accident, too. Someone got

a little careless—you know how it is. Nothing to worry about, though. You've been through it before when they opened a port too soon."

Doc knew enough about that—if that's what it was. "Sure, we can handle that, Palmer. But I thought No. 1 was closing down at five-thirty tonight. Anyhow, how come they haven't installed the safety ports on it? You told me they had, six months ago."

"I didn't say it was No. 1, or that it was a manual port. You know, new equipment for new products." Palmer looked up at someone else, and his upper arms made a slight movement before he looked down at the vision cell again. "I can't go into it now, Dr. Ferrel; accident's throwing us off schedule, you see—details piling up on me. We can talk it over later, and you probably have to make arrangements now. Call me if you want anything."

The screen darkened and the phone clicked off abruptly, just as a muffled word started. The voice hadn't been Palmer's. Ferrel pulled his stomach in, wiped the sweat off his hands again, and went out into the surgery with careful casualness. Damn Palmer, why couldn't the fool give enough information to make decent preparations possible? He was sure 3 and 4 alone were operating, and they were supposed to be foolproof. Just what had happened?

Jenkins jerked up from a bench as he came out, face muscles tense and eyes filled with a nameless fear. Where he had been sitting, a copy of the *Weekly Ray* was lying open at a chart of symbols which meant nothing to Ferrel, except for the penciled line under one of the reactions. The boy picked it up and stuck it back on a table.

"Routine accident," Ferrel reported as naturally as he could, cursing himself for having to force his voice. Thank the Lord, the boy's hands hadn't trembled visibly when he was moving the paper; he'd still be useful if surgery were necessary. Palmer had said nothing of that, of course—he'd said nothing about entirely too much. "They're bringing a few men over for radiation burns, according to Palmer. Everything ready?"

Jenkins nodded tightly. "Quite ready, sir, as much as we can be for—routine accidents at 3 and 4! . . . Isotope R. . . . Sorry, Dr. Ferrel, I didn't mean that. Should we call in Dr. Blake and the other nurses and attendants?"

"Eh? Oh, probably we can't reach Blake, and Palmer

doesn't think we need him. You might have Nurse Dodd locate Meyers—the others are out on dates by now if I know them, and the two nurses should be enough, with Jones; they're better than a flock of the others anyway." Isotope R? Ferrel remembered the name but nothing else. Something an engineer had said once—but he couldn't recall in what connection—or had Hokusai mentioned it? He watched Jenkins leave and turned back on an impulse to his office where he could phone in reasonable privacy.

"Get me Matsuura Hokusai." He stood, drumming on the table impatiently until the screen finally lighted and the little Japanese looked out of it. "Hoke, do you know what they were turning out over at 3 and 4?"

The scientist nodded slowly, his wrinkled face as expressionless as his unaccented English. "Yess, they are make I-713 for the weevil. Why you assk?"

"Nothing; just curious. I heard rumors about an Isotope R and wondered if there was any connection. Seems they had a little accident over there, and I want to be ready for whatever comes of it."

For a fraction of a second, the heavy lids on Hokusai's eyes seemed to lift, but his voice remained neutral, only slightly faster. "No connection, Dr. Ferrel, they are not make Issotope R, very much assure you. Besst you forget Issotope R. Very sorry. Dr. Ferrel, I must now see accident. Thank you for call. Good-bye." The screen was blank again, along with Ferrel's mind.

Jenkins was standing in the door, but had either heard nothing or seemed not to know about it. "Nurse Meyers is coming back," he said. "Shall I get ready for curare injections?"

"Uh—might be a good idea." Ferrel had no intention of being surprised again, no matter what the implication of the words. Curare, one of the greatest poisons, known to South American primitives for centuries and only recently synthesized by modern chemistry, was the final resort for use in cases of radiation injury that was utterly beyond control. While the infirmary stocked it for such emergencies, in the long years of Doc's practice it had been used only twice; neither experience had been pleasant. Jenkins was either thoroughly frightened or overly zealous—unless he knew something he had no business knowing.

"Seems to take them long enough to get the men here—can't be too serious, Jenkins, or they'd move faster."

"Maybe." Jenkins went on with his preparations, dissolving dried plasma in distilled, de-aerated water, without looking up. "There's the litter siren now. You'd better get washed up while I take care of the patients."

Doc listened to the sound that came in as a faint drone from outside, and grinned slightly. "Must be Beel driving; he's the only man fool enough to run the siren when the runways are empty. Anyhow, if you'll listen, it's the out trip he's making. Be at least five minutes before he gets back." But he turned into the washroom, kicked on the hot water and began scrubbing vigorously with the strong soap.

Damn Jenkins! Here he was preparing for surgery before he had any reason to suspect the need, and the boy was running things to suit himself, pretty much, as if armed with superior knowledge. Well, maybe he was. Either that, or he was simply half crazy with old wives' fears of anything relating to atomic reactions, and that didn't seem to fit the case. He rinsed off as Jenkins came in, kicked on the hot-air blast and let his arms dry, then bumped against a rod that brought out rubber gloves on little holders. "Jenkins, what's all this Isotope R business, anyway? I've heard about it somewhere— probably from Hokusai. But I can't remember anything definite."

"Naturally—there isn't anything definite. That's the trouble." The young doctor tackled the area under his fingernails before looking up; then he saw Ferrel was slipping into his surgeon's whites that had come out on a hanger, and waited until the other was finished. "R's one of the big maybe problems of atomics. Purely theoretical, and none's been made yet—it's either impossible or can't be done in small control batches, safe for testing. That's the trouble, as I said; nobody knows anything about it, except that—if it can exist—it'll break down in a fairly short time into Mahler's Isotope. You've heard of that?"

Doc had—twice. The first had been when Mahler and half his laboratory had disappeared with accompanying noise. He'd been making a comparatively small amount of the new product designed to act as a starter for other reactions. Later, Maicewicz had tackled it on a smaller scale, and that time only two rooms and three men had gone up in dust particles. Five or six years later, atomic theory had been extended to the point where any student could find why the apparently safe product decided to become pure helium and energy in approximately one billionth of a second.

"How long a time?"

"Half a dozen theories, and no real idea." They'd come out of the washrooms, finished except for their masks. Jenkins ran his elbow into a switch that turned on the ultraviolets that were supposed to sterilize the entire surgery, then looked around questioningly. "What about the supersonics?"

Ferrel kicked them on, shuddering as the bone-shaking harmonic hum indicated their activity. He couldn't complain about the equipment, at least. Ever since the last accident, when the State Congress developed ideas, there'd been enough gadgets lying around to stock up several small hospitals. The supersonics were intended to penetrate through all solids in the room, sterilizing where the UV light couldn't reach. A whistling note in the harmonics reminded him of something that had been tickling around in the back of his mind for minutes.

"There was no emergency whistle, Jenkins. Hardly seems to me they'd neglect that if it were so important."

Jenkins grunted skeptically and eloquently. "I read in the papers a few days ago where Congress was thinking of moving all atomic plants—meaning National, of course—out into the Mojave Desert. Palmer wouldn't like that . . . There's the siren again."

Jones, the male attendant, had heard it, and was already running out the fresh stretcher for the litter into the back receiving room. Half a minute later, Beel came trundling in the detachable part of the litter. "Two," he announced. "More coming up as soon as they can get to 'em, Doc."

There was blood spilled over the canvas, and a closer inspection indicated its source in a severed jugular vein, now held in place with a small safety pin that had fastened the two sides of the cut with a series of little pricks around which the blood had clotted enough to stop further loss.

Doc kicked off the supersonics with relief and indicated the man's throat. "Why wasn't I called out instead of having him brought here?"

"Hell, Doc, Palmer said bring 'em in and I brought 'em—I dunno. Guess some guy pinned up this fellow so they figured he could wait. Anything wrong?"

Ferrel grimaced. "With a split jugular, nothing that stops the bleeding's wrong, orthodox or not. How many more, and what's wrong out there?"

"Lord knows, Doc. I only drive 'em. I don't ask questions.

So long!" He pushed the new stretcher up on the carriage, went wheeling it out to the small two-wheeled tractor that completed the litter. Ferrel dropped his curiosity back to its proper place and turned to the jugular case, while Dodd adjusted her mask. Jones had their clothes off, swabbed them down hastily, and wheeled them out on operating tables into the center of the surgery.

"Plasma!" A quick examination had shown Doc nothing else wrong with the jugular case, and he made the injection quickly. Apparently the man was only unconscious from shock induced by loss of blood, and the breathing and heart action resumed a more normal course as the liquid filled out the depleted blood vessels. He treated the wound with a sulphonamide derivative in routine procedure, cleaned and sterized the edges gently, applied clamps carefully, removed the pin, and began stitching with the complicated little motor needle—one of the few gadgets for which he had any real appreciation. A few more drops of blood had spilled, but not seriously, and the wound was now permanently sealed. "Save the pin, Dodd. Goes in the collection. That's all for this. How's the other, Jenkins?"

Jenkins pointed to the back of the man's neck, indicating a tiny bluish object sticking out. "Fragment of steel, clear into the medulla oblongata. No blood loss, but he's been dead since it touched him. What me to remove it?"

"No need—mortician can do it if they want. . . . If these are a sample, I'd guess it as a plain industrial accident, instead of anything connected with radiation."

"You'll get that, too, Doc." It was the jugular case, apparently conscious and normal except for pallor. "We weren't in the converter house. Hey, I'm all right! . . . I'll be—"

Ferrel smiled at the surprise on the fellow's face. "Thought you were dead, eh? Sure, you're all right, if you'll take it easy. A torn jugular either kills you or else it's nothing to worry about. Just pipe down and let the nurse put you to sleep, and you'll never know you got it."

"Lord! Stuff came flying out of the air-intake like bullets out of a machine gun. Just a scratch, I thought; then Jake was bawling like a baby and yelling for a pin. Blood all over the place—then here I am, good as new."

"Uh-huh." Dodd was already wheeling him off to a ward room, her grim face wrinkled into a half-quizzical expression over the mask. "Doctor said to pipe down, didn't he? Well!"

As soon as Dodd vanished, Jenkins sat down, running his

hand over his cap; there were little beads of sweat showing
where the goggles and mask didn't entirely cover his face.
" 'Stuff came flying out of the air-intake like bullets out of a
machine gun,' " he repeated softly. "Dr. Ferrel, these two
cases were outside the converter—just by-product accidents.
Inside—"

"Yeah." Ferrel was picturing things himself, and it wasn't
pleasant. Outside, matter tossed through the air ducts; inside— He left it hanging, as Jenkins had. "I'm going to call
Blake. We'll probably need him."

II

"Give me Dr. Blake's residence—Maple 2337," Ferrel said
quickly into the phone. The operator looked blank for a second, starting and then checking a purely automatic gesture
toward the plugs. "Maple 2337, I said."

"I'm sorry, Dr. Ferrel, I can't give you an outside line. All
trunk lines are out of order." There was a constant buzz from
the board, but nothing showed in the panel to indicate
whether from white inside lights or the red trunk indicators.

"But—this is an emergency, operator. I've got to get in
touch with Dr. Blake!"

"Sorry, Dr. Ferrel. All trunk lines are out of order." She
started to reach for the plug, but Ferrel stopped her.

"Give me Palmer, then—and no nonsense! If his line's
busy, cut me in, and I'll take the responsibility."

"Very good." She snapped at her switches. "I'm sorry,
emergency call from Dr. Ferrel. Hold the line and I'll reconnect you." Then Palmer's face was on the panel, and this
time the man was making no attempt to conceal his expression of worry.

"What is it, Ferrel?"

"I want Blake here—I'm going to need him. The operator
says—"

"Yeah," Palmer nodded tightly, cutting in. "I've been trying to get him myself, but his house doesn't answer. Any idea
of where to reach him?"

"You might try the Bluebird or any of the other nightclubs
around there." Damn, why did this have to be Blake's
celebration night? No telling where he could be found by this
time.

Palmer was speaking again. "I've already had all the nightclubs and restaurants called, and he doesn't answer. We're paging the movie houses and theaters now—just a second. . . . Nope, he isn't there, Ferrel. Last reports, no response."

"How about sending out a general call over the radio?"

"I'd . . . I'd like to, Ferrel, but it can't be done." The manager had hesitated for a fraction of a second, but his reply was positive. "Oh, by the way, we'll notify your wife you won't be home. Operator! You there? Good, reconnect the Governor!"

There was no sense in arguing into a blank screen, Doc realized. If Palmer wouldn't put through a radio call, he wouldn't, though it had been done once before. "All trunk lines are out of order. . . . We'll notify your wife. . . . Reconnect the Governor!" They weren't even being careful to cover up. He must have repeated the words aloud as he backed out of the office, still staring at the screen, for Jenkins' face twitched into a maladjusted grin.

"So we're cut off. I knew it already; Meyers just got in with more details." He nodded toward the nurse, just coming out of the dressing room and trying to smooth out her uniform. Her almost pretty face was more confused than worried.

"I was just leaving the plant, Dr. Ferrel, when my name came up on the outside speaker, but I had trouble getting here. We're locked in! I saw them at the gate—guards with sticks. They were turning back everyone that tried to leave, and wouldn't tell why, even. Just general orders that no one was to leave until Mr. Palmer gave his permission. And they weren't going to let me back in at first. Do you suppose . . . do you know what it's all about? I heard little things that didn't mean anything, really, but—"

"I know just about as much as you do, Meyers, though Palmer said something about carelessness with one of the ports on No. 3 or 4," Ferrel answered her. "Probably just precautionary measures. Anyway, I wouldn't worry about it yet."

"Yes, Dr. Ferrel." She nodded and turned back to the front office, but there was no assurance in her look. Doc realized that neither Jenkins nor himself was a picture of confidence at the moment.

"Jenkins," he said, when she was gone, "if you know anything I don't, for the love of Mike, out with it! I've never seen anything like this around here."

Jenkins shook himself, and for the first time since he'd
been there, used Ferrel's nickname. "Doc, I don't—that's why
I'm in a blue funk. I know just enough to be less sure than
you can be, and I'm scared as hell!"

"Let's see your hands." The subject was almost a monoma-
nia with Ferrel, and he knew it, but he also knew it wasn't
unjustified. Jenkins' hands came out promptly, and there was
no tremble to them. The boy threw up his arm so the sleeve
slid beyond the elbow, and Ferrel nodded; there was no sweat
trickling down from the armpits to reveal a worse case of
nerves than showed on the surface. "Good enough, son; I
don't care how scared you are—I'm getting that way myself—but with Blake out of the picture, and the other nurses
and attendants sure to be out of reach, I'll need everything
you've got."

"Doc?"

"Well?"

"If you'll take my word for it, I can get another nurse
here—and a good one, too. They don't come any better, or
any steadier, and she's not working now. I didn't expect
her—well, anyhow, she'd skin me if I didn't call when we
need one. Want her?"

"No trunk lines for outside calls," Doc reminded him. It
was the first time he'd seen any real enthusiasm on the boy's
face, and however good or bad the nurse was, she'd obviously
be of value in bucking up Jenkins' spirits. "Go to it, though;
right now we can probably use any nurse. Sweetheart?"

"Wife." Jenkins went toward the dressing room. "And I
don't need the phone; we used to carry ultra-short-wave personal radios to keep in touch, and I've still got mine here.
And if you're worried about her qualifications, she handed instruments to Bayard at Mayo's for five years—that's how I
managed to get through medical school!"

The siren was approaching again when Jenkins came back,
the little tense lines about his lips still there, but his whole
bearing somehow steadier. He nodded. "I called Palmer, too,
and he O.K.'d her coming inside on the phone without wondering how I'd contacted her. The switchboard girl has standing orders to route all calls from us through before anything
else, it seems."

Doc nodded, his ear cocked toward the drone of the siren
that drew up and finally ended on a sour wheeze. There was
a feeling of relief from tension about him as he saw Jones

appear and go toward the rear entrance; work, even under the pressure of an emergency, was always easier than sitting around waiting for it. He saw two stretchers come in, both bearing double loads, and noted that Beel was babbling at the attendant, the driver's usually phlegmatic manner completely gone.

"I'm quitting; I'm through tomorrow! No more watching 'em drag out stiffs for me—not that way. Dunno why I gotta go back, anyhow; it won't do 'em any good to get in further, even if they can. From now on, I'm driving a truck, so help me I am!"

Ferrel let him rave on, only vaguely aware that the man was close to hysteria. He had no time to give to Beel now as he saw the raw red flesh through the visor of one of the armor suits. "Cut off what clothes you can, Jones," he directed. "At least get the shield suits off them. Tannic acid ready, nurse?"

"Ready." Meyers answered together with Jenkins, who was busily helping Jones strip off the heavily armored suits and helmets.

Ferrel kicked on the supersonics again, letting them sterilize the metal suits—there was going to be no chance to be finicky about asepsis; the supersonics and ultraviolet tubes were supposed to take care of that, and they'd have to do it, to a large extent, little as he liked it. Jenkins finished his part, dived back for fresh gloves, with a mere cursory dipping of his hands into antiseptic and rinse. Dodd followed him, while Jones wheeled three of the cases into the middle of the surgery, ready for work; the other had died on the way in.

It was going to be messy work, obviously. Where metal from the suits had touched, or come near touching, the flesh was burned—crisped, rather. And that was merely a minor part of it, as was the more than ample evidence of major radiation burns, which had probably not stopped at the surface, but penetrated through the flesh and bones into the vital interior organs. Much worse, the writhing and spasmodic muscular contractions indicated radioactive matter that had been forced into the flesh and was acting directly on the nerves controlling the motor impulses. Jenkins looked hastily at the twisting body of his case, and his face blanched to a yellowish white; it was the first real example of the full possibilities of an atomic accident he'd seen.

"Curare," he said finally, the word forced out, but level. Meyers handed him the hypodermic and he inserted it, his

hand still steady—more than normally steady, in fact, with
that absolute lack of movement that can come to a living organism only under the stress of emergency. Ferrel dropped
his eyes back to his own case, both relieved and worried.

From the spread of the muscular convulsions, there could
be only one explanation—somehow, radioactives had not
only worked their way through the air grills, but had been
forced through the almost airtight joints and sputtered
directly into the flesh of the men. Now they were sending out
radiations into every nerve, throwing aside the normal orders
from the brain and spinal column, setting up anarchic orders
of their own that left the muscles to writhe and jerk, one
against the other, without order or reason, or any of the normal restraints the body places upon itself. The closest parallel
was that of a man undergoing metrozol shock for schizophrenia, or a severe case of strychnine poisoning. He injected
curare carefully, metering out the dosage according to the
best estimate he could make, but Jenkins had been acting under a pressure that finished the second injection as Doc
looked up from his first. Still, in spite of the rapid spread of
the drug, some of the twitching went on.

"Curare," Jenkins repeated, and Doc tensed mentally; he'd
still been debating whether to risk the extra dosage. But he
made no counter-order, feeling slightly relieved this time at
having the matter taken out of his hands; Jenkins went back
to work, pushing up the injections to the absolute limit of
safety, and slightly beyond. One of the cases had started a
weird minor moan that hacked on and off as his lungs and
vocal cords went in and out of synchronization, but it quieted
under the drug, and in a matter of minutes the three lay still,
breathing with the shallow flaccidity common to curare treatment. They were still moving slightly, but where before they
were perfectly capable of breaking their own bones in
uncontrolled efforts, now there was only motion similar to a
man with a chill.

"God bless the man who synthesized curare," Jenkins muttered as he began cleaning away damaged flesh, Meyers assisting.

Doc could repeat that; with the older, natural product, true
standardization and exact dosage had been next to impossible.
Too much, and its action on the body was fatal; the patient
died from "exhaustion" of his chest muscles in a matter of
minutes. Too little was practically useless. Now that the dan-

ger of self-injury and fatal exhaustion from wild exertion was over, he could attend to such relatively unimportant things as the agony still going on—curare had no particular effect on the sensory nerves. He injected neo-heroin and began cleaning the burned areas and treating them with the standard tannic-acid routine, first with a sulphonamide to eliminate possible infection, glancing up occasionally at Jenkins.

He had no need to worry, though; the boy's nerves were frozen into an unnatural calm that still pressed through with a speed Ferrel made no attempt to equal, knowing his work would suffer for it. At a gesture, Dodd handed him the little radiation detector, and he began hunting over the skin, inch by inch, for the almost microscopic bits of matter; there was no hope of finding all now, but the worst deposits could be found and removed; later, with more time, a final probing could be made.

"Jenkins," he asked, "how about I-713's chemical action? Is it basically poisonous to the system?"

"No. Perfectly safe except for radiation. Eight in the outer electron ring, chemically inert."

That, as least, was a relief. Radiations were bad enough in and of themselves, but when coupled with metallic poisoning, like the old radium or mercury poisoning, it was even worse. The small colloidally fine particles of I-713 in the flesh would set up their own danger signal, and could be scraped away in the worst cases; otherwise, they'd probably have to stay until the isotope exhausted itself. Mercifully, its half-life was short, which would decrease the long hospitalization and suffering of the men.

Jenkins joined Ferrel on the last patient, replacing Dodd at handing instruments. Doc would have preferred the nurse, who was used to his little signals, but he said nothing, and was surprised to note the efficiency of the boy's cooperation. "How about the breakdown products?" he asked.

"I-713? Harmless enough, mostly, and what isn't harmless isn't concentrated enough to worry about. That is, if it's still I-713. Otherwise—"

Otherwise, Doc finished mentally, the boy meant there'd be no danger from poisoning, at least. Isotope R, with an uncertain degeneration period, turned into Mahler's Isotope, with a complete breakdown in a billionth of a second. He had a fleeting vision of men, filled with a fine dispersion of that, suddenly erupting over their body with a violence that could never be described; Jenkins must have been thinking the same thing. For a few seconds, they stood there, looking at each other silently, but neither chose to speak of it. Ferrel reached for the probe, Jenkins shrugged, and they went on with their work and their thoughts.

It was a picture impossible to imagine, which they might or might not see; if such an atomic blowup occurred, what would happen to the laboratory was problematical. No one knew the exact amount Maicewicz had worked on, except that it was the smallest amount he could make, so there could be no good estimate of the damage. The bodies on the operating tables, the little scraps of removed flesh containing the minute globules of radioactive, even the instruments that had come in contact with them, were bombs waiting to explode. Ferrel's own fingers took on some of the steadiness that was frozen in Jenkins as he went about his work, forcing his mind onto the difficult labor at hand.

It might have been minutes or hours later when the last dressing was in place and the three broken bones of the worst case were set. Meyers and Dodd, along with Jones, were taking care of the men, putting them into the little wards, and the two physicians were alone, carefully avoiding each other's eyes, waiting without knowing exactly what they expected.

Outside, a droning chug came to their ears, and the thump of something heavy moving over the runways. By common impulse they slipped to the side door and looked out, to see the rear end of one of the electric tanks moving away from them. Night had fallen some time before, but the gleaming lights from the big towers around the fence made the plant stand out in glaring detail. Except for the tank moving away, though, other buildings cut off their view.

Then, from the direction of the main gate, a shrill whistle cut the air and there was the sound of men's voices, though the words were indistinguishable. Sharp, crisp syllables followed, and Jenkins nodded slowly to himself. "Ten'll get you a hundred," he began, "that— Uh, no use betting. It is."

Around the corner a squad of men in state militia uniform marched briskly, bayoneted rifles on their arms. With efficient precision, they spread out under a sergeant's direction, each taking a post before the door of one of the buildings, one approaching the place where Ferrel and Jenkins stood.

"So that's what Palmer was talking to the Governor about," Ferrel muttered. "No use asking them questions, I suppose; they know less than we do. Come on inside where we can sit down and rest. Wonder what good the militia can do here—unless Palmer's afraid someone inside's going to crack and cause trouble."

Jenkins followed him back to the office and accepted a cigarette automatically as he flopped back into a chair. Doc was discovering just how good it felt to give his muscles and nerves a chance to relax, and realizing that they must have been far longer in the surgery than he had thought. "Care for a drink?"

"Uh—is it safe, Doc? We're apt to be back in there any minute."

Ferrel pulled a grin onto his face and nodded. "It won't hurt you—we're just enough on edge and tired for it to be burned up inside for fuel instead of reaching our nerves. Here." It was a generous slug of rye he poured for each, enough to send an almost immediate warmth through them, and to relax their overtensed nerves. "Wonder why Beel hasn't been back long ago?"

"That tank we saw probably explains it; it got too tough for the men to work in just their suits, and they've had to start excavating through the converters with the tanks. Electric, wasn't it, battery powered? . . . So there's enough radiation loose out there to interfere with atomic-powered machines, then. That means whatever they're doing is tough and slow work. Anyhow, it's more important that they damp the action than get the men out, if they only realize it—Sue!"

Ferrel looked up quickly to see the girl standing there, already dressed for surgery, and he was not too old for a little glow of appreciation to creep over him. No wonder Jenkins' face lighted up. She was small, but her figure was shaped like that of a taller girl, not in the cute or pert lines usually associated with shorter women, and the serious competence of her expression hid none of the liveliness of her face. Obviously she was several years older than Jenkins, but as he stood up to greet her, her face softened and seemed somehow youthful beside the boy's as she looked up.

"You're Dr. Ferrel?" she asked, turning to the older man. "I was a little late—there was some trouble at first about letting me in—so I went directly to prepare before bothering you. And just so you won't be afraid to use me, my credentials are all here."

She put the little bundle on the table, and Ferrel ran through them briefly; it was better than he'd expected. Technically she wasn't a nurse at all, but a doctor of medicine, a

so-called nursing doctor; there'd been the need for assistants
midway between doctor and nurse for years, having the general training and abilities of both, but only in the last decade
had the actual course been created, and the graduates were
still limited to a few. He nodded and handed them back.

"We can use you, Dr.—"

"Brown—professional name, Dr. Ferrel. And I'm used to
being called just Nurse Brown."

Jenkins cut in on the formalities. "Sue, is there any news
outside about what's going on here?"

"Rumors, but they're wild, and I didn't have a chance to
hear many. All I know is that they're talking about evacuating the city and everything within fifty miles of here, but it
isn't official. And some people were saying the Governor was
sending in troops to declare martial law over the whole section, but I didn't see any except here."

Jenkins took her off, then, to show her the Infirmary and
introduce her to Jones and the two other nurses, leaving Ferrel to wait for the sound of the siren again, and to try putting
two and two together to get sixteen. He attempted to make
sense out of the article in the *Weekly Ray*, but gave it up finally; atomic theory had advanced too far since the sketchy
studies he'd made, and the symbols were largely without
meaning to him. He'd have to rely on Jenkins, it seemed. In
the meantime, what was holding up the litter? He should
have heard the warning siren long before.

It wasn't the litter that came in next, though, but a group
of five men, two carrying a third, and a fourth supporting the
fifth. Jenkins took the carried man over, Brown helping him;
it was similar to the former cases, but without the actual
burns from contact with hot metal. Ferrel turned to the men.

"Where's Beel and the litter?" He was inspecting the supported man's leg as he asked, and began work on it without
moving the fellow to a table. Apparently a lump of radioactive matter the size of a small pea had been driven half an
inch into the flesh below the thigh, and the broken bone was
the result of the violent contractions of the man's own
muscles under the stimulus of the radiation. It wasn't pretty.
Now, however, the strength of the action had apparently
burned out the nerves around, so the leg was comparatively
limp and without feeling; the man lay watching, relaxed on
the bench in a half-comatose condition, his eyes popping out
and his lips twisted into a sick grimace, but he did not flinch

as the wound was scraped out. Ferrel was working around a small leaden shield, his arms covered with heavily leaded gloves, and he dropped the scraps of flesh and isotope into a box of the same metal.

"Beel—he's out of this world, Doc," one of the others answered when he could tear his eyes off the probing. "He got himself blotto, somehow, and wrecked the litter before he got back. Couldn't take it, watching us grapple 'em out—and we hadda go after 'em without a drop of hooch!"

Ferrel glanced at him quickly, noticing Jenkins' head jerk around as he did so. "You were getting them out? You mean you didn't come from in there?"

"Heck, no, Doc. Do we look that bad? Them two got it when the stuff decided to spit on 'em clean through their armor. Me, I got me some nice burns, but I ain't complaining—I got a look at a couple of stiffs, so I'm kicking about nothing!"

Ferrel hadn't noticed the three who had traveled under their own power, but he looked now, carefully. They were burned, and badly, by radiations, but the burns were still new enough not to give them too much trouble, and probably what they'd just been through had temporarily deadened their awareness of pain, just as a soldier on the battlefield may be wounded and not realize it until the action stops. Anyway, atomjacks were not noted for sissiness.

"There's almost a quart in the office there on the table," he told them. "One good drink apiece—no more. Then go up front and I'll send Nurse Brown in to fix up your burns as well as can be for now." Brown could apply the unguents developed to heal radiation burns as well as he could, and some division of work that would relieve Jenkins and himself seemed necessary. "Any chance of finding any more living men in the converter housings?"

"Maybe. Somebody said the thing let out a groan half a minute before it popped, so most of 'em had a chance to duck into the two safety chambers. Figure on going back there and pushing tanks ourselves unless you say no; about half an hour's work left before we can crack the chambers, I guess, then we'll know."

"Good. And there's no sense in sending in every man with a burn, or we'll be flooded here; they can wait and it looks as if we'll have plenty of serious stuff to care for. Dr. Brown, I guess you're elected to go out with the men—have one of them drive the spare litter Jones will show you. Salve down

all the burn cases, put the worst ones off duty, and just send
in the ones with the jerks. You'll find my emergency kit in
the office, there. Someone has to be out there to give first aid
and sort them out—we haven't room for the whole plant in
here."

"Right, Dr. Ferrel." She let Meyers replace her in assisting
Jenkins, and was gone briefly to come out with his bag.
"Come on, you men. I'll hop the litter and dress down your
burns on the way. You're appointed driver, mister. Somebody
should have reported that Beel person before, so the litter
would be out there now."

The spokesman for the others upended the glass he'd filled,
swallowed, gulped, and grinned down at her. "O. K., doctor,
only out there you ain't got time to think—you gotta do.
Thanks for the shot, Doc, and I'll tell Hoke you're appointing
her out there."

They filed out behind Brown as Jones went out to get the
second litter, and Doc went ahead with the quick-setting plastic cast for the broken leg. Too bad there weren't more of
those nursing doctors; he'd have to see Palmer about it after
this was over—if Palmer and he were still around. Wonder
how the men in the safety chambers about which he'd completely forgotten, would make out? There were two in each
converter housing, designed as an escape for the men in case
of accident, and supposed to be proof against almost anything. If the men had reached them, maybe they were all
right; he wouldn't have taken a bet on it, though. With a
slight shrug, he finished his work and went over to help
Jenkins.

The boy nodded down at the body on the table, already
showing extensive scraping and probing. "Quite a bit of spitting clean through the armor," he commented. "These words
were just a little too graphic for me. I-713 couldn't do that."

"Hm-m-m." Doc was in no mood to quibble on the subject. He caught himself looking at the little box in which the
stuff was put after they worked what they could out of the
flesh, and jerked his eyes away quickly. Whenever the lid was
being dropped, a glow could be seen inside. Jenkins always
managed to keep his eyes on something else.

They were almost finished when the switchboard girl announced a call, and they waited to make the few last touches
before answering, then filed into the office together. Brown's
face was on the screen, smudged and with a spot of rouge

standing out on each cheek. Another smudge appeared as she brushed the auburn hair out of her eyes with the back of her wrist.

"They've cracked the converter safety chambers, Dr. Ferrel. The north one held up perfectly, except for the heat and a little burn, but something happened in the other; oxygen valve stuck, and all are unconscious, but alive. Magma must have sprayed through the door, because sixteen or seventeen have the jerks, and about a dozen are dead. Some others need more care than I can give—I'm having Hokusai delegate men to carry those the stretchers won't hold, and they're all piling up on you in a bunch right now!"

Ferrel grunted and nodded. "Could have been worse, I guess. Don't kill yourself out there, Brown."

"Same to you." She blew Jenkins a kiss and snapped off, just as the whine of the litter siren reached their ears.

In the surgery again, they could see a truck showing behind it, and men lifting out bodies in apparently endless succession.

"Get their armor off, somehow, Jones—grab anyone else to help you that you can. Curare, Dodd, and keep handing it to me. We'll worry about everything else after Jenkins and I quiet them." This was obviously going to be a mass-production sort of business, not for efficiency, but through sheer necessity. And again, Jenkins with his queer taut steadiness was doing two for one that Doc could do, his face pale and his eyes almost glazed, but his hands moving endlessly and nervelessly on with his work.

Sometime during the night Jenkins looked up at Meyers, and motioned her back. "Go get some sleep, nurse; Miss Dodd can take care of both Dr. Ferrel and myself when we work close together. Your nerves are shot, and you need the rest. Dodd, you can call her back in two hours and rest yourself."

"What about you, doctor?"

"Me—" He grinned out of the corner of his mouth, crookedly. "I've got an imagination that won't sleep, and I'm needed here." The sentence ended on a rising inflection that was false to Ferrel's ear, and the older doctor looked at the boy thoughtfully.

Jenkins caught his look. "It's O. K., Doc; I'll let you know when I'm going to crack. It was O. K. to send Meyers back, wasn't it?"

"You were closer to her than I was, so you should know

better than I." Technically, the nurses were all directly under his control, but they'd dropped such technicalities long before. Ferrel rubbed the small of his back briefly, then picked up his scalpel again.

A faint gray light was showing in the east, and the wards had overflowed into the waiting room when the last case from the chambers was finished as best he could be. During the night, the converter had continued to spit occasionally, even through the tank armor twice, but now there was a temporary lull in the arrival of workers for treatment. Doc sent Jones after breakfast from the cafeteria, then headed into the office where Jenkins was already slumped down in the old leather chair.

The boy was exhausted almost to the limit from the combined strain of the work and his own suppressed jitters, but he looked up in mild surprise as he felt the prick of the needle. Ferrel finished it, and used it on himself before explaining. "Morphine, of course. What else can we do? Just enough to keep us going, but without it we'll both be useless out there in a few more hours. Anyhow, there isn't as much reason not to use it as there was when I was younger, before the counter-agent was discovered to kill most of its habit-forming tendency. Even five years ago, before they had that, there were times when morphine was useful, Lord knows, though anyone who used it except as a last resort deserved all the hell he got. A real substitute for sleep would be better, though; wish they'd finish up the work they're doing on that fatigue eliminator at Harvard. Here, eat that!"

Jenkins grimaced at the breakfast Jones laid out in front of him, but he knew as well as Doc that the food was necessary, and he pulled the plate back to him. "What I'd give an eye tooth for, Doc, wouldn't be a substitute—just half an hour of good old-fashioned sleep. Only, damn it, if I knew I had time, I couldn't do it—not with R out there bubbling away."

The telephone annunciator clipped in before Doc could answer. "Telephone for Dr. Ferrel; emergency! Dr. Brown calling Dr. Ferrel!"

"Ferrel answering!" The phone girl's face popped off the screen, and a tired-faced Sue Brown looked out at them. "What is it?"

"It's that little Japanese fellow—Hokusai—who's been running things out here, Dr. Ferrel. I'm bringing him in with an acute case of appendicitis. Prepare surgery!"

Jenkins gagged over the coffee he was trying to swallow,

and his choking voice was halfway between disgust and hysterical laughter. "Appendicitis, Doc! My God, what comes next?"

III

It might have been worse. Brown had coupled in the little freezing unit on the litter and lowered the temperature around the abdomen, both preparing Hokusai for surgery and slowing down the progress of the infection so that the appendix was still unbroken when he was wheeled into the surgery. His seamed Oriental face had a grayish cast under the olive, but he managed a faint grin.

"Verry ssorry, Dr. Ferrel, to bother you. Verry ssorry. No ether, pleasse!"

Ferrel grunted. "No need of it, Hoke; we'll use hypothermy, since it's already begun. Over here, Jones. . . . And you might as well go back and sit down, Jenkins."

Brown was washing, and popped out again, ready to assist with the operation. "He had to be tied down, practically, Dr. Ferrel. Insisted that he only needed a little mineral oil and some peppermint for his stomach-ache! Why are intelligent people always the most stupid?"

It was a mystery to Ferrel, too, but seemingly the case. He tested the temperature quickly while the surgery hypothermy equipment began functioning, found it low enough, and began. Hoke flinched with his eyes as the scalpel touched him, then opened them in mild surprise at feeling no appreciable pain. The complete absence of nerve response with its accompanying freedom from post-operative shock was one of the great advantages of low-temperature work in surgery. Ferrel laid back the flesh, severed the appendix quickly, and removed it through the tiny incision. Then, with one of the numerous attachments, he made use of the ingenious mechanical stitcher and stepped back.

"All finished, Hoke, and you're lucky you didn't rupture—peritonitis isn't funny, even though we can cut down on it with the sulphonamides. The ward's full, so's the waiting room, so you'll have to stay on the table for a few hours until we can find a place for you; no pretty nurse, either—until the two other girls get here some time this morning. I dunno what we'll do about the patients."

"But, Dr. Ferrel, I am hear that now ssurgery—I sshould be up, already. There iss work I am do."

"You've been hearing that appendectomy patients aren't confined now, eh? Well, that's partly true. Johns Hopkins began it quite awhile ago. But for the next hour, while the temperature comes back to normal, you stay put. After that, if you want to move around a little, you can; but no going out to the converter. A little exercise probably helps more than it harms, but any strain wouldn't be good."

"But, the danger—"

"Be hanged, Hoke. You couldn't help now, long enough to do any good. Until the stuff in those stitches dissolves away completely in the body fluids, you're to take it easy—and that's two weeks, about."

The little man gave in, reluctantly. "Then I think I ssleep now. But besst you sshould call Mr. Palmer at once, pleasse! He musst know I am not there!"

Palmer took the news the hard way, with an unfair but natural tendency to blame Hokusai and Ferrel. "Damn it, Doc, I was hoping he'd get things straightened out somehow—I practically promised the Governor that Hoke could take care of it; he's got one of the best brains in the business. Now this! Well, no help, I guess. He certainly can't do it unless he's in condition to get right into things. Maybe Jorgenson, though, knows enough about it to handle it from a wheel chair, or something. How's he coming along—in shape to be taken out where he can give directions to the foremen?"

"Wait a minute." Ferrel stopped him as quickly as he could. "Jorgenson isn't here. We've got thirty-one men lying around, and he isn't one of them; and if he'd been one of the seventeen dead, you'd know it. I didn't know Jorgenson was working, even."

"He had to be—it was his process! Look, Ferrel, I was distinctly told that he was taken to you—foreman dumped him on the litter himself and reported at once! Better check up, and quick—with Hoke only half able, I've got to have Jorgenson!"

"He isn't here—I know Jorgenson. The foreman must have mistaken the big fellow from the south safety for him, but that man had black hair inside his helmet. What about the three hundred-odd that were only unconscious, or the fifteen-sixteen hundred men outside the converter when it happened?"

Palmer wiggled his jaw muscles tensely. "Jorgenson would

have reported or been reported fifty times. Every man out there wants him around to boss things. He's gotta be in your ward."

"He isn't, I tell you! And how about moving some of the fellows here into the city hospitals?"

"Tried—hospitals must have been tipped off somehow about the radioactives in the flesh, and they refuse to let a man from here be brought in." Palmer was talking with only the surface of his mind, his cheek muscles bobbing as if he were chewing his thoughts and finding them tough. "Jorgenson—Hoke—and Kellar's been dead for years. Not another man in the whole country that understands this field enough to make a decent guess, even; I get lost on page six myself. Ferrel, could a man in a Tomlin five-shield armor suit make the safety in twenty seconds, do you think, from—say beside the converter?"

Ferrel considered it rapidly. A Tomlin weighed about four hundred pounds, and Jorgenson was an ox of a man, but only human. "Under the stress of an emergency, it's impossible to guess what a man can do, Palmer, but I don't see how he could work his way half that distance."

"Hm-m-m, I figured. Could he live, then, supposing he wasn't squashed? Those suits carry their own air for twenty-four hours, you know, to avoid any air cracks, pumping the carbon-dioxide back under pressure and condensing the moisture out—no openings of any kind. They've got the best insulation of all kinds we know, too."

"One chance in a billion, I'd guess; but again, it's darned hard to put any exact limit on what can be done—miracles keep happening, every day. Going to try it?"

"What else can I do? There's no alternative. I'll meet you outside No. 4 just as soon as you can make it, and bring everything you need to start working at once. Seconds may count!" Palmer's face slid sideways and up as he was reaching for the button, and Ferrel wasted no time in imitating the motion.

By all logic, there wasn't a chance, even in a Tomlin. But, until they knew, the effort would have to be made; chances couldn't be taken when a complicated process had gone out of control, with now almost certainty that Isotope R was the result—Palmer was concealing nothing, even though he had stated nothing specifically. And obviously, if Hoke couldn't handle it, none of the men at other branches of National

Atomic or at the smaller partially independent plants could make even a halfhearted stab at the job.

It all rested on Jorgenson, then. And Jorgenson must be somewhere under that semi-molten hell that could drive through the tank armor and send men back into the infirmary with bones broken from their own muscular anarchy!

Ferrel's face must have shown his thoughts, judging by Jenkins' startled expression. "Jorgenson's still in there somewhere," he said quickly.

"Jorgenson! But he's the man who— Good Lord!"

"Exactly. You'll stay here and take care of the jerk cases that may come in. Brown, I'll want you out there again. Bring everything portable we have, in case we can't move him in fast enough; get one of the trucks and fit it out; and be out with it about twice as fast as you can! I'm grabbing the litter now." He accepted the emergency kit Brown thrust into his hands, dumped a caffeine tablet into his mouth without bothering to wash it down, then was out toward the litter. "No. 4, and hurry!"

Palmer was just jumping off a scooter as they cut around No. 3 and in front of the rough fence of rope strung out quite a distance beyond 4. He glanced at Doc, nodded, and dived in through the men grouped around, yelling orders to right and left as she went, and was back at Ferrel's side by the time the litter had stopped.

O. K., Ferrel, go over there and get into armor as quickly as possible! We're going in there with the tanks, whether we can or not, and be damned to the quenching for the moment. Briggs, get those things out of there, clean out a roadway as best you can, throw in the big crane again, and we'll need all the men in armor we can get—give them steel rods and get them to probing in there for anything solid and big or small enough to be a man—five minutes at a stretch; they should be able to stand that. I'll be back pronto!"

Doc noted the confused mixture of tanks and machines of all descriptions clustered around the walls—or what was left of them—of the converter housing, and saw them yanking out everything along one side, leaving an opening where the main housing gate had stood, now ripped out to expose a crane boom rooting out the worst obstructions. Obviously they'd been busy at some kind of attempt at quenching the action, but his knowledge of atomics was too little even to guess at what it was. The equipment set up was being pushed aside by tanks without dismantling, and men were running up into the roped-in section, some already armored, others dragging on part of their armor as they went. With the help of one of the atomjacks, he climbed into a suit himself, wondering what he could do in such a casing if anything needed doing.

Palmer had a suit on before him, though, and was waiting beside one of the tanks, squat and heavily armored, its front equipped with both a shovel and a grapple swinging from movable beams. "In here, Doc." Ferrel followed him into the housing of the machine and Palmer grabbed the controls as he pulled on a shortwave headset and began shouting orders through it toward the other tanks that were moving in on their heavy treads. The dull drone of the motor picked up, and the tank began lumbering forward under the manager's direction.

"Haven't run one of these since that show-off at a picnic seven years ago," he complained, as he kicked at the controls and straightened out a developing list to left. "Though I used to be pretty handy when I was plain engineer. Damned static around here almost chokes off the radio, but I guess enough gets through. By the best guess I can make, Jorgenson should have been near the main control panel when it started, and have headed for the south chamber. Half the distance, you figure?"

"Possibly, probably slightly less."

"Yeah! And then the stuff may have tossed him around. But we'll have to try to get there." He barked into the radio again. "Briggs, get those men in suits as close as you can and have them fish with their rods about thirty feet to the left of the pillar that's still up—can they get closer?"

The answer was blurred and pieces missing, but the general idea went across. Palmer frowned. "O. K., if they can't make it, they can't; draw them back out of the reach of the stuff and hold them ready to go in. . . . No, call for volunteers! I'm offering a thousand dollars a minute to every man that gets a stick in there, double to his family if the stuff gets him, and ten times that—fifty thousand—if he locates Jorgenson! . . . Look out, you blamed fool!" The last was to one of the men who'd started forward, toward the place, jumping from one piece of broken building to grab at a pillar and swing off in his suit toward something that looked like a standing position; it toppled, but he managed a leap that carried him to another lump, steadied himself, and began probing through the mess. "Oof! You with the crane—stick it in where you

can grab any of the men that pass out, if it'll reach—good!
Doc, I know as well as you that the men have no business in
there, even five minutes; but I'll send in a hundred more if
it'll find Jorgenson!"

Doc said nothing—he knew there'd probably be a hundred
or more fools willing to try, and he knew the need of them.
The tanks couldn't work their way close enough for any careful investigation of the mixed mass of radioactives, machinery, building debris, and destruction, aside from which they
were much too slow in such delicate probing; only men
equipped with the long steel poles could do that. As he
watched, some of the activity of the magma suddenly caused
an eruption, and one of the men tossed up his pole and doubled back into a half circle before falling. The crane operator
shoved the big boom over and made a grab, missed, brought
it down again, and came out with the heaving body held by
one arm, to run it back along its track and twist it outward
beyond Doc's vision.

Even through the tank and the suit, heat was pouring in,
and there was a faint itching in those parts where the armor
was thinnest that indicated the start of a burn—though not as
yet dangerous. He had no desire to think what was happening
to the men who were trying to worm into the heart of it in
nothing but armor; nor did he care to watch what was happening to them. Palmer was trying to inch the machine
ahead, but the stuff underneath made any progress difficult.
Twice something spat against the tank, but did not penetrate.

"Five minutes are up," he told Palmer. "They'd all better
go directly to Dr. Brown, who should be out with the truck
now for immediate treatment."

Palmer nodded and relayed the instructions. "Pick up all
you can with the crane and carry them back! Send in a new
bunch, Briggs, and credit them with their bonus in advance.
Damn it, Doc, this can go on all day; it'll take an hour to pry
around through this mess right here, and then he's probably
somewhere else. The stuff seems to be getting worse in this
neighborhood, too, from what accounts I've had before. Wonder if that steel plate could be pushed down?"

He threw in the clutch engaging the motor to the treads
and managed to twist through toward it. There was a slight
slipping of the lugs, then the tractors caught, and the nose of
the tank thrust forward; almost without effort, the fragment
of housing toppled from its leaning position and slid forward.

The tank growled, fumbled, and slowly climbed up onto it and ran forward another twenty feet to its end; the support settled slowly, but something underneath checked it, and they were still again. Palmer worked the grapple forward, nosing a big piece of masonry out of the way, and two men reached out with the ends of their poles to begin probing, futilely. Another change of men came out, then another.

Briggs' voice crackled erratically through the speaker again. "Palmer, I got a fool here who wants to go out on the end of your beam, if you can swing around so the crane can lift him out to it."

"Start him coming!" Again he began jerking the levers, and the tank buckled and heaved, backed and turned, ran forward and repeated it all, while the plate that was holding them flopped up and down on its precarious balance.

Doc held his breath and began praying to himself; his admiration for the men who'd go out in that stuff was increasing by leaps and bounds, along with his respect for Palmer's ability.

The crane boom bobbed toward them, and the scoop came running out, but wouldn't quite reach; their own tank was relatively light and mobile compared to the bigger machine, but Palmer already had that pushed out to the limit, and hanging over the edge of the plate. It still lacked three feet of reaching.

"Damn!" Palmer slapped open the door of the tank, jumped forward on the tread, and looked down briefly before coming back inside. "No chance to get closer! Wheeoo! Those men earn their money."

But the crane operator had his own tricks, and was bobbing the boom of his machine up and down slowly with a motion that set the scoop swinging like a huge pendulum, bringing it gradually closer to the grapple beam. The man had an arm out, and finally caught the beam, swinging out instantly from the scoop that drew backward behind him. He hung suspended for a second, pitching his body around to a better position, then somehow wiggled up onto the end and braced himself with his legs. Doc let his breath out and Palmer inched the tank around to a forward position again. Now the pole of the atomjack could cover the wide territory before them, and he began using it rapidly.

"Win or lose, that man gets a triple bonus," Palmer muttered. "Uh!"

The pole had located something, and was feeling around to determine size; the man glanced at them and pointed frantically. Doc jumped forward to the windows as Palmer ran down the grapple and began pushing it down into the semi-molten stuff under the pole; there was resistance there, but finally the prong of the grapple broke under and struck on something that refused to come up. The manager's hands moved the controls gently, making it tug from side to side; reluctantly, it gave and moved forward toward them, coming upward until they could make out the general shape. It was definitely no Tomlin suit!

"Lead hopper box! Damn—Wait, Jorgenson wasn't anybody's fool; when he saw he couldn't make the safety, he might . . . maybe—" Palmer slapped the grapple down again, against the closed lid of the chest, but the hook was too large. Then the man clinging there caught the idea and slid down to the hopper chest, his armored hands grabbing at the lid. He managed to lift a corner of it until the grapple could catch and lift it the rest of the way, and his hands started down to jerk upward again.

The manager watched his motions, then flipped the box over with the grapple, and pulled it closer to the tank body; magma was running out, but there was a gleam of something else inside.

"Start praying, Doc!" Palmer worked it to the side of the tank and was out through the door again, letting the merciless heat and radiation stream in.

But Ferrel wasn't bothering with that now; he followed, reaching down into the chest to help the other two lift out the body of a huge man in a five-shield Tomlin! Somehow, they wangled the six-hundred-odd pounds out and up on the treads, then into the housing, barely big enough for all of them. The atomjack pulled himself inside, shut the door and flopped forward on his face, out cold.

"Never mind him—check Jorgenson!" Palmer's voice was heavy with the reaction from the hunt, but he turned the tank and sent it outward at top speed, regardless of risk. Contrarily, it bucked through the mass more readily than it had crawled in through the cleared section.

Ferrel unscrewed the front plate of the armor on Jorgenson as rapidly as he could, though he knew already that the man was still miraculously alive—corpses don't jerk with force enough to move a four-hundred-pound suit appreciably. A side glance, as they drew beyond the wreck of the con-

verter housing, showed the men already beginning to set up
equipment to quell the atomic reaction again, but the armor
front plate came loose at last, and he dropped his eyes back
without noticing details, to cut out a section of clothing and
make the needed injections; curare first, then neo-heroin, and
curare again, though he did not dare inject the quantity that
seemed necessary. There was nothing more he could do until
they could get the man out of his armor. He turned to the
atomjack, who was already sitting up, propped against the
driving seat's back.

" 'Snothing much, Doc," the fellow managed. "No jerks,
just burn and that damned heat! Jorgenson?"

"Alive at least," Palmer answered, with some relief. The
tank stopped, and Ferrel could see Brown running forward
from beside a truck. "Get that suit off you, get yourself
treated for the burn, then go up to the office where the check
will be ready for you!"

"Fifty-thousand check?" The doubt in the voice registered
over the weakness.

"Fifty thousand plus triple your minute time, and cheap;
maybe we'll toss in a medal or a bottle of Scotch, too. Here,
you fellows give a hand."

Ferrel had the suit ripped off with Brown's assistance and
paused only long enough for one grateful breath of clean,
cool air before leading the way toward the truck. As he
neared it, Jenkins popped out, directing a group of men to
move two loaded stretchers onto the litter, and nodding jerkily at Ferrel. "With the truck all equipped, we decided to
move out here and take care of the damage as it came up—
Sue and I rushed them through enough to do until we can
find more time, so we could give full attention to Jorgenson.
He's still living!"

"By a miracle. Stay out here, Brown, until you've finished
with the men from inside, then we'll try to find some rest for
you."

The three huskies carrying Jorgenson placed the body on
the table set up, and began ripping off the bulky armor as the
truck got under way. Fresh gloves came out of a small steril-
izer, and the two doctors fell to work at once, treating the
badly burned flesh and trying to locate and remove the worst
of the radioactive matter.

"No use." Doc stepped back and shook his head. "It's all
over him, probably clear into his bones in places. We'd have
to put him through a filter to get it all out!"

Palmer was looking down at the raw mass of flesh, with all the layman's sickness at such a sight. "Can you fix him up, Ferrel?"

"We can try, that's all. Only explanation I can give for his being alive at all is that the hopper box must have been pretty well above the stuff until a short time ago—very short—and this stuff didn't work in until it sank. He's practically dehydrated now, apparently, but he couldn't have perspired enough to keep from dying of heat if he'd been under all that for even an hour—insulation or no insulation." There was admiration in Doc's eyes as he looked down at the immense figure of the man. "And he's tough; if he weren't, he'd have killed himself by exhaustion, even confined inside that suit and box, after the jerks set in. He's close to having done so, anyway. Until we can find some way of getting that stuff out of him, we don't dare risk getting rid of the curare's effect—that's a time-consuming job, in itself. Better give him another water and sugar intravenous, Jenkins. Then, if we do fix him up, Palmer, I'd say it's a fifty-fifty chance that all this hasn't driven him stark crazy."

The truck had stopped, and the men lifted the stretcher off and carried it inside as Jenkins finished the injection. He went ahead of them, but Doc stopped outside to take Palmer's cigarette for a long drag, and let them go ahead.

"Cheerful!" The manager lighted another from the butt, his shoulders sagging. "I've been trying to think of one man who might possibly be of some help to us, Doc, and there isn't such a person—anywhere. I'm sure now, after being in there, that Hoke couldn't do it. Kellar, if he were still alive, could probably pull the answer out of a hat after three looks—he had an instinct and genius for it; the best man the business ever had, even if his tricks did threaten to steal our work out from under us and give him the lead. But—well, now there's Jorgenson—either he gets in shape, or else!"

Jenkins' frantic yell reached them suddenly. "Doc! Jorgenson's dead! He's stopped breathing entirely!"

Doc jerked forward into a full run, a white-faced Palmer at his heels.

IV

Dodd was working artificial respiration and Jenkins had the oxygen mask in his hands, adjusting it over Jorgenson's face, before Ferrel reached the table. He made a grab for the pulse that had been fluttering weakly enough before, felt it flicker feebly once, pause for about three times normal period, lift feebly again, and then stop completely. "Adrenlin!"

"Already shot it into his heart, Doc! Cardiacine, too!" The boy's voice was bordering on hysteria, but Palmer was obviously closer to it than Jenkins.

"Doc, you gotta—"

"Get the hell out of here!" Ferrel's hands suddenly had a life of their own as he grabbed frantically for instruments, ripped bandages off the man's chest, and began working against time, when time had all the advantages. It wasn't surgery—hardly good butchery; the bones that he cut through so ruthlessly with savage strokes of an instrument could never heal smoothly after being so mangled. But he couldn't worry about minor details now.

He tossed back the flap of flesh and ribs that he'd hacked out. "Stop the bleeding, Jenkins!" Then his hands plunged into the chest cavity, somehow finding room around Dodd's and Jenkins', and were suddenly incredibly gentle as they located the heart itself and began working on it, the skilled, exact massage of a man who knew every function of the vital organ. Pressure here, there, relax, pressure again; take it easy, don't rush things! It would do no good to try to set it going as feverishly as his emotions demanded. Pure oxygen was feeding into the lungs, and the heart could safely do less work. Hold it steady, one beat a second, sixty a minute.

It had been perhaps half a minute from the time the heart stopped before his massage was circulating blood again; too little time to worry about damage to the brain, the first part to be permanently affected by stoppage of the circulation. Now, if the heart could start again by itself within any reasonable time, death would be cheated again. How long? He had no idea. They'd taught him ten minutes when he was studying medicine, then there'd been a case of twenty minutes once, and while he was interning it had been pushed up to a record of slightly over an hour, which still stood; but that was an exceptional case. Jorgenson, praise be, was a normally healthy and vigorous specimen, and his system had been in first-class condition, but with the torture of those long hours, the radioactive, narcotic and curare all fighting against him, still one more miracle was needed to keep his life going.

Press, massage, relax, don't hurry it too much. There! For

a second, his fingers felt a faint flutter, then again; but it stopped. Still, as long as the organ could show such signs, there was hope, unless his fingers grew too tired and he muffed the job before the moment when the heart could be safely trusted by itself.

"Jenkins!"

"Yes, sir!"

"Ever do any heart massage?"

"Practiced it in school, sir, on a model, but never actually. Oh, a dog in dissection class, for five minutes. I . . . I don't think you'd better trust me, Doc."

"I may have to. If you did it on a dog for five minutes, you can do it on a man, probably. You know what hangs on it—you saw the converter and know what's going on."

Jenkins nodded, the tense nod he'd used earlier. "I know—that's why you can't trust me. I told you I'd let you know when I was going to crack—well, it's damned near here!"

Could a man tell his weakness, if he were about finished? Doc didn't know; he suspected that the boy's own awareness of his nerves would speed up such a break, if anything, but Jenkins was a queer case, having taut nerves sticking out all over him, yet a steadiness under fire that few older men could have equaled. If he had to use him, he would; there was no other answer.

Doc's fingers were already feeling stiff—not yet tired, but showing signs of becoming so. Another few minutes, and he'd have to stop. There was the flutter again, one—two—three! Then it stopped. There had to be some other solution to this; it was impossible to keep it up for the length of time probably needed, even if he and Jenkins spelled each other. Only Michel at Mayo's could—Mayo's! If they could get it here in time, that wrinkle he'd seen demonstrated at their last medical convention was the answer.

"Jenkins, call Mayo's—you'll have to get Palmer's O. K., I guess—ask for Kubelik, and bring the extension where I can talk to him!"

He could hear Jenkins' voice, level enough at first, then with a depth of feeling he'd have thought impossible in the boy. Dodd looked at him quickly and managed a grim smile, even as she continued with the respiration; nothing could make her blush, though it should have done so.

The boy jumped back. "No soap, Doc! Palmer can't be located—and that post-mortem misconception at the board won't listen."

Doc studied his hands in silence, wondering, then gave it up; there'd be no hope of his lasting while he sent out the boy. "O. K., Jenkins, you'll have to take over here, then. Steady does it, come on in slowly, get your fingers over mine. Now, catch the motion? Easy, don't rush things. You'll hold out—you'll have to! You've done better than I had any right to ask for so far, and you don't need to distrust yourself. There, got it?"

"Got it, Doc. I'll try, but for Pete's sake, whatever you're planning, get back here quick! I'm not lying about cracking! You'd better let Meyers replace Dodd and have Sue called back in here; she's the best nerve tonic I know."

"Call her in then, Dodd." Doc picked up a hypodermic syringe, filled it quickly with water to which a drop of another liquid added a brownish-yellow color, and forced his tired old legs into a reasonably rapid trot out of the side door and toward Communications. Maybe the switchboard operator was stubborn, but there were ways of handling people.

He hadn't counted on the guard outside the Communications Building, though. "Halt!"

"Life or death; I'm a physician."

"Not in here—I got orders." The bayonet's menace apparently wasn't enough; the rifle went up to the man's shoulder, and his chin jutted out with the stubbornness of petty authority and reliance on orders. "Nobody sick here. There's plenty of phones elsewhere. You get back—and fast!"

Doc started forward and there was a faint click from the rifle as the safety went off; the darned fool meant what he said. Shrugging, Ferrel stepped back—and brought the hypodermic needle up inconspicuously in line with the guard's face. "Ever see one of these things squirt curare? It can reach before your bullet hits!"

"Curare?" The guard's eyes flicked to the needle, and doubt came into them. The man frowned. "That's the stuff that kills people on arrows, ain't it?"

"It is—cobra venom, you know. One drop on the outside of your skin and you're dead in ten seconds." Both statements were out-and-out lies, but Doc was counting on the superstitious ignorance of the average man in connection with poisons. "This little needle can spray you with it very nicely, and it may be a fast death, but not a pleasant one. Want to put down the rifle?"

A regular might have shot; but the militiaman was taking no chances. He lowered the rifle gingerly, his eyes on the needle, then kicked the weapon aside at Doc's motion. Ferrel approached, holding the needle out, and the man shrank backward and away, letting him pick up the rifle as he went past to avoid being shot in the back. Lost time! But he knew his way around this little building, at least, and went straight toward the girl at the board.

"Get up!" His voice came from behind her shoulder and she turned to see the rifle in one of his hands; the needle in the other, almost touching her throat. "This is loaded with curare, deadly poison, and too much hangs on getting a call through to bother with physician's oaths right now, young lady. Up! No plugs! That's right; now get over there, out of the cell—there, on your face, cross your hands behind your back, and grab your ankles—right! Now if you move, you won't move long!"

Those ganster pictures he'd seen were handy, at that. She was thoroughly frightened and docile. But, perhaps, not so much so she might not have bungled his call deliberately. He had to do that himself. Darn it, the red lights were trunk lines, but which plug—try the inside one, it looked more logical; he'd seen it done, but couldn't remember. Now, you flip back one of these switches—uh-uh, the other way. The tone came in assuring him he had it right, and he dialed operator rapidly, his eyes flickering toward the girl lying on the floor, his thoughts on Jenkins and the wasted time running on.

"Operator, this is an emergency. I'm Walnut, 7654; I want to put in a long-distance call to Dr. Kubelik, Mayo's Hospital, Rochester, Minnesota. If Kubelik isn't there, I'll take anyone else who answers from his department. Speed is urgent."

"Very good, sir." Long-distance operators, mercifully, were usually efficient. There were the repeated signals and clicks of relays as she put it through, the answer from the hospital board, more wasted time, and then a face appeared on the screen; but not that of Kubelik. It was a much younger man.

Ferrel wasted no time in introduction. "I've got an emergency case here where all Hades depends on saving a man, and it can't be done without that machine of Dr. Kubelik's; he knows me, if he's there—I'm Ferrel, met him at the convention, got him to show me how the thing worked."

"Kubelik hasn't come in yet, Dr. Ferrel; I'm his assistant.

But, if you mean the heart and lung exciter, it's already boxed and supposed to leave for Harvard this morning. They've got a rush case out there, and may need it—"

"Not as much as I do."

"I'll have to call—Wait a minute, Dr. Ferrel, seems I remember your name now. Aren't you the chap with National Atomic?"

Doc nodded. "The same. Now, about that machine, if you'll stop the formalities—"

The face on the screen nodded, instant determination showing, with an underlying expression of something else. "We'll ship it down to you instantly, Ferrel. Got a field for a plane?"

"Not within three miles, but I'll have a truck sent out for it. How long?"

"Take too long by truck if you need it down there, Ferrel; I'll arrange to transship in air from our special speedster to a helicopter, have it delivered wherever you want. About—um, loading plane, flying a couple hundred miles, transshipping— about half an hour's the best we can do."

"Make it the square of land south of the infirmary, which is crossed visibly from the air. Thanks!"

"Wait, Dr. Ferrel!" The younger man checked Doc's cut- off. "Can you use it when you get it? It's tricky work."

"Kubelik gave quite a demonstration and I'm used to tricky work. I'll chance it—have to. Too long to rouse Kube- lik himself, isn't it?"

"Probably. O. K., I've got the telescript reply from the shipping office, it's starting for the plane. I wish you luck!"

Ferrel nodded his thanks, wondering. Service like that was welcome, but it wasn't the most comforting thing, mentally, to know that the mere mention of National Atomic would cause such an about-face. Rumors, it seemed, were spreading, and in a hurry, in spite of Palmer's best attempts. Good Lord, what was going on here? He'd been too busy for any serious worrying or to realize, but—well, it had gotten him the exciter, and for that he should be thankful.

The guard was starting uncertainly off for reinforcements when Doc came out, and he realized that the seemingly endless call must have been over in short order. He tossed the rifle well out of the man's reach and headed back toward the infirmary at a run, wondering how Jenkins had made out—it had to be all right!

Jenkins wasn't standing over the body of Jorgenson; Brown

was there instead, her eyes moist and her face pinched in and white around the nostrils that stood out at full width. She looked up, shook her head at him as he started forward, and went on working at Jorgenson's heart.

"Jenkins cracked?"

"Nonsense! This is woman's work, Dr. Ferrel, and I took over for him, that's all. You men try to use brute force all your life and then wonder why a woman can do twice as much delicate work where strong muscles are a nuisance. I chased him out and took over, that's all." But there was a catch in her voice as she said it, and Meyers was looking down entirely too intently at the work of artificial respiration.

"Hi, Doc!" It was Blake's voice that broke in. "Get away from there; when this Dr. Brown needs help, I'll be right in there. I've been sleeping like a darned fool all night, from four this morning on. Didn't hear the phone, or something, didn't know what was going on until I got to the gate out there. You go rest."

Ferrel grunted in relief; Blake might have been dead drunk when he finally reached home, which would explain his not hearing the phone, but his animal virility had soaked it out with no visible sign. The only change was the absence of the usual cocky grin on his face as he moved over beside Brown to test Jorgenson. "Thank the Lord you're here, Blake. How's Jorgenson doing?"

Brown's voice answered in a monotone, words coming in time to the motions of her fingers. "His heart shows signs of coming around once in a while, but it doesn't last. He isn't getting worse from what I can tell, though."

"Good. If we can keep him going half an hour more, we can turn all this over to a machine. Where's Jenkins?"

"A machine? Oh, the Kubelik exciter, of course. He was working on it when I was there. We'll keep Jorgenson alive until then, anyway, Dr. Ferrel."

"Where's Jenkins?" he repeated sharply, when she stopped with no intention of answering the former question.

Blake pointed toward Ferrel's office, the door of which was now closed. "In there. But lay off him, Doc. I saw the whole thing, and he feels like the deuce about it. He's a good kid, but only a kid, and this kind of hell could get any of us."

"I know all that." Doc headed toward the office, as much for a smoke as anything else. The sight of Blake's rested face was somehow an island of reassurance in this sea of fatigue and nerves. "Don't worry, Brown, I'm not planning on lacing him down, so you needn't defend your man so carefully. It was my fault for not listening to him."

Brown's eyes were pathetically grateful in the brief flash she threw him, and he felt like a heel for the gruffness that had been his first reaction to Jenkins' absence. If this kept on much longer, though, they'd all be in worse shape than the boy, whose back was toward him as he opened the door. The still, huddled shape did not raise its head from its arms as Ferrel put his hand onto one shoulder, and the voice was muffled and distant.

"I cracked, Doc—high, wide and handsome, all over the place. I couldn't take it! Standing there, Jorgenson maybe dying because I couldn't control myself right, the whole plant blowing up, all my fault. I kept telling myself I was O. K., I'd go on, then I cracked. Screamed like a baby! Dr. Jenkins— *nerve* specialist!"

"Yeah. . . . Here, are you going to drink this, or do I have to hold your blasted nose and pour it down your throat?" It was crude psychology, but it worked, and Doc handed over the drink, waited for the other to down it, and passed a cigarette across before sinking into his own chair. "You warned me, Jenkins, and I risked it on my own responsibility, so nobody's kicking. But I'd like to ask a couple of questions."

"Go ahead—what's the difference?" Jenkins had recovered a little, obviously, from the note of defiance that managed to creep into his voice.

"Did you know Brown could handle that kind of work? And did you pull your hands out before she could get hers in to replace them?"

"She told me she could. I didn't know before. I dunno about the other; I think . . . yeah, Doc, she had her hands over mine. But—"

Ferrel nodded, satisfied with his own guess. "I thought so. You didn't crack, as you put it, until your mind knew it was safe to do so—and then you simply passed the work on. By that definition, I'm cracking, too. I'm sitting in here, smoking, talking to you, when out there a man needs attention. The fact that he's getting it from two others, one practically fresh, the other at a least a lot better off than we are, doesn't have a thing to do with it, does it?"

"But it wasn't that way, Doc. I'm not asking for grandstand stuff from anybody."

"Nobody's giving it to you, son. All right, you screamed—

why not? It didn't hurt anything. I growled at Brown when I came in for the same reason—exhausted, overstrained nerves. If I went out there and had to take over from them, I'd probably scream myself, or start biting my tongue—nerves have to have an outlet; physically, it does them no good, but there's a psychological need for it." The boy wasn't convinced, and Doc sat back in the chair, staring at him thoughtfully. "Ever wonder why I'm here?"

"No, sir."

"Well, you might. Twenty-seven years ago, when I was about your age, there wasn't a surgeon in this country—or the world, for that matter—who had the reputation I had; any kind of surgery, brain, what have you. They're still using some of my techniques . . . uh-hum, thought you'd remember when the association of names hit you. I had a different wife then, Jenkins, and there was a baby coming. Brain tumor—I had to do it, no one else could. I did it, somehow, but I went out of that operating room in a haze, and it was three days later when they'd tell me she'd died; not my fault—I know that now—but I couldn't realize it then.

"So, I tried setting up as a general practitioner. No more surgery for me! And because I was a fair diagnostician, which most surgeons aren't, I made a living, at least. Then, when this company was set up, I applied for the job, and got it; I still had a reputation of sorts. It was a new field, something requiring study and research, and damned near every ability of most specialists plus a general practitioner's, so it kept me busy enough to get over my phobia of surgery. Compared to me, you don't know what nerves or cracking means. That little scream was a minor incident."

Jenkins made no comment, but lighted the cigarette he'd been holding. Ferrel relaxed farther into the chair, knowing that he'd be called if there was any need for his work, and glad to get his mind at least partially off Jorgenson. "It's hard to find a man for this work, Jenkins. It takes too much ability at too many fields, even though it pays well enough. We went through plenty of applicants before we decided on you, and I'm not regretting our choice. As a matter of fact, you're better equipped for the job than Blake was—your record looked as if you'd deliberately tried for this kind of work."

"I did."

"Hm-m-m." That was the one answer Doc had least expected; so far as he knew, no one deliberately tried for a job at Atomics—they usually wound up trying for it after comparing their receipts for a year or so with the salary paid by National. "Then you knew what was needed and picked it up in toto. Mind if I ask why?"

Jenkins shrugged. "Why not? Turnabout's fair play. It's kind of complicated, but the gist of it doesn't take much telling. Dad had an atomic plant of his own—and a darned good one, too, Doc, even if it wasn't as big as National. I was working in it when I was fifteen, and I went through two years of university work in atomics with the best intentions of carrying on the business. Sue—well, she was the neighbor girl I followed around, and we had money at the time; that wasn't why she married me, though. I never did figure that out—she'd had a hard enough life, but she was already holding down a job at Mayo's, and I was just a raw kid. Anyway—

"The day we came home from our honeymoon, dad got a big contract on a new process we'd worked out. It took some swinging, but he got the equipment and started it. . . . My guess is that one of the controls broke through faulty construction; the process was right! We'd been over it too often not to know what it would do. But, when the estate was cleared up, I had to give up the idea of a degree in atomics, and Sue was back working at the hospital. Atomic courses cost real money. Then one of Sue's medical acquaintances fixed it for me to get a scholarship in medicine that almost took care of it, so I chose the next best thing to what I wanted."

"National and one of the biggest competitors—if you can call it that—are permitted to give degrees in atomics," Doc reminded the boy. The field was still too new to be a standing university course, and there were no better teachers in the business than such men as Palmer, Hokusai and Jorgenson. "They pay a salary while you're learning, too."

"Hm-m-m. Takes ten years that way, and the salary's just enough for a single man. No, I'd married Sue with the intention she wouldn't have to work again; well, she did until I finished internship, but I knew if I got the job here I could support her. As an atomjack, working up to an engineer, the prospects weren't so good. We're saving a little money now, and someday maybe I'll get a crack at it yet. . . . Doc, what's this all about? You babying me out of my fit?"

Ferrel grinned at the boy. "Nothing else, son, though I was curious. And it worked. Feel all right now, don't you?"

"Mostly, except for what's going on out there—I got too much of a look at it from the truck. Oh, I could use some sleep, I guess, but I'm O. K. again."

"Good." Doc had profited almost as much as Jenkins from the rambling off-trail talk, and had managed more rest from it than from nursing his own thoughts. "Suppose we go out and see how they're making out with Jorgenson? Um, what happened to Hoke, come to think of it?"

"Hoke? Oh, he's in my office now, figuring out things with a pencil and paper since we wouldn't let him go back out there. I was wondering—"

"Atomics? . . . Then suppose you go in and talk to him; he's a good guy, and he won't give you the brush-off. Nobody else around here apparently suspected this Isotope R business, and you might offer a fresh lead for him. With Blake and the nurses here and the men out of the mess except for the tanks, there's not much you can do to help on my end."

Ferrel felt more at peace with the world than he had since the call from Palmer as he watched Jenkins head off across the surgery toward his office; and the glance that Brown threw, first toward the boy, then back at Doc, didn't make him feel worse. That girl could say more with her eyes than most women could with their mouths! He went over toward the operating table where Blake was now working the heart massage with one of the fresh nurses attending to respiration and casting longing glances toward the mechanical lung apparatus; it couldn't be used in this case, since Jorgenson's chest had to be free for heart attention.

Blake looked up, his expression worried. "This isn't so good, Doc. He's been sinking in the last few minutes. I was just going to call you. I—"

The last words were drowned out by the bull-throated drone that came dropping down from above them, a sound peculiarly characteristic of the heavy Sikorsky freighters with their modified blades to gain lift. Ferrel nodded at Brown's questioning glance, but he didn't choose to shout as his hands went over those of Blake and took over the delicate work of simulating the natural heart action. As Blake withdrew, the sound stopped, and Doc motioned him out with his head.

"You'd better go to them and oversee bringing in the apparatus—and grab up any of the men you see to act as porters—or send Jones for them. The machine is an experimental model, and pretty cumbersome; must weigh seven-eight hundred pounds."

"I'll get them myself—Jones is sleeping."

There was no flutter to Jorgenson's heart under Doc's deft manipulations, though he was exerting every bit of skill he possessed. "How long since there was a sign?"

"About four minutes, now. Doc, is there still a chance?"

"Hard to say. Get the machine, though, and we'll hope."

But still the heart refused to respond, though the pressure and manipulation kept the blood circulating and would at least prevent any starving or asphyxiation of the body cells. Carefully, delicately, he brought his mind into his fingers, trying to woo a faint quiver. Perhaps he did, once, but he couldn't be sure. It all depended on how quickly they could get the machine working now, and how long a man could live by manipulation alone. That point was still unsettled.

But there was no question about the fact that the spark of life burned faintly and steadily lower in Jorgenson, while outside the man-made hell went on ticking off the minutes that separated it from becoming Mahler's Isotope. Normally, Doc was an agnostic, but now, unconsciously, his mind slipped back into the simple faith of his childhood, and he heard Brown echoing the prayer that was on his lips. The second hand of the watch before him swung around and around and around again before he heard the sound of men's feet at the back entrance, and still there was no definite quiver from the heart under his fingers. How much time did he have left, if any, for the difficult and unfamiliar operation required?

His side glance showed the seemingly innumerable filaments of platinum that had to be connected into the nerves governing Jorgenson's heart and lungs, all carefully coded, yet almost terrifying in their complexity. If he made a mistake anywhere, it was at least certain there would be no time for a second trial; if his fingers shook or his tired eyes clouded at the wrong instant, there would be no help from Jorgenson. Jorgenson would be dead!

V

"Take over massage, Brown," he ordered. "And keep it up no matter what happens. Good. Dodd, assist me, and hang onto my signals. If it works, we can all rest afterward."

Ferrel wondered grimly with that part of his mind that was off by itself whether he could justify his boast to Jenkins of having been the world's greatest surgeon; it had been true once, he knew with no need for false modesty, but that was long ago, and this was at best a devilish job. He'd hung on with a surge of the old fascination as Kubelik had performed it on a dog at the convention, and his memory for such details was still good, as were his hands. But something else goes into the making of a great surgeon, and he wondered if that were still with him.

Then, as his fingers made the microscopic little motions needed and Dodd became another pair of hands, he ceased wondering. Whatever it was, he could feel it surging through him, and there was a pure joy to it somewhere, over and above the urgency of the work. This was probably the last time he'd ever feel it, and if the operation succeeded, probably it was a thing he could put with the few mental treasures that were still left from his former success. The man on the table ceased to be Jorgenson, the excessively gadgety infirmary became again the main operating theater of that same Mayo's which had produced Brown and this strange new machine, and his fingers were again those of the Great Ferrel, the miracle boy from Mayo's, who could do the impossible twice before breakfast without turning a hair.

Some of his feeling was devoted to the machine itself. Massive, ugly, with parts sticking out in haphazard order, it was more like something from an inquisition chamber than a scientist's achievement, but it worked—he'd seen it functioning. In that ugly mass of assorted pieces, little currents were generated and modulated to feed out to the heart and lungs and replace the orders given by a brain that no longer worked or could not get through, to coordinate breathing and beating according to the need. It was a product of the combined genius of surgery and electronics, but wonderful as the exciter was, it was distinctly secondary to the technique Kubelik had evolved for selecting and connecting only those nerves and nerve bundles necessary, and bringing the almost impossible into the limits of surgical possibility.

Brown interrupted, and that interruption in the midst of such an operation indicated clearly the strain she was under. "The heart fluttered a little then, Dr. Ferrel."

Ferrel nodded, untroubled by the interruption. Talk, which bothered most surgeons, was habitual in his own little staff, and he always managed to have one part of his mind reserved for that while the rest went on without noticing. "Good. That gives us at least double the leeway I expected."

His hands went on, first with the heart which was the more

pressing danger. Would the machine work, he wondered, in this case? Curare and radioactives, fighting each other, were an odd combination. Yet, the machine controlled the nerves close to the vital organ, pounding its message through into the muscles, where the curare had a complicated action that paralyzed the whole nerve, establishing a long block to the control impulses from the brain. Could the nerve impulses from the machine be forced through the short paralyzed passages? Probably—the strength of its signals was controllable. The only proof was in trying.

Brown drew back her hands and stared down uncomprehendingly. "It's beating, Dr. Ferrel! By itself . . . it's beating!"

He nodded again, though the mask concealed his smile. His technique was still not faulty, and he had performed the operation correctly after seeing it once on a dog! He was still the Great Ferrel! Then, the ego in him fell back to normal, though the lift remained, and his exultation centered around the more important problem of Jorgenson's living. And, later, when the lungs began moving of themselves as the nurse stopped working them, he had been expecting it. The detail work remaining was soon over, and he stepped back, dropping the mask from his face and pulling off his gloves.

"Congratulations, Dr. Ferrel!" The voice was guttural, strange. "A truly great operation—truly great. I almost stopped you, but now I am glad I did not; it was a pleasure to observe you, sir." Ferrel looked up in amazement at the bearded smiling face of Kubelik, and he found no words as he accepted the other's hand. But Kubelik apparently expected none.

"I, Kubelik, came, you see; I could not trust another with the machine, and fortunately I made the plane. Then you seemed so sure, so confident—so when you did not notice me, I remained in the background, cursing myself. Now, I shall return, since you have no need of me—the wiser for having watched you. . . . No, not a word; not a word from you, sir. Don't destroy your miracle with words. The 'copter awaits me, I go; but my admiration for you remains forever!"

Ferrel still stood looking down at his hand as the roar of the 'copter cut in, then at the breathing body with the artery on the neck now pulsing regularly. That was all that was needed; he had been admired by Kubelik, the man who thought all other surgeons were fools and nincompoops. For a second or so longer he treasured it, then shrugged it off.

"Now," he said to the others, as the troubles of the plant

fell back on his shoulders, "all we have to do is hope that Jorgenson's brain wasn't injured by the session out there, or by this continued artifically maintained life, and try to get him in condition so he can talk before it's too late. God grant us time! Blake, you know the detail work as well as I do, and we can't both work on it. You and the fresh nurses take over, doing the bare minimum needed for the patients scattered around the wards and waiting room. Any new ones?"

"None for some time; I think they've reached a stage where that's over with," Brown answered.

"I hope so. Then go round up Jenkins and lie down somewhere. That goes for you and Meyers, too, Dodd. Blake, give us three hours if you can, and get us up. There won't be any new developments before then, and we'll save time in the long run by resting. Jorgenson's to get first attention!"

The old leather chair made a fair sort of bed, and Ferrel was too exhausted physically and mentally to be choosy—too exhausted to benefit as much as he should from sleep of three hours' duration, for that matter, though it was almost imperative he try. Idly, he wondered what Palmer would think of all his safeguards had he known that Kubelik had come into the place so easily and out again. Not that it mattered; it was doubtful whether anyone else would want to come near, let alone inside the plant.

In that, apparently, he was wrong. It was considerably less than the three hours when he was awakened to hear the bull-roar of a helicopter outside. But sleep clouded his mind too much for curiosity and he started to drop back into his slumber. Then another sound cut in jerking him out of his drowsiness. It was the sharp sputter of a machine gun from the direction of the gate, a pause and another burst; an eddy of sleep-memory indicated that it had begun before the helicopter's arrival, so it could not be that they were gunning. More trouble, and while it was none of his business, he could not go back to sleep. He got up and went out into the surgery, just as a gnomish little man hopped out from the rear entrance.

The fellow scooted toward Ferrel after one birdlike glance at Blake, his words spilling out with a jerky self-importance that should have been funny, but missed it by a small margin; under the surface, sincerity still managed to show. "Dr. Ferrel? Uh, Dr. Kubelik—Mayo's, you know—he reported you were shorthanded; stacking patients in the other rooms. We volunteered for duty—me, four other doctors, nine nurses. Probably should have checked with you, but couldn't get a phone through. Took the liberty of coming through directly, fast as we could push our 'copters."

Ferrel glanced through the back, and saw that there were three of the machines, instead of the one he'd thought, with men and equipment piling out of them. Mentally he kicked himself for not asking for help when he'd put through the call; but he'd been used to working with his own little staff for so long that the ready response of his profession to emergencies had been almost forgotten. "You know you're taking chances coming here, naturally? Then, in that case, I'm grateful to you and Kubelik. We've got about forty patients here, all of whom should have considerable attention, though I frankly doubt whether there's room for you to work."

The man hitched his thumb backward jerkily. "Don't worry about that. Kubelik goes the limit when he arranges things. Everything we need with us, practically all the hospital's atomic equipment; though maybe you'll have to piece us out there. Even a field hospital tent, portable wards for every patient you have. Want relief in here or would you rather have us simply move out the patients to the tent, leave this end to you? Oh, Kubelik sent his regards. Amazing of him!"

Kubelik, it seemed, had a tangible idea of regards, however dramatically he was inclined to express them; with him directing the volunteer force, the wonder was that the whole staff and equipment hadn't been moved down. "Better leave this end," Ferrel decided. "Those in the wards will probably be better off in your tent as well as the men now in the waiting room; we're equipped beautifully for all emergency work, but not used to keeping the patients here any length of time, so our accommodations that way are rough. Dr. Blake will show you around and help you get organized in the routine we use here. He'll get help for you in erecting the tent, too. By the way, did you hear the commotion by the entrance as you were landing?"

"We did, indeed. We saw it, too—bunch of men in some kind of uniform shooting a machine gun; hitting the ground, though. Bunch of other people running back away from it, shaking their fists, looked like. We were expecting a dose of the same, maybe; didn't notice us, though."

Blake snorted in half amusement. "You probably would have gotten it if our manager hadn't forgotten to give orders covering the air approach; they must figure that's an official route. I saw a bunch from the city arguing about their relatives in here when I came in this morning, so it must have been that." He motioned the little doctor after him, then turned his neck back to address Brown. "Show him the results while I'm gone, honey."

Ferrel forgot his new recruits and swung back to the girl. "Bad?"

She made no comment, but picked up a lead shield and placed it over Jorgenson's chest so that it cut off all radiation from the lower part of his body, then placed the radiation indicator close to the man's throat. Doc looked once; no more was needed. It was obvious that Blake had already done his best to remove the radioactive from all parts of the body needed for speech, in the hope that they might strap down the others and block them off with local anesthetics; then the curare could have been counteracted long enough for such information as was needed. Equally obviously, he'd failed. There was no sense in going through the job of neutralizing the drug's block only to have him under the control of the radioactive still present. The stuff was too finely dispersed for surgical removal. Now what? He had no answer.

Jenkins' lean-sinewed hand took the indicator from him for inspection. The boy was already frowning as Doc looked up in faint surprise, and his face made no change. He nodded slowly. "Yeah. I figured as much. That was a beautiful piece of work you did, too. Too bad. I was watching from the door and you almost convinced me he'd be all right, the way you handled it. But—So we have to make out without him; and Hoke and Palmer haven't even cooked up a lead that's worth a good test. Want to come into my office, Doc? There's nothing we can do here."

Ferrel followed Jenkins into the little office off the now emptied waiting room; the men from the hospital had worked rapidly, it seemed. "So you haven't been sleeping, I take it? Where's Hokusai now?"

"Out there with Palmer; he promised to behave, if that'll comfort you. . . . Nice guy, Hoke; I'd forgotten what it felt like to talk to an atomic engineer without being laughed at. Palmer, too. I wish—" There was a brief lightening to the boy's face and the first glow of normal human pride Doc had seen in him. Then he shrugged, and it vanished back into his taut cheeks and reddened eyes. "We cooked up the wildest kind of a scheme, but it isn't so hot."

Hoke's voice came out of the doorway, as the little man came in and sat down carefully in one of the three chairs. "No, not sso hot! It iss fail, already. Jorgensson?"

"Out, no hope there! What happened?"

Hoke spread his arms, his eyes almost closing. "Nothing. We knew it could never work, not sso? Misster Palmer, he iss come ssoon here, then we make planss again, I am think now, besst we sshould move from here. Palmer, I—mosstly we are theoreticianss; and, excusse, you alsso, doctor. Jorgensson wass the production man. No Jorgensson, no—ah—ssoap!"

Mentally, Ferrel agreed about the moving—and soon! But he could see Palmer's point of view; to give up the fight was against the grain, somehow. And besides, once the blowup happened, with the resultant damage to an unknown area, the pressure groups in Congress would be in, shouting for the final abolition of all atomic work; now they were reasonably quiet, only waiting an opportunity—or, more probably, at the moment were already seizing on the rumors spreading to turn this into their coup. If, by some streak of luck, Palmer could save the plant with no greater loss of life and property than already existed, their words would soon be forgotten, and the benefits from the products of National would again outweigh all risks.

"Just what will happen if it all goes off?" he asked.

Jenkins shrugged, biting at his inner lip as he went over a sheaf of papers on the desk, covered with the scrawling symbols of atomics. "Anybody's guess. Suppose three tons of the army's new explosives were to explode in a billionth—or at least, a millionth—of a second? Normally, you know, compared to atomics, that stuff burns like any fire, slowly and quietly, giving its gases plenty of time to get out of the way in an orderly fashion. Figure it one way, with this all going off together, and the stuff could drill a hole that'd split open the whole continent from Hudson Bay to the Gulf of Mexico, and leave a lovely sea where the Middle West is now. Figure it another, and it might only kill off everything within fifty miles of here. Somewhere in between is the chance we count on. This isn't U-235, you know."

Doc winced. He'd been picturing the plant going up in the air violently, with maybe a few buildings somewhere near it, but nothing like this. It had been purely a local affair to him, but this didn't sound like one. No wonder Jenkins was in that state of suppressed jitters; it wasn't too much imagination, but too much cold, hard knowledge that was worrying him. Ferrel looked at their faces as they bent over the symbols once more, tracing out point by point their calculations in the hope of finding one overlooked loophole, then decided to leave them alone.

The whole problem was hopeless without Jorgenson, it seemed, and Jorgenson was his responsibility; if the plant went, it was squarely on the senior physician's shoulders. But there was no apparent solution. If it would help, he could cut it down to a direct path from brain to speaking organs, strap down the body and block off all nerves below the neck, using an artificial larynx instead of the normal breathing through vocal cords. But the indicator showed the futility of it; the orders could never get through from the brain with the amount of radioactive still present throwing them off track—even granting that the brain itself was not affected, which was doubtful.

Fortunately for Jorgenson, the stuff was all finely dispersed around the head, with no concentration at any one place that was unquestionably destructive to his mind; but the good fortune was also the trouble, since it could not be removed by any means known to medical practice. Even so simple a thing as letting the man read the questions and spell out the answers by winking an eyelid as they pointed to the alphabet was hopeless.

Nerves! Jorgenson had his blocked out, but Ferrel wondered if the rest of them weren't in as bad a state. Probably, somewhere well within their grasp, there was a solution that was being held back because the nerves of everyone in the plant were blocked by fear and pressure that defeated its own purpose. Jenkins, Palmer, Hokusai—under purely theoretical conditions, any one of them might spot the answer to the problem, but sheer necessity of finding it could be the thing that hid it. The same might be true with the problem of Jorgenson's treatment. Yet, though he tried to relax and let his mind stray idly around the loose ends and seemingly disconnected knowledge he had, it returned incessantly to the necessity of doing something, and doing it now!

Ferrel heard weary footsteps behind him and turned to see Palmer coming from the front entrance. The man had no business walking into the surgery, but such minor rules had gone by the board hours before.

"Jorgenson?" Palmer's conversation began with the same

old question in the usual tone, and he read the answer from Doc's face with a look that indicated it was no news. "Hoke and that Jenkins kid still in there?"

Doc nodded, and plodded behind him toward Jenkins' office; he was useless to them, but there was still the idea that in filling his mind with other things, some little factor he had overlooked might have a chance to come forth. Also, curiosity still worked on him, demanding to know what was happening. He flopped into the third chair, and Palmer squatted down on the edge of the table.

"Know a good spiritualist, Jenkins?" the manager asked. "Because if you do, I'm about ready to try calling back Kellar's ghost. The Steinmetz of atomics—so he had to die before this Isotope R came up, and leave us without even a good guess at how long we've got to crack the problem. Hey, what's the matter?"

Jenkins' face had tensed and his body straightened back tensely in the chair, but he shook his head, the corner of his mouth twitching wryly. "Nothing. Nerves, I guess. Hoke and I dug out some things that give an indication on how long this runs, though. We still don't know exactly, but from observations out there and the general theory before, it looks like something between six and thirty hours left; probably ten's closer to being correct!"

"Can't be much longer. It's driving the men back right now! Even the tanks can't get in where they can do the most good, and we're using the shielding around No. 3 as a headquarters for the men; in another half hour, maybe they won't be able to stay that near the thing. Radiation indicators won't register any more, and it's spitting all over the place, almost constantly. Heat's terrific; it's gone up to around three hundred centigrade and sticks right there now, but that's enough to warm up 3, even."

Doc looked up. "No. 3?"

"Yeah. Nothing happened to that batch—it ran through and came out I-713 right on schedule, hours ago." Palmer reached for a cigarette, realized he had one in his mouth, and slammed the package back on the table. "Significant data, Doc; if we get out of this, we'll figure out just what caused the change in No. 4—if we get out! Any chance of making those variable factors work, Hoke?"

Hoke shook his head, and again Jenkins answered from the notes. "Not a chance; sure, theoretically, at least, R should have a period varying between twelve and sixty hours before turning into Mahler's Isotope, depending on what chains of reactions or subchains it goes through; they all look equally good, and probably are all going on in there now, depending on what's around to soak up neutrons or let them roam, the concentration and amount of R together, and even high or low temperatures that change their activity somewhat. It's one of the variables, no question about that."

"The sspitting iss prove that," Hoke supplemented.

"Sure. But there's too much of it together, and we can't break it down fine enough to reach any safety point where it won't toss energy around like rain. The minute one particle manages to make itself into Mahler's, it'll crash through with energy enough to blast the next over the hump and into the same thing instantly, and that passes it on to the next, at about light speed! If we *could* get it juggled around so some would go off first, other atoms a little later, and so on, fine—only we can't do it unless we can be sure of isolating every blob bigger than a tenth of a gram from every other one! And if we start breaking it down into reasonably small pieces, we're likely to have one decide on the short transformation subchain and go off at any time; pure chance gave us a concentration to begin with that eliminated the shorter chains, but we can't break it down into small lots and those into smaller lots, and so on. Too much risk!"

Ferrel had known vaguely that there were such things as variables, but the theory behind them was too new and too complex for him; he'd learned what little he knew when the simpler radioactives proceeded normally from radium to lead, as an example, with a definite, fixed half-life, instead of the super-heavy atoms they now used that could jump through several different paths, yet end up the same. It was over his head, and he started to get up and go back to Jorgenson.

Palmer's words stopped him. "I knew it, of course, but I hoped maybe I was wrong. Then—we evacuate! No use fooling ourselves any longer. I'll call the Governor and try to get him to clear the country around; Hoke, you can tell the men to get the hell out of here! All we ever had was the counteracting isotope to hope on, and no chance of getting enough of that. There was no sense in making I-231 in thousand-pound batches before. Well—"

He reached for the phone, but Ferrel cut in. "What about the men in the wards? They're loaded with the stuff, most of them with more than a gram apiece dispersed through them.

They're in the same class with the converter, maybe, but we can't just pull out and leave them!"

Silence hit them, to be broken by Jenkins' hushed whisper. "My God! What damned fools we are. I-231 under discussion for hours, and I never thought of it. Now you two throw the connection in my face, and I still almost miss it!"

"I-231? But there iss not enough. Maybe twenty-five pound, maybe less. Three and a half days to make more. The little we have would be no good, Dr. Jenkinss. We forget that already." Hoke struck a match to a piece of paper, shook one drop of ink onto it, and watched it continue burning for a second before putting it out. "Sso. A drop of water for sstop a foresst fire. No."

"Wrong, Hoke. A drop to short a switch that'll turn on the real stream—maybe. Look, Doc, I-231's an isotope that reacts atomically with R—we've checked on that already. It simply gets together with the stuff and the two break down into non-radioactive elements and a little heat, like a lot of other such atomic reactions; but it isn't the violent kind. They simply swap parts in a friendly way and open up to simpler atoms that are stable. We have a few pounds on hand, can't make enough in time to help with No. 4, but we do have enough to treat every man in the wards, *including Jorgenson!*"

"How much heat?" Doc snapped out of his lethargy into the detailed thought of a good physician. "In atomics you may call it a little; but would it be small enough in the human body?"

Hokusai and Palmer were practically riding the pencil as Jenkins figured. "Say five grams of the stuff in Jorgenson, to be on the safe side, less in the others. Time for reaction . . . hm-m. Here's the total heat produced and the time taken by the reaction, probably, in the body. The stuff's water-soluble in the chloride we have of it, so there's no trouble dispersing it. What do you make of it, Doc?"

"Fifteen to eighteen degrees temperature rise at a rough estimate. Uh!"

"Too much! Jorgenson couldn't stand ten degrees right now!" Jenkins frowned down at his figures, tapping nervously with his hand.

Doc shook his head. "Not too much! We can drop his whole body temperature first in the hypothermy bath down to eighty degrees, then let it rise to a hundred, if necessary, and still be safe. Thank the Lord, there's equipment enough. If

they'll rip out the refrigerating units in the cafeteria and im-
provise baths, the volunteers out in the tent can start on the
other men while we handle Jorgenson. At least that way we
can get the men all out, even if we don't save the plant."

Palmer stared at them in confusion before his face galva-
nized into resolution. "Refrigerating units—volunteers—tent?
What—O. K., Doc, what do you want?" He reached for the
telephone and began giving orders for the available I-231 to
be sent to the surgery, for men to rip out the cafeteria
cooling equipment, and for such other things as Doc requested. Jenkins had already gone to instruct the medical staff in
the field tent without asking how they'd gotten there, but was
back in the surgery before Doc reached it with Palmer and
Hokusai at his heels.

"Blake's taking over out there," Jenkins announced. "Says
if you want Dodd, Meyers, Jones or Sue, they're sleeping."

"No need. Get over there out of the way, if you must
watch," Ferrel ordered the two engineers, as he and Jenkins
began attaching the freezing units and bath to the sling on
the exciter. "Prepare his blood for it, Jenkins; we'll force it
down as low as we can to be on the safe side. And we'll have
to keep tabs on the temperature fall and regulate his heart
and breathing to what it would be normally in that condition;
they're both out of his normal control, now."

"And pray," Jenkins added. He grabbed the small box out
of the messenger's hand before the man was fully inside the
door and began preparing a solution, weighing out the
whitish powder and measuring water carefully, but with the
speed that was automatic to him under tension. "Doc, if this
doesn't work—if Jorgenson's crazy or something—you'll have
another case of insanity on your hands. One more false hope
would finish me."

"Not one more case; four! We're all in the same boat.
Temperature's falling nicely—I'm rushing it a little, but it's
safe enough. Down to ninety-six now." The thermometer under Jorgenson's tongue was one intended for hypothermy
work, capable of rapid response, instead of the normal fever
thermometer. Slowly, with agonizing reluctance, the little
needle on the dial moved over, down to ninety, then on. Doc
kept his eyes glued to it, slowing the pulse and breath to the
proper speed. He lost track of the number of times he sent
Palmer back out of the way, and finally gave up.

Waiting, he wondered how those outside in the field hospital were doing? Still, they had ample time to arrange their makeshift cooling apparatus and treat the men in groups—ten hours probably; and hypothermy was a standard thing, now. Jorgenson was the only real rush case. Almost imperceptibly to Doc, but speedily by normal standards, the temperature continued to fall. Finally it reached seventy-eight.

"Ready, Jenkins, make the injection. That enough?"

"No. I figure it's almost enough, but we'll have to go slow to balance out properly. Too much of this stuff would be almost as bad as the other. Gauge going up, Doc?"

It was, much more rapidly than Ferrel liked. As the injection coursed through the blood vessels and dispersed out to the fine deposits of radioactive, the needle began climbing past eighty, to ninety, and up. It stopped at ninety-four and slowly began falling as the cooling bath absorbed heat from the cells of the body. The radioactivity meter still registered the presence of Isotope R, though much more faintly.

The next shot was small, and a smaller one followed. "Almost," Ferrel commented. "Next one should about do the trick."

Using partial injections, there had been need for less drop in temperature than they had given Jorgenson, but there was small loss to that. Finally, when the last minute bit of the I-213 solution had entered the man's veins and done its work, Doc nodded. "No sign of activity left. He's up to ninety-five, now that I've cut off the refrigeration, and he'll pick up the little extra temperature in a hurry. By the time we can counteract the curare, he'll be ready. That'll take about fifteen minutes, Palmer."

The manager nodded, watching them dismantling the hypothermy equipment and going through the routine of cancelling out the curare. It was always a slower job than treatment with the drug, but part of the work had been done already by the normal body processes, and the rest was a simple, standard procedure. Fortunately, the neo-heroin would be nearly worn off, or that would have been a longer and much harder problem to eliminate.

"Telephone for Mr. Palmer. Calling Mr. Palmer. Send Mr. Palmer to the telephone." The operator's words lacked the usual artificial exactness, and were only a nervous sing-song. It was getting her, and she wasn't bothered by excess imagination, normally. "Mr. Palmer is wanted on the telephone."

"Palmer." The manager picked up an instrument at hand, not equipped with vision, and there was no indication to the caller. But Ferrel could see what little hope had appeared at the prospect of Jorgenson's revival disappearing. "Check! Move out of there, and prepare to evacuate, but keep quiet about that until you hear further orders! Tell the men Jorgenson's about out of it, so they won't lack for something to talk about."

He swung back to them. "No use, Doc, I'm afraid. We're already too late. The stuff's stepped it up again, and they're having to move out of No. 3 now. I'll wait on Jorgenson, but even if he's all right and knows the answer, we can't get in to use it!"

VI

"Healing's going to be a long, slow process, but they should at least grow back better than silver ribs; never take a pretty X-ray photo, though." Doc held the instrument in his hand, staring down at the flap opened in Jorgenson's chest, and his shoulders came up in a faint shrug. The little platinum filaments had been removed from around the nerves to heart and lungs, and the man's normal impulses were operating again, less steadily than under the exciter, but with no danger signals. "Well, it won't much matter if he's still sane."

Jenkins watched him begin stitching the flap back, his eyes centered over the table out toward the converter. "Doc, he's got to be sane! If Hoke and Palmer find it's what it sounds like out there, we'll have to count on Jorgenson. There's an answer somewhere, has to be! But we won't find it without him."

"Hm-m-m. Seems to me you've been having ideas yourself, son. You've been right so far, and if Jorgenson's out—" He shut off the stitcher, finished the dressings, and flopped down on a bench, knowing that all they could do was wait for the drugs to work on Jorgenson and bring him around. Now that he relaxed the control over himself, exhaustion hit down with full force; his fingers were uncertain as he pulled off the gloves. "Anyhow, we'll know in another five minutes or so."

"And heaven help us, Doc, if it's up to me. I've always had a flair for atomic theory; I grew up on it. But he's the production man who's been working at it week in and week out, and it's his process, to boot. . . . There they are now! All right for them to come back here?"

But Hokusai and Palmer were waiting for no permission.

At the moment, Jorgenson was the nerve center of the plant, drawing them back, and they stalked over to stare down at him, then sat where they could be sure of missing no sign of returning consciousness. Palmer picked up the conversation where he'd dropped it, addressing his remarks to both Hokusai and Jenkins.

"Damn that Link-Stevens postulate! Time after time it fails, until you figure there's nothing to it; then, this! It's black magic, not science, and if I get out, I'll find some fool with more courage than sense to discover why. Hoke, are you positive it's the *theta* chain? There isn't one chance in ten thousand of that happening, you know; it's unstable, hard to stop, tends to revert to the simpler ones at the first chance."

Hokusai spread his hands, lifted one heavy eyelid at Jenkins questioningly, then nodded. The boy's voice was dull, almost uninterested. "That's what I thought it had to be, Palmer. None of the others throws off that much energy at this stage, the way you described conditions out there. Probably the last thing we tried to quench set it up in that pattern, and it's in a concentration just right to keep it going. We figured ten hours was the best chance, so it had to pick the six-hour short chain."

"Yeah." Palmer was pacing up and down nervously again, his eyes swinging toward Jorgenson from whatever direction he moved. "And in six hours, maybe all the population around here can be evacuated, maybe not, but we'll have to try it. Doc, I can't even wait for Jorgenson now! I've got to get the Governor started at once!"

"They've been known to practice lynch law, even in recent years," Ferrel reminded him grimly. He'd seen the result of one such case of mob violence when he was practicing privately, and he knew that people remain pretty much the same year after year; they'd move, but first they'd demand a sacrifice. "Better get the men out of here first, Palmer, and my advice is to get yourself a good long distance off; I heard some of the trouble at the gate, and that won't be anything compared to what an evacuation order will do."

Palmer grunted. "Doc, you might not believe it, but I don't give a continental about what happens to me or the plant right now."

"Or the men? Put a mob in here, hunting your blood, and the men will be on your side, because they know it wasn't your fault, and they've seen you out there taking chances yourself. That mob won't be too choosy about its targets, either, once it gets worked up, and you'll have a nice vicious brawl all over the place. Besides, Jorgenson's practically ready."

A few minutes would make no difference in the evacuation, and Doc had no desire to think of his partially crippled wife going through the hell evacuation would be; she'd probably refuse, until he returned. His eyes fell on the box Jenkins was playing with nervously, and he stalled for time. "I thought you said it was risky to break the stuff down into small particles, Jenkins. But that box contains the stuff in various sizes, including one big piece we scraped out, along with the contaminated instruments. Why hasn't it exploded?"

Jenkins' hand jerked up from it as if burned, and he backed away a step before checking himself. Then he was across the room toward the I-231 and back, pouring the white powder over everything in the box in a jerky frenzy. Hokusai's eyes had snapped fully open, and he was slopping water in to fill up the remaining space and keep the I-231 in contact with everything else. Almost at once, in spite of the low relative energy release, it sent up a white cloud of steam faster than the air conditioner could clear the room; but that soon faded down and disappeared.

Hokusai wiped his forehead slowly. "The ssuits—armor of the men?"

"Sent 'em back to the converter and had them dumped into the stuff to be safe long ago," Jenkins answered. "But I forgot that box, like a fool. Ugh! Either blind chance saved us or else the stuff spit out was all one kind, some reasonably long chain. I don't know nor care right—"

"S'ot! Nnnuh . . . Whmah nahh?"

"Jorgenson!" They swung from the end of the room like one man, but Jenkins was the first to reach the table. Jorgenson's eyes were open and rolling in a semiorderly manner, his hands moving sluggishly. The boy hovered over his face, his own practically glowing with the intensity behind it. "Jorgenson, can you understand what I'm saying?"

"Uh." The eyes ceased moving and centered on Jenkins. One hand came up to his throat, clutching at it, and he tried unsuccessfully to lift himself with the other, but the aftereffects of what he'd been through seemed to have left him in a state of partial paralysis.

Ferrel had hardly dared hope that the man could be rational, and his relief was tinged with doubt. He pushed Palmer back, and shook his head. "No, stay back. Let the boy handle it; he knows enough not to shock the man now, and you don't. This can't be rushed too much."

"I—uh. . . . Young Jenkins? Whasha doin' here? Tell y'ur dad to ge' busy ou' there!" Somewhere in Jorgenson's huge frame, an untapped reserve of energy and will sprang up, and he forced himself into a sitting position, his eyes on Jenkins, his hand still catching at the reluctant throat that refused to cooperate. His words were blurry and uncertain, but sheer determination overcame the obstacles and made the words understandable.

"Dad's dead now, Jorgenson. Now—"

" 'Sright. 'N' you're grown up—'bout twelve years old, y'were. . . . The plant!"

"Easy, Jorgenson." Jenkins' own voice managed to sound casual, though his hands under the table were white where they clenched together. "Listen, and don't try to say anything until I finish. The plant's still all right, but we've got to have your help. Here's what happened."

Ferrel could make little sense of the cryptic sentences that followed, though he gathered that they were some form of engineering shorthand; apparently, from Hokusai's approving nod, they summed up the situation briefly but fully, and Jorgenson sat rigidly still until it was finished, his eyes fastened on the boy.

"Hellova mess! Gotta think . . . yuh tried—" He made an attempt to lower himself back, and Jenkins assisted him, hanging on feverishly to each awkward, uncertain change of expression on the man's face. "Uh . . . da' sroat! Yuh . . . uh . . . urrgh!"

"Got it?"

"Uh!" The tone was affirmative, unquestionably, but the clutching hands around his neck told their own story. The temporary burst of energy he'd forced was exhausted, and he couldn't get through with it. He lay there, breathing heavily and struggling, then relaxed after a few more half-whispered words, none intelligently articulated.

Palmer clutched at Ferrel's sleeve. "Doc, isn't there anything you can do?"

"Try." He metered out a minute quantity of drug doubtfully, felt Jorgenson's pulse, and decided on half that amount. "Not much hope, though; that man's been through hell, and it wasn't good for him to be forced around in the first place. Carry it too far, and he'll be delirious if he does talk. Anyway, I suspect it's partly his speech centers as well as the throat."

But Jorgenson began a slight rally almost instantly, trying again, then apparently drawing himself together for a final attempt. When they came, the words spilled out harshly in forced clearness, but without inflection.

"First . . . variable . . . at . . . twelve . . water . . . stop." His eyes, centered on Jenkins, closed, and he relaxed again, this time no longer fighting off the inevitable unconsciousness.

Hokusai, Palmer and Jenkins were staring back and forth at one another questioningly. The little Japanese shook his head negatively at first, frowned, and repeated it, to be imitated almost exactly by the manager. "Delirious ravings!"

"The great white hope Jorgenson!" Jenkins' shoulders dropped and the blood drained from his face, leaving it ghastly with fatigue and despair. "Oh, damn it, Doc, stop staring at me! I can't pull a miracle out of a hat!"

Doc hadn't realized that he was staring, but he made no effort to change it. "Maybe not, but you happen to have the most active imagination here, when you stop abusing it to scare yourself. Well, you're on the spot now, and I'm still giving odds on you. Want to bet, Hoke?"

It was an utterly stupid thing, and Doc knew it; but somewhere during the long hours together, he'd picked up a queer respect for the boy and a dependence on the nervousness that wasn't fear but closer akin to the reaction of a rear-running thoroughbred on the home stretch. Hoke was too slow and methodical, and Palmer had been too concerned with outside worries to give anywhere nearly full attention to the single most urgent phase of the problem; that left only Jenkins, hampered by his lack of self-confidence.

Hoke gave no sign that he caught the meaning of Doc's heavy wink, but he lifted his eyebrows faintly. "No, I think I am not bet. Dr. Jenkins, I am to be command!"

Palmer looked briefly at the boy, whose face mirrored incredulous confusion, but he had neither Ferrel's ignorance of atomic technique nor Hokusai's fatalism. With a final glance at the unconscious Jorgenson, he started across the room toward the phone. "You men play, if you like. I'm starting evacuation immediately!"

"Wait!" Jenkins was shaking himself, physically as well as mentally. "Hold it, Palmer! Thanks, Doc. You knocked me out of the rut, and bounced my memory back to something I picked up somewhere; I think it's the answer! It has to work—nothing else can at this stage of the game!"

"Give me the Governor, operator." Palmer had heard, but he went on with the phone call. "This is no time to play crazy hunches until after we get the people out, kid. I'll admit you're a darned clever amateur, but you're no atomicist!"

"And if we get the men out, it's too late—there'll be no one left in here to do the work!" Jenkins' hand snapped out and jerked the receiver of the plug-in telephone from Palmer's hand. "Cancel the call, operator; it won't be necessary. Palmer, you've got to listen to me; you can't clear the whole middle of the continent, and you can't depend on the explosion to limit itself to less ground. It's a gamble, but you're risking fifty million people against a mere hundred thousand. Give me a chance!"

"I'll give you exactly one minute to convince me, Jenkins, and it had better be good! Maybe the blowup won't hit beyond the fifty-mile limit!"

"Maybe. And I can't explain in a minute." The boy scowled tensely. "O. K., you've been bellyaching about a man named Kellar being dead. If he were here, would you take a chance on him? Or on a man who'd worked under him on everything he tried?"

"Absolutely, but you're not Kellar. And I happen to know he was a lone wolf; didn't hire outside engineers after Jorgenson had a squabble with him and came here." Palmer reached for the phone. "It won't wash, Jenkins."

Jenkins' hand clamped down on the instrument, jerking it out of reach. "I wasn't *outside* help, Palmer. When Jorgenson was afraid to run one of the things off and quit, I was twelve; three years later, things got too tight for him to handle alone, but he decided he might as well keep it in the family, so he started me in. I'm Kellar's stepson!"

Pieces clicked together in Doc's head then, and he kicked himself mentally for not having seen the obvious before. "That why Jorgenson knew you, then? I thought that was funny. It checks, Palmer."

For a split second, the manager hesitated uncertainly. Then he shrugged and gave in. "O. K., I'm a fool to trust you, Jenkins, but it's too late for anything else, I guess. I never forgot that I was gambling the locality against half the continent. What do you want?"

"Men—construction men, mostly, and a few volunteers for dirty work. I want all the blowers, exhaust equipment, tubing,

booster blowers and everything ripped from the other three
converters and connected as close to No. 4 as you can get.
Put them up some way so they can be shoved in over the
stuff by crane—I don't care how; the shop men will know
better than I do. You've got sort of a river running off behind
the plant; get everyone within a few miles of it out of there,
and connect the blower outlets down to it. Where does it end,
anyway—some kind of a swamp, or morass?"

"About ten miles farther down, yes; we didn't bother keeping the drainage system going, since the land meant nothing
to us, and the swamps made as good a dumping ground as
anything else." When the plant had first used the little river
as an outlet for their waste products, there'd been so much
trouble that National had been forced to take over all adjacent land and quiet the owners' fears of the atomic activity
in cold cash. Since then, it had gone to weeds and rabbits,
mostly. "Everyone within a few miles is out, anyway, except
a few fishers or tramps that don't know we use it; I'll have
militia sent in to scare them out."

"Good. Ideal, in fact, since the swamps will hold stuff
longer in there where the current's slow. Now, what about
that superthermite stuff you were producing last year. Any
around?"

"Not in the plant. But we've got tons of it at the warehouse, still waiting for the army's requisition. That's pretty
hot stuff to handle, though. Know much about it?"

"Enough to know it's what I want." Jenkins indicated the
copy of the *Weekly Ray* still lying where he'd dropped it, and
Doc remembered skimming through the nontechnical part of
the description. It was made up of two superheavy atoms,
kept separate. By itself, neither was particularly important or
active, but together they reacted with each other atomically
to release a tremendous amount of raw heat and comparatively little unwanted radiation. "Goes up around twenty
thousand centigrade, doesn't it? How's it stored?"

"In ten-pound bombs that have a fragile partition; it breaks
with shock, starting the action. Hoke can explain it—it's his
baby." Palmer reached for the phone. "Anything else? Then,
get out and get busy! The men will be ready for you when
you get there! I'll be out myself as soon as I can put through
your orders."

Doc watched them go out, to be followed in short order by
the manager, and was alone in the infirmary with Jorgenson

and his thoughts. They weren't pleasant; he was both too far outside the inner circle to know what was going on and too much mixed up in it not to know the dangers. Now he could have used some work of any nature to take his mind off useless speculations, but aside from a needless check of the foreman's condition, there was nothing for him to do.

He wriggled down in the leather chair, making the mistake of trying to force sleep, while his mind chased out after the sounds that came in from outside. There were the drones of crane and tank motors coming to life, the shouts of hurried orders, and above all, the jarring rhythm of pneumatic hammers on metal, each sound suggesting some possibility to him without adding to his knowledge. The "Decameron" was boring, the whiskey tasted raw and rancid, and solitaire wasn't worth the trouble of cheating.

Finally, he gave up and turned out to the field hospital tent. Jorgenson would be better off out there, under the care of the staff from Mayo's, and perhaps he could make himself useful. As he passed through the rear entrance, he heard the sound of a number of helicopters coming over with heavy loads, and looked up as they began settling over the edge of the buildings. From somewhere, a group of men came running forward, and disappeared in the direction of the freighters. He wondered whether any of those men would be forced back into the stuff out there to return filled with radioactive; though it didn't matter so much, now that the isotope could be eliminated without surgery.

Blake met him at the entrance of the field tent, obviously well satisfied with his duty of bossing and instructing the others. "Scram, Doc. You aren't necessary here, and you need some rest. Don't want you added to the casualties. What's the latest dope from the pow-wow front?"

"Jorgenson didn't come through, but the kid had an idea, and they're out there working on it." Doc tried to sound more hopeful than he felt. "I was thinking you might as well bring Jorgenson in here; he's still unconscious, but there doesn't seem to be anything to worry about. Where's Brown? She'll probably want to know what's up, if she isn't asleep."

"Asleep when the kid isn't? Uh-huh. Mother complex, has to worry about him." Blake grinned. "She got a look at him running out with Hoke tagging at his heels, and hiked out after him, so she probably knows everything now. Wish Anne'd chase me that way, just once— Jenkins, the wonder boy! Well, it's out of my line; I don't intend to start worrying until they pass out the order. O. K., Doc, I'll have Jorgenson out here in a couple of minutes, so you grab yourself a cot and get some shut-eye."

Doc grunted, looking curiously at the refinements and well-equipped interior of the field tent. "I've already prescribed that, Blake, but the patient can't seem to take it. I think I'll hunt up Brown, so give me a call over the public speaker if anything turns up."

He headed toward the center of action, knowing that he'd been wanting to do it all along, but hadn't been sure of not being a nuisance. Well, if Brown could look on, there was no reason why he couldn't. He passed the machine shop, noting the excited flurry of activity going on, and went past No. 2, where other men were busily ripping out long sections of big piping and various other devices. There was a rope fence barring his way, well beyond No. 3, and he followed along the edge, looking for Palmer or Brown.

She saw him first. "Hi, Dr. Ferrel, over here in the truck. I thought you'd be coming soon. From up here we can get a look over the heads of all these other people, and we won't be tramped on." She stuck down a hand to help him up, smiled faintly as he disregarded it and mounted more briskly than his muscles wanted to. He wasn't so old that a girl had to help him yet.

"Know what's going on?" he asked, sinking down onto the plank across the truck body, facing out across the men below toward the converter. There seemed to be a dozen different centers of activity, all crossing each other in complete confusion, and the general pattern was meaningless.

"No more than you do. I haven't seen my husband, though Mr. Palmer took time enough to chase me here out of the way."

Doc centered his attention on the 'copters, unloading, rising, and coming in with more loads, and he guessed that those boxes must contain the little thermodyne bombs. It was the one thing he could understand, and consequently the least interesting. Other men were assembling the big sections of piping he'd seen before, connecting them up in almost endless order, while some of the tanks hooked on and snaked them off in the direction of the small river that ran off beyond the plant.

"Those must be the exhaust blowers, I guess," he told Brown, pointing them out. "Though I don't know what any of the rest of the stuff hooked on is."

"I know—I've been inside the plant Bob's father had." She lifted an inquiring eyebrow at him, went on as he nodded. "The pipes are for exhaust gases, all right, and those big square things are the motors and fans—they put in one at each five hundred feet or less of piping. The things they're wrapping around the pipe must be the heaters to keep the gases hot. Are they going to try to suck all that out?"

Doc didn't know, though it was the only thing he could see. But he wondered how they'd get around the problem of moving in close enough to do any good. "I heard your husband order some thermodyne bombs, so they'll probably try to gassify the magma; then they're pumping it down the river."

As he spoke, there was a flurry of motion at one side, and his eyes swung over instantly, to see one of the cranes laboring with a long framework stuck from its front, holding up a section of pipe with a nozzle on the end. It tilted precariously, even though heavy bags were piled everywhere to add weight, but an inch at a time it lifted its load, and began forcing its way forward, carrying the nozzle out in front and rather high.

Below the main exhaust pipe was another smaller one. As it drew near the outskirts of the danger zone, a small object ejaculated from the little pipe, hit the ground, and was a sudden blazing inferno of glaring blue-white light, far brighter than it seemed, judging by the effect on the eyes. Doc shielded his, just as someone below put something into his hands.

"Put 'em on. Palmer says the light's actinic."

He heard Brown fussing beside him, then his vision cleared, and he looked back through the goggles again to see a glowing cloud spring up from the magma, spread out near the ground, narrowing down higher up, until it sucked into the nozzle above, and disappeared. Another bomb slid from the tube, and erupted with blazing heat. A sideways glance showed another crane being fitted, and a group of men near it wrapping what might have been oiled rags around the small bombs; probably no tubing fitted them exactly, and they were padding them so pressure could blow them forward and out. Three more dropped from the tube, one at a time, and the fans roared and groaned, pulling the cloud that rose into the pipe and feeding it down toward the river.

Then the crane inched back out carefully as men uncoupled its piping from the main line, and a second went in to replace it. The heat generated must be too great for the machine to stand steadily without the pipe fusing, Doc decided; though they couldn't have kept a man inside the heavily armored cab for any length of time, if the metal had been impervious. Now another crane was ready, and went in from another place; it settled down to a routine of ingoing and outcoming cranes, and men feeding materials in, coupling and uncoupling the pipes and replacing the others who came from the cabs. Doc began to feel like a man at a tennis match, watching the ball without knowing the rules.

Brown must have had the same idea, for she caught Ferrel's arm and indicated a little leather case that came from her handbag. "Doc, do you play chess? We might as well fill our time with that as sitting here on edge, just watching. It's supposed to be good for nerves."

He seized on it gratefully, without explaining that he'd been city champion three years running; he'd take it easy, watch her game, handicap himself just enough to make it interesting by the deliberate loss of a rook, bishop or knight, as was needed to even the odds— Suppose they got all the magma out and into the river; how did that solve the problem? It removed it from the plant, but far less than the fifty-mile minimum danger limit.

"Check," Brown announced. He castled, and looked up at the half-dozen cranes that were now operating. "Check! Checkmate!"

He looked back again hastily, then, to see her queen guarding all possible moves, a bishop checking him. Then his eye followed down toward her end. "Umm. Did you know you've been in check for the last half-dozen moves? Because I didn't."

She frowned, shook her head, and began setting the men up again. Doc moved out the queen's pawn, looked out at the workers, and then brought out the king's bishop, to see her take it with her king's pawn. He hadn't watched her move it out, and had counted on her queen's to block his. Things would require more careful watching on this little portable set. The men were moving steadily and there was a growing clear space, but as they went forward, the violent action of the thermodyne had pitted the ground, carefully as it had been used, and going became more uncertain. Time was slipping by rapidly now.

"Checkmate!" He found himself in a hole, started to nod; but she caught herself this time. "Sorry, I've been playing my

king for a queen. Doctor, let's see if we can play at least one
game right."

Before it was half finished, it became obvious that they
couldn't. Neither had chess very much on the mind, and the
pawns and men did fearful and wonderful things, while the
knights were as likely to jump six squares as their normal L.
They gave it up, just as one of the cranes lost its precarious
balance and toppled forward, dropping the long extended
pipe into the bubbling mass below. Tanks were in instantly,
hitching on and tugging backward until it came down with a
thump as the pipe fused, releasing the extreme forward load.
It backed out on its own power, while another went in. The
driver, by sheer good luck, hobbled from the cab, waving an
armored hand to indicate he was all right. Things settled back
to an excited routine again that seemed to go on endlessly,
though seconds were dropping off too rapidly, turning into
minutes that threatened to be hours far too soon.

"Uh!" Brown had been staring for some time, but her little
feet suddenly came down with a bang and she straightened
up, her hand to her mouth. "Doctor, I just thought; it won't
do any good—all this!"

"Why?" She couldn't know anything, but he felt the faint
hopes he had go downward sharply. His nerves were dulled,
but still ready to jump at the slightest warning.

"The stuff they were making was a superheavy—it'll sink
as soon as it hits the water, and all pile up right there! It
won't float down river!"

Obvious, Ferrel thought; too obvious. Maybe that was why
the engineers hadn't thought of it. He started from the plank,
just as Palmer stepped up, but the manager's hand on his
shoulder forced him back.

"Easy, Doc, it's O. K. Umm, so they teach women *some*
science nowadays, eh, Mrs. Jenkins . . . Sue . . . Dr. Brown,
whatever your name is? Don't worry about it, though—the
old principle of Brownian movement will keep any colloid
suspended, if it's fine enough to be a real colloid. We're sucking it out and keeping it pretty hot until it reaches the
water—then it cools off so fast it hasn't time to collect in particles big enough to sink. Some of the dust that floats around
in the air is heavier than water, too. I'm joining the bystanders, if you don't mind; the men have everything under control, and I can see better here than I could down there, if
anything does come up."

Doc's momentary despair reacted to leave him feeling

more sure of things than was justified. He pushed over on the plank, making room for Palmer to drop down beside him. "What's to keep it from blowing up anyway, Palmer?"

"Nothing! Got a match?" He sucked in on the cigarette heavily, relaxing as much as he could. "No use trying to fool you, Doc, at this stage of the game. We're gambling, and I'd say the odds are even; Jenkins thinks they're ninety to ten in his favor, but he has to think so. What we're hoping is that by lifting it out in a gas, thus breaking it down at once from full concentration to the finest possible form, and letting it settle in the water in colloidal particles, there won't be a concentration at any one place sufficient to set it all off at once. The big problem is making sure we get every bit of it cleaned out here, or there may be enough left to take care of us and the nearby city! At least, since the last change, it's stopped spitting, so all the man have to worry about is burn!"

"How much damage, even if it doesn't go off all at once?"

"Possibly none. If you can keep it burning slowly, a million tons of dynamite wouldn't be any worse than the same amount of wood, but a stick going off at once will kill you. Why the dickens didn't Jenkins tell me he wanted to go into atomics? We could have fixed all that—it's hard enough to get good men as it is!"

Brown perked up, forgetting the whole trouble beyond them, and went into the story with enthusiasm, while Ferrel only partly listened. He could see the spot of magma growing steadily smaller, but the watch on his wrist went on ticking off minutes remorselessly, and the time was growing limited. He hadn't realized before how long he'd been sitting there. Now three of the crane nozzles were almost touching, and around them stretched the burned-out ground, with no sign of converter, masonry, or anything else; the heat from the thermodyne had gassified everything, indiscriminately.

"Palmer!" The portable ultrawave set around the manager's neck came to life suddenly. "Hey, Palmer, these blowers are about shot; the pipe's pitting already. We've been doing everything we can to replace them, but that stuff eats faster than we can fix. Can't hold up more'n fifteen minutes more."

"Check, Briggs. Keep 'em going the best you can." Palmer flipped a switch and looked out toward the tank standing by behind the cranes. "Jenkins, you get that?"

"Yeah. Surprised they held out this long. How much time

till deadline?" The boy's voice was completely toneless, neither hope nor nerves showing up, only the complete weariness of a man almost at his limit.

Palmer looked and whistled. "Twelve minutes, according to the minimum estimate Hoke made! How much left?"

"We're just burning around now, trying to make sure there's no pocket left; I hope we've got the whole works, but I'm not promising. Might as well send out all the I-231 you have and we'll boil it down the pipes to clear out any deposits on them. All the old treads and parts that contacted the R gone into the pile?"

"You melted the last, and your cranes haven't touched the stuff directly. Nice pile of money's gone down that pipe—converter, machinery, everything!"

Jenkins made a sound that was expressive of his worry about that. "I'm coming in now and starting the clearing of the pipe. What've you been paying insurance for?"

"At a lovely rate, too! O. K., come on in, kid; and if you're interested, you can start sticking A. E. after the M. D., anytime you want. Your wife's been giving me your qualifications, and I think you've passed the final test, so you're now an atomic engineer, duly graduated from National!"

Brown's breath caught, and her eyes seemed to glow, even through the goggles, but Jenkins' voice was flat. "O. K., I expected you to give me one if we don't blow up. But you'll have to see Dr. Ferrel about it; he's got a contract with me for medical practice. Be there shortly."

Nine of the estimated twelve minutes had ticked by when he climbed up beside them, mopping off some of the sweat that covered him, and Palmer was hugging the watch. More minutes ticked off slowly, while the last sound faded out in the plant, and the men stood around, staring down toward the river or at the hole that had been No. 4. Silence. Jenkins stirred, and grunted.

"Palmer, I know where I got the idea, now. Jorgenson was trying to remind me of it, instead of raving, only I didn't get it, at least consciously. It was one of Dad's, the one he told Jorgenson was a last resort, in case the thing they broke up about went haywire. It was the first variable Dad tried. I was twelve, and he insisted water would break it up into all its chains and kill the danger. Only Dad didn't really expect it to work!"

Palmer didn't look up from the watch, but he caught his breath and swore. "Fine time to tell me that!"

"He didn't have your isotopes to heat it up with, either," Jenkins answered mildly. "Suppose you look up from that watch of yours for a minute, down the river."

As Doc raised his eyes, he was aware suddenly of a roar from the men. Over to the south, stretching out in a huge mass, was a cloud of steam that spread upward and out as he watched, and the beginnings of a mighty hissing sound came in. Then Palmer was hugging Jenkins and yelling until Brown could pry him away and replace him.

"Ten miles or more of river, plus the swamps, Doc!" Palmer was shouting in Ferrel's ear. "All that dispersion, while it cooks slowly from now until the last chain is finished, atom by atom! The *theta* chain broke, unstable and now there's everything there, too scattered to set itself off! It'll cook the river bed up and dry it, but that's all!"

Doc was still dazed, unsure of how to take the relief. He wanted to lie down and cry or to stand up with the men and shout his head off. Instead, he sat loosely, gazing at the cloud. "So I lose the best assistant I ever had! Jenkins, I won't hold you; you're free for whatever Palmer wants."

"Hoke wants him to work on R—he's got the stuff for his bomb now!" Palmer was clapping his hands together slowly, like an excited child watching a steam shovel. "Heck, Doc, pick out anyone you want until your own boy gets out next year. You wanted a chance to work him in here, now you've got it. Right now I'll give you anything you want."

"You might see what you can do about hospitalizing the injured and fixing things up with the men in the tent behind the infirmary. And I think I'll take Brown in Jenkins' place, with the right to grab him in an emergency, until that year's up."

"Done." Palmer slapped the boy's back, stopping the protest, while Brown winked at him. "Your wife likes working, kid; she told me that herself. Besides, a lot of the women work here where they can keep an eye on their men; my own wife does, usually. Doc, take these two kids and head for home, where I'm going myself. Don't come back until you get good and ready, and don't let them start fighting about it!"

Doc pulled himself from the truck and started off with Brown and Jenkins following, through the yelling, relief-crazed men. The three were too thoroughly worn out for any exhibition themselves, but they could feel it. Happy ending! Jenkins and Brown where they wanted to be, Hoke with his bomb, Palmer with proof that atomic plants were safe where they were, and he—well, his boy would start out right, with himself and the widely differing but competent Blake and Jenkins to guide him. It wasn't a bad life, after all.

Then he stopped and chuckled. "You two wait for me, will you? If I leave here without making out that order of extra disinfection at the showers, Blake'll swear I'm growing old and feeble-minded. I can't have that."

Old? Maybe a little tired, but he'd been that before, and with luck would be again. He wasn't worried. His nerves were good for twenty years and fifty accidents more, and by that time Blake would be due for a little ribbing himself.

BARRIER

Astounding SF,

September

by Anthony Boucher (William Anthony Parker White)

*One of the premier Renaissance men in the
science fiction world, Anthony Boucher was a man
of wide interests and many talents. An influential
and excellent book reviewer in both the mystery (as
"H.H. Holmes") and sf fields (as Boucher and
"Holmes"), his non-sf mystery* Rocket to the
Morgue *(1429) contained several thinly veiled
and humorous references to the world of science
fiction and sf fandom. As a writer within the* genre
*he seemed more at home with fantasy, although he
produced a number of excellent science fiction stories, including "The Quest for Saint Aquin"
(1951), and "Q.U.R." (1943). However, it was
as an editor that Boucher made his greatest contribution, for, along with J. Francis McComas, he
was founding co-editor of* The Magazine of Fantasy
and Science Fiction, *one of the "Big Three" of the
post-World War II era. "Barrier" illustrates his
wide-ranging interests in its excellent combination
of the theme of time travel and the science of
linguistics.*

("Rocket to the Morgue", as Marty points out, was a *roman
á clef* in which the chief fun was picking out who the various
fictional characters represented in real life. None represented
me—one mark against Tony. However, I *was* mentioned
when Tony said that various characters sat about discussing
various sf topics, including "Asimov's positronic robots" and
misspelled my name. It wasn't till over a decade later that I
actually met Tony but I had long since forgiven him, for I
had submitted a number of stories to him and his rejec-

tions—when he rejected—were so kind that it would have taken a heart of stone to bear resentment.—I.A.)

The first difficulty was with language.

That is only to be expected when you jump five hundred years, but it is nonetheless perplexing to have your first casual query of: "What city is this?" answered by the sentence: "Stappers will get you. Or be you Slanduch?"

It was signficant that the first word John Brent heard in the State was "Stappers." But Brent could not know that then. It was only some hours later and fifty years earlier that he was to learn the details of the Stapper system. At the moment all that concerned him was food and plausibility.

His appearance was plausible enough. Following Derringer's advice he had traveled naked—"the one costume common to all ages," the scientist had boomed; "Which would astonish you more, lad; a naked man, or an Elizabethan courtier in full apparel?"—and commenced his life in the twenty-fifth century by burglary and the theft of a complete outfit of clothing. The iridescent woven plastics tailored in a half-clinging, half-flowing style looked precious to Brent, but seemed both comfortable and functional.

No man alive in 2473 would have bestowed a second glance on the feloniously clad Brent, but in his speech, he realized at once, lay danger. He pondered the alternatives presented by the stranger. Stappers would get him unless he was Slanduch. Whatever Stappers were, things that "get you" sounded menacing. "Slanduch," he replied.

The stranger nodded. "That bees O.K.," he said, and Brent wondered what he had committed himself to. "So what city is this?" he repeated.

"*Bees*," the stranger chided. "Stappers be more severe now since Edict of 2470. Before they doed pardon some irregularities, but now none even from Slanduch."

"I be sorry," said Brent humbly, making a mental note that irregular verbs were for some reason perilous. "But for the third time—"

He had thought the wall beside them was solid. He realized now that part of it, at least, was only a deceptive glass-like curtain that parted to let forth a tall and vigorous man, followed by two shorter aides. All three of these wore robes similar to the iridescent garments of Brent and his companion, but of pure white.

The leader halted and barked out, "George Starvel?"

Brent saw a quiet sort of terror begin to grow on his companion's face. He nodded and held out his wrist.

The man in white glanced at what Brent decided must be an identification plaque. "Starvel," he announced, "you speaked against Barrier."

Starvel trembled. "Cosmos knows I doed not."

"Five mans know that you doed."

"Never. I only sayed—"

"You only! Enough!"

The rod appeared in the man's hand only for an instant. Brent saw no flame or discharge; but Starvel was stretched out on the ground and the two aides were picking him up as callously as though he were a log.

The man turned toward Brent, who was taking no chances. He flexed his legs and sprang into the air. His fingertips grasped the rim of the balcony above them, and his feet shot out into the white-robed man's face. His arm and shoulder muscles tensed to their utmost. The smooth plastic surface was hell to keep a grip on. Beneath, he could see his adversary struggling blindly to his feet and groping for the rod. At last, desperately, Brent swung himself up and over the edge.

There was no time to contemplate the beauties of the orderly terrace garden. There was only time to note that there was but one door, and to make for it. It was open and led to a long corridor. Brent turned to the nearest of the many identical doors. Apartments? So—he was taking a chance; whatever was behind that door, the odds were better than with an armed policeman you'd just kicked in the face. Brent had always favored the devil you don't know—or he'd never have found himself in this strange world. He walked toward the door, and it opened.

He hurried into an empty room, glancing back to see the door shut by itself. The room had two other doors. Each of them opened equally obligingly. Bathroom and bedroom. No kitchen. (His stomach growled a comment.) No people. And no exit from the apartment but the door he had come through.

He forced himself to sit down and think. Anything might happen before the Stapper caught up with him, for he had no doubt that was what the white-robed man must be.

What had he learned about the twenty-fifth century in this brief encounter?

You must wear an identification plaque. (Memo: How to get one?) You must not use irregular verbs (or nouns; the Stapper had said "mans"). You must not speak against Barrier, whoever or whatever that meant. You must beware white-robed men who lurk behind false walls. You must watch out for rods that kill (query: or merely stun?). Doors open by selenium cells (query: how do they lock?). You must—

The door opened. It was not the Stapper who stood there, but a tall and majestic woman of, at a guess, sixty. A noble figure—"Roman matron" were the words that flashed into Brent's mind.

The presence of a total stranger in her apartment seemed nowise disconcerting. She opened her arms in a broad gesture of welcome. "John Brent!" she exclaimed in delighted recognition. "It beed so long!"

"I don't want a brilliant young scientific genius!" Derringer had roared when Brent answered his cryptically worded ad. "I've got 'em here in the laboratory. They've done grand work on the time machine. I couldn't live without 'em, and there's not a one of 'em I'd trust out of this century. Not out of this decade. What I want is four things: A knowledge of history, for a background of analogy to understand what's been going on; linguistic ability, to adjust yourself as rapidly as possible to the changes in language; physical strength and dexterity, to get yourself out of the scrapes that are bound to come up; and social adaptability. A chimpanzee of reasonably subhuman intelligence could operate the machine. What counts is what you'll be able to do after you get there."

The knowledge of history and the physical qualities had been easy to demonstrate. The linguistic ability was a bit more complex; Derringer had contrived an intricate series of tests involving adjustment to phonetic changes and the capacity to assimilate the principles of a totally fictitious language invented for the occasion. The social adaptability was measured partly by an aptitude test, but largely Brent guessed, by Derringer's own observation during the weeks of preparation after his probationary hiring.

He had passed all four requirements with flying colors. At least Derringer had grinned at him through the black beard and grunted the reluctant "Good man!" that was his equivalent of rhapsodic praise. His physical agility had already stood him in good stead, and his linguistic mind was rapidly assimilating the new aspects of the language (there were phonetic alterations as well as the changes in vocabulary and inflection—he was particularly struck by the fact that the vowels *a* and *o* no longer possessed the diphthongal off-glide so characteristic of English, but were pure vowels like the Italian *e* and *o*), but his social adaptability was just now hitting a teriffic snag.

What the hell do you do when a Roman matron whom you have never seen, born five hundred years after you, welcomes you by name and exclaims that it haves beed a long time? (This regular past participle of *be*, Brent reflected, gives the speaker something of the quality of a Bostonian with a cold in the nose.)

For a moment he toyed with the rash notion that she might likewise be a time traveler, someone whom he had known in 1942. Derringer had been positive that this was the first such trip ever attempted; but someone leaving the twentieth century later might still be an earlier arrival in the twenty-fifth. He experimented with the idea.

"I suppose," Brent ventured, "you could call five hundred years a long tine, in its relative way."

The Roman matron frowned. "Do not jest, John. Fifty years be not five hundred. I will confess that first five years seemed at times like five centuries, but after fifty—one does not feel so sharply."

Does was of course pronounced *dooze*. All *r*'s, even terminal, were lightly trilled. These facts Brent noted in the back of his mind, but the fore part was concerned with the immediate situation. If this woman chose to accept him as an acquaintance—it was nowise unlikely that his double should be wandering about in this century—it meant probably protection from the Stapper. His logical mind protested, "Could this double have your name?" but he shushed it.

"Did you," he began, and caught himself. "Doed you see anyone in the hall—a man in white?"

The Roman matron moaned. "Oh, John! Do Stappers seek you again? But of course. If you have comed to destroy Barrier, they must destroy you."

"Whoa there!" Brent had seen what happened to one person who had merely "speaked against Barrier." "I didn't . . . doedn't . . . say anything against Barrier."

The friendliness began to die from her clear blue eyes.

"And I believed you," she said sorrowfully. "You told us of this second Barrier and sweared to destroy it. We thinked you beed one of us. And now—"

No amourt of social adaptability can resist a sympathetic and dignified woman on the verge of tears. Besides, this apartment was for the moment a valuable haven, and if she thought he was a traitor of some sort—

"Look," said Brent. "You see, I am—there isn't any use at this moment trying to be regular—I am not whoever you think I am. I never saw you before. I couldn't have. This is the first instant I've ever been in your time."

"If you wish to lie to me, John—"

"I'm not lying. And I'm not John—at least not the one you're thinking of. I'm John Brent, I'm twenty-eight years old, and I was born in 1914—a good five and a half centuries ago."

According to all the time travel fiction Brent had ever read, that kind of statement ranks as a real stunner. There is a deathly hush and a wild surmise and the author stresses the curtain-line effect by inserting a line space.

But the Roman matron was unmoved. The hush and the surmise were Brent's an instant later when she said with anguished patience, "I know, John, I know."

"Derringer left this one out of the rule book," Brent grunted. "Madam, you have, as they say, the better of me. What does A do now?"

"You *do* be same John!" she smiled. "I never beed able to understand you."

"We have much in common," Brent observed.

"And because I can't understand you, I know you be you." She was still smiling. It was an odd smile; Brent couldn't place its precise meaning. Not until she leaned toward him and for one instant gently touched his arm.

He needed friends. Whatever her wild delusions, she seemed willing to help him. But he still could not quite keep from drawing back as he recognized the tender smile of love on this dignified ancient face.

She seemed to sense his withdrawal. For a moment he feared a gathering anger. Then she relaxed, and with another smile, a puzzled but resigned smile, said, "This be part of not understanding you, I guess. Cosmos knows but you be so young, John, still so *young* . . ."

She must, Brent thought with sudden surprise, have been a very pretty girl.

The door opened. The man who entered was as tall as the Stapper, but wore the civilian's iridescent robes. His long beard seemed to have caught a little of their rainbow influence; it was predominantly red, but brown and black and white glinted in it. The hair on his head was graying. He might have been anywhere from forty-five to a vigorous and well-preserved seventy.

"We have a guest, sister?" he asked politely.

The Roman matron made a despairing gesture. "You don't recognize him? And John—you don't know Stephen?"

Stephen slapped his thigh and barked—a sound that seemed to represent a laugh of pleasure. "Cosmos!" he cried. "John Brent! I told you, Martha. I knew he wouldn't fail us."

"Stephen!" she exclaimed in shocked tones.

"Hang the irregularities! Can't I greet John with the old words that comed—no, by Cosmos—*came* from the same past he came from? See, John—don't I talk the old language well? I even use article—pardon me, *the* article."

Brent's automatic mental notebook recorded the fact, which he had already suspected, that an article was as taboo as an irregular verb. But around this self-governing notation system swirled utter confusion. It might possibly have been just his luck to run into a madwoman. But two mad brains in succession with identical delusions were too much. And Stephen had known he was from the past.

"I'm afraid," he said simply, "this is too much for me. Suppose we all sit down and have a drink of something and talk this over."

Stephen smiled. "You remember our bond, eh? And not many places in State you'll find it. Even fewer than before." He crossed to a cabinet and returned with three glasses of colorless liquid.

Brent seized his eagerly and downed it. A drink might help the swirling. It might—

The drink had gone down smoothly and tastelessly. Now, however, some imp began dissecting atoms in his stomach and shooting off a bombardment stream of particles that zoomed up through his throat into his brain, where they set off a charge of explosive of hitherto unknown power. Brent let out a strangled yelp.

Stephen barked again. "Good bond, eh, John?"

Brent managed to focus his host through the blurring lens of his tears. "Sure," he nodded feebly. "Swell. And now let me try to explain—"

The woman looked sadly at her brother. "He denies us, Stephen. He sayes that he haves never seed me before. He forgets all that he ever sweared about Barrier."

A curious look of speculation came into Stephen's brown eyes. "Bees this true, John? You have never seed us before in your life?"

"But, Stephen, you know—"

"Hush, Martha. I sayed in *his* life. Bees it true, John?"

"It bees. God knows it bees. I have never seen . . . seed either of you in my life."

"But Stephen—"

"I understand now, Martha. Remember when he telled us of Barrier and his resolve?"

"Can I forget?"

"How doed he know of Barrier? Tell me that."

"I don't know," Martha confessed. "I have wondered—"

"He knowed of Barrier then because he bees here now. He telled me then just what we must now tell him."

"Then for heaven's sake," Brent groaned, "tell me."

"Your pardon, John. My sister bees not so quick to grasp source of these temporal confusions. More bond?" He had the bottle in his hand when he suddenly stopped, thrust it back in the cabinet, and murmured, "Go into bedroom."

Brent obeyed. This was no time for displaying initiative. And no sooner had the bedroom door closed behind him than he heard the voice of the Stapper. (The mental notebook recorded that apartment buildings must be large, if it had taken this long for the search to reach here.)

"No," Stephen was saying. "My sister and I have beed here for past half-hour. We seed no one."

"State thanks you," the Stapper muttered, so casually that the phrase must have been an official formula. His steps sounded receding. Then they stopped, and there was the noise of loud sniffs.

"Dear God," thought Brent, "have they crossed the bulls with bloodhounds?"

"Bond," the Stapper announced.

"Dear me," came Martha's voice. "Who haves beed in here today, Stephen?"

"I'm homeopath," said the Stapper. "Like cures like. A little bond might make me forget I smelled it."

There was a bark from Stephen and a clink of glasses. No noise from either of them as they downed the liquor. Those, sir, were men. (Memo: Find out why such unbelievable rot-gut is called *Bond*, of all things.)

"State thanks you," said the Stapper, and laughed. "You know George Starvel, don't you?"

A slightly hesitant "Yes" from Stephen.

"When you see him again, I think you'll find he haves changed his mind. About many things."

There was silence. Then Stephen opened the bedroom door and beckoned Brent back into the living room. He handed him a glass of bond and said, "I will be brief."

Brent, now forewarned, sipped at the liquor and found it cheerfully warming as he assimilated the new facts.

In the middle of the twenty-fourth century, he learned, civilization had reached a high point of comfort, satisfaction, achievement—and stagnation. The combination of atomic power and De Bainville's revolutionary formulation of the principles of labor and finance had seemed to solve all economic problems. The astounding development of synthetics had destroyed the urgent need for raw materials and colonies and abolished the distinction between haves and have-nots among nations. Schwarzwalder's *Compendium* had achieved the dream of the early Encyclopedists—the complete systematization of human knowledge. Farthing had regularized the English language, an achievement paralleled by the work of Zinsmeister, Timofeov, and Tamayo y Sárate in their respective tongues. (These four languages now dominated the earth. French and Italian had become corrupt dialects of German, and the Oriental languages occupied in their own countries something the position of Greek and Latin in nineteenty-century Europe, doomed soon to the complete oblivion which swallowed up those classic tongues in the twenty-first.)

There was nothing more to be achieved. All was known, all was accomplished. Nakamura's Law of Spatial Acceleration had proved interplanetary travel to be impossible for all time. Charnwood's Law of Temporal Metabolism had done the same for time travel. And the Schwarzwalder *Compendium*, which everyone admired and no one had read, established such a satisfactory and flawless picture of knowledge that it was obviously impossible that anything remained to be discovered.

It was then that Dyce-Farnsworth proclaimed the Stasis of Cosmos. A member of the Anglo-Physical Church, product of the long contemplation by English physicists of the metaphysical aspects of science, he came as the prophet needed to pander to the self-satisfaction of the age.

He was curiously aided by Farthing's laws of regularity. The article, direct or indirect, Farthing had proved to be completely unnecessary—had not languages as world-dominant as Latin in the first centuries and Russian in the twenty-first found no need for it?—and semantically misleading. "Article," he had said in his final and comprehensive study *This Bees Speech*, "bees prime corruptor of human thinking."

And thus the statement so beloved in the twentieth century by metaphysical-minded scientists and physical-minded divines, "God is the cosmos," became with Dyce-Farnsworth, "God bees cosmos," and hence, easily and inevitably, "God bees Cosmos," so that the utter scientific impersonality became a personification of Science. Cosmos replaced Jehovah, Baal and Odin.

The love of Cosmos was not man nor his works, but Stasis. Man was tolerated by Cosmos that he might achieve Stasis. All the millennia of human struggle had been aimed at this supreme moment when all was achieved, all was known, and all was perfect. Therefore this supernal Stasis must at all costs be maintained. Since Now was perfect, any alteration must be imperfect and taboo.

From this theory logically evolved the State, whose duty was to maintain the perfect Stasis of Cosmos. No totalitarian government had ever striven so strongly to iron out all doubt and dissension. No religious bigotry had ever found heresy so damnable and worthy of destruction. The Stasis must be maintained.

It was, ironically, the aged Dyce-Farnsworth himself who, in a moment of quasi-mystical intuition, discovered the flaw in Charnwood's Law of Temporal Metabolism. And it was clear to him what must be done.

Since the Stasis of Cosmos did not practice time travel, any earlier or later civilization that did so must be imperfect. Its emissaries would sow imperfection. There must be a Barrier.

The mystic went no further than that dictum, but the scientists of the State put his demand into practical terms. "Do not ask how at this moment," Stephen added. "I be not man to explain that. But you will learn." The first Barrier was a failure. It destroyed itself and to no apparent result. But now, fifty years later, the fears of time travel had grown.

The original idea of the imperfection of emissaries had been lost. Now time travel was in itself imperfect and evil. Any action taken against it would be praise to Cosmos. And the new Barrier was being erected.

"But John knows all this," Martha protested from time to time, and Stephen would shake his head sadly and smile sympathetically at Brent.

"I don't believe a word of it," Brent said at last. "Oh, the historical outline's all right. I trust you on that. And it works out sweetly by analogy. Take the religious fanaticism of the sixteenth century, the smug scientific self-satisfaction of the nineteeth, the power domination of the twentieth—fuse them and you've got your State. But the Barrier's impossible. It can't work."

"Charnwood claimed there beed no principle on which time travel can work. And here you be."

"That's different," said Brent vaguely. "But this talk of destroying the Barrier is nonsense. There's no need to."

"Indeed there bees need, John. For two reasons: one, that we may benefit by wisdom of travelers from other ages; and two, that positive act of destroying this Barrier, worshiped now with something like fetishism, bees strongest weapon with which we can strike against State. For there be these few of us who hope to save mankind from this fanatical complacency that race haves falled into. George Starvel beed one," Stephen added sadly.

"I saw Starvel—But that isn't what I mean. There's no need because the Barrier won't work."

"But you telled us that it haved to be destroyed," Martha protested. "That it doed work, and that we—"

"Hush," said Stephen gently. "John, will you trust us far enough to show us your machine? I think I can make matters clearer to Martha then."

"If you'll keep me out of the way of Stappers."

"That we can never guarantee—yet. But day will come when mankind cans forget Stappers and State, that I swear." There was stern and noble courage in Stephen's face and bearing as he drained his glass to that pledge.

"I had a break when I landed here," John Brent explained on the way. "Derringer equipped the machine only for temporal motion. He explained that it meant running a risk; I might find that the coastline had sunk and I'd arrive under water, or God knows what. But he hadn't worked out the synchronized adjustments for tempo-spatial motion yet, and he wanted to get started. I took the chance, and luck was good. Where the Derringer lab used to be is now apparently a deserted warehouse. Everything's dusty and there's not a sign of human occupation."

Stephen's eyes lit up as they approached the long low building of opaque bricks. "Remember, Martha?"

Martha frowned and nodded.

Faint light filtered through the walls to reveal the skeletal outlines of the machine. Brent switched on a light on the panel which gave a dim glow.

"There's not much to see even in a good light," he explained. "Just these two seats—Derringer was planning on teams when he built it, but decided later that one man with responsibility only to himself would do better—and this panel. These instruments are automatic—they adjust to the presence of another machine ahead of you in the time line. The only control the operator bothers with is this." He indicated the double dial set at 2473.

"Why doed you choose this year?"

"At random. Derringer set the outer circle at 2400—half a millennium seemed a plausible choice. Then I spun the inner dial blindfolded. When this switch here is turned, you create a certain amount of temporal potential, positive or negative—which is as loose as applying those terms to magnetic poles, but likewise as convenient. For instance if I turn it to here"—he spun the outer dial to 2900—"you'll have five hundred years of positive potential which'll shoot you ahead to 2973. Or set it like this, and you'll have five centuries of negative, which'll pull you back practically to where I started from."

Stephen frowned. "*Ahead* and *back* be of course nonsense words in this connection. But they may be helpful to Martha in visualizing it. Will you please show Martha the back of your dial?"

"Why?" There was no answer. Brent shrugged and climbed into the seat. The Roman matron moved around the machine and entered the other seat as he loosed the catch on the dial and opened it as one did for oiling.

Stephen said, "Look well, my dear. What be the large wheels marked of?"

"Aceroid, of course. Don't you remember how Alex—"

"Don't remember, Martha. Look. What *be* they?"

Martha gasped. "Why, they . . . they be aluminum."

"Very well. Now don't you understand—*Ssh!*" He broke
off and moved toward the doorway. He listened there a moment, then slipped out of sight.

"What does he have?" Brent demanded as he closed the
dial. "The ears of an elkhound?"

"Stephen haves hyper-acute sense of hearing. He bees
proud of it, and it haves saved us more than once from Stappers. When people be engaged in work against State—"

A man's figure appeared again in the doorway. But its
robes were white. "Good God!" Brent exclaimed. "Jiggers,
the Staps!"

Martha let out a little squeal. A rod appeared in the Stapper's hand. Brent's eyes were so fixed on the adversary that
he did not see the matron's hand move toward the switch until she had turned it.

Brent had somehow instinctively shut his eyes during his
first time transit. *During*, he reflected, is not the right word.
At the time of? Hardly. How can you describe an event of
time movement without suggesting another time measure perpendicular to the time line? At any rate, he had shut them in
a laboratory in 1942 and opened them an instant later in a
warehouse in 2473.

Now he shut them again, and kept them shut. He had to
think for a moment. He had been playing with the dial—
where was it set when Martha jerked the switch? 1973, as
best he remembered. And he had now burst into that world
in plastic garments of the twenty-fifth century, accompanied
by a Roman matron who had in some time known him for
fifty years.

He did not relish the prospect. And besides he was bothered by that strange jerking, tearing sensation that had
twisted his body when he closed his eyes. He had felt nothing
whatsoever on his previous trip. Had something gone wrong
this time? Had—

"It doesn't work!" said Martha indignantly.

Brent opened his eyes. He and Martha sat in the machine
in a dim warehouse of opaque brick.

"We be still here," she protested vigorously.

"Sure we're still here." Brent frowned. "But what you
mean is, we're still *now*."

"You talk like Stephen. What do you mean?"

"Or are we?" His frown deepened. "If we're still now,

where is that Stapper? He didn't vanish just because you pulled a switch. How old is this warehouse?"

"I don't know. I think about sixty years. It beed fairly new when I beed a child. Stephen and I used to play near here."

"Then we could have gone back a few decades and still be here. Yes, and look—those cases over there. I'd swear they weren't here before. After. Whatever. *Then*, when we saw the Stapper." He looked at the dial. It was set to 1973. And the warehouse was new some time around 2420.

Brent sat and stared at the panel.

"What bees matter?" Martha demanded. "Where be we?"

"Here, same like always. But what bothers me is just *when* we are. Come on; want to explore?"

Martha shook her head. "I want to stay here. And I be afraid for Stephen. Doed Stappers get him? Let's go back."

"I've got to check up on things. Something's gone wrong, and Derringer'll never forgive me if I don't find out what and why. You stay here if you want."

"Alone?"

Brent suppressed several remarks concerning women, in the abstract and the particular. "Stay or go, I don't care. I'm going."

Martha sighed. "You have changed so, John—"

In front of the warehouse was an open field. There had been buildings there when Brent last saw it. And in the field three young people were picnicking. The sight reminded Brent that it was a long time since he'd eaten.

He made toward the trio. There were two men and a girl. One man was blond, the other and the girl were brilliantly red-headed. The girl had much more than even that hair to recommend her. She— Brent's eyes returned to the red-headed man. There was no mistaking those deep brown eyes, that sharp and noble nose. The beard was scant, but still there was no denying—

Brent sprang forward with an eager cry of "Stephen!"

The young man looked at him blankly. "Yes," he said politely. "What do you want?"

Brent mentally kicked himself. He had met Stephen in advanced age. What would the Stephen of twenty know of him? And suddenly he began to understand a great deal. The confusion of that first meeting started to fade away.

"If I tell you," he said rapidly, "that I know that you be Stephen, that you have sister Martha, that you drink bond despite Stappers, and that you doubt wisdom of Barrier, will you accept me as a man you can trust?"

"Cosmic eons!" the blond young man drawled. "Stranger knows plenty, Stephen. If he bees Stapper, you'll have your mind changed."

The scantily bearded youth looked a long while into Brent's eyes. Then he felt in his robe, produced a flask and handed it over. Brent drank and returned it. Their hands met in a firm clasp.

Stephen grinned at the others. "My childs, I think stranger brings us adventure. I feel like someone out of novel by Varnichek." He turned to Brent. "Do you know these others, too?"

Brent shook his head.

"Krasna and Alex. And your name?"

"John Brent."

"And what can we do for you, John?"

"First tell me year."

Alex laughed, and the girl smiled. "And how long have you beed on a bonder?" Alex asked.

A bonder, Brent guessed, would be a bond bender. "This bees my first drink," he said, "since 1942. Or perhaps since 2473, according as how you reckon."

Brent was not disappointed in the audience reaction this time.

It's easy to see what must have happened, Brent wrote that night in the first entry of the journal Derringer had asked him to keep. He wrote longhand, an action that he loathed. The typewriter which Stephen had kindly offered him was equipped with a huge keyboard bearing the forty-odd characters of the Farthing phonetic alphabet, and Brent declined the loan.

We're at the first *Barrier—the one that failed. It was dedicated to Cosmos and launched this afternoon. My friends were among the few inhabitants not ecstatically present at the ceremony. Since then they've collected reports for me. The damned contrivance had to be so terrifically overloaded that it blew up. Dyce-Farnsworth was killed and will be a holy martyr to Cosmos forever.*

But in an infinitesimal fraction of a second between the launching and the explosion, the Barrier existed. That was enough.

If you, my dear Dr. Derringer, were ever going to see this journal, the whole truth would doubtless flash instantaneously through your mind like the lightning in the laboratory of the Mad Scientist. (And why couldn't I have met up with a Mad Scientist instead of one who was perfectly sane and accurate . . . up to a point? Why, Dr. Derringer, you fraud, you didn't even have a daughter!)

But since this journal, faithfully kept as per your instructions, is presumably from now on for my eyes alone, I'll have to try to make clear to my own uninspired mind just what gives with this Barrier, which broke down, so that it can't protect the Stasis, but still irrevocably stops me from going back.

Any instant in which the Barrier exists is impassable: a sort of roadblock in time. Now to achieve Dyce-Farnsworth's dream of preventing all time travel, the Barrier would have to go on existing forever, or at least into the remote future. Then as the Stasis goes on year by year, there'd always be a Barrier-instant ahead of it in time protecting it. Not merely one roadblock, but a complete abolition of traffic on the road.

Now D-F has failed. The future's wide open. But there in the recent past, at the instant of destruction, is the roadblock that keeps me, my dear Dr. Derringer, from ever beaming on your spade beard again.

Why does it block me? I've been trying to find out. Stephen is good on history, but lousy on science. The blond young Alex reverses the combination. From him I've tried to learn the theory back of the Barrier.

The Barrier established in that fractional second, a powerful magnetic field in the temporal dimension. As a result, any object moving along the time line is cutting the magnetic field. Hysteresis sets up strong eddy currents which bring the object, in this case me, to an abrupt halt. Cf. that feeling of twisting shock that I had when my eyes were closed.

I pointed out to Alex that I must somehow have crossed this devilish Barrier in going from 1942 to 2473. He accounts for that apparent inconsistency by saying that I was then traveling with the time stream, though at a greater rate; the blockage lines of force were end-on and didn't stop me.

Brent paused and read the last two paragraphs aloud to the young scientist who was tinkering with the traveling machine. "How's that, Alex? Clear enough?"

"It will do." Alex frowned. "Of course we need whole new vocabulary for temporal concepts. We fumble so helplessly in analogies—" He rose. "There bees nothing more I can do for this now. Tomorrow I'll bring out some tools from shop, and see if I can find some acreoid gears."

"Good man. I may not be able to go back in time from here; but one thing I can do is go forward. Forward to just before they launch that second Barrier. I've got a job to do."

Alex gazed admiringly at the machine. "Wonderful piece of work. Your Dr. Derringer bees great man."

"Only he didn't allow for the effects of tempo-magnetic hysteresis on his mechanism. Thank God for you, Alex."

"Willn't you come back to house?"

Brent shook his head. "I'm taking no chances on curious Stappers. I'm sticking here with Baby. See that the old lady's comfortable, will you?"

"Of course. But tell me; who bees she? She willn't talk at all."

"Nobody. Just a temporal hitchhiker."

Martha's first sight of the young Stephen had been a terrible shock. She had stared at him speechlessly for long minutes, and then gone into a sort of inarticulate hysteria. Any attempt at explanation of her status, Brent felt, would only make matters worse. There was nothing to do but leave her to the care—which seemed both tender and efficient—of the girl Krasna, and let her life ride until she could resume it normally in her own time.

He resumed his journal.

Philological notes: Stapper, as I should have guessed, is a corruption of Gestapo. Slanduch, which poor Starvel suggested I might be, had me going for a bit. Asking about that, learned that there is more than one State. This, the smuggest and most fanatical of them all, embraces North America, Australia and parts of Eastern Asia. Its official language is, of course, Farthingized English. Small nuclear groups of English-speaking people exist in the other States, and have preserved the older and irregular forms of speech. (Cf. American mountaineers, and Spanish Jews in Turkey.) A Slanduch belongs to such a group.

It took me some time to realize the origin of this word, but it's obvious enough: Auslandsdeutsche, the Germans who existed similarly cut off from the main body of their culture. With these two common loan words suggesting a marked domination at some time of the German language, I asked

Alex—and I must confess almost fearfully—"Then did Germany win the war?"

He not unnaturally countered with, "Which war?"

"The Second World War. Started in 1939."

"Second?" Alex paused. "Oh, yes. Stephen once told me that they—you used to have numbers for wars before historians simply called 1900's Century of Wars. But as to who winned which . . . who remembers?"

Brent paused, and wished for Stephen's ears to determine the nature of that small noise outside. Or was it pure imagination? He went on:

These three—Stephen, Alex and Krasna—have proved to be the ideal hosts for a traveler of my nature. Any devout believer in Cosmos, any loyal upholder of the Stasis would have turned me over to the Stappers for my first slip in speech or ideas.

They seem to be part of what corresponds to the Underground Movements of my own century. They try to accomplish a sort of boring from within, a subtle sowing of doubts as to the Stasis. Eventually they hope for more positive action; so far it is purely mental sabotage aimed at—

It was a noise. Brent set down his stylus and moved along the wall as quietly as possible to the door. He held his breath while the door slid gently inward. Then as the figure entered, he pounced.

Stappers have close-cropped hair and flat manly chests. Brent released the girl abruptly and muttered a confused apology.

"It bees only me," she said shyly. "Krasna. Doed I startle you?"

"A bit," he confessed. "Alex and Stephen warned me what might happen if a Stapper stumbled in here."

"I be sorry, John."

"It's all right. But you shouldn't be wandering around alone at night like this. In fact, you shouldn't be mixed up in this at all. Leave it to Stephen and Alex and me."

"Mans!" she pouted. "Don't you think womans have any right to fun?"

"I don't know that fun's exactly the word. But since you're here, milady, let me extend the hospitality of the camp. Alex left me some bond. That poison grows on you. And tell me, why's it called that?"

"Stephen telled me once, but I can't— Oh yes. When they prohibited all drinking because drinking makes you think world bees better than it really bees and of course if you make yourself different world that bees against Stasis and so they prohibited it but they keeped on using it for medical purposes and that beed in warehouses and pretty soon no one knowed any other kind of liquor so it bees called bond. Only I don't see why."

"I don't suppose," Brent remarked, "that anybody in this century has ever heard of one Gracie Allen, but her spirit is immortal. The liquor in the warehouses was probably kept under government bond."

"Oh—" she said meekly. "I'll remember. You know everything, don't you?"

Brent looked at her suspiciously, but there was no irony in the remark. "How's the old lady getting on?"

"Fine. She bees sleeping now at last. Alex gived her some dormitin. She bees nice, John."

"And yet your voice sounds worried. What's wrong?"

"She bees so much like my mother, only, of course, I don't remember my mother much because I beed so little when Stappers taked my father and then my mother doedn't live very long but I do remember her some and your old lady bees so much like her. I wish I haved knowed my mother goodlier, John. She beed dear. She—" She lowered her voice in the tone of one imparting a great regret. "She cooked."

Brent remembered their tasteless supper of extracts, concentrates and synthetics, and shuddered. "I wish you had known her, Krasna."

"You know what cooking means? You go out and you dig up roots and you pick leaves off of plants and some people they even used to take animals, and then you apply heat and—"

"I know. I used to be a fair-to-middling cook myself, some five hundred years ago. If you could lead me to a bed of coals, a clove of garlic, and a two-inch steak, milady, I'd guarantee to make your eyes pop."

"Garlic? Steak?" Her eyes were wide with wonder. "What be those?"

Brent explained. For ten minutes he talked of the joys of food, of the sheer ecstatic satisfaction of good eating that passes the love of woman, the raptures of art, or the wonders of science. Then her questions poured forth.

"Stephen learns things out of books and Alex learns things in lab but I can't do that so goodly and they both make fun of me only you be real and I can learn things from you, John, and it bees wonderful. Tell me——"

And Krasna, with a greedy ear, listened.

"You know," Brent muttered, more to himself than to Krasna as he finished his exposition of life lived unstatically, "I never gave a particular damn about politics, but now I look back at my friends that liked Hitler and my friends that loved Stalin and my friends that thought there was much to be said for Franco . . . if only the boys could avoid a few minor errors like killing Jews or holding purge trials. This was what they all wanted: the Perfect State—the Stasis. God, if they could see——!"

At his feet Krasna stirred restlessly. "Tell me more," she said, "about how womans' garments beed unstatic."

His hands idled over her flowing red hair. "You've got the wrong expert for that, milady. All I remember, with the interest of any red-blooded American boy, is the way knees came and went and breasts came and stayed. You know, I've thought of the first point in favor of Stasis: a man could never catch hell for not noticing his girl's new dress."

"But why?" Krasna insisted. "Why doed they change—*styles?*" He nodded. "—change styles so often?"

"Well, the theory—not that I ever quite believed it—was to appeal to men."

"And I always wear the same dress—well, not *same*, because I always put on clean one every morning and sometimes in evening too—but it always looks same, and every time you see me it will be same and——" She broke off suddenly and pressed her face against his knee.

Gently he tilted her head back and grinned down at her moist eyes. "Look," he said. "I said I never believed it. If you've got the right girl, it doesn't matter what she wears."

He drew her up to him. She was small and warm and soft and completely unstatic. He was at home with himself and with life for the first time in five hundred years.

The machine was not repaired the next day, nor the next. Alex kept making plausible, if not quite intelligible technical excuses. Martha kept to her room and fretted, but Brent rather welcomed the delay. There was no hurry; leaving this time several days later had no effect on when they reached 2473. But he had some difficulty making that point clear to the matron.

This delay gave him an opportunity to see something of the State in action, and any information acquired was apt to be useful when the time came. With various members of Stephen's informal and illicit group he covered the city. He visited a Church of Cosmos and heard the official doctrine on the failure of the Barrier—the Stasis of Cosmos did not permit time travel, so that even an attempt to prohibit it by recognizing its existence affronted Cosmos. He visited libraries and found only those works which had established or upheld the Stasis, all bound in the same uniform format which the Cosmic Bibliological Committee of 2407 had ordained as ideal and static. He visited scientific laboratories and found brilliant young dullards plodding away endlessly at what had already been established; imaginative research was manifestly perilous.

He heard arid stretches of intolerable music composed according to the strict Farinelli system, which forbade, among other things, any alteration of key or time for the duration of a composition. He went to a solly, which turned out to be a deceptively solid three-dimensional motion picture, projected into an apparently screenless arena (*Memo*: ask Alex how?) giving something the effect of what Little Theater groups in his day called Theater in the Round. But only the images were roundly three-dimensional. The story was a strictly one-dimensional exposition of the glories of Stasis, which made the releases of Ufa or Artkino seem relatively free from propaganda. Brent, however, suspected the author of being an Undergrounder. The villain, even though triumphantly bested by the Stappers in the end, had all the most plausible and best written speeches, some of them ingenious and strong enough to sow doubts in the audience.

If, Brent thought disgustedly, anything could sow doubts in this smug herd of cattle. For the people of the State seemed to take the deepest and most loving pride in everything pertaining to the State and to the Stasis of Cosmos. The churches, the libraries, the laboratories, the music, the sollies, all represented humanity as its highest peak. We have attained perfection, have we not? Then all this bees perfect, and we love it.

"What we need," he expostulated to Alex and Stephen one night, "is more of me. Lots more. Scads of us pouring in from all ages to light firecrackers under these dopes. Every art and every science has degenerated far worse than anything did in the Dark Ages. Man cannot be man without striving, and all striving is abolished. God, I think if I lived in this age and believed in the Stasis, I'd become a Stapper. Better their arrogant cruelty than the inhuman indifference of everybody else."

"I have brother who bees Stapper," said Stephen. "I do not recommend it. To descend to level of cows and foxes bees one thing. To become jackals bees another."

"I've gathered that those rods paralyze the nerve centers, right? But what happens to you after that?"

—"It bees not good. First you be treated according to expert psychoanalytic and psychometric methods so as to alter your concepts and adjust you to Stasis. If that fails you be carefully reduced to harmless idiocy. Sometimes they find mind that bees too strong for treatment. He bees killed, but Stappers play with him first."

"It'll never happen to me." Alex said earnestly. "I be prepared. You see this?" He indicated a minute plastic box suspended around his neck. "It contains tiny amount of radioactive matter sensitized to wavelength of Stappers' rods. They will never change my mind."

"It explodes?"

Alex grinned. "Stay away from me if rods start waving."

"It seems," Brent mused, "as though cruelty were the only human vice left. Games are lost, drinking is prohibited—and that most splendid of vices, imaginative speculation, is unheard of. I tell you, you need lots of me."

Stephen frowned. "Before failure of Barrier, we often wondered why we never seed time travelers. We doubted Charnwood's Law and yet— We decided there beed only two explanations. Either time travel bees impossible, or time travelers cannot be seed or intervene in time they visit. Now, we can see that Barrier stopped all from future, and perhaps you be only one from past. And still—"

"Exactly," said Alex. "And still. If other travelers came from future, why beed they not also stopped by Barrier? One of our friends searched Stapper records since breakdown of Barrier. No report on strange and unidentified travelers anywhere."

"That means only one thing." Stephen looked worried. "Second Barrier, Barrier you told us of, John, must be successful."

"The hell it will be. Come on, Alex. I'm getting restless. When can I start?"

Alex smiled. "Tomorrow. I be ready at last."

"Good man. Among us, we are going to blow this damned Stasis back into the bliss of manly and uncertain striving. And in fifty years we'll watch it together."

Krasna was waiting outside the room when Brent left. "I knowed you willed be talking about things I doedn't understand."

"You can understand this, milady. Alex has got everything fixed, and we leave tomorrow."

"We?" said Krasna brightly, hopefully.

Brent swore to himself. "We, meaning me and the old lady. The machine carries only two. And I do have to take her back to her own time."

"Poor thing," said Krasna. Her voice had gone dead.

"Poor us," said Brent sharply. "One handful of days out of all of time . . ." For one wild moment a possibility occurred to him. "Alex knows how to work the machine. If he and the old—"

"No," said Krasna gravely. "Stephen sayes you have to go and we will meet you there. I don't understand. . . . But I will meet you, John, and we will be together again and we will talk and you will tell me things like first night we talked and then—"

"And then," said Brent, "we'll stop talking. Like this."

Her eyes were always open during a kiss. (Was this a custom of Stasis, Brent wondered, or her own?) He read agreement in them now, and hand in hand they walked, without another word, to the warehouse, where Alex was through work for the night.

One minor point for the Stasis, Brent thought as he dozed off that night, was that it had achieved perfectly functioning zippers.

"Now," said Brent to Stephen after what was euphemistically termed breakfast, "I've got to see the old lady and find out just what the date is for the proposed launching of the second Barrier."

Stephen beamed. "It bees such pleasure to hear old speech, articles and all."

Alex had a more practical thought. "How can you set it to one day? I thinked your dial readed only in years."

"There's a vernier attachment that's accurate—or should

be, it's never been tested yet—to within two days. I'm allowing a week's margin. I don't want to be around too long and
run chances with Stappers."

"Krasna will miss you."

"Krasna's a funny name. You others have names that were
in use back in my day."

"Oh, it bees not name. It bees only what everyone calls
red-headed girls. I think it goes back to century of Russian
domination."

"Yes," Alex added. "Stephen's sister's real name bees Martha, but we never call her that."

John Brent gaped. "I . . . I've got to go see the old lady,"
he stammered.

From the window of the gray-haired Martha-Krasna he
could see the red-headed Krasna-Martha outside. He held on
to a solid and reassuring chair and said, "Well, madam, I
have news. We're going back today."

"Oh, thank Cosmos!"

"But I've got to find out something from you. What was
the date set for the launching of the second Barrier?"

"Let me see—I know it beed holiday. Yes, it beed May 1."

"My, my! May Day a holiday now? Workers of the World
Unite, or simply Gathering Nuts in May?"

"I don't understand you. It bees Dyce Farnsworth's birthday, of course. But then I never understand . . ."

In his mind he heard the same plaint coming from fresh
young lips. "I . . . I understand now, madam." he said clumsily. "Our meeting—I can see why you—" Damn it, what
was there to say?

"Please," she said. There was, paradoxically, a sort of pathetic dignity about her. "I do not understand. Then at littlest
let me forget."

He turned away respectfully. "Warehouse in half an
hour!" he called over his shoulder.

The young Krasna-Martha was alone in the warehouse
when Brent got there. He looked at her carefully, trying to
see in her youthful features the worn one of the woman he
had just left. It made sense.

"I comed first," she said, "because I wanted to say good-
bye without others."

"Good-bye, milady," Brent murmured into her fine red
hair. "In a way, I'm not leaving you because I'm taking you
with me and still I'll never see you again. And you don't un-

derstand that, and I'm not sure you've ever understood anything I've said, but you've been very sweet."

"And you will destroy Barrier? For me?"

"For you, milady. And a few billion others. And here come our friends."

Alex carried a small box which he tucked under one of the seats. "Dial and mechanism beed repaired days ago," he grinned. "I've beed working on this for you, in lab which I was supposed to be re-proving Tsvetov's hypothesis. Temporal demagnetizer—guaranteed. Bring this near Barrier and field will be breaked. Your problem bees to get near Barrier."

Martha, the matron, climbed into the machine. Martha, the girl, turned away to hide watering eyes. Brent set the dial to 2473 and adjusted the vernier to April 24, which gave him a week's grace. "Well, friends," he faltered. "My best gratitude—and I'll be seeing you in fifty years."

Stephen started to speak, and then suddenly stopped to listen. "Quick, Krasna, Alex. Behind those cases. Turn switch quickly, John."

Brent turned the switch, and nothing happened. Stephen and Krasna were still there, moving toward the cases. Alex darted to the machine. "Cosmos blast me! I maked disconnection to prevent anyone's tampering by accident. And now—"

"Hurry, Alex," Stephen called in a whisper.

"Moment—" Alex opened the panel and made a rapid adjustment. "There, John. Good-bye."

In the instant before Brent turned the switch, he saw Stephen and Krasna reach a safe hiding place. He saw a Stapper appear in the doorway. He saw the flicker of a rod. The last thing he saw in 2423 was the explosion that lifted Alex's head off his shoulders.

The spattered blood was still warm in 2473.

Stephen, the seventy-year-old Stephen with the long and parti-colored beard, was waiting for them. Martha dived from the machine into his arms and burst into dry sobbing.

"She met herself," Brent explained. "I think she found it pretty confusing."

Stephen barked: "I can imagine. It bees only now that I have realized who that woman beed who comed with you and so much resembled our mother. But you be so late. I have beed waiting here since I evaded Stappers."

"Alex—" Brent began.

"I know. Alex haves gived you magnetic disruptor and

losed his life. He beed not man to die so young. He beed good friend . . . And my sister haves gived and losed too I think." He gently stroked the gray hair that had once been red. "But these be fifty-year-old sorrows. I have lived with my unweeped tears for Alex; they be friends by now too. And Martha haves weeped her tears for . . ." He paused then: "Why have you beed so long?"

"I didn't want to get here too long before May Day— might get into trouble. So I allowed a week, but I'll admit I might be a day or so off. What date is it?"

"This bees May 1, and Barrier will be launched within hour. We must hurry."

"My God—" Brent glared at the dial. "It can't be that far off. But come on. Get your sister home and we'll plunge on to do our damnedest."

Martha roused herself. "I be coming with you."

"No, dear," said Stephen. "We can do better alone."

Her lips set stubbornly. "I be coming. I don't understand anything that happens, but you be Stephen and you be John, and I belong with you."

The streets were brightly decorated with banners bearing the double loop of infinity, the sacred symbol of Cosmos that had replaced crescent, swastika and cross. But there was hardly a soul in sight. What few people they saw were all hurrying in the same direction.

"Everyone will be at dedication," Stephen explained. "Tribute to Cosmos. Those who stay at home must beware Stappers."

"And if there's hundreds of thousands thronging the dedication, how do we get close to Barrier to disrupt it?"

"It bees all arranged. Our group bees far more powerful than when you knowed it fifty years ago. Slowly we be honeycombing system of State. With bribery and force when necessary, with persuasion when possible, we can do much. And we have arranged this."

"How?"

"You be delegate from European Slanduch. You speak German?"

"Well enough."

"Remember that haves beed regularized, too. But I doubt if you need to speak any. Making you Slanduch will account for irregular slips in English. You come from powerful Slanduch group. You will be gladly welcomed here. You will oc-

cupy post of honor. I have even accounted for box you carry.
It bees tribute you have bringed to Cosmos. Here be your papers and identity plaque."

"Thanks." Brent's shorter legs managed to keep up with
the long strides of Stephen, who doubled the rate of the moving sidewalk by his own motion. Martha panted along reso-
lutely. "But can you account for why I'm so late? I set my
indicator for April 24, and here we are rushing to make a
date on May 1."

Stephen strode along in thought, then suddenly slapped his
leg and barked. "How many months in 1942?"

"Twelve, of course."

"Ha! Yes, it beed only two hundred years ago that thir-
teen-month calendar beed adopted. Even months of twenty-
eight days each, plus Year Day, which belongs to no month.
Order, you see. Now invaluable part of Stasis—" He concentrated frowningly on mental arithmetic. "Yes, your indicator
worked exactly. May 1 of our calendar bees April 24 of
yours."

Chalk up one slip against Derringer—an unthinking confidence in the durability of the calendar. And chalk up one,
for Brent's money, against the logic of the Stasis; back in the
twentieth century, he had been an advocate of calendar reform, but a stanch upholder of the four-quarter theory
against the awkward thirteen months.

They were nearing now the vast amphitheater where the
machinery of the Barrier had been erected. Stappers were
stopping the few other travelers and forcing them off the
moving sidewalk into the densely packed crowds, faces aglow
with the smug ecstasy of the Stasis, but Brent's Slanduch credentials passed the three through.

The representative of the German Slanduch pushed his
way into the crowd of eminent dignitaries just as Dyce-Farnsworth's grandson pressed the button. The magnificent mass
of tubes and wires shuddered and glowed as the current
pulsed through it. Then the glow became weird and arctic.
There was a shaking, a groaning, and then, within the space
of a second, a cataclysmic roar and a blinding glare. Something heavy and metallic pressed Brent to the ground.

The roar blended into the excited terror of human voices.
The splendid Barrier was a mass of twisted wreckage. It was
more wreckage that weighted Brent down, but this was different. It looked strangely like a variant of his own machine.

And staring down at him from a warped seat was the huge-eyed head of a naked man.

A woman in a metallic costume equally strange to this age and to Brent's own straddled the body of Dyce-Farnsworth's grandson, who had met his ancestor's martyrdom. And wherever Brent's eyes moved he saw another strange and outlandish—no, out-time-ish—figure.

He heard Martha's voice. "It bees clear that Time Barrier haves been erected and destroyed by outside force. But it haves existed and created impenetrable instant of time. These be travelers from all future."

Brent gasped. Even the sudden appearance of these astounding figures was topped by Martha's speaking perfect logical sense.

Brent wrote in his journal: *The Stasis is at least an admirably functional organism. All hell broke loose there for a minute, but almost automatically the Stappers went into action with their rods—odd how that bit of crook's chant has become perfectly literal truth—and in no time had the situation well in hand.*

They had their difficulties. Several of the time intruders were armed, and managed to account for a handful of Stappers before the nerve rays paralyzed them. One machine was a sort of time-traveling tank and contrived to withstand siege until a suicide squad of Stappers attacked it with a load of what Stephen tells me was detonite; we shall never know from what sort of a future the inhabitants of that tank came to spatter their shredded flesh about the amphitheater.

But these events were mere delaying action, token resistance. Ten minutes after the Barrier had exploded, the travelers present were all in the hands of the Stappers, and cruising Stapper bands were efficiently combing all surrounding territory.

(The interesting suggestion comes amazingly from Martha that while all time machines capable of physical movement were irresistibly attracted to the amphitheater by the tempo-magnetic field, only such pioneer and experimental machines as my Derringer, which can move only temporally, would be arrested in other locations. Whether or not this theory is correct, it seems justified by the facts. Only a few isolated reports have come in of sudden appearances elsewhere at the instant of the Barrier's explosion; the focus of arrivals of the time travelers was the amphitheater.)

The Chief of Stappers mounted the dais where an infinity-bedecked banner now covered the martyred corpse of young Dyce-Farnsworth, and announced the official ruling of the Head of State: that these intruders and disrupters of the Stasis were to be detained—tested and examined and studied until it became apparent what the desire of Cosmos might be.

(The Head of State, Stephen explained, is a meaningless figurehead, part high priest and—I paraphrase—part Alexander Throttlebottom. The Stasis is supposedly so perfect and so self-sustaining that his powers are as nominal as those of the pilot of a ship in drydock, and all actual power is exercised by such subordinates as the Editor of State and the Chief of Stappers.)

Thanks to Stephen's ingenuity, this rule for the treatment of time travelers does not touch me. I am simply a Slanduch envoy. Some Stapper search party has certainly by now found the Derringer machine in the warehouse, which I no longer dare approach.

With two Barriers now between me and 1942, it is obvious that I am keeping this journal only for myself. I am stuck here—and so are all the other travelers, for this field, far stronger than the first, has wrecked their machines beyond the repairing efforts of a far greater talent than poor Alex. We are all here for good.

And it must be for good.

I still believe firmly what I said to Stephen and Alex: that this age needs hundreds of me to jolt it back into humanity. We now have, if not hundreds, at least dozens, and I, so far as we yet know, am the only one not in the hands of the Stappers. It is my clearest duty to deliver those others, and with their aid to beat some sense into this Age of Smugness.

"But how?" Brent groaned rhetorically. "How am I going to break into the Stappers' concentration camp?"

Martha wrinkled her brows. "I think I know. Let me work on problem while longer; I believe I see how we can at littlest make start."

Brent stared at her. "What's happened to you, madam? Always before you've shrunk away from every discussion Stephen and I have had. You've said we talk of things you know nothing about. And now, all of a sudden—boom!—you're right in the middle of things and doing very nicely thank you. What's got into you?"

"I think," said Martha smiling, "you have hitted on right phrase, John."

Brent's puzzled expostulation was broken off by Stephen's entrance. "And where have you been?" he demanded. "I've been trying to work out plans, and I've got a weird feeling Martha's going to beat me to it. What have you been up to?"

Stephen looked curiously at his sister. "I've beed out galping. Interesting results, too."

"Galping?"

"You know. Going about among people, taking samples of opinion, using scientific methods to reduce carefully choosed samples to general trends."

"Oh." (Mr. Gallup thought Brent, has joined Captain Boycott and M. Guillotin as a verb.) "And what did you learn?"

"People be confused by arrival of time travelers. If Stasis bees perfect, they argue; why be such arrivals allowed? Seeds of doubt be sowed, and we be carefully watering them. Head of State haves problem on his hands. I doubt if he can find any solution to satisfy people."

"If only," Brent sighed, "there were some way of getting directly at the people. If we could see these travelers and learn what they know and want, then somehow establish contact between them and the people, the whole thing ought to be a pushover."

It was Martha who answered. "It bees very simple, John. You be linguist."

"Yes. And how does that—"

"Stappers will need interpreters. You will be one. From there on you must develop your own plans, but that will at littlest put you in touch with travelers."

"But the State must have its own linguists who—"

Stephen barked with pleasure and took up the explanation. Since Farthing's regularization of English, the perfect immutability of language had become part of the Stasis. A linguist now was a man who knew Farthing's works by heart, and that was all. Oh, he might also be well acquainted with Zinsmeister German, or Tamayo y Sárate Spanish; but he knew nothing of general linguistic principles, which are apt to run completely counter to the fine theories of these great synthesists, and he had never had occasion to learn adaptability to a new language. Faced by the strange and incomprehensible tongues of the future, the State linguist would be helpless.

It was common knowledge that only the Slanduch had any true linguistic aptitude. Brought up to speak three lan-

guages—Farthing-ized English, their own archaic dialect, and
the language of the country in which they resided—their
tongues were deft and adjustable. In ordinary times, this aptitude was looked on with suspicion; but now there would
doubtless be a heavy demand for Slanduch interpreters, and a
little cautious wire-pulling could land Brent the job.

"And after that," said Stephen, "as Martha rightly ob-
serves, you be on your own."

"Lead me to it," grinned John Brent.

The rabbitty little State linguist received Brent effusively.
"Ah, thank Cosmos!" he gasped. "Travelers be driving me
mad! Such gibberish you have never heared! Such irregularities! Frightful! You be Slanduch?"

"I be. I have speaked several languages all my life. I can
even speak pre-Zinsmeister German." And he began to recite
*Die Lorelei. "Die Luft ist kühl und es dunkelt, und ruhig
fliesst der Rhein—"*

"Terrible! *Ist!* Such vile irregularity! And articles! But
come, young man. We'll see what you can do with these temporal barbarians!'   '

There were three travelers in the room Brent entered, with
the shocked linguist and two rodded Stappers in attendance.
One of the three was the woman he had noticed in that first
cataclysmic instant of arrival, a strapping Amazonic blonde
who looked as though she could break any two unarmed
Stappers with her bare fingers. Another was a neat little man
with a curly and minute forked beard and restless hands. The
third—

The third was hell to describe. They were all dressed now
in the conventional robes of the Stasis, but even in these
familiar garments he was clearly not quite human. If man is
a featherless biped, then this was a man; but men do not usually have greenish skin with vestigial scales and a trace of a
gill opening behind each ear.

"Ask each of them three things," the linguist instructed
Brent. "When he comes from, what his name bees, and what
be his intentions."

Brent picked Tiny Beard as the easiest looking start. "O. K.
You!" He pointed, and the man stepped forward. "What part
of time do you come from?"

"A pox o' thee, sirrah, and the goodyears take thee! An
thou wouldst but hearken, thou might'st learn all."

The State linguist moaned. "You hear, young man? How can one interpret such jargon?"

Brent smiled. "It bees O. K. This bees simply English as it beed speaked thousand years ago. This man must have beed aiming at earlier time and prepared himself . . . Thy pardon, sir. These kerns deem all speech barbaric save that which their own conceit hath evolved. Bear with me and all will be well."

"Spoken like a true knight!" the traveler exclaimed. "Forgive my rash words, sir. Surely my good daemon hath led thee hither. Thou wouldst know—"

"Whence comest thou?"

"From many years hence. Thousands upon thousands of summers have yet to run their course ere I—"

"Forgive me, sir; but of that much we are aware. Let us be precise."

"Why then, marry, sir, 'tis from the fifth century."

Brent frowned. But to attempt to understand the gentleman's system of dating would take too much time at the moment. "And thy name, sir?"

"Kruj, sir. Or as thou wouldst be formal and courtly, Kruj Krujil Krujilar. But let Kruj suffice thee."

"And what most concerneth these gentlemen here is the matter of thine intentions. What are thy projects in this our earlier world?"

"My projects?" Kruj coughed. "Sir, in thee I behold a man of feeling, of sensibility, a man to whom one may speak one's mind. Many projects have I in good sooth, most carefully projected for me by the Zhurmandril. Much must I study in these realms of the great Elizabeth—though 'sblood! I know not how they seem so different from my conceits! But one thing above all else do I covet. I would to the Mermaid Tavern."

Brent grinned. "I fear me, sir, that we must talk at greater length. Much hast thou mistaken and much must I make clear. But first I must talk with these others."

Kruj retired, frowning and plucking at his shred of beard. Brent beckoned to the woman. She strode forth so vigorously that both Stappers bared their rods.

"Madam," Brent ventured tentatively, "what part of time do you come from?"

"Evybuy taws so fuy," she growled. "Bu I unnasta. Wy cachoo unnasta *me?*"

Brent laughed. "Is that all that's the trouble? You don't mind if I go on talking like this, do you?"

"Naw. You taw howeh you wanna, slonsoo donna like I dih taw stray."

Fascinating, Brent thought. All final consonants lost, and many others. Vowels corrupted along lines indicated in twentieth-century colloquial speech. Consonants sometimes restored in liaison as in French.

"What time do you come from, then?"

"Twenny-ni twenny-fie. N were am I now?"

"Twent-four seventy-three. And your name, madam?"

"Mimi."

Brent had an incongruous vision of this giantess dying operatically in a Paris garret. "So. And your intentions here?"

"Ai gonno intenchuns. Juh wanna see wha go."

"You will, madam, I assure you. And now—" He beckoned to the green-skinned biped, who advanced with a curious lurching motion like a deep-sea diver.

"And you, sir. When do you come from?"

"Ya studier langue earthly. Vyerit todo langue isos. Ou comprendo wie govorit people."

Brent was on the ropes and groggy. The familiarity of some of the words made the entire speech even more incomprehensible. "Says which?" he gasped.

The green man exploded. "Ou existier nada but dolts, cochons, duraki v this terre? Nikovo parla langue earthly? Potztausend Sapperment en la leche de tu madre and I do mean you!"

Brent reeled. But even reeling he saw the disapproving frown of the State linguist and the itching fingers of the Stappers. He faced the green man calmly and said with utmost courtesy, " 'Twas brillig and the slithy toves did gyre and gimble over the rivering waters of the hither-and-thithering waters of pigeons on the grass alas." He turned to the linguist. "He says he won't talk."

Brent wrote in the never-to-be-read journal: *It was Martha again who solved my green man for me. She pointed out that he was patently extraterrestrial. (Apparently Nakamura's Law of Spatial Acceleration is as false as Charnwood's Law of Temporal Metabolism.) The vestigial scales and gills might well indicate Venus as his origin. He must come from some far distant future when the earth is overrun by inhabitants of other planets and terrestrial culture is all but lost. He had prepared himself for time travel by studying the speech of earth—langue earthly—reconstructed from some larger equivalent of the Rosetta Stone, but made the mistake of thinking that there was only one earthly speech, just as we tend imaginatively to think of Martian or Venusian as a single language. As a result, he's talking all earthly tongues at once. Martha sees a marked advantage in this, even more than in Mimi's corrupt dialect—*

"Thou, sir," said Brent to Kruj on his next visit, "art a linguist. Thou knowest speech and his nature. To wit, I would wager that thou couldst with little labor understand this woman here. One who hath so mastered our language in his greatest glory—"

The little man smirked. "I thank thee sir. In sooth since thou didst speak with her yestereven I have already made some attempts at converse with her."

Mimi joined in. "He taws fuy, but skina cue."

"Very well then. I want you both, and thee in particular, Kruj, to hearken to this green-skinned varlet here. Study his speech, sir, and learn what thou may'st."

"Wy?" Mimi demanded belligerently.

"The wench speaks sooth. Wherefore should we so?"

"You'll find out. Now let me at him."

It was slow, hard work, especially with the linguist and the Stappers ever on guard. It meant rapid analysis of the possible origin of every word used by the Venusian, and a laborious attempt to find at random words that he would understand. But in the course of a week both Brent and the astonishingly adaptable Kruj had learned enough of this polyglot *langue earthly* to hold an intelligible conversation. Mimi was hopelessly lost, but Kruj occasionally explained matters to her in her own corrupt speech, which he had mastered by now as completely as Elizabethan.

It had been Stephen's idea that any project for the liberation of the time travelers must wait until more was learned of their nature. "You be man of good will, John. We trust you. You and mans like you can save us. But imagine that some travelers come from worlds far badder even than ours. Suppose that they come seeking only power for themselves? Suppose that they come from civilization of cruelty and be more evil than Stappers?"

It was a wise point, and it was Martha who saw the solution in the Venusian's amazing tongue. In that mélange of languages, Brent could talk in front of the linguist and the Stappers with complete safety. Kruj and the Venusian, who must have astonishing linguistic ability to master the speech of another planet even so perversely, could discuss matters with the other travelers, and could tell him anything he needed to know before all the listening guards of the State.

All this conversation was, of course, theoretically guided by the linguist. He gave questions to Brent and received plausible answers, never dreaming that his questions had not been asked.

As far as his own three went, Brent was satisfied as to the value of their liberation. Mimi was not bright, but she seemed to mean well and claimed to have been a notable warrior in her own matriarchal society. It was her feats in battle and exploration that had caused her to be chosen for time travel. She should be a useful ally.

Kruj was indifferent to the sorry state of the world until Brent mentioned the tasteless and servile condition of the arts. Then he was all afire to overthrow the Stasis and bring about a new renaissance. (Kruj, Brent learned, had been heading for the past to collect material for a historical epic on Elizabethan England, a fragment of prehistoric civilization that had always fascinated him.)

Of the three, Nikobat, the Venusian, seemed the soundest and most promising. To him, terrestrial civilization was a closed book, but a beautiful one. In the life and struggles of man he found something deep and moving. The aim of Nikobat in his own world had been to raise his transplanted Venusian civilization to the levels, spiritual and scientific, that had once been attained by earthly man and it was to find the seed of inspiration to accomplish this that he had traveled back. Man degenerate, man self-complacent, man smug, shocked him bitterly, and he swore to exert his best efforts in the rousing.

Brent was feeling not unpleased with himself as he left his group after a highly successful session. Kruj was accomplishing much among the other travelers and would have a nearly full report for him tomorrow. And once that report had been made, they could attempt Martha's extraordinary scheme of rescue. He would not have believed it ordinarily possible, but both he and Stephen were coming to put more and more trust in the suggestions of the once scatterbrained Martha. Stephen's own reports were more than favorable. The Underground was boring beautifully from within. The people of the

State were becoming more and more restless and doubting.
Slowly these cattle were resuming the forms of men.

Brent was whistling happily as he entered the apartment
and called out a cheery "Hi!" to his friends. But they were
not there. There was no one in the room but a white-clad
Stapper, who smiled wolfishly as he rose from a chair and
asked, "You be time traveler, be you not?"

This was the most impressive Stapper that Brent had yet
seen—impressive even aside from the startling nature of his
introductory remark. The others, even the one he had kicked
in the face, or the one who killed Alex, Brent had thought of
simply as so many Stappers. This one was clearly an individual. His skin was exceptionally dark and smooth and hairless,
and two eyes so black that they seemed all pupil glowed out
of his face.

Brent tried to seem casual. "Nonsense. I be Slanduch envoy from Germany, staying here with friends and doing service for State. Here bees my identification."

The Stapper hardly glanced at it. "I know all about your
linguistic services, John Brent. And I know about machine
finded in deserted warehouse. It beed only machine not
breaked by Barrier. Therefore it comed not from Future, but
from Past."

"So? We have travelers from both directions? Poor devil
will never be able to get back to own time then." He wondered if this Stapper were corruptible; he could do with a
drink of bond.

"Yes, he bees losed here in this time like others. And he
foolishly works with them to overthrow Stasis."

"Sad story. But how does it concern me? My papers be in
order. Surely you can see that I be what I claim?"

The Stapper's eyes fixed him sharply. "You be clever, John
Brent. You doubtless traveled naked and clothed yourself as
citizen of now to escape suspicion. That bees smartest way.
How you getted papers I do not know. But communication
with German Slanduch will disprove your story. You be
losed, Brent, unless you be sensible."

"Sensible? What the hell do you mean by that?"

The Stapper smiled slowly. "Article," he drawled.

"I be sorry. But that proves nothing. You know how difficult it bees for us Slanduch to keep our speech entirely regular."

"I know." Suddenly a broad grin spread across the Stapper's face and humanized it. "I have finded this Farthing speech hellishly difficult myself."

"You mean you, too, be Slanduch?"

The Stapper shook his head. "I, too, Brent, be traveler."

Brent was not falling for any such trap. "Ridiculous! How can traveler be Stapper?"

"How can traveler be Slanduch envoy? I, too, traveled naked, and man whose clothes and identification I stealed beed Stapper. I have finded his identity most useful."

"I don't believe you."

"You be stubborn, Brent. How to prove—" He gestured at his face. "Look at my skin. In my century facial hair haves disappeared; we have breeded away from it. Where in this time could you find skin like that?"

"A sport. Freak of chromosomes."

The black eyes grew even larger and more glowing. "Brent, you must believe me. This bees no trap for you. I need you. You and I, we can do great things. But how to convince you"—he snapped his fingers. "I know!" He was still for a moment. The vast eyes remained opened but somehow veiled, as though secret calculations were going on behind them. His body shivered. For a moment of strange delusion Brent thought he could see the chair through the Stapper's body. Then it was solid again.

"My name," said the Stapper, with the patience of a professor addressing a retarded class, "bees Bokor. I come from tenth century after consummation of terrestrial unity, which bees, I believe, forty-third reckoning from date of birth of Christian god. I have traveled, not with machine, but solely by use of Vunmurd formula, and, therefore, I alone of all travelers stranded here can still move. Hysteresis of Barrier arrests me, but cannot destroy my formula as it shatters machines."

"Pretty story."

"Therefore I alone of travelers can still travel. I can go back by undestroyed formula and hit Barrier again. If I hit Barrier twice, I exist twice in that one point of time. Therefore each of two of me continues into present."

"So now you be two?" Brent observed skeptically. "Obviously I be too sober. I seem to be seeing single."

Bokor grinned again. Somehow this time it didn't seem so humanizing. "Come in!" he called.

The Stapper in the doorway fixed Brent with his glowing black eyes and said, "Now do you believe that I be traveler?"

Brent gawped from one identical man to the other. The one in the doorway went on. "I need you."

"It isn't possible. It's a gag. You're twin Stappers, and you're trying to—"

Bokor in the chair said, "Do I have to do it again?"

Brent said, "You may both be Stappers. You may turn out to be a whole damned regiment of identical multiple births. I don't give a damn; I want some bond. How about you boys?"

The two Bokors downed their drinks and frowned. "Weak," they said.

Brent shook his head feebly. "All right. We'll skip that. Now what the sweet hell do you need me for?"

Bokor closed his eyes and seemed to doze. Bokor Sub-One said, "You have plans to liberate travelers and overthrow Stasis. As Stapper I have learned much. I worked on changing mind of one of you Underground friends."

"And you want to throw your weight in with us? Good, we can use a Stapper. Or two. But won't the Chief of Stappers be bothered when he finds he has two copies of one man?"

"He will never need to see more than one. Yes, I want to help you—up to a point. We will free travelers. But you be innocent, Brent. We will not overthrow Stasis. We will maintain it—as ours."

Brent frowned. "I'm not sure I get you. And I don't think I like it if I do."

"Do not be fool, Brent. We have opportunity never before gived to man, we travelers. We come into world where already exists complete and absolute State control, but used stupidly and to no end. Among us all we have great knowledge and power. We be seed sowed upon fallow ground. We can spring up and ungulf all about us." The eyes glowed with black intensity. "We take this Stasis and mold it to our own wishes. These dolts who now be slaves of Cosmos will be slaves of us. Stapper, whose identity I have, bees third in succession to Chief of Stappers. Chief and other two will be killed accidentally in revolt of travelers. With power of all Stappers behind me, I make you Head of State. Between us we control this State absolutely."

"Nuts," Brent snorted. "The State's got too damned much control already. What this world needs is a return to human freedom and striving."

"Innocent," Bokor Sub-One repeated scornfully. "Who gives damn what world needs? Only needs which concern man be his own, and his strongest need bees always for power. Here it bees gived us. Other States be stupid and self-complacent like this. We know secrets of many weapons, we travelers. We turn our useless scholastic laboratories over to their production. Then we attack other States and subject them to us as vassals. And then the world itself bees ours, and all its riches. Alexander, Caesar, Napoleon, Hitler, Gospodinov. Tirazhul—never haves world knowed conquerors like us."

"You can go to hell," said Brent lightly but firmly. "All two of you."

"Do not be too clever, my friend. Remember that I be Stapper and can—"

"You be two Stappers, which may turn out to be a little awkward. But you could be a regiment of Stappers, and I still wouldn't play ball. Your plan stinks, Bokor, and you know what you can do with it."

Bokor Sub-One took the idiom literally. "Indeed I do know, Brent. It willed have beed easier with your aid, but even without you it will succeed." He drew out his rod and contemplated it reflectively. "No," he murmured, "there bees no point to taking you in and changing your mind. You be harmless to me, and your liberation of travelers will be useful."

The original Bokor opened his eyes. "We will meet again, Brent. And you will see what one man with daring mind can accomplish in this world." Bokor and Bokor Sub-One walked to the door and turned. "And for bond," they spoke in unison, in parody of the conventional Stapper's phrase, "State thanks you."

Brent stood alone in the room, but the black-eyed domination of the two Bokors lingered about him. The plan was so damned plausible, so likely to succeed if put into operation. Man has always dreamed of power. But damn it, man has always dreamed of love, too, and of the rights of his fellow man. The only power worthy of man is the power of all mankind struggling together toward a goal of unobtainable perfection.

And what could Bokor do against Kruj and Mimi and Nikobat and the others that Kruj reported sympathetic?

Nevertheless there had been a certainty in those vast eyes that the double Bokor knew what he could do.

The release of the travelers was a fabulous episode. Stephen had frowned and Brent had laughed when Martha said

simply, "Only person who haves power to release them bees
Head of State by will of Cosmos. Very well. We will persuade him to do so." But she insisted, and she had been so
uncannily right ever since the explosion of the second Barrier
that at last, when Kruj had made his final report, Brent ac-
compained her on what he was certain was the damnedest
fool errand he'd got himself into yet.

Kruj's report was encouraging. There were two, perhaps
three, among the travelers who had Bokorian ideas of taking
over the State for their own purposes. But these were far out-
weighed by the dozens who saw the tremendous possibilities
of a reawakening of mankind. The liberation was proved a
desirable thing, but why should the Head of State so readily
loose disrupters of his Stasis?

Getting to see the Head of State took the best part of a
day. There were countless minor officials to be interviewed,
all of them guarded by Stappers who looked upon the supposed Slanduch envoy with highly suspicious eyes. But one by
one, with miraculous consistency, these officials beamed upon
Brent's errand and sent him on with the blessing of Cosmos.

"You wouldn't like to pinch me?" he murmured to Martha
after the fifth such success. "This works too easy. It can't be
true."

Martha looked at him blankly and said, "I don't understand it. But what be we going to say?"

Brent jumped. "Hey! Look, madam. This was all your
idea. You were going to talk the Head of State into—"

But a Stapper was already approaching to conduct them to
the next office, and Brent fell silent.

It was in the anteroom of the Head of State that they met
Bokor. Just one of him this time. He smiled confidentially at
Brent and said, "Shocking accident today. Stapper killed in
fight with prisoner. Odd thing—Stapper been second in succession to Chief of Stappers."

"You're doing all right," said Brent.

"I be curious to see what you plan here. How do you hope
to achieve this liberation? I talked with Head of State yesterday and he bees strongly opposed."

"Brother," said Brent sincerely, "I wish I knew."

In a moment Bokor ushered them into the sanctum sanctorum of the Head of State. This great dignitary was at first
glance a fine figure of a man, tall and well built and noble. It
was only on second glance that you noticed the weak lips and

the horribly empty eyes. The stern and hawk-nosed Chief of Stappers stood beside him.

"Well!" the latter snapped. "Speak your piece!"

Brent faltered and glanced at Martha. She looked as vacant and helpless as ever she had before the Barrier. He could only fumble on and pray that her unrevealed scheme would materialize.

"As you know, sir," he began, "I, as interpreter, have beed in very close contact with travelers. Having in my mind good of Cosmos and wishing to see it as rich and fully developed as possible, it seems to me that much may be accomplished by releasing travelers so that they may communicate with people." He gulped and swore at himself for venturing such an idiotic request.

The empty eyes of the Head of State lit up for a moment. "Excellent idea," he boomed in a dulcet voice. "You have permission of State and Cosmos. Chief, I give orders that all travelers be released."

Brent heard Bokor's incredulous gasp behind him. The Chief of Stappers muttered "Cosmos!" fervently. The Head of State looked around him for approval and then reverted to formal vacancy.

"I thank State," Brent managed to say, "for this courageous move."

"What bees courageous?" the Head demanded. His eyes shifted about nervously. "What have I doed? What have I sayed?"

The Chief of Stappers bowed. "You have proclaimed freedom of travelers. May I, too, congratulate you on wisdom of action?" He turned to Bokor. "Go and give necessary orders."

Martha did not say a word till they were outside. Then she asked, "What happened? Why in Cosmos' name doed he consent?"

"Madam, you have me there. But you should know. It was all your idea."

Understanding came back to her face. "Of course. It bees time now that you know all about me. But wait till we be back in apartment. Stephen haves right to know this, too. And Martha," Martha added.

They had left Bokor behind them in the sanctum, and they met Bokor outside the building. That did not worry Brent, but he was admittedly perturbed when he passed a small group of people just off the sidewalk and noticed that its core was a third Bokor. He pulled Martha off the moving path and drew near the group.

Bokor was not being a Stapper this time. He was in ordinary iridescent robes. "I tell you I know," he was insisting vigorously. "I am . . . I be Slanduch from State of South America, and I can tell you deviltry they be practicing there. Armament factories twice size of laboratories of Cosmos. They plan to destroy us; I know."

A Stapper shoved his way past Brent. "Here now!" he growled. "What bees going on here?"

Bokor hesitated. "Nothing, sir. I was only—"

"*Was,* huh?"

"Pardon, sir. *Beed.* I be Slanduch, you see, and—"

One of the men in the crowd interrupted. "He beed telling us what all State needs to know—plans of State of South America to invade and destroy us."

"Hm-m-m!" the Stapper ejaculated. "You be right, man. That sounds like something to know. Go on, you."

Bokor resumed his rumor mongering, and the Stapper lent it official endorsement by his listening silence. Brent moved to get a glimpse of the Stapper's face. His guess was right. It was another Bokor.

This significant byplay had delayed them enough so that Brent's three travelers had reached the apartment before them. When they arrived, Stephen was deep in a philosophical discussion with the Venusian of the tragic nobility of human nature, while Kruj and Mimi were experimenting with bond. Their respective civilizations could not have been markedly alcoholic; Kruj had reached the stage of sweeping and impassioned gestures, while Mimi beamed at him and giggled occasionally.

All three had discarded the standardized robes of the Stasis and resumed, in this friendly privacy, the clothes in which they had arrived—Kruj a curiously simplified and perverted version of the ruffled court costume of the Elizabethan era he had hoped to reach, Mimi the startling armor of an unfamiliar metal which was her uniform as Amazon warrior, and Nikobat a bronze-colored loincloth against which his green skin assumed an odd beauty.

Brent introduced Martha's guests to their hostess and went on, "Now for a staff meeting of G.H.Q. We've got to lay our plans carefully, because we're up against some stiff opposition. There's one other traveler who—"

"One moment," said Martha's voice. "Shouldn't you introduce me, too?"

"I beg your pardon, madam. I just finished that task of courtesy. And now—"

"I be sorry," her voice went on. "You still do not understand. You introduced Martha, yes—but not me."

Stephen turned to the travelers. "I must apologize for my sister. She haves goed through queer experiences of late. She traveled with our friend John and meeted herself in her earlier life. I fear that shock has temporarily—and temporally—unbalanced her."

"Can none of you understand so simple thing?" the woman's voice pleaded. "I be simply using Martha's voice as instrument of communication. I can just as easily—"

" 'Steeth!" Kruj exclaimed. " 'Tis eke as easy and mayhap more pleasant to borrow this traveler's voice for mine explications."

"Or," Mimi added, "I cou taw li thih, but I do' like ih vey muh."

Stephen's eyes popped. "You mean that you be traveler without body?"

"Got it in one," Brent heard his own voice saying. "I can wander about any way I damned please. I picked the woman first because her mind was easy to occupy, and I think I'll go on using her. Brent here's a little hard to keep under control."

Stephen nodded. "Then all good advice Martha haves beed giving us—"

"Bees mine, of course." The bodiless traveler was back in Martha now.

Brent gasped. "And now I see how you wangled the release of the travelers. You got us in by usurping the mind and speech of each of the minor officials we tackled, and then ousted the Head of State and Chief of Stappers to make them give their consent."

Martha nodded. "Exactly."

"This is going to be damned useful. And where do you come from, sir? Or is it madam?"

"I come from future so far distant that even our Venusian friend here cannot conceive of it. And distinction between *sir* and *madam* bees then meaningless."

The dapper Kruj glanced at the hulking Amazon beside him. " 'Twere a pity," he murmured.

"And your intentions here, to go on with the State linguist's questionnaire?"

"My intentions? Listen, all of you. We cannot shape ends. Great patterns be shaped outside of us and beyond us. I beed historian in my time. I know patterns of mankind even down to minute details. And I know that Stephen here bees to lead people of this Age of Smugness out of their stupidity and back to humanity."

Stephen coughed embarrassedly. "I have no wish to lead. But for such cause man must do what he may."

"That bees ultimate end of this section of pattern. That bees fixed. All that we travelers can do bees to aid him as wisely as we can and to make the details of the pattern as pleasing as may be. And that we will do."

Stephen must have been so absorbed in this speech that his hearing was dulled. The door opened without warning, and Bokor entered.

" 'Swounds!" Kruj cried out. "A Stapper!"

Stephen smiled. "Why fear Stappers? You be legally liberated."

"Stapper, hell!" Brent snorted. "Well, Bokor? You still want to declare yourself in with your racket?"

Bokor's deep eyes swept the room. He smiled faintly. "I merely wished to show you something, Brent. So that you know what you be up against. I have finded two young scientists dissatisfied with scholastic routine of research for Cosmos. Now they work under me and they have maked for me—this." He held a bare rod in his hand.

"So it's a rod. So what next?"

"But it bees different rod, Brent. It does not paralyze. It destroys." The point of the rod wavered and covered in turn each individual in the room. "I want you to see what I can accomplish."

"You suvvabih!" Mimi yelled and started to rise.

"State thanks you, madam, for making up my mind. I will demonstrate on you. Watch this, Brent, and realize what chance you have against me." He pointed the rod firmly at Mimi.

"Do something!" Martha screamed.

It all happened at once, but Brent seemed to see it in slow motion even as he moved. Mimi lunged forward furiously and recklessly. Kruj dived for her feet and brought her to the floor out of the line of fire. At the same time Brent threw himself forward just as Bokor moved, so that the rod now pointed directly at Brent. He couldn't arrest his momentum. He was headed straight at Bokor's new instrument of death. And then the rod moved to Bokor's own head.

There was no noise, no flash. But Bokor's body was lying on the floor, and the head was nowhere.

"That beed hard," said Martha's voice. "I haved to stay in his mind long enough to actuate rod, but get out before death. Matter of fractions of seconds."

"Nice work, sir-madam," Brent grunted. He looked down at the corpse. "But that was only one of him."

Brent quoted in his journal: *Love, but a day, and the world has changed! A week, to be more exact, but the change is nonetheless sudden and impressive.*

Our nameless visitant from the future—they seem to need titles as little as sexes in that time—whom I have for convenience labeled Sirdam, has organized our plans about the central idea of interfering as little as possible—forcing the inhabitants of the Stasis to work out their own salvation. The travelers do not appear openly in this great change. We work through Stephen's associates.

There are some 40 of us (I guess I count as a traveler; I'm not too sure what the hell my status is by now), which means each of us can take on five or ten of Stephen's boys (and girls), picking the ones whose interests lie closest to his own special fields. That means a working force of Undergrounders running somewhere above 200 and under 500 . . . fluctuating constantly as people come under or escape from Stapper observation, as new recruits come in, or (as will damnably happen despite every precaution) as one of our solid old-timers gets his mind changed and decides Stasis bees perfect after all.

The best single example to show the results we obtain is the episode of Professor Harrington, whose special department of so-called learning is the preservation of the Nakamura Law of Spatial Acceleration, which had so conclusively proved to the founders of the Stasis the impossibility of interplanetary travel.

This fell obviously within Nikobat's field. A young scientist affiliated with the Underground—a nephew, I have since learned, of Alex's—expounded the Nakamura doctrine as he had learned and re-proved it. It took the Venusian less than five minutes to put his finger on the basic flaw in the statement—the absolute omission, in all calculations, of any con-

sideration of galactic drift. Once this correction was applied to the Nakamura formulas, they stood revealed as the pure nonsense which, indeed, Nikobat's very presence proved them.

It was not Nikobat but the young man who placed this evidence before Professor Harrington. The scene must have been classic. "I saw," the young man later told us—they are all trying desperately to unlearn Farthing-ized English—"his mouth fall open and gap spread across his face as wide as gap he suddenly finded in universe."

For the professor was not stupid. He was simply so conditioned from childhood to the acceptance of the Stasis of Cosmos that he had never questioned it. Besides, he had doubtless had friends whose minds were changed when they speculated too far.

Harringon's eyes lit up after the first shock. He grabbed pencil and paper and furiously checked through the revised equations again and again. He then called in a half dozen of his best students and set them to what was apparently a routine exercise—interpolating variations for galactic drift in the Nakamura formulas.

They ended as astonished as their instructor. The first one done stared incredulously at his results and gasped, "Nakamura beed wrong!"

That was typical. The sheep are ready to be roused, each in his individual way. Kruj has been training men to associate with the writers of the Stasis. The man's knowledge of literature of all periods; and especially of his beloved Elizabethan Age, is phenomenal and his memory something superhuman. And four writers out of five who hear his disciples discourse on the joys of creative language and quote from the Elizabethan dramatists and the King James Bible will never be content again to write Stasis propaganda for the sollies or the identically bound books of the State libraries.

I have myself been contributing a fair amount to the seduction of the world by teaching cooks. I was never in my own time acknowledged as better than a fair-to-middling non-professional, but here I might be Escoffier or Brillat-Savarin. We steal plants and animals from the scientific laboratories, and in our hands they become vegetables and meat; and many a man in the street, who doesn't give a damn if his science is false and his arts synthetic, has suddenly realized that he owes the State a grudge for feeding him on concentrates.

The focus of everything is Stephen. It's hard to analyze why. Each of us travelers has found among the Undergrounders someone far more able in his own special field, yet all of us, travelers and Undergrounders alike, unquestioningly acknowledge Stephen as our leader. It may be the sheer quiet kindliness and goodness of his nature. It may be that he and Alex, in their organization of this undercover group of instinctive rebels, were the first openly to admit that the Stasis was inhuman and to do something about it. But from whatever cause, we all come to depend more and more on the calm reliability of Stephen.
Nikobat says—

Brent broke off as Kruj Krujil Krujilar staggered into the room. The little man was no longer dapper. His robes were tattered, and their iridescence was overlaid with the solid red of blood. He panted his first words in his own tongue, then recovered himself. "We must act apace, John. Where is Stephen?"

"At Underground quarters. But what's happened?"

"I was nearing the building where they do house us travelers when I beheld hundreds of people coming along the street. Some wore our robes, some wore Stappers'. And they all—" He shuddered. "They all had the same face—a brown hairless face with black eyes."

Brent was on his feet. "Bokor!" The man had multiplied himself into a regiment. One man who was hundreds—why not thousands? millions?—could indeed be a conqueror. "What happened?"

"They entered the building. I knew that I could do nothing there, and came to find you and Stephen and the bodiless one. But as I came along the street, lo! on every corner there was yet another of that face, and always urging the people to maintain the Stasis and destroy the travelers. I was recognized. By good hap those who set upon me had no rods, so I escaped with my life."

Brent thought quickly. "Martha is with Stephen, so Edam is probably there, too. Go to him at once and warn him. I'm going to the travelers' building and see what's happened. Meet you at the headquarters as soon as I can." Kruj hesitated. "Mimi—"

"I'll bring her with me if I can. Get going."

The streets were mad. Wild throngs jammed the moving

roadways. Somewhere in the distance mountainous flames
leaped up and their furious glitter gleamed from the eyes of
the mob. These were the ordinary citizens of Stasis, no longer
cattle, or rather cattle stampeded.

A voice blared seemingly out of the heavens. Brent recognized the public address system used for vital State messages.
"Revolt of travelers haves spreaded to amphitheater of Cosmos. Flames lighted by travelers now attack sacred spot.
People of Cosmos: Destroy travelers!"

There was nothing to mark Brent superficially as a traveler. He pushed along with the job, shouting as rapidly as any
other. He could make no headway. He was borne along on
these foaming human waves.

Then in front of him he saw three Bokors pushing against
the mob. If they spied him—His hands groped along the wall.
Just as a Bokor looked his way, he found what he was seeking—one of the spying niches of the Stappers. He slipped
into safety then peered out cautiously.

From the next door he saw a man emerge whom he knew
by sight—a leading dramatist of the sollies, who had
promised to be an eventual convert of Kruj's disciples. Three
citizens of the mob halted him as he stepped forth.

"What bees your name?"

"Where be you going?"

The solly writer hesitated. "I be going to amphitheater.
Speaker have sayed—"

"When do you come from?"

"Why, from now."

"What bees your name?"

"John—"

"Ha!" the first citizen yelled. "Stappers have telled us to
find this John. Tear him to pieces; he bees traveler."

"No, truly. I be no traveler; I be writer of sollies."

One of the citizens chortled cruelly. "Tear him for his bad
sollies!"

There was one long scream—

Fire breeds fire, literally as well as metaphorically. The
dwelling of the travelers was ablaze when Brent reached it. A
joyous mob cheered and gloated before it.

Brent started to push his way through, but a hand touched
his arm and a familiar voice whispered, "Ach-tung! Ou vkho-
dit."

He interpreted the warning and let the Venusian draw him aside. Nikobat rapidly explained.

"The Stappers came and subdued the whole crowd with paralyzing rods. They took them away—God knows what they'll do with them. There's no one in there now; the fire's just a gesture."

"But you— How did you—"

"My nerve centers don't react the same. I lay doggo and got away. Mimi escaped, too; her armor has deflecting power. I think she's gone to warn the Underground."

"Then come on."

"Don't stay too close to me," Nikobat warned. "They'll recognize me as a traveler; stay out of range of rods aimed at me. And here. I took these from a Stapper I strangled. This one is a paralyzing rod; the other's an annihilator."

The next half-hour was a nightmare—a montage of flames and blood and sweating bodies of hate. The Stasis of Stupidity was becoming a Stasis of Cruelty. Twice groups of citizens stopped Brent. They were unarmed; Bokor wisely kept weapons to himself, knowing that the fangs and claws of an enraged mob are enough. The first group Brent left paralyzed. The second time he confused his weapons. He had not meant to kill.

He did not confuse his weapons when he bagged a brace of Bokors. But what did the destruction of two matter? He fought his way on, finally catching up with Nikobat at their goal. As they met, the voice boomed once more from the air. "Important! New Chief of Stappers announced that officers of Chief of Stappers and Head of State be henceforth maked one. Under new control, travelers will be wiped out and Stasis preserved. Then on to South America for glory of Cosmos!"

Brent shuddered. "And we started out so beautifully on our renaissance!"

Nikobat shook his head. "But the bodiless traveler said that Stephen was to destroy the Stasis. This multiple villain cannot change what has happened."

"Can't he? We're taking no chances."

The headquarters of the Underground was inappositely in a loft. The situation helped. The trap entrance was unnoticeable from below and had gone unheeded by the mobs. Brent delivered the proper raps, and the trap slid open and dropped a ladder. Quickly they mounted.

The loft was a sick bay. A half-dozen wounded members of Stephen's group lay groaning on the floor. With them was Kruj. Somewhere the little man had evaded the direct line of an annihilator, but lost his hand. Blood was seeping out of his bandages, and Mimi, surprising feminine and un-Amazonic, held his unconscious head in her lap.

"You don't seem to need warning," Brent observed.

Stephen shook his head. "We be trapped here. Here we be safe for at littlest small while. If we go out—"

Brent handed him his rods. "You're the man we've got to save, Stephen. You know what Sirdam's said—it all depends on you. Use these to protect yourself, and we'll make a dash for it. If we can lose ourselves in the mob as ordinary citizens there's a chance of getting away with it. Or"—he turned to Martha-Sirdam—"have you any ideas?"

"Yes. But only as last resort."

Nikobat was peering out the window. "It's the last resort now," he said. "There's a good fifty of those identical Stappers outside, and they're headed here. They act as though they know what this is."

Brent was looking at Stephen, and he saw a strange thing. Stephen's face was expressionless, but somewhere behind his eyes Brent seemed to sense a struggle. Stephen's body trembled with an effort of will, and then his eyes were clear again. "No," he said distinctly. "You do not need to control me. I understand. You be right. I will do as you say." And he lifted the annihilator rod.

Brent started forward, but his muscles did not respond to his commands. Force his will though he might, he stood still. It was the bodiless traveler who held him motionless to watch Stephen place the rod to his temple.

"This bees goodest thing that I can do for mans," said Stephen simply. Then his headless corpse thumped on the floor.

Brent was released. He dashed forward, but vainly. There was nothing men could do for Stephen now. Brent let out a choking gasp of pain and sorrow.

Then the astonished cries of the Undergrounders recalled him from his friend's body. He looked about him. Where was Nikobat? Where were Kruj and Mimi?

A small inkling of the truth began to reach him. He hurried to the window and looked out.

There were no Bokors before the house. Only a few citizens staring dazedly at a wide space of emptiness.

At that moment the loud-speaker sounded. "Announcement," a shocked voice trembled. "Chief of Stappers haves just disappeared." And in a moment it added, "Guards report all travelers have vanished."

The citizens before the house were rubbing their eyes like men coming out of a nightmare.

"But don't you see, madam— No? Well, let me try again." Brent was not finding it easy to explain her brother's heroic death to an untenanted Martha. "Remember what your inhabitant told us? The Stasis was overthrown by Stephen."

"But Stephen bees dead."

"Exactly. So listen: All these travelers came from a future wherein Stephen had overthrown the Stasis so that when Stephen destroyed himself, as Sirdam realized, he likewise destroyed that future. A world in which Stephen died unsuccessful is a world that cannot be entered by anyone from the other future. Their worlds vanished and they with them. It was the only way of abolishing the menace of the incredibly multiplied Bokor."

"Stephen bees dead. He cans not overthrow Stasis now."

"My dear madam—Hell, skip it. But the Stasis is drained nonetheless in this new world created by Stephen's death. I've been doing a little galping on my own. The people are convinced now that the many exemplars of Bokor were some kind of evil invader. They rebound easy, the hordes; they dread the memory of those men and they dread also the ideas of cruelty and conquest to which the Bokors had so nearly converted them.

"But one thing they can't rebound from is the doubts and the new awarenesses that we planted in their minds. And there's what's left of your movement to go on with. No, the Stasis is damned, even if they are going to erect yet another Barrier."

"Oh," Martha shuddered. "You willn't let them."

Brent grinned. "Madam, there's damned little letting I can do. They're going to, and that's that. Because, you see, all the travelers vanished."

"But why—"

Brent shrugged and gave up. "Join me in some bond?" It was clear enough. The point of time which the second Barrier blocked existed both in the past of the worlds of Nikobat and Sirdam, and in the past of this future they were now entering. But if this future road stretched clear ahead, then travelers— a different set from a different future, but travelers nonetheless—would have appeared at the roadblock. The vanishing. Bokors and Nikobat and the rest would have been replaced by another set of stranded travelers.

But no one, in this alternate unknown to Sirdam in which Stephen died a failure, had come down the road of the future. There was a roadblock ahead. The Stasis would erect another Barrier . . . and God grant that some scientific successor to Alex would create again the means of disrupting it. And the travelers from this coming future—would they be Sirdams to counsel and guide man, or Bokors to corrupt and debase him?

Brent lifted his glass of bond. "To the moment after the next Barrier!" he said.

THE TWONKY

Astounding,

September

by ("Lewis Padgett") Henry Kuttner and C. L. Moore

The most famous man and wife writing team in the history of science fiction, Henry Kuttner and Catherine L. Moore produced a large body of outstanding work from their marriage in 1940 through the early 1950s. Although Kuttner had written a number of excellent stories before 1940 under his own name and a bewildering number of pseudonyms, his reputation was less than that of Moore's, who had become an established star in the 1930s with her "Northwest Smith" and "Jirel of Joiry" series. As many historians have pointed out, Kuttner's best solo work was of the highest standards, although after his marriage almost all of the stories published under either of their names or their pseudonyms (of which "Pagett" was the most famous and important) were joint efforts in the truest sense. Their most prolific period was the mid-to-late 1940s, and we will encounter them frequently in future volumes of this series.

"The Twonky" was somewhat lost in the September, 1942 Astounding because that issue also contained Boucher's "Barrier" and del Rey's "Nerves," but it is an excellent and clever story about children, radio, and a most peculiar form of social control. It was later filmed (The Twonky, 1952), but this adaptation failed to capture the real spirit of the story.

(I have, on a few occasions, collaborated and I have always found the process to be a difficult one. I find it very difficult to accept someone else's views in connection with

622

something I am doing; and I invariably fail to understand why someone else should ever question my own views which are so transparently correct. Yet Kuttner and Moore not only carried through a very successful collaboration, and so intimate a one apparently that it is impossible to tell exactly who wrote what, but managed to maintain a successful marriage at the same time. —Of course, someone is bound to ask how I can collaborate with Marty in this series of anthologies. The answer is easy: Marty is so good-natured, and so willing to do the scutwork—writing for permissions, keeping the books, handling the correspondence—that I would have to be an idiot not to be able to maintain a perfectly loving collaboration.—I. A.)

The turnover at Mideastern Radio was so great that Mickey Lloyd couldn't keep track of his men. It wasn't only the draft; employees kept quitting and going elsewhere, at a higher salary. So when the big-headed little man in overalls wandered vaguely out of a storeroom, Lloyd took one look at the brown dungaree suit—company provided—and said mildly, "The whistle blew half an hour ago. Hop to work."

"Work-k-k?" The man seemed to have trouble with the word.

Drunk? Lloyd, in his capacity as foreman, couldn't permit that. He flipped away his cigarette, walked forward, and sniffed. No, it wasn't liquor. He peered at the badge on the man's overalls.

"Two-oh-four, m-mm. Are you new here?"

"New. Huh?" The man rubbed a rising bump on his forehead. He was an odd-looking little chap, bald as a vacuum tube, with a pinched-pallid face and tiny eyes that held dazed wonder.

"Come on, Joe. Wake up!" Lloyd was beginning to sound impatient. "You work here, don't you?"

"Joe," said the man thoughtfully. "Work. Yes, I work. I make them." His words ran together oddly, as though he had a cleft palate.

With another glance at the badge, Lloyd gripped Joe's arm and ran him through the assembly room. "Here's your place. Hop to it. Know what to do?"

The other drew his scrawny body erect. "I am—expert," he remarked. "Make them better than Ponthwank."

"O.K.," Lloyd said. "Make 'em, then." And he went away.

The man called Joe hesitated, nursing the bruise on his

head. The overalls caught his attention, and he examined them wonderingly. Where—oh, yes. They had been hanging in the room from which he had first emerged. His own garments had, naturally, dissipated during the trip—what trip?

Amnesia, he thought. He had fallen from the . . . the something . . . when it slowed down and stopped. How odd this huge, machine-filled barn looked. It struck no chord of remembrance.

Amnesia, that was it. He was a worker. He made things. As for the unfamiliarity of his surroundings, that meant nothing. He was still dazed. The clouds would lift from his mind presently. They were beginning to do that already.

Work. Joe scuttled around the room, trying to goad his faulty memory. Men in overalls were doing things. Simple, obvious things. But how childish—how elemental! Perhaps this was a kindergarten.

After a while Joe went out into a stock room and examined some finished models of combination radio-phonographs. So that was it. Awkward and clumsy, but it wasn't his place to say so. No. His job was to make Twonkies.

Twonkies? The name jolted his memory again. Of course he knew how to make Twonkies. He'd made them all his life—had been specially trained for the job. Now they were using a different model of Twonky, but what the hell! Child's play for a clever workman.

Joe went back into the shop and found a vacant bench. He began to build a Twonky. Occasionally he slipped off and stole the material he needed. Once, when he couldn't locate any tungsten, he hastily built a small gadget and made it.

His bench was in a distant corner, badly lighted, though it seemed quite bright to Joe's eyes. Nobody noticed the console that was swiftly growing to completion there. Joe worked very, very fast. He ignored the noon whistle, and, at quitting time, his task was finished. It could, perhaps, stand another coat of paint—it lacked the Shimmertone of a standard Twonky. But none of the others had Shimmertone. Joe sighed, crawled under the bench, looked in vain for a relax-opad, and went to sleep on the floor.

A few hours later he woke up. The factory was empty. Odd! Maybe the working hours had changed. Maybe—Joe's mind felt funny. Sleep had cleared away the mists of amnesia, if such it had been, but he still felt dazed.

Muttering under his breath, he sent the Twonky into the stock room and compared it with the others. Superficially it was identical with a console radio-phonograph combination of the latest model. Following the pattern of the others, Joe had camouflaged and disguised the various organs and reactors.

He went back into the shop. Then the last of the mists cleared from his mind. Joe's shoulders jerked convulsively.

"Great Snell!" he gasped. "So that was it! I ran into a temporal snag!"

With a startled glance around, he fled to the storeroom from which he had first emerged. The overalls he took off and returned to their hook. After that, Joe went over to a corner, felt around in the air, nodded with satisfaction and seated himself on nothing, three feet above the floor. Then Joe vanished.

"Time," said Kerry Westerfield, "is curved. Eventually it gets back to the same place where it started. That's duplication." He put his feet up on a conveniently outjutting rock of the chimney and stretched luxuriously. From the kitchen Martha made clinking noises with bottles and glasses.

"Yesterday at this time I had a Martini," Kerry said. "The time curve indicates that I should have another one now. Are you listening, angel?"

"I'm pouring," said the angel distantly.

"You get my point, then. Here's another. Time describes a spiral instead of a circle. If you call the first cycle a, the second one's a *plus* 1—see? Which means a double Martini tonight."

"I know where that would end," Martha remarked, coming into the spacious, oak-raftered living room. She was a small, dark-haired woman with a singularly pretty face and a figure to match. Her tiny gingham apron looked slightly absurd in combination with slacks and silk blouse. "And they don't make infinity-proof gin. Here's your Martini." She did things with the shaker and manipulated glasses.

"Stir slowly," Kerry cautioned. "Never shake. Ah—that's it." He accepted the drink and eyed it appreciatively. Black hair, sprinkled with gray, gleamed in the lamplight as he sipped the Martini. "Good. Very good."

Martha drank slowly and eyed her husband. A nice guy, Kerry Westerfield. He was forty-odd, pleasantly ugly, with a wide mouth and an occasional sardonic gleam in his gray eyes as he contemplated life. They had been married for twelve years, and liked it.

From outside, the late faint glow of sunset came through the windows, picking out the console cabinet that stood against the wall by the door. Kerry peered at it with appreciation.

"A pretty penny," he remarked. "Still—"

"What? Oh. The men had a tough time getting it up the stairs. Why don't you try it, Kerry?"

"Didn't you?"

"The old one was complicated enough," Martha said, in a baffled manner. "Gadgets. They confuse me. I was brought up on an Edison. You wound it up with a crank, and strange noises came out of a horn. That I could understand. But now—you push a button, and extraordinary things happen. Electric eyes, tone selections, records that get played on both sides, to the accompaniment of weird groanings and clickings from inside the console—probably you understand those things. I don't even want to. Whenever I play a Crosby record in a superdooper like that, Bing seems embarrassed."

Kerry ate his olive. "I'm going to play some Sibelius." He nodded toward a table. "There's a new Crosby record for you. The latest."

Martha wriggled happily. "Can I, maybe, huh?"

"Uh-huh."

"But you'll have to show me how."

"Simple enough," said Kerry, beaming at the console. "Those babies are pretty good, you know. They do everything but think."

"I wish it'd wash dishes," Martha remarked. She set down her glass, got up and vanished into the kitchen.

Kerry snapped on a lamp nearby and went over to examine the new radio, Mideastern's latest model, with all the new improvements. It had been expensive—but what the hell? He could afford it. And the old one had been pretty well shot.

It was not, he saw, plugged in. Nor were there any wires in evidence—not even a ground. Something new, perhaps. Built-in antenna and ground. Kerry crouched down, looked for a socket and plugged the cord into it.

That done, he opened the doors and eyed the dials with every appearance of satisfaction. A beam of bluish light shot out and hit him in the eyes. From the depths of the console a faint, thoughtful clicking proceeded. Abruptly it stopped. Kerry blinked, fiddled with dials and switches, and bit at a fingernail.

The radio said, in a distant voice, "Psychology pattern checked and recorded."

"Eh?" Kerry twirled a dial. "Wonder what that was? Amateur station—no, they're off the air. Hm-m-m." He shrugged and went over to a chair beside the shelves of albums. His gaze ran swiftly over the titles and composers' names. Where was the "Swan of Tuonela"? There it was, next to "Finlandia." Kerry took down the album and opened it in his lap. With his free hand he extracted a cigarette from his pocket, put it between his lips, and fumbled for the matches on the table beside him. The first match he lit went out.

He tossed it into the fireplace and was about to reach for another when a faint noise caught his attention. The radio was walking across the room toward him. A whiplike tendril flicked out from somewhere, picked up a match, scratched it beneath the table top—as Kerry had done—and held the flame to the man's cigarette.

Automatic reflexes took over. Kerry sucked in his breath, and exploded in smoky, racking coughs. He bent double, gasping and momentarily blind.

When he could see again, the radio was back in its accustomed place.

Kerry caught his lower lip between his teeth. "Martha," he called.

"Soup's on," her voice said.

Kerry didn't answer. He stood up, went over to the radio and looked at it hesitantly. The electric cord had been pulled out of its socket. Kerry gingerly replaced it.

He crouched to examine the console's legs. They looked like finely finished wood. His exploratory hand told him nothing. Wood—hard and brittle.

How in hell—

"Dinner!" Martha called.

Kerry threw his cigarette into the fireplace and slowly walked out of the room. His wife, setting a gravy boat in place, stared at him.

"How many Martinis did you have?"

"Just one," Kerry said in a vague way. "I must have dozed off for a minute. Yeah. I must have."

"Well, fall to," Martha commanded. "This is the last chance you'll have to make a pig of yourself on my dumplings, for a week, anyway."

Kerry absently felt for his wallet, took out an envelope,

and tossed it toward his wife. "Here's your ticket, angel. Don't lose it."

"Oh? I rate a compartment!" Martha thrust the pasteboard back into its envelope and gurgled happily. "You're a pal. Sure you can get along without me?"

"Huh? Hm-m-m—I think so." Kerry salted his avocado. He shook himself and seemed to come out of a slight daze. "Sure, I'll be all right. You trot off to Denver and help Carol have her baby. It's all in the family."

"We-ell, my only sister—" Martha grinned. "You know how she and Bill are. Quite nuts. They'll need a steadying hand just now."

There was no reply. Kerry was brooding over a forkful of avocado. He muttered something about the Venerable Bede.

"What about him?"

"Lecture tomorrow. Every term we bog down on the Bede, for some strange reason. Ah, well."

"Got your lecture ready?"

Kerry nodded. "Sure." For eight years he had taught at the University, and he certainly should know the schedule by this time!

Later, over coffee and cigarettes, Martha glanced at her wrist watch. "Nearly train time. I'd better finish packing. The dishes—"

"I'll do 'em." Kerry wandered after his wife into the bedroom and made motions of futile helpfulness. After a while, he carried the bags down to the car. Martha joined him, and they headed for the depot.

The train was on time. Half an hour after it had pulled out, Kerry drove the car back into the garage, let himself into the house and yawned mightily. He was tired. Well, the dishes, and then beer and a book in bed.

With a puzzled look at the radio, he entered the kitchen and did things with water and soap chips. The hall phone rang. Kerry wiped his hands on a dish towel and answered it.

It was Mike Fitzgerald, who taught psychology at the University.

"Hiya, Fitz."

"Hiya. Martha gone?"

"Yeah. I just drove her to the train."

"Feel like talking, then? I've got some pretty good Scotch. Why not run over and gab a while?"

"Like to," Kerry said, yawning again, "but I'm dead. Tomorrow's a big day. Rain check?"

"Sure. I just finished correcting papers, and felt the need of sharpening my mind. What's the matter?"

"Nothing. Wait a minute." Kerry put down the phone and looked over his shoulder, scowling. Noises were coming from the kitchen. What the hell!

He went along the hall and stopped in the doorway, motionless and staring. The radio was washing the dishes.

After a while he returned to the phone. Firzgerald said, "Something?"

"My new radio," Kerry told him carefully. "It's washing the dishes."

Fitz didn't answer for a moment. His laugh was a bit hesitant. "Oh?"

"I'll call you back," Kerry said, and hung up. He stood motionless for a while, chewing his lip. Then he walked back to the kitchen and paused to watch.

The radio's back was toward him. Several limber tentacles were manipulating the dishes, expertly sousing them in hot, soapy water, scrubbing them with the little mop, dipping them into the rinse water and then stacking them neatly in the metal rack. Those whip-lashes were the only sign of unusual activity. The legs were apparently solid.

"Hey!" Kerry said.

There was no response.

He sidled around till he could examine the radio more closely. The tentacles emerged from a slot under one of the dials. The electric cord was dangling. No juice, then. But what—

Kerry stepped back and fumbled out a cigarette. Instantly the radio turned, took a match from its container on the stove, and walked forward. Kerry blinked, studying the legs. They couldn't be wood. They were bending as the . . . the thing moved, elastic as rubber. The radio had a peculiar sidling motion unlike anything else on earth.

It lit Kerry's cigarette and went back to the sink, where it resumed the dishwashing.

Kerry phoned Fitzgerald again. "I wasn't kidding. I'm having hallucinations or something. That damned radio just lit a cigarette for me."

"Wait a minute—" Fitzgerald's voice sounded undecided. "This is a gag—eh?"

"No. And I don't think it's an hallucination, either. It's up your alley. Can you run over and test my knee-jerks?"

"All right," Fitz said. "Give me ten minutes. Have a drink ready."

He hung up, and Kerry, laying the phone back into its cradle, turned to see the radio walking out of the kitchen toward the living room. Its square, boxlike contour was subtly horrifying, like some bizarre sort of hobgoblin. Kerry shivered.

He followed the radio, to find it in its former place, motionless and impassive. He opened the doors, examining the turntable, the phonograph arm, and the other buttons and gadgets. There was nothing apparently unusual. Again he touched the legs. They were not wood, after all. Some plastic, which seemed quite hard. Or—maybe they were wood, after all. It was difficult to make certain, without damaging the finish. Kerry felt a natural reluctance to use a knife on his new console.

He tried the radio, getting local stations without trouble. The tone was good—unusually good, he thought. The phonograph—

He picked up Halvorsen's "Entrance of the Boyards" at random and slipped it into place, closing the lid. No sound emerged. Investigation proved that the needle was moving rhythmically along the groove, but without audible result. Well?

Kerry removed the record as the doorbell rang. It was Fitzgerald, a gangling, saturnine man with a leathery, wrinkled face and a tousled mop of dull-gray hair. He extended a large, bony hand.

"Where's my drink?"

" 'Lo Fitz. Come in the kitchen. I'll mix. Highball?"

"Highball."

"O. K." Kerry led the way. "Don't drink it just yet, though. I want to show you my new combination."

"The one that washes dishes?" Fitzgerald asked. "What else does it do?"

Kerry gave the other a glass. "It won't play records."

"Oh, well. A minor matter, if it'll do the housework. Let's take a look at it." Fitzgerald went into the living room, selected "Afternoon of a Faun," and approached the radio. "It isn't plugged in."

"That doesn't matter a bit," Kerry said wildly.

"Batteries?" Fitzgerald slipped the record in place and adjusted the switches. "Now we'll see." He beamed triumphantly at Kerry. "Well? It's playing now."

It was.

Kerry said. "Try that Halvorsen piece. Here." He handed the disk to Fitzgerald, who pushed the reject switch and watched the lever arm lift.

But this time the phonograph refused to play. It didn't like "Entrance of the Boyards."

"That's funny," Fitzgerald grunted. "Probably the trouble's with the record. Let's try another."

There was no trouble with "Daphnis and Chloe." But the radio silently rejected the composer's "Bolero."

Kerry sat down and pointed to a nearby chair. "That doesn't prove anything. Come over here and watch. Don't drink anything yet. You, uh, you feel perfectly normal?"

"Sure. Well?"

Kerry took out a cigarette. The console walked across the room, picking up a match book on the way, and politely held the flame. Then it went back to its place against the wall.

Fitzgerald didn't say anything. After a while he took a cigarette from his pocket and waited. Nothing happened.

"So?" Kerry asked.

"A robot. That's the only possible answer. Where in the name of Petrarch did you get it?"

"You don't seem much surprised."

"I am, though. But I've seen robots before— Westinghouse tried it, you know. Only this—" Fitzgerald tapped his teeth with a nail. "Who made it?"

"How the devil should I know?" Kerry demanded. "The radio people, I suppose."

Fitzgerald narrowed his eyes. "Wait a minute. I don't quite understand—"

"There's nothing to understand. I bought this combination a few days ago. Turned in the old one. It was delivered this afternoon, and—" Kerry explained what had happened.

"You mean you didn't know it was a robot?"

"Exactly. I bought it as a radio. And . . . and . . . the damn thing seems almost alive to me."

"Nope." Fitzgerald shook his head, rose, and inspected the console carefully. "It's a new kind of robot. At least—" he hesitated. "What else is there to think? I suggest you get in touch with the Mideastern people tomorrow and check up."

"Let's open the cabinet and look inside," Kerry suggested.

Fitzgerald was willing, but the experiment proved impossible. The presumably wooden panels weren't screwed into place, and there was no apparent way of opening the console. Kerry found a screwdriver and applied it, gingerly at first, then with a sort of repressed fury. He could neither pry free a panel nor even scratch the dark, smooth finish of the cabinet.

"Damn!" he said finally. "Well, your guess is as good as mine. It's a robot. Only I didn't know they could make 'em like this. And why in a radio?"

"Don't ask me," Fitzgerald shrugged. "Check up tomorrow. That's the first step. Naturally I'm pretty baffled. If a new sort of specialized robot has been invented, why put it in a console? And what makes those legs move? There aren't any casters."

"I've been wondering about that, too."

"When it moves, the legs look—rubbery. But they're not. They're hard as . . . as hardwood. Or plastic."

"I'm afraid of the thing," Kerry said.

"Want to stay at my place tonight?"

"N-no. No. I guess not. The—robot—can't hurt me."

"I don't think it wants to. It's been helping you, hasn't it?"

"Yeah," Kerry said, and went off to mix another drink.

The rest of the conversation was inconclusive. Fitzgerald, several hours later, went home rather worried. He wasn't as casual as he had pretended, for the sake of Kerry's nerves. The impingement of something so entirely unexpected on normal life was subtly frightening. And yet, as he had said, the robot didn't seem menacing—

Kerry went to bed, with a new detective mystery. The radio followed him into the bedroom and gently took the book out of his hand. Kerry instinctively snatched for it.

"Hey!" he said. "What the devil—"

The radio went back into the living room. Kerry followed, in time to see the book replaced on the shelf. After a bit Kerry retreated, locking his door, and slept uneasily till dawn.

In dressing gown and slippers, he stumbled out to stare at the console. It was back in its former place, looking as though it had never moved. Kerry, rather white around the gills, made breakfast.

He was allowed only one cup of coffee. The radio appeared, reprovingly took the second cup from his hand, and emptied it into the sink.

That was quite enough for Kerry Westerfield. He found his hat and topcoat and almost ran out of the house. He had a horrid feeling that the radio might follow him, but it didn't, luckily for his sanity. He was beginning to be worried.

During the morning he found time to telephone Mideastern. The salesman knew nothing. It was a standard model combination—the latest. If it wasn't giving satisfaction, of course, he'd be glad to—"

"It's O.K.," Kerry said. "But who made the thing? That's what I want to find out."

"One moment, sir." There was a delay. "It came from Mr. Lloyd's department. One of our foremen."

"Let me speak to him, please."

But Lloyd wasn't very helpful. After much thought, he remembered that the combination had been placed in the stock room without a serial number. It had been added later.

"But who *made* it?"

"I just don't know. I can find out for you, I guess. Suppose I ring you back."

"Don't forget," Kerry said, and went back to his class. The lecture on the Venerable Bede wasn't too successful.

At lunch he saw Fitzgerald, who seemed relieved when Kerry came over to his table. "Find out any more about your pet robot?" the psychology professor demanded.

No one else was within hearing. With a sigh Kerry sat down and lit a cigarette. "Not a thing. It's a pleasure to be able to do this myself." He drew smoke into his lungs. "I phoned the company."

"And?"

"They don't know anything. Except that it didn't have a serial number."

"That may be significant," Fitzgerald said.

Kerry told the other about the incident of the book and the coffee, and Fitzgerald squinted thoughtfully at his milk. "I've given you some psych tests. Too much stimulation isn't good for you."

"A detective yarn!"

"Carrying it a bit to extremes, I'll admit. But I can understand *why* the robot acted that way—though I dunno how it managed it." He hesitated. "Without intelligence, that is."

"Intelligence?" Kerry licked his lips. "I'm not so sure that it's just a machine. And I'm not crazy."

"No, you're not. But you say the robot was in the front room. How could it tell you were reading?"

"Short of X-ray vision and superfast scanning and assimilative powers, I can't imagine. Perhaps it doesn't want me to read anything."

"You've said something," Fitzgerald grunted. "Know much about theoretical—machines—of that type?"

"Robots?"

"Purely theoretical. Your brain's a colloid, you know. Compact, complicated—but slow. Suppose you work out a gadget with a multimillion radioatom unit embedded in an insulating material—the result is a brain, Kerry. A brain with a tremendous number of units interacting at light-velocity speeds. A radio tube adjusts current flow when it's operating at forty million separate signals a second. And—theoretically—a radioatomic brain of the type I've mentioned could include perception, recognition, consideration, reaction and adjustment in a hundred-thousandth of a second."

"Theory."

"I've thought so. But I'd like to find out where your radio came from."

A page came over. "Telephone call for Mr. Westerfield."

Kerry excused himself and left. When he returned, there was a puzzled frown knitting his dark brows. Fitzgerald looked at him inquiringly.

"Guy named Lloyd, at the Mideastern plant. I was talking to him about the radio."

"Any luck?"

Kerry shook his head. "No. Well, not much. He didn't know who had built the thing."

"But it was built in the plant?"

"Yes. About two weeks ago—but there's no record of who worked on it. Lloyd seemed to think that was very, very funny. If a radio's built in the plant, they *know* who put it together."

"So?"

"So nothing, I asked him how to open the cabinet, and he said it was easy. Just unscrew the panel in back."

"There aren't any screws," Fitzgerald said.

"I know."

They looked at one another.

Fitzgerald said, "I'd give fifty bucks to find out whether that robot was really built only two weeks ago."

"Why?"

"Because a radioatomic brain would need training. Even in such matters as the lighting of a cigarette."

"It saw me light one."

"And followed the example. The dish-washing—hm-m-m. Induction, I suppose. If that gadget has been trained, it's a robot. If it hasn't—" Fitzgerald stopped.

Kerry blinked. "Yes?"

"I don't know what the devil it is. It bears the same relation to a robot that we bear to *eohippus*. One think I do know, Kerry; it's very probable that no scientist today has the knowledge it would take to make a . . . a thing like that."

"You're arguing in circles," Kerry said. "It *was* made."

"Uh-huh. But how—when—and by whom? That's what's got me worried."

"Well, I've a class in five minutes. Why not come over tonight?"

"Can't. I'm lecturing in the Hall. I'll phone you after, though."

With a nod Kerry went out, trying to dismiss the matter from his mind. He succeeded pretty well. But dining alone in a restaurant that night, he began to feel a general unwillingness to go home. A hobgoblin was waiting for him.

"Brandy," he told the waiter. "Make it double."

Two hours later a taxi let Kerry out at his door. He was remarkably drunk. Things swam before his eyes. He walked unsteadily toward the porch, mounted the steps with exaggerated care, and let himself into the house.

He switched on a lamp.

The radio came forward to meet him. Tentacles, thin, but strong as metal, coiled gently around his body, holding him motionless. A pang of violent fear struck through Kerry. He struggled desperately and tried to yell, but his throat was dry.

From the radio panel a beam of yellow light shot out, blinding the man. It swung down, aimed at his chest. Abruptly a queer taste was perceptible under Kerry's tongue.

After a minute or so, the ray clicked out, the tentacles flashed back out of sight, and the console returned to its corner. Kerry staggered weakly to a chair and relaxed, gulping.

He was sober. Which was quite impossible. Fourteen brandies infiltrate a definite amount of alcohol into the system. One can't wave a magic wand and instantly reach a state of sobriety. Yet that was exactly what had happened.

The robot—was trying to be helpful. Only Kerry would have preferred to remain drunk.

He got up gingerly and sidled past the radio to the bookshelf. One eye on the combination, he took down the detective novel he had tried to read on the preceding night. As he had expected, the radio took it from his hand and replaced it on the shelf. Kerry, remembering Fitzgerald's words, glanced at his watch. Reaction time, four seconds.

He took down a Chaucer and waited, but the radio didn't stir. However, when Kerry found a history volume, it was gently removed from his fingers. Reaction time, six seconds.

Kerry located a history twice as thick.

Reaction time, ten seconds.

Uh-huh. So the robot did read the books. That meant X-ray vision and superswift reactions. Jumping Jehoshaphat!

Kerry tested more books, wondering what the criterion was. *Alice in Wonderland* was snatched from his hand; Millay's poems were not. He made a list, with two columns, for future reference.

The robot, then, was not merely a servant. It was a censor. But what was the standard of comparison?

After a while he remembered his lecture tomorrow, and thumbed through his notes. Several points needed verification. Rather hesitantly he located the necessary reference book— and the robot took it away from him.

"Wait a minute," Kerry said. "I *need* that." He tried to pull the volume out of the tentacle's grasp, without success. The console paid no attention. It calmly replaced the book on its shelf.

Kerry stood biting his lip. This was a bit too much. The damned robot was a monitor. He sidled toward the book, snatched it, and was out in the hall before the radio could move.

The thing was coming after him. He could hear the soft padding of its . . . its feet. Kerry scurried into the bedroom and locked the door. He waited, heart thumping, as the knob was tried gently.

A wire-thin cilia crept through the crack of the door and fumbled with the key. Kerry suddenly jumped forward and shoved the auxiliary bolt into position. But that didn't help, either. The robot's precision tools—the specialized antenna— slid it back; and then the console opened the door, walked into the room, and came toward Kerry.

He felt a touch of panic. With a little gasp he threw the

book at the thing, and it caught it deftly. Apparently that was all that was wanted, for the radio turned and went out, rocking awkwardly on its rubbery legs, carrying the forbidden volume. Kerry cursed quietly.

The phone rang. It was Fitzgerald.

"Well? How'd you make out?"

"Have you got a copy of Cassen's *Social Literature of the Ages?*"

"I don't think so—no. Why?"

"I'll get it in the University library tomorrow, then." Kerry explained what had happened. Fitzgerald whistled softly.

"Interfering, is it? Hm-m-m. I wonder—"

"I'm afraid of the thing."

"I don't think it means you any harm. You say it sobered you up?"

"Yeah. With a light ray. That isn't very logical."

"It might be. The vibrationary equivalent of thiamin chloride."

"Light?"

"There's vitamin content in sunlight, you know. That isn't the important point. It's censoring your reading—and apparently it reads the books, with superfast reactions. That gadget, whatever it is, isn't merely a robot."

"You're telling me," Kerry said grimly. "It's a Hitler."

Fitzgerald didn't laugh. Rather soberly, he suggested, "Suppose you spend the night at my place?"

"No," Kerry said, his voice stubborn. "No so-and-so radio's going to chase me out of my house. I'll take an ax to the thing first."

"We-ell—you know what you're doing, I suppose. Phone me if . . . if anything happens."

"O. K.," Kerry said, and hung up. He went into the living room and eyed the radio coldly. What the devil was it—and what was it trying to do? Certainly it wasn't merely a robot. Equally certainly, it wasn't alive, in the sense that a colloid brain is alive.

Lips thinned, he went over and fiddled with the dials and switches. A swing band's throbbing erratic tempo came from the console. He tried the short-wave band—nothing unusual there. So?

So nothing. There was no answer.

After a while he went to bed.

At luncheon the next day he brought Cassen's *Social Literature* to show Fitzgerald.

"What about it?"

"Look here," Kerry flipped the pages and indicated a passage. "Does this mean anything to you?"

Fitzgerald read it. "Yeah. The point seems to be that individualism is necessary for the production of literature. Right?"

Kerry looked at him. "I don't know."

Eh?"

"My mind goes funny."

Fitzgerald rumpled his gray hair, narrowing his eyes and watching the other man intently. "Come again. I don't quite—"

With angry patience, Kerry said, "This morning I went into the library and looked at this reference. I read it all right. But it didn't mean anything to me. Just words. Know how it is when you're fagged out and have been reading a lot? You'll run into a sentence with a lot of subjunctive clauses, and it doesn't percolate. Well, it was like that."

"Read it now," Fitzgerald said quietly, thrusting the book across the table.

Kerry obeyed, looking up with a wry smile. "No good."

"Read it aloud. I'll go over it with you, step by step."

But that didn't help. Kerry seemed utterly unable to assimilate the sense of the passage.

"Semantic block, maybe," Fitzgerald said, scratching his ear. "Is this the first time it's happened?"

"Yes . . . no. I don't know."

"Got any classes this afternoon? Good. Let's run over to your place."

Kerry thrust away his plate. "All right. I'm not hungry. Whenever you're ready—"

Half an hour later they were looking at the radio. It seemed quite harmless. Fitzgerald wasted some time trying to pry a panel off, but finally gave it up as a bad job. He found pencil and paper, seated himself opposite Kerry, and began to ask questions.

At one point he paused. "You didn't mention that before."

"Forgot it, I guess."

Fitzgerald tapped his teeth with the pencil. "Hm-m-m. The first time the radio acted up—"

"It hit me in the eye with a blue light—"

"Not that. I mean—what it said."

Kerry blinked. "What *it* said?" He hesitated. " 'Psychology pattern checked and noted,' or something like that. I thought I'd tuned in on some station and got part of a quiz program or something. You mean—"

"Were the words easy to understand? Good English?"

"No, now that I remember it," Kerry scowled. "They were slurred quite a lot. Vowels stressed."

"Uh-huh. Well, let's get on." They tried a word-association test.

Finally Fitzgerald leaned back, frowning. "I want to check this stuff with the last tests I gave you a few months ago. It looks funny to me—damned funny. I'd feel a lot better if I knew exactly what memory was. We've done considerable work on mnemonics—artificial memory. Still, it may not be that at all."

"Eh?"

"That—machine. Either it's got an artificial memory, has been highly trained or else it's adjusted to a different *milieu* and culture. It has affected you—quite a lot."

Kerry licked dry lips. "How?"

"Implanted blocks in your mind. I haven't correlated them yet. When I do, we may be able to figure out some sort of answer. No, that thing isn't a robot. It's a lot more than that."

Kerry took out a cigarette; the console walked across the room and lit it for him. The two men watched with a faint shrinking horror.

"You'd better stay with me tonight," Fitzgerald suggested.

"No," Kerry said. He shivered.

The next day Fitzgerald looked for Kerry at lunch, but the younger man did not appear. He telephoned the house, and Martha answered the call.

"Hello! When did you get back?"

"Hello, Fitz. About an hour ago. My sister went ahead and had her baby without me—so I came back." She stopped, and Fitzgerald was alarmed at her tone.

"Where's Kerry?"

"He's here. Can you come over, Fitz? I'm worried."

"What's the matter with him?"

"I . . . I don't know. Come right away."

"O. K.," Fitzgerald said, and hung up, biting his lips. He was worried. When, a short while later, he rang the Westerfield bell, he discovered that his nerves were badly out of control. But sight of Martha reassured him.

He followed her into the living room. Fitzgerald's glance went at once to the console, which was unchanged; and then to Kerry, seated motionless by a window. Kerry's face had a blank, dazed look. His pupils were dilated, and he seemed to recognize Fitzgerald only slowly.

"Hello, Fitz," he said.

"How do you feel?"

Martha broke in. "Fitz, what's wrong? Is he sick? Shall I call the doctor?"

Fitzgerald sat down. "Have you noticed anything funny about that radio?"

"No. Why?"

"Then listen." He told the whole story, watching incredulity struggle with reluctant belief on Martha's face. Presently she said, "I can't quite—"

"If Kerry takes out a cigarette, the thing will light it for him. Want to see how it works?"

"No-no. Yes. I suppose so." Martha's eyes were wide.

Fitzgerald gave Kerry a cigarette. The expected happened.

Martha didn't say a word. When the console had returned to its place, she shivered and went over to Kerry. He looked at her vaguely.

"He needs a doctor, Fitz."

"Yes." Fitzgerald didn't mention that a doctor might be quite useless.

"What is that thing?"

"It's more than a robot. And it's been readjusting Kerry. I told you what's happened. When I checked Kerry's psychology patterns, I found that they'd altered. He's lost most of his initiative."

"Nobody on earth could have made that—"

Fitzgerald scowled. "I thought of that. It seems to be the product of a well-developed culture, quite different from ours. Martian, perhaps. It's such a specialized thing that it naturally fits into a complicated culture. But I do not understand why it looks exactly like a Mideastern console radio."

Martha touched Kerry's hand. "Camouflage?"

"But why? You were one of my best pupils in psych, Martha. Look at this logically. Imagine a civilization where a gadget like that has its place. Use inductive reasoning."

"I'm trying to. I can't think very well. Fitz, I'm worried about Kerry."

"I'm all right," Kerry said.

Fitzgerald put his fingertips together. "It isn't a radio so much as a monitor. In this other civilization, perhaps every man has one, or maybe only a few—the ones who need it. It keeps them in line."

"By destroying initiative?"

Fitzgerald made a helpless gesture. "I don't know! It worked that way in Kerry's case. In others—I don't know."

Martha stood up. "I don't think we should talk any more. Kerry needs a doctor. After that we can decide upon that." She pointed to the console.

Fitzgerald said, "It'd be rather a shame to wreck it, but—" His look was significant.

The console moved. It came out from its corner with a sidling, rocking gait and walked toward Fitzgerald. As he sprang up, the whiplike tentacles flashed out and seized him. A pale ray shone into the man's eyes.

Almost instantly it vanished; the tentacles withdrew, and the radio returned to its place. Fitzgerald stood motionless. Martha was on her feet, one hand at her mouth.

"Fitz!" Her voice shook.

He hesitated. "Yes? What's the matter?"

"Are you hurt? What did it do to you?"

Fitzgerald frowned a little. "Eh? Hurt? I don't—"

"The radio. What did it do?"

He looked toward the console. "Something wrong with it? Afraid I'm not much of a repair man, Martha."

"Fitz." She came forward and gripped his arm. "Listen to me." Quick words spilled from her mouth. The radio. Kerry. Their discussion—

Fitzgerald looked at her blankly, as though he didn't quite understand. "I guess I'm stupid today. I can't quite understand what you're talking about."

"The radio—you know! You said it changed Kerry—" Martha paused, staring at the man.

Fitzgerald was definitely puzzled. Martha was acting strangely. Queer! He'd always considered her a pretty level-headed girl. But now she was talking nonsense. At least, he couldn't figure out the meaning of her words—there was no sense to them.

And why was she talking about the radio? Wasn't it satisfactory? Kerry had said it was a good buy, with a fine tone and the latest gadgets in it. Fitzgerald wondered, for a fleeting second, if Martha had gone crazy.

In any case, he was late for his class. He said so. Martha didn't try to stop him when he went out. She was pale as chalk.

Kerry took out a cigarette. The radio walked over and held a match.

"Kerry!"

"Yes, Martha?" His voice was dead.

She stared at the . . . the radio. Mars? Another world—another civilization? What was it? What did it want? *What was it trying to do?*

Martha let herself out of the house and went to the garage. When she returned, a small hatchet was gripped tightly in her hand.

Kerry watched. He saw Martha walk over to the radio and lift the hatchet. Then a beam of light shot out, and Martha vanished. A little dust floated up in the afternoon sunlight.

"Destruction of life-form threatening attack," the radio said, slurring the words together.

Kerry's brain turned over. He felt sick, dazed and horribly empty. Martha—

His mind—churned. Instinct and emotion fought with something that smothered them. Abruptly the dams crumbled, and the blocks were gone, the barriers down. Kerry cried out hoarsely, inarticulately, and sprang to his feet.

"Martha!" he yelled.

She was gone. Kerry looked around. Where—

What had happened? He couldn't remember.

He sat down in the chair again, rubbing his forehead. His free hand brought up a cigarette, an automatic reaction that brought instant response. The radio walked forward and held a lighted match ready.

Kerry made a choking, sick sound and flung himself out of the chair. He remembered now. He picked up the hatchet and sprang toward the console, teeth bared in a mirthless rictus.

Again the light beam flashed out.

Kerry vanished. The hatchet thudded onto the carpet.

The radio walked back to its place and stood motionless once more. A faint clicking proceeded from its radioatomic brain.

"Subject basically unsuitable," it said, after a moment.

"Elimination has been necessary." *Click!* "Preparation for next subject completed."
Click.

"We'll take it," the boy said.

"You won't be making a mistake," smiled the rental agent. "It's quiet, isolated, and the price is quite reasonable."

"Not so very," the girl put in. "But it *is* just what we've been looking for."

The agent shrugged. "Of course an unfurnished place would run less. But—"

"We haven't been married long enough to get any furniture," the boy grinned. He put an arm around his wife. "Like it, hon?"

"Hm-m-m. Who lived here before?"

The agent scratched his cheek. "Let's see. Some people named Westerfield, I think. It was given to me for listing just about a week ago. Nice place. If I didn't own my own house, I'd jumpt at it myself."

"Nice radio," the boy said. "Late model, isn't it?" He went over to examine the console.

"Come along," the girl urged. "Let's look at the kitchen again."

"O. K., hon."

They went out of the room. From the hall came the sound of the agent's smooth voice, growing fainter. Warm afternoon sunlight slanted through the windows.

For a moment there was silence. Then—
Click!

QRM-INTERPLANETARY

Astounding,

October

by George O. Smith (1911-   )

George O. Smith is a trained electronics engineer who successfully translated his technical expertise to prose fiction with this interesting tale, which was his first published science fiction story. It proved to be so popular that it resulted in an important series, the Venus Equilateral *stories (first collected 1947). Among his other ten or so novels, the most important is* The Fourth R *(1959), one of the most neglected and best superman treatments of the last several decades.*

Although "QRM-Interplanetary" was not the first story of space communications techniques, it was the most noteworthy before Arthur C. Clarke turned his attention to the subject a few years after it appeared in the pages of Astounding.

(We all have our peculiar characteristics—I shudder when I think of my own—and George's is that he is an inveterate interrupter. This is true not only in informal conversation but even in the case where he is in the audience listening to a formal speech. It does tend to break the line of thought and weaken the thrust of the argument when you're the speaker and can therefore be harrowing. I remember once, when I was speaking at a convention and it was Cyril Kornbluth who was interrupting. I stopped him cold when I said, "Cyril, you're the poor man's George O. Smith." I don't think he ever forgave me.—I.A.)

Korvus, the Magnificent, Nilamo of Yoralen, picked up the telephone in his palace and said: "I want to talk to Wilneda. He is at the International Hotel in Detroit, Michigan."

"I'm sorry, sir," came the voice of the operator. "Talking is not possible, due to the fifteen-minute transmission lag between here and Terra. However, teletype messages are welcome."

Her voice originated fifteen hundred miles north of Yoralen, but it sounded as though she might be in the next room. Korvus thought for a moment and then said, "Take this message: 'Wilneda: Add to order for mining machinery one type 56-XXD flier to replace washed-out model. And remember, alcohol and energy will not mix!' Sign that Korvus."

"Yes, Mr. Korvus."

"Not *mister!*" yelled the monarch. "I am Korvus the Magnificent! I am Nilamo of Yoralen!"

"Yes, your magnificence," said the operator humbly. It was more than possible that she was stifling a laugh, which knowledge made the little man of Venus squirm in wrath. But there was nothing he could do about it, so he wisely said nothing.

To give Korvus credit, he was not a pompous little man. He was large—for a Venusian—which made him small according to the standards set up by the Terrestrians. He, as Nilamo of Yoralen, had extended the once-small kingdom outward to include most of the Palanortis Country, which extended from 23.0 degrees north latitude to 61.7 degrees, and almost across the whole, single continent that was the dry land of Venus.

So Korvus' message to Terra zoomed across the fifteen hundred rocky miles of Palanortis to Northern Landing. It passed high across the thousand-foot-high trees and over the mountain ranges. It swept over open patches of water, and across intervening cities and towns. It went with the speed of light and in a tight beam from Yoralen to Northern Landing, straight as a die and with person-to-person clarity. The operator in the city that lay across the North Pole of Venus clicked on a teletype, reading back the message as it was printed.

Korvus told her: "That is correct."

"The message will be in the hands of your representative Wilneda within the hour."

The punched tape from Operator No. 7's machine slid along the line until it entered a coupling machine.

The coupling machine worked furiously. It accepted the tapes from seventy operators as fast as they could set them. It selected the messages as they entered the machine, placing a

mechanical preference upon whichever message happened to
be ahead of the others on the moving tapes. The master tape
moved continuously at eleven thousand words per minute,
taking teletype messages from everywhere in the Northern
Hemisphere of Venus to Terra and Mars. It was a busy
machine; even at eleven thousand words per minute it often
got hours behind.

The synchronous-keyed signal from the coupling machine
left the operating room and went to the transmission room. It
was amplified and sent out of the city to a small, squat building at the outskirts of Northern Landing. It was hurled at the
sky out of a reflector antenna by a thousand-kilowatt transmitter.

The wave seared against the Venusian Heaviside Layer. It
fought and it struggled. And, as is the case with strife, it lost
heavily in the encounter. The beam was resisted fiercely. Infil-
trations of ionization tore at the radio beam, stripping and
trying to beat it down.

But man triumphed over nature. The megawatt of energy
that came in a tight beam from the building at Northern
Landing emerged from the Heaviside Layer as a weak, pif-
fling signal. It wavered and it crackled. It wanted desperately
to lie down and sleep. Its directional qualities were impaired,
and it wobbled badly. It arrived at the relay station tired and
worn.

One million watts of ultra-high frequency energy at the
start, it was measurable in microvolts when it reached a space
station only five hundred miles above the city of Northern
Landing.

The signal, as weak and as wobbly as it was, was taken in
by eager receptors. It was amplified. It was dehashed, desta-
ticked and deloused. And once again, one hundred decibels
stronger and infinitely cleaner, the signal was hurled out on a
tight beam from a gigantic parabolic reflector.

Across sixty-seven million miles of space went the signal.
Across the orbit of Venus it went in a vast chord, and arrived
at the Venus Equilateral Station with less trouble than the
original transmission through the Heaviside Layer. The signal
was amplified and demodulated. It went into a decoupler
machine where the messages were sorted mechanically and
sent, each to the proper channel, into other coupler machines.
Beams from Venus Equilateral were directed at Mars and at
Terra.

The Terra beam ended at Luna. Here it again was placed

in the two-compartment beam and from Luna it punched down at Terra's Layer, emerging into the atmosphere of Terra as weak and as tired as it had been when it had come out of the Venusian Heaviside Layer. It entered a station in the Bahamas, was stripped of the interference, and put upon the land beams. It entered decoupling machines that sorted the messages as to destination. These various beams spread out across the face of Terra, the one carrying Korvus' message finally coming into a station at Ten Mile Road and Woodward. From this station, at the outskirts of Detroit, it went upon land wires downtown to the International Hotel.

The teletype machine in the office of the hotel began to click rapidly. The message to Wilneda was arriving.

And fifty-five minutes after the operator told Korvus that less than an hour would ensue, Wilneda was saying, humorously, "So, Korvus was drunk again last night—"

Completion of Korvus' message to Wilneda completes also one phase of the tale at hand. It is not important. There were a hundred and fifty other messages that might have been accompanied in the same manner, each as interesting to the person who likes the explanation of the interplanetary communication service. But this is not a technical journal. A more complete explanation of the various phases that a message goes through in leaving a city on Venus to go to Terra may be found in the *Communications Technical Review*, Volume XXVII, number 8, pages 411 to 716. Readers more interested in the technical aspects are referred to the article.

It so happens that Korvus' message was picked out of a hundred-odd messages because of one thing only. At the time that Korvus' message was in transit through the decoupler machines at the Venus Equilateral Relay Station, something of a material nature was entering the air lock of the station.

It was an unexpected visit.

Don Channing looked up at the indicator panel in his office and frowned in puzzlement. He punched a buzzer and spoke into the communicator on his desk.

"Find out who that is, will you, Arden?"

"He isn't expected," came back the voice of Arden Westland.

"I know that. But I've been expecting someone ever since John Peters retired last week. You know why."

"You hope to get his job," said the girl in an amused voice.

"I hope you do. So that someone else will sit around all day trying to make you retire so that he can have your job!"

"Now look, Arden, I've never tried to make Peters retire."

"No, but when the word came that he was thinking of it, you began to think about taking over. Don't worry, I don't blame you." There was quite a protracted silence, and then her voice returned. "The visitor is a gentleman by the name of Francis Burbank. He came out in a flitter with a chauffeur and all."

"Big shot, hey?"

"Take it easy. He's coming up the office now."

"I gather that he desires audience with me?" asked Don.

"I think that he's here to lay down the law! You'll have to get out of Peter's office, if his appearance is any guide."

Some more silence followed. The communicator was turned off at the other end, which made Channing fume. He would have preferred to hear the interchange of words between his secretary and the newcomer. Then, instead of having the man announced, the door opened and the stranger entered. He came to the point immediately.

"You're Don Channing? Acting Director of Venus Equilateral?"

"I am."

"Then I have some news for you, Dr. Channing. I have been appointed Director by the Interplanetary Communications Commission. You are to resume your position as Electronics Engineer."

"Oh?" said Channing. "I sort of believed that I would be offered *this* position."

"There was a discussion of that procedure. However, the commission decided that a man of more commercial training would better fill the position. The Communications Division has been operating at too small a profit. They felt that a man of commercial experience could cut expenses and so on to good effect. You understand their reasoning, of course," said Burbank.

"Not exactly."

"Well, it is like this. They know that a scientist is not usually the man to consider the cost of experimentation. Scientists build thousand-ton cyclotrons to convert a penny's worth of lead into one and one-tenth cents' worth of lead and gold. And they use three hundred dollars' worth of power and a million-dollar machine to do it with.

"They feel that a man with training like that will not know

the real meaning of the phrase 'cutting expenses.' A new broom sweeps clean, Dr. Channing. There must be many places where a man of commercial experience can cut expenses. I, as Director, shall do so."

"I wish you luck," said Channing.

"Then, there is no hard feeling?"

"I can't say that. It is probably not your fault. I cannot feel against you, but I do feel sort of let down at the decision of the commission. I have had experience in this job."

"The commission may appoint you to follow me. If your work shows a grasp of commercial operations, I shall so recommend."

"Thanks," said Channing dryly. "May I buy you a drink?"

"I never drink. And I do not believe in it. If it were mine to say, I'd prohibit liquor from the premises. Venus Equilateral would be better off without it."

Don Channing snapped the communicator. "Miss Westland, will you come in?"

She entered, puzzlement on her face.

"This is Mr. Burbank. His position places him in control of this office. You will, in the future, report to him directly. The report on the operations, engineering projects and so on that I was to send in to the commission this morning will, therefore, be placed in Mr. Burbank's hands as soon as possible."

"Yes, Dr. Channing." Her eyes held a twinkle, but there was concern and sympathy in them, too. "Shall I get them immediately?"

"They are ready?"

"I was about to put them on the tape when you called."

"Then give them to Mr. Burbank." Channing turned to Burbank. "Miss Westland will hand you the reports I mentioned. They are complete and precise. A perusal of them will put you in grasp of the situation here at Venus Equilateral better than will an all-afternoon conference. I'll have Miss Westland haul my junk out of here. You may consider this as your office, it having been used by Dr. Peters. And, in the meantime, I've got to check up on some experiments on the ninth level." Channing paused. "You'll excuse me?"

"Yes, if Miss Westland knows where to find you."

"She will. I'll inform her of my whereabouts."

"I may want to consult you after I read the reports."

"That will be all right. The autocall can find me anywhere on Venus Equilateral, if I'm at the place Miss Westland calls."

Don Channing stopped at Arden's desk. "I'm booted," he told her.

"Leaving Venus Equilateral?" she asked with concern.

"No, blonde and beautiful, I'm just shunted back to my own office."

"Can't I go with you?" pleaded the girl.

"Nope. You are to stay here and be a nice, good-looking Mata Hari. This bird seems to think that he can run Venus Equilateral like a bus or a factory. I know the type, and the first thing he'll do is to run the place into a snarl. Keep me informed of anything complicated, will you?"

"Sure. And where are you going now?"

"I'm going down to get Walt Franks. We're going to inspect the transparency of a new type of glass."

"I didn't know that optical investigations come under your jurisdiction."

"This investigation will consist of a visit to the ninth level."

"Can't you take me along?"

"Not today," he grinned. "Your new boss does not believe in the evils of looking through the bottom of a glass. We must behave with decorum. We must forget fun. We are now operating under a man who will commercialize electronics to a fine art."

"Don't get stewed. He may want to know where the electrons are kept."

"I'm not going to drink that much. Walt and I need a discussion," he said. "And in the meantime, haul my spinach out of the office, will you, and take it back to the electronics office? I'll be needing it back there."

"O.K., Don," she said. "I'll see you later."

Channing left to go to the ninth level. He stopped long enough to collect Walt Franks.

Over a tall glass of beer, Channing told Franks of Burbank's visit. And why.

Only one thing stuck in Franks' mind. "Did you say that he might close Joe's?" asked Franks.

"He said that if it were in his power to do so, he would."

"Heaven forbid. Where will we go to be alone?"

"Alone?" snorted Channing. The barroom was half filled with people, being the only drinking establishment for sixty-odd million miles.

"Well, you know what I mean."

"I could smuggle in a few cases of beer," suggested Don.

"Couldn't we smuggle him out?"

"That would be desirable. But I think he is here to stay. Darn it all, why do they have to appoint some confounded political pal to a job like this? I'm telling you, Walt, he must weigh two hundred if he weighs a pound. He holds his stomach on his lap when he sits down."

Walt looked up and down Channing's slender figure. "Well, he won't be holding Westland on his lap if it is filled with stomach."

"I never hold Westland on my lap—"

"No?"

"—during working hours!" Channing finished. He grinned at Franks and ordered another beer. "And how is the Office of Beam Control going to make out under the new regime?"

"I'll answer that after I see how the new regime treats the Office of Beam Control," answered Franks. "I doubt that he can do much to bugger things up in my office. There aren't many cheaper ways to direct a beam, you know."

"Yeah. You're safe."

"But what I can't understand is why they didn't continue you in that job. You've been handling the business ever since last December, when Peters got sick. You've been doing all right."

"Doing all right just means that I've been carrying over Peters' methods and ideas. What the commission wants, apparently, is something new. Ergo, the new broom."

"Personally, I like that one about the old shoes being more comfortable," said Franks. "If you say the right word, Don, I'll slip him a dose of high voltage. That should fix him."

"I think that the better way would be to *work* for the bird. Then when he goes, I'll have his recommendation."

"Phooey," snorted Franks. "They'll just appoint another political pal. They've tried it before and they'll try it again. I wonder what precinct he carries."

The telephone rang in the bar, and the bartender, after answering, motioned to Walt Franks. "You're wanted in your office," said the bartender. "And besides," he told Channing, "if I'm going to get lunch for three thousand people, you'd better trot along, too. It's nearly eleven o'clock, you know, and the first batch of two hundred will be coming in."

Joe was quite inaccurate as to the figures. The complement of Venus Equilateral was just shy of twenty-seven hundred. They worked in three eight-hour shifts, about nine hundred to a shift. They had their breakfast, lunch and dinner hours staggered so that at no time were there more than about two hundred people in the big lunchroom. The bar, it may be mentioned, was in a smaller room at one end of the much larger cafeteria.

The Venus Equilateral Relay Station was a modern miracle of engineering if you liked to believe the books. Actually, Venus Equilateral was an asteroid that had been shoved into its orbit about the sun, forming a practical demonstration of the equilateral triangle solution of the Three Moving Bodies. It was a long cylinder, about three miles in length by about a mile in diameter.

In 1946, the United States Army Signal Corps succeeded in sending forth and receiving in return a radar signal from the moon. This was an academic triumph; at that time such a feat had no practical value. It's value came later when the skies were opened up for travel; when men crossed the void of space to colonize the nearer planets, Mars and Venus.

They found, then, that communications back and forth depended upon the initial experiment in 1946.

But there were barriers, even in deep space. The penetration of the Heaviside Layer was no great problem. That had been done. But they found that Sol, our sun, was often in the path of the communications beam because the planets all make their way around Sol at different rates of speed.

All too frequently Mars is on the opposite side of the sun from Terra, or Sol might lie between Venus and Mars. Astronomically, this situation where two planets lie on opposite sides of the sun is called Major Opposition, which is an appropriate name even though those who named it were not thinking in terms of communications.

The concept of Sol being between two planets and interfering with communication does not mean a true physical alignment. The sun is a tremendous generator of radiothermal energy, so that communication begins to fail when the other planet is 15 to 20 degrees from the sun. Thus, from 30 to 40 degrees of opposition passage, Venus Equilateral is a necessary relay station.

To circumvent this natural barrier to communications, mankind made use of one of the classic solutions of the problem of the Three Moving Bodies, in which it is stated that three celestial objects at the corners of an equilateral triangle will so remain, rotating about their common center of gravity. This equilateral position between the sun and any planet is called the "Trojan" position because it has been known for some time that a group of asteroids precedes and follows Jupiter around in its orbit. The "Trojan" comes from the fact that these asteroids bear the well-known names of the heroes of the famous Trojan War.

To communicate around the sun, then, it is only necessary to establish a relay station in the Trojan position of the desired planet. This will be either ahead or behind the planet in its orbit; and the planet, the sun, and the station will form an equilateral triangle.

So was born the Venus Equilateral Relay Station.

Little remained of the original asteroid. At the present time, the original rock had been discarded to make room for the ever-growing personnel and material that were needed to operate the relay station. What had been an asteroid with machinery was now a huge pile of machinery with people. The insides, formerly of spongy rock, were now neatly cubed off into offices, rooms, hallways, and so on, divided by sheets of steel. The outer surface, once rugged and forbidding, was now all shiny steel. The small asteroid, a tiny thing, was gone, the station having overflowed the asteroid soon after men found that uninterrupted communication *was* possible between the worlds.

Now the man-made asteroid carried twenty-seven hundred people. There were stores, offices, places of recreation, churches, marriages, deaths and everything but taxes. Judging by its population, it was a small town.

Venus Equilateral rotated about its axis. On the inner surface of its double-walled shell were the homes of the people—not cottages, but apartmental cubicles, one, two, three, six rooms. Centrifugal force made a little more than one Earth G of artificial gravity. Above this shell of apartments, the offices began. Offices, recreation centers, and so on. Up in the central position, where the gravity was nil or near-nil, the automatic machinery was placed: the servogyroscopes and their beam finders, the storerooms, the air plant, the hydroponic farms, and all other things that needed little or no gravity for well-being.

This was the Venus Equilateral Relay Station, 60 degrees ahead of the planet Venus, on Venus' orbit. Often closer to Terra than Venus, the relay station offered a perfect place to relay messages through whenever Mars or Terra was on the other side of the sun. It was seldom idle, for it was seldom that Mars and Venus were in such a position that direct communications between all the three planets was possible.

This was the center of Interplanetary Communications. This was the main office. It was the heart of the solar system's communication line, and as such, it was well manned. Orders for everything emanated from Venus Equilateral. It was a delicate proposition, Venus Equilateral was, and hence the present-on-all-occasions official capacities and office staff.

This was the organization that Don Channing hoped to direct. A closed corporation with one purpose in mind: interplanetary communication!

Channing wondered if the summons for Walt Franks was an official one. Returning to the electronics office, Don punched the communicator and asked, "Is Walt in there?"

Arden's voice came back, "No, but Burbank is in Franks' office. Wanna listen?"

"Eavesdropper! Using the communicator?"

"Sure."

"Better shut it off," Don warned. "Burbank isn't foolish, you know, and there are pilot lights and warning flags on those things to tell if someone has the key open. I wouldn't want to see you fired for listening in."

"All right, but it was getting interesting."

"If I'm betting on the right horse," said Channing, "this will be interesting for all before it is finished."

Seven days went by in monotonous procession. Seven days in a world of constant climate. One week, marked only by the changing of work shifts and the clocks that marked off the eight-hour periods. Seven days unmarred by rain or cold or heat. Seven days of uninterrupted sunshine that flickered in and out of the sealed viewports with eye-searing brilliance, coming and going as the station rotated.

But in the front offices, things were not serene. Not that monotony ever set in seriously in the engineering department, but that sacred sanctum of all-things-that-didn't-behave-as-they-should found that even their usual turmoil was worse. There was nothing that a person could set his fingers on directly. It was more of a quiet, undercover nature. On Monday, Francis Burbank sent around a communiqué removing the option of free messages for the personnel. On Tuesday, he remanded the years-long custom of permitting the supply ships to carry, free, packages from friends at home. On Wednesday, Burbank decided that there should be a curfew on the one and only beer emporium. "Curfew" was a revision made after he found that complete curtailing of all alcoholic beverages might easily lead to a more moral problem; there being little enough to do with one's spare time. On Thursday, he set up a stiff-necked staff of censors for the moving picture house. On Friday, he put a tax on cigarettes and candy. On Saturday, he installed time clocks in all the laboraties and professional offices, where previous to his coming men had come for work a half-hour late and worked an hour overtime at night.

On Sunday—

Don Channing stormed into the Director's office with a scowl on his face.

"Look," he said, "for years we have felt that any man, woman or child who was willing to come out here was worth all the freedom and consideration that we could give them. What about this damned tax on cigarettes? And candy? And who told you to stop our folks from telling their folks that they are still in good health? And why stop them from sending packages of candy, cake, mementoes, clothing, soap, mosquito dope, liquor, or anything else? And did you ever think that a curfew is something that can be applied only when time is one and the same for all? On Venus Equilateral, Mr. Burbank, six o'clock in the evening is two hours after dinner for one group, two hours after going to work for the second group, and mid-sleep for the third. Then this matter of cutting all love scenes, drinking, female vampires, banditry, bedroom items, murders and sweater girls out of the movies? We are a selected group and well prepared to take care of our morality. Any man or woman going offside would be heaved out quick. Why, after years of personal freedom, do we find ourselves under the authority of a veritable dictatorship?"

Francis Burbank was not touched. "I'll trouble you to keep to your own laboratory," he told Channing. "Perhaps your own laxity in matters of this sort is the reason why the commission preferred someone better prepared. You speak of many things. There will be more to come. I'll answer some of your questions. Why should we permit our profits to be eaten up by people sending messages, cost-free, to their acquaintances all over the minor planets? Why should valuable space for valuable supplies be taken up with personal favors between friends? And if the personnel wants to smoke and drink, let them pay for the privilege! It will help to pay for the high price of shipping the useless items out from the nearest planet—as well as saving of previous storage space!"

"But you're breeding ill will among the employees," Channing objected.

"Any who prefer to do so may leave!" snapped Burbank.

"You may find it difficult to hire people to spend their lives in a place that offers no sight of a sky or breath of fresh air. The people here may go home to their own planets to find that smell of fresh, spring air is more desirable than a climate that never varies from the personal optimum. I wonder, occasionally, if it might not be possible to instigate some sort of cold snap for a rainy season just for the purpose of bringing to the members of Venus Equilateral some of the surprises that are to be found in Chicago or New York. Hell, even Canalopsis has an occasional rainstorm!"

"Return to your laboratory," said Burbank coldly. "And let me run the station. Why should we spend useful money to pamper people? I don't care if Canalopsis does have an occasional storm, we are not on Mars, we are in Venus Equilateral. You tend to your end of the business and I'll do as I deem fitting for the station!"

Channing mentally threw up his hands and literally stalked out of the office. Here was a close-knit organization being shot full of holes by a screwball. He stamped down to the ninth level and beat upon the closed door of Joe's. The door remained closed.

Channing beat with his knuckles until they bled. Finally a door popped open down the hallway fifty yards and a man looked out. His head popped in again, and within thirty seconds the door to Joe's opened and admitted Channing.

Joe clapped the door shut behind Channing quickly.

"What in hell are you operating, Joe—a speakeasy?"

"The next time you want in," Joe informed him, "knock on 902 twice, 914 once and then here four times. We'll let you in. And now, don't say anything too loud." Joe put a finger to his lips and winked broadly. "Even the walls listen," he said in a stage whisper.

He led Channing into the room and put on the light. There was a flurry of people who tried to hide their glasses under the table. "Never mind," called Joe. "It's only Dr. Channing."

The room relaxed.

"I want something stiff," Channing told Joe. "I've just gone three rounds with His Nibs and come out cold."

Some people within earshot asked about it. Channing explained what had transpired. The people seemed satisfied that Channing had done his best for them. The room relaxed into routine.

The signal knock came on the door and was opened to admit Walt Franks and Arden Westland. Franks looked as though he had been given a stiff workout in a cement mixer.

"Scotch," said Arden. "And a glass of brew for the lady."

"What happened to him?"

"He's been trying to keep to Burbank's latest suggestions."

"You've been working too hard," Channing chided him gently. "This is the wrong time to mention it, I suppose, but did that beam slippage have anything to do with your condition—or was it vice versa?"

"You know that I haven't anything to do with the beam controls personally," said Franks. He straightened up and faced Channing defiantly.

"Don't get mad. What was it?"

"Mastermind, up there, called me in to see if there were some manner or means of tightening the beam. I told him, sure, we could hold the beam to practically nothing. He asked me why we didn't hold the beam to a parallel and save the dispersed power. He claimed that we could reduce power by two to one if more of it came into the station instead of being smeared all over the firmament. I, foolishly, agreed with him. He's right. You could. But only if everything is immobilized. I've been trying to work out some means of controlling the beam magnetically so that it would compensate for the normal variations due to magnetic influences. So far I've failed."

"It can't be done. I know, because I worked on the problem for three years with some of the best brains in the system. To date, it is impossible."

A click attracted their attention. It was the pneumatic tube. A cylinder dropped out of the tube, and Joe opened it and handed the enclosed paper to Franks.

He read:

WALT:
   I'M SENDING THIS TO YOU AT JOE'S BECAUSE I KNOW
THAT IS WHERE YOU ARE AND I THINK YOU SHOULD GET
THIS REAL QUICK.

                                        JEANNE S.

Walt smiled wearily and said, "A good secretary is a thing of beauty. A thing of beauty is admired and is a joy forever. Jeanne is both. She is a jewel."

"Yeah, we know. What does the letter say?"

"It is another communiqué from our doting boss. He is removing from my control the odd three hundred men I've got working on Beam Control. He is to assume the responsibility for them himself. I'm practically out of a job."

"Make that two Scotches," Channing told Joe.

"Make it three," chimed in Arden. "I've got to work for him, too!"

"Is that so bad?" asked Channing. "All you've got to do is to listen carefully and do as you're told. We have to answer to the bird, too."

"Yeah," said Arden, "but you fellows don't have to listen to a dopey guy ask foolish questions all day. It's driving me silly."

"What I'd like to know," murmured Franks, "is what is the idea of pulling me off the job? Nuts, I've been on the Beam Control for years. I've got the finest crew of men anywhere. They can actually foresee a shift and compensate for it, I think. I picked 'em myself and I've been proud of my outfit. Now," he said brokenly, "I've got no outfit. In fact, I have darned little crew left at all. Only my dozen lab members. I'll have to go back to swinging a meter myself before this is over."

It was quite a comedown. From the master of over three hundred highly paid, highly prized, intelligent technicians, Walt Franks was now the superintendent of one dozen laboratory technicians. It was a definite cut in his status.

Channing finished his drink and, seeing that Franks' attention was elsewhere, he told Arden: "Thanks for taking care of him, but don't use all your sympathy on him. I feel that I'm going to need your shoulder to cry on before long."

"Any time you want a soft shoulder," said Arden generously, "let me know. I'll come a-running."

Channing went out. He roamed nervously all the rest of the day. He visited the bar several times, but the general air of the place depressed him. From a place of recreation, laughter and pleasantry, Joe's place had changed to a room for reminiscences and remorse, a place to drown one's troubles—or poison them—or to preserve them in alcohol.

He went to see the local moving picture, a piece advertised as being one of the best mystery thrillers since Hitchcock. He found that all of the interesting parts were cut out and that the only thing that remained was a rather disjointed protrayal of a detective finding meaningless clues and ultimately the criminal. There was a suggestion at the end that the detective and the criminal had fought it out, but whether it was with pistols, field pieces, knives, cream puffs or words was left to the imagination. It was also to be assumed that he and the heroine, who went into a partial blackout every time she sat down, finally got acquainted enough to hold hands after the picture.

Channing stormed out of the theater after seeing it and finding that the only cartoon had been barred because it showed an innocuous cow without benefit of shorts.

He troubled Joe for a bottle of the best and took to his apartment in disappointment. By eight o'clock in the evening Don Channing was asleep with all his clothing on. The bed rolled and refused to stay on an even keel, but Channing found a necktie and tied himself securely in the bed and died off in a beautiful, boiled cloud.

He woke to the tune of a beautiful hangover, gulped seven glasses of water, staggered to the shower. Fifteen lavish minutes of iced needles and some coffee brought him part way back to his own, cheerful self. He headed down the hall toward the elevator.

He found a note in his office directing him to appear at a conference in Burgank's office. Groaning in anguish, Channing went to the Director's office expecting the worst.

It was bad. In fact, it was enough to drive everyone in the conference to drink. Burbank asked opinions on everything, and then tore the opinions apart with little regard to their validity. He expressed his own opinion many times, which was a disgusted sense of the personnel's inability to do anything of real value.

"Certainly," he stormed, "I know you are operating. But have there been any new developments coming out of your laboratory, Mr. Channing?"

Someone was about to tell Burbank that Channing had a doctor's degree, but Don shook his head.

"We've been working on a lot of small items," said Channing. "I cannot say whether there has been any one big thing that we could point to. As we make developments, we put them into service. Added together, they make quite an honest effort."

"What, for instance?" Burbank stormed.

"The last one was the coupler machine improvement that permitted better than ten thousand words per minute."

"Up to that time the best wordage was something like eight thousand words," said Burbank. "I think that you have been resting too long on your laurels. Unless you can bring me something big enough to advertise, I shall have to take measurse. Now *you*, Mr. Warren," continued Burbank. "You are the man who is supposed to be superintendent of maintenance. May I ask why the outer hull is not painted?"

"Because it would be a waste of paint," said Warren. "Figure out the acreage of a surface of a cylinder three miles long and a mile in diameter. It is almost eleven square miles! Eleven square miles to paint from scaffolding hung from the outside itself."

"Use bos'n's chairs," snapped Burbank.

"A bos'n's chair would be worthless," Warren informed Burbank. "You must remember that to anyone trying to operate on the outer hull, the outer hull is a ceiling and directly overhead. Another thing," said Warren, "you paint the hull and you'll run this station by yourself. Why d'ya think we have it shiny?"

"If we paint the hull," persisted Burbank, "it will be more presentable than that nondescript steel color."

"That steel color is as shiny as we could make it," growled Warren. "We want to get rid of as much radiated heat as we can. You slap a coat of any kind of paint on that hull and you'll have plenty of heat in here."

"Ah, that sounds interesting. We'll save heating costs—"

"Don't be an idiot," snapped Warren. "Heating costs, my grandmother's eye. Look, Burbank, did you ever hear of the Uranium Pile? Part of our income comes from refining uranium and plutonium and the preparation of radioisotopes. And— Good Lord, I'm not going to try to explain fission-reacting materials to you; get that first old copy of the Smyth Report and get caught up-to-date.

"The fact remains," continued Warren, cooling somewhat after displaying Burbank's ignorance, "that we have more power than we know what to do with. We're operating on a safe margin by radiating just a little more than we generate. We make up the rest by the old methods of artificial heating.

"But there have been a lot of times when it became necessary to dissipate a lot of energy for diverse reasons and then we've had to shut off the heating. What would happen if we couldn't cool off the damned coffee can? We'd roast to death the first time we got a new employee with a body temperature a degree above normal."

"You're being openly rebellious," Burbank warned him.

"So I am. And if you persist in your attempt to make this place presentable, you'll find me and my gang outright mutinous! Good day, sir!"

He stormed out of the office and slammed the door.

"Take a note, Miss Westland. 'Interplanetary Communications Commission, Terra. Gentlemen: Michael Warren, superintendent of maintenance at Venus Equilateral, has proven to be unreceptive to certain suggestions as to the appearance and/or operation of Venus Equilateral. It is my request that he be replaced immediately. Signed, Francis Burbank, Director.' " He paused to see what effect that message had upon the faces of the men around the table. "Send that by special delivery!"

Johnny Billings opened his mouth to say something, but shut it with a snap. Westland looked up at Burbank, but she said nothing. She gave Channing a sly smile, and Channing smiled back. There were grins about the table, too, for everyone recognized the boner. Burbank had just sent a letter from the interworld-communications relay station by special delivery mail. It would not get to Terra for better than two weeks; a use of the station's facilities would have the message in the hands of the commission within the hour.

"That will be all, gentlemen," Burbank smiled smugly. "Our next conference will be next Monday morning!"

"Mr. Channing," chortled the pleasant voice of Arden Westland, "now that the trifling influence of the boss versus secretary taboo is off, will you have the pleasure of buying me a drink?"

"Can you repeat that word for word and explain it?" grinned Don.

"A man isn't supposed to make eyes at his secretary. A gal ain't supposed to seduce her boss. Now that you are no longer Acting Director and I no longer your stenog, how about some sociability?"

"I never thought that I'd be propositioned by a typewriter jockey," said Channing, "but I'll do it. What time is it? Do we do it openly, or must we sneak over to the apartment and snaffle a snort on the sly?"

"We snaffle. That is, if you trust me in your apartment."

"I'm scared to death," Channing informed her. "But if I should fail to defend my honor, we must remember that it is no dishonor to try and fail."

"That sounds like a nice alibi," said Arden with a smile. "Or a come-on. I don't know which. Or, Mr. Channing, am I being told that my advances might not be welcome?"

"We shall see," Channing said. "We'll have to make a careful study of the matter. I cannot make any statements without first making a thorough examination under all sorts of conditions. Here we are. You will precede me through the door, please."

"Why?" asked Arden.

"So that you cannot back out at the last possible moment. Once I get inside, I'll think about keeping you there!"

"As long as you have some illegal fluid, I'll stay." She tried to leer at Don but failed because she had had all too little experience in leering. "Bring it on!"

"Here's to the good old days," Don toasted as the drinks were raised.

"Nope. Here's to the future," proposed Arden. "Those good old days—all they were was old. If you were back in them, you'd still have to have the pleasure of meeting Burbank."

"*Grrrr,*" growled Channing. "That name is never mentioned in this household."

"You haven't a pix of the old bird turned to the wall, have you?" asked Arden.

"I tossed it out."

"We'll drink to that." They drained glasses. "And we'll have another."

"I need another," said Channing. "Can you imagine that buzzard asking me to invent something big in seven days?"

"Sure. By the same reasoning that he uses to send a letter from Venus Equilateral instead of just slipping it on the Terra beam. Faulty."

"Phoney."

The door opened abruptly and Walt Franks entered. "D'ja hear the latest?" he asked breathlessly.

"No," said Channing.

He was reaching for another glass automatically. He poured, and Walt watched the amber fluid creep up the glass, led by a sheet of white foam.

"Then look!"

Walt handed Channing an official envelope. It was a regular notice to the effect that there had been eleven failures of service through Venus Equilateral.

"Eleven! What makes?"

"Mastermind."

"What's he done?"

"Remember the removal of my jurisdiction over the beam control operators? Well, in the last ten days, Burbank has installed some new features to cut expenses. I think that he hopes to lay off a couple of hundred men."

"What's he doing, do you know?"

"He's shortening the dispersion. He intends to cut the power by slamming more of the widespread beam into the receptor. The tighter beam makes aiming more difficult, you know, because at seventy million miles, every time little Joey of Mars swings his toy horseshoe magnet on the end of his string, the beam wobbles. And at seventy million miles, how much wobbling does it take to send a narrow beam clear off the target?"

"The normal dispersion of the beam from Venus is over a thousand miles wide. It gyrates and wobbles through most of that arc. That is why we picked that particular dispersion. If we could have pointed the thing like an arrow, we'd have kept the dispersion down."

"Right. And he's tightened the beam to less than a hundred miles' dispersion. Now, every time a sunspot gets hit amidships with a lady sunspot, the beam goes off on a tangent. We've lost the beam eleven times in a week. That's more times than I've lost it in three years!"

"O.K.," said Channing. "So what? Mastermind is responsible. We'll sit tight and wait for developments. In any display of abilities, we can spike Mr. Burbank. Have another drink?"

"Got any more? If you've not, I've got a couple of cases cached underneath the bed in my apartment."

"I've plenty," said Channing. "And I'll need plenty. I have exactly twenty-two hours left in which to produce something comparable to the telephone, the electric light, the airplane or the expanding universe! Phooey. Pour me another, Arden."

A knock at the door; a feminine voice interrupted simultaneously. "May I come in?"

It was Walt's secretary. She looked worried. In one hand she waved another letter.

"Another communiqué?" asked Channing.

"Worse. Notice that for the last three hours there have been less than twelve percent of messages relayed!"

"Five minutes' operation out of an hour," said Channing. "Where's that from?"

"Came out on the Terra beam. It's marked number seventeen, so I guess that sixteen other tries have been made."

"What has Mastermind tried this time?" Channing stormed. He tore out of the room and headed for the Director's office on a dead run. On the way, he hit his shoulder on the door, caromed off the opposite wall, righted himself, and was gone in a flurry of flying feet. Three heads popped out of doors to see who was making the noise.

Channing skidded into Burbank's office on his heels. "What gives?" he snapped. "D'ya realize that we've lost the beam? What have you been doing?"

"It is a minor difficulty," said Burbank calmly. "We will iron it out presently."

"Presently! Our charter doesn't permit interruptions of service of that magnitude. I ask again: What are you doing?"

"You, as Electronics Engineer, have no right to question me. I repeat, we shall iron out the difficulty presently."

Channing snorted and tore out of Burbank's office. He headed for the Office of Beam Control, turned the corner on one foot and slammed the door roughly.

"Chuck!" he yelled. "Chuck Thomas! Where are you?"

No answer. Channing left the beam office and headed for the master control panels, out near the airlock end of Venus Equilateral. He found Thomas stewing over a complicated piece of apparatus.

"Chuck, for the love of Michael, what in the devil is going on?"

"Thought you knew," answered Thomas. "Burbank had the crew install photoelectric mosaic banks on the beam controls. He intends to use the photomosaics to keep Venus, Terra and Mars on the beam."

"Great Sniveling Scott! They tried that in the last century and tossed it out three days later. Where's the crew now?"

"Packing for home. They've been laid off!"

"Get 'em back! Put 'em to work. Turn off those darned photomosaics and use the manual again. We've lost every beam we ever had."

A sarcastic voice came in at this point. "For what reason do you interfere with my improvements?" sneered the voice. "Could it be that you are accepting graft from the employees to keep them on the job by preventing the installation of superior equipment?"

Channing turned on his toe and let Burbank have one. It was a neat job, coming up at the right time and connecting sweetly. Burbank went over on his head.

"Get going," Channing snapped at Thomas.

Charles Thomas grinned. It was not Channing's one-ninety that decided him to comply. He left.

Channing shook Burbank's shoulder. He slapped the man's face. Eyes opened, accusing eyes rendered mute by a very sore jaw, tongue and throat.

"Now listen," snapped Channing. "Listen to every word! Mosaic directors are useless. Know why? It is because of the lag. At planetary distances, light takes an appreciable time to reach. Your beam wobbles. Your planet swerves out of line because of intervening factors; varying magnetic fields, even the bending of light due to gravitational fields will shake the beam microscopically. But, Burbank, a microscopic discrepancy is all that is needed to bust things wide open. You've got to have experienced men to operate the beam controls. Men who can think. Men who can, from experience, reason that this fluctuation will not last, but will swing back in a few seconds, or that this type of swerving will increase in magnitude for a half-hour, maintain the status and then return, pass through zero and find the same level on the minus side.

"Since light and centimeter waves are not exactly alike in performance, a field that will serve one may not affect the other as much. Ergo, your photomosaic is useless. The photoelectric mosiac is a brilliant gadget for keeping a plane in a spotlight or for aiming a sixteen-inch gun, but it is worthless for anything over a couple of million miles. So I've called the men back to their stations. And don't try anything foolish again without consulting the men who are paid to think!"

Channing got up and left. As he strode down the stairs to the apartment level, he met many of the men who had been laid off. None of them said a word, but all of them wore bright, knowing smiles.

By Monday morning, however, Burbank was himself again. The rebuff given him by Don Channing had worn off and he was sparkling with ideas. He speared Franks with the glitter in his eyes and said, "If our beams are always on the center, why is it necessary to use multiplex diversity?"

Franks smiled. "You're mistaken," he told Burbank. "They're not always on the button. They vary. Therefore, we use diversity transmission so that if one beam fails momentarily, one of the other beams will bring the signal in. It is analogous to tying five or six ropes onto a hoisted stone. If one breaks, you have the others."

"You have them running all the time, then?"

"Certainly. At several minutes of time lag in transmission, to try and establish a beam failure of a few seconds' duration is utter foolishness."

"And you disperse the beam to a thousand miles wide to keep the beam centered at any variation?" Burbank shot at Channing.

"Not for *any* variation. Make that any *normal* gyration and I'll buy it."

"Then why don't we disperse the beam to two or three

thousand miles and do away with diversity transmission?" asked Burbank triumphantly.

"Ever heard of fading?" asked Channing with a grin. "Your signal comes and goes. Not gyration; it just gets weaker. It fails for want of something to eat, I guess, and takes off after a wandering cosmic ray. At any rate, there are many times per minute that one beam will be right on the nose and yet so weak that our strippers cannot clean it enough to make it usable. Then the diversity system comes in handy. Our coupling detectors automatically select the proper signal channel. It takes the one that is the strongest and subdues the rest within itself."

"Complicated?"

"It was done in the heyday of radio—1935 or so. Your two channels come in to a common detector. Automatic volume-control voltage comes from the single detector and is applied to all channels. This voltage is proper for the strongest channel, but is too high for the ones receiving the weaker signal, blocking them by rendering them insensitive. When the strong channel fades and the weak channel rises, the detector follows down until the two signal channels are equal and then it rises with the stronger channel."

"I see," said Burbank. "Has anything been done about fading?"

"It is like the weather, according to Mark Twain," smiled Channing. " 'Everybody talks about it, but nobody does anything about it.' About all we've learned is that we can cuss it out and it doesn't cuss back."

"I think it should be tried," said Burbank.

"If you'll pardon me, it has been tried. The first installation at Venus Equilateral was made that way. It didn't work, though we used more power than all of our diversity transmitters together. Sorry."

"Have you anything to report?" Burbank asked Channing.

"Nothing. I've been more than busy investigating the trouble we've had in keeping the beams centered."

Burbank said nothing. He was stopped. He hoped that the secret of his failure was not generally known, but he knew at the same time that when three hundred men are aware of something interesting, some of them will see to it that all the others involved will surely know. He looked at the faces of the men around the table and saw suppressed mirth in every one of them. Burbank writhed in inward anger. But he was a good poker player. He didn't show it at all.

He then went on to other problems. He ironed some out,

others he shelved for the time being. Burbank was a good businessman. But like so many other businessmen, Burbank had the firm conviction that if he had the time to spare and at the same time was free of the worries and paperwork of his position, he could step into the laboratory and show the engineers how to make things hum. He was infuriated every time he saw one of the engineering staff sitting with hands behind head, lost in a gazy, unreal land of deep thought. Though he knew better, he was often tempted to raise hell because the man was obviously loafing.

But give him credit. He could handle business angles to perfection. In spite of his tangle over the beam control, he had rebounded excellently and had ironed out all of the complaints that had poured in. Ironed it out to the satisfaction of the injured party as well as the Interplanetary Communications Commission, who were interested in anything that cost money.

He dismissed the conference and went to thinking. And he assumed the same pose that infuriated him in other men under him: hands behind head, feet upon desk.

The moving-picture theater was dark. The hero reached longing arms to the heroine, and there was a sort of magnetic attraction. They approached one another. But the spark misfired. It was blacked out with a nice slide of utter blackness that came from the screen and spread its lightlessness all over the theater. In the ensuing darkness, several osculations resounded that were more personal and more satisfying than the censored clinch. The lights flashed on and several male heads moved back hastily. Female lips smiled happily. Some of them parted in speech.

One of them said: "Why, Mr. Channing!"

"Shut up, Arden," snapped the man. "People will think that I've been kissing you."

"If someone else was taking advantage of the situation," she said, "you got gypped. I thought I was kissing you and I cooked with gas!"

"Did you ever try that before?" asked Channing interestedly.

"Why?" she asked.

"I liked it. I merely wondered, if you'd worked it on other men, what there was about you that kept you single."

"They all died after the first application," she said. "They couldn't take it."

"Let me outta here! I get the implication. I am the first bird that hasn't died, hey?" He yawned luxuriously.

"Company or the hour?" asked Arden.

"Can't be either," he said. "Come on, let's break a bottle of beer open. I'm dry!"

"I've got a slight headache," she told him. "From what, I can't imagine."

"I haven't a headache, but I'm sort of logy."

"What have you been doing?" asked Arden. "Haven't seen you for a couple of days."

"Nothing worth mentioning. Had an idea a couple of days ago and went to work on it."

"Haven't been working overtime or missing breakfast?"

"Nope."

"Then I don't see why you should be ill. I can explain my headache away by attributing it to eyestrain. Since Billyboy came here, and censored the movies to the bone, the darned things flicker like anything. But eyestrain doesn't create an autointoxication. So, my fine fellow, what have you been drinking?"

"Nothing that I haven't been drinking since I first took to my second bottlehood some years ago."

"You wouldn't be suffering from a hangover from that hangover you had a couple of weeks ago?"

"Nope. I swore off. Never again will I try to drink a whole quart of Two Moons in one evening. It got me."

"It had you for a couple of days." Arden laughed. "All to itself."

Don Channing said nothing. He recalled, all too vividly, the rolling of the tummy that ensued after that session with the only fighter that hadn't yet been beaten: Old John Barleycorn.

"How are you coming on with Burbank?" asked Arden. "I haven't heard a rave for—well, ever since Monday morning's conference. Three days without a nasty dig at Our Boss. That's a record."

"Give the devil his due. He's been more than busy placating irate citizens. That last debacle with the beam control gave him a real Moscow winter. His reforms came to a stop whilst he entrenched. But he's been doing an excellent job of squirming out from under. Of course, it has been helped by the fact that even though the service was rotten for a few hours, the customers couldn't rush out to some other agency to get communications with the other planets."

"Sort of: 'Take us, lousy as we are?' "

"That's it."

Channing opened the door to his apartment and Arden went in. Channing following, and then stopped cold.

"Great Jeepers!" he said in an awed tone. "If I didn't know—"

"Why, Don! What's so startling?"

"Have you noticed?" he asked. "It smells like the inside of a chicken coop in here!"

Arden sniffed. "It does sort of remind me of something that died and couldn't get out of its skin." She smiled. "I'll hold my breath. Any sacrifice for a drink."

"That isn't the point. This is purified air. It should be as sweet as a baby's breath."

"Some baby," whistled Arden. "What's baby been drinking?"

"It wasn't cow juice. What I've been trying to put over is that the air doesn't seem to have been changed in here for nine weeks."

Channing went to the ventilator and lit a match. The flame bent over, flickered, and went out.

"Air intake is O.K.," he said. "Maybe it is I. Bring on that bottle, Channing; don't keep the lady waiting."

He yawned again, deeply and jaw-stretchingly. Arden yawned, too, and the thought of both of them stretching their jaws to the breaking-off point made both of them laugh foolishly.

"Arden, I'm going to break one bottle of beer with you, after which I'm going to take you home, kiss you good night and toss you in your own apartment. Then I'm coming back here and I'm going to hit the hay!"

Arden took a long, deep breath. "I'll buy that," she said. "And tonight, it wouldn't take much persuasion to induce me to snooze right here in this chair!"

"Oh, fine," Don cheered. "That would fix me up swell with the neighbors. I'm not going to get shot-gunned into anything like that!"

"Don't be silly," said Arden.

"From the look in your eye," said Channing, "I'd say that you were just about to do that very thing. I was merely trying to dissolve any ideas that you might have."

"Don't bother," she said pettishly. "I haven't any ideas. I'm as free as you are, and I intend to stay that way!"

Channing stood up. "The next thing we know, we'll be fighting," he observed. "Stand up, Arden. Shake."

Arden stood up, shook herself, and then looked at Chan-

ning with a strange light in her eyes. "I feel sort of dizzy,"
she admitted. "And everything irritates me."

She passed a hand over her eyes wearily. Then, with a visible effort, she straightened. She seemed to throw off her momentary ill feeling instantly, and she smiled at Channing, and
was her normal self in less than a minute.

"What is it?" she asked. "Do you feel funny, too?"

"I do!" he said. "I don't want that beer. I want to snooze."

"When Channing would prefer snoozing to boozing he is
sick," she said. "Come on, fellow, take me home."

Slowly they walked down the long hallway. They said
nothing. Arm in arm they went, and when they reached
Arden's door, their good-night kiss lacked enthusiasm. "See
you in the morning," said Don.

Arden looked at him. "That was a little flat. We'll try it
again—tomorrow or next week."

Don Channing's sleep was broken by dreams. He was
warm. His dreams depicted him in a humid, airless chamber,
and he was forced to breathe that same stale air again and
again. He awoke in a hot sweat, weak and feeling—lousy!

He dressed carelessly. He shaved hit-or-miss. His morning
coffee tasted flat and sour. He left the apartment in a bad
mood, and bumped into Arden at the corner of the hall.

"Hello," she said. "I feel rotten. But you have improved.
Or is that passionate breathing just a lack of fresh air!"

"Hell! That's it!" he said.

He snapped up his wristwatch, which was equipped with a
stopwatch hand. He looked about, and finding a man sitting
on a bench, apparently taking it easy while waiting for someone, Channing clicked the sweep hand into gear. He started
to count the man's respiration.

"What gives?" asked Arden. "What's 'It'? Why are you so
excited? Did I say something?"

"You did," said Channing after fifteen seconds. "That
bird's respiration is better than fifty! This whole place is filled
to the gills with carbon dioxide. Come on, Arden, let's get going!"

Channing led the girl by several yards by the time that
they were within sight of the elevator. He waited for her, and
then sent the car upward at a full throttle. Minutes passed,
and they could feel that stomach-rising sensation that comes
when gravity is lessened. Arden clasped her hands over her
middle and hugged. She squirmed and giggled.

"You've been up to the axis before," said Channing. "Take long, deep breaths."

The car came to a stop with a slowing effect. A normal braking stop would have catapulted them against the ceiling.

"Come on," he grinned at her, "here's where we make time!"

Channing looked up at the little flight of stairs that led to the innermost level. He winked at Arden and jumped. He passed up through the opening easily. "Jump," he commanded. "Don't use the stairs."

Arden jumped. She sailed upward, and as she passed through the opening, Channing caught her by one arm and stopped her flight. "At that speed you'd go right on across," he said.

She looked up, and there, about two hundred feet overhead, she could see the opposite wall.

Channing snapped on the lights. They were in a room two hundred feet in diameter and three hundred feet long. "We're at the center of the station," Channing informed her. "Beyond that bulkhead is the air lock. On the other side of the other bulkhead, we have the air plant, the storage spaces and several rooms of machinery. Come on," he said.

He took her by the hand and with a kick he propelled himself along on a long, curving course to the opposite side of the inner cylinder. He gained the opposite bulkhead as well.

"Now, that's what I call traveling," said Arden. "But my tummy goes *whoosh, whoosh* every time we cross the center."

Channing operated a heavy door. They went in through rooms full of machinery and into rooms stacked to the center with boxes; stacked from the wall to the center and then packed with springs. Near the axis of the cylinder, things weighed so little that packing was necessary to keep them from floating around.

"I feel giddy," said Arden.

"High in oxygen," said he. "The CO_2 drops to the bottom, being heavier. Then, too, the air is thinner up here because centrifugal force swings the whole out to the rim. Out there we are so used to 'down' that here, a half-mile above—or to the center, rather—we have trouble in saying, technically, what we mean. Watch!"

He left Arden standing and walked rapidly around the inside of the cylinder. Soon he was standing on the steel plates directly over her head. She looked up, and shook her head.

"I know why," she called, "but it still makes me dizzy. Come down from up there or I'll be sick."

Channing made a neat dive from his position above her head. He did it merely by jumping upward from his place toward her place, apparently hanging head- down from the ceiling. He turned a neat flip-flop in the air and landed easily beside her. Immediately, for both of them, things became right-side-up again.

Channing opened the door to the room marked AIR PLANT. He stepped in, snapped on the lights, and gasped in amazement.

"Hell!" he groaned.

The place was empty. Completely empty. Absolutely and irrevocably vacant. Oh, there was some dirt on the floor and some trash in the corners, and a trail of scratches on the floor to show that the life-giving air plant had been removed, hunk by hunk, out through another door at the far end of the room.

"Whoa, Tillie!" screamed Don. "We've been stabbed! Arden, get on the type and have— No wait a minute until we find out a few more things about this!"

They made record time back to the office level. They found Burbank in his office, leaning back, and talking to someone on the phone.

Channing tried to interrupt, but Burbank removed his nose from the telephone long enough to snarl, "Can't you see I'm busy? Have you no manners or respect?"

Channing, fuming inside, swore inwardly. He sat down with a show of being calm and folded his hands over his abdomen like the famed statue of Buddha. Arden looked at him, and for all the trouble they were in, she couldn't help giggling. Channing, tall, lanky and strong, looked as little as possible like the popular, pudgy figure of the sitting Buddha.

A minute passed.

Burbank hung up the phone.

"Where does Venus Equilateral get its air from?" snapped Burbank.

"That's what I want—"

"Answer me, please. I'm worried."

"So am I. Something—"

"Tell me first, from what source does Venus Equilateral get its fresh air?"

"From the air plant. And that is—"

"There must be more than one," said Burbank thoughtfully.

"There's only one."

"There *must* be more than one. We couldn't live if there weren't," said the Director.

"Wishing won't make it so. There is only one."

"I tell you, there must be another. Why, I went into the one up at the axis day before yesterday and found that instead of a bunch of machinery, running smoothly, purifying air, and sending it out to the various parts of the station, all there was was a veritable jungle of weeds. Those weeds, Mr. Channing, looked as though they must have been put in there years ago. Now, where did the air-purifying machinery go?"

Channing listened to the latter half of Burbank's speech with his chin at half-mast. He looked as though a feather would knock him clear across the office.

"I had some workmen clear the weeds out. I intend to replace the air machinery as soon as I can get some new material sent from Terra."

Channing managed to blink. It was an effort. "You had workmen toss the weeds out . . ." he repeated dully. "The weeds . . ."

There was silence for a minute. Burbank studied the man in the chair as though Channing were a piece of statuary. Channing was just as motionless.

"Channing, man, what ails you—" Burbank began. The sound of Burbank's voice aroused Channing from his shock.

Channing leaped to his feet. He landed on his heels, spun and snapped at Arden: "Get on the type. Have 'em slap as many oxy-drums on the fastest ship they've got! Get 'em here at full throttle. Tell 'em to load up the pilot and crew with gravanol and not to spare the horsepower! Scram!"

Arden gasped. She fled from the office.

"Burbank, what did you think an air plant was?" snapped Channing.

"Why, isn't it some sort of purifying machinery?" asked the wondering Director.

"What better purifying machine is there than a plot of grass!" shouted Channing. "Weeds, grass, flowers, trees, alfalfa, wheat or anything that grows and uses chlorophyll. We breathe oxygen, exhale CO_2. Plants inhale CO_2 and exude oxygen. An air plant means just that. It is a specialized type of Martian sawgrass that is chlorophyll. We breathe oxygen, exhale CO_2. Plants inhaling dead air and revitalizing it. And you've tossed the weeds out!" Channing snorted in anger. "We've spent years getting that plant so that it will grow just right. It got so good that the CO_2 detectors weren't even needed. The balance was so adjusted that they haven't even

been turned on for three of four years. They were just another source of unnecessary expense. Why, save for a
monthly inspection, that room isn't even opened, so efficient
is the Martian sawgrass. We, Burbank, are losing oxygen!"

The Director grew white. "I didn't know," he said.

"Well, you know now. Get on your horse and do something. At least, Burbank, stay out of my way while I do
something."

"You have a free hand," said Burbank. His voice sounded
beaten.

Channing left the office of the Director and headed for the
chem lab. "How much potassium chlorate, nitrate, sulphate,
and other oxygen-bearing compounds have you?" he asked.
"That includes mercuric oxide, spare water, or anything else
that will give us oxygen if broken down."

A ten-minute wait followed until the members of the chem
lab took a hurried inventory.

"Good," said Channing. "Start breaking it down. Collect
all the oxygen you can in containers. This is the business! It
has priority! Anything, no matter how valuable, must be
scrapped if it can facilitate the gathering of oxygen. God
knows, there isn't by half enough—not even a tenth. But try,
anyway."

Channing headed out of the chemistry laboratory and into
the electronics lab. "Jimmie," he shouted, "get a couple of
stone jars and get an electrolysis outfit running. Fling the hydrogen out of a convenient outlet into space and collect the
oxygen. Water, I mean. Use tap water, right out of the faucet."

"Yeah, but—"

"Jimmie, if we don't breathe, what chance have we to go
on drinking? I'll tell you when to stop."

"O.K., Doc," said Jimmie.

"And look. As soon as you get that running, set up a CO_2
indicator and let me know the percentage at the end of each
hour! Get me?"

"I take it that something has happened to the air plant?"

"It isn't functioning," said Channing shortly. He left the
puzzled Jimmie and headed for the beam control room. Jimmie continued to wonder about the air plant. How in the
devil could an air plant cease functioning unless it were—
dead! Jimmie stopped wondering and began to operate on his
electrolysis setup furiously.

Channing found the men in the beam control room worried and ill at ease. The fine coordination that made them ex-

pert in their line was ebbing. The nervous work demanded perfect motor control, excellent perception and a fine power of reasoning. The perceptible lack of oxygen at this high level was taking its toll already.

"Look, fellows, we're in a mess. Until further notice, take five-minute shifts. We've got about thirty hours to go. If the going gets tough, drop it to three-minute shifts. But, fellows, keep those beams centered until you drop!"

"We'll keep 'em going if we have to call our wives up here to run 'em for us," said one man. "What's up?"

"Air plant's sour. Losing oxy. Got a shipload coming out from Terra, be here in thirty hours. But upon you fellows will rest the responsibility of keeping us in touch with the rest of the system. If you fail, we could call for help until hell freezes us all in—and no one would hear us!

"We'll keep 'em rolling," said a little fellow who had to sit on a tall stool to get even with the controls.

Channing looked out of the big, faceted plexiglass dome that covered one entire end of the Venus Equilateral Station. "Here messages go in and out," he mused. "The other end brings us things that take our breath away."

Channing was referring to the big air lock at the other end of the station, three miles away, right through the center.

At the center of the dome, there was a sighting 'scope. It kept Polaris on a marked circle, keeping the station exactly even with the Terrestrial North. About the periphery of the dome, looking out across space, the beam-control operators were sitting, each with a hundred-foot parabolic reflector below his position, outside the dome, and under the rim of the transparent bowl. These reflectors shot the interworld signals across space in tight beams, and the men, half the time anticipating the vagaries of space warp, kept them centered on the proper, shining speck in that field of stars.

Above his head the stars twinkled. Puny man, setting his will against the monstrous void. Puny man, dependent upon atmosphere. " 'Nature abhors a vacuum,' said Spinoza," groaned Channing. "Nuts! If nature abhorred a vacuum, why did she make so much of it!"

Arden Westland entered the apartment without knocking. "I'd give my right arm up to here for a cigarette," she said, marking above the elbow with the other hand.

"Na-hah," said Channing. "Can't burn oxygen."

"I know. I'm tired, I'm cold and I'm ill. Anything you can do for a lady?"

"Not as much as I'd like to do," said Channing. "I can't help much. We ve got most of the place stopped off with the airtight doors. We've been electrolyzing water, baking $KCIO_3$ and everything else we can get oxy out of. I've a crew of men trying to absorb the CO_2 content and we are losing. Of course, I've known all along that we couldn't support the station on the meager supplies we have on hand. But we'll win in the end. Our micro-cosmic world is getting a shot in the arm in a few hours that will reset the balance."

"I don't see why we didn't prepare for this emergency," said Arden.

"This station is well balanced. There are enough people here and enough space to make a little world of our own. We can establish a balance that is pretty darned close to perfect. The imperfections are taken care of by influxes of supplies from the system. Until Burbank upset the balance, we could go on forever, utilizing natural purification of air and water. We grow a few vegetables and have some meat critters to give milk and steak. The energy to operate Venus Equilateral is supplied from the uranium pile. Atomic power, if you please. Why should we burden ourselves with a lot of cubic feet of supplies that would take up room necessary to maintain our balance? We are not in bad shape. We'll live, though we'll all be a bunch of tired, irritable people who yawn in one another's faces."

"And after it is over?"

"We'll establish the balance. Then we'll settle down again. We can take up where we left off," said Don.

"Not quite. Venus Equilateral has been seared by fire. We'll be tougher and less tolerant of outsiders. If we were a closed corporation before, we'll be tighter than a vacuum-packed coffee can afterwards. And the first bird that cracks us will get hissed at."

Three superliners hove into sight at the end of thirty-one hours. They circled the station, signaling by helio. They approached the air lock end of the station and made contact. The air lock was opened and spacesuited figures swarmed over the South End Landing Stage. A stream of big oxygen tanks was brought into the air lock, admitted, and taken to the last bulwark of people huddled on the fourth level.

From one of the ships came a horde of men carrying huge square trays of dirt and green, growing sawgrass.

For six hours, Venus Equilateral was the scene of wild, furious activity. The dead air was blown out of bad areas, and the hissing of oxygen tanks was heard in every room.

Gradually the people left the fourth level and returned to their rightful places. The station rang with laughter once more, and business, stopped short for want of breath, took a deep lungful of fresh air and went back to work.

The superliners left. But not without taking a souvenir. Francis Burbank went with them. His removal notice was on the first ship, and Don Channing's appointment as Director of Venus Equilateral was on the second.

Happily he entered the Director's office once more. He carried with him all the things he had removed just a few short weeks before. This time he was coming to stay.

Arden entered the office behind him. "Home again?" she asked.

"Yep," he grinned at her. "Open file B, will you, and break out a container of my favorite beverage?"

"Sure thing," she said.

There came a shout of glee. "Break out four glasses," she was told from behind. It was Walt Franks and Joe.

Arden proposed the toast. "Here's to a closed corporation," she said.

They drank on that.

She went over beside Don and took his arm. "You see?" she said, looking up into his eyes. "We aren't the same. Things have changed since Burbank came, and went. Haven't they?"

"They have," laughed Channing. "And now that you are my secretary, it is no longer proper for you to shine up to me like that. People will talk."

"What's he raving about?" asked Joe.

Channing answered, "It is considered highly improper for a secretary to make passes at her boss. Think of what people will say; think of his wife and kids."

"You have neither."

"People?" asked Channing innocently.

"No—you ape—the other."

"Maybe so," Don nodded, "but it is still in bad taste for a secretary—"

"No man can use that tone of voice on me!" stormed Arden with a glint in her eye. "I resign! You can't call me a secretary!"

"But Arden, darling—"

Arden relaxed in the crook of Channing's arm. She winked at Walt and Joe. "Me," she said, "I've been promoted!"

THE WEAPONS SHOP

Astounding,

December

by A. E. van Vogt

A. E. van Vogt started what became The Weapons Shop *series with "The Seesaw" and in this novelette gave the science fiction world one of those phrases that achieve instant fame—"The right to buy weapons is the right to be free." The Weapons Shops represent forces operating behind the scenes who periodically attempt to balance and sometimes defeat the powers who are in control in the society in which the action takes place. Here van Vogt (like Heinlein in much of his fiction) is really presenting us with a libertarian answer to the problems of centralized bureaucracy and imperial government. And while this may be a simplistic answer, in this case it is filled with the sense of wonder for which van Vogt is renowned.*

The series appeared in book form as The Weapon Makers *(1946) and* The Weapon Shops of Isher *(1951).*

(I can never hear the phrase, "The right to buy weapons is the right to be free" without wanting to start an argument. I know that liberty is dead if *only* the government can make use of weapons, but that is only true if the governed are also deprived of due process of law. And what of the alternative—when weapons are available to every hood, every nitwit, every self-proclaimed liberator and guerrilla. We see the results everywhere these days when all you have to do is plant a bomb or shoot unarmed people from ambush to be a hero—I. A.)

The village at night made a curiously timeless picture. Fara walked contentedly beside his wife along the street. The air was like wine; and he was thinking dimly of the artist who had come up from Imperial City and made what the telestats called—he remembered the phrase vividly—"a symbolic painting reminiscent of a scene in the electrical age of seven thousand years ago."

Fara believed that utterly. The street before him with its weedless, automatically tended gardens, its shops set well back among the flowers, its perpetual hard, grassy sidewalks and its street lamps that glowed from every pore of their structure—this was a restful paradise where time had stood still.

And it was like being a part of life that the great artist's picture of this quiet, peaceful scene before him was now in the collection of the empress herself. She had praised it, and naturally the thrice-blest artist had immediately and humbly begged her to accept it.

What a joy it must be to be able to offer personal homage to the glorious, the divine, the serenely gracious and lovely Innelda Isher, one thousand one hundred eightieth of her line.

As they walked, Fara half turned to his wife, In the dim light of the nearest street lamp, her kindly, still youthful face was almost lost in shadow. He murmured softly, instinctively muting his voice to harmonize with the pastel shades of night:

"She said—our empress said—that our little village of Glay seemed to her to have in it all the wholesomeness, the gentleness, that constitutes the finest qualities of her people. Wasn't that a wonderful thought, Creel? She must be a marvelously understanding woman. I—"

He stopped. They had come to a side street, and there was something about a hundred and fifty feet along it that—

"Look!" Fara said hoarsely.

He pointed with rigid arm and finger at a sign that glowed in the night, a sign that read:

FINE WEAPONS

**THE RIGHT TO BUY WEAPONS IS THE RIGHT
TO BE FREE**

Fara had a strange, empty feeling as he stared at the blazing sign. He saw that other villagers were gathering. He said finally, huskily, "I've heard of these shops. They're places of infamy, against which the government of the empress will act one of these days. They're built in hidden factories, and then transported whole to towns like ours and set up in gross defiance of property rights. That one wasn't there an hour ago."

Fara's face hardened. His voice had a harsh edge in it, as he said, "Creel, go home."

Fara was surprised when Creel did not move off at once. All their married life she had had a pleasing habit of obedience that had made cohabitation a wonderful thing. He saw that she was looking at him wide-eyed, and that it was a timid alarm that held her there. She said, "Fara, what do you intend to do? You're not thinking of—"

"Go home!" Her fear brought out all the grim determination in his nature. "We're not going to let such a monstrous thing desecrate our village. Think of it"—his voice shivered before the appalling thought—"this fine, old-fashioned community, which we had resolved always to keep exactly as the empress has it in her picture gallery, debauched now, ruined by this . . . this thing— But we won't have it; that's all there is to it."

Creel's voice came softly out of the half-darkness of the street corner, the timidity gone from it: "Don't do anything rash, Fara. Remember it is not the first new building to come into Glay—since the picture was painted."

Fara was silent. This was a quality of his wife of which he did not approve, this reminding him unnecessarily of unpleasant facts. He knew exactly what she meant. The gigantic, multitentacled corporation, Automatic Atomic Motor Repair Shops, Inc., had come in under the laws of the state with their flashy building, against the wishes of the village council—and had already taken half of Fara's repair business.

"That's different!" Fara growled finally. "In the first place people will discover in good time that these new automatic repairers do a poor job. In the second place it's fair competition. But this weapon shop is a defiance of all the decencies that make life under the House of Isher such a joy. Look at the hypocritical sign: 'The right to buy weapons—' Aaaaahh!"

He broke off with: "Go home, Creel. We'll see to it that they sell no weapons in this town."

He watched the slender woman-shape move off into the shadows. She was halfway across the street when a thought occurred to Fara. He called, "And if you see that son of ours hanging around some street corner, take him home. He's got to learn to stop staying out so late at night."

The shadowed figure of his wife did not turn; and after watching her for a moment moving along against the dim background of softly glowing street lights, Fara twisted on his heel, and walked swiftly toward the shop. The crowd was growing larger every minute and the night pulsed with excited voices.

Beyond doubt, here was the biggest thing that had ever happened to the village of Glay.

The sign of the weapon shop was, he saw, a normal-illusion affair. No matter what his angle of view, he was always looking straight at it. When he paused finally in front of the great display window, the words had pressed back against the store front, and were staring unwinkingly down at him.

Fara sniffed once more at the meaning of the slogan, then forgot the simple thing. There was another sign in the window, which read:

THE FINEST ENERGY WEAPONS IN THE KNOWN UNIVERSE

A spark of interest struck fire inside Fara. He gazed at that brilliant display of guns, fascinated in spite of himself. The weapons were of every size, ranging from tiny little finger pistols to express rifles. They were made of every one of the light, hard, ornamental substances: glittering glassein, the colorful but opaque Ordine plastic, viridescent magnesitic beryllium. And others.

It was the very deadly extent of the destructive display that brought a chill to Fara. So many weapons for the little village of Glay, where not more than two people to his knowledge had guns, and those only for hunting. Why, the thing was absurd, fantastically mischievous, utterly threatening.

Somewhere behind Fara, a man said: "It's right on Lan Harris' lot. Good joke on that old scoundrel. Will he raise a row!"

There was a faint titter from several men, that made an odd patch of sound on the warm, fresh air. And Fara saw that the man had spoken the truth. The weapon shop had a forty-foot frontage. And it occupied the very center of the green, gardenlike lot of tight-fisted old Harris.

Fara frowned. The clever devils, the weapon-shop people, selecting the property of the most disliked man in town, coolly taking it over and giving everybody an agreeable titillation. But the very cunning of it made it vital that the trick shouldn't succeed.

He was still scowling anxiously when he saw the plump figure of Mel Dale, the mayor. Fara edged toward him hurriedly, touched his hat respectfully, and said, "Where's Jor?"

"Here." The village constable elbowed his way through a little bundle of men. "Any plans?" he said.

"There's only one plan," said Fara boldly. "Go in and arrest them."

To Fara's amazement, the two men looked at each other, then at the ground. It was the big constable who answered shortly, "Door's locked. And nobody answers our pounding. I was just going to suggest we let the matter ride until morning."

"Nonsense!" His very astonishment made Fara impatient. "Get an ax and we'll break the door down. Delay will only encourage such riffraff to resist. We don't want their kind in our village for so much as a single night. Isn't that so?"

There was a hasty nod of agreement from everybody in his immediate vicinity. Too hasty. Fara looked around puzzled at eyes that lowered before his level gaze. He thought: "They are all scared. And unwilling." Before he could speak, Constable Jor said, "I guess you haven't heard about those doors or these shops. From all accounts, you can't break into them."

It struck Fara with a sudden pang that it was he who would have to act here. He said, "I'll get my atomic cutting machine from my shop. That'll fix them. Have I your permission to do that, Mr. Mayor?"

In the glow of the weapon-shop window, the plump man was sweating visibly. He pulled out a handkerchief and wiped his forehead. He said, "Maybe I'd better call the commander of the Imperial garrison at Ferd, and ask them."

"No!" Fara recognized evasion when he saw it. He felt himself steel; the conviction came that all the strength in this village was in him. "We must act ourselves. Other communities have let these people get in because they took no decisive action. We've got to resist to the limit. Beginning now. This minute. Well?"

The mayor's "All right!" was scarcely more than a sigh of sound. But it was all Fara needed.

He called out his intention to the crowd; and then, as he pushed his way out of the mob, he saw his son standing with some other young men staring at the window display.

Fara called, "Cayle, come and help me with the machine."

Cayle did not even turn; and Fara hurried on, seething. That wretched boy! One of these days he, Fara, would have to take firm action there. Or he'd have a no-good on his hands.

The energy was soundless—and smooth. There was no sputter, no fireworks. It glowed with a soft, pure white light, almost caressing the metal panels of the door—but not even beginning to sear them.

Minute after minute, the dogged Fara refused to believe the incredible failure, and played the boundlessly potent energy on that resisting wall. When he finally shut off his machine, he was perspiring freely.

"I don't understand it," he gasped. "Why—no metal is supposed to stand up against a steady flood of atomic force. Even the hard metal plates used inside the blast chamber of a motor take the explosions in what is called infinite series, so that each one has unlimited rest. That's the theory, but actually steady running crystallizes the whole plate after a few months."

"It's as Jor told you," said the mayor. "These weapon shops are—big. They spread right through the empire, *and* they *don't recognize the empress.*"

Fara shifted his feet on the hard grass, disturbed. He didn't like this kind of talk. It sounded—sacrilegious. And besides it was nonsense. It must be. Before he could speak, a man said somewhere behind him, "I've heard it said that that door will open only to those who cannot harm the people inside."

The words shocked Fara out of his daze. With a start, and for the first time, he saw that his failure had had a bad psychological effect. He said sharply, "That's ridiculous! If there were doors like that, we'd all have them. We—"

The thought that stopped his words was the sudden realization that *he* had not seen anybody try to open the door; and

with all this reluctance around him it was quite possible
that—

He stepped forward, grasped at the doorknob and pulled.
The door opened with an unnatural weightlessness that gave
him the fleeting impression that the knob had come loose in
his hand. With a gasp, Fara jerked the door wide open.

"Jor!" he yelled. "Get in!"

The constable made a distorted movement—distorted by
what must have been a will to caution, followed by the instant realization that he could not hold back before so many.
He leaped awkwardly toward the open door—and it closed in
his face.

Fara stared stupidly at his hand, which was still clenched.
And then, slowly, a hideous thrill coursed along his nerves.
The knob had—withdrawn. It had twisted, become viscous
and slipped amorphously from his straining fingers. Even the
memory of that brief sensation gave him a feeling of abnormal things.

He grew aware that the crowd was watching with a silent
intentness. Fara reached again for the knob, not quite so eagerly this time; and it was only a sudden realization of his reluctance that made him angry when the handle neither turned
nor yielded in any way.

Determination returned in full force, and with it came a
thought. He motioned to the constable. "Go back, Jor, while
I pull."

The man retreated, but it did no good. And tugging did
not help. The door would not open. Somewhere in the crowd,
a man said darkly, "It decided to let you in, then it changed
its mind."

"What foolishness are you talking!" Fara spoke violently.
"*It* changed its mind. Are you crazy? A door has no sense."

But a surge of fear put a half-quaver into his voice. It was
the sudden alarm that made him bold beyond all his normal
caution. With a jerk of his body, Fara faced the shop.

The building loomed there under the night sky, in itself
bright as day, huge in width and length, and alien, menacing,
no longer easily conquerable. The dim queasy wonder came
as to what the soldiers of the empress would do if they were
invited to act. And suddenly—a bare, flashing glimpse of a
grim possibility—the feeling grew that even they would be
able to do nothing.

Abruptly, Fara was conscious of horror that such an idea

could enter his mind. He shut his brain tight, said wildly, "The door opened for me once. It will open again."

It did. Quite simply it did. Gently, without resistance, with that same sensation of weightlessness, the strange, sensitive door followed the tug of his fingers. Beyond the threshold was dimness, a wide, darkened alcove. He heard the voice of Mel Dale behind him, the mayor saying, "Fara, don't be a fool. What will you do inside?"

Fara was vaguely amazed to realize that he had stepped across the threshold. He turned, startled, and stared at the blur of faces "Why—" he began blankly; then he brightened; he said, "Why, I'll buy a gun, of course."

The brilliance of his reply, the cunning implicit in it, dazzled Fara for half a minute longer. The mood yielded slowly, as he found himself in the dimly lighted interior of the weapon shop.

It was preternaturally quiet inside. Not a sound penetrated from the night from which he had come, and the startled thought came that the people of the shop might actually be unaware that there was a crowd outside.

Fara walked forward gingerly on a rugged floor that muffled his footsteps utterly. After a moment, his eyes accustomed themselves to the soft lighting, which came like a reflection from the walls and ceilings. In a vague way, he had expected ultranormality; and the ordinariness of the atomic lighting acted like a tonic to her tensed nerves.

He shook himself angrily. Why should there be anything really superior? He was getting as bad as those credulous idiots out in the street.

He glanced around with gathering confidence. The place looked quite common. It was a shop, almost scantily furnished. There were showcases on the walls and on the floor, glitteringly lovely things, but nothing unusual, and not many of them—a few dozens. There was in addition a double, ornate door leading to a back room—

Fara tried to keep one eye on that door, as he examined several showcases, each with three or four weapons either mounted or arranged in boxes or holsters.

Abruptly, the weapons began to excite him. He forgot to watch the door, as the wild thought struck that he ought to grab one of those guns from a case, and then the moment someone came, force him outside where Jor would perform the arrest and—

Behind him, a man said quietly, "You wish to buy a gun?"

Fara turned with a jump. Brief rage flooded him at the way his plan had been wrecked by the arrival of the clerk.

The anger died as he saw that the intruder was a fine-looking, silver-haired man, older than himself. That was immeasurably disconcerting. Fara had an immense and almost automatic respect for age, and for a long second he could only stand there gaping. He said at last, lamely, "Yes, yes, a gun."

"For what purpose?" said the man in his quiet voice.

Fara could only look at him blankly. It was too fast. He wanted to get mad. He wanted to tell these people what he thought of them. But the age of this representative locked his tongue, tangled his emotions. He managed speech only by an effort of will:

"For hunting." The plausible word stiffened his mind. "Yes, definitely for hunting. There is a lake to the north of here," he went on more fulsomely, glibly, "and—"

He stopped, scowling, startled at the extent of his dishonesty. He was not prepared to go so deeply into prevarication. He said curtly, "For hunting."

Fara was himself again. Abruptly, he hated the man for having put him so completely at a disadvantage. With smoldering eyes he watched the old fellow click open a showcase, and take out a green-shining rifle.

As the man faced him, weapon in hand, Fara was thinking grimly, "Pretty clever, having an old man as a front." It was the same kind of cunning that had made them choose the property of Miser Harris. Icily furious, taut with his purpose, Fara reached for the gun; but the man held it out of his reach, saying, "Before I can even let you test this, I am compelled by the by-laws of the weapon shops to inform you under what circumstances you may purchase a gun."

So they had private regulations. What a system of psychology tricks to impress gullible fools! Well, let the old scoundrel talk. As soon as he, Fara, got hold of the rifle, he'd put an end to hypocrisy.

"We weapons makers," the clerk was saying mildly, "have evolved guns that can, in their particular ranges, destroy any machine or object made of what is called matter. Thus whoever possesses one of our weapons is the equal and more of any soldier of the empress. I say more because each gun is the center of a field of force which acts as a perfect screen against immaterial destructive forces. That screen offers no resistance to clubs or spears or bullets, or other material substances, but it would require a small atomic cannon to penetrate the superb barrier it creates around its owner.

"You will readily comprehend," the man went on, "that such a potent weapon could not be allowed to fall, unmodified, into irresponsible hands. Accordingly, no gun purchased from us may be used for aggression or murder. In the case of the hunting rifle, only such specified game birds and animals as we may from time to time list in our display windows may be shot. Finally, no weapon can be resold without our approval. Is that clear?"

Fara nodded dumbly. For the moment, speech was impossible to him. The incredible, fantastically stupid words were still going round and around in his head. He wondered if he ought to laugh out loud, or curse the man for daring to insult his intelligence so tremendously.

So the gun mustn't be used for murder or robbery. So only certain birds and animals could be shot. And as for reselling it, suppose—suppose he bought this thing, took a trip of a thousand miles, and offered it to some wealthy stranger for two credits—who would ever know?

Or suppose he held up the stranger. Or shot him. How could the weapon shop ever find out? The thing was so ridiculous that—

He grew aware that the gun was being held out to him stock first. He took it eagerly, and had to fight the impulse to turn the muzzle directly on the old man. Mustn't rush this, he thought tautly. He said, "How does it work?"

"You simply aim it, and pull the trigger. Perhaps you would like to try it on a target we have."

Fara swung the gun up. "Yes," he said triumphantly, "and you're it. Now, just get over there to the front door, and then outside."

He raised his voice: "And if anybody's thinking of coming through the back door, I've got that covered, too."

He motioned jerkily at the clerk. "Quick now, move! I'll shoot! I swear I will."

The man was cool, unflustered. "I have no doubt you would. When we decided to attune the door so that you could enter despite your hostility, we assumed the capacity for homicide. However, this is our party. You had better adjust yourself accordingly, and look behind you—"

There was silence. Finger on trigger, Fara stood motionless. Dim thoughts came of all the *half-things* he had heard in his days about the weapon shops: that they had secret supporters in every district, that they had a private and ruthless hidden government, and that once you got into their clutches, the only way out was death and—

But what finally came clear was a mind picture of himself, Fara Clark, family man, faithful subject of the empress, standing here in this dimly lighted store, deliberately fighting an organization so vast and menacing that— He must have been mad.

Only—here he was. He forced courage into his sagging muscles. He said, "You can't fool me with pretending there's someone behind me. Now, get to that door. And *fast!*"

The firm eyes of the old man were looking past him. The man said quietly, "Well, Rad, have you all the data?"

"Enough for a primary," said a young man's baritone voice behind Fara. "Type A-7 conservative. Good average intelligence, but a Monaric development peculiar to small towns. One-sided outlook fostered by the Imperial schools present in exaggerated form. Extremely honest. Reason would be useless. Emotional approach would require extended treatment. I see no reason why we should bother. Let him live his life as it suits him."

"If you think," Fara said shakily, "that that trick voice is going to make me turn, you're crazy. That's the left wall of the building. I know there's no one there."

"I'm all in favor, Rad," said the old man, "of letting him live his life. But he was the prime mover of the crowd outside. I think he should be discouraged."

"We'll advertise his presence," said Rad. "He'll spend the rest of his life denying the charge."

Fara's confidence in the gun had faded so far that, as he listened in puzzled uneasiness to the incomprehensible conversation, he forgot it completely. He parted his lips, but before he could speak, the old man cut in, persistently, "I think a little emotion might have a long-run effect. Show him the palace."

Palace! The startling word tore Fara out of his brief paralysis. "See here," he began, "I can see now that you lied to me. This gun isn't loaded at all. It's—"

His voice failed him. Every muscle in his body went rigid. He stared like a madman. *There was no gun in his hands.*

"Why, you—" he began wildly. And stopped again. His mind heaved with imbalance. With a terrible effort he fought off the spinning sensation, thought finally, tremblingly: Somebody must have sneaked the gun from him. That meant—there was someone behind him. The voice was no mechanical thing. Somehow, they had—

He started to turn—and couldn't. What in the name of—He struggled, pushing with his muscles. And couldn't move, couldn't budge, couldn't even—

The room was growing curiously dark. He had difficulty seeing the old man and— He would have shrieked then if he could. Because the weapon shop was gone. He was—

He was standing in the sky above an immense city.

In the sky, and nothing beneath him, nothing around him but air, and blue summer heaven, and the city a mile, two miles below.

Nothing, nothing— He would have shrieked, but his breath seemed solidly embedded in his lungs. Sanity came back as the remote awareness impinged upon his terrified mind that he was actually standing on a hard floor, and that the city must be a picture somehow focused directly into his eyes.

For the first time, with a start, Fara recognized the metropolis below. It was the city of dreams, Imperial City, capital of the glorious Empress Isher— From his great height, he could see the gardens, the gorgeous grounds of the silver palace, the official Imperial residence itself—

The last tendrils of his fear were fading now before a gathering fascination and wonder; they vanished utterly as he recognized with a ghastly thrill of uncertain expectancy that the palace was drawing nearer at great speed.

"Show him the palace," they had said. Did that mean, could it mean—

That spray of tense thoughts splattered into nonexistence, as the glittering roof flashed straight at his face. He gulped, as the solid metal of it passed through him, and then other walls and ceilings.

His first sense of imminent and mind-shaking desecration came as the picture paused in a great room where a score of men sat around a table at the head of which sat—a young woman.

The inexorable, sacrilegious, limitlessly powered cameras that were taking the picture swung across the table, and caught the woman full face.

It was a handsome face, but there was passion and fury twisting it now, and a very blaze of fire in her eyes, as she leaned forward, and said in a voice at once familiar—how often Fara had heard its calm, measured tones on the telestats—and distorted. Utterly distorted by anger and an insolent certainty of command. That caricature of a beloved voice slashed across the silence as clearly as if he, Fara, was there in that room: "I want that skunk killed, do you understand? I don't care how you do it, but I want to hear by tomorrow night that he's dead."

The picture snapped off and instantly—it was as swift as that—Fara was back in the weapon shop. He stood for a moment, swaying, fighting to accustom his eyes to the dimness; and then—

His first emotion was contempt at the simpleness of the trickery—a motion picture. What kind of a fool did they think he was, to swallow something as transparently unreal as that? He'd—

Abruptly, the appalling lechery of the scheme, the indescribable wickedness of what was being attempted here brought red rage.

"Why, you scum!" he flared. "So you've got somebody to act the part of the empress, trying to pretend that— Why, you—"

"That will do," said the voice of Rad; and Fara shook as a big young man walked into his line of vision. The alarmed thought came that people who would besmirch so vilely the character of her imperial majesty would not hesitate to do physical damage to Fara Clark. The young man went on in a steely tone, "We do not pretend that what you saw was taking place this instant in the palace. That would be too much of a coincidence. But it was taken two weeks ago; the woman *is* the empress. The man whose death she ordered is one of her many former lovers. He was found murdered two weeks ago; his name, if you care to look it up in the new files, is Banton McCreddie. However, let that pass. We're finished with you now and—"

"But I'm not finished," Fara said in a thick voice. "I've never heard or seen so much infamy in all my life. If you think this town is through with you, you're crazy. We'll have a guard on this place day and night, and nobody will get in or out. We'll—"

"That will do." It was the silver-haired man; and Fara stopped out of respect for age, before he thought. The old man went on: "The examination has been most interesting. As an honest man, you may call on us if you are ever in trouble. That is all. Leave through the side door."

It was all. Impalpable forces grabbed him, and he was shoved at a door that appeared miraculously in the wall, where seconds before the palace had been.

He found himself standing dazedly in a flower bed, and there was a swarm of men to his left. He recognized his fellow townsmen and that he was—outside.

The incredible nightmare was over.

"Where's the gun?" said Creel, as he entered the house half an hour later.

"The gun?" Fara stared at his wife.

"It said over the radio a few minutes ago that you were the first customer of the new weapon shop. I thought it was queer, but—"

He was eerily conscious of her voice going on for several words longer, but it was the purest jumble. The shock was so great that he had the horrible sensation of being on the edge of an abyss.

So that was what the young man had meant: "Advertise! We'll advertise his presence and—"

Fara thought: His reputation! Not that his was a great name, but he had long believed with a quiet pride that Fara Clark's motor repair shop was widely known in the community and countryside.

First, his private humiliation inside the shop. And now this—lying—to people who didn't know why he had gone into the store. Diabolical.

His paralysis ended, as a frantic determination to rectify the base charge drove him to the telestat. After a moment, the plump, sleepy face of Mayor Mel Dale appeared on the plate. Fara's voice made a barrage of sound, but his hopes dashed, as the man said, "I'm sorry, Fara. I don't see how you can have free time on the telestat. You'll have to pay for it. They did."

"They did!" Fara wondered vaguely if he sounded as empty as he felt.

"And they've just paid Lan Harris for his lot. The old man asked top price, and got it. He just phoned me to transfer the title."

"Oh!" The world was shattering. "You mean nobody's going to do anything. What about the Imperial garrison at Ferd?"

Dimly, Fara was aware of the mayor mumbling something

about the empress' soldiers refusing to interfere in civilian matters.

"Civilian matters!" Fara exploded. "You mean these people are just going to be allowed to come here whether we want them or not, illegally forcing the sale of lots by first taking possession of them?"

A sudden thought struck him breathless. "Look, you haven't changed your mind about having Jor keep guard in front of the shop?"

With a start, he saw that the plump face in the telestat plate had grown impatient. "Now, see here, Fara," came the pompous words, "let the constituted authorities handle this matter."

"But you're going to keep Jor there," Fara said doggedly.

The mayor looked annoyed, said finally peevishly: "I promised, didn't I? So he'll be there. And now—do you want to buy time on the telestat? It's fifteen credits for one minute. Mind you, as a friend, I think you're wasting your money. No one has ever caught up with a false statement."

Fara said grimly, "Put two on, one in the morning, one in the evening."

"All right. We'll deny it completely. Good night."

The telestat went blank; and Fara sat there. A new thought hardened his face. "That boy of ours—there's going to be a showdown. He either works in my shop, or he gets no more allowance."

Creel said: "You've handled him wrong. He's twenty-three and you treat him like a child. Remember, at twenty-three you were a married man."

"That was different," said Fara. "I had a sense of responsibility. Do you know what he did tonight?"

He didn't quite catch her answer. For the moment, he thought she said, "No; in what way did you humiliate him first?"

Fara felt too impatient to verify the impossible words. He rushed on: "He refused in front of the whole village to give me help. He's a bad one, all bad."

"Yes," said Creel in a bitter tone, "he is all bad. I'm sure you don't realize how bad. He's as cold as steel, but without steel's strength or integrity. He took a long time, but he hates even me now, because I stood up for your side so long, knowing you were wrong."

"What's that?" said Fara, startled; then gruffly: "Come, come, my dear, we're both upset. Let's go to bed."

He slept poorly.

There were days then when the conviction that this was a personal fight between himself and the weapon shop lay heavily on Fara. Grimly, though it was out of his way, he made a point of walking past the weapon shop, always pausing to speak to Constable Jor and—

On the fourth day, the policeman wasn't there.

Fara waited patiently at first, then angrily: then he walked hastily to his shop, and called Jor's house. No, Jor wasn't home. He was guarding the weapon store.

Fara hesitated. His own shop was piled with work, and he had a guilty sense of having neglected his customers for the first time in his life. It would be simple to call up the mayor and report Jor's dereliction. And yet—

He didn't want to get the man into trouble—

Out in the street, he saw that a large crowd was gathering in front of the weapon shop. Fara hurried. A man he knew greeted him excitedly: "Jor's been murdered, Fara!"

"Murdered!" Fara stood stock-still, and at first he was not clearly conscious of the grisly thought that was in his mind: Satisfaction! A flaming satisfaction. Now, he thought, even the soldiers would have to act. They—

With a gasp, he realized the ghastly tenor of his thoughts. He shivered, but finally pushed the sense of shame out of his mind. He said slowly, "Where's the body?"

"Inside."

"You mean, those . . . scum—" In spite of himself, he hesitated over the epithet; even now, it was difficult to think of the fine-faced, silver-haired old man in such terms. Abruptly, his mind hardened; he flared: "You mean those scum actually killed him, then pulled his body inside?"

"Nobody saw the killing," said a second man beside Fara, "but he's gone, hasn't been seen for three hours. The mayor got the weapon shop on the telestat, but they claim they don't know anything. They've done away with him, that's what, and now they're pretending innocence. Well, they won't get out of it as easily as that. Mayor's gone to phone the soldiers at Ferd to bring up some big guns and—"

Something of the intense excitement that was in the crowd surged through Fara, the feeling of big things brewing. It was the most delicious sensation that had ever tingled along his nerves, and it was all mixed with a strange pride that he had been so right about this, that he at least had never doubted that here was evil.

He did not recognize the emotion as the full-flowering joy that comes to a member of a mob. But his voice shook, as he said, "Guns? Yes, that will be the answer, and the soldiers will have to come, of course."

Fara nodded to himself in the immensity of his certainty that the Imperial soldiers would now have no excuse for not acting. He started to say something dark about what the empress would do if she found out that a man had lost his life because the soldiers had shirked their duty, but the words were drowned in a shout:

"Here comes the mayor! Hey, Mr. Mayor, when are the atomic cannons due?"

There was more of the same general meaning, as the mayor's sleek, all-purpose car landed lightly. Some of the questions must have reached his honor, for he stood up in the open two-seater and held up his hand for silence.

To Fara's astonishment, the plump-faced man looked at him with accusing eyes. The thing seemed so impossible that, quite instinctively, Fara looked behind him. But he was almost alone; everybody else had crowded forward.

Fara shook his head, puzzled by that glare; and then, astoundingly, Mayor Dale pointed a finger at him, and said in a voice that trembled, "There's the man who's responsible for the trouble that's come upon us. Stand forward, Fara Clark, and show yourself. You've cost this town seven hundred credits that we could ill afford to spend."

Fara couldn't have moved or spoken to save his life. He just stood there in a maze of dumb bewilderment. Before he could even think, the mayor went on, and there was quivering self-pity in his tone, "We've all known that it wasn't wise to interfere with these weapon shops. So long as the Imperial government leaves them alone, what right have we to set up guards, or act against them? That's what I've thought from the beginning, but this man . . . this . . . this Fara Clark kept after all of us, forcing us to move against our wills, and so now we've got a seven-hundred-credit bill to meet and—"

He broke off with, "I might as well make it brief. When I called the garrison, the commander just laughed and said that Jor would turn up. And I had barely disconnected when there was a money call from Jor. He's on Mars."

He waited for the shouts of amazement to die down. "It'll

take three weeks for him to come back by ship, and we've got to pay for it, and Fara Clark is responsible. He—"

The shock was over. Fara stood cold, his mind hard. He said finally, scathingly, "So you're giving up and trying to blame me all in one breath. I say you're all fools."

As he turned away, he heard Mayor Dale saying something about the situation not being completely lost, as he had learned that the weapon shop had been set up in Glay because the village was equidistant from four cities, and that it was the city business the shop was after. This would mean tourists, and accessary trade for the village stores and—

Fara heard no more. Head high, he walked back toward his shop. There were one or two catcalls from the mob, but he ignored them.

He had no sense of approaching disaster, simply a gathering fury against the weapon shop, which had brought him to this miserable status among his neighbors.

The worst of it, as the days passed, was the realization that the people of the weapon shop had no personal interest in him. They were remote, superior, undefeatable. That unconquerableness was a dim, suppressed awareness inside Fara.

When he thought of it, he felt a vague fear at the way they had transferred Jor to Mars in a period of less than three hours, when all the world knew that the trip by fastest spaceship required nearly three weeks.

Fara did not go to the express station to see Jor arrive home. He had heard that the council had decided to charge Jor with half of the expense of the trip, on the threat of losing his job if he made a fuss.

On the second night after Jor's return, Fara slipped down to the constable's house, and handed the officer one hundred seventy-five credits. It wasn't that he was responsible, he told Jor, but—

The man was only too eager to grant the disclaimer, provided the money went with it. Fara returned home with a clearer conscience.

It was on the third day after that the door of his shop banged open and a man came in. Fara frowned as he saw who it was: Castler, a village hanger-on. The man was grinning.

"Thought you might be interested, Fara. Somebody came out of the weapon shop today."

Fara strained deliberately at the connecting bolt of a hard

plate of the atomic motor he was fixing. He waited with a gathering annoyance that the man did not volunteer further information. Asking questions would be a form of recognition of the worthless fellow. A developing curiosity made him say finally, grudgingly, "I suppose the constable promptly picked him up."

He supposed nothing of the kind, but it was an opening.

"It wasn't a man. It was a girl."

Fara knitted his brows. He didn't like the idea of making trouble for women. But—the cunning devils! Using a girl, just as they had used an old man as a clerk. It was a trick that deserved to fail, the girl probably a tough one who needed rough treatment. Fara said harshly, "Well, what's happened?"

"She's still out, bold as you please. Pretty thing, too."

The bolt off, Fara took the hard plate over to the polisher, and began patiently the long, careful task of smoothing away the crystals that heat had seared on the once shining metal. The soft throb of the polisher made the background to his next words:

"Has anything been done?"

"Nope. The constable's been told, but he says he doesn't fancy being away from his family for another three weeks, and paying the cost into the bargain."

Fara contemplated that darkly for a minute, as the polisher throbbed on. His voice shook with suppressed fury, when he said finally, "So they're letting them get away with it. It's all been as clever as hell. Can't they see that they musn't give an inch before these . . . these transgressors. It's like giving countenance to sin."

From the corner of his eye, he noticed that there was a curious grin on the face of the other. It struck Fara suddenly that the man was enjoying his anger. And there was something else in that grin; something—a secret knowledge.

Fara pulled the engine plate away from the polisher. He faced the ne'er-do-well, scathed at him, "Naturally, that sin part wouldn't worry you much."

"Oh," said the man nonchalantly, "the hard knocks of life make people tolerant. For instance, after you know the girl better, you yourself will probably come to realize that there's good in all of us."

It was not so much the words, as the curious I've-got-secret-information tone that made Fara snap: "What do you mean—if I get to know the girl better! I won't even speak to the brazen creature."

"One can't always choose," the other said with enormous casualness. "Suppose he brings her home."

"Suppose who brings who home?" Fara spoke irritably. "Castler, you—"

He stopped; a dead weight of dismay plumped into his stomach; his whole being sagged. "You mean—" he said.

"I mean," replied Castler with a triumphant leer, "that the boys aren't letting a beauty like her be lonesome. And, naturally, your son was the first to speak to her."

He finished: "They're walkin' together now on Second Avenue, comin' this way, so—"

"Get out of here!" Fara roared. "And stay away from me with your gloating. Get out!"

The man hadn't expected such an ignominious ending. He flushed scarlet, then went out, slamming the door.

Fara stood for a moment, every muscle stiff; then, with an abrupt, jerky movement, he shut off his power, and went out into the street.

The time to put a stop to that kind of thing was—now!

He had no clear plan, just that violent determination to put an immediate end to an impossible situation. And it was all mixed up with his anger against Cayle. How could he have had such a worthless son, he who paid his debts and worked hard, and tried to be decent and to live up to the highest standards of the empress?

A brief, dark thought came to Fara that maybe there was some bad blood on Creel's side. Not from her mother, of course—Fara added the mental thought hastily. *There* was a fine, hard-working woman, who hung on to her money, and who would leave Creel a tidy sum one of these days.

But Creel's father had disappeared when Creel was only a child, and there had been some vague scandal about his having taken up with a telestat actress.

And now Cayle with this weapon-shop girl. A girl who had let herself be picked up—

He saw them, as he turned the corner onto Second Avenue. They were walking a hundred feet distant, and heading away from Fara. The girl was tall and slender, almost as big as Cayle, and, as Fara came up, she was saying, "You have the wrong idea about us. A person like you can't get a job in our organization. You belong in the Imperial Service, where they can use young men of good education, good appearance and no scruples. I—"

Fara grasped only dimly that Cayle must have been trying to get a job with these people. It was not clear; and his own mind was too intent on his purpose for it to mean anything at the moment. He said harshly, "Cayle!"

The couple turned, Cayle with the measured unhurriedness of a young man who has gone a long way on the road to steellike nerves; the girl was quicker, but withal dignified.

Fara had a vague, terrified feeling that his anger was too great, self-destroying, but the very violence of his emotions ended that thought even as it came. He said thickly, "Cayle, get home—at once."

Fara was aware of the girl looking at him curiously from strange, gray-green eyes. No shame, he thought, and his rage mounted several degrees, driving away the alarm that came at the sight of the flush that crept into Cayle's cheeks.

The flush faded into a pale, tight-lipped anger, Cayle half-turned to the girl, said, "This is the childish old fool I've got to put up with. Fortunately, we seldom see each other; we don't even eat together. What do you think of him?"

The girl smiled impersonally. "Oh, we know Fara Clark; he's the backbone of the empress in Glay."

"Yes," the boy sneered. "You ought to hear him. He thinks we're living in heaven; and the empress is the divine power. The worst part of it is that there's no chance of his ever getting that stuffy look wiped off his face."

They walked off; and Fara stood there. The very extent of what had happened had drained anger from him as if it had never been. There was the realization that he had made a mistake so great that—

He couldn't grasp it. For long, long now, since Cayle had refused to work in his shop, he had felt this building up to a climax. Suddenly, his own uncontrollable ferocity stood revealed as a partial product of that—deeper—problem.

Only, now that the smash was here, he didn't want to face it—

All through the day in his shop, he kept pushing it out of his mind, kept thinking, would this go on now, as before, Cayle and he living in the same house, not even looking at each other when they met, going to bed at different times, getting up, Fara at 6:30, Cayle at noon? Would *that* go on through all the days and years to come?

When he arrived home, Creel was waiting for him. She

said, "Fara, he wants you to loan him five hundred credits, so that he can go to Imperial City."

Fara nodded wordlessly. He brought the money back to the house the next morning, and gave it to Creel, who took it into the bedroom.

She came out a minute later. "He says to tell you good-bye."

When Fara came home that evening, Cayle was gone. He wondered whether he ought to feel relieved or—what?

The days passed. Fara worked. He had nothing else to do, and the gray thought was often in his mind that now he would be doing it till the day he died. Except—

Fool that he was—he told himself a thousand times how big a fool—he kept hoping that Cayle would walk into the shop and say, "Father, I've learned my lesson. If you can ever forgive me, teach me the business, and then you retire to a well-earned rest."

It was exactly a month to a day after Cayle's departure that the telestat clicked on just after Fara had finished lunch. "Money call," it sighed, "money call."

Fara and Creel looked at each other. "Eh," said Fara finally, "money call for us."

He could see from the gray look in Creel's face the thought that was in her mind. He said under his breath: "Damn that boy!"

But he felt relieved. Amazingly relieved! Cayle was beginning to appreciate the value of parents and—

He switched on the viewer. "Come and collect," he said.

The face that came on the screen was heavy-jowled, beetle-browed—and strange. The man said, "This is Clerk Pearton of the Fifth Bank of Ferd. We have received a sight draft on you for ten thousand credits. With carrying charges and government tax, the sum required will be twelve thousand one hundred credits. Will you pay it now or will you come in this afternoon and pay it?"

"B-but . . . b-but—" said Fara. "W-who—"

He stopped, conscious of the stupidity of the question, dimly conscious of the heavy-faced man saying something about the money having been paid out to one Cayle Clark that morning in Imperial City. At last, Fara found his voice:

"But the bank had no right," he expostulated, "to pay out the money without my authority. I—"

The voice cut him off coldly: "Are we then to inform our

central that the money was obtained under false pretenses? Naturally, an order will be issued immediately for the arrest of your son."

"Wait . . . wait—" Fara spoke blindly. He was aware of Creel beside him, shaking her head at him. She was as white as a sheet, and her voice was a sick, stricken thing, as she said, "Fara, let him go. He's through with us. We must be as hard—let him go."

The words rang senselessly in Fara's ears. They didn't fit into any normal pattern. He was saying:

"I . . . I haven't got— How about my paying . . . installments? I—"

"If you wish a loan," said Clerk Pearton, "naturally we will be happy to go into the matter. I might say that when the draft arrived, we checked up on your status, and we are prepared to loan you eleven thousand credits on indefinite call with your shop as security. I have the form here, and if you are agreeable, we will switch this call through the registered circuit, and you can sign at once."

"Fara, no."

The clerk went on: "The other eleven hundred credits will have to be paid in cash. Is that agreeable?"

"Yes, yes, of course, I've got twenty-five hund—" He stopped his chattering tongue with a gulp; then: "Yes, that's satisfactory."

The deal completed, Fara whirled on his wife. Out of the depths of his hurt and bewilderment, he raged: "What do you mean, standing there and talking about not paying it? You said several times that I was responsible for his being what he is. Besides, we don't know why he needed the money. He—"

Creel said in a low, dead tone: "In one hour, he's stripped us of our life work. He did it deliberately, thinking of us as two old fools, who wouldn't know any better than to pay it."

Before he could speak, she went on, "Oh, I know I blamed you, but in the final issue, I knew it was he. He was always cold and calculating, but I was weak, and I was sure that if you handled him in a different . . . and besides I didn't want to see his faults for a long time. He—"

"All I see," Fara interrupted doggedly, "is that I have saved our name from disgrace."

His high sense of duty rightly done lasted until midafternoon, when the bailiff from Ferd came to take over the shop.

"But what—" Fara began.

The bailiff said, "The Automatic Atomic Repair Shops,

Limited, took over your loan from the bank, and are foreclosing. Have you anything to say?"

"It's unfair," said Fara. "I'll take it to court. I'll—"

He was thinking dazedly: *If the empress ever learned of
this, she'd . . . she'd—*

The courthouse was a big, gray building; and Fara felt
emptier and colder every second, as he walked along the gray
corridors. In Glay, his decision not to give himself into the
hands of a bloodsucker of a lawyer had seemed a wise act.
Here, in these enormous halls and palatial rooms, it seemed
the sheerest folly.

He managed, nevertheless, to give an articulate account of
the criminal act of the bank in first giving Cayle the money,
then turning over the note to his chief competitor, apparently
within minutes of his signing it. He finished with: "I'm sure,
sir, the empress would not approve of such goings-on against
honest citizens. I—"

"How dare you," said the cold-voiced creature on the
bench, "use the name of her holy majesty in support of your
own gross self-interest?"

Fara shivered. The sense of being intimately a member of
the empress' great human family yielded to a sudden chill
and a vast mind-picture of the ten million icy courts like this,
and the myriad malevolent and heartless men—*like this*—
who stood between the empress and her loyal subject, Fara.

He thought passionately: If the empress knew what was
happening here, how unjustly he was being treated, she
would—

Or would she?

He pushed the crowding, terrible doubt out of his mind—
came out of his hard reverie with a start, to hear the Cadi
saying, "Plaintiff's appeal dismissed, with costs assessed at
seven hundred credits, to be divided between the court and
the defense solicitor in the ratio of five to two. See to it that
the appellant does not leave till the costs are paid. Next
case—"

Fara went alone the next day to see Creel's mother. He
called first at "Farmer's Restaurant" at the outskirts of the
village. The place was, he noted with satisfaction in the
thought of the steady stream of money flowing in, half full,
though it was only midmorning. But madame wasn't there.
Try the feed store.

He found her in the back of the feed store, overseeing the weighing out of grain into cloth measures. The hard-faced old woman heard his story without a word. She said finally, curtly, "Nothing doing, Fara. I'm one who has to make loans often from the bank to swing deals. If I tried to set you up in business, I'd find the Automatic Atomic Repair people getting after me. Besides, I'd be a fool to turn money over to a man who lets a bad son squeeze a fortune out of him. Such a man has no sense about worldly things.

"And I won't give you a job because I don't hire relatives in my business." She finished: "Tell Creel to come and live at my house. I won't support a man, though. That's all."

He watched her disconsolately for a while, as she went on calmly superintending the clerks who were manipulating the old, no longer accurate measuring machines. Twice her voice echoed through the dust-filled interior, each time with a sharp: "That's overweight, a gram at least. Watch your machine."

Though her back was turned, Fara knew by her posture that she was still aware of his presence. She turned at last with an abrupt movement and said, "Why don't you go to the weapon shop? You haven't anything to lose and you can't go on like this."

Fara went out, then, a little blindly. At first the suggestion that he buy a gun and commit suicide had no real personal application. But he felt immeasurably hurt that his mother-in-law should have made it.

Kill himself? Why, it was ridiculous. He was still only a young man, going on fifty. Given the proper chance, with his skilled hands, he could wrest a good living even in a world where automatic machines were encroaching everywhere. There was always room for a man who did a good job. His whole life had been based on that credo.

Kill himself—

He went home to find Creel packing. "It's the common sense thing to do," she said. "We'll rent the house and move into rooms."

He told her about her mother's offer to take her in, watching her face as he spoke. Creel shrugged.

"I told her 'No' yesterday," she said thoughtfully. "I wonder why she mentioned it to you."

Fara walked swiftly over to the great front window overlooking the garden, with its flowers, its pool, its rockery. He tried to think of Creel away from this garden of hers, this home of two thirds a lifetime, Creel living in rooms—and knew what her mother had meant. There was one more hope—

He waited till Creel went upstairs, then called Mel Dale on the telestat. The mayor's plump face took on an uneasy expression as he saw who it was.

But he listened pontifically, said finally, "Sorry, the council does not loan money; and I might as well tell you, Fara—I have nothing to do with this, mind you—but you can't get a license for a shop any more."

"W-what?"

"I'm sorry!" The mayor lowered his voice. "Listen, Fara, take my advice and go to the weapon shop. These places have their uses."

There was a click, and Fara sat staring at the blank face of the viewing screen.

So it was to be—death!

He waited until the street was empty of human beings, then slipped across the boulevard, past a design of flower gardens, and so to the door of the shop. The brief fear came that the door wouldn't open, but it did, effortlessly.

As he emerged from the dimness of the alcove into the shop proper, he saw the silver-haired old man sitting in a corner chair, reading under a softly bright light. The old man looked up, put aside his book, then rose to his feet.

"It's Mr. Clark," he said quietly. "What can we do for you?"

A faint flush crept into Fara's cheeks. In a dim fashion, he had hoped that he would not suffer the humiliation of being recognized; but now that his fear was realized, he stood his ground stubbornly. The important thing about killing himself was that there be no body for Creel to bury at great expense. Neither knife nor poison would satisfy that basic requirement.

"I want a gun," said Fara, "that can be adjusted to disintegrate a body six feet in diameter in a single shot. Have you that kind?"

Without a word, the old man turned to a showcase, and brought forth a sturdy gem of a revolver that glinted with all the soft colors of the inimitable Ordine plastic. The man said in a precise voice, "Notice the flanges on this barrel are little more than bulges. This makes the model ideal for carrying in a shoulder holster under the coat; it can be drawn very swiftly because, when properly attuned, it will leap toward the reaching hand of its owner. At the moment it is attuned to me. Watch while I replace it in its holster and—"

The speed of the draw was absolutely amazing. The old man's fingers moved; and the gun, four feet away, was in them. There was no blur of movement. It was like the door the night that it had slipped from Fara's grasp, and slammed noiselessly in Constable Jor's face. *Instantaneous!*

Fara, who had parted his lips as the old man was explaining, to protest the utter needlessness of illustrating any quality of the weapon except what he had asked for, closed them again. He stared in a brief, dazed fascination; and something of the wonder that was here held his mind and his body.

He had seen and handled the guns of soldiers, and they were simply ordinary metal or plastic things that one used clumsily like any other material substance, not like this at all, not possessed of a dazzling life of their own, leaping with an intimate eagerness to assist with all their superb power the will of their master. They—

With a start, Fara remembered his purpose. He smiled wryly, and said, "All this is very interesting. But what about the beam that can fan out?"

The old man said calmly, "At pencil thickness, this beam will pierce any body except certain alloys of lead up to four hundred yards. With proper adjustment of the firing nozzle, you can disintegrate a six-foot object at fifty yards or less. This screw is the adjustor."

He indicated a tiny device in the muzzle itself. "Turn it to the left to spread the beam, to the right to close it."

Fara said, "I'll take the gun. How much is it?"

He saw that the old man was looking at him thoughtfully; the oldster said finally, slowly, "I have previously explained our regulations to you, Mr. Clark. You recall them, of course?"

"Eh!" said Fara, and stopped, wide-eyed. It wasn't that he didn't remember them. It was simply—

"You mean," he gasped, "those things actually apply. They're not—"

With a terrible effort, he caught his spinning brain and blurring voice. Tense and cold, he said, "All I want is a gun that will shoot in self-defense, but which I can turn on myself if I have to or—want to."

"Oh, suicide!" said the old man. He looked as if a great

understanding had suddenly dawned on him. "My dear sir, we have no objection to your killing yourself at any time. That is your personal privilege in a world where privileges grow scanter every year. As for the price of this revolver, it's four credits."

"Four cre . . . only four credits!" said Fara.

He stood, absolutely astounded, his whole mind snatched from its dark purpose. Why, the plastic alone was—and the whole gun with its fine, intricate workmanship—twenty-five credits would have been dirt cheap.

He felt a brief thrill of utter interest; the mystery of the weapon shops suddenly loomed as vast and important as his own black destiny. But the old man was speaking again:

"And now, if you will remove your coat, we can put on the holster—"

Quite automatically, Fara complied. It was vaguely startling to realize that, in a few seconds, he would be walking out of here, equipped for self-murder, and that there was now not a single obstacle to his death.

Curiously, he was disappointed. He couldn't explain it, but somehow there had been in the back of his mind a hope that these shops might, just might—what?

What indeed? Fara sighed wearily—and grew aware again of the old man's voice, saying:

"Perhaps you would prefer to step out of our side door. It is less conspicuous than the front."

There was no resistance in Fara. He was dimly conscious of the man's fingers on his arm, half guiding him; and then the old man pressed one of several buttons on the wall—so that's how it was done— and there was the door.

He could see flowers beyond the opening; without a word he walked toward them. He was outside before he realized it.

Fara stood for a moment in the neat little pathway, striving to grasp the finality of his situation. But nothing would come except a curious awareness of many men around him; for a long second, his brain was like a log drifting along a stream at night.

Through that darkness grew a consciousness of something wrong; the wrongness was there in the back of his mind, as he turned leftward to go to the front of the weapon store.

Vagueness transformed to a shocked, startled sound. For—he was not in Glay, and the weapon shop *wasn't* where it had been. In its place—

A dozen men brushed past Fara to join a long line of men farther along. But Fara was immune to their presence, their strangeness. His whole mind, his whole vision, his very being was concentrating on the section of machine that stood where the weapon shop had been.

A machine, oh, a machine—

His brain lifted up, up in his effort to grasp the tremendousness of the dull-metaled immensity of what was spread here under a summer sun beneath a sky as blue as a remote southern sea.

The machine towered into the heavens, five great tiers of metal, each a hundred feet high; and the superbly streamlined five hundred feet ended in a peak of light, a gorgeous spire that tilted straight up a sheer two hundred feet farther, and matched the very sun for brightness.

And it *was* a machine, not a building, because the whole lower tier was alive with shimmering lights, mostly green, but sprinkled colorfully with red and occasionally a blue and yellow. Twice, as Fara watched, green lights directly in front of him flashed unscintillatingly into red.

The second tier was alive with white and red lights, although there were only a fraction as many lights as on the lowest tier. The third section had on its dull-metal surface only blue and yellow lights; they twinkled softly here and there over the vast area.

The fourth tier was a series of signs that brought the beginning of comprehension. The whole sign was:

WHITE	—	BIRTHS
RED	—	DEATHS
GREEN	—	LIVING
BLUE	—	IMMIGRATION TO EARTH
YELLOW	—	EMIGRATION

The fifth tier was also all sign, finally explaining:

POPULATIONS

SOLAR SYSTEM	19,174,463,747
EARTH	11,193,247,361
MARS	1,097,298,604
VENUS	5,141,053,811
MOONS	1,742,863,971

The numbers changed, even as he looked at them, leaping

up and down, shifting below and above what they had first been. People were dying, being born, moving to Mars, to Venus, to the moons of Jupiter, to Earth's moon, and others coming back again, landing minute by minute in the thousands of spaceports. Life went on in its gigantic fashion—and here was the stupendous record. Here was—

"Better get in line," said a friendly voice beside Fara. "It takes quite a while to put through an individual case, I understand."

Fara stared at the man. He had the distinct impression of having had senseless words flung at him. "In line?" he started—and stopped himself with a jerk that hurt his throat.

He was moving forward, blindly, ahead of the younger man, thinking a curious jumble that this must have been how Constable Jor was transported to Mars—when another of the man's words penetrated.

"Case?" said Fara violently. "Individual case!"

The man, a heavy-faced, blue-eyed young chap of around thirty-five, looked at him curiously: "You must know why you're here," he said. "Surely, you wouldn't have been sent through here unless you had a problem of some kind that the weapon shop courts will solve for you; there's no other reason for coming to Information Center."

Fara walked on because he was in the line now, a fast-moving line that curved him inexorably around the machine; and seemed to be heading him toward a door that led into the interior of the great metal structure.

So it was a building as well as a machine.

A problem, he was thinking, why, of course, he had a problem, a hopeless, insoluble, completely tangled problem so deeply rooted in the basic structure of Imperial civilization that the whole world would have to be overturned to make it right.

With a start, he saw that he was at the entrance. And the awed thought came: In seconds he would be committed irrevocably to—what?

Inside was a long, shining corridor, with scores of completely transparent hallways leading off the main corridor. Behind Fara, the young man's voice said, "There's one, practically empty. Let's go."

Fara walked ahead; and suddenly he was trembling. He had already noticed that at the end of each side hallway were some dozen young women sitting at desks, interviewing men and . . . and, good heavens, was it possible that all this meant—

He grew aware that he had stopped in front of one of the girls.

She was older than she had looked from a distance, over thirty, but good-looking, alert. She smiled pleasantly, but impersonally, and said, "Your name, please?"

He gave it before he thought and added a mumble about being from the village of Glay. The woman said, "Thank you. It will take a few minutes to get your file. Won't you sit down?"

He hadn't noticed the chair. He sank into it; and his heart was beating so wildly that he felt choked. The strange thing was that there was scarcely a thought in his head, nor a real hope; only an intense, almost mind-wrecking excitement.

With a jerk, he realized that the girl was speaking again, but only snatches of her voice came through that screen of tension in his mind:

"—Information Center is . . . in effect . . . a bureau of statistics. Every person born . . . registered here . . . their education, change of address . . . occupation . . . and the highlights of their life. The whole is maintained by . . . combination of . . . unauthorized and unsuspected liaison with . . . Imperial Chamber of Statistics and ... . through medium of agents . . . in every community—"

It seemed to Fara that he was missing vital information, and that if he could only force his attention and hear more— He strained, but it was no use; his nerves were jumping madly and—

Before he could speak, there was a click, and a thin, dark plate slid onto the woman's desk. She took it up and examined it. After a moment, she said something into a mouthpiece, and in a short time two more plates precipitated out of the empty air onto her desk. She studied them passively, looked up finally.

"You will be interested to know," she said, "that your son, Cayle, bribed himself into a commission in the Imperial army with five thousand credits."

"Eh?" said Fara. He half rose from his chair, but before he could say anything, the young woman was speaking again, firmly, "I must inform you that the weapon shops take no action against individuals. Your son can have his job, the money he stole; we are not concerned with moral correction. That must come naturally from the individual, and from the people as a whole—and now if you will give me a brief account of your problem for the record and the court."

Sweating, Fara sank back into his seat; his mind was heaving; most desperately, he wanted more information about Cayle. He began: "But . . . but what . . . how—" He caught himself; and in a low voice described what had happened. When he finished, the girl said, "You will proceed now to the Name Room; watch for your name, and when it appears go straight to Room 474. Remember, 474—and now, the line is waiting, if you please—"

She smiled politely, and Fara was moving off almost before he realized it. He half turned to ask another question, but an old man was sinking into his chair. Fara hurried on, along a great corridor, conscious of curious blasts of sound coming from ahead.

Eagerly, he opened the door; and the sound crashed at him with all the impact of a sledgehammer blow.

It was such a colossal, incredible sound that he stopped short, just inside the door, shrinking back. He stood then trying to blink sense into a visual confusion that rivaled in magnitude that incredible tornado of noise.

Men, men, men everywhere; men by the thousands in a long, broad auditorium, packed into rows of seats, pacing with an abandon of restlessness up and down aisles, and all of them staring with a frantic interest at a long board marked off into squares, each square lettered from the alphabet, from A, B, C and so on to Z. The tremendous board with its lists of names ran the full length of the immense room.

The Name Room, Fara was thinking shakily, as he sank into a seat—and his name would come up in the C's, and then—

It was like sitting in at a no-limit poker game, watching the jewel-precious cards turn up. It was like playing the exchange with all the world at stake during a stock crash. It was nerve-racking, dazzling, exhausting, fascinating, terrible, mind-destroying, stupendous. It was—

It was like nothing else on the face of the earth.

New names kept flashing on to the twenty-six squares; and men would shout like insane beings and some fainted, and the uproar was absolutely shattering; the pandemonium raged on, one continuous, unbelievable sound.

And every few minutes a great sign would flash along the board, telling everyone:

"WATCH YOUR OWN INITIALS."

Fara watched, trembling in every limb. Each second it seemed to him that he couldn't stand it an instant longer. He wanted to scream at the room to be silent; he wanted to jump up to pace the floor, but others who did that were yelled at hysterically, threatened wildly, hated with a mad, murderous ferocity.

Abruptly, the blind savagery of it scared Fara. He thought unsteadily: "I'm not going to make a fool of myself. I—"

"Clark, Fara—" winked the board. "Clark, Fara—"

With a shout that nearly tore off the top of his head, Fara leaped to his feet. "That's me!" he shrieked. "Me!"

No one turned; no one paid the slightest attention. Shamed, he slunk across the room where an endless line of men kept crowding into a corridor beyond.

The silence in the long corridor was almost as shattering as the mind-destroying noise it replaced. It was hard to concentrate on the idea of a number—474.

It was completely impossible to imagine what could lie beyond—474.

The room was small. It was furnished with a small, business-type table and two chairs. On the table were seven neat piles of folders, each pile a different color. The piles were arranged in a row in front of a large, milky-white globe, that began to glow with a soft light. Out of its depths, a man's baritone voice said, "Fara Clark?"

"Yes," said Fara.

"Before the verdict is rendered in your case," the voice went on quietly, "I want you to take a folder from the blue pile. The list will show the Fifth Interplanetary Bank in its proper relation to yourself and the world, and it will be explained to you in due course."

The list, Fara saw, was simply that, a list of the names of companies. The names ran from A to Z, and there were about five hundred of them. The folder carried no explanation; and Fara slipped it automatically into his side pocket, as the voice came again from the shining globe: "It has been established," the words came precisely, "that the Fifth Interplanetary Bank perpetrated upon you a gross swindle, and that it is further guilty of practicing scavengery, deception, blackmail and was accessory in a criminal conspiracy.

"The bank made contact with your son, Cayle, through what is quite properly known as a scavenger, that is, an employee who exists by finding young men and women who are normally capable of drawing drafts on their parents or other victims. The scavenger obtains for this service a commission of eight percent, which is always paid by the person making the loan, in this case your son.

"The bank practiced deception in that its authorized agents deceived you in the most culpable fashion by pretending that it had already paid out the ten thousand credits to your son, whereas the money was not paid over until your signature had been obtained.

"The blackmail guilt arises out of a threat to have your son arrested for falsely obtaining a loan, a threat made at a time when no money had exchanged hands. The conspiracy consists of the action whereby your note was promptly turned over to your competitor.

"The bank is accordingly triple-fined, thirty-six thousand three hundred credits. It is not in our interest, Fara Clark, for you to know how this money is obtained. Suffice to know that the bank pays it, and that of the fine the weapon shops allocate to their own treasury a total of one half. The other half—"

There was a *plop;* a neatly packaged pile of bills fell onto the table. "For you," said the voice; and Fara, with trembling fingers, slipped the package into his coat pocket. It required the purest mental and physical effort for him to concentrate on the next words that came:

"You must not assume that your troubles are over. The re-establishment of your motor repair shop in Glay will require force and courage. Be discreet, brave and determined, and you cannot fail. Do not hesitate to use the gun you have purchased in defense of your rights. The plan will be explained to you. And now, proceed through the door facing you—"

Fara braced himself with an effort, opened the door and walked through.

It was a dim, familiar room that he stepped into, and there was a silver-haired, fine-faced man who rose from a reading chair, and came forward in the dimness, smiling gravely.

The stupendous, fantastic, exhilarating adventure was over; and he was back in the weapon shop of Glay.

He couldn't get over the wonder of it—this great and fascinating organization established here in the very heart of a ruthless civilization, a civilization that had in a few brief weeks stripped him of everything he possessed.

With a deliberate will, he stopped that glowing flow of thought. A dark frown wrinkled his solidly built face; he said,

"The . . . judge—" Fara hesitated over the name, frowned again, annoyed at himself, then went on: "The judge said that, to reestablish myself I would have to—"

"Before we go into that," said the old man quietly, "I want you to examine the blue folder you brought with you."

"Folder?" Fara echoed blankly. It took a long moment to remember that he had picked up a folder from the table in Room 474.

He studied the list of company names with a gathering puzzlement, noting that the name of Automatic Atomic Motor Repair Shops was well down among the A's, and the Fifth Interplanetary Bank only one of several great banks included. Fara looked up finally:

"I don't understand," he said; "are these the companies you have had to act against?"

The silver-haired man smiled grimly, shook his head. "That is not what I mean. These firms constitute only a fraction of the eight hundred thousand companies that are constantly in our books."

He smiled again, humorlessly: "These companies all know that, because of us, their profits on paper bear no relation to their assets. What they don't know is how great the difference really is; and, as we want a general improvement in business morals, not merely more skillful scheming to outwit us, we prefer them to remain in ignorance."

He paused, and this time he gave Fara a searching glance, said at last: "The unique feature of the companies on this particular list is that they are every one wholly owned by Empress Isher."

He finished swiftly: "In view of your past opinions on that subject, I do not expect you to believe me."

Fara stood as still as death, for—he did believe with unquestioning conviction, completely, finally. The amazing, the unforgivable thing was that all his life he had watched the march of ruined men into the oblivion of poverty and disgrace—and blamed *them*.

Fara groaned. "I've been like a madman," he said. "Everything the empress and her officials did was right. No friendship, no personal relationship could survive with me that did not include belief in things as they were. I suppose if I started to talk against the empress I would receive equally short shrift."

"Under no circumstances," said the old man grimly, "must you say anything against her majesty. The weapon shops will not countenance any such words, and will give no further aid to anyone who is so indiscreet. The reason is that, for the moment, we have reached an uneasy state of peace with the Imperial government. We wish to keep it that way; beyond that I will not enlarge on our policy.

"I am permitted to say that the last great attempt to destroy the weapon shops was made seven years ago, when the glorious Innelda Isher was twenty-five years old. That was a secret attempt, based on a new invention; and failed by purest accident because of our sacrifice of a man from seven thousand years in the past. That may sound mysterious to you, but I will not explain.

"The worst period was reached some forty years ago when every person who was discovered receiving aid from us was murdered in some fashion. You may be surprised to know that your father-in-law was among those assassinated at that time."

"Creel's father!" Fara gasped. "But—"

He stopped. His brain was reeling; there was such a rush of blood to his head that for an instant he could hardly see.

"But," he managed at last, "it was reported that he ran away with another woman."

"They always spread a vicious story of some kind," the old man said; and Fara was silent, stunned.

The other went on: "We finally put a stop to their murders by killing the three men from the top down, *excluding* the royal family, who gave the order for the particular execution involved. But we do not again want that kind of bloody murder.

"Nor are we interested in any criticism of our toleration of so much that is evil. It is important to understand that *we do not interfere in the main stream of human existence.* We right wrongs; we act as a barrier between the people and their more ruthless exploiters. Generally speaking, we help only honest men; that is not to say that we do not give assistance to the less scrupulous, but only to the extent of selling them guns—which is a very great aid indeed, and which is one of the reasons why the government is relying almost exclusively for its power on an economic chicanery.

"In the four thousand years since the brilliant genius Walter S. DeLany invented the vibration process that made the weapon shops possible, and laid down the first principles of weapon shop political philosophy, we have watched the tide of government swing backward and forward between democ-

racy under a limited monarchy to complete tyranny. And we
have discovered one thing:

"*People always have the kind of government they want.*
When they want change, they must change it. As always we
shall remain an incorruptible core—and I mean that literally;
we have a psychological machine that never lies about a
man's character—I repeat, an incorruptible core of human
idealism, devoted to relieving the ills that arise inevitably under any form of government.

"But now—your problem. It is very simple, really. You
must fight, as all men have fought since the beginning of time
for what they valued, for their just rights. As you know, the
Automatic Repair people removed all your machinery and
tools within an hour of foreclosing on your shop. This
material was taken to Ferd, and then shipped to a great warehouse on the coast.

"We recovered it, and with our special means of transpor-
tation have now replaced the machines in your shop. You
will accordingly go there and—"

Fara listened with a gathering grimness to the instructions,
nodded finally, his jaw clamped tight.

"You can count on me," he said curtly. "I've been a stubborn man in my time; and though I've changed sides, I
haven't changed *that.*"

Going outside was like returning from life to—death; from
hope to—reality.

Fara walked along the quiet streets of Glay at darkest
night. For the first time it struck him that the weapon shop
Information Center must be halfway around the world, for it
had been day, brilliant day.

The picture vanished as if it had never existed, and he
grew aware again, preternaturally aware of the village of
Glay asleep all around him. Silent, peaceful—yet ugly, he
thought, ugly with the ugliness of evil enthroned.

He thought: The right to buy weapons—and his heart
swelled into his throat; the tears came to his eyes.

He wiped his vision clear with the back of his hand,
thought of Creel's long dead father, and strode on, without
shame. Tears were good for an angry man.

The shop was the same, but the hard metal padlock yielded
before the tiny, blazing, supernal power of the revolver. One
flick of fire; the metal dissolved—and he was inside.

It was dark, too dark to see, but Fara did not turn on the
lights immediately. He fumbled across to the window control,

turned the windows to darkness vibration, and then clicked on the lights.

He gulped with awful relief. For the machines, his precious tools that he had seen carted away within hours after the bailiff's arrival, were here again, ready for use.

Shaky from the pressure of his emotion, Fara called Creel on the telestat. It took a little while for her to appear; and she was in her dressing robe. When she saw who it was she turned a dead white.

"Fara, oh, Fara, I thought—"

He cut her off grimly: "Creel, I've been to the weapon shop. I want you to do this: go straight to your mother. I'm here at my shop. I'm going to stay here day and night until it's settled that I *stay*. . . . I shall go home later for some food and clothing, but I want you to be gone by then. Is that clear?"

Color was coming back into her lean, handsome face. She said: "Don't you bother coming home, Fara. I'll do everything necessary. I'll pack all that's needed into the carplane, including a folding bed. We'll sleep in the back room of the shop."

Morning came palely, but it was ten o'clock before a shadow darkened the open door; and Constable Jor came in. He looked shamefaced.

"I've got an order here for your arrest," he said.

"Tell those who sent you," Fara replied deliberately, "that I resisted arrest—with a gun."

The deed followed the words with such rapidity that Jor blinked. He stood like that for a moment, a big, sleepy-looking man, staring at that gleaming, magical revolver; then:

"I have a summons here ordering you to appear at the great court of Ferd this afternoon. Will you accept it?"

"Certainly."

"Then you will be there?"

"I'll send my lawyer," said Fara. "Just drop the summons on the floor there. Tell them I took it."

The weapon shop man had said, "Do not ridicule by word any legal measure of the Imperial authorities. Simply disobey them."

Jor went out, and seemed relieved. It took an hour before Mayor Mel Dale came pompously through the door.

"See here, Fara Clark," he bellowed from the doorway. "You can't get away with this. This is defiance of the law."

Fara was silent as His Honor waddled farther into the building. It was puzzling, almost amazing, that Mayor Dale

would risk his plump, treasured body. Puzzlement ended as
the mayor said in a low voice, "Good work, Fara; I knew
you had it in you. There's dozens of us in Glay behind you,
so stick it out. I had to yell at you just now, because there's a
crowd outside. Yell back at me, will you? Let's have a real
name calling. But, first, a word of warning: the manager of
the Automatic Repair Shop is on his way here with his body-
guards, two of them—"

Shakily, Fara watched the mayor go out. The crisis was at
hand. He braced himself, thought: *Let them come, let
them*—

It was easier than he had thought—for the men who entered the shop turned pale when they saw the holstered
revolver. There was a violence of blustering, nevertheless,
that narrowed finally down to:

"Look here," the man said, "we've got your note for twelve
thousand one hundred credits. You're not going to deny you
owe that money."

"I'll buy it back," said Fara in a stony voice, "for exactly
half, not a cent more."

The strong-jawed young man looked at him for a long
time. "We'll take it," he said finally, curtly.

Fara said, "I've got the agreement here—"

His first customer was old man Miser Lan Harris. Fara
stared at the long-faced oldster with a vast surmise, and his
first, amazed comprehension came of how the weapon shop
must have settled on Harris' lot—by arrangement.

It was an hour after Harris had gone that Creel's mother
stamped into the shop. She closed the door.

"Well," she said, "you did it, eh? Good work. I'm sorry if I
seemed rough with you when you came to my place, but we
weapon-shop supporters can't afford to take risks for those
who are not on our side.

"But never mind that. I've come to take Creel home. The
important thing is to return everything to normal as quickly
as possible."

It was over; incredibly it was over. Twice, as he walked
home that night, Fara stopped in midstride, and wondered if
it had not all been a dream. The air was like wine. The little
world of Glay spread before him, green and gracious, a
peaceful paradise where time had stood still.

MIMIC

Astonishing Stories,

December

by Donald A. Wollheim (1914-   )

*Although he is best known as a leading editor
and publisher, Donald A. Wollheim has written
some twenty science fiction novels and has had one
collection (*Two Dozen Dragon Eggs, *1969) of
stories, many of them for the young adult market.
One of the major figures in the early history of fandom and an original Futurian, he worked at Avon
Books and then edited the science fiction line at
Ace before starting DAW Books in 1971. Also a
noted anthologist, his* Annual World's Best SF *(previously* World's Best SF) *has maintained a consis-
tently high standard.*

*"Mimic," addresses an important sf theme that
would later be treated by writers as diverse as Mark
Clifton and Philip K. Dick, and is (arguably) Don
Wollheim's finest science fiction story.*

(Don Wollheim was the quintessential science fiction fan,
at the time when the "fan movement" was in its classic phase.
He was articulate, cutting and opinionated and the paper on
which he wrote his letters invariably scorched at the edges.
I've often thought that if he didn't bleed off his writing talents in denouncing his fellow fans, he would have become a
remarkable science fiction writer. "Mimic," for instance, has
stayed with me for nearly forty years, and I strongly suggested its inclusion even though Don *is* the original publisher of this
series, and we might be accused of trying to curry favor.—That
would be a ridiculous accusation, by the way, for it is impossible to
curry favor with the irascible Don.—I. A.)

It is less than five hundred years since an entire half of the
world was discovered. It is less than two hundred years since

the discovery of the last continent. The sciences of chemistry and physics go back scarcely one century. The science of aviation goes back forty years. The science of atomics is being born.

And yet we think we know a lot.

We know little or nothing. Some of the most startling things are unknown to us. When they are discovered, they may shock us to the bone.

We search for secrets in the far islands of the Pacific and among the ice fields of the frozen North, while under our very noses, rubbing shoulders with us every day, there may walk the undiscovered. It is a curious fact of nature that that which is in plain view is oft best hidden.

I have always known of the man in the black cloak. Since I was a child he has always lived on my street, and his eccentricities are so familiar that they go unmentioned except among the casual visitor. Here, in the heart of the largest city in the world, in swarming New York, the eccentric and the odd may flourish unhindered.

As children we had hilarious fun jeering at the man in black when he displayed his fear of women. We watched, in our evil, childish way, for those moments; we tried to get him to show anger. But he ignored us completely and soon we paid him no further heed, even as our parents did.

We saw him only twice a day. Once in the early morning, when we would see his six-foot figure come out of the grimy dark hallway of the tenement at the end of the street and stride down toward the elevated to work—again when he came back at night. He was always dressed in a long, black cloak that came to his ankles, and he wore a wide-brimmed black hat down far over his face. He was a sight from some weird story out of the old lands. But he harmed nobody, and paid attention to nobody.

Nobody—except perhaps women.

When a woman crossed his path, he would stop in his stride and come to a dead halt. We could see that he closed his eyes until she had passed. Then he would snap those wide, watery blue eyes open and march on as if nothing had happened.

He was never known to speak to a woman. He would buy some groceries, maybe once a week, at Antonio's—but only when there were no other patrons there. Antonio said once that he never talked, he just pointed at things he wanted and paid for them in bills that he pulled out of a pocket somewhere under his cloak. Antonio did not like him, but he never had any trouble from him either.

Now that I think of it, nobody ever did have any trouble with him.

We got used to him. We grew up on the street; we saw him occasionally when he came home and went back into the dark hallway of the house he lived in.

He never had visitors, he never spoke to anyone. And he had once built something in his room out of metal.

He had once, years ago, hauled up some long flat metal sheets, sheets of tin or iron, and they had heard a lot of hammering and banging in his room for several days. But that had stopped and that was all there was to that story.

Where he worked I don't know and never found out. He had money, for he was reputed to pay his rent regularly when the janitor asked for it.

Well, people like that inhabit big cities and nobody knows the story of their lives until they're all over. Or until something strange happens.

I grew up, I went to college, I studied.

Finally I got a job assisting a museum curator. I spent my days mounting beetles and classifying exhibits of stuffed animals and preserved plants, and hundreds and hundreds of insects from all over.

Nature is a strange thing, I learned. You learn that very clearly when you work in a museum. You realize how nature uses the art of camouflage. There are twig insects that look exactly like a leaf or a branch of a tree. Exactly.

Nature is strange and perfect that way. There is a moth in Central America that looks like a wasp. It even has a fake stinger made of hair, which it twists and curls just like a wasp's stinger. It has the same colorings and, even though its body is soft and not armored like a wasp's, it is colored to appear shiny and armored. It even flies in the daytime when wasps do, and not at night like all other moths. It moves like a wasp. It knows somehow that it is helpless and that it can survive only by pretending to be as deadly to other insects as wasps are.

I learned about army ants, and their strange imitators.

Army ants travel in huge columns of thousands and hundreds of thousands. They move along in a flowing stream several yards across and they eat everything in their path. Everything in the jungle is afraid of them. Wasps, bees, snakes, other ants, birds, lizards, beetles—even men run away, or get eaten.

But in the midst of the army ants there also travel many other creatures—creatures that aren't ants at all, and that the army ants would kill if they knew of them. But they don't know of them because these other creatures are disguised. Some of them are beetles that look like ants. They have false markings like ant thoraxes and they run along in imitation of ant speed. There is even one that is so long it is marked like three ants in single file! It moves so fast that the real ants never give it a second glance.

There are weak caterpillars that look like big armored beetles. There are all sorts of things that look like dangerous animals. Animals that are the killers and superior fighters of their groups have no enemies. The army ants and the wasps, the sharks, the hawk, and the felines. So there are a host of weak things that try to hide among them—to mimic them.

And man is the greatest killer, the greatest hunter of them all. The whole world of nature knows man for the irresistible master. The roar of his gun, the cunning of his trap, the strength and agility of his arm place all else beneath him.

Should man then be treated by nature differently from the other dominants, the army ants and the wasps?

It was, as often happens to be the case, sheer luck that I happened to be on the street at the dawning hour when the janitor came running out of the tenement on my street shouting for help. I had been working all night mounting new exhibits.

The policeman on the beat and I were the only people besides the janitor to see the thing that we found in the two dingy rooms occupied by the stranger of the black cloak.

The janitor explained—as the officer and I dashed up the narrow, rickety stairs—that he had been awakened by the sound of heavy thuds and shrill screams in the stranger's rooms. He had gone out in the hallway to listen.

When we got there, the place was silent. A faint light shone from under the doorway. The policeman knocked, there was no answer. He put his ear to the door and so did I. We heard a faint rustling—a continuous slow rustling as of a breeze blowing paper.

The cop knocked again, but there was still no response.

Then, together, we threw our weight at the door. Two hard blows and the rotten old lock gave way. We burst in.

The room was filthy, the floor covered with scraps of torn

paper, bits of detritus and garbage. The room was unfurnished, which I thought was odd.

In the corner there stood a metal box, about four feet square. A tight-box, held together with screws and ropes. It had a lid, opening at the top, which was down and fastened with a sort of wax seal.

The stranger of the black cloak lay in the middle of the floor—dead.

He was still wearing the cloak. The big slouch hat was lying on the floor some distance away. From the inside of the box the faint rustling was coming.

We turned over the stranger, took the cloak off. For several instants we saw nothing amiss and then gradually—horribly—we became aware of some things that were wrong.

His hair was short and curly brown. It stood straight up in its inch-long length. His eyes were open and staring. I noticed first that he had no eyebrows, only a curious dark line in the flesh over each eye.

It was then I realized he had no nose. But no one had ever noticed that before. His skin was oddly mottled. Where the nose should have been there were dark shadowings that made the appearance of a nose, if you only just glanced at him. Like the work of a skillful artist in a painting.

His mouth was as it should be and slightly open—but he had no teeth. His head perched upon a thin neck.

The suit was—not a suit. It was part of him. It was his body.

What we thought was a coat was a huge black wing sheath, like a beetle has. He had a thorax like an insect, only the wing sheath covered it and you couldn't notice it when he wore the cloak. The body bulged out below, tapering off into the two long, thin hind legs. His arms came out from under the top of the "coat." He had a tiny secondary pair of arms folded tightly across his chest. There was a sharp, round hole newly pierced in his chest just above the arms, still oozing a watery liquid.

The janitor fled gibbering. The officer was pale but standing by his duty. I heard him muttering under his breath an endless stream of Hail Marys over and over again.

The lower thorax—the "abdomen"—was very long and insectlike. It was crumpled up now like the wreckage of an airplane fuselage.

I recalled the appearance of a female wasp that had just laid eggs—her thorax had had that empty appearance.

The sight was a shock such as leaves one in full control. The mind rejects it, and it is only in afterthought that one can feel the dim shudder of horror.

The rustling was still coming from the box. I motioned to the white-faced cop and we went over and stood before it. He took the nightstick and knocked away the waxen seal.

Then we heaved and pulled the lid open.

A wave of noxious vapor assailed us. We staggered back as suddenly a stream of flying things shot out of the huge iron container. The window was open, and straight out into the first glow of dawn they flew.

There must have been dozens of them. They were about two or three inches long and they flew on wide gauzy beetle wings. They looked like little men, strangely terrifying as they flew—clad in their black suits, with their expressionless faces and their dots of watery blue eyes. And they flew out on transparent wings that came from under their black beetle coats.

I ran to the window, fascinated, almost hypnotized. The horror of it had not reached my mind at once. Afterward I have had spasms of numbing terror as my mind tries to put the things together. The whole business was so utterly unexpected.

We knew of army ants and their imitators, yet it never occurred to us that we too were army ants of a sort. We knew of stick insects and it never occurred to us that there might be others that disguise themselves to fool, not other animals, but the supreme animal himself—man.

We found some bones in the bottom of that iron case afterwards. But we coudn't identify them. Perhaps we did not try very hard. They might have been human. . . .

I suppose the stranger of the black cloak did not fear women so much as it distrusted them. Women notice men, perhaps, more closely than other men do. Women might become suspicious sooner of the inhumanity, the deception. And then there might perhaps have been some touch of instinctive feminine jealousy. The stranger was disguised as a man, but its sex was surely female. The things in the box were its young.

But it is the other thing I saw when I ran to the window that has shaken me the most. The policeman did not see it. Nobody else saw it but me, and I only for an instant.

Nature practices deceptions in every angle. Evolution will

create a being for any niche that can be found, no matter how unlikely.

When I went to the window, I saw the small cloud of flying things rising up into the sky and sailing away into the purple distance. The dawn was breaking and the first rays of the sun were just striking over the housetops.

Shaken, I looked away from that fourth-floor tenement room over the roofs of lower buildings. Chimneys and walls and empty clotheslines made the scenery over which the tiny mass of horror passed.

And then I saw a chimney, not thirty feet away on the next roof. It was squat and of red brick and had two black pipe ends flush with its top. I saw it suddenly vibrate, oddly. And I saw its red brick surface seem to peel away, and the black pipe openings turn suddenly white.

I saw two big eyes staring into the sky.

A great, flat-winged thing detached itself silently from the surface of the real chimney and darted after the cloud of flying things.

I watched until all had lost themselves in the sky.